THE SUBSTITUTE

Book I

Tionne Rogers

Cover image: John Singer Sargent. "Grand Canal", c. 1902, National Gallery of Art, Washington, DC, Watercolour over graphite, Alicia Mellon Bruce Collection.

ISBN. 978-1-105-63763-6

To Higashi and Stacey Jo
for their support and good advise

To my family
for their unconditional love

PART I

The Duke

Chapter 1

December 28th, 2001

    I still can't believe I'm here. I really need to get a grip on all the things that happened so far. Ten days ago I was working at the pub, the finals just done and fortunately (not too bad if I say so), successfully passed and now look at me, I'm in old Europe travelling with my best friend.

    Maybe I should introduce myself before I explain a bit further how I got here. I was born in New York almost twenty years ago, but I have no memories of the city. My father moved to Argentina when I was three years old and since then, I was living in a private school nearby Buenos Aires. I didn't know my mother, as she died in childbirth. Perhaps that was the reason my father was never much around. He was always travelling and sending presents from abroad. Now and then he would come to visit me, but he never stayed too long. When I was seven he committed suicide without any kind of explanation. How could it be? Honestly, I never knew why. The school's headmaster just broke the news to me; Jerôme de Lisle was found dead in his flat in Paris and the investigation had ruled it out as a suicide a week ago. A solicitor had been appointed as my tutor and I was supposed to remain in the school, since I had no living relatives anywhere.

    Even if I could not say that I deeply loved my father, hell, you should know people to have any kind of feelings toward them; it was awkwardly devastating for me. I just shut everything and everybody out. Not like an autistic person, but I couldn't form any kind of ties with the rest of the class. I just sat there, did my homework and stayed out of trouble, more like a machine than a child. Was I angry with the world? No, I think not, but I had firmly determined that I would form no attachments with anybody. I simply kept my relationships to the point of being polite.

    Living in a boarding school is not so bad after all. I could have ended up in an orphanage and that would have been really bad. I can't complain at all. St. Peter's was among the most expensive and good schools around. Teachers were distant but nice, and since I was not a troublemaker, they left me alone. The school was for boys only and in the old British tradition, with many of the teachers imported from the United Kingdom My fellow students came from the wealthiest families and our happy micro society was well organised according to money. Being an orphan with a trust fund to pay for my education would have not ranked me on the top, but on the other hand, I had the mysterious allure of a French passport, so I was not "one of the natives."

    However, as usual I'm jumping parts and the idea of this diary is to organise my thoughts. So let's start again.

    I bought this notebook; better call it Diary, some days ago, before Christmas. I came to Europe with Fefo, Fedérico Martiarena Alvear, for the record, who is my best friend since school days. He was also sent to St. Peter's, but in his case was some sort of last chance. He's a little older than me; three years to be exact. He was failing class after class, mostly out of boredom. His mother, a Senator, thought that a boarding school would give him some "structure," in his life. He joined us when I was

9

thirteen years old, in the second year of high school. We were in the same class, as he had failed the last course of primary school and then made the first year twice. I was more or less an outcast since I had no family, but nobody was really too interested in me to take the trouble to hassle me.

Our tutor stuck us together; I was supposed to keep him out of trouble, and he should get me out of my cocoon (I was really happy in there!). At the beginning we didn't get along; hell, we were more than crossed that we had to sit together in class and share a room. I absolutely hated his blaring radio at study hours, and he loathed to be seen in the company of a "dwarf". The first months were like a cold war between us, with us not speaking to each other, and he just crossing the teachers more and more... well, furious would be a better description. He had the bloody habit of smoking and drinking, and I suppose the teachers knew it.

One June night, I think the principal decided he had enough of Fefo and conducted one of his famous "search parties". The man was really impressive, and I still become completely nervous around him. With another two teachers and tutor (did he forget or could he not find the sniffing dogs?), they stormed in our room and started their merry search through our things. A Playboy magazine was immediately discarded; no one was shocked by that. Cigarettes were already consumed and, even if they were more frantic than a Spaniard searching for El Dorado, they found nothing. When they were leaving surrounded by a cloud of defeat (and we were almost glowing with satisfaction and the prospect of a good story to tell the other boys), Mr. Sour (our principal, not his real name but quite appropriate), turned on his footsteps and with an evil grin said "I think nobody could be so foolish as to hide something in his desk, but let's give you a chance, gentlemen". There, like the jewels of the Crown, was a Jack Daniel's bottle, blinding us with its reflection.

The storm just broke on our heads and was aimed entirely at Fedérico. In the middle of the shouting I said, "It's mine". Of course nobody heard me, too busy shouting and secretly congratulating themselves that they would get rid of the boy who was more trouble than the money they were making out of his family.

"It's mine," I repeated louder, perhaps a bit stronger than my usual self, "sir," I hastily added, who knows, maybe a gentleman's manners would lessen the punishment. For a moment, I was the centre of the universe; all eyes wide open, especially those from Fedérico. Needless to say, I got the special escort service to the Principal's office. All hell broke loose in there; I got the routine of the good and bad teacher telling me how daft I was for covering someone like Fefo. It was unthinkable that a good student like me would do something like this. I would be expelled and that would be the end of me, etc., etc., etc., I tried to keep my cool—no need to embarrass myself by crying when that was all what I wanted to do—look contrite and keep my head down and my mouth shut to every question that could reveal that I had no bloody idea regarding the bottle's provenance. Had these people never heard about Human Rights?

Finally, they let me go, not really believing me, but with the secret hope that Fefo would screw it up later. As punishment I got lots of hours of extra work, lost all privileges for the rest of the year—no going out on weekends and no TV for the rest of the year—but that was a small price to pay to be the hero of the school. Nobody really thought I would keep my mouth shut, and perhaps would crack under the pressure and describe the system to smuggle things into the school. The most surprised was Fefo.

We were separated. After all, the general impression among the teachers was that he was the bad apple, and I was corrupted—yeah, yeah, I can do rubbish and still look innocent—but we became best friends. Once he asked me why I risked my head for him, but I could only answer him: "earn it". Funny, he did.

Of course he did not become a model student, but he had the good grace of stay out of trouble and copy from my homework since then. Perhaps I'm giving a wrong impression of him. He's not an angel and I'm the first one to admit it, but he's a good person. Crazy and impulsive, sort of a lady killer, but he will always be there for you and taught me lots of things like an older brother, like: my first cigarette; what to do on a date; driving, which I'm still not so good at; fighting; and most importantly, to keep my ground. Okay, running to the discos in the slums of Buenos Aires was not my idea of fun, but here, if you come from a long list of landlords, it's the usual thing to do... and the girls are not too bad considering everything around. He helped me out of my shell, and I helped him to survive high school.

In the beginning of December 2000, we graduated. OK, I did it, since he still had some subjects to pass, but the ceremony was for the whole class. My trust fund was almost finished, but somehow it had managed to last several Argentinean crises. Anyhow, it would not last enough to support me during university. I wanted to study Economics and Social Work, and I needed a job. Fefo spoke with a cousin of his and got me a stable job in a book shop that was also a restaurant built over an old cinema. Since in Argentina, the unemployment rate was quite high at that time, it was sort of a miracle. He also helped me to rent a small flat near work and the university—a shoe box to be honest—by convincing his mother to be my collateral.

In July 2001 we accomplished a small miracle; Fefo passed his two last subjects with a little help from me, and could register to attend the University next year. Naturally, he would go to a private one, not the public one like me, which is free and sometimes chaotic. I was perfectly aware that Economics was meant to be my first subject—hey, I have the particular habit of eating—and Social Work was a side career—too much altruistic to live only for that.

Please don't misunderstand me. I like helping people and the work in the slums with the church (honestly when you go there for the first time, you feel like shit if you don't do something, and I firmly believed that with hard work, things could improve for people), but I know deeply in my heart that I would not survive such a hard life. One of the things that struck me hard during my escapades to these very poor discos located in the outskirts-slums was the people. I mean, most of them had no place to drop dead; the drugs, crime and indifference slowly killing them, but some of them were still fighting to get out.

It would be nice to call me an idealist and not an idiot. When my school fellows were trying to convince a poor girl "to service them" for a beer or even for a dinner, I felt dirty because I honestly believed that it was abusive, no matter if the girls were more than happy to comply.

Maybe I was the romantic type, or perhaps I attended too many religion classes, but I could not bring myself to have a one-night stand; I wanted a full commitment and a family and since I was perfectly aware that I had nothing to offer to a girl, I was not really into that type of hunt. Sometimes, I think I was born an old man, stuck in the nineteenth century. According to Fefo I was a lost cause who would probably marry a girl from the parish, work as an accountant and raise many children till I would die of boredom, boring other people in the process; "even your name is old, Guntram, whoever heard of it?" Strangely, and no matter if it sounded dull, the idea was appealing to me.

Coming back to the present story, and why I bought you, Diary, let me say that 2001 was a good year for me. I worked as a waiter from 9 a.m to 4 p.m. in one of the best book stores ever; the manager was nice to me, co-workers were also students —we used to cover each other—and I could go to University in the night shift. I was taking six classes per term and had to run a bit to make ends meet, but I was satisfied with myself. My flat was OK, in a good neighbourhood, near both university buildings and work. Money was a little short, but I had enough for rent, books and some food. My day started at 7 a.m. and finished not earlier than 11 p.m. The Fortune Goddess was smiling upon me. I was not surprised when Fefo came that suffocating summer evening to tell me the good news.

We were going to Europe! The "must do Argentinean Cultural Tour" designed to brush up a little the countryman inside of all of us. Fefo's mother decided that he and this servant, as the necessary caboose, will visit the main attractions; Paris, London, Rome, Milan, Venice, Florence, Munich and Berlin. In order to avoid trouble, we will be on a tight budget (ever heard of hostels and students rail-pass?), cheap flight and so on. Fefo's Mother honoured me with a long speech on the value of virtue, good manners and temperance and in theory, I would have to pass these noble virtues to my young charge.

Excuse me? I'm 19 and he's 23 years old. I have to chaperone Fefo? No way! However the Senator and her Prodigal Son were sitting in my humble living, kitchen room, completely convinced that it was such a great plan. For me, the idea was so ridiculous, hilarious.

"Come on Guntram, say yes, I will behave accordingly. You always dreamed visiting those places."

He had a point there, and, even if it was not mentioned, my chances of making such a big trip were close to none. "I have to work this summer," I said feebly, steadfastly rowing with my teaspoon in my cup.

"Nonsense Guntram, Everything is arranged with Martín. You'll get holidays from mid December onwards. It's an opportunity for you," the mighty Senator and mother told (ordered) me.

"It's an offer you can't reject", my friend added, winking at me.

Chapter 2

So here I'm in Venice. We were in Paris for five days, but Fefo decided to go after the Italian sun much to my chagrin. Hey, some French is getting into my head, who knows; maybe I would be able to show my French passport without embarrassing myself, as I never excelled at French lessons. I bought the folder, mostly because I liked its hard cover with the small rabbit from the Dame à la Licorne on it. I was lucky enough as to be dumped by Fefo in the Quartier Latin and ran to visit the Cluny Museum where there was this wonderful set of tapestries, before the employees closed early. All right, it's not a good idea to visit a Museum on December 23rd. On the 24th, I went to Mass in the Notre Dame Cathedral—my ears hurt from Fefo's laughing when I told him about my plans—and then I just wandered the city, watching people hurrying themselves to get home and trying to understand what they were saying.

Somehow I felt like I was living in a dream, such a wonderful city full of light and so elegant was a sharp and painful contrast to the scenes of my own turbulent Buenos Aires, after the President's fall from power. The metro and the walking to the hostel, took me out of the melancholy that was almost engulfing me. The muslin kebab vendor, who also spoke no French at all—well, not the Alliance Française French, I learnt at school—waved his hand at me. "*Ajourd'hui fiesta eh*?" He said laughing truly happy mixing languages. It was impossible not to fall into his contagious smile, and he lifted my spirits. He arrived to Paris twenty-four years ago from Fez.

In the hostel, all the students were preparing for a huge Christmas party. Fefo as usual had found other Argentinean people and some Americans too. He was also making friends with several French girls, telling horror stories about the crisis—who said it was bad for all of us? I swear, he could make money out of a stone. It was only 7 p.m. and they were already drinking. The idea was to stay in the hotel till twelve and then go to a disco in Pigalle, where the "hot girls" are (?) I'm a quiet person and by midnight, I had enough of the noise, the smoke, the booze, the chat mixing English, French, and Spanish and just wanted to crawl into my bed hoping the headache would lessen.

"Fefo, I'm going straight to bed. I'm dead," I shouted to him.

"What?"

"Bed. Now." Damn music, too loud for my taste.

"No way, come with us. Come on, don't be a grandpa. It's gonna be real fun."

"Exactly. The less I know, the less I need lie about when Mummy Dear asks me about your "cultural exploits". See you in the morning."

"The only ones who are going to bed are you and those two American soldiers from Germany."

"See? I have to oblige to with my fellow citizens."

"OK. Don't forget to ask them for your warm milk. Maybe they even have a bottle with them," he said with a grin bigger than the Cheshire Cat.

Internal debate: should I give him the finger or just throw an insult in Spanish? Considering the amount of ladies present, classical swearing is better. "Go to Hell, idiot."

"Sleep tight darling," he just turned his back and attention to the girls, as drunk as him, giggling all the time. Hello? I'm still here.

Next morning, I was a little surprised that I had not heard the usual stampede of Fefo coming back. I swear, the word "subtle," Is not in his vocabulary. He was not in the room and probably found some place to sleep. I tossed around my things, looking for a pair of faded jeans, a polo shirt and a blue pullover; located the trekking boots under my bunk—Argentinean tradition when travelling; always get the biggest shoes. You never know if you have to kick the cows—I was ready to take over Christmas day (and don't come with this silly notion than being an orphan made me depressed on that day, had enough of that crap with the School Councillor) so I went for breakfast.

Not surprisingly, the cafeteria was almost empty—no queue, great! How considerate. I spotted the two American soldiers sitting at a table and after making the universal hello sign with the head, they waved at me, indicating that my presence was accepted. They were okay guys, a little on the shy and silent side, but I was no better.

"Hey Günther, you went to bed early too," the blond shouted. I believe his name was Edward.

"Guntram is the name. Don't worry it's not a usual one."

"Has your friend returned?" Wow, direct and to the point. The one, who was built like Schwarzenegger asked.

"Haven't seen him so far," I shrugged away. "If he's not back by nightfall, I'll be concerned. Why do you ask?"

"How old are you?" Is it questioning time or was I enlisted and somebody forgot to tell me? I gave Arnie a blank stare and half expected he would develop his line of thought for stupid me, the civilian.

"Look Guntram, you must be very young and have no experience but such things can be dangerous to play with. You are in a foreign country," Edward explained to me gently.

"I'm afraid I don't follow you. What do you mean by dangerous? We were not drinking so much anyway. And I'm legal, I'm nineteen years old." Without preamble they were both chuckling like I had made the biggest joke.

"Didn't you realise that those girls were looking for a clean transport for their stuff?"

I'm lost now. Transport?

"You really don't get it, do you? It's common in places like this that a beautiful girl comes to a student, makes friends and then, in a moment, they put their drug cargo in his bag, so he carries it for them. Normally, they offer to share the earnings or a hot night. The guy goes with the parcel to another city, and they follow him. If he's caught, they escape," Edward explained softly for innocent (dumb) me.

"This is nonsense, who would be such an idiot as to knowingly carry drugs? I think you two are overdoing it," I said secretly hurt as they would think that Fefo would be so stupid and who the hell let these two meddle into our business?

"Sit down and don't raise your voice," the huge one stated firmly. "One thing you learn in the Army is when you can trust your buddies. Your life depends on it, and believe me your chit-chat friend is not to be trusted. He will get you into a lot of trouble. Finish your breakfast."

Nobody can deny that they know how to give orders, like teachers, for example. I just sat there, frozen, silent with my head almost inside of the cereal bowl. Edward's hand reached to touch my left arm, and I was shocked that he was softly smiling at me.

"Don't worry, you will find someone who's better for you. Believe me, I know. I was also in a bad relationship till I met Frank."

I could have fallen from the chair, but fortunately there were armrests on both sides. Brain connecting to ears. Those two were an item? No way, I've seen gay people. They go on parades and have lots of friends. I even got some invitations from aged guys in big cars when I was coming late at night from University. How they can mistake a student, dressed with jeans, old pullover and carrying a monstrous backpack, with a taxi boy (they work in my area), is beyond me, but they do.

"No, no, no, I think you're mistaken. Fedérico is my best pal—nothing else," I retorted quickly, nearly hyperventilating and losing all colour in the face.

The Frank-Arnie guy just snorted at me. Yeah, yeah, you are also cool, like a gorilla.

"Thank you for your company at breakfast, but I'm afraid I have delayed you for too long. Good morning, gentlemen," I said, rising from my saviour chair. No need to lose manners if you are already trying to avoid a scene.

"The Queen Victoria could have not said it better."

To hell with manners! I don't care if they are big and trained to kill. This is too much. I stopped dead in my tracks and turned around, with a killer glare, ready to give them a piece of my mind before we kill each other (or better they would clean the floor with my body), Edward was again softly smiling at me, and I could see no evil or mockery in his eyes. That disturbed me even more.

No need to say that I made it in record time, the 500 metres to the metro station. I went again to Notre Dame and from there started to walk alongside the Seine River direction Orsay. The breeze did nothing to calm me down. I was in turmoil, how could those two think that I was on their side of the game? I've said nothing that could give that impression. Maybe my voice was too soft? No, it's a normal tenor tone. Perhaps it's the fact that I'm not too tall, at 5' 6", which is good. My features were nothing out of the ordinary; big blue eyes and light brown hair, inherited from my father's side of the family, and small nose and full lips from my mother, a dimple on my chin, like all Libras have. I wear normal, plain clothes—nothing fancy—I mean I almost look like a librarian without the glasses. Maybe it was that my experience with girls was close to zero. All right, now you know my biggest secret. Not even Fefo knows about it. All the images of these disgusting guys in their cars asking for boys came rushing back to my mind. I was nothing like those boys. OK, I was not the biggest alpha male in the pack, but to be a quiet, mousy guy doesn't mean you're gay.

Okay, final test. I tried to picture in my mind the image of Fedérico and then I closed my eyes and imagined myself kissing him full in the lips. The bile rose up to my throat just by imagining his rough cheeks with a beard and his breath reeking of cigarettes or alcohol. That was definitely not a turn on. I'm not gay or ever could be. Sorry guys I'm not playing on your field.

With my new life purpose found, I started to go back to the hostel. I walked alongside the River (don't ask me if it was the right or the left as I always confuse them), just enjoying the city. Honestly, I don't know how much I walked. At some point I was in front of Les Invalides and somehow I finished in the Quartier Latin.

Despite today everything was closed, I was hoping to go tomorrow to the Louvre, if I could drag Fedérico along.

I found a metro station and carefully checked the connections to get back to the hostel. If there's something good about Paris, no matter where you are, you can get wherever you want with the subway. First, the map looks to newcomers like a big spaghetti dish, but with patience, and if you follow the desired line with your finger, you can find your way in this labyrinth.

I arrived late in the afternoon only to find Fedérico and two really nice looking girls sitting in our room. Both were tall and blond, like those models you see on TV. Both dressed casually but you could see those were expensive clothes and real jewellery, nothing like me. Even though I was tired, I put a smile on my face and politely greeted them in my school-days French.

"Oh, you must be the other Argentinean friend. How are you?" The one with shorter hair and musical voice said. I fell immediately under her spell but lucky me, I started to become red under her scrutinizing stare. That girl, let's better say woman, was like an X-ray machine, praising me without reserves. I swallowed hard.

"Very well, Madam. Thank you" Great! Now I sound like a five year old! Act matured, idiot, I chastised myself.

"I'm afraid your friend neglected to introduce us... or is it that you already forgot our names, dear?"

"I'm sorry. So much beauty makes me overlook my manners. Anne Marie (that's the tall one with short hair) Chantal (longer hair, bigger front) the baby over there is Guntram de Lisle." Fedérico introduced me.

Can you please stop teasing about my age? It's not my fault you're overgrown.

"Your last name is French, but your accent is not," Anne Marie said as a matter of fact, giving me another of her piercing looks. Oh, you're a clever one, right?

"My parents were French and I lived most of my life in Argentina," I blurted out. Excellent. I told the story of my life in one sentence. What else will I say now? Wait, I can still say age, occupation, plans for the future. Not everything is lost! And look how nicely this floor is polished.

I lifted my eyes for a second just to catch a lightning fast exchange of looks between the two girls (women) and the slight denial sign Chantal made toward me. That's mean girls, you could at least give me another five seconds before you discard me; I have some primeval male pride left in me.

Chantal gracefully stood up, shaking her head delicately in a sexy way that made me open my mouth. I swear, these French women are something out of this world. If you walk through Paris you will never see one who doesn't look interesting or like a princess.

"Bye Fedérico, see you at the train station."

Train station? No, no, no. We are supposed to go to the Louvre tomorrow. I shot an inquisitive glare toward my friend, hoping he would give me a hint. Nothing. I was totally and completely ignored as he showed both girls (women) to the door.

"Nice looking, huh? He stated after closing the door.

"Care to explain what's going on? I missed the train part tomorrow," I fired back

"Yup, we are going to Milan," he said as if he were commenting the weather report.

"We? I don't remember when I changed plans. We have a paid reservation for mid-January in Milan," I retorted, perfectly aware where we were going with this talk —he has another great idea like running all over Europe after two girls—and I should have to run after him. Not my idea of a holiday at all.

"Come on, don't be such an old lady," he whined making his best puppy eyes. Damn, that was low, but two can play too.

"What are we going to say to Mummy Dear? She planned all our schedules, and if we miss something, there would be hell on earth," ha, ha, got you! He seemed thoughtful for an entire minute. Then, the skies opened, and an idea landed on his thick head.

"You are going to continue with the schedule. After all, you like this mummies stuff around here. I, on the other hand, have an anthropological approach toward Europe." One single gesture of his hand cut my attempt to protest. "You will go on the twenty-seventh night to Venice as planned, register in the morning at the hotel for both of us and I will meet you there before January 2nd. Then, we will continue to collect museum brochures. Anyhow I don't think I'm going to be able to keep up with those two tigresses in bed for longer than that."

That was too much information! Gruesome. One night and he already had the two of them in bed? And now he was running with those two, leaving me alone. Hope he remembers to leave some money.

"What do they do for a living?" I asked, hoping the utter defeat in my voice would be not so noticeable and that his mother would not skin me alive if something might happen to her little ray of sunshine. After all, she comes from a long line of landlords who had the hobby of collecting indigenous people ears.

"They are art students."

"Are you kidding?" Those two are nearing their thirties and no way an artist could afford such pieces. "Where do they study?" I shot back as fast as I could— nothing like a good attack in warfare.

Fedérico let out a long sigh and put on his face of "time for an explanation from Big Brother to hopeless Dwarf". Great, I can't wait any longer for your wisdom.

"You see, Guntram", he started with his best grown up voice, "when you are presented with an opportunity like I was yesterday, you don't ask many questions. They look old enough to take care for themselves and think for a minute how much it would cost me in Buenos Aires a week with not one, but two hot looking Parisians girls. It's not like I'm going to marry one of them."

"Incredible, your dick directs your actions."

"As for most men; you will understand when your time comes." Has he grown a pair of ears like Yoda or what?

"Do whatever you want but don't come back crying if something goes wrong. I will continue with the trip as planned and pray that your mother doesn't call because I will not lie for you."

"Right, works for me. I'm going out for dinner".

"Right, suit yourself." Now I was pissed. Did he just hint something about my sexuality—or lack thereof? Fuck.

"Later."

"Later."

I started to rummage through my rucksack. I was upset and hungry; a bad combination for a guy. Where was that damn apple and the biscuits left from yesterday? I was fuming. And now, I was not jealous, but it felt so unfair that he was leaving me for two perfect unknown women. This was supposed to be our big adventure. Together. Like brothers.

That selfish bastard ate my apple.

Chapter 3

Next morning, he just put his things together and left. We said our goodbyes, but we were still sore from yesterday's fight. When he was leaving, he said something like "you are a man who thinks everything beforehand. Too much for my liking. Try to act some more, or you're going to spend your whole life in a cave."

That hurt me deeply. I can make decisions when the time is right. I know I take my time to do it, but wouldn't you do it also? I have no security net like the rest of you. I'm perfectly aware that I have no family, no real friends—and I can lie as much as I want to myself, but I know Fedérico will continue with his life after this trip and I with mine, we're just too different— no place to call home, just a shitty apartment, no sound finances. In one sentence: I'm free as a bird and that scares me like nothing else. Isn't it ironic? Most people complain that they're bound to something, and here I'm desperately looking for something/someone to form any kind of attachments, but so afraid to lose everything again.

However, life is too short to depress myself. I still have two more days in Paris, all to myself. Today, I will visit the Quai d'Orsay Museum and the Army Museum. I can't think about going to the Louvre, I'm still too worked up. I had breakfast, not minding at all the others. I emptied my tray, left it in its place and defied the cold winter morning toward the metro. This jacket, it's not so "winter proof" as the tag claims.

Well, Diary, Les Invalides is an overwhelming place. It makes you feel small. I was interested in watching the weapons' collections. After all, I've never seen the real things in "live" so to speak. In the interior yard was the artillery; magnificent and terrifying in their deadly beauty. I tried to stay as long as possible there, but the dying sun made me direct my footsteps toward the small entrance that led to a staircase up to the first level, where the collections were stored. I climbed up, opened and closed the wooden door as softly as I could. Believe me, you don't want to wake up the French guard who's there. They can throw really dirty glares at you. Nobody was there and that should not have been a surprise because in the entire hour I've been here, I only saw two or three persons going to Napoleon's Tomb.

I directed my gaze through the room and there, on the other side, was a small half open door, revealing a wooden and battered desk. One very old man was there. Better say something if I don't want to give him a heart attack when he realises he has a visitor. I walked toward him, making the floor creak a little more than necessary and said softly *"Bonsoir, Monsieur"*.

"Billet, s'il vous plait," was his answer. While I was fumbling with the pockets of my jacket, I glimpsed for a second a really large man inside of the room. He was bigger than the American soldier, maybe over six feet tall? Is it possible to be so tall? I couldn't see his face, since he turned his back to me on purpose. Where is the famous French Politeness? My hand finally found the all access paper, and I showed it to the old man.

He immediately started the drill for wild tourists; *"Il est interdit de..."* Naturally, I shut my ears trying to look interested, a survival skill I picked in my school days. When he was finished and clearly reminded me that he was closing at five o'clock sharp, I started to look at the incredible muskets and passing through several rooms and showcases. I don't know why but I couldn't help feeling this prickling sensation on the back of my neck of being watched which was ridiculous because I heard nobody else coming and the old guy should be making a tea for himself.

Way to go Guntram, apart from being neurotic, now you can add paranoia to you own private list of virtues. I sat in the last room trying to watch a documentary on World War II, but this sensation was becoming harder and harder to ignore. True or not, it made me nervous. At quarter to five I had enough and went straightforward for the door. Not even bothering to say *"Au revoir et merci,"* I pulled the heavy thing.

"Monsieur, un moment s'il vous plaît. J'aurais bessoin des quelques renseigments pour une enquête. Vôtre nom, prénom et lieu de naissance."

Honestly, I found this an odd thing to ask for and for a second I thought to give it all wrong but, alas, he had the pen and the folder already opened for me, and he looked like one of these grandfathers you can't say no to. I wrote down all what he asked.

"Vous êtes français?" He asked me with a puzzled look on his face.

"Partly, I'm American too. My father was French, but this is the first time I'm in France. I was born in New York, but I live in Argentina. I hardly use my French passport, since I butcher your language every time I speak it."

"Then your blood is French. The language can be learned. You are certainly not an American. Thibaudet *à vôtre service,"* he said with a small bow of the head and closed the door fast. Speaking of mood swings!

I decided to walk toward the Eiffel Tower, cross the Seine, direction the Arc de Triomph and later see Champs Elysèes by night. The night was cold, but the lights in the street gave it a magical air. Somehow, I still had this feeling of someone watching me, and it didn't disappear till I reached the hostel.

Next day, I spent the whole day in the Louvre, but I had an increasing sense of being watched. I didn't get rid of it until I took the night train to Venice.

So Diary this is how you ended up with me. I plan, and plan is the key word here, to write a bit every evening, mostly to organise my thoughts and keep a memory of this trip. Who knows when I would be able to come back to Europe again.

* * *

Venice

Night trains are not the best idea. I mean the train in and of itself was modern and comfortable and incredibly on time. It's very difficult to sleep in those seats or *couchettes*, it's noisy and the train stops everywhere. Nevertheless, the morning view of the train crossing the lagoon toward Venice was wonderful and made the trip worthy.

Coming out of the railway station was another thing. I was certainly not prepared to see boats instead of buses waiting for the people. I made the queue and bought a ticket toward the Rialto Bridge. Line 1, here I go.

* * *

I left the hostel after leaving my rucksack there. Another thing for the traveler; *Palazzo* does not mean palace in Italian; it's building as I discovered this morning when I arrived at our Palazzo/Hostel from the XVII century. The part where you get off from the *vaporetto* in the Rialto Stop is true. Continuing straight direction San Polo, also true. Passing the Fish Market, more or less true (it's hidden), but if you follow the street up to its end, you get there. I had to swallow when I saw it. Hard. I counted up to ten and rang the bell because with the prices I've seen so far, at least this was a roof.

I entered into what used to be a foyer a long time ago. In front of me there was a stairwell (not to heaven really). The lights and the painting in the walls were missing, and why on earth were those wooden sticks laying there? I tread carefully, not really wanting to be hit by the scorched ceiling and climbed up the stairs.

The host was a funny looking man, all smiles. He took my passport and mumbled something like *americano*. I kept a straight face while he was making the check in. With all the dignity I could gather, I informed him that my friend would arrive in the next days.

He rose an eyebrow and almost chuckling said "Blonde or brunette?"

"Blonde and two," I replied, realizing within the moment that Federico's stocks had just sky-rocketed.

"Not coming back," he assured me with the same certainty that the sun rises every morning. "Do you want to go to the Peggy Guggenheim Museum?"

"Sorry?"

"The Museum all Americans visit here," he clarified for the tourist. "Are you not American, uh?"

"I was hoping to go to San Marco or the Academia." Why is he looking at me, as if I've grown a horn on the head. Doesn't he know his own cities main attractions?

"You are the first one to ask for that in a long time."

"San Marco, Mosaics, *Palazzo Ducale, Piazza, Duomo*?" Maybe he didn't understand me.

Chapter 4

Another thing I learned here is, that following directions is a relative matter. Straight is not always straight and left and right can be misleading. I have no idea how to move in a mediaeval city, with channels everywhere on top! Please give me back my nice square Renaissance towns, with long avenues, back home. Fortunately, I remembered the first rule of tourism; follow the masses. In their infinite wisdom, they know where the food and the fun is.

After several turns, up to the point of getting dizzy, I got to main square. There it was: the Cathedral, the Palazzo Ducale, the Tower and the Lion. I had enough time to make a visit to the Palace because the idea was to meet Fedérico at 4 p.m. somewhere in the square and continue from there.

When I left the palace, the sun was shining over the square. I still had some free time left before 4:00, but it wasn't enough to do something else like visiting the Cathedral. I located a nice spot on a bench, sunny, and after the extremely cold cellars and prison from the Venetian Dukes, any source of heat was more than welcome. I went straightforward to it, evading the bird food sellers for the hundreds of doves that were pestering the place. I sat and took out of my backpack a very cheap paperback copy of *Le Rouge et le Noir,* I bought some time ago. If you don't learn French with Stendhal, then you're a hopeless case.

I tried to read but the birds in Venice are real bullies. I mean; they are bigger than normal doves, have an attitude and are convinced that tourists are supposed to feed them as much as they want. If you refuse, they bring more friends in and start to peck at your shoes. Forget about shouting or stamping your foot on the ground— they're unimpressed.

After a while of our happy moment together, reading the same sentence for like ten times, doves and me, I realised a few things. One: the doves had given up and two: the sun was away. Well, the sun was blocked to be precise, by a huge man; big, like 6'2", dark coat, short hair and with a love for his gym.

"Is Julien out of his father's house?" he asked in English with a baritone voice which sent shivers through my spine.

"Not yet," I whispered. He just made the gesture to sit beside me and I was clever enough as to move as fast as possible, or otherwise he would have crushed me. Are Europeans not supposed to be sophisticated and polite?

"Stendhal was a good diplomat, but I prefer Lampedussa's view on the subject. Attaining power is relatively easy. To keep it is the hardest thing," he stated looking directly into my eyes. For a second, I felt like I was seven again and forgot to study for the test. I gulped and quickly recovered myself; I didn't want a literature or politics lecture! OK, let's make a stupid remark, so he gets the hint and disappears. Didn't your mother tell you not to speak with strangers? Probably not, with your gorilla size, strangers go elsewhere.

"Really? I thought it was an adventure novel. I have the comic," I replied with my best dork face. Was that a flash of anger that quickly passed through his eyes? Now it's working.

"Already degraded to comic?" He softly said with that polite tone that teachers use before starting to shout. He's going to be a tough one. Next level of pissing people off; before I could open my mouth to make the second great phrase, his piercing stare abruptly stopped me. Without the blinding sun, I now had a clear view of his face. Although it was a handsome one, the aura of power and danger around him increased my nervousness of him. My first impression was that he the result of a coupling between a lion and a cobra. His features were strong, aristocratic and masculine, steely blue eyes like the stormy sky, brown hair, around his forties, but it was hard to tell and an unmistakably air of superiority. He sat on that miserable bench like on a throne, and I was immediately correcting my slouched but comfortable posture.

"Konrad von Lintorff," he introduced himself extending his hand toward me. I shook it without realising what I was doing and automatically replied, "Guntram de Lisle". A second later I was chastising myself; not only I had revealed my name to a perfect stranger, but I have given him another topic; "what a strange name you have". My parents must have been high when they chose it.

"Do you take your Christian name after the King or the Opera?"

"I don't know," I admitted dumbfounded. Right, excellent Guntram. Escaping from the Literature class to the History one. Is there any willing wall who would let me hit my head against it?

"It's an old Frankish name, but you don't have a French accent when you speak English," he stated. Why does everybody immediately assume I'm French? I don't deny my roots, but I'm much closer to Argentina than to France or the United States.

"I was born in New York but lived most of my life in Buenos Aires. My father was French and my mother partly German, I think, I'm not sure," I dutifully repeated under his scrutinizing eyes. Or was it my grandmother? Yes, it was her. My mother was French.

"Pumpkin, there you are!" Somebody yelled at the top of his lungs. There was this fine example of the Gaucho race and for once, and only this time, I was happy to hear his embarrassing name calling.

"Hi there, I'm glad you could understand the map and make it," I retorted and gave Fefo a hug.

"You're so hilarious. You should start an acting career," was his reply, patting my back with more strength than necessary. "I came to tell you I have business elsewhere and can't see you till tomorrow. Were you already at the cave? Creepy. My mother hates us, pumpkin."

I'm slow. I need some time to process and by the look of the whole story, it seems I was brushed away, all over again.

"I could come," I said hopefully, knowing how pathetic I sounded, like the smallest brother left behind.

"Better not. It's for grown ups," he whispered. "You could stay with your friend here... Mister?" he shouted clearly and loudly. I think the winged lion on top of that tower didn't hear you well.

Do you dare to call yourself my brother, my friend? You threw me into the snakes' pit without a second thought! Tomorrow I'm killing you because now it would be bloody and messy.

"Konrad, *Herzog* von Lintorff," he curtly said, looking not thrilled and not shaking hands at all.

"Fedérico Martiarena Alvear. How do you do?"

Awkward moment. The German was not so loquacious as my first impression, and the soft whistle of Fefo after hearing he was a Duke was not helping at all. He just made a short movement with the head, giving him a blank stare.

"I have to run. Take care and don't get into trouble." With that, he sprinted away, leaving me at the mercy of killer doves and a stony German. Time to make an exit.

I turned around to face him. I had to lift my head, since my great 5'6" allowed me to reach, with lots of luck, his shoulder, and opened my mouth to say the usual goodbye.

"Do you want to visit the Correr Museum?"

Yeah, but not with you. "I don't want to take more of your time." That should do. Aristocrats are touchy if you believe novels.

"I insist."

Nope, does not work. Let's try tactic number two. Play the imbecile. Just when I was going to elaborate something with McDonald's...

"Rest assured I will enjoy our time together," he cut me before I could say something else, giving me a very small smile while his eyes lit a gentle light. "Besides, your friend has just appointed me your guardian." He was clearly amused with the task. "I hope you don't bite," he chuckled as I found the situation utterly absurd.

We entered inside of the big building and I went to the ticket office, but he held me strongly by the arm.

"There is no need for that. I'm one of the patrons."

Wow. He's truly loaded.

"Come. I'll show you the map room and the coin collection. Later we can see the paintings."

I was in awe when I saw the rich room, full with showcases and maps. It was the first time I saw something like that. I slowly walked around, taking in every little detail of the pages and books laying in display. At some point, I remembered my companion and lifted up my gaze to find him intensely looking in my direction. I don't know why I blushed and immediately fixed my eyes on the shelves.

A middle aged man in a dark blue suit approached us and whispered something in his ear. "Send a curator here," he curtly ordered, his lips drawing a thin line. It was the first time I saw a museum clerk run fast, with only one look from him, radiating displeasure, I totally sympathized with the poor man. I guess the Duke is used to be obeyed and his wrath must be something to be seen.

"I'm afraid the Director needs to have a word with me."

"Oh, thank you very much for the visit; it's been a honour to meet you, Duke." (Well, protocol lessons were not a total waste of time).

"Please call me Konrad. Someone will accompany you and hopefully I can rejoin you for the painting rooms."

"I don't want to be a nuisance, sir," I said. Who knows? Maybe I can escape now.

"Konrad, and, no, it will be an insult to the Venetians if you don't allow them to show you their glorious past," he shot back at me, leaving no place for discussion.

Perhaps in Europe aristocrats are not so out of office as I used to believe. His cold, imposing stare makes our school principal look like a little mouse.

A really kind old lady was picking me up and started the tour. I was afraid I'd say something silly or out of place, but if I did, she was nice as not to show it. She led me through the rooms and bore with me for two hours. Honestly, I don't know because time flew by. We waited for fifteen minutes at the entrance of the painting rooms, but our own German didn't make an appearance. She nervously told me to continue with her, and I could feel that she was not happy disobeying the order.

I was mesmerized by an icon, I think that is the word, depicting the Tree of Life. I had no idea what it was, but it was beautiful with those vibrant colours and full of energy.

"Do you like it, Guntram?" Someone whispered in my right ear, making me jump out of my bones. I tried to regain my composure.

"Yes, indeed," I looked around to see that my guide had vanished into the thin air.

"Why do you like it?" The German asked.

"I don't know much about art. It intrigues me."

"But there must be a reason for you to like it," he pressed. Yes, he does not take "no" for an answer. Time to embarrass myself, except this time I didn't want to look like the ignorant country boy I already look like.

"The figures are alive," I blurted out, expecting a laugh.

"True. That is the essence of art," he said softly, giving me a comforting look.

"I realise now how ignorant I am."

"That's a good start," silence engulfed us. I tried to break the tension by looking somewhere else, but I couldn't shake the feeling of his eyes on my back. It was nerve-raking. We are in a Museum! Can't you find something else to do? I looked through the window at the column and strangely the doves flying around like a whirlwind gave me a sense of peace. The Piazza was losing the frenetic river of tourists and slowly settling down. The waiters at the Florian Café made a huge contrast to the imposed calm of the sunset, madly running to remove the outside tables and get rid of the last coffee clients as they prepared the inside tables for dinner.

"I think it's enough for today. Let's have something to eat," he said to me, taking me out of my reverie and pulling me by the arm, as if I were a rag doll with a gentle but firm grip; time to reaffirm my grounds in a polite way, sort of.

"Please, I don't want to impose myself any further," I said putting some emphasis on the "I don't want" part; perhaps he now gets the message.

"Nonsense," was his eloquent answer as he quickly pulled me toward the stairway exit, and look now, we were on the street! Civility was not really working at all with this meddling giant!

"It's unfortunate that my house is not open yet, and taking someone so young as you to a hotel would be totally inappropriate," he said as matter of fact, as he led me with ease through the street maze and not falling miserably into dead ends like I do. Excuse me? In which century does he live? Has nobody told him that nowadays is okay to go to hotel restaurants and that there is no shame in sitting in the parterre of theatres? I honestly tried to slow him down by dragging my feet, but a sharp look from him made me change my mind. All right, you win, only because I'm hungry; the

25

chances that I find Fefo and go to dine at our favourite fast food chain are truly slim and finally I'm totally fed up with said food.

We stopped at a small door and two small windows with no visible sign at all —an opium smoking room perhaps? No, no such luck. Nothing remotely exciting ever happens to me!

We entered into a warm and lavishly furnished room. I looked toward the dining room and failed to notice that he had already taken my jacket away. A girl with a dark uniform discreetly appeared behind us and took our coats. I turned around and saw that he was dressed in a grey breasted suit with a matching tie and black handmade shoes. Everything looked expensive and exclusive. I couldn't help to feel ashamed of my plain blue jeans and brown sweater. A waiter led us to a small table in the back part of the room. He took the seat against the wall in a way so that the entire restaurant fitted into his view field.

A menu landed in my hands, and I opened it only to see it was written in German. Of all places in Italy have I ended in "Little Germany"?

"The usual," he said and in less than a millisecond, I lost my menu. "Are you allowed to drink?" he asked me.

"I'm not sure. I will be twenty next October," was my reply, hoping I would get some wine. Preferably, one of those real Italian Chianti I've read so much about.

"Mineral water, Carlo."

Without any preamble, he started to elaborate on the history of Venice. Strangely, his words, softly intoned, his German accent or the precision of his sentences, never repeating a concept, had a hypnotic effect on me. The warmth of the room also relaxed me, and I started to feel less afraid of his unmistakable dangerous aura around him. After a few minutes, I started to look discreetly around and I saw that at the next table, two giants with dark suits were sitting. It struck me that, even if we were in a restaurant, they only had coffee and water. They also looked oddly familiar, but I couldn't place their faces.

"My bodyguards. You saw them at the Museum. The one on the left is Hendrick and the other is Ferdinand," I opened my eyes and most certainly gaped. I didn't know if I was surprised for the fact that he needed protection with his size and short temper (almost pitied the poor soul who would try to mug him), or because he considered it necessary to have them. "I own several banks and companies," was the following explanation.

"I see," was my insightful answer. With that he considered "twenty questions" season open, and I was going to be the main game piece.

"Do you live with your parents in Buenos Aires?"

"My parents died when I was a child," I slowly said finding a new interest in the delicate porcelain dish, expecting he would proceed to the next level. It's such a painful matter that I simply don't want to speak about and much less with a total stranger.

"How did they die?" European sophistication is overvalued, believe me. Did nobody tell you that a proper talk with strangers revolves around the weather and nothing more?

"I would prefer to switch the topic if you don't mind. It's something I don't normally speak about".

"Did you lose them recently?"

26

Forget it Guntram. He's an idiot who can't take a hint. Now the mercury is officially at the top.

"If it's so important for you to know, no. My mother died in childbirth, so I have no recollection of her and my father decided to jump from a window when I was seven. Since then and till I turned eighteen, I lived in a private school in Buenos Aires. Happy now?" I said screeching my teeth while I was throwing daggers with my eyes. Medusa is a kind girl compared to me.

"Why did he kill himself?" He pressed on, his gaze intensively fixed on me. You don't know when to stop, do you? What do you want? Should I tell you that my father blamed me for my mother's dead? That I loathed him for not being brave enough as to stay with me? That I secretly envied him because he had the guts to jump while I'm still around?

"Honestly I don't know. I was in school at the time he died in Paris. No suicide note. He left all his affairs in order before doing it. He even named a solicitor as my guardian and established a trust fund to pay for my education," I painfully articulated, my throat suddenly dry.

"I'm sorry for your loss," he said, gently taking my hand and caressing my knuckles in a soothing way. I continued to stare at my dish, the food losing all its glamour. I fished the water cup and took several sips to calm myself down.

"What do you do for a living?"

That's more like it—a safe topic. "I work as a waiter and go to the public University at night. I finished the introductory course for Economics and Social Work. Fortunately, in Argentina you don't have to pay for a career, and with my salary, I can afford a small flat in the area."

"It's hard these days to find someone so young and mature who can support himself and believes in progressing in life."

Please, please, I'm getting all flushed. Stop with the praising... or better not, don't get much of it anyhow. I resumed my attack on the dish. Whatever it is, tastes fantastic.

"Why are you studying Social Work? It's not a popular choice of career."

"Since I was fourteen, the priest in the school used to take all the class to help people in one of the slums. He said we needed to have contact with reality and be more humble. I liked the people and they made a great impression on me and I still go on weekends, to help with the kitchen and teach children to read. Honestly, I don't want to think what I'm going to find there when I get back with all this political turmoil," I answered happily. See? It's not so hard to have a chit chat with me.

I only received silence as an answer. For a moment, he seemed to be deep in his thoughts. I took a good look at his face. High cheekbones, strong nose, full lips, said blue eyes that now seemed much darker, very thin lines around them. His eyes are really something with those long eyelashes to make them look bigger. He certainly looks handsome and manly, all women must drool over him. Wait a minute! From where did that come from? I'm not into men! I'm straight and guys are not supposed to look beautiful. I blushed a second time, and he caught me this time completely unaware.

"What is your relationship with that boy (deep disgust pouring from his voice at that word), that was on the Piazza?

"Fedérico? We came together to Europe. We have a special friendship. We fool around since I was thirteen," was my explanation. One of his men smashed his coffee cup rather strongly against the dish staring at me, visibly shocked. Why does Konrad look like a volcano about to explode? In a flash his hot fury became a cold anger, visibly radiating from himself. Careful boy, it's real china and your boss would not be happy if you break it, and he has to pay for it. Anyhow, labour relations are not my problem, so I elaborated further. "We shared a bedroom in the school and, even if it took some time to connect, we became best buddies, and he's always fooling around. It might be shocking for strangers at the beginning, but it's very common there. I admit he can embarrass me sometimes, but I'm used to it. Teachers were also punishing us for that, but what else can you do in a boarding school?"

"I'm not surprised about that. It's criminal with someone like yourself, considering you were thirteen, and he looks much older," he answered, his lips pressed together in an almost invisible line, his voice deep with the German accent more noticeable than ever. I looked around and his bodyguards were also looking completely pissed off. It's not my fault that you Germans are such serious people!

"There is nothing to be ashamed of. Once, he called me Pigeon in front of his mother and that was certainly embarrassing. We are always joking around, I know, I should grow up, but I'm still nineteen. He was quite wild in the classroom. Once, he released a pig in the library," I defended myself, now obfuscated that the three of them were accusingly looking at me, with their German air of superiority. "Did you not play the fool in school-days? Fooling around," I clarified for these happiness-haters.

The two bodyguards are human after all! They were chuckling almost to the point of tears. That greased pig was something incredible. Pity we lost our going out rights for two months after it and had to peel a lot of potatoes for a long week.

"Did you mean "to banter"?" Was his question, as he threw an assassin's side glance at his men. They reverted in less than a second to their usually grouchy personalities.

"Yes, that's right. I'm sorry if you heard his name calling. He tends to do that a lot."

"English is not your first language, I see."

"Not really. I think mostly in Spanish."

"To fool around refers to engage in casual sex. You fool around with a prostitute," he explained with his best tone for little children.

I needed a black hole to jump in. A big one that allows no matter to escape from its guts. I turned violently red and wanted to die in shame. Why teachers teach you how to read Shakespeare, but leave out of the lesson with the really important words?

"I'd better order dessert before you take permanent residence under the table," he said visibly amused at my reaction.

Can he read my mind? Probably not. I must look totally mortified. Diabolically, the thought of my whole class "fooling around" crossed my mind, and it's really funny. Germans must be thinking that we had quite a party going on! Yuk, Me and Fefo!

"You probably should buy a copy of American Psycho to enlarge your English vocabulary," his tone was this time playful.

"We read *The Catcher in the Rye* for that matter. Maybe I should update myself," I answered while doing my best to recover from one of the biggest and most shameful moments of my life so far. I was saved by the army of waiters who took the dishes away and cleaned the table. The following dessert trolley looked really good and there, partly hidden was an apple cake portion, with almonds, exactly as I like. I haven't seen one of those in years—since I was six or seven! Funny the things we remember.

I asked for it and while it was served, I lifted my sight in his direction to catch his gaze intensely fixed upon me. I paused in my attack on the cake, secretly annoyed they had forgotten to sprinkle some cinnamon on it. I know it's not usual in this type of desserts, but that was a thing I had in common with my father; cinnamon on everything with apples.

"Something wrong?"

"Oh, it's very childish. I wonder if they had some cinnamon, but probably the chef would kill me for ruining his creation.

"We could ask for some *Zimt*," his gaze was clouded for a moment as he fixed it on my eyes, like if he were trying to absorb me. He swallowed hard.

"Please, it's not necessary. It just came to my memory that this cake is very similar to what my father and I used to eat on weekends. He would sprinkle cinnamon more than is humanly healthy, and it's a habit I took from him," was my amused reply.

The rest of the dinner was in relative peace. He didn't seem interested in engaging in further conversation, and I could understand him. Who would want to spend more than the minimum required time with a teenager? Coffee was served as he was so deep in his reflections, that I was starting to fidget a little in my chair. He realised it.

"I think your bedtime is past due. I'll take you to your hotel."

"That's hardly necessary. If you would be so kind as to direct me to the Rialto, I can find my way from there."

"I'm afraid you will fall deep into a canal. It's not safe for someone so young to wander these streets alone; walking would be good."

Remember I told you he has a particular way of letting you know he doesn't take no for an answer? He must have a lot of problems with rejection. Anyhow, we started to walk back to my luxurious hotel with the two goons in tow, at a discreet distance. The night was really cold now, and I put my hands in my pockets.

"Don't do that. It's unbecoming," he frowned, his voice cold, sending shivers through my spine. I hastily took them out.

"I'm cold." My voice was sounding like a five year old baby. No better, think of a three year old. He approached me, his walking oddly reminding me of a huge predator, a wolf. Silently, he took my hands into his leather gloved ones and drew them into his lips. Not kissing them, mind you! I was utterly astonished by his strange, out of place behaviour, but I didn't feel insulted or want to start a fight. My heart began to hammer quickly, but I remembered that my father used to do the same when I was running a fever and this man could be his age for what I knew. With my new found mantra "it's like with papa," I disentangled my fingers from his hands.

He just stared directly into my eyes, his boring holes into mine. I gulped nervously as he silently put his own gloves out, and effortlessly he clasped one of my hands and slipped the glove in, caressing slowly my fingers at the same time. I found his movement utterly erotic and became absolutely restless fidgeting against his hold.

"It's not a good idea to be in an European winter without gloves," he released

29

me. Where are his bodyguards? Is it my imagination or have they vanished? Well, guys, your boss is about to get in trouble, and you're not here—nasty you. This is definitely not fatherly. Time to go home... to the hotel or wherever takes me away from here!

I stood there, frozen in my place from the shock. "I can't take them. You will be cold instead of me," was my slurred reply, slowly articulated.

He shrugged as if nothing had happened and resumed his walking to the hotel. Maybe I misunderstood everything. You know, these Europeans noblemen are more free than we, peasants from the Pampas. I admit that I'm a bit obsessed with the sex thing. Not having (none, in fact), much makes you see signs where there are none. It's the first symptom of sex deprivation, according to Fefo. So lost in my thoughts I was, that I nearly toppled on him when we arrived at my castle.

"So, I guess it's goodbye. Thank you for the dinner..."

"Have you been to San Marco?"

Sorry? No, I wasn't but if this was another trick to glue himself to me again, he had it coming otherwise. "I'm going there tomorrow or the day after with some friends." Yeah Fefo, it's culture time for you! I was secretly pleased I wasn't totally lying and getting rid of him at the same time.

"Excellent. Tomorrow I can take you to Torcello to see the mosaics in the Church. They're fantastic, more meaningful than those of San Marco. Sadly, they're away from the tourists and not well known."

How did I get into this mess? Beat me if I know, right into the hole again. Time to think fast and make an excuse because he's driving me more and more mad with his grandeur airs and inappropriate touches and I don't care if they're Europeans! I breathed deeply and prepared my answer.

"Tomorrow at ten o'clock. Where we met. Good night" A firm and fast hand shake, like men do, and he just turned his back to me and walked away, not even waiting for my answer! Bloody hell. You can wait sitting. I can also be rude, you know.

Furious, I went to bed. As usual, Fefo was not there. His rucksack was comfortably resting on top of mine. Great! Now my T-shirts are crumpled!

Chapter 5

December 29th , 2001

Breakfast, against my original impression of the place, was very good. Not fancy, but a lot to eat, and for a guy that is important—essential. So there I was happily munching on toast when the owner, Marcello, burst into the room with, "There you are. Your Argentinean friend left a message. You're supposed to meet him in San Marco's square this morning at ten. He has a nice girl for you!" It's not necessary to wink, you know. I got the idea. I'm slow, but not totally retarded.

The gods of tourism hate me. If I don't show up, he will complain till the end of days that I abandoned him in a foreign country... poor baby! My toast tasted now dry and bitter. I reassured myself with the thought that San Marco is big and full of people. I should be able to evade the German pest and meet Fefo. Perhaps, I misunderstood what transpired last night. It was dark, he had wine, I was cold, I don't know the customs here and finally who would be so crazy as to take an interest in me? A rich guy like him could have remotely no interest in a poor thing like me. I have no cultural background, no money nor style. I should get no hopes... *What?* I'm totally insane. I'm thinking like a woman. He's a man! I swear there's something in the water.

Disgusted beyond words with myself, I picked up my jacket and backpack. If he gets romantic again he will get it full in the face, was my firm determination. 'Wouldn't you like it, uh?' my meddling little inner voice said. "Are you not supposed to tell the right path?" I chided it.

I briskly walked through the streets. Merchants, move away because this tourist is upset and penniless. I crossed the Rialto Bridge without looking at the myriad of glass things chaotically piled up. I found the sign to redirect me to San Marco. As expected the Piazza was full with people and bully doves, terrifying innocent tourists. Could Fefo not be a little bit more specific? This crowd was starting to give me a headache.

Somebody pinched my backside. Yes, backside as in ass. I turned around like a fury ready to give a punch to the pervert.

"You're slow, eh. I bet I could do it twice in a row."

"Fedérico, I swear you're an asshole."

"Ouch... woke up sore because I was not there to hold you, baby?" My dearest friend mocked me. This was not the moment to taunt me.

Yes, it was not the moment because I saw, from the corner of my eye, a very tall German, with a dark coat, standing beside me and most probably hearing my idiotic friend saying something like "don't be so mad at me. I know you need a strong man by your side. I will not leave you alone ever again," I don't remember it too well because I was too furious. Great, even the Japanese tourists understand Spanish and believe they're about to see another proof of the Western Decadence. Who knows, maybe they even get nice pictures to take home!

I threw a side glance and I didn't need to be a genius to realise, that as mentioned-above German was furious in a composed, calm, mature and more dangerous way than I'd ever be. His face showed no emotion but his eyes were something else. I suppose he doesn't like to be caught in the middle of a cheap comedy too.

"Would just you shut up? I'm sick of your foolishness," I yelled at him switching to English. He stopped and I thought for a minute that I could be imposing.

"Jeez, you have a bad morning," he shrugged. "Anyway, I came to tell you that we're finished, my love," he chuckled this time, dazzling us with his English skills.

"Great, I'm impressed. Your wits are greater with each passing day." My voice was sharp and icy.

"Really bad today. However, I'll go with the girls tonight to a party and we'll head up for New Year in Rome. You can't come, it's for people older than twenty-one. It's for grown up people."

I'm totally pissed off. Truly. He throws me out me? *Pendejo*.

"Don't worry. You could always find someone older to look after you, who would be more than happy to support you and visit mausoleums. Honestly, we are not exactly the best buddies for this trip," he stated, this time, completely serious.

What did he say exactly? I really hope it's not what I think. I felt a cold fury descending upon me. Not the kind that makes you yell, but the one that makes you gut you enemy and smile at it.

"I have no worries. I only hope that I don't have to drag your ass out of a European jail. I will stick to the original plan. Feel free to join me whenever your whores are through with you," I said, turning my back on him and grabbing my backpack not even bothering to wait for an answer, running the stony German over.

Still agitated I sat on the opposite corner of the square. For once the doves did not come, perhaps the fact that I nearly kicked one was a good move. I was too busy fuming when I felt someone sitting beside me.

"It's hard when you realise friends are not up to your expectations," he told me softly.

"I never expected he would tell me something like this. We had fights, clearly, but I don't understand why is he so mean to me," I slowly articulated. "We were best friends in school. I covered him more times than I can count."

"Are you certain that he was really a good friend? Loneliness can make us see things that in fact are not there."

I looked at him totally perplexed. With one single phrase, that man, saw through me to my core; my biggest fear. I'm not the best when it comes to making friends. I have no real enemies but on the other hand my only friend thinks I'm retarded and never misses the opportunity to remind me how poor I am. I've known deep down that Fedérico's friendship at school had something more to do with having his homework done than a real appreciation for me.

"I've seen his type many times. Young, rich, arrogant, expecting the world to bend to their will. No real morals behind."

"That he's rich, I have no doubts, but to accuse him of low morals is somewhat extreme."

"Perhaps you should reconsider where you place your loyalties. Respect and truth are essential in any kind of relationship, no matter if it's for business, friendship or love. Forgive me for saying so, but I consider you allow too much informality in this friendship," he said with an acid tone.

"I think I don't follow you completely. Friends are supposed to be trusted, therefore we can be informal. Besides, we're in our twenties. We banter, go to rock concerts and make foolish things."

"I beg to differ. You trust each other, but it does not mean that one can permanently poke at the other. It wears the friendship out, because the person finally believes that the other is no better than the joke perpetrated."

Even if his talk seemed like it came out of the XIX century, he was right. Fefo never took me very seriously, perhaps because I was younger. I sat gloomy, staring at the Piazza's shinning tones, the cathedral's domes, almost blinding me with their glare. I kept silent.

"Nevertheless a quarrel between young people is not so permanent as it is among older persons like myself. Young ones forgive easily. Come, if I see correctly we had an appointment this morning before it was so rudely interrupted."

"Appointment," he said, not "date," I clarified for my own sake. The perspective of sitting the whole day depressed or worse, wandering around the streets like a stray dog, was not an appealing one. Yeah, I felt lost. He had just sounded so normal and sensible, that it was almost ridiculous to think that he wasn't a normal fellow. Guys go all the time on fishing trips and nobody thinks wrong, and refusing him would not help at all considering:

1. His tendency to ignore anything against his wishes.
2. His ability to get his way.
3. Even if I could get rid of him, I still would have to look for something else to do. I stood up, very sure of my decision.

"All right, let's go now."

He started to walk with long strides toward the cathedral with me almost running behind. Passed by the *vaporetto* stops and stopped in front of the pier of the Danieli Hotel, "a hotel around San Marco" were his words. There was a ship, well a small yacht would be more appropriate. I know nothing about these things, with three people inside. Two clearly were the bodyguards and the other must be the driver. He jumped in easily as I stood there hesitating; does he always travel with a full army?

"Guntram, come," he said in an imperial tone. I complied. As I was preparing myself to make the small jump into the boat, he pulled me by the arm with ease, and slightly moving his head, indicated me where I was supposed to sit, and as expected, he placed himself next to me over the seat/bench located on the back.

We left the city behind, my pleasure and excitement soaring at the beauty of the lagoon. It was majestic, and with a sense of aloofness, we passed by Murano, full with the water buses and people hurrying to see the artisans.

The chirping of a mobile phone pulled me out of my reverie. One of the big guys quickly pulled it out of his coat and answered it in German as he looked sheepishly at Konrad. He made a gesture to his boss as if he wanted to take it.

"No calls today," was the icy answer. He lifted one eyebrow, a silent message of "don't mess around".

"*Entschuldigung. Zürich.*" Now I believe he was upset as he stood up, took the phone and went straight into the lower part of the ship.

The two mountains in human form advanced toward me and sat one on each side of me. Take it easy fellows, I'm not going to steal the flag! Both looked at me with an expression that would have made an executioner jealous. I don't know if it was the need to breathe now being compressed by the two of them, but I couldn't take more of their silence and stares.

"Do you see monkeys on my face?"

"No. Only one," mountain number one said. Is this the world famous German sense of humour? Can't wait to get another example!

"Don't be so restless boy," mountain number two smirked. "We wanted to fool around a little with you."

"I see you already had your tea time together, girls," I hate completely to be reminded of a stupid mistake. They burst into laughter.

"Pay me," the second mountain snorted, truly satisfied with himself. "I was right. He has a lot of spirit despite his size. Like a small *Dachs*."

"It's really not my fault that you come from the land of giants and eat anabolic meat," I grunted. Are you not supposed to be quiet and look like trained assassins?

"We were not trying to offend you, just testing. What is the English word for *Dachs*...? Badger? They're all teeth and bite hard; very difficult to hunt them down."

Me? Bite? Please! You're very wrong, but better don't tell them so they respect me a little.

"This morning, Heindrik was telling us that you looked like an adorable child with your little orphan Annie story, but I said the Duke would never waste his time with a doll boy or fall for it. We bet who was right and I won," mountain number two told me, with a satisfied grin plastered all over his big face.

"I'm not a wimp and I don't have to give an explanation of my past life to you two. I couldn't care less if you believe it or not," I said now incensed. "Finally, I don't understand why are you so interested in me, when your job is to take care of your boss."

"Exactly. For a minute I thought I would lose my €10 since your story was true, but luckily for me you have some character."

"Have you checked my background? Are you out of your mind?"

"The Duke is an important and wealthy person. We can't risk some punk coming out of thin air to get in the middle to cause havoc," mountain number one interfered with a disgusted look in his eyes. "Don't look so shocked. It's standard procedure. Be glad everything you said is true. The Duke would have not been pleased if you would have lied to him," his tone was dry.

I glared at them, but they didn't seem to be impressed. "You are blowing everything out of proportion. He's just showing me a Church and nothing else. Is being paranoid in your job description?"

"We just follow orders."

Orders? As if they come from The Supreme Boss? That's not reassuring at all. Was he checking my background and why on earth would he do that? As long as I see, we visit the mosaics and then he goes back to his bank and I to Rome. I couldn't avoid feeling upset at the idea that those gorillas assumed I was some kind of gold digger trying to catch their precious boss.

Fuck! If they think that, it means said boss likes to play on the other street! I rose my horrified sight to them, recognition clear in my eyes, a "no, no" choking in my throat.

"It's not what you're thinking," I slurred so fast that even I could not understand myself.

Both smiled in a smug manner. Mountain number two, after throwing a quick glance toward the inside cabin, cleared his throat. "You're not his usual type of girl or boy, but on the other hand, they don't last more than one night and certainly don't get dinner or a guided tour, so my opinion could be wrong."

I turned my back unable to hear more of their nonsense. I became distracted by the glistening waters and the reeds slowly moving in the wind.

"Something wrong?" I jumped at his deep voice. "I apologise for the disturbance, but some of my little lambs became restless in my absence," he said with a smug smile. Why do I think there's lamb ribs on the menu today?

"Nothing, just thinking," his eyes pierced me, mistrust clearly radiating, but he didn't press the issue and I was grateful for that. I was so on the edge, trying to process. I wish I had Federíco's experience with romance because in the moment having kissed one of his cousins is not helpful at all.

We reached our destination and departed the yacht. He had to shake me lightly to get me out of my reverie. I briefly apologized for my lack of attention and meekly followed him along the deserted road to the church. Like in the Correr Museum, there was somebody from the Administration waiting to greet him. Not surprisingly he was one of the sponsors. Two options: He adores Venice or he has a lot of money.

Nothing really prepared me for the view of the mosaics. They depicted Christ's Descent into Hell, the Resurrection of the Dead and the Final Judgement in a vivid and hypnotic way. I gaped at the pictures and lost track of time, admiring the figures and how they shone and looked like they were about to move. I think he said something to me, but I didn't listen really. I was stunned in front of such beauty.

"It's almost one o'clock," he said gently tugging at my sleeve.

"Already? Sorry I didn't realise the time."

We walked in comfy silence out of the building. He mentioned something about going to eat to a *Locanda*, whatever it is, and I softly mumbled my acceptance. I was becoming more and more agitated after the calm feel inside the Church. We crossed a small bridge over a stream surrounded by reeds, a big willow tree, and frogs.

"I enjoy very much your company."

"I also," I whispered, all my inner alarms ringing loud and clear again.

"Would you accompany me tonight to my house?"

Right to the point. No doubt. Is that "accompany" as in let's have dinner or let's trash around the bed sheets? The best would be to brighten this muddy mess before I have a heart attack. Such said organ is beating so fast that I'm afraid it would break my chest. Unfortunately, he mistook my silence for shyness.

"I would take care of you. I would do nothing that could hurt you. You're precious to me," he said, closing the distance between us. Fuck, I need to think fast, but my brain was too distracted with the hammering of my heart.

"I'm not into men," I blurted out, becoming red as a tomato and finding a wonderful spot to look at on the ground. My diplomatic skills amaze me with each passing day.

"I know."

What kind of bizarre answer is that? Are you not supposed to yell or be upset that you were stood up on a small island? I lifted my gaze to find him looming over me. I was forced to twist my neck in order to be able to see him. He cupped my face into his huge hands. I tried to revolve a little but it was impossible. He had me firmly within his clasp.

"I understand this is all new to an inexperienced youth like yourself. I was half expecting your denial, but I'm willing to wait, within a reasonable time frame, that you become my lover. I will provide, take care and see that no harm falls upon you, as long as you respect me and behave according to your status. As I said, you are the most adorable thing that has caught my attention in years. You have to be mine and I have every intention to win you over."

Who needs a soap opera writer when you have Konrad von Lintorff making a love declaration? God, it looks like a contract. No, I'm not thinking romantically, far from that. It's just, I couldn't avoid feeling somewhat disappointed that the first time somebody tells me is in love with me, I could feel the long shadows of lawyers behind my back, looming over me. Now it's time to squirm really. He was almost on top of me with his big hands pressing the sides of my face. I rose my hands to his chest and pushed him hard, but he didn't move an inch.

"I'm not gay or plan to be one," I said, with unwavering resolution lacing my voice, which came out raspy. I needed to drink something or I was going to throw up. That sentence should do.

No, it didn't. He regarded me with a hungry look in his eyes, assessing the situation, and launched himself toward me like a rabid alpha wolf. I had no time to put some distance as he effortlessly trapped me with one iron arm around my waist as the other firmly grab me by the base of my skull. His lips collided with mine with so much force that I couldn't mount a counter-attack. He kissed me despite my muffled protests. I closed my eyes to escape the harsh reality of being kissed by another man, but I couldn't avoid comparing this brutal attack with the kisses I had shared years ago at a party with a sweet blonde from another school. We both were nervous and it was nothing more than small kisses and light touches. She never returned my calls, and according to Fefo, I was a complete idiot for not pressing her to do more.

This was something entirely different. He kissed me in a possessive, animalistic way, increasing his hold over my body. I tried to open my mouth to breath and he used this slight move, to put his tongue inside my mouth, roaming all my insides. I surrendered every wall I had to him and kissed him back. He was a little bit surprised of my lips returning his kiss, but his instant falter, quickly faded away and went back to suck my lips stronger than before. I felt in ecstasy as an unknown fire roved my body. The need for air forced us to break apart, and I softly wailed at the loss of his lips. He kissed me again, this time on my cheek and directed his attention toward my neck with soft butterfly kisses. I had to hold myself with a stronger grip to his body so I wouldn't faint. I felt his lips trailing through my neck and his tongue playfully licking it. He briefly bit me at the crook of my neck, but in a way it wouldn't leave a mark and as suddenly as it had begun, he released me.

I moaned like a child at the loss of contact. Again. And faltered a little. This island was becoming a boat or I was dizzy. He held me by the arm, a look of concern passing through his eyes. I tried to regain my composure, but it was impossible. I frantically looked around for who knows what. Again his hands were cupping my face, his fingers rubbing my temples as if he wanted to placate me. I leaned unintentionally toward his touch deeply comforted and felt a sense of security missing in my life for a long time. Unexplained tears threatened to cloud my eyes.

His furiously ringing mobile phone brought us back to reality. He growled and released me, answering it with a hissed "*was?*" and moved away from me. Reality hit me back. Hard. I've just kissed a man and found it to be the most pleasurable and erotic moment in my entire life! I panicked. I looked at his huge back retreating toward the other side of the bridge and the nausea hit me with all its power. I checked my watch. Five minutes left for the tourists' boat to leave the harbour.

It also takes a lot of courage to run away. Trust me. I heard his faint shout "Guntram", but didn't stop. I needed to get out and fast before the oppressing feeling weaving in my chest exploded.

I caught sight of the saving boat and of Tweedledee and Tweedledum standing by. I gathered all my bravery and went straight toward them. The smaller one tried to stop me but I yelled "out" at him with a tone I didn't know I had. He let me pass.

The *vaporetto* was standing there, at the end of the pier and I ran to catch it before the man would let the moorings go. "Murano", he said. "*Va bene,*" I replied, not really caring where the thing was going or if my Italian was correct.

I slouched in the seat, tired like I have never been before, with a headache mercilessly pounding my brain. Damn! I realised I've forgotten my backpack on his yacht.

Chapter 6

I wandered across the Venetian streets finding everything interesting, up to the last piece of scorched paint on the walls till it became dark. I didn't want to think. By miracle or sheer luck, I found the way back to my hostel and prepared myself to face Fedérico and his most likely obtrusive probing, when he would realise that I've gotten into more trouble than I could handle. Yes, it's not easy to tell to your very straight, manly best friend, that you were kissing another guy and the worst part was that it was enjoyable.

Fedérico left the hotel this morning, I was told by the receptionist, manager and owner; no idea where he was going and much less if he was coming back. All right, it's official, I'm on my own now. I would stick to the original plan hoping he would make an appearance at some point, mostly driven by fear of his mother than by his sense of responsibility. The hotel manager also told me that there was a bunch of Americans planning a party for New Year's Eve, and I should go; "the more the merrier when you're young". Right, but at this moment I felt like Methuselah. Anyhow, I went to meet them.

They were three nice girls in their twenties, real students if you get my meaning, and a boy, older brother no doubt, trying to keep the flock neat, all of them completely excited and yelling at the silliest thing on the TV set. I sat at the table and quietly enjoyed their laughter and planning for tomorrow. Finally, we all decided to go for pizza at a small restaurant nearby per Marcello's advice.

We had dinner at a lively and noisy place. The food was acceptable and prices reasonable, but I couldn't help to compare the shallow conversation we had (is Kylie Minogue hot or not?), with the cultural and fascinating talk with Konrad. I felt bored now, but it wasn't their fault if I was not exactly acting my age. We went back to the hotel, crossing the dark, narrow streets, the three girls in the front happily chatting and we both escorting them, sharing the knowing silence only men can do. At some point, I felt as if we were followed, but when I turned around nobody was there. It didn't help me shake the jitters away.

* * *

December 30th, 2001

It was an uneventful day for a change. I went in the morning to the Academia and to San Rocco Scola. I wandered around a little. My American friends from yesterday's went to the Giudecca and Murano (hope they don't die crushed under the glass animals), I ate at McDonald's (yeah, have to keep the budget tight from now onward), and bought the bottles I was supposed to for tomorrow's big party.

No sign from the German. I should consider this business as over. Probably found something better, so much for his alleged fidelity, I repeated to myself for the hundredth time. Fuck him! I'm going to have fun with people my age and to hell with his overbearing manners. I should consider myself lucky I got rid of him.

* * *

December 31st, 2001

Last day of the year. I checked my e-mails today and no sign from Fefo or his mother. OK. I will be concerned from January 3rd onwards. I miss my backpack a lot. My book was there along with my *Travel Italy* guide. Perhaps I should try to replace it. Today, there's not much to do because everything closes at 2 p.m. I could go to San Marco (finally!) and then wander around a little more. My train will leave tomorrow night for Naples.

I put on my jacket and headed to the door. I went downstairs, crossed our foyer noticing somebody put the wood pieces away, but the light bulb is still broken; tonight I'll have to be extra careful if I don't want to break my neck with the stairs in case I'm too drunk.

The fresh air hit me as I opened the front door. I directed my tracks toward the Rialto when I heard a voice with thick German accent saying "*Dachs*! I mean, Guntram, I have your backpack."

I turned around to see one of the bodyguards from yesterday. No, the previous day, I corrected myself. It's Tweedledum. I should ask his name, really.

"Hello." No need to be impolite, even if your boss is a bastard.

"I'm sorry I couldn't bring it earlier. Plenty of work yesterday," he chuckled. Well, today you don't look so intimidating. Losing your charm perhaps?

"Thank you," I replied and turned to go away. What else is there to say? He caught me by the arm. Are all these Germans all happy grabbing people?

"Do you want to come to spend Silvester with us? We are gathering tonight to have some drinks and then watch the fireworks," he blurted.

"I don't think is very appropriate. Your boss and I didn't part on the best terms," he looked puzzled at me but only for a fleeting moment.

"The Duke is in Zurich now. Chopping heads… if they're lucky," he smirked with an evil grin. "Anyway, we're in holidays. I know, as a soldier, it's hard to be alone far away from home for the festivities. You can come with us; we don't bite hard," he laughed loudly this time.

"Thank you, but I have already plans with some other students. We're having dinner here and then maybe go to the Piazza," I explained. The last thing I want to do is spend New Year's Eve with four or more drunken gorillas.

"OK, then. Don't worry. Look, here you have our address if you should change your opinion. You're a good kid and we really don't mind having you around," he said this time seriously.

"Goodbye and thank you again."

"I go in that direction also." OK, it runs in the family. You don't shake them out with ease.

We walked several meters in heavy silence. I have enough. You won. I admit I wouldn't last too long in a police interrogation.

"Did you work long for Mr. Lintorff?" I finally said, unable to cope with the silence. He looked happy that I've asked.

"I served the *Herzog* for seven years already," he stated very proud of himself.

"You say 'work for' in English," I teased him. "To serve sounds something like out from the Middle Ages."

"We serve him," he repeated emphatically, looking sternly into my eyes. "It's an honour to do so."

I stood petrified. Time to disappear. I mumbled something about going the other way, and he let me go without much trouble.

* * *

I came back at 7 p.m., ready to shake the dark mood lingering in me the whole day. He kissed me, didn't get something else and went back to his business? That man has no heart. He makes out with me, and I don't recall asking him to do it, and since he gets nothing else, prefers to visit his bank and send my things back with one of his goons? It's not that I was expecting flowers or a box of chocolates, but a little explanation or talk would have been in order. Mind you!

My new friends were already sitting at the table when I arrived. Some others were also there and the laughter was more than contagious. I took a glass of wine; *Prosecco* it's called and believe me, it's really good. I didn't refuse two other glasses. We had some pieces of *pannettone* as dinner (yes, mothers of the world, horrify yourselves!), and lots of alcohol. The conversation revolved around music, universities, films and all the important topics of our age. It's good to be back in the land of youth again.

The clock struck 11:30 and they decided to go to San Marco. The fireworks there are supposed to be impressive. I was a little dizzy (one more glass and I would be out for the rest of the night. I know, I better stop before I lose all control).

The square was full with people roaming the place, armed with champagne bottles and firecrackers. Some were dancing and most yelling. My party strategically located themselves in the right side of the square, facing the Cathedral and the Tower where you can see the fireworks best. We resumed the drinking with the girls now frankly tipsy. There was a bewitching brunette who had every intention of kissing me, and I didn't oppose. Pity she kissed the other boy too, and then an older guy. However, after flirting with many, she came back to peck me on my cheek, like a sister. "You're really something hot!" She said laughing. That girl was really trashed.

The cathedral's clock stroke the twelfth hour and the whole place became a pandemonium with couples kissing, fireworks over us, bottles rolling at our feet and strangers dancing. It was so amusingly loud!

I had no idea which time it was, but the square was slowly being vacated. I withdrew myself to one of the galleries to catch myself before returning to the hotel. Needless to say that my friends were lost somewhere in this huge disco San Marco had turned into. I leaned against one of the columns, the action moving in a slow motion in front of my eyes. Yes, I was a bit trashed. Not of the point of starting to cry, but to the point of needing support. I closed my eyes with the vain hope, the pounding headache would vanish. I took a deep breath and opened my eyes to find a broad shouldered German glaring at me. Even now, I could tell he was not happy.

"You are drunk," he stated with his best School Headmaster persona.

Nooo? Really? "Do you always come to such brilliant conclusions on your own?" I blurted out. OK, I'm over the tipsy phase and completely into the trashed one. Now he really seemed furious, in his calm, composed and terrifying way. However, I'm too drunk to care if he has no sense of humour. I started to walk over him, but I faltered having lost the backing of my column. He caught me before I fell on my face —literally.

"If you can't hold your alcohol like a man, then you shouldn't drink," he clarified sternly for irresponsible me. "Come. I'll take you to your hotel before you fall into a canal."

Why does he never wait for an answer before acting? Why should this time be different? His strides this time were too big, and I was nearly tumbling down in my effort to keep up. Of course he was not helping at all with his iron grip on my left arm and his dragging of the rest of my body. The evil headache slowed me down and tried several times to stall, but he would have none of it. He pulled me along harder.

We finally arrived at my hotel. To put the key in the lock proved to be a huge task for me. I could hear his low growl as he took it away and easily slid it in. Lucky bastard, you're bigger. Therefore, alcohol takes longer to affect you. I tread in and out of the blue I said hesitantly.

"About Torcello..."

"It was nothing," he silenced me, waving his hand.

"Then, why the hell are you here?" I answered back, headache forgotten, fury welcomed.

Again he violently launched himself against me and in less than a second had me pinned against the dirty wall. He lifted me effortlessly and sat me over a small pillar I'd not seen before, positioning himself rather forcefully between my legs. I tried to push him away, but my hands froze midway as his mouth clashed against mine, his sharp teeth slicing my lower lip. I felt the coppery taste of blood in my tongue for a brief moment, as he started to suck it, avidly. The hungry, almost desperate kisses from a man who looked like an iceberg made me lose all composure. I kissed him back this time without reservations, my tongue battling with his to feel a taste of the expensive spirits that was still lingering in his mouth.

We kissed like there was no tomorrow. I put my arms around his neck drawing him toward my body, completely lost in the incredible wanton feeling engulfing me. His expert hand opened with ease my zipper and took my throbbing erection, massaging it with slow movements, alternating with small touches to the tip of it. His masturbation was something like I have never experienced previously, and I was increasingly feeling more and more dizzy. At some point his strong left arm encircled my hips and pushed me towards his own groin. The minute my aching member touched his powerful erection, I ejaculated staining his hand with my seed.

He rose his stained fingers towards my mouth and whispered in my ear "suck them" sending chills through my back. I obediently took the one by one in my mouth, licking them with my tongue and sucking hard. The salty taste of my own sperm, instead of repulsing me as I would have thought some time ago, drove me mad with desire, and I kissed him deeply for the first time, ravishing at the idea that he was also enjoying my taste. We parted panting heavily. "Come home with me," he sinfully breathed in my ear.

I panicked. I pushed him harder than ever, effectively scurrying myself like a snake, running upstairs to the security of my hotel hearing at the distance his frustrated grunt of "Guntram".

Chapter 7

New Year, New Resolutions. First and most important; forget Konrad von Lintorff. What happened yesterday is past. I was totally drunk, as the actual hangover can testify. Second and no less important; get a girlfriend as soon as I'm back in Argentina, and get laid. This was a horrible mistake; a product of my daft romantic notions of unending love and all that crap. Tonight, I'll take the train to Naples, and it's over. Forever.

I dressed myself and went to the breakfast room. The other single student sitting there looked as bad as I. We growled at each other in sympathy. *Prosecco* and champagne are not a good combination. I slowly sat, hoping the boat would stop rocking me, but, no chance. The piercing sound of the doorbell nearly made me puke, and I threw an evil look at the idiot who had rung it and now was stamping in our place.

It was a policeman. And then, two other more and a dog. They all were speaking very quickly in Italian.

Two of them headed directly toward me as the other plus dog went straight into my room. I was really surprised and almost paralysed when one of them addressed me.

"Can you please show us your passport, sir?"

"I have it in my jacket in my room. Is something wrong?"

"Lead us, please".

When we entered into my room, the dog was sniffing everything and everywhere. I went for my coat and took my passport out. One of the policemen took a long look at it and asked,

"Where were you last night?"

"At a party here and then in San Marco's square. I came back very late. I really don't remember. Why?"

"All clear here," the one with Rin Tin Tin shouted.

"Yes, the hotel owner says so. And in the previous days, on 29th and 30th ?"

"I went to Torcello with a friend, walked around the city, and on the 30th to the Academia and San Rocco," I said sheepishly, now totally lost.

"When have you seen for the last time Fedérico Martiarena Alvear?"

"Is he into troubles?"

"Answer the question, sir"

"Morning of the 29th. We had a quarrel and he said he would go to Rome. Is he hurt?"

"Can your friend say that you went with him to Torcello?"

"I don't know. You must ask him. His name is *Herzog* Konrad von Lintorff and his two bodyguards, they saw me. He was staying at the Daniele."

"Danieli. You must accompany us to the station to give a brief declaration".

"I refuse to go till you inform me, what are the charges against me."

"You're not under arrest, sir. You have to testify in a drug trafficking inquiry concerning Fedérico Martiarena Alvear."

"What??"

One of the policemen said something in Italian to the one who was questioning me.

"Your friend is accused of trafficking three kilos of pure cocaine. He and two other students were caught in a disco near the University."

"This is some kind of mistake. Fedérico would never do something like that. He has no need for that."

"Well, he asserts you provided the drugs on December 27th, bringing them from Paris."

I had all the symptoms of a heart attack—a real one. I sat on the bed utterly shocked. My heart beat so fast that it was hurting and my ears had a funny buzzing noise inside.

"It's impossible! I was at the Louvre at that time, not here. I arrived on the 28th! I have my rail pass stamped if you want it," I muttered.

"We know, the hotel owner confirmed it and your luggage is clear from drugs. So please, get your coat and come with us to make a routine statement."

"What about Fedérico, is he all right?" My mind already playing scenes from Miami Vice through my head.

"I would not be concerned about someone who drags me into a major drugs case," the silent police said very formally.

True to their word they only wanted a statement. When I arrived in Europe, where I was, with whom I was and who I've met, and what I've done in Venice. OK, the hot parts were left out. After they were finished typing, a police officer led me to a small windowless room, like those on the TV series and left me there for three hours.

The door was violently opened by a huge, bald man.

"I'm deputy Rossi, in charge of the investigation. You are free to go. Consider yourself lucky that a man like Lintorff backed your story. Normally, these persons throw the likes of you to the trash when they're finished."

I stood up, cramps running up in my legs. "Can you please tell me something about my friend?"

"*Incommunicato*. Get a solicitor from his consulate if you want to be helpful." With that I was escorted out of the police station.

Outside, I realised that it was more than five o'clock, as the sun was already gone. I shivered from cold and went to find a phone parlour to make contact with the Consulate in Milan.

First, I tried to reach Fedérico's mother, but she was away in the Senate in the middle of a crisis. She was unreachable, since they were trying to force the President out and get a new one from the governors' league. Her secretary told me that she would try to get in contact with the ambassador, but since the original one had resigned several days ago and the appointed one had yet to arrive, she thought it would be hopeless. The best I could do was to go back to the police station and see if I could find out something else.

I dragged myself back to the station, night already falling upon me. I entered the building and there I met The Front Desk Officer, yes with capital letters. One fat, middle aged man was behind it and decided that it was time to phone the minute I approached him. I stood by waiting for him to finish, but then he had the urgent need to go for a coffee.

"Please, could I have a word with you?" I slowly pleaded him, cornering the man against the coffee machine. I had enough of his evasiveness.

"*Non parlo inglese*," was the brief answer as he was extremely busy looking for the sugar.

"*Seguro que entiende español*," I was trying to control my temper.

"Look kid, go home. Get a real lawyer and then come back."

"The consulate is empty at this point and his family is trying to get one. There should be someone I can speak to… perhaps there's a way to bail him out," I replied trying to hide the desperation in my voice.

"Bail for that? Where do you think you are, in the South?" The man exploded. "The magistrate will be informed the day after tomorrow, and we'll see."

"I didn't mean to be disrespectful." Better I pacify him, or he will throw me out. "I just don't know what to do. I can get no solicitor or even know one here."

"If I were you, I'd get out of here as fast as I can. Your friend—the word enhanced with imaginary quotation marks—tells only lies, and you're gonna get caught in the middle again."

"Fine. May I speak with detective Rossi?"

"Stubborn little pest. Sit and wait," he mumbled. I decided it would be best to obey him and sat on the wooden bench there to wait, who knows for what.

I must have fell asleep as the next thing I remember was the strong shaking of Detective Rossi. I sat up from my slouched position, moved the hair from my face in a futile attempt to wake up. Rossi extended a plastic cup toward me, and I took it. Latte machiatto, why does everybody think that I'm a baby who can't hold a real coffee?

"Thank you," I whispered.

"You're welcome," I drank the coffee in silence, as he was deeply thinking. "I want to help your friend, and I don't really think I could, once the lawyers are here to make things more complicated.

"I don't understand."

"Lawyers tend to entangle things more and more and that could work or not, leaving your friend in more trouble than he already is. I don't believe he's the main player here, and I want to catch the others. Would you help him out?"

"I don't see how. We split in Paris, right after Christmas."

"Tell me whatever you remember. It would certainly help."

"He went away with two French girls we met at the party in the hostel. I think their names were Chantal and Anne Marie, no last name, art students. They went later to a disco in Pigalle, but I wasn't going there because I was very tired and drunk," he softly chuckled, encouraging me to carry on. "Next day, the girls were in our room and he wanted to go to Milan. I was not invited, of course, and we agreed to meet here from the 28th onward.

"Did you get a good look at the girls, could you work with a sketch artist to make a portrait?"

"I don't know. They both looked alike, as a Claudia Schiffer's copy," was my uncertain reply.

"Then you really took a good look, boy," he retorted smugly.

"Wait. Before I do anything else for you, I think you owe me an explanation."

"Well, here's the pretty story so far. A snitch told us about a large quantity of cocaine to be smuggled into Venice for the New Year's parties. This is a small city and criminality here is very low. It's suicidal for a dealer to come here. We investigated and found your friend selling doses near the University. When we raid the flat he had, we found also three kilos of pure cocaine. He swears that you brought the thing here, and that he was just storing it for you. He only admits that he was selling the 160 g, we found him with. Don't look so shocked. You're gonna have a heart attack. We know it's almost impossible to smuggle five kilos in a rucksack on a train nowadays. You see, after September 11th, all baggage is carefully checked in airports and train stations. Most probably the drugs came by car."

"Why do you say five kilos now when you first spoke about three?"

"The French girls and the two remaining kilos are missing. Come on, you have to work now."

He led me into a small, well illuminated room where there was already a woman sitting, about thirty years old, brunette and with a full set of pencils. She smiled gently and made a gesture, so I would sit in front of her.

Several hours later I was almost dead on my feet, and she looked fresh as a rose. She triumphantly showed me her two sketches, and I gasped at them. They were almost good as a photo. This woman has earned all my respect, since she could recreated them out of my initial sentence, "blonde, big boobs".

Detective Rossi entered and looked at the pictures.

"Good, now we can identify them. Come on Guntram. Take a look at these shots."

Identify? I didn't like the word at all. Don't look at the table, there's nothing good in his Manila paper folder. "May I see Fedérico now?" My throat was dry and raspy, a lump was forming in my stomach.

"Not yet, tomorrow perhaps. Come on Guntram, just look at the pictures, tell me if those are the girls, and we are finished. You've done very well so far."

I took a pained look at the folder and slowly opened, feeling both police officers stares fixed on me. I put my hand fast in my hand trying to suffocate the need to throw all the contents of my stomach up.

"Yeah, that happens if you're in water. Do you recognise them?"

I nodded, my face adopted a green shadow while I was fighting the urge to vomit. The taste of bile was overwhelming.

"What happened?" I was horrified, unable to understand what those deep gashes around their necks were and the bruises all over their perfect faces.

"We think they stole the cocaine from somebody, tried to sell it with your friend and the original owner decided to finish the business. Martiarena can consider himself lucky that we arrested him before the one who killed the girls got him," he said as if this would be the most normal thing in the world. "Marina, can you get a cup of tea for the boy?" She rose from her chair, shyly smiled to me and left the room.

"You should go back to your hotel when you feel better. Look, it's nine, go for breakfast and then home. If we need something else, we will contact you."

"My hotel reservation finished yesterday, and I don't think they will be thrilled to have me back. I think I should look for something else in the city."

"Not now, everything is full," he stared at the ceiling for a long moment.

"Why don't you go to your friend's house? He certainly might have room for you."

"It's not a good idea. He's a very strict man and probably furious he got in the middle of a drug case. He's a banker, you know."

"Nobody can really blame you for this mess. You just got in the middle. Go to him and stay there, huh? If we need something, his lawyer will tell you."

I went out of the police station and went again to the phone parlour. Of course I couldn't contact with the consulate in Milan and tried the Embassy in Rome with similar luck. I checked my e-mails and there was a raging message from Federíco's mother. She blamed me of all the mess because of my utter stupidity for not being able to take care of him. She would be arriving on the 4th to Milan. I was supposed to pick her up. With what money I wondered? At the moment, I have travellers check and € 40 cash. I hope she likes the train.

Once again, out in the streets, I noticed I was lost again. No idea where I was or where to go, and I didn't really want to think about it. I put my hands in my pockets and there was a piece of paper. "Calle del Dose da Ponte, near Palazzo Corner" Suddenly it dawned on me, that it was the address the gentle gorilla had given me, but it had no number. I asked around and they told me it was in the direction of the Accademia.

I wandered and wandered debating with myself. What could I possibly tell him? Certainly, he had always been kind to me, but I've been taking advantage of the situation and here I was coming again to ask for a favour but I really had no choice. I prayed that he would give advice before he would kick me out of his house. I arrived at the huge, imposing renaissance mansion, like one of those that you see from the vaporetto in the Grand Canal and wondered if they were museums or foundations. Since what appeared to be the main entrance was by the water, I went to a side one and rang the bell.

An intimidating man with a butler's uniform opened it and asked something in German. I was befuddled and just turned around to go away when I heard a well-known voice laughing. "Well, if it's the international drug dealer from the Pampas. Come here Dachs!"

I got a bear hug and was dragged inside to a kitchen where there were also three more mountain-men. "You should have told me your party was much better than ours!"

"Silence! The lad is in no shape for your idiotic prattle," the older one exclaimed, Ferdinand if I remember correctly. "Where were you all day? Goran has been looking for you," he firmly told me, putting his big hands on top of my shoulders. And who the heck is Goran? "The Duke is in a meeting, but he will see you later. Have you eaten something yesterday?"

"Yes, I had a coffee at the police station."

He chided me with a gesture and made me sit in front of the table where there were the other two. Hendrick was one and the other I didn't know. As if they had read my mind, the "funny one" said "I'm Michael and that one over there, is Alexei from Russia. Here, eat your sandwich." Ferdinand had disappeared.

"Where were you yesterday night? Goran had a really hard time trying to find you. For a moment, I thought I would have to go out and help him," Michael said barely containing his laughter.

"At the police station making sketches with an artist." Was my mechanical answer, eating in such a manner the sandwich that had materialized out of nowhere.

"The Duke is upset," he informed cheerily.

"I'm sorry he got mixed into this mess. It was never my intention to get him into this," I tried to defend myself, not very convincingly.

"Oh, no. It's not that. He's upset you didn't come right after the police set you free. Not to mention the default with Argentina's bonds. The offices at Zurich are having a hard time with him on their necks, and that's without calculating loses," he told with a secretive voice. I looked at him now totally stunned. I went back to my sandwich, not really wanting to chat. He smirked and started to speak in German with the other two.

The severe butler announced that the Duke would see me in his studio. I followed him across a series of corridors and rooms exquisitely decorated in a XVII or XVIII century style, but not so heavy as the original ones. The high ceilings made me feel small and the oppressive feeling in my heart and guts were not helping at all. Too soon for my taste we arrived at a grand dark wooden door, easily and soundlessly opened by the servant. He entered and announced briefly my name, as if we were in a royal audience.

Chapter 8

I gathered some courage from I don't know where and advanced up to the middle of the room. Konrad was sitting behind a huge desk reading some papers. He never lifted his gaze toward me, only made a small gesture with the hand to stop my advance. I took a look around, not moving an inch of my body. He took his time to finish reading the documents, signing them with a pen and putting them in a leather folder. After they were handed to the butler, his stormy blue eyes seriously looked directly into mine.

The butler passed beside me, closing the door without a sound. I waited for him to open fire. The tension was so palpable as I realised what a big mistake I'd made by coming to him.

"Guntram, don't fidget, it's unbecoming. Come over here," I advanced toward the guillotine like my ancestors did and stopped in front of the desk, exactly as you do when you're called to the Principal's office.

"Why my name was involved in one of the most notorious drugs cases this city had in the last ten years?" he slowly articulated punctuating every word.

"I'm deeply sorry you were brought into this. The police caught me unaware and I just didn't think when I said your name. They wanted to know where I'd been and with whom and I just said it. I do hope they have not troubled you much," was my answer, now totally afraid of him and his stern look. All his body was tense like he would jump over me at the slightest chance, and knowing our history together that was quite possible. I'd been a complete moron for coming to him for help. I should be grateful if he would let me go away unharmed.

"What really upsets me the most is, that even if I gave you a serious warning about this person, you would not only disregarded it, but persisted in your association with him."

What? You only said he should respect me, nothing about not being friends! Better keep quiet as I sense he's looking for an excuse to lash out. "I didn't have the opportunity to terminate our association as you call it," I defended myself feebly.

"Drugs, prostitution, murder and let's do not forget trafficking. Counsellor Gandini has been working on your case very hard."

"I was never accused of anything!" I exploded. This is too much. I'm not guilty of Fedérico's actions. Perhaps you can accuse me of not being hard enough on him, but I was not carrying several kilos of cocaine. "I was only asked to make a statement."

"A statement which they would have used against you! Don't you realise that most probably they think you are that boy's accomplice or that you might have even murdered those two prostitutes because of the missing drugs?" He shouted enraged, his face showing his disbelief at my sentence.

The memory of the photos hit me with full force and tears veiled my eyes. I tried unsuccessfully to fight them back and stuttered "I had to identify the bodies and don't even know their last names." My face lost all colour and suddenly the floor decided to rock me. I totally lost my control and burst into tears, covering my eyes in a vain attempt to hide the growing embarrassment engulfing me. A grown up man crying like a baby!

He extended his hand over the desk and pulled me softly, forcing me to circle the table and stand in front of him without the safety barrier of the desk. I was more than shocked when he yanked me strongly and I landed without grace on top of his lap. I pushed with my two hands against his chest, but he encircled me with his arms and compelled me to lean against him. Again all my defences were dropped and I simply cried like a baby. He let me stay there venting all the stress I'd accumulated during the last day. He caressed my hair with soothing movements and without uttering a single word the whole time.

"I'm sorry I ruined your jacket."

"Nonsense. I was concerned about you," he replied softly, handing me his handkerchief.

"Are you not furious with me?"

"I'm most upset, but not for the reasons you're thinking about."

"I don't understand. I honestly didn't want to get you in the middle."

"I'm upset that you didn't obey me; that this boy complicated things more and more with his lies and finally that you disappeared after leaving the police station and didn't come to me. Did you think I would deny myself to you? Your lack of trust toward me is the most disturbing matter here."

I was speechless. "I was trying to contact the Argentinean consulate and his mother. I didn't want to take advantage of you any longer. Since I came to Europe, you have been the only kind person to me."

"Guntram, I was not lying when I said that I would protect and provide for you. It offends me deeply that you take my words so lightly, but alas that could the fault of this lawless times' education. I'm forty-four years old and way past the age for playing. If I told you about my interest for you, it was because I truly want the opportunity to start a relationship with you. You are everything I've dreamed of for a lover and a companion in life. Your beauty and innocence along with this steel core in you, makes you perfect for me. I want to love you and that you love me back. And don't tell me again that you're not interested in men because we both know it's a falsehood given our two past experiences. You're just afraid of it because of your purity. We can go through this together and we will."

Without any further preambles, he kissed me, this time tenderly as if I were something precious and valuable that could be broken at the smallest vibration. I clung to his lips like a drowning man and put my arms around his neck. He didn't deepen the kiss and abruptly as he had started, he stopped. I was now disoriented while he chastely kissed anew my forehead.

"Come now. I understand you're tired and feel lost. Friederich will take you to your room and you can bathe, change your clothes and sleep a little before dinner."

"I can't stay here. It's too much. Besides, my clothes are at the police station. They had to test something," I babbled too overwhelmed with what has just transpired.

Did he still want me and why did I feel that it was the right thing to do, to kiss him? He has a smashing personality, rich like the devil, chauvinist, stern, unable to accept dissent, much older than me and most probably I was his newest pet project. Nevertheless, he was the only person who had looked at me with such true adoration in his eyes in my whole life and I just simply loved it.

Not even bothering to start an argument, he put me off his lap and playfully gave me a not so mild smack in my bottom "Go upstairs before you anger Friederich and he can be meaner than myself."

Outside his office, studio as it was called, the serious big black bird, Friederich was waiting for me. He showed me the way to a guest room. "The one from the Duke is at the end of the corridor, near your own," I was ushered to a bedroom the size of my flat with a full bathroom inside, and a view over the main canal. I ran toward the window, like a child to watch the ships.

"Please, don't delay young sir, you still have to bathe and sleep," I was discretely reminded by the butler, busy now by putting on top of the four posted king size bed a folded pyjama. Jesus, nanny time was over for me many years ago! I threw him an incensed glare, but he didn't seem fazed.

Showering and shaving can do wonders. I felt much better after it and put the fluffy towel around me and went out to get some clothes on. My clothes from the previous day had vanished and there was only the pyjamas. My options were a nice pyjama or a nice white towel. Better pyjama.

A few seconds after I had finished putting the clothes on, which fitted me perfectly and a pair of closed slippers, the butler came back for inspection. I think I passed it, as he made a grimace almost like a smile and presented me with a tray with milk and cookies. It was my turn to make a face; I'm a grown up! I stopped eating cookies and warm milk more than a decade ago! But on the other hand, the thing looked very good so I took the tray from his hands and went to the big window where a couch was strategically placed. I took a sip and immediately felt a strange bitter taste in the milk.

"It has a little bourbon to help you sleep. You might be overtired, sir."

Well, definitely this was not for children. I finished the milk and some of the cookies as I was watching the busy ships at midday. The butler was occupied fumbling in the closet with some clothes, but I didn't pay attention. I yawned and put the tray back on top of the small desk with a chair and went straight to bed. The butler was faster than me and lifted the padded covers before I could slide in. He then closed the shutters and sleep overtook me.

* * *

Some hours later, five if my watch was accurate, I woke up, a little bit disoriented. This nice soft Egyptian cotton sheets and fluffy covers are not usual in hostels, not to mention the size of this bed. Knowing I could not stay for the rest of the year, even if that was my biggest desire, I jumped out of bed and started the search for my clothes. They were still missing. Just when I was facing myself with the dilemma of wandering in a strange house in pyjamas or staying there till the end of time, I saw a neat pile of clothes arranged on top of the small bureau with a small note saying "Mr. de Lisle". It was a pair of grey wool trousers, a white cotton shirt (one of the good ones), light blue pullover, underwear with grey socks and black leather shoes. I got dressed astonished by the fact that everything was my size, even the shoes that were one of the more comfortable things I ever had. To be honest, the taste in fashions was a little bit gloomy and I was disappointed with the fact that there were no jeans.

When I was about to leave the room I heard a soft knock on the door.

"I see you are up, sir. The Duke would like to see you in the office," Friederich informed me at the same time he took a good look at me, perhaps to check if everything was in its place and I didn't have a Metallica T-shirt hidden somewhere. Satisfied, he turned around and I, as usual, trotted behind him, trying to be as quiet as possible. This house had something that reminded me of a Museum.

"You look much better now. Come now, counsellor Gandini is waiting for us in the office," Konrad greeted me, standing at the bottom of the marble staircase.

"I must thank you for the clothes. It's very thoughtful to you," I softly started, sudden shyness overtaking me. He had changed his grey business suit from the morning to something more informal, a tweed brown jacket, beige shirt, a scarf and matching brown trousers. Even in "casual" clothes, he looked regal and imposing. I suppose some people are born with a crown on their heads and the rest of us can only gape at them.

"Nonsense, my dear. Come, let's finish this unpleasant business with the Counsellor Gandini. He's certain that we can get your name out of the investigation before it goes to the judge," he said kissing me lightly, like a child on the forehead and taking me firmly by the waist. He released me the moment we arrived to a door and opened it with ease.

Inside of an immense room, almost like a library, but without the books, there was a huge desk, two chairs in front of it and a round table aside, with a man sitting at the desk fondling with papers. I think the furniture was mahogany. The man quickly stood up in Konrad's presence and gathered his papers, a light smile on his lips and eyes. He was round and wore a conservative suit.

"Well, if it isn't my mysterious client. Come over here boy. The prosecutor still wants to make a face-to-face between you and the main defendant. I know it's bothersome, but he demands it before he clears you out."

"I would like to thank you for your help," I said extending my right hand.

"Not at all, boy. I'm robbing the Duke in this case, but don't tell him," he chuckled, shaking my hand with full force. "Fortunately, your friend is totally determined to get you in the mess. My bill will not look so outrageous. The Argentinean lawyers who take over this mess, will have a hard time."

"Is there any chance for him to come out?"

"With a good lawyer with connections like myself for example, yes. After all, they only found him with 160 grams cocaine. The rest could be indicted to the dead girls. But it's none of my business and I had enough of him yesterday. However, is very strange the fact that he's so bent on placing the blame on you, when you obviously were not even in the country. Perhaps he's trying to win time and force the police to look elsewhere."

My guilty expression didn't go unnoticed to Konrad whose gaze was fixed at me all the time.

"Is there any reason why he would do something like this, Guntram? He growled at me his darkened blue eyes petrifying me in my place. The light mood imposed by the chatty lawyer vanished into thin air and even this nice, fat man, looked threateningly at me. I gulped. Time to acknowledge my own idiocy.

"I think there's a reason," I trailed.

"Better say it here in front of a lawyer."

"When I was thirteen-years-old, we were together in school and the principal caught us with a bottle of whiskey. I said it was mine when in fact I've never seen the thing. He wanted to expel Fedérico and I took the blame so he wouldn't do it. I don't think Fedérico would accuse me of something so serious. There must be some kind of mistake or the police might be lying. I swear I have nothing to do with all this."

The lawyer snorted, visibly entertained by my story. Konrad continued to stare at me, slowly breathing.

"Boy, don't ever enter into the law business because you'll get burned," he laughed openly at me. "I'm giving you two pieces of advice for free. First, never take the blame for somebody else. You have enough with your own troubles. Second, choose better friends because had it not been for his Excellency's intervention, you would be the next dish in prison," I opened my mouth to protest.

"Please, save it," he interrupted me, waving his hand. "Who do you think they will believe? A poor student or the child of a Senator highly related?" His last words hit me full in my core, like a punch in the stomach. Had Fedérico really tried to betray me in such a way?

I was speechless on the brink of tears. I regained my composure the best as I could. I cleared my throat and asked if he could do something for Fedérico, considering his mother would come tomorrow. "No", was his answer after silently checking with his boss.

"Let's go and finish this unsavoury issue," Konrad said. Both men went for the exit to be met by Friederich with their coats. The butler helped them in while I was still there, paralysed. "Guntram, don't stall," he scolded me. I hurried to meet them. Friederich literally shoved me into a black coat.

Too fast to my liking, we arrived to the central police station in front of the train station. Gandini took me by the arm and quickly climbed the stairs to the main entrance. He spoke briefly with the man in the reception and then both men led me to a windowless room with a desk and two chairs.

"You'll see your friend now," the policeman said in good English.

I paced in the suffocating room, like a caged lion. Was it my imagination or was the dammed thing becoming hotter and smaller? The door opened and a policeman brought Fefo handcuffed. He released him as he was supposed to.

"How are you?" I asked anxiously. He looked like crap with his clothes dirty and his face haggard due to the sleep deprivation.

"Hello Pumpkin, came to see me finally."

I chose to overlook his banter. "Your mother arrives tomorrow. She will get the lawyers to work on the case better than I could ever do".

"Why didn't you tell them the truth? You could have done it, for old time sake," he scolded me.

I was lost. Really. "Don't understand. If you think I'm going to repeat the bottle number, you're mistaken. This is too big and serious."

"Clearly, you found somebody else to pound you into the mattress and out with me," he shouted at me now.

"What? Are you drunk or something?"

"It was your fucking idea since the beginning. You got those two girls and convinced them to take the stuff from their boss and come here to sell it at a better price. But you picked that rich guy up in the streets, and fuck all of us and the deal. He gives you more money, it seems by the way you're dressed," he ranted incensed, furious at me.

I was shocked, spaced into another dimension and nobody made the effort to tell me. I felt dizzy, nauseous and my ears were filled with a thundering sound. I needed to sit down before I fall.

"Whore! So much for your promises of unending love. I'm going to kill you!" He jumped at me, throwing me and the chair in the process. He got two punches at me, before three policemen stormed in and dragged him out, still shouting.

Gandini stood by me and offered me his hand to stand up. "Couldn't hope to get it better," he confided in me smugly, whispering in my ear. Another man, dressed in a suit entered, looking at me without much interest. It was the prosecutor, my lawyer told me later.

"Obviously, this young man has nothing to do with this. There is no physical evidence against him or anything to support the defendant's accusations against him. Gandini, for once your customer might be truly not guilty. You have to pay dinner for me and my family. I have to make you sweat somehow," he teased.

"He certainly has a big family. Goodbye to my profits with this case," Gandini laughed back. I was totally stunned. They were making jokes even if my friend had clearly lost his mind and attacked me!

"Papers will be ready tomorrow. But tell your client he's officially out and clean."

The lawyer led me out of the police station and we stood facing the wind.

"Where's the Duke?" I inquired.

"He preferred to walk home by the canal. He was really upset about something," the ship's driver informed me.

Chapter 9

I ran as fast as I could for about five minutes over the deserted streets. If you wonder Diary why I did it, the answer is I had no bloody idea. I just needed to be with him, to get his comfort and his kisses. I was overwhelmed and exhausted beyond measure. I needed him like I never needed someone before. When I heard of my father's suicide I swallowed the pain and wallowed into it. Now, I didn't want to do it. I needed his calm voice and his strong arms and perhaps, his shoulder to cry on over Fedérico's betrayal.

I caught sight of him far away, his silhouette is unmistakable. "Konrad wait, please!" I cried. He stopped dead in his tracks, but didn't turn to me. I quickly closed the distance among us and briefly touched his right arm and he turned to me. Even with the low light I could see his eyes looking at me with a mix of fury and reproach.

"Konrad, you have to help him. He's not himself. He doesn't know what he's saying...," I pleaded with my best puppy eyes.

"Whore! That's what you are!" he roared. My mouth fell open and I tried to look for the words to defend myself but I was rendered mute from the shock at his reaction.

"You play the innocent lamb, when in fact you're a miserable snake," he took me by the arms and started to shake me violently. "You tried to fool me with your act of the poor virginal boy," and then he backhanded me. Hard. Really hard, like when you hit a rock. I fell onto the pavement, my hand touching the right side of my face, something cool dripping from my lower lip.

"I offered you my love, my protection, even waited for you to be ready to accept me, and how do you repay me? You shamelessly sit in front of your lover, let him yell at you, like the whore you are, and now you ask me to help him. You can't even deny it!" he shouted completely out of himself and viciously kicking me in the ribs.

I tried to stand up and run (I'm perfectly aware that my chances in a fight with him are near zero), but he caught me by the hair. He pulled me strongly backward toward his chest and one of his hands crushed my windpipe with full force. I tried to elbow him on the stomach so he would let me go, but it was like hitting a wall. I was terrified and desperate to escape him, revolving against him as the hand increased its force. When I started to see black points in front of my eyes, he threw me away, like a discarded rag doll. I hit again the ground with full force and again he came at me ready to fight more.

"I'm not his lover! Can't you see that he's insane? It must have been the drugs!" I cried desperately.

"Do you take me for an idiot? Look at you, you defend him even if he's lying. Like true lovers do. You're his whore!"

"It's not true," I said this time really crying. "I only want to help him, that's all. He's the only friend I have. I don't know why he said we're lovers. Please, Konrad, you have to believe me. I've never lied to you, and you know that."

"Do you really think I'm going to believe that you're asking my help, out of selflessness, for a man who just tried to send you twenty years to prison? That you two had nothing more than a friendship? Every time I saw him with you, he was touching and calling you his Pumpkin."

My sobs became now open tears. I cried like I never before had. The headache was pounding me like a hammer.

"If you want my help, I want you to be fully mine. No more games. We will finish what we start and we will do it now. No more running away, Guntram. My patience with you is over," he stated this time in a slow and calculating voice, his figure looming over me.

"I swear there's nothing between Fedérico and me. I've never been into men until you and still don't know if this is right to do."

He smirked at me "By the way you kiss? I thought you were an innocent boy. You have probably been fooling around more than I," he stopped when he heard my muffled sobs. "Show me what you're able to do in the bed and maybe I will get your friend out of prison. It's your call," he knelt down beside where I was. "Now," he commanded.

I felt lost. I was confused. Show what? I looked at him with pleading eyes and I saw a flash of anger passing through his. He stood up and turned around and started to walk away from me. I jumped to my feet and ran after him and caught him like a drowning man grasps a plank in the sea. "Tell me what to do," I stammered.

He dragged me to a small street, more like an alley in fact, with almost no light. He pushed me against a wall and opened his coat and pulled down his zipper. "On your knees and suck, boy," his evil aura stronger than ever. I panicked and tried to escape, only to be smashed again the wall, my head hitting it hard. He repeated, "Suck boy, this time you don't run away," I fell on my knees, feeling the little stones pierce them. I was now crying again and trembling like a leaf. I couldn't take my hands to the front of his trousers because I couldn't control them, as much as they were shaking. He bent down and took my hand and directed them into his pants. I pulled his pants open and moved away as best I could the silk brief he had. His penis was fully erect and sprang into life as soon as my hand touched it.

He placed his hand on the back of my neck, most probably to have better control of my head and drew it near his member. "Come, put your lips around the top and gently suck," he explained to me softly as he wouldn't scare me any more. I complied, delicately touching the point with my tongue. I was afraid of biting him or grazing it with my teeth. Then I started to draw circles with it, oddly enjoying the salty spicy taste of his member. He gently removed my hairs from my face and his left hand started to caress the side of my face with slow, relaxing motions. "That's very good, now try to put it entirely inside your mouth," was his next instruction. I tried to open my mouth as much as I could, but the pain from the earlier blow hit me again with full force. I whimpered at the effort and he made a soothing sound with his mouth. I looked up, afraid he would become mad again and hit me or do something worse, but his eyes were kind anew.

"All right, don't worry. We'll try it later. Lick it from the base to the top and put your hand around it," I followed his advice slowly and somehow the situation became pleasurable for us. Licking his hard staff made me feel as if a jolt of electricity was running through my own body, increasing its strength every time I lapped it. Boldly, I returned to the top and opened my mouth as much as I could swallowing only a little bit, but it was enough to drive me crazy with desire.

55

I increased the pace of my sucking totally losing conscience of where I was or what I was doing, his thumb rubbing circles at my temple, my only anchor to reality. I sucked eagerly like a hungry baby and there he exploded into my mouth. I gagged and tried to escape, but his hand firmly held my head against his member. I swallowed the best that I could, finding the taste of his seed to my liking. After he was finished, he released me. I huddled myself against the wall and adapted a foetal position, too stunned and too embarrassed for what I had just done.

"Have you understood finally, Guntram, the idea behind your punishment?"

I didn't bother to answer, too deeply immersed in my own private hell of wonder, lust, shame and hate for what he had coerced me to do. I hated myself more, because in the end, I had enjoyed it.

He pulled me viciously up and threw me against the wall forcing me to use both hands to avoid another slam against it. He forced me to open my legs wide with a kick in the calves, and fast as a lightening, he undid my belt and pulled down my trousers and underwear with one violent jerk. His right hand squeezed my throat hard, and all I could think was that he was going to rape me now.

He slid his member fully erect again between the globes of my bottom, not penetrating me, but hitting the entrance of my anus with force, sliding it in and out at a very fast pace at the same time he was almost strangling me. He ejaculated this time over me and released me, making me fall to the ground. I tried to compose my clothes, but I was so terrified, that I could only start to weep again, coughing reflexively in a futile attempt to alleviate the burning pain in my throat.

He shook me in order to get my attention, and I looked at him totally afraid of what he might do next. This man was a psycho!

"Good, let's see now, if you have finally understood the goal of your punishment and the rules you are going to live under from this moment onward. Obviously, you're too stressed to think clearly, so I will help you. First, why was I angry with you?" He asked his fingernails strongly clasped in my chin forcing me to engage my eyes with his own.

"I'm not Federíco's lover," I said.

"Wrong," I got a full slap on my already pained side. "Try again," he hissed. I searched my brain, but I was too desperate and afraid to think clearly. I remembered that he had been most incensed with the notion of taking him for a fool.

"I tried to fool you and lied to you," I tested.

"Better. Lying or deceiving me is totally forbidden. You belong body and soul to me. Therefore, you have to obey me in everything. What else?"

"I ran away from you."

"Yes, that could be acceptable, but it's not the main offence."

"I don't know honestly, help me out!" I cried.

"All right since you ask for my help, I will tell you, only this time. You put somebody else in the middle of our relationship. I don't know why this punk believes he can burst into our lives and provoke a fight. Finally, he has touched you, and this, I don't consent. Nobody touches you but me. Is that understood, boy?"

"Yes," I quipped.

"Now we'll go through the rules, so we are both certain that we have an understanding. First, nobody or nothing comes between us. Whatever happens, we solve it in private. Second, you belong to me, body and soul. Third, honesty, obedience and modesty are your virtues. Fourth, I will love you and look after you in any way I deem proper. Are we clear now?"

"Yes, I understand," I sobbed, not willing to anger him any more. He gathered me in his arms and held me against his chest as I tried to stop my shaking and crying, and calmed down my ragged breathing. He soothed me, speaking softly in my ear and caressing my hair and back with long movements.

"I do hope you follow the rules henceforth. This punishment is meant to show you your proper place. You have run wild for too long, and now it's time you learn what it means to belong to somebody. Come, let's go home, *Mäuschen*," he finally said, delicately removing me from my plastered position against his chest. I sobbed once more and tried to clean my eyes with my sleeve, but he stopped me in mid-air. "Here, take my handkerchief. Your coat is dirty, and you could hurt your eyes," I accepted it, and dried my tears.

He gracefully stood up and did his trousers and offered me his hand. Why did I take it? I don't know. I was too exhausted to think coherently. I knew he was not a good man nor a gentleman, but a beast waiting for the smallest opportunity to lash out. However, he had offered me shelter and the promise of love. I think, I was mostly tired of being alone since my father died. Life altering decisions are made without much thought, so I took his warm hand. He helped me to rearrange my stained clothes. My doubts assaulted me once again and I took a small step away from him, but his arm trapped me by the waist as fast as an anaconda. I knew better than rebelling so I followed him.

We walked along the Grand Canal once again, in silence. I was trying to organise my thoughts, but it proved to be an impossible task. My mind replayed over and over the scenes of his brutal onslaught on me, mixing them with images of us in the restaurant, his soft and soothing voice explaining to me about the mosaics in Torcello and his first maddening kiss.

Too fast to my liking we arrived to his house. He led me from the back entrance to the main foyer through several rooms. We stood in front of the staircase leading to the bedrooms. He let go of my waist and said "go upstairs and take a shower. You're all dirty," I stood there, motionless. "Come on, go. I'll see you later. I need to arrange a few things," he said, giving me a soft nudge.

I went to my bedroom hoping the butler would not be there. I needed time to be alone. I entered in the already tidied up room. I took off the coat, shoes, trousers, and pullover and left them in a disorderly way on top of the chair. Half-dressed, I went to the bathroom and turned the hot faucet on in the shower. I undressed and caught a glimpse of my face in the mirror. My eyes were completely red and puffy and my left cheek had started to swell. I knew for sure it would be blue tomorrow. However, what scared me the most was the lifeless expression in my eyes. True, I have been in several rabbles in school, but never had someone had punished and humiliated me so much. I felt like I was acting like an automata, still too stunned to react to anything. I brushed my teeth and went into the hot water.

There, realization hit me with full power. I started to cry, not really knowing why, or perhaps not wanting to acknowledge the many reasons I had to cry for. I crumbled in the floor of the shower and started to weep loudly and irrepressibly, covering my face with my hands. My life had turned, and not for good, in less than forty-eight hours. My best friend wanted to frame me with a crime; a crazy, overzealous, violent and with no qualms when it came about using any means to get what he wanted man, had taken a fancy to me, and I had partly enjoyed it. This was what was most disturbing; me, a normal, boring guy, with an ordinary life, felt attracted to some kind of Dr. Jekyll and Mr. Hide.

My options were not good either. The most sensible thing was to escape from him at the slightest chance, but he had sounded so determined to get his way that it would not be easy to do. I also needed his help to get Fedérico out of prison and escaping would not help him. I could always go to the police and denounce that the man who had given me shelter in his house had also beaten me and almost raped me, after I offered myself to him. I could hear the policemen laugh at me. My money was almost gone and there were few chances that I could survive another three weeks on my own, till my plane would get me home (I had one of those cheap flights). Asking for help from Fefo's mother could be an option, and pray that she wouldn't bite my head off. Yes, that would be the most sensible option; speak with her tomorrow and ask for her help to run away from this maniac.

I kept my huddled position under the hot water for some time, wishing the water would wash away all my sorrows and give me a clear mind. The shower abruptly stopped and I found myself wrapped in a big towel. I turned and saw that Konrad was there kneeling on the floor beside me and had started to dry me off at the same time he drew me against his chest. I let him do it. I didn't want to start another fight.

When I was not so dripping wet, he led me to the bedroom and helped me into my pyjamas. On the desk, there was a tray with a steaming cup of chocolate and some grilled sandwiches. He told me to eat and go to bed. I complied as usual, not saying a word. He sat at my side, gently petting my head as I ate.

"I see now that such a severe punishment was too much for a sweet child like you. A stern reprimand would have sufficed, but it's too late for regrets. Guntram, hear me well in this, respect the rules and everything will run smoothly between us. I do want that we reach an understanding. Promise me you won't defy me again, and we can continue our relationship where we left it, before all this happened,"

I looked directly into his eyes and I saw for the first time an emotion that perhaps was real repentance. I quickly turned my gaze down, looking for an answer in the cup of chocolate, but there was none.

"Please let's forget this horrible matter and let's give ourselves a second start," he whispered in my ear, kissing it delicately, trailing kisses down my neck up to my collarbone. He took my stillness for a sign to advance and kissed me softly, testing my lips. I jumped a little in surprise and opened my lips a little, and he stuck his tongue inside me, his kisses, ravaging as they used to be. I was deeply kissed. I felt his desire to possess me, to engulf me again, but this time I was not afraid of it.

I briefly thought to let him kiss me and then he would be disappointed and would leave me, but it was only a stupid passing idea. I needed him more than I was ready to admit. I kissed him back pushing my body against his. He lifted us both and effortlessly led us towards the bed. He threw me on the bed and climbed on top of me without interrupting the kiss and letting me rampage freely in his mouth.

I panicked. Now he was going to take me fully. I tried to push him with my hands, but he would not move, still kissing me. My breathing became agitated and I squirmed under him, and he stopped kissing me. He might have seen the look of pure terror reflected in his eyes because he broke our embrace.

"Don't' be afraid dear. I will do nothing to you, tonight. You're too nervous to enjoy it. You need your rest and to get used to my touch. Our first time must be special and unique. Your purity is a gift you'll give me, and I don't want to spoil it. Sleep well now," he hushed me and gave me a brief last kiss on the mouth. "My bedroom is at the end of the corridor if you need anything."

Finally, I was alone and I let a long sigh escape. I had lost my appetite and decided to slide under the covers to sleep, as fatigue and soreness were finally catching up with me.

Several hours later, I woke up and needed to use the bathroom. I did my thing and went back to bed, but I couldn't sleep in that huge thing. The question tormented me and I knew I would not be able to sleep again, unless I had a true answer. I gathered my courage and went to Konrad's bedroom.

I opened the door and entered hesitantly into his room. I only saw a big window, and while I was trying to adjust my eyesight, I heard a small metallic clunk beside the huge poster bed.

"Guntram?"

"Would you ever hurt me again?" I blurted out my question. He sat on his bed, not turning on the lights, his frame drawing itself against the open window.

"Come to bed Guntram, it's cold," I slid under his covers, and he hugged me, bringing me closer to him. "No, I hope I never have to be this harsh with you ever again," I felt relieved, and snuggled closer to him and let him cuddle me till I fell asleep.

Chapter 10

Next morning, I was awakened by a gentle shake on my shoulder. "Wake up child, it's more than ten o'clock," somebody said.

I immediately sat up in bed, a bit disorientated, realising three important things. First, I was in Konrad's bed (with pyjamas on); Second, Friederich, the butler, was in front of me (therefore, he had guessed where I had slept last night, and I became red as a tomato); Third, and most horrible, I was supposed to pick up Fedérico's mother from Milan Airport at eight in the morning.

I jumped from the bed under the amused sight of Friederich. I was dead now. She would kill me in a slow and painful way!

"I have to go to Malpensa, Milan. Do you know if there are any trains going out now?"

"There's a train to Milan every hour, but if you want to pick up the Senator, you're already late," he sauntered with satisfaction—a genuine one.

"Thank you. I'll get dressed and go," was my answer, a little irked with the black bird. I'm in trouble and he mocks me!

"Goran and counsellor Gandini went for her with the car, early this morning. It's a three-hour journey. They should be here at twelve for lunch. The Duke ordered me to leave you to sleep longer. Nevertheless, I would still advise that you get dressed and have a small breakfast in your room, sir."

I retired to my own room, defeated, to find it already made as if I would have never been there. The staff in this house must have worked in a hotel before. I dressed with the set of clothes I found neatly piled on top of the bed and ate the breakfast (it was really small, coffee, milk and two pieces of toast with marmalade and butter, not much for a grown guy like me).

I went back to Konrad's room to come upon Friederich very busy reorganizing a closet, pulling out suits and rearranging shirts on racks.

"I'm sorry to disturb you, but I wonder if you could tell me where is the Duke?" I asked hesitantly. Had Konrad not said that he was meaner than him?

"His Excellency's agenda is very tight all morning. You can go to the library or the garden and wait there until the Senator arrives or it is lunch time."

"Thank you," I replied, impressed by this man's formality. "Could you tell me where the library is, please?

"Downstairs, the door on the left from the Duke's studio. If you wait, I can take you there," he said fumbling once again with the clothes until he freed almost half of the closet. "Do you think that would be sufficient space for your things, sir?

"I beg your pardon?"

"The Duke instructed me to move your belongings to his room, and I would like to know if this would be sufficient space for you."

This time, instead of pink, I turned red like a ripe tomato. Not only he had seen me in his bed, but now he positively knew what I've been doing (well, technically not yet), with Konrad. I looked down to the wooden floor and mumbled my answer.

"I think, yes."

He looked very amused at my predicament and said "It's fortunate that the

Duke has chosen you as a companion, considering his past record," he told me softly. "Yes, I think also this will suffice till we return to Zurich," he said, back to business.

Excellent! Safe topic ahead, and why has Konrad decided I have to move to his room? Anyhow, the man looks more talkative now, and maybe he could fill in the gaps of what I don't know about his boss.

"Do you live in Zurich?" I asked with my best lamb face.

"Most of the time the Duke resides in Zurich when he's not travelling for business. It was a surprise that he decided to take holidays, and come to Venice for New Year," he explained to me, while moving the suits to another cupboard hidden behind a painted wall. "He has houses in London, New York, Frankfurt, Rome and Paris. I travel with him when he decides to stay in a place more than a week. He has other properties of course, but he never visits them".

"How is Zurich?"

"You will like it. Although it's a big city, it's not noisy or polluted. There's the lake, large trees in the streets, good schools, and you can walk everywhere. The dialect is difficult to understand at the beginning, but can be learned."

"You are not Swiss?"

"No, I was born in Salzburg, and I've been working there for the last decades. Shall we go?"

So much for communication time. I bet I'll have better luck with the monster bodyguards. They seemed more friendly last time I saw them. I was led to the library, which was big, but not so huge as his office (I don't want to imagine the size of the living room or the dining room!). So far I have counted: kitchen, service rooms, studio, office, seven bedrooms on the top floor and who knows what they keep under the roof.

I checked my watch and saw it was only 11:00. Well, one hour to read or prepare something to say to Fedérico's mother. I looked on the shelves trying to find a volume not leather bound or that at least looked cheap (don't want to risk anything being ruined), but most of them were in German or Italian. Finally, I got to the English section, and there, lucky me, they had several, mostly about history (Roman and German). I took one about Roman paintings and started to read but not for long; Tweedledum and the Ferdinand guy stormed into the room.

"Hello, there you are hiding," the "funny one", if you can call him that, affirmed. "Friederich told us we would find you here," he advanced and sat in the leather couch in front of me. The other, Ferdinand, decided to sit at my side, without invitation. He took my chin to inspect my bruised cheek. He said something to the other in German.

"Next time, use spider vein cream the moment you get a punch. It helps to accelerate the healing process, and you won't get this blue shade."

"I hit myself against the bathroom door last night," I hissed upset with their meddling.

"As you say. However, next time, do it. At the moment Michael can get you some make up, so we don't scare the Senator with your face." With this unspoken order, Michael, the monster formerly known as Number Two, rushed to get it.

"My name is Ferdinand von Kleist. I'm Head of Operations for the Duke as you probably already know. The one going away is Michael Dähler and you have already met Alexei Gregorevich Antonov and Heindrik Holgersen from Sweden, but you still haven't met Goran Pavicevic," he asserted in a very formal way.

"Pleased to meet you all." Where is all this leading? Most important, do I want to know or play along with them? I could feel the tension rising as he looked at me intensely. Let's shake the mood because I can't stand another police interrogation session. "More than a group of bodyguards, you all look like the United Nations," I said, lightly.

"We are the inner circle at the moment. There are more, but you don't need to know them. I would like to explain to you a few rules concerning your own safety in this house."

"I will not be here for too long, and I don't want to be any burden to you all," I said defensively. I knew for certain that I was not going to like this. Fortunately, Michael stormed in the room, carrying something in his hand.

"Got this from one of the maidens. You can keep as long as you need it," he told me, his hand extending a small powder box. I muttered a "thank you" and applied a little of the thing into my cheek. "Looks better, but not much," he reassured me while he took his previous place on the couch.

"As I was saying, I want to explain to you some of the rules about safety in this house. The *Herzog* is a very wealthy man, billionaire, if you need to know, and since you are going to be an important part of his life, you are henceforth a source of concern for us, since you could be considered as a target by the Duke's enemies,"

I tried to protest as, with a lot of luck, I was one of his toys till the "young virgin" thrill was over, but he stopped me with a hand gesture. "Let me finish before you say anything. I'm particularly glad the Duke has decided finally to settle down, but I must stress to you what it means."

"First, and most important rule. You don't discuss or speak with anyone outside these house walls or the staff, I have mentioned before, anything you hear or see. The Duke sometimes hosts meetings with very important people, and we don't like any kind of leaks. Furthermore, the Duke is quite jealous of his privacy. Therefore, he hates to have the press around. He tries to keep his profile as low as possible as his position in world finances allows it. He's not like a Rothschild or a Buffet if you understand me."

"Second rule is that you don't leave the house without informing us, Friederich or the Duke of your whereabouts. It's us who decide if you take an escort, or if you can go alone. You will always take this mobile phone with you."

"Third rule is you don't discuss or disobey orders. If some of us says 'get in the car' you do so—immediately. I believe Monika, the Duke's private secretary, will give you a credit card and some cash, but as for the financial details, you'll discuss those with her."

I was shocked, utterly shocked. Have those two lost their minds, coming to boss me around like that? I made a real effort to keep my cool as I gritted, "Excuse me gentlemen, but do you take me for some kind of stray dog that you and your Duke can pick up from the streets and order around?"

"It's for your protection. I think you don't realise so far where you have landed and who is the Duke," Michael said very seriously. He's not so funny when he's 'working'".

"I think you are overdoing it. Do I have to ask permission to go out, like a five year old? I have lived my whole life on my own and please, you are blowing everything out of proportion. Don't you realise how ridiculous everything sounds? I have only known the Duke for two or three days at most, and you are already offering me a credit card and security personal?"

"The Duke has gone through a considerable amount of trouble to keep you at his side, and you're the first we ever saw to sleep in his own bed. Normally, he will take his lovers to a hotel and away with them next morning," Ferdinand stated.

I blushed again; deeply, wishing I could crawl into a dark hole. Does everybody around here discuss what we do or don't do in bed?

"Don't be so obfuscated, kid. We are glad to have you here, and we won't give you troubles as long as you don't become one for us," Michael said, with a fatherly smile. Did I hear a hidden threat there? "You should be happy that a man like him has decided to take you as his lover."

"Are you deaf or just foolish? I'm only a novelty and when the excitement is over, and pretty soon because I'm a boring person, he will throw me out. Besides, are you not upset that your boss is going after another man?"

"What the Duke does is not our business to discuss. He fulfils perfectly his duties toward The Order and that's all that matters. He has done it tirelessly since he took over twenty-two years ago," Ferdinand affirmed, obviously proud of his boss. Wait, did he just said "order"?

"Even Friederich likes you, and that is a first," Michael chuckled. "Normally, he's the one ranting about the Duke's lovers, but with you, he's completely happy, and this morning, he was thanking God, he would not have to deal any more with uptight top models. He really has a lousy job, if you ask me."

"As I see, you have already felt the consequences of crossing the Duke," Ferdinand said, while I opened my mouth to protest, but he didn't give me the chance to do it. "You should be grateful you got away relatively unscathed. I would not do it too often. He's not used to being disobeyed and trust me, you don't want to experience what he's capable of doing when angry," was his stern advise.

"Come on kid, if you'd see the people's list trying to get your place, you'd be astonished," Michael giggled. Was this the German version of the Merry Wives of Windsor?

The door opened and Konrad entered in the room, casually dressed with a trousers and jacket. The two bodyguards jumped to their feet like well-oiled springs and in a sort of military way. I did likewise, without even realising what I was doing. He dismissed the men with a simple gesture of the head, and advanced toward me. He leaned his head and briefly and tenderly kissed me on the lips.

"Did you sleep well, little one?" Without giving me time to reply, he sat on the couch and with a playful pull made me land on his lap. He resumed his kissing, his arms trapping me effectively. Even if that was really nice and I could have continued for as long as ever, I had to have some answers from him. I tried to separate us by gently pushing him away. He looked a bit cross, like a child denied a candy, that I have interrupted the kiss.

"Konrad, we need to talk. I'm completely confused." Let's try the puppy tactics because a frontal attack was a disaster last time I tried.

"Can you not wait for later?" he mumbled trying to catch me again.

"No, please. All this situation is driving me crazy."

"All right. Say what you have in mind. We have about half an hour before the Argentinean woman arrives."

"I'm a mess. Yesterday you beat me and nearly raped me, and today, I have your bodyguards giving me a full list of the things I'm supposed to do since you have almost adopted me as your new pet," I said rather hotly.

"Not pet. Companion," he clarified. Is there any difference?

"You can't enter into my life and rule it like you own it. I can't deny any longer that I'm attracted to you, but this does not give you the right to boss me around like a paid whore."

There, I said it. He looked cross and about to lash out. Shit. I was in real trouble! The time went slowly by as the only sound I could hear was his ragged breathing, as if he was trying to calm himself down.

"I think we have already gone through all this," he finally answered biting the words. "I love you and I don't want anything to happen to you. Anybody could try to kidnap you because of my money. Therefore, you need protection. You are clearly not a whore, and I never treated you like one. I'm only giving a sense of order into your chaotic lifestyle."

"Konrad, I have a life in Argentina, and I will return to it, eventually. On February 3rd to be more precise. I have a job, an university to attend, a flat, friends and many other things. You can't burst into my life just like this."

"You can fly to the country, put your affairs in order and then return to me. I can give you time."

"Have you not considered the notion that maybe I don't think I would be able to have a relationship with you?"

"Why not?"

"Because we are so different one from another!" I yelled and immediately felt ashamed for losing my temper. "There is the age difference," I said much softer. "You're an educated man, and I'm not. You have your life already organised, and I don't. I haven't even finished school! You're a handsome man and I'm a regular guy, one from the bunch. I think you're fascinated by the novelty of getting a virgin in your bed and then that would be it. There's nothing to keep us together."

"Why do you think so low of yourself?" he inquired softly.

"I'm realistic," I said, not really wanting to answer the question. My status in front of his eyes must be extremely low if he thinks I have nothing of value to come back to, and I'm like some kind of puppy he can pick up whenever he feels like it. No need to feel more ashamed than I do at this point.

"I am also. All my life, I achieved everything I proposed myself to, but I never enjoyed a pure love like the one you can offer me. I don't know what makes your self-esteem so low, but you don't realise how unique and beautiful you are. The only thing I'm asking from you, is the chance to start a sound relationship with you. To get to know you, and let you come into my world. Let's take this month before we make any decisions about the future. You have already acknowledged your feelings for me, and I have declared mine for you. At this moment, my greatest wish would be to grow old together. Many dear things were taken away from me in the past in order to become who I am now, and I don't want this any longer," he cupped my face with his hands and looked me in the eyes, as if he wanted to check if I'd understood. I put my arms around his neck and bent my head down to kiss him. He didn't hesitate to respond to my soft pecking, crushing my body against his chest and almost sucking the life out of me with his kissing.

Even if I'm positively sure that this will end bad for me, I long for the opportunity to feel again close to somebody. Perhaps I should take the risk for once in my life and ride the wave the best as I can. Some trains pass you by, once in a lifetime. If he could be a little less overbearing with me, I think we could be together.

A soft knock on the door pulled me out of my bliss—yeah, he's a hell of a kisser, and maybe I'm gay although the idea of another man touching me who is not Konrad makes me want to puke—I tried to disentangle from his arms, but he kept me firmly on his lap while he said "Come in". I could officially die of shame!

The Russian bodyguard, Alexei entered with a phone in his hand. He barely looked at me and with a blank expression said "My Duke, Goran is on the phone and wishes instructions."

"How's the weather?"

"Stormy."

What? It looks very sunny from the window. Better be quiet, I'm already quite noticeable sitting in a grown man's lap to make myself further known.

"Hotel then," he said, nonchalantly. The big blond Russian disappeared as fast as he had entered. Time to give a piece of my mind to Konrad because he seems quite determined to pick up things where he left them before the interruption.

"Why did you do that?" I asked, not letting him to catch me again.

"Did what?"

"Make this lovers' scene in front of your people?" I clarified, now serious.

"Because we are that; the faster they acknowledge it, the better for us. I have nothing to be ashamed of. Do you?" There was a dangerous glint dangling in his eyes.

"Maybe here in Europe things are more advanced than in Latin America, but two men kissing is not something you show on the streets, unless you want to go to the police station to do some explanation. I'm not into all this gay pride day or whatever it's called that many of them proclaim. One thing is to kiss you and another completely different is to start a promiscuous lifestyle for me, shouting it to the whole world."

"I'm glad we agree on something. I'm not into this propaganda for the gays' rights or anything like that. I defend my privacy as much as I can, and believe me not all 'gay people' as you call them, are dancing in the streets with feathers on their head."

"I have to be honest with you. I don't know if I'm into men at all. Wait! Let me finish. When I was in the school, I never felt the need to look at the other boys in the swimming pool or drool over them like a gay is supposed to do since infancy. I even think that women's bodies are far more beautiful than our ones. To make out with another guy makes me want to puke."

"What did you feel the first time I kissed you, in Torcello? Did you feel disgusted?"

"No, it felt great, the right thing to do, but I don't understand it, really. It's just you whom I like to kiss me," I answered slowly, hiding my head in his shoulder.

His big hand caressed my head in circles, playing with my hair as he whispered in my left ear, "Then I should be grateful. Love is love regardless of the gender. When you truly fall in love, the rest of the world ceases to exist. You only want to belong to this person and nothing else. That you already feel like that for me bodes very well for our future."

"Do you feel like this for me? I'm afraid that all your declarations are only nice words. You must have hundreds of people waiting in line to catch you, someone much better than me."

He burst into laughter. Not what I was expecting, and it hurt.

"My dear *Maus*, I will not deny that many have been after me, mostly because of money, sadly, but the truth is that I have to be concerned you'll run away with someone better. I will have to be careful with young ladies around you. A face like yours could cause a disaster," he chuckled. "All right, I will not kiss you, for the moment, in public but understand that my employees are not an audience."

"Could you try to be a little less pushy? You're always telling me what to do." If it's compromise time, let's use it!

"I'm used to being obeyed, and if I tell something to you is with best intentions. I know better than you this world, and it would be really sad if something bad would happen to you. I can try to listen to your protests if that helps you to cope with it."

It's not really what I had in mind, but maybe it would do, for the moment. I looked around, distracted for a moment, and he caught me again by the chin, and seriously asked me with his face of "don't mess around".

"Do you give me your word of respecting and obeying the rules that I set before?"

"Yes, I do."

"Will you do exactly as Ferdinand and the others tell you to?"

"Why do I have to obey them too?" No answer; sharp, expressionless look on his face. That's scary. "All right," I mumbled this time. The idea of five gorillas bossing me around is not nice.

"It would not be so bad, Guntram. They can be reasonable," he playfully told me, poking me in the ribs. I batted his finger away with a soft slap, and he seized my hand and kissed it, giving me one of his flashing smiles and I smiled back at him as I lifted myself from his lap.

"When the Senator arrives, I want that you remain silent. No interruptions, no lashing out if she says something offensive, and only answer if you get a direct question," he said suddenly serious, his eyes piercing me and his regal and intimidating aura back into place, as if the tender man of two minutes ago had never existed. "Gandini and I have to discuss the terms of your 'friend's' release with her, and it will not be pleasant. So please, go to you room or with Ferdinand and the others when I ask you to do so. Is that understood?"

His deadly seriousness hit me full force, but I saw some hope for Fedérico. If his solicitor wanted to help then maybe he could get out of the mess.

"Are you going to help Fedérico? I said, my hope returning to me.

"I promised you that I would try, and I fulfil all my promises. That we are successful or not depends on the Senator."

When I was about to ask what he was trying to tell me, or what he was concocting in that twisted brain of his, the Gandini solicitor burst into the room, without knocking or anything. I was glad to be on the opposite chair!

"That woman is impossible. I'm not surprised everybody wants to fry the Argentineans nowadays." He kept going on in a heated German with Konrad. I sat there, peacefully wondering if it would be too rude if I went back to my book. Yes, it seemed Gandini met our distinguished lady from the north of the country.

"Guntram, take your book and go to the living room. This might take a while," Konrad instructed me in a glacial tone. OK, time to go away. I secured my book under my arm and tilted my head slightly toward Gandini.

The living room was grandiose to say something. Impressive was not enough of a description. Big windows over the canal, the ceiling painted like those baroque paintings like the ones in San Rocco, some big ferns in the corners. Leather brown couches, carpet the size of almost the whole thing, a French marble chimney, some ivory and silver artworks and in the walls some paintings who looked very similar in style to those of Mary Cassatt.

Just when I was about to sit in one of the couches by the window, an unknown butler opened the door to let Fedérico's mother enter the room. I remained standing and frozen in my spot unable to say anything. She looked extremely upset and walked in a straight line toward me.

"Good morning, Madam," I didn't want to piss her off more than she already was and impoliteness is the perfect way to do so.

She didn't waste time or words with me. I got a full slap to the face, nothing that could be compared to Konrad's, but with enough force to make me sway and look downward, burning with the humiliation of receiving the punishment meant for an unruly and lowly servant.

"You're worse than trash! The only thing you had to do was to keep Fedérico out of trouble, and you created them. After your father jumped that god-damned window, they should have also thrown you out, you useless prick!" She cried now completely hysterical and raising the hand for a second blow.

"Madam, resorting to violence will not solve the situation," a very stern German growled. "Guntram is a guest in my house, and I will not tolerate any offence toward him."

Well, to have a bear the size of Konrad at your side is not so bad after all. He has just gotten the great Martina de Alvear to be quiet and look humble for a minute. My stinging cheek was worthy, if you ask me. But the remark about my father's death hurt me more than the slap.

"Please forgive my outburst, sir. I'm under considerable stress at the moment," she said like a queen, easily recovering her poise and taking a good look at him. I supposed she was quite taken with Konrad's appearance. I mean, when he's upset, his eyes glint in a disturbingly attractive manner, even if his face is stoic.

Fortunately, Gandini, partially hidden behind Konrad, decided to intervene. He strategically placed himself between both silent contenders. "Senator, please allow me to introduce you to the Duke." The air was thick with electricity and for a moment, I could smell the aroma of gunpowder too. Another clever man, Friederich, entered to announce lunch was served.

The dining room was also grandiose, more in a baroque style, because the paintings in the ceiling and mirrors in the walls were more ever present than in the living room. The whole thing looked like one of those state banquet rooms. Honestly, I was expecting to see the Queen of England enter at any moment. However, I'm afraid that if you want to impress Martina, you need more than that, because she entered without throwing a second glance, going straight to the place on the right side of the principal seat. I looked a bit lost and Friederich again made a small gesture indicating me the one beside the left one, in the farthest corner.

Friederich and the other butler started to serve the lunch, the first one concentrated on Konrad and Martina, while Gandini and I got the second one. Since I was sitting in direct line with Fedérico's mother's cold and disdaining glance, I decided to focus on my dish and keep quiet as a mouse Who knows, maybe this time I'd get the soup through my nose. Again nobody considered it necessary that I would get some wine.

Gandini started to tell about his cousins in Argentina and what a great time he had when visiting them ten years ago and what a pity that everything was in shambles now. Martina thankfully picked up the queue, and kindly replied and the conversation could carry on versing on politics and possible scenarios. To my surprise, Konrad had a good understanding of the figures in our economy and was quite updated on our local politics. That's the good thing of being on CNN is that you're back on the map! He heard her very mindfully asking whenever something was not perfectly clear. Fedérico was never discussed.

"Your house is very beautiful Duke, do you live here all year long?" Martina inquired.

"Not really. This house was my great grandmother's favourite. Mostly, I'm in Zurich or London."

"I assume you are in the banking business."

"I'm the CEO of five hedge funds and private banks in Switzerland and in the U.K. I control also several middle insurance companies and industries. Farming is a sector I'm not yet familiar with," he said in a kind voice, completely seductive if you ask me.

He should worry that I run away with somebody else? My ass, that bastard is flirting with the wicked witch of the north and the worst part is that she looks great for her age—perfect for him. Better I take care of my apple cake for dessert. Thank God for small consolation prizes!

"My family name dates from the XII century from the Mecklenburg Vorpommern area. Alas during the communist invasion, my grandparents had to move to the South, to Munich, till we went to Vaduz, where my mother came from," he was telling to her so nicely. Better listen well, so I get more information about him. No, I'm not jealous, but he could have told me his C.V in advance and avoid me to hear it, almost snooping.

"Did you study in Switzerland?"

"Partly. I got several tutors until I turned thirteen. I was sent to a boarding school in Bern and later to study Business Administration in Zurich, and made my Thesis at the London School of Economics by paternal demand. I was supposed to take over the family business, and I did it at the age of twenty-two when my father passed away."

Impressive, if you ask me.

"I'm most grateful to you for the interest you took in my son's case."

"You should thank Guntram that he insistently interceded for him. I'm afraid I don't know your son, and my charity cases focus elsewhere."

Ouch! That must have hurt. The Alvears a "charity case"; all of them must be turning in their family vault, and she would cut her tongue out before admitting I could be of some use.

"Yes, Guntram has actively sought to help my son. He was quite loyal," she said through her gritted teeth. It was a pity that I didn't have a camera at the time. But I should not gloat, this is a truly bad moment for her.

"Thank you, Madam," was my quiet reply and only contribution to the talk.

"I think we should have coffee in my studio and discuss the details concerning your son's release. Shall we, Madam?"

We all stood up to let her pass and the two men went directly to the studio, leaving me alone with the butlers. Friederich was the first to break the ice, so to speak.

"Would you like to join the rest of the Duke's men? They're in the kitchen having lunch also."

"I do not want to disturb them. I will stay in the living room, reading, if it's suitable."

"As you wish, sir."

I went back to my book enjoying the restored peace in the living room. I would have preferred to go out, but I wanted to know what was transpiring in that studio. I read for about an hour in silence, relaxing as much as possible till the Barbarian Invasions started anew. At the entrance, Ferdinand, Michael and Heindrik, were standing, imposing as usual.

"Come with us Guntram. You are not going to sit there, miserably, the whole evening. We are about to have coffee in the kitchen," Michael said cheerfully.

"I was reading here," I protested.

"You have to meet Goran also, he's the last one missing from the gang," Michael happily informed me. Oh joy, the last ape!

"No chance I can stay here and read?"

"None. If you are waiting for them, it could take hours."

"Why? I think the lawyer only has to explain his tactic and present his bill."

"The Duke has still to make his demands clear on the matter and discuss the terms for his help," Ferdinand said nonchalantly, as he took me by the arm, pulling me to my feet. Luckily, I was able to grab the book while he pulled me toward the kitchen.

Chapter 11

The kitchen was quite crowded. The bodyguards took by assault the main table, where a dark haired man, not too big, was sitting with a cup of coffee. One nice looking girl with a maiden's uniform, started to place cups and dishes on the table without saying anything to them. Then she brought two different type of cakes along with a coffee pot and a kettle. I sat where they indicated me, next to the dark haired man, who happened to be the famous Goran from Serbia; a really quiet and spooky guy.

They all started to speak at each other in German, and I think in Russian. Whatever was being said, I had no idea. I don't speak a word of Russian or German, so I decided to space out a little, absently drawing a small hedgehog with a pencil on a piece of white paper.

"It looks almost real," Goran said, taking me out from my happy limbo. "Are you an artist?"

"No, far from that. I study Economics and Social Work," I replied with a smile, noticing the others had stopped talking and were looking at me like hungry hyenas. Incredible! One single question and I had opened the hunting season entirely by myself!

"You don't really paint or something?" Heindrik asked, with a thick accent.

"No, I work in a book store with a cafeteria inside, nothing fancy".

"Why did you come to Europe?" Ferdinand barked.

"Holidays. The original idea was to visit the big cities and then go home. But at the moment, I don't know any longer. I think I will return with Fedérico and his mother as soon this nightmare is over."

"I was under the impression you were going to stay here, independently of what happens to that boy," Ferdinand pointed out again, crossing his hands over the bridge of his nose, as the others fixed their gazes on me.

"With all due respect, gentlemen, this is not something to discuss with you at all," I said, now really upset. Your gorilla size and your killer looks don't give you the right to meddle in my life. I'm not going to tell my whole life to five perfect strangers, the kind you cross the street if you see them coming.

"Does the Duke know of this?" Ferdinand inquired softly, changing his bully demeanour into something else, but not reassuring at all.

I took a deep breath before answering. "I can't stay longer because I have a life in my own country. Besides, I will be abusing the Duke's good will. I will not make up my mind based only in two or three days," I returned to my hedgehog not wanting to hear any more from these men. A poignant silence established around the table.

"Are you not in love with him?" Who else but Michael could ask such a blunt question? I stopped drawing, my pencil in mid-air, hesitating, my heart beating strongly and deciding my fate. I should have denied everything and sent those idiots to Hell, but I couldn't do it because it would have been a blatant lie.

"I'm keen on him. He's a cult man with an interesting conversation," I said, hoping it would keep the wolves at bay.

Michael snorted rather loudly and the others laughed openly, all except Ferdinand who looked at me with true hate in his eyes. Sorry man if not all of us drool over your almighty boss, but these things need time.

"For your sake, I hope you are not playing because I will be the one to put an end to it," He barked, all laughter abruptly died.

"What do you expect me to say? I fail to see why this is your business. Take a look at me and you'll see that I'm not much of a threat to your boss, physically or mentally. He's way out of my league. You are overstepping your boundaries," I said really upset, rising my voice a little more than necessary.

"Ferdinand, leave the boy alone. He has no malice." Michael interfered in our duel of looks, half standing from his chair.

"Quiet you! I'm the one who decides here!" The older German roared. "I don't like you at all. Too good to be true. If you even try to hurt the Duke, I swear I'll make you pay slow and painfully."

This was it. Now I'm beyond the point of my usual polite lamb persona. "And this is supposed to frighten me or make me fall in love with your boss? You are very sick if you think that I will throw myself into his bed after only a few days of knowing him. You are demanding something from me that not even he expects. Mind your own business!"

I felt a pair of hands resting on my shoulders. I turned my head to see Friederich standing behind me. He softly said something in German to Ferdinand, and the man magically relaxed his rabid dog attack position.

"I believe the young man should know what he's getting into. It's the fair thing to do," he gravely said, his hands never leaving my shoulders.

"I don't think so," Ferdinand replied flatly.

"I second the motion" Michael said. "Alexei, Heindrik, Goran, go outside." All the men left the room as if they were pursued by the devil himself.

"You have no voice in this!" Ferdinand barked again. "You were not there like us!"

"I'm an associate and I can decide in equal terms as you."

"It will be on your conscience!"

"So be it. Friederich, you must tell because you're the one who knows best and frankly Ferdinand is not up to it."

"I believe that the best we can do for you and him, Guntram, is to tell you more about the Duke's past love life. You should be aware where you're standing. Many years ago, twenty-two to be precise, his Excellency fell madly in love with a currency broker in one of his banks. He had just overtaken his father companies, and was not the man he is today. He was extremely intelligent, but still 'green' so to speak. His father had prepared him for what was expected of him since he was sixteen, but he had not much idea of how low human beings can fall. Anyway, there was this trader, five years older and he was truly a beautiful man, with the face of an angel. Nevertheless, he was ambitious, greedy, with no morals at all, and would stop at nothing in order to advance further his career. He managed to get his way to the Duke and seduced him, almost effortlessly. Before him, the Duke had not much interest in men, well nothing more than some experiences in school."

"When this man entered in his life, he went almost mad with desire. They had a rocky relationship for many years. He was always cheating on him, blackmailing him into giving more positions in the upper scales of the banks and even getting married. The Duke should have ended everything as soon as he found out that he was married, but his love was more strong than his sense of self-preservation. This clearly abusive relationship carried on for almost seven years, till this person thought he could take over everything his Excellency had by betraying him. Fortunately, Ferdinand discovered the plan before he could perpetrate it, and with great pain, he could prove it to the Duke," Friederich told me, pausing to take a sip of water. I moved my head in order to encourage him to continue.

"He ended any kind of relationship with this snake, but he was dead inside. For the last thirteen years, he has only worked, transforming himself into a hard, unforgiving man, unable to build his private life back again. He totally forwent of men, and only had brief encounters with women, not even lasting the night he had paid. He closed completely to the rest of humans."

"This man looked very much like you Guntram. The eye colour, the hair, nose, structure of your body. If it wouldn't be for the age difference, he was twenty-seven when he met the Duke, you two could pass for brothers. But I'm sure that you're nothing like him at all. Your nature is quiet, sweet, shy and compassionate when he was the opposite."

"Since you are here, our Duke has changed. He looks human again, not that money making machine he is nowadays. My only concern is that you could hurt him like the other did. I don't think he would have the strength to survive it. This morning, when I went to his bedroom to wake him up, I found him in the bed already awake, holding you as if you were his most precious belonging. He had spent the whole night without sleeping, just looking at you. You are his chance to live again."

"I don't know if I could meet the expectations you place on me. I know deep inside, that he could not like me for myself, but only because I'm some kind of doppelgänger of long forgotten love," I said slowly, utterly disappointed with Konrad and myself, feeling an oppressive knot in the pitch of my stomach, and the urgent need to run away and cry.

"You see, better get rid of him before he'll destroy us more," Ferdinand barked.

"Yes, Ferdinand, you are right. I should go," I was heartbroken. It seems that love is for people more outgoing, clever and beautiful than me. I rose from the table, much older than before.

"Guntram, I know the story, wait a minute," Michael stopped me. "Try to place yourself in Ferdinand's shoes. He's a childhood friend of the Duke, not a simple servant. He had to pick up the pieces after the collapse. He only wants to ensure that you will not deliberately hurt the Duke."

"I would not hurt him. Why would I do it? He has been kind to me most of the time. But, don't you see that he will be always looking at this person instead of me?"

"I admit that at first glance you two look very similar, but after ten minutes of speaking to you, the resemblance disappears. You two are day and night," Ferdinand said, taking me by the hand. "Please sit down again and listen to us," I tried to disentangle myself from his firm grip, a huge contrast with his softly spoken words. "Now, child tell us the truth, please. Do you think you could love him?"

"I don't know," I hesitated. Those men had just informed me that I was the chosen replacement for someone gone many years ago.

"Yes, you do," Ferdinand pressed me.

"I can't deny that I'm attracted to him. Very. I don't know if this is real love. I never had a girlfriend or boyfriend before. Everything is new and confusing for me. I can promise you that I would do nothing deliberately to harm him, but you can't put all the blame on me if we don't work at all."

Ferdinand stood up, large as life and circled the table toward me, stopping in front of me. I looked up to him, a menacing mountain if ever, waiting for him to make the first move. He lifted me with ease from my elbows, and crushed me against his broad chest, while he patted me on my back rather strongly. "Welcome now, little brother," he said with real tenderness in his voice. I tried to disentangle from his bear hug but it was impossible. Finally, he decided that he had enough of squeezing me and released me.

"You should never discuss what we have told you just now with the Duke. It remains in this room," Michael warned me, deadly serious.

"Why not?"

"Because the mention of his name infuriates him to no end, and you don't want to be on the receiving end of his fury. I know him since we were nine years old, and in this moment he's truly convinced that you are his second chance for love, this time in a clean form." Ferdinand asseverated, his eyes fixated on mine. "He wants to have you and will stop at nothing to do so."

"Come Ferdinand, I thought we have already passed the phase of terrifying the boy," Michael said nervously. Ferdinand let go of me, and I backed a few steps away from him. Even if he's not so keen of skinning me alive, he's truly scary now in his "big brother" form.

"For his sake, I want the boy to understand what kind of man he will be living with from now onward."

"I think I had a proof yesterday," I rebutted still feeling cold shivers running through my back at the memory.

"He's forty-four years old and will not change, no matter what you think or he tells you." Was his final warning before letting me go.

Friederich sat next to me and he started to ask me about my university, job, and what I was doing in the slums. Despite my initial impression that he was a cold hearted man, he was kind in a fatherly fashion. I don't know why Konrad had said that he was mean.

"Do we have some myrrh left? It would be good to burn some in my studio," Konrad surprised us all, his figure almost covering the entrance door of the kitchen. All the men immediately rose, and I also, not so gracefully as them. How those big hulks can move with grace and silently is a mystery.

"Impossible woman," he mumbled frustrated, coming to me and ruffling my hair playfully and sitting in the place strategically vacated beside me "Something left from coffee?" In less than a minute, Friederich served him a cup of coffee and a piece of cherry cake.

"Is she always this stubbornly stupid or is it just for my benefit?" Konrad asked me.

"She is not used to be contradicted," I said softly, the understatement of the year, fearing the worst. Most probably, Martina had pissed him off to no end. She just doesn't know how to retreat or when is the time to do it. I'd bet she had even lectured him on the art of being a responsible parent. "Is there any chance you could help her?"

"Yes, Gandini has taken her to the hotel and he will solve the problem."

"So, is it done, Sire?" Ferdinand asked. Why a head of security will ask his boss something like this? It sounded very strange to me.

"Indeed," he dryly replied, his spoon slowly stirring the coffee. "So, Guntram what have you being doing all this time?" He shot the question at me, not really giving me time to come out of my daze of "what had been done" with Martina.

"Trying to read, having coffee with your men, drawing, telling most of my life story, and being threatened with a slow and painful death if I misbehave," I blurted out. If you are going to lie, do it as close as possible to the truth.

He chuckled. "Indeed. That sounds like a happy afternoon with my staff." The others looked relieved. Great guys, you owe me now. Luckily for us all, he didn't press the issue, distracted with the food and studying my drawing intensely. Now it was my turn to become restless, because I was getting again the feeling of sitting in front of a teacher with the homework not properly done. His fingertip passed slowly over the top of the hedgehog's thorns. Out of his reverie he ordered "Ferdinand, call Lehnder and tell him, that I want those transfers made as quickly as possible. No delays. If the traders have to stay longer, they should do it. I want this business finished before dinner." Needless to say, the huge man went hastily away with the other in tow.

"Were you not in holidays?" I asked smiling. The man must be a workaholic at least and an optimist. It's more than five, see if you get a bank clerk now!

"I am," he chuckled. "Otherwise, I would be there, making sure they don't screw it up twice. All right, let's go for a walk. Friederich, dinner at 8:30 in the private dining room," he stood up as he pulled me up alongside with him.

We went to the foyer and there was waiting for us the second butler with our coats. He helped Konrad to get his and handed him a pair of gloves. Without even looking at the man he said "Thank you," In that tone you should use with the servants when you want them out, exactly as we were told in school, but I've never mastered. The butler disappeared instantly as Konrad took my own overcoat and helped me to slide in and battered my hand away when I tried to do the buttons, taking the task by himself.

"Where are your gloves, Guntram?" He whispered seductively in my ear, bending his head down. When I turned my neck to answer he quickly gave me a brief kiss to muffle my reply. I found his gesture utterly tender and chuckled as my heart melted away. He let me go smiling, obviously satisfied that his small prank had had such a positive return. Who knows, maybe what happened last night was a consequence of a flashback from his hellish previous relationship, and his character was not that blood thirsty beast from the previous night.

"I think I should get you gloves," he half seriously stated.

"It's really not necessary. You have already given me a lot…," I rejected, but his fingertip on my lips prevented me to continue further.

"So, do I presume you prefer my method for warming hands? I also like it," he said with a devious glint in his eyes while I blushed beyond pink. Now he openly laughed at me as he gave me a soft nudge toward the door.

"And the caboose doesn't come along today?" I said, nonchalantly with my best innocent voice. All right it's payback time.

"I will have to defend your virtue by myself. Should I take the sword along?" He intoned with a deep voice. This time, I laughed conceding defeat. He has a strange sense of humour if you ask me.

We went out and he made a gesture with the head toward the right and said, "Peggy Guggenheim Museum?"

"It's not really my taste but we could go if you want."

"What do you like?"

"I'm not much into modern art, I don't understand it really. And since I'm here, I prefer the classical art. I wanted to visit an exhibition from Bronzino they had in Florence, but I don't know any more."

"Yes, but your drawing looks more like a young Dürer."

"Please, he's a genius and I, with lots of luck, can copy decently. I can't even draw comics. The only ones who like my drawings are the children at the school," I chuckled, finding the idea totally ridiculous; love really makes you blind if you think I can remotely draw like Dürer.

"You have almost a photographic quality in your drawing, yet it's somehow different in essence to the original, as if the drawing would have a life of its own."

"This is because I never saw a hedgehog alive, only in books or Animal Planet."

"Then more to my favour. Dürer was drawing mostly from memory, from what he had seen and studied in books, this is why you don't see any kind of indecision in his strokes because he had first understood the intrinsic logic and dynamics of the object. Have you studied art in school?"

"The normal drawing class and almost flunked it. I had, and I quote the teacher 'no feeling or imagination, completely cold and rational copies', so I pursued my artistic career drawing cards for teaching to read. For children, you have to get almost photos, they really don't like abstractions, so they find funny my drawings. You have to draw fast, because they get easily bored, and then it is Hell on earth, believe me."

"You should reconsider about drawing," he said earnestly.

"At the moment I have quite a handful with two careers in the University. I would be glad if I finish Economics and get a paying job," I said in a dreamy way. Yeah, my idea was to get a job, a wife, children and do as much as possible for the others, but now, all this looked far away, and it scared me how this man was altering my life in less than a week.

He said nothing and we continued to walk along the streets, now going to the fine area near San Marco. We walked in comfy silence without a real direction or purpose. I wonder what he would be thinking, but his face was giving no clues at all. Does he think of me? No, I scolded myself. Most probably his mind is on his banks, people like him have a lot on their minds, especially if you look as dashing as him. The tenderness he had shown me in the house vanished, and his stance was like one of a predator; a wild, dangerous, deadly one, with a magnetic appeal.

Konrad stopped in front of a man's shop and opened the door for me. I should inform him at some point, for example, when he's in a fantastic good mood, that I'm not a girl who needs his help. We entered into what looked like a tailor's shop, and a middle aged man rushed to greet Konrad in Italian. They spoke quite fast for my liking, unable to understand anything. The man produced a box from under the counter filled with leather gloves.

"Show me your hand, sir," the man ordered me. I was taken aback because I really was not expecting this. I mechanically extended my hand toward him. "Yes, an eight. Try this, please".

Seeing my more than justifiable hesitation because of the clearly expensive price of the things, Konrad let out a sight of exasperation. "Guntram, it will not be funny when your fingers freeze in this cold. You're not used to it." Defeated I tried the things, marvelled at how soft and flexible the leather was. He resumed his talk in Italian with the man, and gave me a soft push toward the door, making me leave the store.

"Should we not pay?" I inquired.

"He will bring the bill tomorrow when he comes to the house. Martinelli has been a provider for the family for the last forty years," he explained to me as he started to walk backward.

"Konrad, there's something I should discuss with you," he stopped and looked at me, with an expressionless face without saying anything. I took a deep breath, it seemed we were going to clash anyhow.

"Please don't think I'm ungrateful to you, but this whole situation is very violent for me. You paid the lawyer, and I intend to return the money to you as soon as I can, offered me shelter and even the clothes I'm wearing, but this is too much. I'm not at your level and never will be. I know you do this selflessly, but I can't help the feeling that I'm taking advantage of you. So, please, this has to stop," I whispered, my voice almost inaudible. All right, now wait for the explosion; he does not like to be contradicted remember?

He looked at me, seriousness portrayed in his face his lips making a very thin line.

"You should have told me earlier that you preferred to go naked around the house. I've would have been more than happy to accommodate you."

I blushed beyond red, purple to be exact at the image he was throwing at me, and burst into laughter. What else can you do in front of such a blunt answer?

"Seriously."

"I am. This is only money. Besides, I would get jealous if my men were to admire you," he teased me. He took my now gloved hand into his big ones, devouring me with his eyes, "You are only mine to enjoy," he murmured, making time freeze for me. My heart accelerated its beat, and there, in a small, crowded and noisy street in Venice, I knew with a killing certainty that I had fallen in love with him. This time, I had a lump in my throat but it was fine. I closed my hand over his long fingers in a brief, shy clasp only to let them go, almost immediately, as I smiled at him truly for the first time. In response he tugged me almost playing toward him. "Come, let's go home. It's getting late."

Around eight o'clock, we arrived at his residence. Michael was waiting for Konrad with a stack of papers to read and sign. Konrad looked at me, letting out a frustrated sigh, throwing a dirty glance at Michael, who visibly paled at that.

"Let's go to the library so I can wrap these documents up before dinner. Or are you planning also spoiling my digestion, Dähler?" he said through gritted teeth.

"Not at all, my Duke," he answered sheepishly, under my barely contained fun. So, big men like you can get nervous after all?

"Perhaps I should leave you alone to your business," I tested.

"Nonsense. You can sit by me and read your book," he scoffed at me impatiently. I meekly followed him to the library, and sat in front of him on the nice couch, just to allow him a little bit of privacy with his papers. He beckoned with his hand so I would sit beside him.

On the coffee table in front of us, was the Roman art book from the morning, and I briefly wondered how it had appeared there. I took it and started to read as Konrad was already deeply immersed in his papers, reading with an almost frightening fierceness. Now and then, he would give me an mind absently caress on my arm, I think most to check if I was still there, never lifting his eyes from the papers. I had to quench a giggle when Friederich made a theatrical entrance to announce dinner as if we had just won the lottery. But Konrad didn't stop to read. The poor man had to stay there, standing, waiting for him to acknowledge his presence. After five minutes, he conceded defeat and went away silently.

All of a sudden Konrad soundly closed the folder he had been reading, startling me a bit. "All right, dinner it is, about time," he said to me, rising to his full height.

Instead of going to the dining room from noon, we went to a smaller room, almost looking like a winter garden, furnished with a table, some chairs and a terrace with a view over the house garden.

"Normally, I eat here. Only if I have business dinners or to entertain guests, I go to the other one."

We sat and Friederich started to serve dinner in a very efficient way. He poured the water and offered a bottle of red wine to Konrad to try it. He found it to his liking and the butler served it to him while he asked me if I wanted orange or apple juice. My disappointed expression didn't escape Konrad who dryly informed me, "Alcohol and you don't mix together well." At least I was not served a glass of milk! Apple juice is fine.

He started to ask me about my school-days and slowly and easily we engaged in a conversation. He told me about his time in school in Switzerland, like me, and when he was going to the University in Zurich. We spoke a bit over my intended trip, and he told me I should visit Perugia to see the Galleria dell'Umbra if I liked so much Renaissance Art. He, on the other hand, was more interested in Roman history and early Middle Ages. He would have liked to become a historian, but the family business got in the way.

Just when I was thinking how charming he was, Ferdinand burst into the room with a phone in his hand. Not even looking at me, he started to speak in German to a very annoyed Konrad. Their argument lasted for a few minutes before he angrily stood up, making me shrink just a little in my chair.

"I'm afraid you will have to finish dinner alone. Don't wait for me. Go to bed and sleep. I don't know when I will be able to join you." Without even waiting for my answer, he strode away, with Ferdinand almost running behind him.

I was disappointed that he had so abruptly interrupted the dinner and that I should go to bed just like that. OK, I was expecting something else, in the line of what had happened in the hotel "lobby", but it seemed unlikely at the moment. This was really unfair!

I finished the dish not really hungry any more, and refused dessert and coffee (incredible, I've been promoted to adulthood. I wonder if it has any caffeine), under the frown of Friederich. It seems Germans don't take rejection well at all.

I went to the library to fetch my book for a little bedtime reading. On my way, I heard a heated discussion in German between Michael, Ferdinand, Gandini and Konrad behind the closed doors of the office. Oh, I hope I haven't got into more trouble.

Quiet as a mouse, I fetched the volume and went straight to my bedroom, only to remember I was supposed to sleep in Konrad's room now, but I was not really certain that if this would be appropriate any longer. I was dutifully debating with myself on the pros and cons of bed choosing when Friederich came out of nowhere. He ended the debate quite quickly. I should go to the Duke's bedroom as it was arranged this morning.

I obeyed as usual. I put on my pyjamas, folded on the left side of the bed (guess this is my side. I have not many ideas on bed etiquette), brushed my teeth, and got into the huge bed, trying to read.

I did it for several hours, almost up to twelve not really wanting to sleep, a haunting feeling of guilt looming over me. Had other things emerged in Fedérico's case? Why were they shouting, and most importantly again, was Konrad upset with me? I tossed around in the bed until sleep took me over.

At some point during the night, I heard Konrad quietly slide under the covers. I sat up in the bed half asleep with my hair tousled and he hushed me.

"I didn't want to wake you up. It's late."

"What time is it? Are you all right?" I mumbled fighting against my sleep.

"Yes, just some trouble with some transfers. Nothing for you to worry about."

"When I went to the library to look for my book, I think, I heard counsellor Gandini speaking. Am I in trouble again?"

"You, no; not at all. Don't worry, everything has been taken care of. It was a misunderstanding with some bonds and transfers. Sleep now, because tomorrow I would like to go out with you, if my employees allow me to take holidays, that is," he said, pulling me toward him as if I were a big teddy bear. I comfortably cuddled myself against him resting my head in the crook of his arms.

"You are so affectionate my love," he whispered tenderly in my ear as he nuzzled it softly sending shivers through my body as I pressed myself more against his warm body. "But let's know each other more before we take our relationship a step further. God knows I'm dying to make you mine."

Chapter 12

January 5th, 2002

Konrad shook my shoulder softly in the morning "Wake up sleepyhead. It's eight already!" he said cheerfully for sleepy (and grumpy), me. I groaned my discomfort at being awaken so early. After all, we are in holidays and nine o'clock would be a good time. A hard slap on my bottom made the trick.

"I'm up already. This is really impossible!" I protested loudly only to be silenced with one of his devastating kisses. I put my arms around his neck and pulled him toward me as I returned his kiss, sliding myself back into the bed, secretly hoping to get more time to laze. His weight settled along my body as he started to kiss me on the mouth and my neck, making me softly moan.

"Friederich, could you allow us some more privacy?" I heard him saying between our reckless kisses. I jumped immediately out of his embrace, pushing him away with both hands, and there, to my utter mortification, was said butler, busy setting the breakfast table, ignoring us totally. Konrad, on the other side, was laughing like a child at my embarrassment.

"Well, I know now what is required to get you out of bed," he giggled at his prank.

"How old did you say you were?" I shot back angrily.

"And we also know that you're not a morning person, are you?"

I huffed, still upset, picked up what was left of my pride and went to the bathroom to shower and dress myself. Now I know why Germans are not famous for their sense of humour. When I was ready, I went back to the room to find him already sitting at the table, reading something on his laptop. I sat in the chair beside him. Friederich served the coffee and placed two dishes with something like scrambled eggs.

"That was low from you," I complained still cross at him.

"Who started to kiss me without checking first? Do you really think that any man in his right mind would have let the opportunity pass?" he said innocently. "Grow up, Kitten. Men seize every chance they have."

Yeah, he's bloody right, but I don't want to accept defeat so fast. "Yes, you're right, I suppose. I should better not kiss you at all in the mornings. I'm always half asleep and on autopilot," I replied, putting my best contemplative puppy eyed face. I swear I saw a flash of annoyance passing light speed through his eyes, but he quickly recovered his aloof calm. OK, I think we reversed the tables again.

"Perhaps you're not the big eyed dove I originally thought. That might make things more complicated," he said returning to his laptop, ignoring me in his surly mood.

"You are a bad loser!" I laughed trying to sit in his lap, but Konrad stopped me with a stern glance.

"I don't like to be toyed with. Not many people in this world dare to do it, and when they do, they face the consequences," he affirmed with a deep frown marring his forehead.

I looked at him perplexed. How had we moved from childish pranks to threats? Had this something to do with his past lover who was always playing him, if Friederich is to be believed?

"Konrad, I'm lost now. Have I offended you?"

He looked at me for a long moment as if he were gauging the sincerity of my intentions. I held his scrutinizing glance.

"No," he finally said, "I'm under considerable pressure these days."

This time, I forced myself into his lap and caressed his cheek while smiling. "Even if you are grumpy and have a lousy sense of humour, I think I'm falling for you," I whispered, approaching my lips towards his ear.

"That's good," he mumbled as he kissed me and hugged me. We stayed like that for some time.

"What are we doing today?" I asked cheerfully, in an attempt to shake the mood.

"I have to work today."

"Bad loser!"

"Really Guntram, I have to liquidate this mess with Argentina's bonds," he growled.

"Ouch, did we get you in?"

"Like all of us," he answered dryly. "Anyway, Monika has plans for you in the morning. You can go in the afternoon to a Museum. I will be able to join you for dinner."

"Who is Monika?"

"My secretary. She will brief you and take care of some minor issues regarding your stay in Europe. Don't cross her because she will be more than able to hide your body more efficiently than Ferdinand or his men."

"Why does everybody in your staff threatens me with killing me if I move an inch from my assigned place? It's not like I'm going to steal the silver," I whined.

"It's for your own protection. *Auf*, finish your breakfast, I have a plane to catch." He gracefully rose, putting me off and giving me a small slap on my head. He went directly to his dresser, opened one of the doors and selected a light blue tie without hesitation. I, on the other hand, could waste a whole morning trying to make up my mind if I were him. His fingers made the knot with precise movements and he put on a vest and jacket in a dark grey shade, looking like the perfect banker. He closed his laptop and stuffed it into a leather briefcase alongside with some papers. He bent down to give me quick kiss in the forehead and murmured something like "be good", and went away, not even bothering to wait for an answer.

I saw him through the window going into the ship with Ferdinand, Heindrik and two other men more I was not even knowing. I sighed and decided to face the world in the form of a tyrannical woman named Monika.

Downstairs, I bumped literally into Michael, who looked more relaxed than yesterday.

"Are you my baby sitter today?" I asked feigning innocence. If I was going to suffer his bad sense of humour, better start ahead.

"You're not so lucky. You will remain under the gentle, loving and motherly care of Monika," He said very smugly to me.

"I see you're still loafing around here, Dr. Dähler. Don't you have anything to do?" A middle size woman said, with dark hair, striking blue eyes, dressed in a suit, with good but discreet jewellery over her. Michael visibly paled and quietly disappeared, not making a single remark.

"So, you must be Guntram, pleased to meet you. I'm Monika van der Leyden, the Duke's private secretary. I will coordinate all your papers and everything else you might need," she continued saying, offering me her hand as if she were a princess.

I shook her hand carefully and bowed my head under her quizzical gaze. "How do you do, Madam?"

"Very well, thank you. Please, come with me to the office, and we will sort out some paperwork before the tailor comes. This way."

We entered into a grand salon, the original ballroom, transformed into a provisional office in case the Duke wanted to spend some time in Venice and work, as she told me, decorated with four desks, some chairs, laptops and a few filing cabinets. She went straight to one of the desks and beckoned me to sit in front of her.

"I will need you to sign these papers," she said handing me a handful of forms, all written in German.

"What are they?" Bloody me if I sign something I don't understand.

"These are forms for a credit card, your residence permission application for Switzerland and private health insurance."

"I don't remember asking for those things," I said trying to keep my cool and temper down.

"You did not. The Duke ordered it yesterday," she firmly replied, not even bating an eyelash.

"I'm afraid this is over scaled for a three weeks stay in Europe," I gritted my teeth to ease the tension. "Besides, I have a credit card of my own, health insurance for the trip and a French citizenship. I don't need a visa to go to Switzerland."

"Such kind of details you should discuss with the Duke himself. Now, please sign. I'm only following orders," she explained to me, her eyes shining with a light that was foreboding nothing good for me if I didn't do it.

"My budget can't allow another credit card much less another insurance policy." Excellent, now I have to explain my financial status to an unknown woman!

"This will be on the Duke's account, Guntram," she told me softly.

"I can't accept them. This is too much," I was furious with him. Two or three kisses, and he thinks he can order me around like one of his employees?

"If you don't take them, he will be most upset with me and blame me for your attitude," she started to plead with her blue eyes becoming bigger. I gulped nervously. "I understand this approach might be harsh on you, but if you really don't want them, just don't use them. I really don't want to face his wrath if I fail this simple task."

Do you know that children and women in distress can always get the best out of me?

"All right. I don't want to cause you trouble, but I think this is nonsense and he's wasting his money," I sighed, taking the offered pen and signing the forms. What kind of damage can do a stupid residence in Switzerland? Is not that I have a huge income or taxes to hide or evade from the Argentinean Government.

"Thank you dear," she said flashing me a wonderful smile. I flushed. "I have two grown up boys. One is a medical doctor and the other is studying Civil Engineering. Don't gape at me like that. I'm old enough to be your mother," she laughed. "I take care of the Duke's agenda and his personal needs. From now onwards, you will be under my care too. Whatever you need, please, don't hesitate to tell me. I will organize your paperwork if you decide to attend a school or your international travels. Do you speak German, dear?"

"Not a single word," she wrote something down in her leather bound pad.

"Do you have a driver's license?"

"Yes, but I don't drive up to European Standards," I replied more puzzled than before.

"So, would you need to take some lessons or a few afternoons driving with one of the men would be enough for you? I will need your Argentinean license to exchange it for an European one."

"I can take the bus or walk. There's no need to further trouble you," I said, defensively.

She musically laughed at me "Friederich was right," she said, enigmatically. Does nobody have something better to do in this house than discussing my exploits? "I think it's time for the tailor to arrive. I believe three morning suits, two more for the evening, one more coat and some casual clothes would be enough for the time being. I almost forgot about shoes! Age is catching up with me dear!"

"Ms. Leyden I don't believe it's appropriate from me to spend so much of the Duke's money," I sternly replied. This spending has to stop. It makes me uncomfortable to no end.

"Dear, you can't go around in jeans and T-shirts beside a man like him. You will only be embarrassing him. This is nothing for the Duke's finances, and he's more than happy to pay for it. At the moment, you are properly dressed for city holidays, I admit it, but if you have to go to a dinner or to an opening, this outfit would be completely out of place. Without a jacket and a tie, you can't enter in many places," she punctuated with a sharp voice. "Do I need to repeat the speech I gave my youngest son, five years ago, when he wanted to go with tennis shoes to a job interview in a bank?"

"I see your point and I agree with you." Damn, I'm not such an outcast that I don't know what a dress code is, "but you must understand that for a man is unacceptable to take things from another."

"Please, humour me with this and tonight you can speak with the Duke," she pleaded again, this time batting her big eyelashes. "I assure you there's nothing to be uncomfortable about. He thinks very highly of you, and only wants the best for you. I don't believe that you're a fortune digger, like the many I have to brush away now and then around his Excellency. I see that you're very young indeed, just out of school, right? Let me tell you this as a mother. You think that you're abusing his trust by accepting these gifts, but it's not so. You would be abusing him if you were only asking and not giving. This kind of amount has no value for him. He makes much more in an hour than you could spend in a year, but you give him something he has not being able to find in many years. You can make him feel alive and happy, and for him that is priceless. Do you love him?"

"Yes," I said with a tiny voice, almost imperceptibly. It's not easy to admit to a perfect stranger that you're in love with somebody who happens to be of your own sex!

"I believe you. Now, move young man. I have work to do and a tailor is waiting for you".

The tailor was yesterday's man from the shop. He was not willing to speak English, so I kept my mouth shut as he measured me and made me try one jacket. After he finished with me, Monika came in, and started to fondle through several samples of fabrics. To my utter amusement (I was a little crossed that nobody asked my opinion), the Italian rejected almost everything she chose and triumphantly announced that he "knows the Duke tastes better and he has seen the young man long enough to know what is best. I've been his tailor for more than thirty years," he would choose and we should be quiet.

I had lunch with Monika and Michael, both taunting at each other during the whole meal. I see why Konrad said that she was difficult. This woman had a sharp tongue and the brain of a division general. For a moment, I felt sorry for the poor German as she metaphorically mopped the floor with his pride. To his credit, I had to admit, he wasn't giving up at all, and coming back for more, at every chance he had.

After lunch, Monika had to work and Michael, "should at least pretend that he's able to do it", and disappeared into the office, leaving us alone.

"Things we cope with for love. What a woman," Michael told me. "Why don't you go somewhere, like the Ca' D'Oro Museum. It's nice and quiet, not very far away from here."

"Am I not supposed to ask for permission to cross the street?" I asked, jokingly.

"Can't you swim?" he rebutted me opening big time his eyes.

"Very funny. I can swim and with a map I could reach it. I promise I'll be good, Mum"

"You'd better because Ferdinand will kill me if something happens to you."

"I thought he wanted to skin me alive in the kitchen."

"Not so much anymore. He really welcomed you, if not, he would have never say the words."

"He's quite the military type," I shrugged.

"He started his career in the Army, till he entered into the Duke's service and has a Harvard Business Administration degree. Surprised? Not the mindless killing machine you imagined, huh? I on the other hand, went to the Navy and studied Physics, with a doctor's degree in Astrophysics."

"That's not funny."

"It's true. Should I show you my diploma? I'm telling you because I want that you understand that we are not simple gorillas or frustrated cops," I blushed at his words. He had really caught me this time. Am I so easy to read?

"How did you end up in the security business if you're a scientist?" I asked while was trying to overcome my discomfort.

"Thanks for calling me a scientist, but I'm not. I went to the Navy for almost ten years, served in the Gulf, the Balkans and the Navy paid for my education, but I grew tired of it and came here to work."

"But he said you were a bodyguard."

"Well, we are, sort of," he chuckled. "We are more like advisers. I take care of the strategical outlook for the decision making process and the security around the companies and banks. But if I would get into a fight with the Duke, most probably my ass would be sorry. I'm telling you this so you know you can trust us, and we hope likewise from you. You will meet the others in Zurich."

"What about Alexei, Goran and Heindrik?"

"All from military background. Alexei was KGB, Goran something like a captain in the Serbian Army and Heindrik was in the Swedish Navy. They are the second line and don't make any recommendations. They are real bodyguards."

I was rendered speechless. KGB? Were these guys not supposed to be heartless killers? Am I supposed to feel "safe" around one of them? Keep dreaming man!

"Do you have money with you?"

"Sorry?" My mind was elsewhere with all the information I'd just gotten. No wonder those men look frightening, because they were lethal and happy to be thus.

"How much money do you have in your wallet?" He punctuated every word for stupid me.

"About €40; I'm going to a Museum; should be enough."

He let a growl out and raised his eyes to the ceiling, asking for divine patience. He put his hand in his pocket, took his wallet out and pulled a handful of bills, "Take it and don't argue," he said with his best commanding officer voice.

"This is like €200! It's too much. I have enough with forty," I protested.

"Rule number three: You do as we say. Remember, or should I tell Ferdinand?"

No, better let's keep it quiet. "All right, thanks, but I'm giving it back to you when I return."

"Have a nice time and don't get into trouble. Take the mobile phone with you."

"Yes, Mum," I grunted.

On my way to the Museum, I bought a small drawing notebook and a soft 2B pencil. If I was sent away for the afternoon, presumably I should not return till seven or eight, and that was like five hours away. I should better find something to do inside, like copying something there. Honestly, you learn more about drawing in an hour looking at the paintings here than in full year in the school.

The palace was impressive in and of itself. I think it was a pure Gothic style but I'm not sure. I looked at the collection, and finally decided to draw some parts of Carpaccio paintings. Time flew by as I was so absorbed in the paintings. A beep in my pocket transported me back to earth as I realised I had a message. "Wait in the Museum. I'll be there at 7:30." All right, let's wait for Michael, but when he comes he will hear me. I can find my way back and most certainly I can look after myself. I've been doing it since I was seven!

I continued to draw, this time sitting on one of the benches inside the Museum—I don't want to risk picking up another German—happy in my bubble. Someone placed a heavy hand on my shoulder, and I lifted my gaze to find Konrad there, still dressed like in the morning, but without papers.

"It's you. Hello," I said with a small grin, after all this a very public place.

"Were you expecting someone else?" He replied softly and I think that for a second there was like a flash of anger passing through his eyes. No, it can't be.

"Your man, Michael Dähler. He sent me here after all," he looked more relaxed or a better word would be appeased. He sat beside me, and without a warning, started to look at my sketches, focusing his attention on them. I nudged him, hitting my elbow against his ribs in a frisky way.

"Are you going to waste your time with that when you could watch the real thing?"

"I can't look at anything. I'm dead on my feet," he admitted slowly. "I only want to go home and spend the evening with you. Perhaps we could watch a simple film together."

I rose to my feet and this time I pulled him by his sleeve. "Sounds great."

His, only a little haggard appearance, was more appealing to me than his Super Male Nietzschean persona. We walked home in silence, he purportedly slowing down his big strides so I could look at the houses, the shop windows, and the people with my country boy big eyes.

We arrived to his house only to be intercepted by Friederich, who announced that the Director of the Prima Banca Veneto Lombarda was in the library with Ferdinand.

"Cousin Albert?" Konrad said, not hiding his annoyance at all. "Does he plan to stay for dinner?"

"Certainly, your Excellency."

Konrad let a long sight out. "When it rains, it pours they say. All right we go to the main dining room. Ferdinand and Michael will have to suffer him too. I'm sorry Guntram, but Albert is Geborene [1] and we have to cope with him."

"Dähler defected two hours ago, Sire." Konrad made a shrug and muttered something like "clever man."

"If he's from your family, maybe I should make myself scarce," I suggested.

"No, Guntram, you must stay. Meeting you must be the reason behind his visit."

We went to the library where Ferdinand and another man in his fifties, I would say, were talking. Well, Ferdinand was listening with a stony face to the visitor's prattle. He stood up to attention immediately as he saw Konrad, while the man remained sitting.

"Hello, old thing. You still look well Konrad." Did I hear well? He must be really close family to call him like that.

"How do you do, Albert? Your bank is still in one piece?"

"Almost," he laughed as he embraced Konrad into a bear hug and patted his back strongly. Konrad didn't miss the opportunity to return the hit. "And who is this nice thing, hiding behind your back?"

"His name is Guntram de Lisle, and he is my chosen companion," Konrad affirmed gravely. Albert was totally taken aback, but he quickly hid his surprise, and shook my proffered hand, now taking a really good look at me.

"I have to admit that he's not what I was expecting. Your normal flings are flashier and he even looks from a good breed," he said happily. Is this a compliment and I have to say thanks? No way. Better I keep my mouth shut. He laughed loudly at my awkward pause. "Yes, he's good breed indeed and old school," he said enigmatically, winking an eye to me.

---

[1] Geborene means "born," It's a word used by the German Aristocracy to refer themselves as such. This expression was employed up to World War One.

"I'm expecting an invitation for dinner. Come on, Konrad, I know you can formulate one. We went together to school."

"Would you grant us the pleasure of your company, Albert?" Konrad said gritting his teeth so much that I could almost hear the noise. All right, note to self, Konrad does not like buddy bantering at all.

"Most certainly, gentle knight," he replied with a mocked curtsy. "Come Guntram, let's speak about your country because my cousin has enough of me for the time being," he said pulling me by the arm. "I hope you can lift his dark mood, because, if not, he will bore you to hell," he whispered. "Don't get jealous Konrad, I'll be back to pester you soon."

He led me to the far away sofa, under the window and started to ask about the political situation in Argentina, then about my studies, school, my work in the bookshop and in the slums, religion, etc. A full road test if you ask me, diary.

"Konrad is an honourable man deep in his core. I'm glad he settled down with you. You'll only have to be careful with his character. Don't rub him in the wrong direction, if you understand me," he said in a conspiratorial tone, while Konrad and Ferdinand were lost talking in German on the other side of the room. "My cousin has to be cold, calculating, ruthless, heartless if he wants to keep all what he has achieved. He has to, if he wants to just keep his hedge funds under control."

"You speak of him as if he were Machiavelli's Prince."

"Well, he is but with far more power. Only his three hedge funds are worth 500 billion, not counting the two private banks and companies that belong to him."

"That's like a country," I murmured astonished. I thought he was rich, but nothing like this. I felt like a small ant or a snail compared to him.

"His personal fortune is smaller, about 12 or 15 billion, but he controls this sum of money, and believe me, even if he's on the lowest part of the sharks' top ten, he can shake the market when he wants to do it."

"Now I understand why he's always working, even on holidays, but I can't imagine why he would like to spend his time with me," I replied slowly, more to myself than for Albert's benefit.

"Because he's in love." Now, it was my turn to give him a good look. "I know my cousin since forever. Even if he pretends he's upset at me, we have a good friendship. Today, is the first time I've see him truly in love, not infatuated. Didn't you realise that he checks almost every minute at our direction to see if I'm nasty to you? He would skin me alive if I lay a hand on you."

"I see you are already scaring Guntram with your horror stories about me, Albert."

"No, I haven't got to the Tequila Crisis part yet," he said with a huge grin, "or commented on your wardrobe," he chuckled under Konrad's killer gaze. "Relax cousin, I'm only doing what you should have done as a normal person if you were not such a paranoid. I just told him of the extent of your financial business. Really cousin, you can't take a truly innocent person from the streets, and plunge him into your world without a warning of what he's getting into," he said with a deep seriousness in his voice, looking directly into his cousin's eyes.

"Even if I can agree with your point, you have overstepped your boundaries by talking to Guntram. It's my prerogative to do so."

"I apologize, but if he's going to be part of the family, he deserves to hear the truth. You can't start a sound relationship with an obfuscation."

"Konrad, please. I understand perfectly why you were not telling me. There's no need to. It's your money, not mine and I have no interest to interfere with your affairs," I interceded before things would escalate more. Good, I have his attention, or at least he has diverted it from Albert's throat. "What I don't understand is how you avoided having your picture in Fortune Magazine," I finished using a lighter tone. He roared a laugh and gave me a soft pat on the head.

"I bribed the Editor," he whispered in my ear. "I think we should feed you cousin, so you keep your mouth shut," he told the other man half-jokingly, half menacingly.

"Ten to one, *Rouladen* are the main dish," Albert said not impressed at all.

"Of course, if I have you here, the least the chef can do is cook my favourite dish."

They both laughed like lions. Well maybe Konrad does not dislike him so much, he's only annoyed at his bantering or "lack of respect" as he would say.

At the table, Albert sat at Konrad's right side and Ferdinand to his left. I was sent to sit with Ferdinand, and again, I got no wine at all—apple juice this time. When Ferdinand was telling the story of Albert's stacking a lizard into his practice flute in the fifth grade, we heard a turmoil in the other room. The door burst open and there was Martina, completely furious standing in front of us.

I rose from my chair (lady aboard!), and she came directly towards me, one of Konrad's bodyguards trailing behind her.

"You piece of slime! You set this up with that piece of shit that fucks you every night! He stole 700 million from our government's account!" She shouted completely out of mind. Fast as a cobra she took a glass from the table and threw it to me. Apple juice. I was in shock.

"Lintorff, you knew very well that that money belonged to my province and if it was under my name it was to avoid the embargo on every government's account. I'm going to go to the courts and destroy your bank. You have no idea what mistake you have done with the set up you organized for my son. Your days are numbered."

"Madam keep your voice down or I will ask my men to escort you out," he said with this calm that precedes the tsunami. "Our bank has made the transfers you asked and bought Argentina's Lecops as requested, at a very convenient price if I might say so."

"From your own fucking hedge funds! You took our cash and converted it into worthless papers at a nominal value, when in the market they are at thirty percent! You also got money out of Argentina even if it's forbidden to do so! I will denounce you to the Congress. Be proud Guntram, not only you betrayed your friend, but you stole money meant for poor children!

"Perhaps we should speak properly. What you call "bonds" are in fact "local currencies," issued by your own national government, and they're nominally valued exactly as the peso. We even accepted the market value of 2.5 pesos per dollar on your favour when the official exchange rate is 1.4 pesos. You authorized us to trade currencies. I see no harm done, but if you're willing to present a complaint, you can do it in Zurich. Now leave my house, you have already insulted my guests twice."

Martina launched at Konrad, I supposed to give him a slap or something, but Ferdinand blocked her faster. He firmly took her by the arm, I noticed he was not exerting any pressure and led her out of the room. I stood there, still dripping apple juice and in shock. I could not believe that Konrad had tricked her into buying Lecops. Lord, everybody knew they were pieces of junk, issued by the government to pay debts to their public servants when the real cash was over. Everybody avoided them like the plague! I needed to get out and fast.

"May I be excused?" I said, fighting to get my tears repressed.

"Of course, but do come back for coffee." Konrad said, studying my face intensely. I just turned around and left the room in haste, only to hear Albert saying something in German.

I went to the room and decided to take a shower. I selected some nondescript clothes from the closet and dressed myself again. I searched again, found my backpack there and I checked if I had my passport and papers with me. I still had my travellers checks and plane ticket. Bloody me if I was going to stay with a crook that could take money away from children!

I went downstairs, straight to the door to find it firmly blocked by Goran. He was not so big like the others, but he could be intimidating in his own way. He reminded me of a cold predator.

"Move aside, please. I'm leaving," I said.

"Do you have the Duke's permission?"

"Don't need it or want it. Now move," was my reply, ready to charge against him.

"Guntram, go back to the library; they're having coffee," Michael interrupted us.

"I'm leaving, do you understand?" Is he stupid?

"I said, go to the library. We had enough for one night. The Duke will be furious."

"So his Excellency is upset?" I smirked ironically "What about the rest of us? He just took 700 million from a poor country and he's upset. Life is truly unfair for noblemen."

"Do as you are told or do you want that the Duke lifts his protection over your stupid friend? He still has to make it to the Airport," Michael half shouted at me, his words coming out of his mouth like acid over steel.

"What?"

"He got out of jail, but there's still the mess of the two missing kilos. Perhaps Goran could explain to you how Albanian drug dealers treat slimy rats like your friend. If he's still alive, is because Gandini used all his influences in the judiciary system to save his skin and the Duke paid a lot of money to cover the loses. Don't behave like a brat and go to the library as if nothing has happened," he told me darkly.

"You should give the Duke a chance to explain his actions," Goran added. "Now go, because you don't want me to drag you in there," he said in a deep commanding voice.

"I'll take your backpack before the Duke sees it," Michael growled as he gave me a nudge in the back toward the library. I looked at them furiously, but they seemed impassive. "Move!"

I slowly walked toward the library, stood in front of the huge wooden door, a knot constricting my throat as I knocked on the darkly shinning surface. I smoothed invisible wrinkles in my sweater. Friederich opened the door and let me pass. There, on the couches, the three men were sitting and having coffee. Konrad made a small gesture with the head so I would sit next to him, but I choose to ignore him, placing myself at Ferdinand's side.

"You look better now, Guntram," Albert decided to start a talk to ease the tension, "Have you ever been to Turin?"

I mechanically replied no, and he began to elaborate over his family's castle there, how nice the lake was and now that it had been recently refurnished, we should visit it at our convenience. Konrad asked him about the works and they spoke softly while I was busy trying to process all what had happened in the last hours.

"I think is time to send the children to bed, Konrad," Albert suggested at some point.

"Yes, you're right. It has been a long day for you and Guntram."

Albert laughed without reserves, his laughter increasing my growing headache. He shook hands with us and muttered to me something like "glad to have you here. My cousin almost looks human." Ferdinand went away with him.

Konrad and I were left alone. He returned to his position on the couch and ordered, "Guntram come here, let me hold you. I can tell you're upset."

"Upset? I'm furious with you!" I cried not moving an inch from my position by the door. "I'm going away right now. I can't even stand the look of you!"

He jumped from his couch advancing too fast for my liking. I turned my back to open the door and leave but he was much faster than I, blocking the thing with his right hand and trapping me with the other. He placed both hands on the sides of my body and I knew this moment that the evil maniac was back and I didn't care.

"You'll go nowhere till we clear the subject up," he growled.

"There's nothing to clarify. You knowingly took money that belonged to a poor province and made some more out of it. As if you did not have enough! If they asked you to make these transfers, it was to avoid the international courts to put their hands on it. These people are in horrible need. Don't you see that all international aid is over since Argentina defaulted? You are worse than trash!"

"Are you really telling me that you believe the money was for the poor people in Argentina? Please Guntram, not even you can be so naïve," he snorted. "The embargoes are on the accounts of the national government, not over the provincial ones. So, tell me, why would the money be under the name of private persons? Your Senator was more than happy to use my banks and contacts to hide the money for who knows which purposes. This money would have never reached the poor people!"

"You had no right to sell her those stupid bonds and don't give me this lawful shit of "local currencies" because we both know it's not true. How much did you pay for them? Twenty percent? Thirty percent?"

"An average of fifteen percent of the nominal price. Was hard to get them," he said very calmly, while I was becoming more furious.

"Bastard!" I shouted.

He backhanded me, but not so hard as the first time. Maybe this was his idea of a "corrective"; no blood or choking involved. Nevertheless, I had to lean against the door, the whole room turning around like a tornado.

"Be glad I do nothing more to you. Calm down and listen to me because I will not repeat my words. I fulfilled my part of the agreement, your friend is out of jail with minor charges, only expelled from the European Union. Nothing permanent in his record. Why should I assume the losses for Argentina's lack of accountability? These "bonds" are bad for Argentineans but good for international investors? I only took back a part of what we invested there. It's not about the money."

It was my time to snort in disbelief.

"It's about teaching a lesson of respect to these unruly politicians. A default can happen and it's part of the risk. I accept it but what I don't tolerate is the Argentinean Congress applauding and celebrating the default like they did, telling the world they're the cleverest. The money we recovered was likely coming out of their murky businesses, to be used for campaigning. I took nothing from orphan children. This is a lesson for them and they should be glad that the punishment from my part would be only that. From my other colleagues, I can't say nothing. Grow up, kitten, this is a dark and shady world and you have to be harder than them if you want to achieve something. I don't play fair with people who want to deceive or use me."

"Are you going to give me a lesson in ethics? Excellent," I laughed contemptuously. The nerve of this man! "Now that you have finished, remove your hand from the door. I'm going away," he didn't move an inch, of course.

"You are not moving from here till we finish this conversation. Sit down."

"Let. Me. Go." We stood there, both looking at each other. I was as furious as I've ever been before, and he just studied my face, not showing regret, fury or any other emotion. A man who tricks a woman in need, certainly has no heart or feelings for anything.

Suddenly, he removed his arm, allowing me some room to move.

"Very well, Guntram. If you wish so, you can go now," he said completely cold and went to resume his position on the couch, sitting like a king. I remained by the door, heavily breathing, my brain looking for the obvious deceit in his words. Would he throw Federico and his mother to the lions just as Michael affirmed he would? That German could be well bluffing, but somehow I knew that was not the case. How could an allegedly respectable man like a banker be able to make a deal with drug trafficker?

"Did you set up Federico?"

"No!" He looked genuinely incensed. "I only took the opportunity of recovering part of the money stolen by the government. I didn't plan this and had to improvise all the way," he messed his hair with a nervous movement, the first one I'd seen him do since I met him. "Do you think I would have risked you in a drug case? You have no idea how close you were to finishing in an Italian prison. You would have been dead in less than a month, and that without taking into consideration the Albanians who rule the trade here," he buried his face into his hands, his back hunched, defeated.

"So you did pay them," I painfully articulated, closing my eyes.

"I'm not proud of it. But it was the only way to get them off your back. When your friend accused you of having the drugs, you became a target for them. I couldn't bear the idea of losing you and Goran made the deal. They would have tortured and killed you for that stupid thing."

I closed the distance between us and knelt in front of him taking his hands still glued to his face with mine. I pried them away and saw barely withheld tears in his ice blue eyes. He sobbed as a way to regain his composure, and leaned against the sofa, trying to remove his hands from mine. I held them strongly and put them close to my chest as my anger faded. Without even thinking, I kissed them softly.

"You saved my life. I owe you."

"No, you owe me nothing," he protested. "Goran spoke with them and arranged everything. He knows how to do it. He's from Serbia and understands the logic behind their actions," I leaned my head against the side of his thighs a deep grief engulfing me. He intertwined his fingers in my hair drawing small circles against my skull as I was there, motionless.

"Still it doesn't change the fact that you cheated and lied to a woman in need, not mentioning that we really need that money."

"I admit I was angered with the Argentineans for the default show but, on the other hand, I've been able to get most of the money out of the country before they closed all international transfers. We had important loses in our investments, but it was nothing that could have not been recovered later. When she came to me, I was more preoccupied with solving the problem with the drug traffickers than with her son. Gandini could tell you, he was there. This woman was not much interested in knowing his strategy for getting her son out of jail, but finding out if she could use me to clean her party's dirty money. She didn't want to contribute to Goran's efforts. She would have given you to them as payment. After all, you're nobody to her. I decided to pay the "compensation fee" all by myself, but in exchange she would sign the transfer orders to move that money around, so we could get some commissions out of it. When she left with Gandini to visit the judge, I was more incensed than ever so I planned the scheme with the local currencies."

"You have to realise, Guntram, that I, as a member of the banking community, can't and will not let pass an opportunity to penalize the behaviour of some people against the system. I plan to make businesses in the future in Argentina, but the only way the local ruling class will respect us and keep to their word is if they fear us. This year, Davos' meeting will be a living hell for Argentina," he said completely lost in thoughts. We remained in silence.

"Are you still upset with me?" he asked, cupping my face now into his hands to check my reaction.

"Yes, because you never tell me anything and I'm concerned because you have risked your banks' position. What will you do if she goes to the Swiss Banking Board? You could lose everything."

"First, she would have to explain the money's origin, and second, everything I did is perfectly legal. She's well aware that she can't corner me with that. Why do you think she made the scene? So I would not sleep tonight from remorse? Please Guntram. She attacked me on my weakest point so to speak," he huffed, visibly upset.

"I don't understand."

"She's not stupid. She knows I care deeply for you, therefore she came here to spread lies about starving children and treasons. Do you see now why one of the rules is nobody comes between us? Many will try to poison it in order to attack me." Again I was silent for a long while.

"You must have paid a lot of money if you needed the commissions over 700 million to cover your expenses," I whispered.

"My banks offer an excellent service for a more than reasonable fee," he said, haughtily.

"I'm not opening an account in your bank, so save it," I retorted half-jokingly. I needed to clear the dense air surrounding us.

"Do you have five million?"

"In my Monopoly box, yes."

This time he laughed uncontrollably. "Let's go to bed. We all had enough for one day."

Chapter 13

January 6th, 2002

I was awakened by a series of hungry kisses trailing from my mouth towards my ears. Without opening my eyes, I put my arms around Konrad's neck and pulled him toward me. Unwittingly, I arched my back to allow him better access to my collarbone, where he was very busy chomping the fabric of the pyjama, and my bony hips collided with his manhood as he settled his weight on top of me.

"If Friederich is here, I'll kill you," I muttered while I was delivering my kisses all over his cheek and neck.

"All clear," he chuckled. "You're quite lewd in the mornings, *Maus*," he whispered in my ear as he nibbled my earlobe making me moan softly.

"Don't know the word. You have to elaborate more," I replied feeling my own member become hard and very interested in our dealings.

I opened my eyes to look at him, my hands burning with desire to touch his skin as much as he was touching mine. He let me freely roam his face, his neck and his back without saying anything. I grew bolder as he rearranged his position, his own erection touching mine. I started to undo the buttons of his pyjama to discover his broad chest and truly well-defined abs. I stopped my hands in mid-air, afraid that my boldness would upset him.

"Shh, don't be nervous, take whatever you want," he hushed me, giving me an encouraging kiss on my lips, and half lifting from me, supporting his weight on his arms.

I slid his pyjama top away as I devoured him with my eyes. Even if he was huge in size, his body was harmonic, manly and powerful. I traced the outline of his muscles with my right hand.

"Do you like what you see?

"A lot," was my distracted answer as I bit my lower lip hard. He chuckled and moved away from me. I was disappointed at this contact loss.

"Now is my turn. Show me," he said with a raspy voice.

Again I moistened my lips with my tongue, his eyes almost clouded at my gesture, and I half stood from my laying position in the bed. I was afraid that my body would repulse him, so I slowly started to undo the buttons, looking in his eyes, bearing a strange glare, not losing a single of my fingers' moves. I slid the top in one daft movement, and remained there, motionless, waiting for the verdict. He said and did nothing. He just looked intensely at my much slender chest, but with well-shaped muscles in my stomach.

"This is all what you'll get. There's nothing more," I said, mortified by his lack of response.

He extended his hand touching me first softly in the crook of my neck and then roaming it over my chest, his fingers tracing the contours of my muscles. "You're everything I've dreamed of," he mumbled, devouring me with his adoring eyes. I smiled as a wave of relief hit me.

He jumped on top of me, grabbing me by the arms and kissing me with hunger and desperation, as if he would want to own me in an animalistic and possessive way.

"Your skin is so smooth," he whispered as he roamed his tongue around my neck, sending shivers of pleasure directly to my nether regions. He sucked my right nipple hard, making me moan uncontrollably, his tongue drawing circles around it; I caressed his hair as he was drowning me in waves of pleasure.

His hands sharply pulled down my pyjama pants and he stopped briefly to gauge my reaction. I sighed and moved my hips toward him. Konrad took my member by the base with his hand, rubbing my balls and making me shudder. His mouth engulfed me in one single motion and started to suck hard, with rhythmic movements.

I admit I have little experience, but this was as close to bliss as much as something can be. He was driving me mad with desire with each of his skilled sucks, alternating from the top to the down part, his teeth grazing the sensitive skin.

He introduced a finger into my anus and I jumped in surprise and pain. I tried to squirm but he firmly caught me by my hipbones, sucking harder than before. I moaned and relaxed under his touch as he slowly put it in and out in a rhythm in sync with his strong sucking on my penis. It was a wonderful feeling for me as I found myself dissolving into a pleasure I've never enjoyed before. Suddenly his finger touched a spot inside me that felt like a jolt of electricity roaming my entire self. I had to draw my hand to my mouth to muffle my cry of ecstasy as he increased the speed of his pumping. I couldn't control myself any longer and spilled my seed into his mouth.

I laid there, motionless, raggedly breathing while he kissed me softly on my temples. I returned his kiss, this time hungrily, again tasting myself in his mouth. He leaned his head against my chest and I embraced him, totally grateful for the pleasure he had shown me.

"So it seems I sated you, kitten," he chuckled, his head still on my chest.

"It was incredible," I sighed.

"Only that?"

"What am I supposed to say now, all mighty sex god?" I was a little pissed off with his arrogance.

"Well, acknowledging my status is a start," he laughed reclining his head against my chest anew. We remained like that for a long time, I caressed his head and back, while he made soft sounds like a well satisfied cat. I want to know who is the kitten now?

"Konrad?" I got a grunt as an answer. Not so articulate now, huh? "You didn't get your release," his head come up very fast and he looked at me, quizzically, with one eyebrow lifted. I swallowed hard as I made my decision. "Take me now."

He rose from my body and sat in the bed.

"You are not ready yet," he answered dryly. "You're still too nervous around me. You don't trust me completely and don't deny it because I hate lies."

"I know what I want and I'm willing to go all the way."

"Your first time could be painful and I don't want you running away in panic."

"Would you stop treating me like a child? I ceased to be one when I turned seven," I shouted back. "I have lived on my own since I have memory and make my own decisions. God knows that nobody cares about me." Did he slightly flinch?

"I do care and I don't want to hurt you. If we start, there will be no going back and we will finish what we start, for good or bad," was his stern condition.

"I want you," I said slowly, my gaze fixed onto his eyes. A fleeting doubt passed through them, but it was quickly dismissed. He bent again over me to capture my lips into an excruciating kiss.

"I'll be as careful as I can and I hope I don't have any regrets later," he promised me and I heard a trace of distress dangling from his voice.

He rummaged through his night table to come with a small white tube. Lube I suppose it was. Again I felt a hard pang of fear at the entrance of my stomach, but I dismissed it fast. I wanted this and we had to do it for both our sakes. I had to end this endless game of cat and mouse, and see if I really wanted to have a relationship with him.

Konrad spread some of the liquid gel on top of the fingers of his right hand and told me to lay down on the pillows. I complied feeling again as if I were a small child. I spread my legs to allow him to position better as he removed his trousers and I couldn't help to open big my eyes at his size, his cock largely engorged. There was no way he was going to be able to put his shaft inside of me! He noticed my rising panic and made some calming sounds as he kissed my neck and nuzzled in my collarbone.

"Try to relax. I'll do it as slow as I can so you get used to me. Do you still want to go ahead?"

"I trust you."

"First, I will do what we did before so I can stretch you."

I jumped a little bit at the cold substance he was pouring at my entrance but soon the liquid warmed up and I relaxed a little more. I initiated the kiss this time, opening my mouth to allow him to roam free in my cavity. My tongue battled again for dominance and he let me enter into his mouth. I got lost in the feeling of his taste and the smell of his expensive cologne delicate and oddly familiar at the same time.

Realising that I was soothed by his kisses, Konrad inserted one of his fingers again into me. I was surprised, but it was not as painful as before thanks to the lube. He started to move it slowly as he searched again for my prostate. "You are so tight, relax dear, you're almost hurting me," he whispered in my ears as he inserted his second finger this time pressing that spot that sent waves of pleasure from my entrance to my brain.

He continued massaging me with care for some time, I was too lost in the incredible sensation of his fingers twisting and moving inside of me, soothing me, lulling me, making me feel comfortable in his arms and spreading my legs more to give him more room.

He placed himself between my legs, taking one over his hips, delicately. I was surprised that such a big man, who had so much force, could be more delicate than a girl, treating me as if I were made of porcelain. He took his member in his right hand and pressed it against my anus, but lingered and looked to me as if asking permission to take me.

"I love you, Konrad," I simply said as he bent to kiss me deeply.

Nothing had prepared me for the sharp pain I felt when he entered me, burying his penis in one single motion. I cried into his mouth, my eyes filled with tears. I tried to escape, but he firmly held me in place, clawing his hands into the sides of my pelvis, pinned me with his member now fully and deeply buried inside. I couldn't move, and I felt like an insect punctured against a cardboard. He didn't move at all as he waited for the pain to subside.

"Soon it will feel good, I promise. It's only a little bit longer," he waited till my breathing returned to normal and kissed me again on the mouth "If you need to cry, do it inside me, my love," hesitantly, he started to move, slowly at first, checking every moment if he was causing me more pain. Soon his member found again my pleasure point and the pain started to subside. He concentrated his slamming into this point with slow movements as I relaxed more and more and his movements were more fluid.

When I started to moan and trash around the bed, he again placed his hands on my hips and guided me so my own movements would match the pace he had set. It was a maddening sensation to meet every one of his slams as he increased the pace. My own member was fully erect in a painful way as it was compressed and rocked by Konrad's body.

The pace picked up an incredible speed as he increased the movements with his pelvis, pinning me more and more against the mattress. I couldn't restrain any longer myself and ejaculated with more force than ever before as he reached his climax inside me.

I felt dizzy and spent as he took my head into his hands and covered me with kisses in the aftermath. "You are mine. Say you belong to me."

I looked at him, my eyes almost closed, exhausted like never before and he was looking at me anxiously, waiting for my answer. "I'm yours," I muttered within ragged breaths as I slid into sleep.

Sometime later, I felt Konrad's hands roaming over me feverishly as he turned me onto one side, his body positioning behind my back. I tried to turn around to face him, but the arm around my waist kept me still. I felt his mouth on my cheek kissing me softly. "Stay calm, love," he muttered in my ear as his hand grabbed my leg and threw it over his own hips. He started to suck my neck, his tongue playing with the skin, drawing circles as I became more and more alert. I twisted my head to allow him to kiss me on the mouth, deeply, savouring the fresh mint in his breath.

Without any preparation he inserted himself into me, but this time it wasn't so painful as the first time. I gasped at the pain, but it lessened soon because I was so relaxed. His movements picked up speed as he penetrated me deeper changing the angle. His hand took my member and started to pump it with strong and fast movements. The feeling of him, dominating me totally, was overwhelming and strangely sexy as I let him do me as he wanted. In his possession there was something tender as a man so big and powerful was so dominated by his desire to have me. He left my lips to go back to my neck and bit me hard.

We both climaxed shortly after and remained unmoving, embraced, he still buried inside me. Completely spent, we allowed laziness to overtake us.

The glaring sunlight woke me up and I turned around to check if he was still in the bed. I should have been more careful because I got a real shot of pain from my bottom up to the top of my spine. I sat on the bed, leaning down against the pillows and felt very dizzy, not to mention the cursed pain running through me. The sun was really up, and its reflection on the water hurt my eyes. It was like a hangover, but without the alcohol.

I heard some noises in the bathroom as Konrad emerged from it, completely casually dressed, no suit this morning, but grey trousers, blue shirt and black pullover, hair still damp from the shower and a grin like the Cheshire cat. He bent over the bed and kissed me softly on the forehead.

"Hey lover boy, time to stand up and maybe we can catch lunch."

"Lunch? What time is it?"

"About one more or less," he smirked. "Fortunately, I've taken holidays today, if not we would have had all my staff banging on the door at nine."

I rearranged my stance, only to get another reminder of our previous activities and I grimaced in pain. "You should take a bath. Helps to lessen the pain," he added, sympathetically.

"You are an animal in bed," I grunted. Fuck, it's so late. The whole house must know by now what we have been doing (for real) and the mental image of all his goons coming to check on his poor, defenceless boss in the clutches of a super killer like myself, made me blush deeply.

"It was not the compliment I was expecting, but it will do for the moment," he chuckled. "Yes, Guntram, my staff has a vivid imagination. If they have not realised what we have done by now, they will the minute they see your neck," he added triumphantly to my utter horror. "Come on, take a bath and dress. You must be starving."

"Turn around," I said suddenly blushing.

"Please, there's nothing I have not seen already."

"Anyway. Turn around, please. I'm not putting on a show," I said while I searched between the covers for something to dress. I found his pyjama jacket, and I was glad because it was big enough as to cover me. He laughed and moved away from the bed toward the desk placed over the terrace window.

I put the shirt on and stood on wobbly legs. Honestly, next time I will do it only once, because twice with him is too much for me. This man is like the Energizer bunny! I directed myself toward the closet to look for some clothes.

"Better I read Bloomberg's before I throw you again in the bed."

"Sorry?" I was puzzled by his remark. More? Please I'm sore from before and not that I didn't enjoy it and would like to repeat, but later. Temperance, you know?

"There is nothing sexier than to see your lover with your own clothes," he wolfishly answered, his eyes strangely shinning. "It reinforces your claim on him."

"You will have to wait for tonight because I'm not up to it." Yes, a career as boy toy is not for me.

True to his word the bath really helped and I felt more like myself. I dressed, shaved, brushed my teeth, combed my hair and found myself with the dilemma of a hickey the size of Buenos Aires on the right side of my neck. Even if I closed the shirt, the damn thing would be seen from a mile! I would have to ask for a scarf from Konrad, after all had he not just said how sexy borrowing/lending was? I hope he doesn't charge me interest.

Two strong arms encircled my waist as said culprit started to chomp on my shoulder again, oblivious to my protests.

"Please stop. I can't do it anymore," I pleaded not too strongly or manly, I admit. "You're going to leave more marks," was my protest muffled by his kisses.

"That's the idea behind a mark," he whispered, too busy eating me.

I disentangled myself from his bear hug and turned around to face him, the smell of his cologne entrancing me with its softness and a sense of *déja vu*.

"Can you lend me a scarf? I'm not coming downstairs with this."

"You are so shy my love," he chuckled "But in the bed you're so greedy," he said, lustfully making me blush. "That's every man's desire," he whispered as he held me against his chest for some time.

"I remember now," I suddenly said under his perplexed gaze. "Your cologne smells like my father's! This is why I like it so much. He always wore it when he visited me," he looked at me concerned, with a deep frown in his forehead.

"I hope you don't take me for your father," he barked, his eyes darkening as he held me with more force than necessary against the marble vanity.

"What? No chance. I'm not looking for a father figure, and you don't look like him at all!" I shrugged. "Where did you get it? I haven't smelled it in years."

"A perfumer makes it for me in Milan. I'll give you a scarf if you want it so much," he said dryly.

We went downstairs together. I was not so brave as to do it alone, so I followed him like a good obedient puppy through the corridor toward his studio. Friederich came rushing to ask if we wanted to have lunch, and Konrad agreed to have it in the small dining room. Not a few seconds after the butler disappeared, Ferdinand and Michael rushed in the studio with some folders and started to speak in German, completely ignoring me. I sat happily by the window looking at them not very interested in what they were saying. When they finally left, Konrad beckoned me to approach his desk.

"Come here Guntram, I have something for you."

As I drew nearer him I saw that he pulled out of his desk a green large box and extended it toward me. "Today is Epiphany Day."

"I've totally forgotten. I have nothing for you." Honestly, this is not one of the festivities I care about. When I was in school, it was holidays and all the students were out, with their families; the teachers who were stuck in the school with me, never remembered to give me something. I had better luck for Christmas. I stood there, in awe looking at the package.

"It's only something I got for you in Zurich. Come, open it," he nudged me softly.

I continued to stare at the thing. He pulled me by the sleeve, playfully to shake me from my rapt. I tore the paper to find a polished wooden box with a metal lid. Under his encouraging glance, I opened it to reveal a set of pencils neatly arranged in two trays from Caran d'Ache.

"It's wonderful, it's too much. Thank you very much indeed. I always wanted one of these sets," I replied throwing myself around his neck. He pulled me into his lap without saying anything and I stayed there watching the box dreamily and enjoying the warmth radiating from his body.

"Can I ask you something?"

"Depends on what it is," he replied half seriously, a twitch of a smile hanging from his lips.

"Do you have any news from Fedérico and his mother?" A flash of anger quickly passed across his eyes. Great, Guntram you just spoiled a wonderful moment!

"They took a flight back to Argentina this morning," he replied harshly, not leaving any place for further questions. "This business is over as far as I'm concerned and I don't wish to speak about it ever again. You should do well in forgetting you ever met them," was his stern advise.

"I can't help to be concerned, even if you don't like them. I've known Fedérico for the last eight years. He's the closest thing to a brother that I will ever get."

"You are too naive for your own good," he grunted, dismissing my speech with small shake of his head. "Let's do not waste our time with a pointless argument. I think we should take a few days off together. Travel around Italy for a week or two, before we come back to Zurich."

"So, you are going to start your holidays finally?" I retorted half-jokingly.

"Yes, but you have to make up your mind fast before I get a better offer."

"I was expecting something like that. One hot morning and out. I should go back to San Marco and see what I catch next."

His hand caught my chin with force, painfully digging his fingernails into my flesh. "You should never say something like this ever again. Not even as a joke. You are mine and better don't forget it. You would not like the consequences if you do," he hissed, sending a pang of true fear through my body. We remained silent for several minutes, he not letting my chin go, and I not daring to move an inch in fear he would retaliate like that time, considering how his body was tense and ready to attack.

"My love for you is true and you still play with me, Guntram. This is not a teenagers' foolish game," he stated his magnetic evil aura stronger than ever.

"I understand," I said, hoping this would appease him.

"No, you don't. I have a position in society and obligations to fulfil. You must behave like an adult. You are not a child any more. I will protect you as much as I can, but there will be many trying to undermine your place at my side. You must allow no room for misunderstandings. Your lack of trust toward my decisions could be a great handicap."

"Forgive me if I taunted you. It was not my intention. I thought you were also joking," I said softly, looking at the carpet. His body relaxed visibly, but he didn't let me go.

"Let's eat and then go for a walk," he said, finally releasing me.

The rest of the evening was peaceful. We had lunch alone, not interrupted at all. At three o'clock, we went for a walk, and I was still nervous around him. Was he always like this, exploding for no reason? How could a man, who was so cold and composed in front of others, change so much? I know he's a business like minded person, people running or better say, scurrying away when he's around, with a superhuman intelligence, to the point of being terrifying and the temper of a basilisk.

We walked along the narrow streets without any direction just for the pleasure of it. His sporadic conversation eased a little bit my jitters, but not so much. He suggested we go for a coffee in a small place, not very crowded. We ordered a cappuccino for me and a straight black espresso for him and sat at a table by the corner.

"Why are you so edgy now? Since lunch you have not said more than twenty words."

"I haven't quite figured you out. One moment, you are charming, and the next you change into this frightening person ready to kill. All this makes me nervous. I don't know what sets you off."

"I don't have two personalities, if this is what you're thinking. Normally, I'm a man with severe convictions and many obligations. I can't have the luxury of playing nice or letting offences go unpunished. In this world, is better to be feared than loved. I have to see through the lies of many sharks swimming in my pond. I told you once, that achieving power is something relatively easy. The main problem is to keep a hold on it. I'm not used to be disobeyed or questioned, and when it happens, I react, perhaps too much in your case. What you call my "charming" side is not the norm. With you, I can lower my defences, and enjoy freely your company."

"You have so much and so little at the same time," I muttered more to me than for him. Even if this sounds corny, poor guy, more money than he will ever be able to spend and so much solitude in his life. I mean, I have nothing but I don't have to watch my back. Does he have friends at all?

"We both will have to make adjustments in our characters for this relationship to work. You have been running wild for too long, and you need to get used to the idea of having someone in your life to give you some direction."

Me? Wild? You must be joking. I followed orders my whole life! First the nannies, then my father, the teachers, the manager in the book store and finally you. I'm a complete idiot who is in bed at 11 p.m., because he has to work the next morning. I've never enjoyed the "sex, rock and roll and fun" routine like my student fellows.

"Konrad, If you think that I'm an example of a wild youth, you should really go out more or watch Big Brother for once in your life."

"You are quite good at playing the game of "I'm a serious, responsible young man," In order to avoid problems or be ignored by your guardians, but deep inside, you do whatever you please. If you don't like a situation or think it would become too personal, you flee or hide behind the wall you have built over the years to keep you isolated from the world. You are no better than Victor de l'Aveyron; you can speak and don't smash things like this savage. You are wild in the sense that although you are aware of society rules, you have not internalized them; you play along."

"This morning you shared my bed, but have you shared your feelings with me? I think not. You say you love me, but you don't trust me, so how can this be real love? It sounds more like lust to me. Guntram. Not everybody will abandon you like your father did. I will not let you go. I can't do it."

What set me on fire? The mention of my father's suicide? Comparing me with a half retarded wolf child from the XVIII century? The fact he had figured me out totally in less than a week? That he obviously saw himself as the almighty god who will bring me back to civilization? That he had just implied that I was something like an emotionally handicapped person, resorting to fuck, in order to avoid facing things? That he realised I was terrified of having any contact with other human beings?

"Do you think that half a day of tumbling down between the sheets gives you the right to manipulate and change my life?" I said in a low and dark voice. "If I were in need of a shrink, I would look for one really qualified. You are no better than I. Everybody around you fears you, and I bet you can't have a single real friend. Who's more pathetic? I, with zero relationships at nineteen years old or you at forty-four and close to zero? You have no mercy, compassion or kindness in your heart. You think that possessing someone to be your puppet is love. And when you don't get your way, you resort to violence, threats or bribery. I pity you now," I said going from fury to contempt.

He looked at me, anger boiling between his eyes. Great, now we will have a fight again, only that this time we will end up in the police station. Fortunately, the guys already know me.

The maniac laughed at me, in a musical and harmonious way.

"Incredible, Guntram. This is the first time, I see you showing your true emotions, not what you think people expect you to do."

He's totally crazy and in a disturbing way. Has he not seen me crying like a baby in his office or moaning like a heated whore in his bed?

"If I'm some kind of Rainman, why do you waste your time with me? It seems I'm some kind of dark evil pretender," I grunted, shocked and hurt.

"I never said you were an autistic person. What I described were the survival skills of an intrinsically good person who has alienated himself in order to avoid more suffering. If you continue to live like this, I fear that in ten years, you would be jumping out of a window."

It's horrible to show your inner core to somebody and worse, that said person tells you how you really foresee your own future no matter the lies you told to yourself or the goals you set to escape from it. I took a deep breath, shocked and horrified.

"You also are not surrounded by happiness," I said, willing to hurt him as much as he did.

"I know and I want to change it. I've also severed all ties with humans because I believe that they're treacherous and dangerous creatures. Many years ago, I loved a man with all my soul but he betrayed me in the worst possible way. Since that episode, I devoted my life to expanding the banks of the family. I think you love me but you're too afraid that I would leave you, that you don't want to truly submit into the relationship. *Tu n'es encore pour moi, qu'un petit garçon tout semblable à cent mille petits garçons. Et je n'ai pas besoin de toi. Et tu n'as pas besoin de moi non plus. Je ne suis pour toi qu'un renard semblable à cent mille renards. Mais, si tu m'apprivoises, nous aurons besoin l'un de l'autre. Tu seras pour moi unique au monde. Je serai pour toi unique au monde...* " [2]

Why had he chosen this passage of The Little Prince? It was one of my favourite pieces and I've secretly been envious of that fox who knew the secret of love; to let go of yourself for the other. I was voiceless as my inner walls were crumbling.

"My life would have been entirely different if you would have been ten years ago in my life," he pondered to himself, his eyes clouded.

"Yes, you would be in jail. I was nine," I said softly, taking his hand over the table. If you have not realised by now, I turn to humour when they have struck too close to my heart. He looked at me and smiled bewitchingly. I think he knows he won

---

[2] "To me, you are still nothing more than a little boy who is just like a hundred thousand other little boys. And I have no need of you. And you, on your part, have no need of me. To you, I am nothing more than a fox like a hundred thousand other foxes. But if you tame me, then we shall need each other. To me, you will be unique in all the world. To you, I shall be unique in all the world …"

Antoine de Saint-Exupéry, *Le Petit Prince*, Chap. XXI. 1943.

the game.

"This is why I didn't want to advance further in our relationship. I wanted you to be sure of yourself, and carry it to the end."

"*Ma vie est monotone. Mais, si tu m'apprivoises, ma vie sera comme ensoleillée. Je connaîtrai un bruit de pas qui sera différent de tous les autres. Les autres pas me font rentrer sous terre. Le tien m'appellera hors du terrier, comme une musique.*" [3] I quoted out of the blue, reddening myself once again as he looked at me with adoration in his eyes, melting my heart, as he engulfed my hand into his.

Suddenly, he tore apart his head from my face and looked at the door, where a small man with two big mountains behind, was standing. A dense haze of danger radiated from him as he modified his relaxed position to one of attack. The man, coming to us faltered in his steps, stopping a few meters from Konrad, with his head bent down, submissively.

"Sire, may I approach?" he said with a strange accent to my utter bewilderment.

"Proceed."

"Sire, I'm most honoured that one of your Lieutenants requested my services for you," he humbly said, not really looking at Konrad in the eyes. Well, bankers are strange people if you ask me.

"Your cooperation will not be forgotten," Konrad dismissed the man without a second thought.

"If you allow me to say it, he's very beautiful. He could fetch several million in the market," he said making an imperceptibly gesture towards me.

Konrad glared at him. "Dismissed," he hissed.

"Could my men escort you, Sire?" the man blurted out, visibly alarmed at Konrad's barely checked temper.

"It's not necessary. I trust the city is in order now."

"Most certainly Sire. Good bye."

"Good bye and thank you."

The funny little man almost bowed at Konrad's words, and quickly left us with his two friends.

"That was creepy. Who is he?"

"Nobody. Just business. Let's go home. You still haven't told me where you want to go tomorrow. Even Monika needs some warning to make reservations."

We went home just like he said we should. My head was still in the clouds, thinking on his sweet words. He was right, sure, more than I wanted to admit but was I ready for what he wanted? Originally, I'd thought that sex was what frightened me the most. How wrong I was and he knew it since the first kiss. Intimacy is more difficult to achieve.

Conversation was kept civilised between us during dinner. We decided over Florence and Milan, leaving Rome for later. He could only take ten days at most before returning to work. Monika interrupted us, wishing to know who would be

---

[3] My life is very monotonous (...) But if you tame me, it will be as if the sun came to shine on my life. I shall know the sound of a step that will be different from all the others. Other steps send me hurrying back underneath the ground. Yours will call me, like music, out of my burrow.

Antoine de Saint-Exupéry, *Le Petit Prince*, Chap. XXI. 1943.

coming along. Konrad decided on Heindrik and another two who I was didn't know. The secretary was pleased with the selection and was leaving when Konrad asked her very nicely to send Friederich in.

"I think Friederich has enough of moving for the year. I will send him back to Zurich. He hates to travel. He's only happy in the castle," he told me.

"Do you live in a castle?" I asked, baffled. I know *estancias* that are like castles, but since I've been in Europe, I had to reconsider my idea of big and luxurious.

"It's about thirty minutes from the city. The tower is the only remaining vestige from the XII century. The living quarters were added in the XIX century by the Metternich House. Sadly, it was about to be turned into a spa when my father acquired it forty years ago and needed a complete renovation. The original place from the Lintorff family is in shambles now, after the Allied bombing and the communists' looting later, but as the Metternich family was related to my mother's in a second degree, it was appropriate to buy it," he told me, as if it were the simplest thing in life to buy a castle.

"You will like it. It's not big or grandiose, but it serves our needs perfectly. It's quite discreet and comfortable if you have to organize meetings. Everything you might need, ask Friederich. He rules the house with an iron fist."

I'm not surprised to hear that. A soft knock in the door announced the butler; Konrad gave him the orders and clearly established that I was supposed to share his room.

We talked a little more before going to bed and again I was falling for his soft voice and incredible rich conversation which, even if it was worthy of a university professor, was at the same time modest. You didn't feel as if you were in front of a superior mind. At eleven, he considered it was time to go to bed, and I was more than happy to comply—almost giddy.

We changed into our pyjamas in silence, the tension building up in me with every minute. I brushed my teeth and went to bed where he was already, reading some papers. I slid in and waited for him to take the initiative.

"Do you want to sleep now?" he asked still concentrating on his blasted files.

"Not really. And you?" This should be enough for a horny guy like him, if we consider this morning's performance.

"Good. I have to finish these documents." Not at all what I was expecting. I turned around in the bed disappointed and frankly pissed off. He continued to read for a while. Finally, he turned off his bedside light and turned around to hold me. OK, things were looking definitely better. I squirmed a little bit in his embrace grinding my bottom against his manhood. Time to be naughty.

"Kitten, don't think I don't know what you're up to," was his amused answer to my seduction attempts. Sorry, I didn't get in school the "bedroom etiquette training course"!

"Don't waste your time trying to distract me. Make up sex will not allow you to escape from what I told you today. We need time to know each other," he sounded quite determined.

"I want it. You're not going to hurt me," I said, half pleadingly.

"Have you considered that I could be hurt in the process if you decide you don't want me?"

Chapter 14

January 15th, 2002

Hello diary. Do you remember me? It's me again. I left you alone for almost a week, but for a good reason. Konrad and I were... well... busy. The thing that goes around two people in love. You know, right?

He was right. We needed some time to know each other well before... like three days more or less. I think I have fallen completely for him. OK, sometimes he's so serious and formal, but then there's this sparkle shinning in his eyes when he looks at me that melts me. *Je suis apprivoisé.* But again I'm jumping as usual.

On January 7th morning, we left for Florence with two cars, black Mercedes. In one a driver and us and in the other Heindrik and the other bodyguards. To my credit, I was looking at the landscape as Italy is beautiful, while he was entertained with the contents of a leather briefcase strategically left in the car.

We arrived at noon in Florence, at a hotel in the centre with the name of a *Palazzo*, on the side of the Palazzo Pitti, and it had a wonderful view over the Arno River and the city, with the Duomo looming over it. We went for a walk for the rest of the day, speaking about nothing and everything. For the first time in my life, I felt I could speak up my mind without fearing to be ridiculed or feel ashamed of my own little polishing. With him I feel a sense of freedom I've never had. For once, I didn't have to be the perfect picture of a modern boy. I mean, he didn't laugh outright when I almost fell into a trance at entering at Santa Maria Maggiore, like Fefo would have done. Yes, I'm into "mummies' stuff" more than I thought. We had dinner in the hotel's restaurant and returned to the suite.

There's something I want to tell you Diary. He's different from all the other rich people I met during my school days. Even if he's loaded to an obscene point, he doesn't show it or rub it into your face on purpose. Perhaps this is the result of several generations of money. Everything seems to be natural for him. So, we went back in the suite and he had to read his e-mails while I entertained myself with drawing all the things I saw on the streets.

Without any kind of warning, he stole my sketch folder and started to look at it. Even my protest of "don't touch if you're not buying" was dismissed with a shrug. He went through the pages looking at them sharply, like everything he does, driving me to the edge.

"It's amazing how you change if you feel unrestrained. The first ones are almost academic studies, but do not show your feelings in them. They are like an animated picture of the feelings of the depicted object. Those from today show almost like you had an opinion of the object. Perhaps you might even develop a style."

I recovered my folder "Yeah, right. Next stop Christies'"

"What did change?"

"Don't know what you mean." Warning glare from him. "OK, if you want to know. I feel liberated somehow. You don't judge me like the others and I can do as I truly want without worrying about the consequences."

"I see."

"It's not that I don't care about your opinion anymore," I hastily said. Had he got it all wrong?

"I don't believe that. But I do hope that you will come out of your shell someday."

I was rendered speechless as I pondered what he wanted to tell me.

* * *

Next morning, we went to the Uffizzi and spent the whole day there. He knows a lot about art history and even has a minor collection at home, mostly "scattered from ancestors". We went back to the hotel and stayed in the room until dinner.

As usual he started to look at his computer. If there's a workaholic person, he's one. I took some white paper from the desk and a pencil. Without giving too much thought, I outlined first the contours of his face, adding the shadows that were playing over his cheekbones and lost track of time.

"This is how you see me?" He can make me jump for sure.

"What? Oh, it's not finished and you were not supposed to see it," I replied trying to pry it back from his hands. My chest collided against his back as I futility tried to get it back from his hands. He turned around, threw the folder to the floor and jumped on top of me making me fall on top of the bed.

Our kisses were hungry, ravenous and our breathing ragged and he didn't bother with the buttons of my shirt; they flew away under his fingers, tearing the fabric of my collar. Clothes were discarded in a frenzied heat as we couldn't pull apart our hands from each other. The tingling of my erection became painful with all the tension we had accumulated over the days. He devoured my member with long movements of his mouth, sending waves of pleasure across my body. I was in ecstasy, moaning and buckling my hips to meet the caresses of his tongue on my shaft.

All at once as he had started with his kisses, he stopped sucking me when I was about to get my release. I was lost. Konrad I swear this is not the moment for a talk. I growled menacingly at him.

"So eager my love? Wait, we both have to enjoy it," he chuckled making me turn over in the bed. His hands guided my hips to a four legged position, my rear fully exposed to him as he knelt behind me. One of his hands took my member as he penetrated me with full force. No more of his "gentle love" manner and I didn't want any. I wanted him without restrictions.

I gasped at the intrusion, the pain almost throwing me down but I anchored my arms against the mattress holding my ground. He picked up a fast pace while he pounded me, his hand repeating it as he rubbed my member. I think it was brief but intense. I can't say. Honestly. I was too immersed in the wonderful sensations he was discovering for me. We both reached our climax together.

We slid under the covers, spent and breathless and stayed there, my head resting against his chest, lulled by his quick heartbeat. His big hand toyed with my hair in a loving way and I left a trail of soft kisses over his chest, lapping playfully with his nipple. He laughed. So you are ticklish? Good to know.

"Promise me it will always be like this," I uttered lovingly.

"Guntram, compared to you, I'm an old man," he replied with a hint of humour in his voice.

"Sorry to disagree with you, but your friend down there seems to deny your statement," I deviously grinned at his erection which was growing again.

"I think I still need to be convinced," he looked at me, daring me to do something about it.

I smiled and winked an eye in a shameless way. OK I didn't know I had it in me. Maybe I'm not so dull as I originally believed. I knelt over him and straddled his hips between my tights as I engulfed his member in my mouth and sucking with powerful moves. It felt very good to hear his grunts of pleasure as I played with him, sucking, teasing.

"I need to have you. Mount on top," his voice almost sounding like a plea.

Honestly, I was a little bit afraid to impale myself. "Go slowly dear, don't hurry," he whispered. I took a deep breath and hesitantly I positioned myself over his hard member. With my hand I placed his shaft in my anus and slid it in slowly. His cum from before eased the entrance a lot and his rod pierced me, giving pleasure instead of the expected pain. I started a series of slow motions to accustom to the feeling.

"Now you're in control of the situation," he said softly, letting me do as I pleased. I closed my eyes to enjoy better, picking up the pace as I was engulfed by lust. My moves became frantic as he put his fingers into my mouth to suck them, making him wail.

He depleted himself into me, flooding me like never before. A few seconds later I did the same over his chest, falling boneless over him.

"This is the first time I came with somebody on top of me. Normally, I have to control the situation," he confessed to me as he covered my forehead with kisses. "You have bewitched me."

"Stop whining Lintorff and get used to it. You will have to do it more than once," I joked as I drifted into sleep absolutely tired.

"I have created a monster," he snorted.

Several hours later, I think, somebody wanted round three. Old man, right!

We stayed in Florence for several more days enjoying the city and the bed since the weather was stormy. We went once to Arezzo and on another day to Perugia. Milan will have to remain for later, and let's be honest, even if the city is fantastic, the idea of a day spent lazily in bed with Konrad, is far more appealing.

Chapter 15

January 16th, 2002

Back to reality. He has to return to his business before "my people realise they can live without me and throw me out." On the way back to Zurich, we argued about what I should do next. I mean, he has to work and the time he could devote to me will be very little. His day starts at six and ends at eleven or twelve in the night!

My suggestion, that I should use my return ticket to Buenos Aires, and come back in a few months—hey, I have a life, you know?—fell on dead ears. He would have none of it. I was supposed to move with him to Zurich, and study a career in the University from September onwards since the school year had already started. I could use the time for something really useful like learning German (excuse me?) or taking painting classes (?) because it was a real shame I was not doing it professionally (have you been hit hard on the head?) or attend a summer course to get the feeling of the University, as most of them are in English (really?).

Just as the argument threatened to leave the civilised tone so far employed by him—I was supposed to remain quiet and listen—he came to the idea that I should stay with him in Zurich, and in a week, we would discuss it again. I should not worry or feel pressed by my flight's date in order to make a decision. OK, I have again collided against the thick wall that is his stubbornness.

The rest of the flight was in silence as he plunged into his reports, ignoring all of us. I was fuming, trying to keep my temper in check in front of Monika and Ferdinand, who had come along with Konrad's private jet to "update him". No need to start a noisy and vulgar dispute in front of a lady.

The landing was uneventful (thank God, I hate it), and three black cars were waiting for us. I wanted to drive with Monika or the bodyguards, because I had the feeling that our earlier talk would take a turn for worse. After all, he was playing local and with his rules.

"I can drive with Monika so I'm not in the middle," I suggested to him. A flash of anger passed through his eyes but he kept himself cool. Obviously, he didn't want a scene in front of the underlings gathered there and waiting for him.

"I'll see you at dinner." Great! He's pissed off, but I have gained enough time to mount an offensive. Who am I kidding? I would be lucky if I can organise the defence line.

Monika was more than happy to have me in the car as she bombarded me with questions: How the trip had turned out; if I liked Florence, where we had been; if we had enjoyed our time together (I swear she stressed the word enjoy). Then she started to speak about the Castle, how nice it was, that I should love it with its views and peace around; that she had collected several brochures from the University and that it's one of the best in the world (I have no doubts of that); that I should not be worried about the language because most of the subjects were taught in English, and I would catch up with the German language in no time (not so sure).

The cars left the main highway to take a secondary road which passed through a dense forest till it reached a big gate. We passed it and the trees disappeared

108

as the cars now rode over a gravel path. The building was very simple on its structure, but quite elegant as it had no ornaments like a baroque cream pie. On the right side, was the old tower which had been used as the base to enlarge the castle with an inner courtyard, looking much more like a military fortress than a noble house, which harboured the different wings. Everything was covered in snow giving a mysterious air, and contrary to most castles, which are completely bare of vegetation; this one had solid bushes and trees, adding more privacy.

We left the cars parked outside the courtyard with an archway entrance. Strangely, there were two very old trees inside, facing the open galleries and main door. I was informed later that this part had been originally designed during the XVI century, and the works of the XIX century had tried to be as true to the original as possible. The concept was more Italian than German. Although the Castle was officially bought from a side line of the Metternich House, it had been linked to the Lintorff family in many occasions in the past. Even if they were originally from the Mecklenburg area, after the Thirty Years War, they had moved south to start in the banking business and returned later, in the XIX century, to Prussia to be one of the financiers of the industrialization process.

Monika felt that I needed the introductory course to Konrad's pedigree.

"The Lintorff House was quite modern at its time for being *Uradel*, old nobility. Even if they were dramatically defeated in the Thirty Year War as Catholics, they managed to start anew in Italy, under the protection of the Pope, for the services they have provided him during the war. They settled in Venice, and from there they built their banks. In a way they were more Italian or English than their German counterparts since they had no qualms to involve themselves in trade or finances, when for other noblemen it was totally unthinkable. They were not interested in making blood alliances with the other houses or provide princesses to marry. Like the Liechtensteins, they realised that land was more a liability than an asset, and built their power on money and industry. After Napoleon's defeat and the rise of the Prussian Empire, the Lintorffs came back to Germany, mostly because of their old links to the Hohenzollern Dynasty at the time of the Teutonic Order. They were able to lend capital to the state at a very low interest. They received land, but since they were Catholics, they were never truly happy to be in Protestant land, and were constantly coming back to Austria or Bavaria to marry there.

After World War II, the land was lost and they moved definitively to Vaduz and Zurich where were the main offices. Under Konrad—she said his name as if he were Karl the Great—the two original banks expanded into very successful hedge funds, but this you already know."

"Is the Duke the last of the Family? Does he have brothers or sisters?" I asked

"Unfortunately, the death of his baby brother left the Duchess devastated, and there were no more siblings. Marianne von Liechtenstein retreated from all social activities at that time. It has been agreed that the title will go to the oldest son of Albert von Lintorff, who is the son of his Excellency's uncle, whose line was in charge of the Italian branch, so to speak, of the family businesses. The name will not be lost, but his line yes. As for his fortune, a large part will go into the Church's hands, and the rest we don't know. The Duke has considered the idea of adopting or having children, in order to pass his companies on, but so far, he has not made any decision. I'm most confident that with you here, he will finally make up his mind."

With me around? Is this woman crazy? I'm a man and there's no chance we can have babies together, and adopting me is out of the question. This inheritance is a poisonous gift to whoever gets it. I pity the poor baby on whose head it will befall. And second, his past relationship must have been a real mess if he was not even able to make a convenient marriage like most of his ancestors did in order to secure the succession. Suddenly, I felt very tired and a headache started to dance around me.

"Are you feeling all right?" she asked me looking truly concerned

"Yes. Thank you very much, just tired from the flight. I become completely nervous in planes. I prefer more a train or a boat."

She smiled at me kindly. "I understand you perfectly. I also hate those things and prefer to make my job from here. Fortunately, the Duke allows me to stay most of the times. Do you want that I take you to your room to rest till dinner?"

"That would be very kind of you, Madam."

She led me to the main bedroom where Friederich was already busy with the luggage. Konrad's private quarters were a series of rooms interconnected in the old tower. A big private living room, with a gigantic chimney, sparsely furnished with old pieces that were coming out of museum, some paintings, family portraits. From there was a door leading to his bedroom which had a view over the courtyard, a big bed and a private bathroom and dressing room the size of my flat. In the other side of the living room, there was a door leading to a small guest bedroom and another leading to a private studio and library.

"Friederich, could you later explain to Guntram the management of the house?" Monika said to him in a tone that left no room for discussion "Could you give him some aspirin for his headache?" I swear women and mothers have a sixth sense when it comes to see through you. "Dinner would be at eight and Lehnder, the CEO from one of the hedge funds plus wife, and the President of the Reconstruction Bank for Central Europe and wife, will be coming. It's black tie, dear and very dull. I'll sit you beside Ferdinand's wife, Gertrud, so you don't have to suffer too much. Friederich will help you dress." And just like that, she disappeared, leaving me in the center of the living room at the butler's mercy.

"Would you like a tea, child? You look sick."

"Yes, thank you. I'm not used to this cold weather," I said going to sit in one of the chairs.

"You could rest before dinner or take a warm bath. It helps."

He left me alone, most probably gone to look for tea. A sense of dread permeated my soul. I wasn't sure any more I could take it. This was too much for me. Konrad was back into his cold, overbearing personality, and I wanted to get the first plane back home. I was a simply guy, a student with a small job and a rented flat; not someone who can wear a tuxedo and sit at the same table with a CEO.

Friederich returned with a tray filled with a teapot and a cup. He settled it on top of the table. I served myself the hot beverage and swallowed the aspirin.

"I will explain to you the dynamics of the house tomorrow. You seem very tired."

"I have a monster headache," I said with a shrug. "Could you sit with me a little bit?"

"Certainly sir," he answered with a grandfatherly smile.

"Please don't call me sir. I drives me mad. Everybody calls me Guntram or de Lisle."

"The Duke would not like it. He does not take disrespect well, and your status is close to his in this house."

"I have noticed," I sighed.

"Perhaps I might call you by your Christian name when the Duke is not around," he suggested.

"That would be great," I replied my spirits lifted a bit. We sat around the table as I drank the tea.

"It's very fortunate that everything went well during the holidays. The Duke looks almost ten years younger. It's been a long time since I saw him so full of life."

I don't want to know how he was before, if this is his "brightest" day. Better put some sense into this man. "We almost quarrelled in the plane," I whispered.

"About what?" he asked, raising an eyebrow.

"He has just decided how my life should be from now onwards, and forgot to ask me if I wanted the kind of life he leads," I said in a truly sour mood. Friederich chuckled visibly amused.

"The Duke always had such a strong character. As a child, he was impossible. He can't help it. It's part of his nature to be dominant. He's used to being obeyed and not questioned at all."

"Sounds like a spoiled brat to me," I mumbled at the old man, still upset with Konrad.

"In a way he is. When he's cross about something, his revenge can be... of epic proportions. Should you disagree with him, bear always in mind, that in a negotiation you will not achieve everything you want, that you have to reach a compromise. A frontal attack against him is suicidal. You will only enrage him more. Speak again with him and tell him what it is that you want, and appeal to his generous and protective side," he advised me looking straight into my eyes. "Never forget that the thing he hates most is deceit," he added getting up from his chair. "Rest a little in the main bedroom Guntram. I'll wake you up at half past six."

I laid down over the covers of the bed, having removed jacket and shoes, the pounding in my head decreased to a rhythmic pulse.

* * *

"Hello *Maus*. Did you sleep well? Friederich told me you were feeling under the weather." Konrad's voice woke me up as he laid a trail of short kisses over my neck and cheek. I slowly sat on the bed, my head much better than before, trying to shake the sleep away. I noticed that I was covered with a plaid blanket that was not there before, and that he was already dressed in a double breasted tuxedo looking like a million dollars, like the Americans say.

"Oh God, what time is it?"

"Don't swear," was his sharp scold. "It's almost seven, but you don't have to be downstairs till quarter to eight."

"I'm sorry. I'd better hurry," was my automatic reply as I jumped out of the bed, now completely alert.

"All right, Kitten. I still have to make some phone calls. Meet me in the studio when you're ready."

I took a shower and quickly dressed in the dark blue dinner jacket that was laid out for me. I suppose this is a grant to my young age, not being forced to wear the uncomfortable thing. The bow tie didn't gave me too many problems.

I stopped in front of the polished door to catch my breath before I knocked. I entered and he was sitting, busy with his blackberry. He lifted his gaze and devoured me with his eyes.

"Pity we only have ten minutes left. I don't think you could get dressed again in such a short time."

"You're shameless!" I laughed loudly, half shocked. I crossed the room to give him a brief kiss on his temple. He caught me by the waist.

"How are you feeling?" He asked without releasing his hold from me.

"Overwhelmed to be honest."

"It's only a matter of time and you will get used to this—a week or two. Tonight is relatively easy. Ralf and his wife are not imposing at all, Lehnder you should not worry about, Gertrud, Ferdinand's wife is one of the few nice cousins I have, and Michael Dähler, you know him."

Dinner was not as bad as I expected. I mean, Michael was there and Gertrud was a tall, icy looking blonde in her late forties that despite her aristocratic demeanour, was a very funny woman, bombarding me with questions about the Argentinean countryside and polo teams. The other noble guests ignored me, of course, and I was thankful for that.

Michael told us some of his adventures in the Navy and how he remembered one of the Argentinean Admirals during the sea blockade against Iraq in the 90's. "His ship was in charge of leading the other ships across the sea mines. In such cases, you follow the leader in a straight line like a duck to his mother. They were always making very sharp turns at some point, forcing the other boats to heel like crazy. Once, our Admiral asked him why on earth he was doing this and he just said "so you don't fall asleep." My commanding officer nearly had a heart attack that day, and I really pondered asking for a transfer to Argentina's Navy," he said grinning, to our utter amusement.

The other side of the table was not so funny judging for the stern looks there and the formal tone employed in their conversation in German. I caught Konrad throwing a glimpse at my direction several times.

"Michael you should really tell the story of your mission to the Kabukicho district in Tokyo," Gertrud said quite entertained.

"That was a dangerous and heroic mission to get my men out of there, but I'm afraid your husband and the Duke will take turns to strangle me if I do so. Guntram is under twenty-one," he chuckled.

"Yes, sometimes I believe Ferdinand had no childhood at all. He can be so serious and my cousin is no better. This vacation has done him so good, because he doesn't look so stressed as before. He reminds me, in a way, when we were in our twenties, back in the ice age."

We had coffee in the living room, and I chose to sit on a sofa in a dark corner since Michael had rejoined the men for an all-German round, and the ladies were happily chatting about the next season in Bayreuth and the Vienna Opera Ball from the previous year. Not my talk at all, so I kept my mouth shut as I heard them musically speak in English for my benefit.

At eleven, everybody decided to call it a night and went home. Konrad and I went to bed together and I only got a single kiss and the order of "sleep now, you look like you're about to the get the flu."

Chapter 16

January 17th , 2002

It's true. He gets up at 6 a.m. as I can testify. It's dark and very cold.
"Sleep a little more. I have to train with Heindrik up to seven thirty, and then we can have breakfast together before I leave for the office," was his hushed sentence in my ear as I was falling again into a light slumber.

At 7:15, I could hear Friederich setting the breakfast table in the living room. I can say goodbye to the idea of sleeping late in this house. I got up from the bed and decided to face the world. I washed myself and dressed in a casual way. Well, as casual as you can do it here. Forget about baggy pants or big sweaters. It was grey wool trousers, shirt, striped tie and beige pullover. I can let go of the jacket for now.

"Good morning, Friederich."

"Good morning, Guntram. The Duke will come shortly to prepare himself. I need to get his suit ready," he replied, making a brief and quick but detailed inspection of me.

Like a hurricane, Konrad burst into the room and I saw that he had a small bloodied cut in one of his biceps.

"What happened to you?" I asked horrified.

"Nothing that it's not the product of my own clumsiness. Goran has always something nasty under his sleeve," he muttered, while going for the bathroom leaving me baffled.

"Friederich, does it make any sense for you?"

"Let him be. He's furious at himself, and the cut is not dangerous. Goran's combat style is wild, treacherous and fierce. The Duke should do well in remembering it. When they fight, they do it quite violently and a cut is nothing compared to what they could do to each other," he told me as if it were the most common thing in the world.

"He said he was going to train as in work out."

"It's training as in a military sense. He does it every morning; keeps his senses sharp," he explained to me, hurrying after his boss.

Several minutes later Konrad emerged from the bedroom with long strides, showered and dress in dark conservative suit, and took a seat at the table. He barked several things to Friederich in German. Guess he also has bad mornings.

"You will stay here today with Friederich and Goran. I will be back at seven," he sharply told me as gave me a not so gentle kiss, catching my chin in a strong grip.

I was sort of "deposited", in the library for the morning, with paper, pencils, and books and told to avoid trouble (?) I stayed there because the fire on the chimney was very nice and the idea of going through twenty centimetres of snow in the garden was not appealing at all. I had lunch with Friederich and Goran, the super killer from Serbia. Not much was said, mostly because of Goran's tendency to answer every question with a single word. Five words in a sentence was his record. After eating, the dark haired man asked me if wanted to go to the stables and see the newly-born

Rotweiller pups. I agreed.

We walked around the Castle and went to see the animals, still with their mother. They were really cute puppies, completely black with the fire marks on top of their eyes.

"Mr. Pavicevic, the Duke told me of your doings on my behalf in Venice and I wanted to thank you."

"It was my duty."

"I'm sorry if you had to place yourself in a dangerous situation. After all these people are criminals."

"Don't think about it anymore. It's over." Long pause while he was thinking. "It's getting cold. Let's get you into the house."

Again, I was left in the library, this time with my Stendahl book.

At seven o'clock, Konrad was back in the library, jumping on top of me, and kissing me fiercely.

"Let's have dinner and go to bed," he whispered in my ear as he nibbled my earlobe delicately with his sharp teeth. I moved my neck to give him better access, and he started to kiss me on the collarbone, unbuttoning my shirt with expert fingers.

"Come on, Guntram let's go to bed," I laughed at his sinful proposition expressed in such a crude manner.

"You are really a romantic man. Aren't you?"

"I was offering dinner first," he said with a false insulted expression in his eyes. "But you just lost it due to your delaying. I'm taking you directly to bed."

"Well, I hope they do have a microwave in your noble kitchen," I retorted under his amused glare.

Needless to say, we went to the bedroom and closed the door for a session of hot, steamy sex, and he was like crazy from desire not really wanting to waste any more time. If he plans to come back from work every day like that, the chef can forget about making soufflé.

Two hours later, I laid nearly dead on top of his chest, enjoying his soft petting on my back and the sense of peace in our afterglow, all tension disappeared.

"Are you peaceful now?" he asked me.

"What does it mean?" I growled

"Yesterday, you were quite nervous about coming here; almost shouting with me in the plane."

"Konrad, we need to speak. You can't put my life upside down in two seconds. I have a life back home."

"I said we both would have to make some adjustments to our lifestyles."

"And your contribution would be…," I trailed starting to be upset at his calm demeanour. Fuck it's my life we are speaking about!

"I will try to be home at seven every day." Impressive Konrad. I shot him a deadly glare if this is his idea of a joke. He held my regard unmoved. "I will not whore as much as I did in the past." Wow. What can I say? I'm touched beyond words! "As I said, you can continue your education here, and work under Gertrud's orders since you two got along so well yesterday. She's in charge of the charity projects of the foundation," he finished with a look of "this is the best offer you can get".

I remembered Friederich's words, and took a deep breath when I really wanted to hit him with a pillow. Yes, bad idea, direct combat with a giant of a man who likes to have a good fight in the mornings like other men drink coffee or eat a croissant. Let's resort to diplomacy and logic.

"I hope you see my point Konrad. We have met only two weeks ago and you're asking me to give everything I have, know and cherish away, in one go. I have a job, friends, a University to attend, a flat to pay for, people I like to help and plans for my future. This is a huge sacrifice you're demanding from me, and I don't think I'm ready to do it."

"You live in a rented flat, have a low paying job as a waiter, go to a University whose name is not even ranked in the Top 100 Schools and let's do not dwell on your friends. The only thing I can accept as a stopper for you, is your work for the Church in the slums," he said deadly serious to me as if he were one step from exploding.

"I can't throw everything out through the window! Even if, and I stress the if, I accept your offer of moving here with you, there are simple practical questions to be solved like giving my apartment back, quitting my job, getting my papers from the school, my grades from the University, other documents and personal papers and hundreds of small things that I can't think about at the moment."

"All right. You can go there for a week to put your affairs in order," he conceded. "Next week I have to fly to London and New York for business. You can use that time."

"I need a minimum of a month! Do you have any idea of how horrible the Argentinean bureaucracy can be?" Shit! Have I indirectly agreed to his crazy plan? I'm insane!

"Ten days. No more."

"We are not buying stocks," I retorted dryly. He was not impressed at all with my remark. "All right, I think I could manage in three weeks," I said with my best puppy eyes. Remember the part of appealing to his generosity?

"Fifteen days and it's final, Guntram. Don't try my patience. You leave with me on Monday 21st and will be back in Zurich airport on February 4th. I'll tell Monika to make the arrangements," he said still upset, leaving the bed and starting to get dressed.

I stayed in the bed for some time trying to understand what had transpired. I got "permission" like a five year old to come back to my own home for fifteen lousy days, and in exchange I was supposed to give everything up and move to a country 12,000 kilometres from everything I knew.

Chapter 17

I'm going home today. In the evening! Early in the morning, Konrad went away in his private jet to London. Michael is supposed to take me to the airport and make sure that I don't screw up the flight. Monika booked me a first class ticket despite my protests and I'm a bit edgy. After all, I came on a low budget company and go back like a prince.

The past week was odd. Konrad was still upset the day after the "negotiation". By Friday, he had calmed down and came back from the bank early, in order to take me to a concert in Zurich, and I was more than happy to leave the Castle to see the city, even if it was in darkness.

The concert was in a luxurious hotel in the Centre followed by a dinner for us together in a suite. He said he was too tired to drive home (mind you it's forty minutes and the driver can do it), so he had planned a romantic evening for us. I think that was his way to apologise for his unreasonable behaviour. I was moved by this and his tenderness reminded me of our time together in Florence. Again, I fell under his spell.

Next morning, he showed me the city and even came up with the crazy idea of going to the Zoo. We came home late in the afternoon, and spent our time together, him reading his usual load of papers and me sitting by him, my head snuggled on his lap, almost falling asleep.

"Guntram, promise me you will come back on the 4th."

Not again. Konrad, if I didn't know better, I would think you're being psychotic. I sighed, utterly too tired to start a fight anew. "I do. I'll come on the 4th. And you promise you won't organise a sex party in my absence."

"I will miss you," he muttered softly and shyly.

That night he didn't want to make love even if I really tried to engage him. "I don't want to have casual sex with you," he told me, gritting his teeth so much that I could almost hear them grinding. Instead he almost placed himself on top of me, not leaving much space for breathing and holding me so strongly that my ribs were hurting. He only lessened his hold when I told him that it was painful and not much.

On Sunday, his dark and heavy mood worsened, not speaking with the staff, staying most of the day in his studio and only crossing a few words with me. We had lunch in silence, and not even Michael dreaded to make a joke or comment on the weather. When he left the table he barked at me "since you're going away tomorrow, the least you can do is to stay near me. Come to the office." Not caring at all that Michael was still sitting there. Just like that, he left the dining room in a whirlwind, not even caring for dessert or coffee. I looked at Michael and he made a shrug, not impressed at all by Konrad's outburst. "Now!" He yelled from the distance.

I had to remain quiet as a mouse in his office while he was working. Fortunately I had the pencil box and some paper there. With his temper today, only the brave would get a book to read! The turning of the pages might get to his nerves! Several hours later, with the only interruption for looking for more paper, I heard

Friederich in the bedroom preparing the luggage for us.

At six, he decided he had enough of his affairs and went into the bedroom as a thunderbolt. I followed him, wondering if there was going to be teatime or not. He was looking through what I assumed it was my own luggage.

"The Degas is on the left side and the silver cutlery on the right," I said dryly starting to get annoyed by his borderline behaviour. I swear he low growled at me, like a lion.

"Why are you taking two sweaters? It's summer there."

"Because Zurich is cold in February and I think a Hawaiian shirt would not look good on the VIPs lounge," I retorted pissed off. The nerve of him!

"You don't need three pyjamas!" He roared throwing them out.

"Ask Friederich why the hell he put them in!" I shouted back.

"You are expected to bring clothes in not put them out of this house!" he shouted advancing menacingly toward me.

"Are you even hearing yourself? This is insane, even for your standards!"

He pushed me hard making me tumble over the bed. His strong body trapped me almost immediately, his lips kissing me so fiercely that his teeth tore my lower lip, making it bleed. I clawed his face in a vain attempt to get him away, but he easily grabbed my hands with one of his and put them over my head. His free hand grasped my chin with an iron grip and he bent down to kiss me again. This time I bit him completely furious, trying also to kick him in the stomach. He retaliated with a full blow to my plexus.

The pain was so sharp that I couldn't breathe. He let go of my arms and I rolled to the side, coughing miserably, trying to recover my breath.

"Oh God, what have I done?" he cried horrified. "I never meant to hurt you. Try to relax and breathe in slowly," he said forcing me to adopt a foetal position. He just sat there beside me, patting me softly in the back, hearing my ragged breathing.

"I'm so sorry. I swear I didn't want to hurt you. Can you turn around and sit?" he said, gently lifting me as my breathing was more regular. He held me against his chest as he caressed me with long movements.

"The idea of losing you drives me crazy. I never meant to do this," he repeated, his eyes full of remorse and veiled tears. "Now you would go away and it's my fault."

"Konrad, I have promised to come back. You have to believe me!" I cried like a child, oddly looking for comfort in his arms.

"Guntram, I can't let go of you anymore," he desperately confessed, breaking my heart.

"It's only two weeks. Besides, next week you will be away and for the other you're always at work," I tried to reason, suddenly frightened with the idea that he would go back on his promise. "I will be back before you notice."

We remained there, lying in the bed for a long time, not speaking, unmoving.

* * *

Monday

In the morning Konrad left to the airport where his jet was waiting for him.

He kissed me desperately, crushing me in his arms.

"It's only two weeks," I said softly.

"I hope," he mumbled. Just like that, he went away, not even looking backward once.

After lunch, Michael came to take me to the airport. I was surprised, I was not expecting that he would do it.

"Hi kid. I've been promoted to chauffeur. Get your things, we're leaving," he said with a huge grin on his face.

I said goodbye to Friederich and thanked him for his trouble. "I hope you come back soon," he replied as he took my luggage. Hey, don't spoil me because I'll have to take care of myself from now onwards.

Outside was parked a black Maserati. A true beauty of a car. I whistled at Michael. "Yours?"

"I wish. The Duke will not mind if I use it to take you to the Airport. Who knows, maybe I get a hot stewardess there. OK, final check. Passport?"

"In my pocket."

"Ticket?"

"In the coat, Mum."

"Bomb?"

"We have to come back. Forgot it," I chuckled.

He insisted on taking me to the check in. I can read signs, you know? He gave me a bear hug and listed his final advice. "Behave, don't eat anything you can't pronounce; if you visit the hot girls, take only cash with you and remember sake and California rolls do not mix well."

"All right. Don't do anything I wouldn't do," I chastised.

"Do you want me to die of boredom?" he replied falsely shocked. I laughed. "You have to come back in two weeks and rescue us from the monster you leave here," he said, this time seriously.

First class is something incredible. You can even get a bed to sleep and a nice stewardess or flight attendant as you're supposed to call them now. The only problem with it is that in the seat across the corridor there was a non-descript Austrian sitting from the acquisitions department of the Lintorff Privatbank.

He was quite discreet and most of the time asked things about Argentina. He said he was going there to evaluate some real estate and land purchases and that he will be staying at the Park Hyatt should I need something.

Konrad. You. Are. A. Control. Freak!

Chapter 18

January 24th , 2002

Nothing really prepared me for what I found on my way back. I have missed most of the events on December 21st when the president was thrown out during the riots and looting. More than twenty people officially dead and unofficially, well, the numbers were too large to believe them. If before people were barely scratching a life, now they didn't even have the chance to do it. Unemployment rate at more than 25%, inflation, banks collapsed as nobody could get money out of them and hordes of poor people scavenging paper and tin cans in the trash cans for selling or recycling at sunset. It was constant demonstrations and permanent political turmoil with people meeting in popular assemblies, mostly led by the leftist parties. I was in shock.

When the Austrian and I descended from the plane I said goodbye but he specifically ordered me to use the car sent by the hotel (an armoured 4x4 van), since there was a huge risk of being attacked when we would pass through the poor areas. I thought he was overdoing it, but he was unfortunately right. "Welcome to Colombia", he said to my utter annoyance.

Surprisingly, he could speak Spanish very well and immediately engaged the driver in talk about politics and economics. He was nice enough as to drop me in front of my building, which is no more than twenty blocks from his hotel. Great!

I left my things at home, changed myself because it's very warm and hell if I go there dressed with such fine things I'd be scorned for the rest of my life. I walked to my hopeful workplace. In theory, I should have been back on the 23rd. I greeted my colleagues who were very intrigued about what I had been doing in Europe for almost a month. Keep dreaming I will tell you the whole story. They got the edited version of me visiting some cities and I very vaguely mentioned staying with someone in Zurich.

"Fuck, Guti is now a grown up man!" Valeria shouted in ecstasy, her hair now furiously pink/purple. "You were with a woman!"

"No, such silly ideas you have," I protested indignantly. Well it's the truth. Essentially.

I found out that my morning shift had been changed into a night shift. Shit! OK, I should not be upset because I'm quitting in a week. I'm supposed to work from 4 p.m. to 11 p.m., but it's 12 to be honest. In theory, you get more tips in this shift than in the mornings.

I shopped for some groceries on the way back and passed by the Social Sciences Faculty (it's where I study Social Work), and was surprised to find it open because it was still holidays. But there were the students (the guys from sociology and political sciences for sure), organizing committees to work in the slums and a barter market (no cash, remember? Not even the local currencies/bonds from the provincial governments). It astonished me to no end that most of the people registering were not the usual students, but middle aged men and women from middle class. Perhaps the mess had given them some social awareness.

Back home, I felt the tiredness hitting me. The bell rang and there was my neighbour with the hell dog he has, barking excitedly at me.

"Lola heard you come at noon. You look dead from the flight. I have made spaghetti," he said in a whirlwind, going directly to my kitchenette and rummaging through my cupboard.

"Hello George—Jorge—but he likes to be called George with French accent; helps his business. *Coiffeur*, it's good to see you again," he's a really nice guy, even if sometimes he becomes worse than a mothering hen to me.

"You have to tell everything! Were you in Paris?" he shouted happily as he sat in my good chair.

"Hold your horses. I'll confess, don't worry. Let me first finish putting the things in the refrigerator."

His admiration whistle at my coat put me on guard. When I was looking for an excuse, the phone started to ring.

"Your real loden coat speaks, Guntram. It's the cashmere goat's spirit trying to reach us," he pointed out.

The mobile phone! I've forgotten the damn thing.

"Hello," I said hesitantly.

"Did you have a nice flight kitten?" Konrad said.

"Hi, it was nice. Thank you," I replied as vaguely as possible. Not really the good moment if we considered that George's world famous "gaydar" was working full time. And, no, there's no other room in this flat to escape to.

"Are you settled now?"

"Yes, most of the things are done. Where are you now?"

"George V. Dreadful meetings the whole day," he sighed. "I miss you already."

Not now, Konrad, I have an audience pending of every word I say!

"Me too," I shyly answered. "My work shift was changed to the night," I blurted out, not knowing why I did it.

"I was under the impression you were going to quit," he said with a dangerous edge in his voice.

"It's only a week more, till they find a replacement," I quickly defended myself. "Too much work today?"

"The usual amount. It's not having you tonight that makes me sad."

I smiled touched by his words. "This is low my love, you know that anyway I could have not travelled with you." George was literally glowing with satisfaction as he settled the dishes and glasses. Fuck! He knows for sure. Argh. Ignore him.

"It doesn't make it any easier," told me Konrad.

"I know. What time is there? Must be very late, you should rest."

"I can't sleep."

"I've met your man in the plane. Landau. He gave me a lift to here. That was very thoughtful of him."

"Anything you should need, ask him. His main task is to oversee some purchases and establish contacts with the locals, but he knows how special you are to me," I blushed this time as the bloody dog started to bark like crazy.

"Do you have a dog?" Konrad asked me alarmed. Don't worry I will not put a dog on you Persian rug.

"It belongs to my neighbour. He came to check if I was still in one piece after one month in the Wild Europe. Can I call you tomorrow?"

121

"I see."

"Seven, your time, would be fine for you?"

"Perfect. Good night Guntram."

"Sleep well," I switched off the phone, ready to face the more than all ears *coiffeur*.

"I knew it!" he gloated "Who's the lucky bastard who got you? You have to tell everything. I already envy him. For almost a year, I tried to pair you with some of my friends and nothing and this guy gets you in less than a month!"

"Why do you think it's a he?" I said a little bit crossed. Do I have a sign on my back "Gay"? He lifted an eyebrow mockingly in answer. "Fine. It's a he. His name is Konrad and he's forty-four years old."

"You little hypocrite! I tried to match you with Pedro—who's only thirty— and you told me he was "too old", and now you're shagging someone twice your age," he laughed almost to the point of tears. "By the way you were sounding in the phone, he must be really something in bed," he said with an evil smile. I gaped. "You have so much to learn. When a couple sounds so restrained on the phone, they set on fire the bed. I know," I blushed to no end. "Honestly, you were starting to worry me. Almost twenty, with a face like yours and nobody had done you. Lucky bastard!"

"Would you stop calling him that? He's an honourable person," I rebuked him attacking my pasta.

"How cute. You already defend him" He mocked me. "What does he do for a living?"

"He works in a bank in Zurich," It's true!

"How does he look?"

"Very tall, blond hair, all of it if you need to know, blue eyes, really handsome features. Muscular type, an incredible intelligence and cultivated."

"Does he have a younger brother? Can you give me his phone number?" he asked, making me laugh.

"I always knew you were like me, dear boy. Luckily you found someone good for your first time. Normally, it's not like that," he sighed.

"He wants that I move with him in two weeks—To Zurich," I confessed.

"Then you should start to collect boxes and put your things together. I'll look tomorrow in the saloon if there's something you can use."

"You don't understand. He wants that I definitely move to Zurich to study at the University there."

"What is to understand? It's an opportunity in a lifetime boy! Get your things together and jump on the next plane! Do you really want to stay here? In a poor country, with no real job opportunities unless you have connections, cleaning tables and attending an out dated university? Do you want to be killed in a robbery?" He shouted, looking at me as if I were an alien.

"I don't even know if I'm into men!"

"Well dear, after a month frolicking in his bed, you should already know if you like it or not," he said visibly amused at my outburst. Most likely, he thinks I'm into a denial phase.

"It's that when I look at other men I'm not aroused at all—only with him. I still think girls are much nicer looking than men. He's surrounded by bodyguards, all looking like the Ken doll and I don't find them attractive," I confessed.

122

"Bodyguards? As in plural? Well he's more than the typical bank clerk."

"He owns the bank, but you should keep that secret. He's very discreet."

"You caught a Swiss Banker? And you doubt to go back? Hurry up before someone else snatches him!"

"I need time to think. What if it was only a passing fling and he's only interested because I'm something new?"

"Guntram, the doctor must have dropped you on your head when you were born. We are speaking of a man, more than forty years old, that has the incredible luck of getting a virgin of your beauty, intelligence, loyalty, educated in an elite school and who, on top of all these virtues, does not look at other men, right? That bastard hit the jackpot! If I were him I would have not let you escape here. Do you love him?"

"A lot, even if sometimes he's overbearing," I said blushing deeply for the tenth time. "He was wonderful to me during the mess with the police in Venice."

"You have to explain that. Police and you in the same sentence, is not normal."

"Remember my friend Fedérico?" He made a displeased grimace. He does. "The police caught him with 160 grams of cocaine and he said that I had bought it, when I was not even there in the city and later when I was with Konrad. He supported my side of the story and even paid the lawyer who took care of me. Later, at my urging, he also paid the lawyer for Fedérico," short and official version, the other is too… messy and not really clear for me.

"Are you telling me that a man of his position and money got into the middle of a scandal made by a brat student and even made a statement in your favour at a police station? Shit, what else has the man to do to prove his love for you? Tattoo your name in his ass?"

He has a point.

* * *

Next morning I went to the shanty town to check how things were running. Shitty as usual. Father Patricio was overwhelmed with all the things he had to take care of. No money at all for the soup kitchen and no hope in the near future to get any. I started to help in the school, mostly to entertain the children, before it was time for them to go picking up paper in the late afternoon or cleaning car windshields.

What really irks me most, besides the misery they live in, is the misery of the people who live in front of them. Yes, the slums in Retiro are located in stolen land from the rail roads, running along one of the most expensive areas of the city. The Libertador Avenue and the railways flow like an unbridgeable river separating the wealthy from the poor. On one side, you have Versace and less than a kilometre away, you have children sniffing glue.

I felt very bad. Why could I enjoy a decent life or even one of luxury with Konrad when these kids would not be even turn thirty? Life was truly unfair.

At 4 p.m. I started to work again without much hassle till six when the place was really crowded and didn't empty till 11:45. I was dead on my feet, but still managed to smile to the last customer.

When I hit the bed at almost 1 a.m., I realised that I had totally overlooked to call Konrad as promised and also to load the mobile phone. He will be furious tomorrow! I jumped from the bed to write him a short e-mail. Who knows, maybe it would appease him. Yeah, right!

"My dear Konrad,

I'm terribly sorry for not calling you today. I overlooked the time this afternoon. I went to help Father Patricio in the school and time flew by and I had to run to work and I'm only now back and it must be six in the morning for you. You have every right to be upset with me and I'll call you today at 7:00 if it's OK by you.

Please forgive me,

Guntram"

Today I have less work since I have only to go to the University to ask for a certificate with my grades, take my high school diploma to get an international stamp at the Educational Board and pass by my bank to see if there's any chance I can make an international transfer (yes, pigs can fly), and then to work.

Educational Board. Done. No problem.

Bank. Relatively done. I asked. The clerk laughed at me. Met nice people at the long queue. Anyhow, the original $30,000 dollars were transformed into 42.000 pesos argentinos which now are worth $14,000 dollars at today's exchange rate. Forget about getting the money out of the bank. Only 400 pesos per week. I'm so full of joy!

Around noon, I was able to go to the University and ask for the papers. One week delay. Good, not so bad as I feared it would be. Then and I don't know why I did it, I fulfilled the papers to ask for this year classes in the morning shift. I think I did it out of habit.

At 2:02 p.m., I was able to get a free table in the school's cafeteria and pulled out the mobile phone and called him.

"Lintorff" he barked. OK, maybe the legend about his short temper at work was real.

"Hello Konrad. I wanted to apologise for yesterday's confusion. It was very stupid from me to overlook the time like that," I said meekly.

"I was worried about you, Kitten." Good sign, he calls me Kitten not Guntram.

"I'm sorry really. I think, that coming here and seeing everything so bad was a huge shock for me. I was almost late for work."

"Why are you still working? Have you not sent your resignation letter?" His courteous tone chilled me to my bones.

"I'll do it today. But I can't flee after they kept my job for one extra week. Besides, I have to work," I replied softly.

"Do you need money? Ask Landau if you need anything for the move."

"I don't need money. Thank you," I said mildly upset. I'm not that poor.

"What have you done so far?"

"I went to the Educational Board and got the papers stamped even those of the International Baccalaureate and asked what I needed from my University. Then to my bank to find out that I can't touch my money unless I want to buy a house or a car. No international transfers at the moment."

"Perhaps it's time for you to consider the stability a Swiss/German bank can offer," he said, slightly amused.

"I would love to see if you are so funny after losing 54% of your savings in

124

one go," I retorted harshly.

"I apologise. It was most thoughtless of me."

"I'm also sorry I answered you back so vulgarly. It's not your fault this is a mess."

"So bad?"

"Very. So far the only good thing is that people started to realise that money isn't everything and are helping each other and involved more in the community's problems," I sighed.

"Then, come home. There's nothing left for you there."

"It's only eleven days more and you have an advocate pleading your case almost every day. My neighbour says I should have not even come back and I should take the first plane back before someone else snatches you," I laughed.

"Sensible man. I'm sorry Guntram, but I have to go to a meeting. I will call you tomorrow at 8:00 my time."

"All right. I love you."

"Me too."

* * *

Friday 25th, 2002

I was supposed to quit today and I even went to the manager's office. Stood like an idiot in front of the door till somebody called me and I had to rush back to work.

Later, said manager was gone. It's not really my fault.

Konrad will be… upset. This morning he was quite cross because I have still not hired a moving company for my books and my grandmother's piano (I like the mammoth and I can play it).

And tomorrow, I will be working late at the school. The teachers don't come on weekends and someone has to clean, take care of the children and help with the food. I've been doing it since I was sixteen years old with the other volunteers. Besides, Father Patricio needs to rest a little bit. He's dead on his feet. I should write an e-mail to Konrad so he does not worry if I can't speak with him on the weekend.

"My dear Konrad,

This weekend I will be helping Father Patricio in the school. The teachers don't come and somebody has to help him. I don't think I would be able to call you and I don't plan to take the mobile phone with me. It would be risked to be stolen. Please, before you become angry with me for breaking the rule, bear in mind that I know these people since years and they would do nothing to me, but the phone is another story.

I have to work late Saturday and Sunday.

With love,

Guntram"

Chapter 19

February 28th, 2002
Monday

I'm dead and stayed in bed until 12:00. Around 2:00, I had gathered enough courage as to call him.

"Lintorff," he barked.

"Hello Konrad," I stammered. Great. Prolonged silence as if he's fuming. Most probably.

"So you have finished playing the missionary?" Acid, sarcastic tone. Better play the lamb. With a big light blue ribbon.

"Yes, it was a lot of work. I really would miss the kids when I'm gone. Next weekend, I will say goodbye," I said softly, not willing to anger him. Yeah, I'm afraid even if he's 12,000 km away.

"Did you quit?"

"Tomorrow. I promise."

"Why not today?" Dangerous edge in his voice.

"It's the manager's free day."

"Do you need Monika's help with the moving? Because you haven't started yet." How does he know? I said nothing on the matter.

"It's not necessary to bother her. I'll manage to get a better price. $400 per cubic metre is expensive."

"I see."

"How are you? Are you back home?"

"I'm in St. Petersburg. I have to make some phone calls. Good bye." And he hung up on me.

At eight, I was taking care of my job when I noticed a familiar Austrian sitting in my area. I took a menu and went to check on him.

"Good evening, Mr. Landau. It's a surprise to see you. Will you have dinner?"

"Only a cappuccino and a mineral water. Thank you. It's an interesting concept this book shop. Was this a theatre?"

"A cinema, sir. It was modified three years ago. Please, excuse me."

Several minutes later I went back with the cappuccino and water. I served him and when I was leaving he stopped me.

"The Duke asked me to give you this personally," he said very seriously, handing me a closed envelope. I hesitated to grab it. "Please, take it. He would be most upset with me if you don't do it."

"All right. Thank you, sir."

"It's my pleasure, sir," he answered as he bowed his head.

Inside there was $5,000. Fuck Konrad! I'm sick of you treating me like an unruly child!

* * *

January 29th, 2002

    I didn't call him.
    I didn't quit.
    I'm sick of his bossing me around. This whole relationship is a huge mistake. Distance allows me to see I was infatuated with you, not in love. People in love trust each other. They don't press each other to the point of being suffocated.
    He didn't call me on the next days also.

* * *

February 1st, 2002

    Today is Friday and it's my free night. I'm going out with some friends from the Star Wars Fan Club. Yeah, I'm a fan since I was little and we meet every first Friday of the month in a Burger King to chat and admire our action figures and trading cards. I know I'm old for such things, but I also want to do something stupidly harmless.
    I really need to see people my age who won't get me into trouble. No heated politics from the University, no international drug dealers and specially no CEO's or Super Bankers.
    We met at five at Juan's house as he had a new computer and the latest SW strategy game.
    My mobile phone rang sharply. Why do I still carry this thing along?
    "Hello?" I left the room, looking for privacy since the orgasmic yelling at Dark Knight graphics was too much.
    "What are you doing in that boy's house?"
    "I'm in my meeting for the Star Wars Fan Club. We meet every month. Wait. Are you checking on me?"
    "So, you are there to say good bye to them."
    "No. I came to eat a greasy cold pizza with some friends and play some video games," I answered heatedly.
    "Good. Go home before nine."
    What the fuck? "Sorry to disappoint you, but we plan to eat a burger later and then shed a lot of virtual blood with Counter Strike online or Wolfstein and kill as many Nazis as possible. And to top the night, it'll be group sex with Chewbacca, Jabba and Yoda!" I exploded to that fucking control freak.
    "Have you expressed yourself now Guntram? At ten at home. You have to organise your things for tomorrow," was his arrogant answer.
    "I'm not coming back," I said strangely calmed, never more sure of anything in my short life.
    Silence. Dark silence. My resolve grew stronger.
    "You'd better be at the Zurich Airport on Monday morning," he said in a chilly voice.
    "You are delusional if you think I'm coming back to a man who already beat the shit out of me. Twice. I'm treading on eggs every time I speak with you, afraid you would explode and kill me! It's over!"

Finally I said what has been devouring my inner self since I came back. "Monday morning in Zurich or I will recapture what is mine."

Chapter 20

February 3rd, 2002
Sunday

I'm not taking that plane. What would he do besides yelling at me? He has a lot of messes to care about than losing his time with a stray dog he picked up in a Venetian square.
But why don't I find the thought reassuring?
I will carry on with my life as it was before him.
Even if everything is in chaos, people are changing and involving into politics. Now I believe that the dense haze of corruption surrounding us can be lifted. Life is not shady and dark as he says. People still care for each other and act out of kindness.

* * *

February 11th, 2002 Monday

Not a single word from him in a week. I don't know if I should be worried or relieved. He has just vanished from my life. For the hundredth time I tell myself that it's for the better.
Today I started a Summer Course in the school. *Rethinking the New Argentinean Society under the Post-modern Paradigms of Social Change*. It's not as dull as it sounds and would be nice to meet other young people who believe in creating a fairer system.
Before entering my classroom, I went to the Administrative Office to check if they had my schedule for next term. Unfortunately they had lost my application and I had to do it again. Well, it seems that the new world has still a lot from the previous one's incompetency.
Life becomes normal again. I decided to go home and grab something before work.
At two, I fumbled with the keys on my apartment door, cursing them softly.
I entered in my bright flat to see Konrad sitting on my humble sofa like a king. I turned around to escape only to find my door blocked by Heindrik. He smirked at me and gave me a soft nudge to put me back inside. He closed the door on my face.
Dreading the worst, I turned to face him, crouching there like a lion waiting for the perfect moment to jump at my throat. I was thankful for the door's support.
"Why are you dressed like a beggar from the sixties?" He asked in a soft voice, contempt pouring on every word and sending electricity jolts through my spine.
"I went to school," I gulped nervously, feeling the sour taste of bile in my mouth.
"I see. You have ten minutes to change into something appropriate before you come to the hotel with me."
"I'm going nowhere. We are finished," I muttered gently but certain.

"Since you were unable to sort your things in order, I will have to do it," he kept on, not caring at all for my words.

"It's finished. Please leave my home. I have to go to work," I said softly fearing that he would explode now.

He rose from the sofa. Regally. "You have twenty four hours to prepare yourself before we leave for Zurich. If not, I will do it and you'll regret it. You played with me and now you'll face the consequences," he went for the door with long strides as I moved fast out of his way. He opened and closed the door softly.

I fell to my knees, urgently needing to cry to release the tension. Or shout. Something to ease the constricting feeling in my chest and the heaves I felt rising. He was back and not willing to give up. I started to cry like a baby engulfed by sorrow and despair. Why didn't he leave me alone? I was nothing, had nothing and he wanted everything I had.

Some hours later, I realised that I still had to go to work. I got up from the floor and went to the bathroom to change myself into my uniform. Over the table was the envelope with the money I had left at Landau's hotel reception a week ago. Beside it, there was one of his visit cards. "Hotel Park Hyatt. Tuesday at 8."

I tried to calm myself down. I'm playing local now and he's likely bluffing. What is he going to do? Force me into the VIP Lounge of the airport with a gun?

Chapter 21

February 13th , 2002

My boss wanted to speak with me in private. I climbed up the stairs, trying to remember if I had somehow screwed up.

"Hello Guntram. Take a seat," he said with false joviality. I did as was told.

"There's no easy way to say it so I will go straight to the point. We have just been overtaken by an international group and they want to make a lot of changes, starting by the workforce. They said all of you are unprofessional and prefer people with first class hotel backgrounds. I'm afraid I have to let you go. I will pay you three months salary and write you a nice recommendation letter since you are a good worker."

I was shocked beyond words. He looked at me concerned.

"Sorry kid, but those Germans are very strict and if they say something, you have to comply. Can you send Verónica here?"

I slowly walked home since they didn't want me to do anything more. Normally, you're supposed to be fired on Fridays. Right?

My head hurts like hell. I need an aspirin and to sit in the cold for some time. This damn heat is horrible. I'll take a few days off and on Monday I will start the job hunt again. Rent is paid till the end of the month and I have some savings plus the compensation money.

I went back to my flat and made a tea, drank it mechanically and went to bed hoping my headache would lessen. I fell asleep.

Chapter 22

February 17th, 2002

You diary, are everything I have left now; a notebook and a few photos from my family. I played with fire and got burnt. Carbonized.

I should have known better. A man like him would not bluff or resort to idle threats to get what he wants. Friederich told me once something like "his revenge is epic" and nothing is more true. I slouched farther in the soft leather seat of Konrad's private jet, bringing my knees to my chest.

I looked fearfully up from my notebook to see him sitting with six other men I don't know at his meeting table, papers, blackberries and laptops scattered in disorder over it. Michael was showing some graphics on a screen speaking in German. He's not any more the funny German, but a professional businessman, explaining his latest strategy for Latin America and the importance of the primary sector, if I understood the graphics' legends in English.

Konrad turned his head briefly to look at me and I wanted to disappear. He gave me a smirk of triumph, gloating on his total control over me. I looked down ashamed because he's right.

Last Thursday, I was woken up by a thundering knock at my door. I went to open and there was my landlady, a sixty year old witch, third degree cousin of Fedérico's mother. She never liked me, but she couldn't find another idiot so desperate to pay a cheap rent for the hole she calls a flat.

"Good morning Miss Duran. What can I do for you?" I asked puzzled to have her there, standing like a vulture at the door. Rent was paid.

"Hello Guntram. I will be very grateful if you leave the flat by tonight. I have sold it and the new owner wants to take over before Friday. I will give you a compensation."

"But I have paid rent till the end of the month. You can't kick me out just like that!" I said a little bit louder than necessary.

"We don't have a contract and the house is mine. I will give you $5,000 for your trouble, which is much more than you would pay for a year's rent. You can go to a hotel and then look for something. It's not that you have much to move."

"I'm not moving with such a short notice," I firmly held my ground to the bitch.

"OK, I'll give you $7,000. Listen to me, useless brat. If I haven't tossed you out after what you did to Fedérico, it's because I needed the rent. Now, a nice German gentlemen has offered and paid $65,000 dollars for this shoebox when the market value is now $35,000. He even offered me $25,000 extra if I get you out by tomorrow. Get your things together and piss off before I call my nephews and beat the hell of a disgusting faggot like you."

I was furious. The fucking prick had the nerve to steal my flat! Deep calming breath. And another one.

"Well Miss Duran, you have just gotten another faggot in your flat. That nice German is the one I was bending for in Europe. Ask Martina how he plays and how much he got out of her. And pray that he's happy only with getting me out of here," I sweetly answered.

"Don't worry, I'll take the keys to his hotel with the $7,000 you offered. Nothing would please me more than he loses another $25,000. That, if he pays you at all," I snorted, enjoying to no end the look of her face, eyes almost popping out. I closed the door on her face after getting the money out of her claws. Fuck manners!

I stuffed my clothes and books in a big garbage bag and went to George's apartment to ask him if he could take care of my things for a few days. He wanted to know what the mess was about, but I refused to tell him anything I was too out of my mind to have a normal chat with a nice guy like him.

I gathered all my important papers like passport and ID, school diplomas, my laptop, some CD's and my family's photos and also stuffed them in my backpack. Put all the money together with the keys in a brown envelope. The rest he can clean by himself!

I slammed the door.

I walked the fifteen blocks, under the scorching midday sun, too totally enraged to care. I stomped over the doorman at the entrance of the lobby too focused in getting the receptionist, a tall, fantastically good looking blonde girl.

"Sir?" She looked very nervous at me and made a discreet gesture to the security guard standing there, who rushed toward us. Man, you need to do much more to be at the level of the big scary gorillas I know!

"I would like to leave an envelope for Mr. Landau or Lintorff, it's the same, please," I said through gritted teeth.

"One moment please," she looked more at ease and called by the phone.

Her delay was the cherry on top of the ice cream. I hurled the envelope on her desk and turned around. The least I need is another meeting with the bastard.

At the door I was intercepted by Michael and Goran. Are those two an item? Always together.

"Hey Guntram. Glad you could make it finally," Michael said with a smirk, blockading the door as Goran placed behind me.

"Just leaving some things for your boss. Tell him to enjoy the flat. Goodbye."

"Ouch, come on boy, no need to be upset at us. You can speak with the Duke later. He's meeting the natives at the moment," he chuckled. "Tell me something, is this Che Guevara's Fans Club look you wear fashionable here? Should I get a copy of Mao's red book too?"

"Let me pass. I'm in no mood for your bad sense of humour," I growled.

"It's the heat no doubt," he said as a matter of fact to Goran. "Up to the suite with you and wait there for the Duke," the Serbian lashed out an iron grip on my right elbow and pulled me with him, making me wince a bit in pain.

"Stop it!"

"Go upstairs, order something to drink and wait for the Duke. I see you have brought your things along. Is there something more you might need?" Michael said menacingly.

"Are you planning to make a scandal in a five stars hotel?" I grunted daringly.

"One single blow to your ribs and you will be out before somebody notices.

Do you want that?"

Goran had enough of our diplomatic negotiations. He increased the pressure in my arm to the point of almost breaking the elbow and pulled me along with him. He pushed me into a private lift and in no time, we were on the hotel's top floor.

"The whole floor is rented by us. Don't bother in making a scene," Michael warned me as Goran nearly threw me in a big living room, furnished in a modern style with flat screen TV, dining table, sitting area and wonderful panoramic windows overlooking the city.

"Get a shower, change yourself into a proper attire because this "anti-globalization" look, makes the Duke upset and honestly you don't want to provoke him any further. It's friendly advice, kid. He's very angry at you at the moment and you can't complain at all because he gave you many chances to come back to his good graces," Michael told me, sending a warning glare to me. They both turned around and closed (locked), the door, taking my backpack with them.

A pang of dread went through my heart. He was furious with me and completely convinced that he had "given me the chance to repent". In two days he had already left me jobless, homeless, friendless and who knew what else he had in store in order to "punish" me or bend me to his will. A beating was too simple for the level of the game he was playing with me now. He had fired all my friends at work, making their lives harder and without a second thought.

His revenge is epic I muttered to myself as I sat by the window looking at the passing cars for a long time. The room became darker as the evening wore on. I closed my eyes, exhausted and fell asleep.

A large hand softly petted my hair waking me up. I barely suffocated a small cry to see Konrad crouching in front of the chair, both hands resting on the arms, effectively trapping me.

"You came to me and brought your papers. I might still overlook your past revolt if you apologise," he said looking sharply into my eyes, the shadows of the lights playing on his face. I was afraid of him and sank deeper into the chair trying to put more distance between us. A flash of anger went through his eyes and his lips formed a thin line.

"I see you cling to your stubbornness and don't accept my reign over you. Should I continue with your taming?" He frowned at me.

"Please, this has to stop. I can't continue with your game. I'm sorry if I hurt you with my refusal, but I fear this shall end very badly for me," I whispered, closing my eyes, secretly hoping he would see reason. "I'm most sure you will find someone who is a real equal to you."

He stood up to his full height very fast. I also tried to stand up myself, but a stern look from him made me stay where I was.

"You have nobody else to blame than yourself for what is going to happen," he stated turning around and going for the door.

I jumped to my feet and caught him by the arm. The look of fury I got from him made me release the sleeve in no time. "Please Konrad, don't go. Let's try to talk things over," I pleaded with him, maybe I could still convince him to drop whatever he had planned do now.

He sat in one of the black leather sofas indicating to me to take on the one in front of him.

"Come home with me. Willingly. Everything would be as it was if you fulfil the promise you gave me. "

"I can't. Things have changed," I painfully articulated.

"What changed? You tricked me with your false look of innocence and promises of love!" he roared.

"I didn't lie when I said that I loved you! It's just we can't live together. You are brutal. The last time we were together you knocked the air out of me, remember? You try to control my every move and want me to live in a Mausoleum for a house! You explode if I'm anything less than the perfect picture of what you desire from me. I'm nineteen years old and I want to make mistakes like the others and live my life as I see it fit!" I shouted at him first, but losing my bravado as he was looking more enraged than before.

"So you will forgo a life at my side for this pathetic little country?" he snorted, his face full of scorn.

"Things are changing and will improve," I said softly, looking at the floor.

"My experience so far is, that this a corrupted country on every level, an asset in the moment for me, and that they would sell anything at a very low price. Your politicians even offered a combo so to speak to Landau; Three Senators for one hundred and a high level official in the Central Bank for thirty thousand. Or perhaps you refer to the little soviets organised in the cities by the "concerned citizens," In order to "re-found a new Argentina". This country has no law, education, civility or a little bit of honesty in its people. The minute they make money again, everything would be exactly as before."

His cynical view hurt me more than I wanted to admit. "Still I want to take the risk," I said firmly.

"As you wish," he stood up again.

"What are you going to do now? This is nonsense Konrad. You are not being reasonable."

"Without you I have no restraints to carry on what I want," he shrugged, hunching his shoulders.

"I don't understand. You'll do whatever suits you, like always."

"I would not touch something you like."

"I have nothing you might like," I said contemptuously. "You fired all of us yesterday and today you bought my flat at a ridiculous price if I may say."

"The land where that shanty town you care about so much, is in a valuable location. Many would like to invest there and the railway company is willing to sell to cover the loses derived from the default."

"Good luck because these people have been there for more than fifty years and no government could get them out. Social protest is something no politician wants. You will be just another who loses money there."

"Perhaps their methods were not the most appropriate to deal with the situation. Those shacks are always so vulnerable to accidents and if something would happen there, people should be relocated," he explained to me making me chill at his coldness. "All those illegal and dangerous electrical connections might well spark into flames and if I understood correctly, no fire fighter would enter there because they are afraid to be killed by the inhabitants."

"You wouldn't dare," I said now afraid at the casual tone he was employing.

"Their local leaders are interested and with the appropriate stimulus we can obtain what we want."

"You're bluffing. Your men could not even come two hundred metres near the entrance," I said, relieved to no end. No way he knows the guys who run the drugs and weapons market there. Besides, the place is their perfect hideaway, they would never give it up. Not even the police can enter. If there's a problem, they throw the bodies at the entrance.

He rose from his chair giving me another smirk. He went to the desk and picked up one of the folders laying there, opened and started to read.

"Martínez Orondo, Cucho is name or alias? Don't mind. He's quite a character told me the local intelligence," I lost my colour. The Cucho is the boss and quite paranoid, if you ask me. He tolerates our presence there because her daughter goes to school with us. Nobody sees or speaks with him unless he wants.

"His last deals with the Colombians turned out wrong and a few things were lost. People in Antioch are very upset and would love to have his location. Then we have this Maria Sala, she's the local political leader from the Peronist Party and took quite an active role in the past revolts, but she hasn't paid the "troops" what was promised and she needs cash desperately. Father Patricio Fernández would not be the first priest to be killed there by a task force. This Third World Movement priests still have many enemies. Should I extend more or you can read the files by yourself?" he said handing me the folder.

It contained police files, reports, dates, pictures and three of my drawings from last week. I froze. He looked at me.

"According to the person who got them, the children understand very well the capitalist system. They dribbled till they doubled the original price," he affirmed amused. "Anyway, I don't have to tell you that it's impossible for you to come back as all the small thieves there know that a rich "gringo," Is after you and pays handsomely for everything you might have. You wouldn't last two hours before they cut you into pieces for getting a better price. They don't look very clever. This glue sniffing habit is good for population control."

"As you understand I cannot let go of a project that could result in a return of 300%. But on the other hand, if I would get something else to keep my mind occupied, I would not care about it," he trailed.

"These persons never did anything to you," I whispered truly shocked, petrified, horrified at his coldness.

"Exactly. They mean nothing to me. You are everything. Now, answer me Guntram. Should we proceed to the next level?"

"No. What do you want?" I fixed my bloodied eyes into his triumphant ones.

"That you keep all your promises and obey the rules as they were set. No more petty uprisings."

I nodded unable to speak, a painful knot constricting my throat.

"I can't hear you. Say it out loud."

"I will behave and return to Switzerland with you," I slowly recited, but noticed he was not satisfied so I hastily added, "I belong to you also."

"Go to the bedroom. I still have to make you remember to whom you belong to," he growled. "Move. Now!"

I remained in my seat, petrified like a deer in front of the car lights.

He advanced fast as a lightening towards me and pulled me, as if I were a rag doll, to my feet. A strong push almost sent me flying to the bedroom door and I panicked. I turned around to escape, but he was faster and grabbed me by the neck.

"Ever smelt the aroma of burnt human flesh? It's sweet and intoxicating," he whispered in my ear. I ceased all squirming and went dead in his grasp. "Better. Take your clothes off. Now."

I could have died of shame as I slowly took everything I had off. He just stood there, looking, no emotions in his face. He took his jacket off and carefully placed it on a chair. He came forward opening his fly with a hand. I had to make a supreme effort to remain standing where I was, the king size bed against my shins and keep the tears at bay.

Without a word he turned me around with a swift move and shoved me to the bed. I could barely soften the fall with my hands in a defensive position. He spread my buttocks and with one single and brutal push, penetrated me not even waiting for me to adjust.

He fucked me very hard like an animal. No tenderness, no kisses nothing. Only the mounting made in a surgical way, designed to humiliate and not give pleasure at all. I screamed, but he didn't stop. I tried to escape, but he dug his fingernails into my hips so hard that it bruised me. His rough thrusts hurt like hell and soon I started to bleed, easing them.

He depleted himself deeply inside me with only a groan. I was freely crying, numbed by the excruciating pain and the horror of it. No words can describe a rape. He bent down over my back and bit me hard on the shoulder making me scream again at the pain and the smell of blood running down my collarbone.

He stood up and rearranged his clothes as I was sobbing, trying to control my tears in fear he would retaliate more.

"I do hope that this time you understand what is expected of you and respect and love me as you should. Next time you behave like a leftie slut, I'll give you to my men for their entertainment."

"Take a hot shower and get into your pyjamas They are on the left side of the bed. Order something to eat and don't wait for me. I have work to do." As I stayed unmoving, he lifted me with one arm and shoved me to the bathroom, throwing the clothes inside.

The cold tiles and the bright light got me out of my shock. Shaking, I went into the bath top and the hot water washed the blood and sperm away. My muscles relaxed a little, but I wanted out of the water as soon as possible. I dried myself and picked the pyjamas from the floor. There were no traces of my earlier bleeding. I dressed in the white with light blue stripes pyjama buttoning myself with shaky fingers. I went to the mirror to meet a man with red bloodied eyes and a large half open gash on the right shoulder. I had no marks on my face. I combed my hair in a soothing motion in a useless attempt to calm down.

He was still in the bedroom, with a new suit, the other crumpled in the chair. Hair combed, looking refreshed. I stood hesitantly at the door frame.

"Come Guntram, let me see your shoulder," I approached him, terrified with the idea that he would be looking for another excuse to hurt me more. He loomed over me and I closed my eyes waiting for the blow, but he gently moved the pyjama jacket away to study my shoulder. He went into the bathroom for a brief moment and returned with alcohol and a gauze. He cleaned the wound and patched it very carefully, almost like a mother. He left the things in a table nearby and took my face into his hands.

"I have ordered some meat for you. Eat it because you had nothing since yesterday," he said softly, putting a strand behind my ear. How does he know that? I felt an unbounded fear roaming my guts. "Then go to bed and sleep. Good night," he kissed me briefly on the lips, his tongue caressing them and demanding to enter. I automatically opened my mouth, letting him taste me without reserves. He seemed pleased.

He opened the door to the living room to reveal a covered tray over the dining table. He went for the door to open it to have Ferdinand almost falling over him. The man said something fast in German.

"No, he's not too hurt. See that he eats and sleeps. He's only shaken," he said dryly. A wave of relief washed Ferdinand's face as he entered into the room.

"Come Guntram, sit by me and eat your dinner," he softly said.

"I can't eat. I fear I will throw up."

"You have to try and if you feel sick I'll take it away," he reasoned with me like you do with a small child. I sat where he told me and he put in front of me a dish with a sirloin and vegetables. "I don't know how you can have vegetarian people in Argentina. It's very good this meat."

I started to eat slowly, my eyes glued to the china.

"You should never do something so stupid again. Defying him like that is very dangerous. The night you fought with him he was devastated, but the next morning he was already planning how to get you back. He can't let go of you because you are his soul. Don't look at me like that. If there's somebody who could make him a better person, that is you. He would do anything and stop at nothing to keep you at his side."

"I fear him. I left him because I was afraid of his temper and now I'm terrified. I don't know how I'm going to survive it."

"What made you change your mind? You were very much in love of him in Zurich."

"He's too much for me. Distance made me realise it. He absorbs me totally. He doesn't let me breath without his permission."

"I think you were overwhelmed by everything and ran to what you knew without much thinking. Forget the money he has, his position, just for a moment, and think back when you first realised you loved him and tell me when it was."

"When he came to me during the bonds mess and showed me he was tired, frustrated and lost without me."

"Well, he's like that, deep in his core. He has to hide it in order to survive, but with you he can be sure you will not judge or use it against him. Please Guntram, give him another chance to win your love back. I swear that if he ever hurts you again like tonight, I will get you out of here and take you where he would never find you," he gravely said, and I believed all of his words.

"You want to help people. Think in all the good things you could do with his power. He only wants your companionship and love. Remember of you time together."

"I don't know. I love him, but I'm afraid of his reactions. He's like a psycho."

138

"He does it because he's a desperate man who sees the love of his life sliding through his fingers. Don't give him cause to believe it and he will be very good to you."

"I might try," I replied almost inaudible.

"That's the spirit, child. Finish the meat and I'll get you a cognac, you need it."

"He doesn't let me drink." Somehow he will know I was drinking and will punish me.

"That is because you were completely drunken on New Year's Eve and he feared you would end in a coma!"

He made me sit on the big sofa in front of the TV with the drink. Animal Planet it was. I started to feel drowsy and put my head against the arm chair, finally relaxing, lulled by the TV. I think he covered me with a blanket despite we were in February.

At some point, someone ruffled my hair. It was Konrad. Without saying a word, he picked me up in his arms as if I weighed nothing. He shushed my protests and carried me to the big bed, placing me on the left side, tucking the covers around me as I fell asleep again.

Chapter 23

February 15th, 2002. Friday

Next morning, I woke up to the sunlight bathing the room to find myself cuddled in his arms. I slowly moved in order to disentangle myself, but he tightened his embrace. Bad move. I closed my eyes again not willing to wake him.

"You look much better this morning *Maus*. Come, out of the bed. Even if I would like it, we can't stay here forever," he greeted me with a soft kiss on my forehead. He rose from the bed and went to the bathroom. Half an hour later he emerged showered and shaved with only a towel around his hips. Fuck, I've almost forgotten how good he looks! I'm officially insane; lusting after the man who raped me yesterday. Stockholm Syndrome it's called.

He bent on the bed to kiss me again and I let him stick his tongue up to my larynx. He softly chuckled.

"You will not convince me to stay. Up with you and get dressed for breakfast. Outside we don't have Friederich, but Michael, Ferdinand, Goran and Alexei are waiting for us," he said while he dressed quickly into a light blue shirt and grey suit.

"Do you know where my clothes are?" I asked shyly.

"If I wouldn't know you better, I would think you're quite the party boy," he teased me. "Some of your things are in the left closet. Friederich packed them. Complain to him if something is missing," he said fumbling with a box, finally getting a very expensive watch out. "If you see a Lange und Söhne watch with moon phases around, it's mine. Please put it back with the others. Hurry up and we might get breakfast together," he left the bedroom and I let a big sigh out, relieved to no end that he was away, even for a brief moment.

I stood up, went to the bathroom and washed myself. I chose some beige trousers (forget about jeans or baggy trendy shirts in a closet designed by Konrad), a light blue shirt and a sport jacket with brown shoes. I was still surprised that he would leave watches like those (I mean, those German things are worth more than $40.000 dollars and I know it, because Fedérico told me), in the room and not in the safe box.

There I saw something shinning between the mattress and the headboard. The watch. I picked up and went to the living room.

The men were already sitting and having breakfast and the chair on Konrad's left side was empty. They greeted me as if nothing had happened ever and moved to indicate where I should sit. A butler appeared from nowhere and asked me if I wanted coffee. They started to speak in German, ignoring me. When they stopped for a second, I tried to get Konrad's attention.

"I found your watch. Should you not put it in the safe box? We're not in Europe and things tend to get lost here," I whispered.

"You did? Thank you. Don't worry, the safe box is full with the laptop and papers. Leave it with the others and let's trust the strangers generosity. Now, eat something because there's nothing till who knows when."

I complied and then went to put the thing back in the box and found my backpack in the closet. I took my wallet and put it in my trousers. The bloody envelope was still there and I left it in Konrad's closet.

In the living room the men were already gathering papers and jackets. I noticed that Alexei and Goran were both carrying weapons. Walther P99, if I'm correct. Knowing already Konrad's way of doing businesses, I wasn't so surprised any longer. I noticed Michael taking an apple and putting it into his pocket. I tried to hide my grin.

"Dähler put that back," Ferdinand said in a sullen tone.

"Forget it. It's not my fault the Army knows nothing about Logistics like we sailors do," he replied as a deep frown marred Ferdinand's features.

A man I didn't know entered and announced that the cars were ready. At the hotel's esplanade there were three big black SUVs, most probably armoured judging by the size of the wheels. Goran rushed to open the door in the middle one for Konrad. I stayed behind uncertain.

"Go into the middle one, you drive with me and Goran," Konrad softly nudged me inside.

In the other two, the other three men plus Landau and two nice looking girls, dressed like secretaries distributed themselves. I started to become uneasy about our destination, even if my reason was telling me that with the girls there, he would do nothing nasty to me.

"We're visiting a house in the countryside that I want to buy for holidays. Landau showed me the pictures a week ago and I liked it. It's located a 120 km from here, in Lobos. It's called Estancia La Candelaria," he explained to me as he sat next to me.

I know the place. It belongs to the grandfather of two friends of mine from the school. The Dollenbergs, Germans of course. Where else would Konrad go? I even spent two summer holidays there because the youngest brother, Juan, was in the same class as I. Now he's studying in England. He and his brother Pablo were brought up by their grandfather and if I remember well he had passed away a few years ago. Surely they wouldn't remember me. The house was truly impressive with the forest around it, the lake and the garden.

The cars took the highway, the main road that goes to the airport and Cañuelas. We passed through impoverished areas and I was shocked for the amount of street vendors, buses that were about to fall in pieces, the bad shape of the road, crumbling down social buildings. It was nothing comparable to what I remembered from my visit here, no more than five years ago. Some of the places were scary to pass by and I could understand why the Europeans were so concerned about their safety.

After an hour driving in silence, because Konrad was busy focusing on the landscape and the people we saw along the road, we arrived to the familiar, flanked with trees, private lane to the main house. It was as I remembered; a large colonial structure that was later enlarged with a very strange Gothic structure, almost looking like a tower with windows. All painted in the traditional creole pink, with a lake on the back part (swans included). Does Konrad like this? I have my doubts.

Pablo Dollenberg and his foreman, Martiniano were standing in front of the main door. He came to politely greet Konrad and his men in German and when he started to turn around to proceed with the house show, he shouted completely happy.

"It can't be. It's you Guti!" He gave me a bear hug. "Martiniano, do you remember my brother's friend from school?"

"Of course, I remember *Niño* Guntram. It's been a long time, sir," the old man greeted me, smiling and shaking my hand. "Herr Dollenberg was very fond of you."

"I see we all know each other," Konrad said a little bit stiff in front of the Argentineans effusive greetings and that the fact that we were speaking in Spanish.

"Of course we all know. Guntram went to school with Juan, my brother and came here for holidays three or four years ago. My grandfather held him in his highest esteem. We still keep some of the drawings of the house and the animals you left behind. Grandfather even framed two of them and kept them in his room. He passed away of Alzheimer and one of the few things he still remembered was Guntram. Later when he was not able to speak any more, he would spend hours looking at the drawings. Come in, María has to see you," he said turning his back to Konrad. Strangely he was not displeased at such an etiquette gap.

"Sorry, I almost forgot you are here to visit the property. Today we have some tourists around, but they should not bother us because they're hunting with the Indians." Look of shock from the Germans. "Yeah, retired people like that we put a show on and some of the workers help us by dressing like Indians in the summer or gauchos in the winter. They show the horses, a little bit of archery and *boleadoras*. The tourists are happy with it and it's good to do it before lunch. We also have some farming for them to enjoy the countryside life."

"I see. Is the estate used as a hotel?"

"Almost. We have guests on the weekends but mostly is tourism for the day. The house in itself is 2,500 square meters with a six hundred acres area. One hundred acres are occupied by the gardens and the forest which was planted one hundred fifty years ago, when they built the monstrosity we have just seen. The original part of the house dates from 1790, and it had been refurnished ten years ago. My grandfather acquired in 1946 at a low price since it was only the house and some land, not the originally 10,000 acres it had. We never used it for farming or cattle since he was an engineer and worked in Buenos Aires. In the 90's he transformed it into a hotel in order to cut the costs down."

"The land is not good?"

"The land is very good but the ratio costs/size is wrong. We have five hundred acres to put cattle, goats and pigs and some corn. It's not enough. The minimum size for a decent living is eight hundred acres. The costs of fertilizers and vaccines are impossible and it's in dollars now, without adding taxes. The hotel supports part of the land. To make it profitable, I should sell the land to my neighbours, but they have no money."

Pablo showed us the house, traditionally decorated under Luciana's—his wife—design as she was an interior decorator. I was surprised to hear that he was selling the furniture with the house and he wanted a written work contract for seven of the people on his staff.

"I must insist on this Duke, where would people go like Martiniano and his wife or several of the old workers if I sell now? They've been with my family for more than forty years and are about to retire."

"This would not pose an inconvenience. I don't plan to use the house more than a month per year. Should we discuss the terms of the sale?"

"It's almost time for lunch. You and your people should stay and we can discuss after it. You can't deprive me of the pleasure of seeing an old friend like Guntram."

"In that case, thank you," he answered, not too upset that his agenda had just been turned upside down.

We all sat at the large dining table, including the bodyguards and girls, Goran and Alexei going to the other side with the girls, leaving the other side to Pablo, Konrad, Ferdinand and Landau.

"So Guntram, have you started to paint professionally? He shot without preamble not even after the meat was served. I gulped nervously.

"Not really, I study Economics and Social Work."

"Are you kidding me? You, of all people in Economics? That's a real waste. In school everybody thought you were going to be an artist. After all, it was the only thing you were really enjoying to do."

"I like numbers," I defended myself

"So?"

"Then I study Economics," I retorted a little pissed off. He snorted and decided to grant Konrad an opinion of my past school days.

"I know him from our school time. He was in my brother's class. I never saw a person so shy and good natured as him. He never fought or was mean to anybody. He would pass through the classes studying very hard, getting the best grades, but he never showed any emotions at all. Heck, I think I never heard your voice till you came to visit us. Have you ever seen one of his drawings, my Duke? My wife loves them and she should know because she studied Art in France."

"Yes, I have seen several copies from things he had seen," Konrad replied, frankly interested.

"Could you believe that he miserably flunked the Art class? The teacher finally passed him so she wouldn't have to suffer him any longer. She was a very bent on that we should "paint with the heart" (big snort). Well you can imagine how it was, male teenagers throwing paint like in a happening from the sixties." Both men chuckled at the image, producing a huge desire in me to crawl under the table. "Anyway, she said to my brother's class, this was not going to work at all and that they should have to do a better job to pass it. All the students convinced Guntram to make most of their homework. She never realised all of the drawings were made by the same hand. He could change styles without problems. But for some unknown reason, he was never presenting his own works."

"You draw sixteen different views of the same flower vase and you'll see if you want to make number seventeen," I growled, praying inwardly he would shut up.

"Why did you do it?" Ferdinand asked.

"I didn't like her and her way of understanding art," I growled again, feeling miserable in my corner.

"The principal had to speak with the teacher and they both had to catch Guntram and force him to paint in front of them so she could grade his work. Beat me if that's not an artist's temper! I believe that the only happy moments for my grandfather in the end, were when he was looking at your stuff. Juan and I are very grateful for that," I kept my eyes downcast, embarrassed to no end.

"Luciana will kill me if I don't get your email or phone number. She has an

American colleague who wanted to buy some paints from you. Even if you don't sell, think about it. Cash is always welcomed."

"Thank you. I'll give it to you."

"Good. Coming back must have been a shock for you. I mean, after Europe, landing in the mess is hard," he commented happily, almost making me choke on the ice cream. Not that subject please.

"It was all right. People seem to be more concerned about the others and want to help," I replied softly.

He laughed heartlessly.

"Guntram, you are from another planet if you believe something can change here. It's the same as before, but without money. Give them five months to recover something and they all will be back to their old self. The Peronist party is back in power and corrupt as ever or more because they're desperate to get money to keep the troops happy. You were not here during the riots. It wasn't a few people escaping the gases in Plaza de Mayo or a few looting the supermarkets. It was much worse. We were close to a civil war and had it not be for the Army and some local leaders, today we would not be speaking here."

"Did you know how well organized was the looting by some politicians to get the useless president we had out? No, you didn't. Some of them were distributing *paco* (it's a cheap form of cocaine), transporting people from the settlements in the outskirts, and that is a category below the slums gentlemen, to attack the supermarkets in the low and middle class areas. They provided even weapons for them and put the police off the streets. The problem was that the situation got out of control and these poor devils started to attack private houses. The only way to stop it was with the Army. They chose an area in the south and started to shoot with machine guns against the looters to set an example. The bodies are in unidentified graves. It was the only way to calm them down. The press never said a word about it. You can imagine at which level all was planned."

"But the main remaining problem, is the social hatred created around us. My wife, Luciana was caught in the middle of the first skirmishes downtown. She's six months pregnant, but she's blonde and "white". A horde of these animals, who were destroying a McDonald's, saw her and started to kick her just because she was an "uptown girl". By sheer miracle, she didn't lose the baby and now she's in Uruguay with her aunt waiting for the baby to come, so we can move to London and start again."

"I wasn't aware of it. I'm terribly sorry," I whispered, all colour drawn from my face.

"If you can, leave this country. You're French, you should have no problems. This will become worse. The ones in power are the same as before."

A long silence engulfed the table.

"I believe we should discuss business before I think it over and run away," Konrad said, breaking the dark mood looming over all of us.

"You are right, Duke but I'm afraid my price has been lowered with my speech," Pablo said, getting up from the table.

Both men plus one of the girls went into the Library. Ferdinand, Landau and Michael started to work on their computers not minding at all what I was doing. I went to sit down by the lake, enjoying the peace of the place drifting away again in my thoughts, wondering what Konrad was after now; nothing good likely.

"So here you are. Come Guntram, it's getting late," Konrad said, sitting beside me and pulling me toward him, grabbing me by the waist. "It's quite beautiful here. I can understand why you didn't want to leave it. There's something about this country that finally traps and bounds you to it."

"Is it finished?" I asked fearfully.

"Yes, the money will be transferred to a London based account to avoid the risk it could be trapped in Buenos Aires. We argued a little over the price, but we reached an agreement."

"Why did you buy this?"

"Because I understood that I can't cut all your roots off and expect that you are happy about it. I see now, that we should come once per year, for holidays, so you can see your people," he explained looking into my surprised eyes. "Guntram, I told you we should make adjustments to make this work well. I know that I have to respect your past."

I was speechless, astonished to no end.

"Did you just buy a house in the middle of the countryside for holidays?"

"Yes, so we can come in July or August for two or three weeks. It's relatively near downtown and in the way to the airport. Would need some security reforms and the pink paint would have to go away. Don't stare at me as if I had done something crazy. It was only 1.6 million dollars. The forest around alternating with the open spaces is very appealing to me."

"Only 1.6 million?" I stammered. Wow.

"Does it make you happy? To come here?" He asked solicitous.

"Yes, I would like to come here. I'm crushed that you did it."

"I want that you're happy with me. You are truly important to me and I don't want that we ever repeat the past two weeks. Once you've learnt your place, everything will be perfect. I'll do anything to prevent you escaping again," he said softly, chilling my bones and heart as he kissed me on the lips.

I felt lost. How could he say that he loves me and then he rapes me to ensure his possession. This man was utterly out of his mind. I had to find a way to run away from him... to the Colombian jungle because I'm certain he could find me anywhere.

"Come, we have to return. I have several meetings scheduled for this late evening and night with local officials and politicians. They have discovered they need international support if they want to come back to the markets. Could you drive with Michael or Ferdinand? I need to prepare the meetings with Landau."

"Yes, of course," I replied, secretly glad to be free from him again, even for an hour.

We went back to the cars, where most of the people were already ready to leave. Pablo gave me a big hug and asked for my e-mail again. "You take a treasure with you, sir," he affirmed strangely serious. Having second thoughts about the sale? No chance Konrad would go back. He takes all.

"I know. Good bye, Mr. Dollenberg, the lawyers will take care from now on," he shook hands with him as he entered inside the car with Landau and Michael behind him.

I got to ride with Ferdinand and Goran. Alexei, lucky bastard got the two nice secretaries. I sat quiet as a mouse, looking through the window at the landscape while Ferdinand was busy with some papers.

"You're certainly quiet, aren't you?" Goran asked me.

"Sorry, I didn't mean to be rude," I replied automatically. "I was distracted."

"It's hard to leave your country. I know. For me leaving Serbia, even if we were just out of war, was hard. I still want to come back to Krajina despite now it's Croatian territory. The first months are the worse, but one day you get up and realise that you have to leave things behind or you'll get crazy and start anew."

"Do you have relatives there?"

"Not any more. I had a brother, but he was killed by the Croats during the war."

"I'm sorry."

"Don't be. It's not your fault and I have already settled the matter. You have the advantage of not having relatives here."

"Goran, leave the boy alone," Ferdinand interrupted us. "This is a matter for the Duke to sort out."

"Will he keep his word to Dollenberg?" I asked directly to Ferdinand

"I don't see why not," he retorted sharply, surely pissed off that I was not worshipping his Excellency. "The price was right and he likes the estate."

"Given the past experience with Fedérico's mother, forgive me if I doubt a little. The Dollenbergs are good people," I counter attacked using a sarcastic and acid tone with him.

"Exactly. He has nothing against them. The sooner you learn that the Duke only retaliates when he's challenged, the better for you. He's not the bad man you now think he is. He has more integrity in his finger than most of the people you call friends."

"I can't believe my ears. You were there last night!"

"You are still sore and sulky from your last punishment and wallow in hatred and misery when in fact, you should be grateful that he has given you a second chance. For him, this punishment was sufficient and would never mention this matter again. He has forgiven you for the pain you caused him and even mended his wrong conduct. All this mess was caused by your doubts and not fulfilling your promise. You should learn your lesson and take this opportunity. Not many men are as generous as to forgive completely and move on. You, on the other hand, are now thinking on how to take revenge on him. I saw it in your eyes today! Remember what you promised me yesterday!" Ferdinand exploded finally.

"I'm not doing anything like this. I'm only thinking how to survive this psycho!"

"Easy. Start anew."

I said nothing. Fuck him.

"This morning he treated you exactly as before. No reproaches or second intention lines at you. Most couples after a fight start a cold war with poisoned darts. He did not," he pressed on.

Well, that's called bipolar disorder in my town. I remained silent.

"Guntram, for all our sakes, let go of your fear and forgive him if he has hurt you and move on," Goran said very gently. "It's a hard life for living it in hatred, planning revenge because when you achieve it, you realise it was the only driving force in your life and you're only an empty shell. You have a pure soul, don't sully it."

"I said I will try, not that I will do it, Ferdinand. Forgive me if I want to save my skin."

"And I swore that if he lays a finger on you, I will get you out. You have to trust our word since you are one of us now, little brother."

"Is it true, your word?"

"With God as my witness," Goran crossed himself at Ferdinand's words.

"I'll do my best to overcome my more than reasonable fear of him."

"I know it will not be easy, but when you learned to walk you fell many times and yet you finally managed to do it," Ferdinand said squeezing my hand in a fatherly way. "Now lift up this dark mood and stop sulking."

We rode the rest of the trip in silence. We arrived to the hotel and Konrad said that he had to get changed for his meetings. I went with him to the suite and stayed in the living room, sitting in the big leather sofa in front of the TV, my mind still in turmoil. He came out of the bedroom wearing a dark blue suit and fumbling with the tie. He stood in front of me to study me.

"I spoke with Ferdinand," I slowly started, unable to cope with his piercing glare. "He said that I've hurt you a lot but you have completely forgiven me. Is it true?"

"Ferdinand should mind his own business," he growled with a low voice. I looked at him with big eyes silently pleading him to answer. "Yes, my world crumbled down after that call. With you, I had regained my life. I felt truly happy and complete, but in one second all was taken away," he admitted sitting next to me. "I exploded in rage and only wanted to get you back, no matter the costs. So, I planned to come here and recover what was mine, my soul," his hands messed his hair so perfectly combed and I felt grief and guilt engulfing me. Finally, I had been the one to make the deeper cut. I put my hand on his arm in a soothing way.

"I'm sorry. I didn't think that I could hurt you so much." This time my apology was heartfelt.

"It's not all your fault. I blame myself for not being more severe with you and directly forbid you to come here, despite I knew that this was a huge temptation and you were still scared and adjusting yourself to your new life. I was not strong enough as to face your momentary wrath if I postponed your trip and would have come with you," he slowly admitted.

"But Konrad, you can't control my every move," I whispered, half expecting his anger.

"I don't want to. I failed you in the way I introduced you to my life. Too fast and too harsh and this provoked the crisis. I forgot that you're only nineteen years old and I expected you to behave like a thirty year old."

I was completely dumbfounded as my image of the evil man I thought he was, crumbled down. "I don't know what to say. We both screw it up."

"Can you please forgive me also?"

"Yes," I mumbled throwing myself into his arms. He embraced me hard, not letting me go and placing soft kisses over my head.

"Let's start all over again, my dear. No regrets or ill thoughts between us. How I wish I didn't have to go out tonight and could stay with you."

"Don't worry, we have the rest of our lives together," I said clutching his neck. He kissed me on the lips in a tender and desperate way, all at the same time.

"Tomorrow we will spend the day together and you will show me your city. I have to dine with many blasted politicians and I will be back late. Don't wait for me," he kissed me and left.

Chapter 24

February 16th, 2002. Saturday

"You are truly a sleepyhead," an amused Konrad said, as he gently shook me.

He had really come back very late and slid into the bed, snuggling close to me and immediately falling asleep. How he could be active again was a mystery.

"It's Saturday and very early in the morning. Don't you take a day off at some point?"

"It's eight o'clock," he answered falsely shocked. "It's late. I have meetings and if I hurry I might be free at eleven. Should I tickle you?"

"No, thanks," I replied shooting him a warning glare which only made him smile. "You have spoilt the fun of sleeping." Now I was sitting in the bed as he went to shower and change.

We had breakfast together, without an audience till Ferdinand stormed in, completely upset saying something in German. Here we go again.

"Yes, I have given the men leave until tomorrow at ten. The men deserve it. They have been working nonstop for a month. I will go around with Guntram after 12."

"You can't be serious. This could be dangerous!" he shouted.

"Ferdinand, the men are exhausted. I can't ask more of them. You should also go out and get something for Gertrud and the children. You're overreacting and I can protect myself."

"I still protest."

"Guntram will stay with Alexei in the morning and perhaps drive to his flat to look for something he might have forgotten." Great, I have a date with a big Russian was my sarcastic thought. "Then we will eat something, walk around, have dinner and come back."

"I don't trust the people here."

"I also don't, but they have more to lose if they try something than us. Now you have your orders."

The Russian picked me up later with one of the monster trucks they love to use and drove me to my former apartment; he had the keys, of course. These KGB boys are always ready. George was truly happy to see the big boy (he might be around thirty-five years old and like most Russians, has a baby face till the vodka catches up with them).

"We have to come back," Alexei interrupted us abruptly, tired of George's insistent prodding. He picked up my things and ran away to the car.

"Pity he doesn't want to play," he sighed.

"Lucky you that he didn't want to hit you. I'm going to miss you and maybe that noisy dog you have too."

"Good bye my boy. Call me if you need expert advice."

"I will and thanks for everything," I said giving him a big hug. He was the only one to say good bye to me in Argentina.

At 11:30, Konrad returned from his last meeting and went to change from his suit into beige trousers, white shirt and tweed jacket. In this casual outfit he looks younger and attractive like a devil. I had to refrain myself from salivating.

"Can I ask you something personal?" I playfully said.

"If you want to know where I hide my money, no."

"Nothing so personal. Have you ever considered wearing jeans?"

"No. I'm not John Wayne."

"Sometimes you look as coming out of the Middle Ages," I chuckled at his answer. He's a hopeless case.

* * *

We took one of the monster trucks and he decided to drive, leaving the chauffeur at the hotel. We drove around the city and went to have lunch at the docks, Puerto Madero, transformed into a trendy area in the 90's. He wanted to have meat, of course, all gringos die for it and I didn't complain because the natives (or adopted ones), also like it. He said that his firm wanted to buy one of the warehouses to establish permanent offices.

"I thought you didn't like Argentineans," I asked puzzled.

"I still don't like them, but it doesn't prevent the country to be a good investment opportunity. It has vast misused natural resources and with the crises the prices are extremely low. Agribusiness and Mining are what we're concentrating on now. We will not enter into the industry because the technological update and labour costs are too high to make a profit in less than seven years. Furthermore, we will have the local politicians meddling permanently in our affairs.

"No Real Estate development for the moment?" I asked hopefully.

"None, as long we keep our arrangement," his seriousness frightened me once more.

He continued to elaborate on the richness of the countryside and what a lousy ruling class we have, their long term thinking no more than the next election. They were like children demanding everything and giving nothing in return. They had not really understood the meaning of what the default had meant for the economical establishment and were astonished that they were almost kicked out from Davos Conference this year.

He wanted later to walk around the docks and then we should see downtown. He had passed several times with the car, but he never had the chance to see it in peace. I laughed a little bit at the idea that he wanted to make the tourists' visit.

"Normally, you go around the city before buying anything," I joked lightly.

"I did. Read several books and the reports from Landau before coming here. All the acquired land has been evaluated by experts and honestly, I don't know much about cows or intend to learn. Besides, it was not such a huge investment. We're only taking positions."

"How much if it's not too much to ask?" Not really expecting an answer.

"I start at three hundred and then maybe continue to five hundred millions (if I'm very happy with the returns), from my own capital. I will not risk the bank. This is still too unstable."

"With such amount you could get half of the Patagonia," I stammered, trying not to gape too much.

"Yes. But I prefer to concentrate on Buenos Aires and the Littoral provinces," he simply stated to my utter astonishment. "How well do you know this man Dollenberg?"

"Not much. I know his brother who is a nice person, honest, not the cleverest in the class, but very outgoing. I met Pablo briefly because he was older and didn't like Fedérico and wasn't allowing his brother come to near him. I was surprised to be invited by them one summer. He was polite, but distant with me as you should be to younger midgets. He was always busy with the farm tasks and very serious about everything. His grandfather was a real gentleman and very clever and I could speak with him for hours. He fought in the war and later moved here."

"I was thinking to offer him a position in the new brand here. We need some agricultural experts and even if he's young, he could work in the second line. The problem is that he's so determined to leave the country."

"I can't blame him for that. He almost lost his child."

We walked in silence for a long time until he decided to go back to the car and to the hotel.

In the living room, we started to watch a film and like a teenager, he took my hand. My heart rushed at the same time I felt a pang of desire in my nether regions. I tried to think in something ugly like two dead skunks I saw once in the countryside, but it didn't work at all. Embarrassed, I turned my gaze down to ignore the wonderful heat his body was emanating. His hand took my chin and lifted it, forcing me to look into his eyes, the perfect picture of caring and tenderness. He bent his body to kiss me and this time I couldn't restrain myself any longer.

We kissed like two animals in heat, he holding me as my head felt dizzy under his experienced kisses and my sloppy ones. Without realising we landed over his big bed, his body on top of mine. Like before I rearranged my pelvis to allow him to accommodate himself between my legs, his manhood resting on mine, my right leg trapping his thigh and rubbing my interiors. Trapping him with my legs always had driven him crazy with pleasure and I wanted to make love and forget that horrible previous night.

He interrupted his kiss, making me growl desperately at his rejection. I fought to keep his body plastered to mine, lacing my arms around his neck, but he was stronger.

"Let me give you pleasure today," he enigmatically said. Were we not doing that before? However, go back to work boy, I wanted to say.

"Let me undress you".

"Do as you like Konrad." My laboured voice managed to say.

His skilled fingers started to unbutton my shirt as he softly kissed and licked every part of my skin released from the clothes. His tongue swirled around my nipples making me moan softly and my hands plunged into his hair. He sucked hard in a slow motion fuelling my erection to the point of being painful. He trailed a series of soft kisses down my stomach to my navel, where he played again with his tongue.

Suddenly he stopped again almost making me cry in disappointment. He smiled, giving me a comforting gaze as he took my ankle and slowly pulled the sock off. He massaged my calf with round moves, making me relax in a funny way since my toes were curling in extreme tension.

"You are so sensitive my love," he chuckled as he did the same on the other leg. Well, stop you being so appreciative and do something more before I explode of sexual frustration.

"You are so beautiful, almost like an angel," he whispered in my ear. No need to become romantic now, I'm already in bed and needy. I grunted my appreciation, hoping he would get the idea and continue what he was doing so well so far.

"Would you let me cover your eyes? I only want that you enjoy the pleasure freely. Nothing will happen unless you want it," he asked, his eyes locked onto mine. This was unexpected and frightening at the same time. Would he do it again? He saw my fear in my eyes and slowly, almost in a motherly tone said, "Please, maybe this would be a way for you to trust again in me. I swear to stop if you want."

"Take your clothes off before you do it," I don't want any reminder of that night.

He looked at me startled, but said nothing as he rose from the bed and quickly disrobed himself exposing his magnificent body to me. Life is unfair. Really. I smiled at him encouraging his next move, secretly hoping he would forget his original idea and jump my bones.

He went to the dresser and took one of his ties as I sat on the bed.

"That's Italian silk," I protested none too convincingly.

"Better. I can take it to work for a good memory," he mischievously retorted, making me blush as he tided the silk tie around my eyes.

My heartbeat increased in expectation and fear but he remained still for a long moment. Suddenly, I felt his lips kissing my face in a soft and loving manner. I relaxed again as he shoved me softly against the mattress and started anew with his trail of kisses inflaming my blood with expectation toward his next move.

I felt his hands opening my trousers and throwing them out in one swift movement. I caught my breath as he took some time to ponder his next course of action. I felt his weight slightly crushing my body and a strong scent of almonds invaded my nostrils going directly to my brain.

"It's a scented oil, nothing more. You smell naturally like apples," he said sending shivers to my spine.

His mouth engulfed my member in one move not wasting more time on kisses or caressing. He sucked me hard, a milking feeling running through all my body as I moaned completely lost in the pleasure he was giving me. His fingers brushed softly against my balls, playfully rolling them while his mouth engulfed me once and again.

I couldn't hold it much longer and climaxed into his mouth. I felt ashamed of my low resistance and childish eagerness.

"Now, there's nothing to worry about. It's perfectly fine," he shushed me, driving slow comforting circles with his thumbs in my cheeks.

"I was too fast," I said desperately, feeling like an ass.

"Would you let me take you? Only if you really want it, don't feel pressed to do anything you don't want. I've missed you so much," strangely, but when you're blinded, you can hear much better people's intonations and his voice sounded very pleading and needy, like a lost child.

"Do it. I love you," I said shyly.

He accommodated my back against the pillows to an almost sitting position. A wave of almonds again hit my nose and I felt his fingers tracing the shape of my chest with the liquid making me lose all sense. I felt the intrusion of his fingers into me and I let a small cry of ecstasy.

He started to slowly stretch me with delicate moves, not urging, not pressing, only waiting for me to enjoy the pleasure he was giving me and I was taking without restrictions. My bones felt as if they were turning into jelly.

He took my legs and put them over his shoulder to have better access to me. I shuddered in anticipation as I felt my bottom being placed over his lap. His member lingered for an instant at my entrance as if asking permission and I bucked my hips toward him to easy the penetration.

Konrad penetrated me softly and almost hesitantly as if he were afraid to hurt me, sliding in inch by inch. The pace he set was slow and giving me waves of pleasure with each thrust as my body adjusted to his length. His thrusting carried on for several minutes, changing the angle several times flooding me with maddening pleasure till I started to accelerate my hips moves to encourage him to pick up the pace. Now his banging against my rear was frantic and my mouth only emitted strangled cries of delight. He came deep inside of me, hard and filling me with his warm liquor.

We both rested, panting for a few minutes, I caressing in a loving way his head against my chest as he hold me. At some point he abandoned me to go to the bathroom and came back with a towel to clean us both. He helped me to get the blindfold off as he kissed me. Together we slid under the covers as I felt completely weary from the tension of the past month. I closed my eyes and felt him hold me and snuggle against me as I fell asleep.

It was dark when I woke up still in Konrad's arms. I carefully turned around not willing to wake him up, but he reinforced his hold on me still completely out. I drew my hand towards his face to touch the left side of his face. Fast as the light speed, he caught my hand in a painful and strong grip digging his nails into my wrist. I yelped more surprised than anything. He released me and muttered an apology, visibly embarrassed.

"It seems you're not a morning person also," I said trying to lift his mood.

"An evening person would be more correct. Let's get some meat."

"You're going to die from a clogged artery if you continue your attack on our cattle," I smirked.

"It's a pleasant road to death," he chuckled as he rose from the bed, pulling me with him.

We took a shower and went for round number two. Life it's too short to lose time. It was incredible, so full of love and caring. I was a total fool for not coming back to him before. School and work could be replaced easily, but a man like him not. His temper was short, but I firmly believed it could be changed and he wanted to change since he had made amendments and reflected on my reasons for breaking up. Yes, I was grateful he had not given me up.

Trying to comb my hair or drying myself was an impossible task. He was touching me everywhere and trying to steal kisses, behaving worse than a horny teenager.

"Stop it please, you have more hands than an octopus!" I protested amused at his behaviour. He let me go not too happy, but secretly pleased with my comparison.

Again I was enthralled by his cologne as he put it on. It was so similar to my father's. "What's in it? In the cologne, I mean."

He was taken aback by my question but quickly recovered from the shock and shrugged nonchalantly "Not sure, should ask the perfumer. I just like it. Do you want it?"

"No, it would be too much," I chuckled as I pried the bottle from his hand and smelled. "It looks like there's some apple in it. Funny," I said as I let the thing aside catching a glimpse of relief in Konrad's eyes. "Don't worry, I'm not stealing your perfume also. I have already half of your closet space."

"It would be very nice of you if you would wear it for me," he softly said.

I hesitated a little. It was somehow spooky to use something so similar to my father's but his expression hanging literally from my words made me decide. "Yes, I will but don't complain later if the bottle is empty."

We finished dressing and went to get the car. He wanted to know San Telmo, a popular tango neighbourhood, completely crowded with tourists on a Saturday night. What else can you do if you are with a gringo in your own city and he wants to see the tango girls?"

We had to park a few blocks away from the restaurant since there was no parking place available and strangely there were no tourists or locals in the area. Guess the crisis is bigger than I originally thought. This area is nice in the daylight, but at night you have to be careful because many of the houses, built in the early XIX century when the south area was rich until the Yellow Jack wiped most of the population out and the rich people escaped to the northern areas, are now more or less in shambles. Many of the houses are intruded or transformed into *conventillos* or tenements. The tourists like it because there's an antiquities market, artists and typical colonial style houses.

We ordered dinner (meat if you have any doubts), and ate in peace.

"Do you remember your father?" He asked me, almost making me choke on a piece. What on earth was this question about? I didn't want to speak about this.

"Not much. He was never around. Coming once per month or less and staying for a few days. He would bring me a present and play with me the whole time he was there," I softly smiled at the memory of playing horses with him.

"What kind of a man was he?"

"Physically very much like me, I guess. I have photos from my family if you want to see them. He was very nice to me, playing and I guess spoiling me a lot, when he was around. I think he worked in a bank in Paris, but I'm not sure. I never understood why he did it. He never seemed to be depressed or in trouble when he was around, but I suppose you don't tell such things to children. He told me once that he loved my mother very much and that I had inherited her peaceful character. He had a lot of energy and was quite decided whereas I take a lot of time to make a decision."

"I believe that once you reach a decision and are convinced of it, you'll be stubborn as a mule."

I feigned an offended look at him.

"You said he worked in a bank, which one was it?"

"Honestly I don't know. When I turned eighteen, the lawyer in charge of my affairs turned everything to me... in a box. There were only pictures, letters of him and my mother, my grandmother's piano. By the way, if the bitch who sold you the flat tells you it's hers, don't believe it. There was nothing about his work. The lawyer told me that he only saw him once when he established the trustee fund for me. Before he had the accident, he sold his flat and transferred the money into my account."

"I'll tell Monika to take care of the piano."

"I was more concerned about my twelve inch action figures from Star Wars from the seventies." Time to put you on the edge and it seems to have worked because you have settled the cutlery down and look a little bit alarmed. "They would look great in the showcases you have in the blue living room. I think those gold and white china pots could be moved elsewhere," I said with complete seriousness.

"Those "pots" as you called them were made by Böttger himself. They were a gift from King Augustus to a grandmother from my mother's side," he was barely concealing his contempt. Let's rub him a little more was my thought.

"I see, if they're a family souvenir we can let them in peace. But they look quite horrible. The Chinese painted them much better," I said in a merry tone.

"Well considering that Böttger discovered the art of porcelain in less than twenty years while for the Chinese took several centuries, we can't complain so much. It was fashion to copy this kind of motives and Meissen had no good painters yet," he explained, taking a deep breath in.

"If you like them so much, it's fine, but the others figures, the hunters scene, the animals and this tailor on top of the goat are somewhat extreme. My figures will erase that baroque air."

"Those are original figures, modelled by Kaendler, dating from 1735 to 1760. My grand grandmother got them as presents for her services to the King of Poland," he intoned with his best face of heir to the Holy Roman Empire and barely keeping his anger under control.

"I see. She got them on the battlefield," I quickly retorted making him blush for the first time. I laughed openly. "I will never take on the Meissen pieces, don't be so upset. Sometimes you can be so serious that it's impossible to resist to pull a joke on you," he also laughed now at himself.

"It could have been much worse, Konrad. Imagine if she would have gotten the Monkey's Band."

"She did. All of them. They are at the house in Paris. You knew all the time what they were," he lightly accused me.

"Most of them. I would have gone after them, not the silvery if I wanted to steal something," I chuckled, relieved to no end that he had not reacted like a psycho as he had done in Venice. "Our last Art teacher thought we were a lost cause and we got the introductory course to shopping at Christie's. She had worked many years in London and since her retirement decided to recruit new customers."

"Yet your figures still have to make it to Zurich," he trailed maliciously.

"I have no concerns. They're good, hard American plastic. Classical, all of them."

At about eleven, we decided to go back to the hotel both tired, and I was not very coherent really with the glass of wine he let me have. We walked down Defensa, Carlos Calvo to Humberto Primo where we had the car parked. Since the street was deserted I let him hold my hand only briefly. Sorry we're not in Europe.

Four men in their thirties, sporty dressed cut our path and I thought "well, we get mugged" and tried to keep my cool. They were looking like the low class robbers after your wallet for another fix. Not even asking for the money or the watches, two of them jumped on me and one of them hit me violently on the right side of the face with a chain and as I fell to the ground he repeated the operation with the chain to my midsection, causing a huge burning pain all over my body. *Pegale fuerte al putito para que el gringo de mierda se vaya* (hit hard the little fag so the fucking gringo goes away), shouted one of the other two who had grabbed Konrad by the arms. One of the men stomped with full force on my left hand giving me a horrible pain.

Konrad took the opportunity the other two gave him, momentarily distracted by the show I was providing, to revolve and in two swift moves threw them off of his back. I heard a faint sound of bones breaking as he slammed one of them against a wall and his fist connected with the other's face. I don't know exactly what happened because he was so fast, but he had the three of them in the ground wailing in pain.

The one who had hit me pulled me up, grabbing me from the hair and put a knife against my throat. Konrad seemed to hesitate for a little while, but the man started to cut me slowly and he pulled out a semi-automatic weapon and fired, hitting the man in the shoulder. We both fell to the ground; Konrad coming to him with a determined gesture to finish him, but the stampede provoked by the others in their haste to escape, made him look at them and fired a second chance, this time hitting another in the leg.

I was horrified and I thought he was going to kill the two down men. "Please, Konrad, stop," I pleaded. My voice full of pain seemed to get him out of his killing trance and pulled me from the ground and away from the whining hurt men.

He almost carried me to the car and put me in, driving fast to the hotel. I was in pain and said to him several times that we should call the police, but he didn't pay attention to me. He half dragged me to our room under the aghast look of the doorman at my state.

"Goran, come to my room," he barked into his mobile phone. He advanced toward me with long strides and I covered unwillingly in the sofa he had laid me down. He growled low and said "Guntram please, don't be childish, I have to see your wounds."

"You shot two men down," I stammered, still scared out of my soul. "Call the police at least!"

"I would have put the four of them down. They hurt you," he calmly said. I had to put my hand in my mouth to prevent vomiting my dinner over the carpet. I started to hyperventilate as he closed the distance between us.

"Stay away. Don't come any closer." My head was hurting me like crazy and every breath made my side erupt in a burst of painful flames.

"Guntram, this is the first time you see someone shot. I understand you're nervous, but please calm down, close your eyes, think of something else and let me see the extent of your injuries so we can treat them," he affirmed in a cold voice.

"You could have killed them! They only were some poor devils trying to get money out of a tourist! You could have given them the wallet and they would have gone away!" I shouted back almost crying.

"Should I give them the money before or after they kicked you in the ground?" he asked coldly, a clear brief hint of annoyance at my outburst in his voice. "Now, be reasonable and let me look. You are bleeding on your cheek and you have six centimetres superficial cut on your throat."

I look at him disoriented and placed my hand into my face to find it dirtied with dried blood. I gasped at the sight of it and almost cried with horror. He took the chance my momentary breakdown gave him to sit by me and held me by the hands, making me shriek when he touched my sprained wrist.

"It's OK, don't worry, I will settle this matter in no time, hush child," he tried to appease me as he pulled me toward his chest. I cried there like a baby as he held me.

Goran came in without jacket or tie and stood in front of us looking bewildered.

"We were attacked by four men. I want you to find them. Use the locals to help you. Don't involve the others yet. Get a doctor for Guntram; they focused on him. It was a message and I intend to return the favour."

"How can you say that? They were four junkies after your Rolex," I said. God, does he have to be such a paranoid?

"Be quiet. They knew us and focused on you when the logical step would have been to neutralize me. It was made to look like a mugging," he grunted at me, making me flinch with his harsh words. "What did they tell you?"

"Nothing."

"Guntram. I have no patience left. Speak up!" he barked menacingly.

"Perhaps you would like to tell me, without the Duke's presence." Goran suggested. I nodded my agreement and Konrad huffed as he left the room. I told Goran what they had shouted.

"Please Goran, you have to stop this. You have not seen him. He would have killed them all," I pleaded with him.

"It's all right Guntram. I'll send the doctor for you and you'll stay with the Duke for the time being. You need your rest and he needs to see that you're fine," he softly said, easing my fears a little.

"You promise you will speak with him?"

"Of course I will speak with him. He has to give me the description of what I should look for," he said, leaving me more scared than before.

Goran and Konrad disappeared for a good half an hour. At some point Konrad returned with a man who was the doctor. He checked upon me, cleaned both wounds and dressed them; bandaged the sprained wrist and said I should get a look at it in Switzerland. I should not sleep for the next five hours to avoid a commotion and if I felt dizzy or wanted to throw up I should be taken immediately to a hospital. He handed me several painkillers and left with Konrad.

Some time, in the middle of the night, Konrad returned to check upon me. He almost forced me into my pyjamas and then put me in bed.

"Stay with me, please."

"I'll come back in half an hour, kitten. You should rest now."

"What are you doing? I know you're up to something bad with those men. Let the police deal with them."

"Kitten, stay out of my businesses. I will do what I deem necessary."

Chapter 25

Konrad left the room, and did not turn around when I called his name again. I tried to stand up, but the sharp pain on my side made me lay down again. I must have fallen asleep, as my next memory of him was when he gently shook me to wake me up for breakfast.

I sat up in the bed, a little bit dizzy. I tried to gather my thoughts, but it was a hard task. "Please, help me with the…shirt buttons, as my left hand is immobilized," I articulated slowly, still trying to get the room to stop moving.

"You do not need to be dressed that much. Just eat and return to bed, till it's time for our flight."

"Were we not supposed to fly at noon?" I could tell he was after something and nasty.

"It's just a delay, Guntram, nothing to worry about. Here, put this on and join me in the living room," Konrad said, as he handed me a night-shirt from the hotel and hastily left the bedroom.

Fortunately, there was nobody in the living room and the breakfast table was set for two. I glanced at the clock and noticed that it was after nine. I was unsuccessful in hiding my wince as I sat, and dutifully started to eat the bowl of cereal even if I felt like gagging. We remained in silence mostly because he was checking his laptop, and the dark aura of his cold fury was too dense to break.

Ferdinand's shout at the door startled me, "Scheisse, Guntram. What is it now?" I looked down at my cereal. Michael and Alexei were also with him gaping at me.

"Some of the natives are not happy with our presence here," Konrad growled, as Ferdinand rushed to check on me, like a mother hen. I think he was glad that Konrad was not guilty this time. "Goran will give his report in an hour or less. We must express our point of view explicitly on the matter, gentlemen."

"As you wish, my Duke," Michael said. "Is it broken?" He asked me, pointing to my wrist.

"Only sprained—would be better in a few weeks," I mumbled.

"This time, Konrad, the message should be really clear. I'm afraid these natives don't understand anything but force," Ferdinand said heatedly, surprising me with his use of his Duke's Christian name, in a tone that sounded like he was challenging Konrad's opinion.

"I intend to show our strength this time. They have elevated the stakes to a new level."

"Konrad, they were only four junkies. Let the police deal with them," I protested, but nobody bothered to hear me.

"I have personally taken care of them, Sire," Goran announced, as he entered the room. "The local help will need…much more training until they meet our needs."

I was stunned by Goran's words, and even more by Konrad's response.

"Good work. Then gentlemen, it is up to us to repair this handicap and show how we deal with our enemies. Alexei Gregorevich, Guntram is your responsibility from now till we reach Zurich. We will leave at six. Complete all our preparations," he said, as he rose from his chair.

I stood up, too, appalled by Konrad's behaviour. "What are you talking about? You sound like a mobster from Chicago!"

"Guntram, I have told you once before. Do not interfere in my affairs. This was a planned assault, and it has to be stopped before it escalates further. It is for your own good," Konrad barked through his gritted teeth, with his fury barely contained.

I looked at the five of them. They were not bankers, CEO's nor even bodyguards. They were all trained assassins who had smelled blood in the waters. The Germans from the Army and Navy, the Serb from who knows which militia and the KGB monster. I took a step backward, afraid of them and what I was getting into. "I'm not coming with you. I don't like what you're implying," I muttered, now afraid.

"Guntram, this is not the time to be difficult. Go get some rest and leave it to us," Konrad said, as he advanced toward me.

I fled toward the door, but Alexei caught me with both arms. I squirmed hard against him; the pain became unbearable, but my will to run away kept me fighting against a mountain that didn't even seem disturbed. I felt a sharp prick on my left biceps and quickly turned around to see Konrad giving a small syringe back to Michael. The world started to spin as black dots danced in front of my eyes. I staggered, but he caught me in his arms before I hit the ground. I looked at him accusingly, and even fisted his jacket a bit.

"Shh, easy Guntram. You're still in shock and can only hurt yourself more. The doctor left this, if you had a nervous breakdown. You will sleep for a few hours, and then we will go home," he whispered softly, as he picked me up easily, and tucked me back in the bed. I fought to keep my eyes open, but I couldn't.

* * *

In the afternoon somebody shook me aggressively. It was Alexei.

"Wake up. You have been sleeping for more than six hours. We have to go now. I'll help you with the clothes."

I made a supreme effort to sit in the bed and briefly considered playing sick, but I realised that the Russian would drag me in my pyjamas to wherever he wanted to go. I noticed that the closets were empty and the bags put away. Alexei had laid, over a chair, a simple pair of grey pants, light blue shirt and blue pullover with underwear and dark shoes. There was also an informal grey tweed jacket.

"I'll roast like a chicken inside of those things!" I protested.

"Don't wear the pullover for the moment," he explained to me as if I were a five year old boy. "Hurry up, clean yourself and get dressed. Are you hungry?"

"No."

"Good, you can eat while aboard the plane then."

I complied, the best as I could. One side of my face, had turned into a deep blue-violet colour, and fortunately the bandage on my neck and on my cheek didn't allow me to see more. My wrist was throbbing, and for a minute, I thought about those bastards who did it. A wave of nausea hit me again, and I had to lay my head against the tiles for support. I really hoped that those crazy Germans had done nothing too serious to these poor devils.

"Do you feel well?" The Russian startled me, gently touching my shoulder.

"Just dizzy. Could you help me with the buttons, please?"

"No problem. Once, I broke all my left hand fingers. It took me six months to get them working fine again," I honestly did not want to know the circumstances.

He carefully helped me with my clothes, and led me to the car. There was one chauffeur and another man I did not know. I got into it, still a bit dazed and completely tired even though I had been sleeping for so long. The drive to the airport was fine, I think, because I had trouble keeping my eyes open. Finally, I gave up and leaned my head against the window, lulled by the sound of the motor.

"Hey, you're going to miss a beauty," Alexei said jovially, as he practically dragged me out of the car.

We stood in the shadow of a big plane—like the type you use for commercial flights—and I gaped at the monster, while I fought against my fatigue, almost making me fall asleep on my feet.

"It's a Boeing Business Jet. It's based on the 737. The Duke also has a Dassault Falcon 900 for short distances, but I think he wants to change it for the Airbus 380, when it's released." Alexei informed me, as he led me to the stairs without giving me the chance to realise where we were going, to revolt or try anything stupid.

Alexei ushered me into a big seating area full of light coloured leather sofas lined against the windows and several work tables, flat-screen TVs and a wood-panelled bar.

"This is the common area. Beyond this area is the private meeting room, restaurant, a small office and, finally, the Duke's bedroom with a private bathroom. The commoners have to use the other two bathrooms. It accommodates up to twenty-five people and seven crew members. The rest have to walk or swim," he chuckled, visibly amused. "The advantage is that you can fly a little bit over 6,000 miles non-stop."

"Can I sit? I'm not feeling well at all," I whispered almost dying with the headache.

"Sure, sit here," he said almost dropping me in one of the individual sofas which felt like heaven. He accommodated himself in front of me. "Marie!" he called, almost making me jump.

A good-looking girl in her late thirties appeared, dressed like a stewardess.

"Mr. Antonov?" She asked politely.

"Get him a coffee and a gin tonic for me."

After a few minutes, she came back and handed him his drink and moved a small wooden table in front of me to set the coffee... with milk. I muttered thanks and she vanished again.

"Do you know where he is?" I asked.

"Will be here at six o'clock. German precision. They really did a good number on you."

"Don't remind me. I still feel it, and I don't know why I'm so tired. What was in that?"

"Just a mild sedative. Should have worn out by now. Perhaps, we will have to take you to the hospital. Did they use a chain or something like that?"

"Chain I think, not sure."

"How unprofessional," he smirked. "Why don't you rest some more? I think we will be served dinner, once we're in air. Today, we have Marie, Elizabeth and

Charles. I'm going to speak with the pilots."

Again, I was left alone for some time. Through the window, I saw a small caravan of four black vans approaching. Then the gang emerged from those vehicles, in addition to six other men I had never seen before. Landau was there speaking with Konrad and Ferdinand. The rest looked utterly bored. I dozed again.

"Are you feeling better?" Konrad asked me, as he touched my forehead lightly.

"Yes, just tired, thank you. Where were you?"

"Around. The captain says we can take off at 7 p.m."

"You haven't answered my question."

"Then don't ask things you don't want an answer," he retorted sharply, with a threatening glint dancing in his eyes, as he placed both hands on the side-arms of the seat, trapping me. "What is done is past, and you should not be concerned any longer about those men. You should consider yourself very lucky they didn't cut your throat or break your skull open. It's not my fault, that some people think they can exact revenge on me in such a stupid way, not expecting any retaliation from me. I trust, this time, they have learned."

"Are you accusing Fedérico's mother of yesterday's attack?" I looked into his eyes, hoping to catch any sign of deception, but they were expressionless and steely. This is beyond normal paranoia.

"Everything points to that direction. Why would they bother to go after you instead of me and hit you in a way to "teach me a lesson"? They didn't touch me, so they wouldn't lose the contracts this stupid country believes would get through me. It's a personal vendetta against you and I, done by a stupid woman with too much power in her hands."

"What did you do?" I whispered, now terrified as the potential scenarios went through my head. I'm aware that he is more than capable of using terrible violence and has the means and the will to do it. He would have killed those men on-the-spot, and his men were a bunch of fanatics worshipping him.

"Just gave her to the local wolves," he said, giving me a smile that froze the blood in my veins. "You're too kind for this game. Don't get into it. Leave it to us," he rose from his spot, as I looked at him horrified.

"Hey, Guntram, you look slightly better than in the morning," Michael interrupted us. He ruffled my hair and sat on the couch next to me and he started to fumble his briefcase, producing a laptop. Konrad took the opportunity to disappear into his office. "Don't tell the boss, I have "Age of Empires" here. Do you want to play?"

"No, thank you. I still feel very dizzy," It was the truth, but the irony of the situation was too overwhelming. I sat there looking through the window.

"OK, then I have to work if I don't find a good excuse."

"Sir, would you like to have dinner? The others are already in the dining room." One of the girls stood in front of me with her studied plastic smile. I didn't want dinner. I wanted to be left alone but there was no chance of it, so I followed her to the front part of the plane.

The dining room was lined with wood panels, two big oak tables and chairs. Most of the men were already sitting. In one of the tables, seated along with Goran and Alexei, were the six guys I had not been introduced to. Michael, Ferdinand,

Landau were at the other table, which had two available seats. One at the head and the other at the head's left. Ferdinand indicated that I should sit on the left side of the head.

A few minutes later, Konrad entered the room and everybody, including me, stood up. This reminded me of how it was in the school, when the Principal entered the room. Konrad sat at the head and made a gesture allowing us to reclaim our seats. Two ladies and a man started to serve the dinner.

I ate mechanically, keeping my answers to a "yes" or "no" and not much more. Fortunately, they left me in peace and started to speak in German.

When dinner was over, Konrad and the others decided to have a meeting and returned to the main room. I followed them and sat in a corner far away, alone in my misery. I had nothing left.

"Guntram, are you all right?" Konrad asked, disrupting my thoughts and making me almost jump. When had he moved so close to me? I didn't remember. "Come to my office, if you still want to draw. The men would like to sleep. It's getting late."

What? Is he out of his mind? I'm not drawing! I opened my mouth to answer, but I saw that I had a folder and small box of pencils on my lap. Where did those things come from? I was shocked, but regained my composure quickly. I stood up, but sickness almost threw me down. I gulped, and managed to get to his office and sat in one of the chairs. He came behind me, and placed himself behind his desk. It's not like I'm going to bite you, you know.

Fuck! Somebody messed with the pencils. They're in complete chaos! I started to put them back in place. Now, they're all set. I laid against the backrest, satisfied.

The warm colours are totally wrong! I renewed my efforts to reorganize the pencils.

"Guntram, What are you exactly doing?"

Could you not see, asshole? "Setting the pencils in a chromatic order," I answered, upset. Apart from being a murderer, are you also blind or retarded? I started for the third time.

"It doesn't make much sense," he stood next to me, looking concerned. Hypocrite. Were you so merciful to those poor junkies?

I jumped to my feet. "Get away from me! Monster. You even have stains of blood on your shirt!" I pushed him hard away from me, but as usual he caught me effortlessly. I struggled against his hold, and everything went black.

Chapter 26

February 26th, 2002

"Hello. Do you understand me?"

I tried to focus my eyes on the doctor and a nurse standing against a blinding light. Where was I?

"Nod your head if you don't feel up to speaking yet," I nodded. "Good. We had to operate on your brain to alleviate the pressure. The blow you received in Buenos Aires got us very concerned, as it caused a respectable-sized concussion. What is the last thing you remember?"

"I was on a plane," he wrote something down in his pad.

"Excellent. Your vitals seem very good, but I still want to keep you here for a few more days for further evaluation."

"Where is here?"

"*Zürich. Klinik Hirschbaum*. These hits on the head can be tricky. Everything seems fine but then it's not."

"What date is it today?"

"February 26th, still the same year," he told me with an amused smile. "I'll let you see the Duke for ten minutes, and then he's out till tomorrow."

Konrad entered as soon as the doctor and the nurse left the room. He looked... haggard and very pale.

"You don't look very well," I said.

"Says the one who was in a hospital bed for eight days. Hello, Maus," he sat on the chair beside the bed. I turned my head to get a better look at him.

"What happened?" I whispered.

"We only have five minutes before the nurse from Hell casts me out. Don't worry about it. It's over."

"Please tell me. The doctor mentioned brain surgery?" I raised my hand and found something like a bandage on my head. My wrist was not throbbing any more. That was good.

"Twice, to alleviate the intra-cranial pressure; we don't know when you started to have hallucinations, but you collapsed five hours before we landed in Zurich. Doctors had to induce you into a pharmacological coma to give your brain a chance to recover."

"I had hallucinations?"

"You were hysterical about how I was covered in blood, and bit Goran hard. You could not distinguish colours and heard voices—or at least that's what we gathered. That hit on your head was much worse than the doctor in Argentina originally estimated. The swelling must have been increasing, and affecting your abilities since that moment. Even your personality changed; you yelled at us all morning, and bit Goran in the evening."

"I have to apologise to him. I've never wanted to do such a thing," I said, embarrassed to no end. "The other six guys you had on the plane must be thinking I'm a psycho," I muttered.

"If it's any consolation to you, there was nobody else in that plane aside from Ferdinand, Michael, Goran, Alexei and me; and the three stewardesses."

"Not even Landau?"

"He's still in Buenos Aires, taking care of the new office."

"I'm confused," I whispered. Had nothing been real? Not possible; I was sure of what I heard and saw.

"You must rest now, and then you'll come home with me," he rose and softly kissed me on the forehead, looking at me with eyes full of love. "I have to go now. The nurses have had enough of me this past week. I'll return tomorrow morning before going to my office. Sleep well."

Chapter 27

March 2nd, 2002

I returned to the Castle today. Doctor Van Horn released me at midday and I was glad to leave. Please don't misunderstand me. The doctors were kind, the food was good, and the nurses were nice and motherly; but the constant pestering from Michael, Monika, Ferdinand, Goran, Heindrik, Friederich and Alexei (and don't forget the biggest German of all), was driving me crazy.

They were visiting me in shifts. The first one in the morning is Konrad, and he stayed with me till 10:30. Then I got Goran or Heindrik. At 12:30, Michael came (and he'd always been kind enough to smuggle something else besides the hospital food for me), and he stayed until Monika kicks him out at 3:00. She stayed with me till 6:00, fussing over me. Then her boss and Ferdinand came, but they only stayed till 7:00. Konrad kept me company till 10:00 when the nurse, Anke, literally kicked him out. I have a growing respect for that woman.

This morning, the doctor left me three different kinds of pills and strict orders to take them. I'm supposed to return to his office in two weeks for a check-up and to take life easy: lots of rest, fresh air, not much reading or stress and sleep as much as I can. This man wants to turn me into a marmot!

"Ready to go?" The fine Serbian man stood at the door.

"More than ever. Let's go before the doctor finds more tests for me," I smiled to him.

"Where is your muzzle?"

"I have apologized to you several times. Don't you know the concept of forgiveness?" I said, embarrassed and somehow crossed that he was bringing the subject up again.

"Just checking that I'm driving the nice Guntram and not his evil twin," he chuckled, finding it terribly humorous that I was blushing.

"It wasn't so bad. You have all blown everything out of proportion," I retorted.

"Nobody, since kindergarten, has managed to bite me."

"I'm terribly sorry for that. Didn't know what I was doing."

"We all noticed. You're very funny when you sing ABBA songs."

"Did I do that?" I was petrified, and mortified. He laughed at me till he almost bent double. I guess he got me. Well, we can call it even.

"Of course not. Are sure you don't want to eat here?"

"No, I've had enough."

I said goodbye to Anke and Lisa. They were both truly nice women.

Goran drove me to the house. Friederich was waiting for us, and he seemed happy to see me. He gave me a light hug, which was more emotionally demonstrative than he had ever been with me. "We were very concerned about you, Guntram. The Duke did not even come home that week. He stayed in the hospital or in his office."

I was moved. I never thought he would do something like that. I felt so bad for thinking all those stupid ideas about him murdering and taking revenge. I acknowledge he had been a psycho for taking away my flat and job, but on the other hand he was so in love that he couldn't live without me and had almost thrown everything away to come and get me back. Remorse was biting me hard in the heart, because I had been totally unfair to him.

I had lunch with both men. The house was oddly silent without the other men there. Friederich thought it was inappropriate for me to sit with them in the service area, but I didn't want to be alone. He eventually allowed me in the service area, but I still sat away from the rest of the servants. Later, Goran took me for a walk in the snow, for only an hour.

I stayed the rest of the day in the library reading and drawing with pencil only. Yeah, I know it sounds boring, but I was feeling tired after the walk. I think I dozed again on the leather couch, because Konrad's kisses took me by surprise. While he was choking me with his hungry kisses and touches, I noticed it was already dark outside.

"Should we take this to the bedroom?" I said, doing my best to match his eagerness. He abruptly stopped and looked at me half seriously.

"It seems you do feel better, Kitten, but no. The doctor said you have to take it easy for the next two weeks."

"It's not fair!" I whimpered and tried to kiss him. "I was nice the whole day: ate everything, walked around and stayed here without causing trouble to your staff. Come on, just a little bit."

"Nothing would please me more, but you have to recover fully before doing more. Anyway, I have a letter for you from Dollenberg. He sent it to me, since he did not get a response from your email account and was worried. I told him of the accident and I hope you don't mind."

"I have totally forgotten about him. I haven't even checked my e-mails. Did everything go all right between you two?"

"You can do it tomorrow. Your laptop is in my studio upstairs. The doctor forbade you from reading and stressing your brain out any more. And yes, everything was satisfactory in our business. The transaction is done and your friend, even though he's young, behaves like a gentleman." After searching in his briefcase, he handed me a folder.

"His grandfather would have drowned him in the lake if he turned out less than that. I'll reply to his e-mail tomorrow," I said, putting it away for later.

"I think it's time to dine. I'll have Friederich serve now, so we can retire early," he stood up and left me alone.

I took the letter and I was surprised to see it written in English. Well, maybe it was a way to be polite to Konrad. There was a small note attached addressed to him explaining that he was concerned, as Pablo could not contact me.

Dear Guntram,

I was deeply concerned when I heard the news of your accident in Buenos Aires. My wife and I are praying for your speedy recovery. Honestly, I'm glad that you moved away from this city. Things are calm these days, but you never know how long the peace will last.

Our baby decided to take the Concord and visit us earlier than expected—as in, yesterday. It's a healthy good looking boy, Juan Ignacio, who

fortunately looks like his mother. When you feel well, please send me a few lines so I can overload your e-mail account with photos of him.
My useless brother sends his regards as well, and would like to write to you.
Best wishes, Pablo

"He had a baby. How long was I out?" I asked Konrad, when he returned to the room.

"He spoke with me two days ago and the letter was written yesterday. Monika has already sent something for the baby. You can't stop a woman from shopping if she hears the word 'baby'."

"Thank you very much. It was very kind of you," I looked gratefully into his eyes, almost drowning in them.

"Nonsense. There's now another German to pay for my pension."

He made me laugh. I stood up to embrace him and this one was stronger than necessary, as if he needed to release the tension built up during the last weeks. I touched the side of his face. "It was bad for you, wasn't it?"

"I've had better days, Kitten," he murmured, as he held me tighter and pushed my head against his chest with his big hand.

"I thought horrible things about you after the attack. I'm terribly sorry about that," my voice trailed off, regret almost choking me.

"You didn't think anything. It was the concussion. Forget this mess and let's think about our future," I had to go on tiptoes to kiss him this time.

"Monika has been collecting brochures from the Career Center at the University here, and for the summer courses for this year, so you can start reviewing them. Don't frown. You know it's for the best. You need to start organising yourself here. But don't hurry, because you're still recovering," he sternly advised me.

"But I don't even speak German!"

"Most of the subjects are taught in English, and the language can be learned in no time. Why don't you take some German lessons in the morning and some private painting courses?"

"That would really be a waste of money!" I protested.

"No. You have an incredible talent for drawing. It's a shame that you don't recognise it, and try to hide it. It's about time you do something about it."

"You say that because you're in love with me, and not really thinking," I heard a big and unprincely snort for an answer.

"Humour me."

"Fine," It's a total waste of money. Perhaps after the teacher throws me out, he would see reason.

"Don't pout like a child."

"I still have six months left as a nasty teenager," I retorted, as he heaved a long sigh.

"I hope I'll survive them, or the University straightens you out."

During dinner, I was graciously informed that he would be taking two days off from work from Thursday to Saturday. Thereafter, on Sunday night, he would fly to Beijing and Shanghai for meetings and a brief inspection of the Shanghai offices. He would then return, if nothing else arose, in the middle of Thursday night.

167

"You should not be concerned. Monika managed to find a German Teacher, who will come in the mornings every day to instruct you. She's also from Buenos Aires. Monika spoke quite highly of her," I was astonished. Had he already booked a teacher for me, when only few minutes ago he was telling me to think about learning that blasted language?

"I was under the impression that I still had to make a decision on the matter," I said softly, jabbing the fish with more force than required.

"Oh yes, she's flexible on the method you would like to use," he replied to me, as though the matter had already been decided – when it had not! It's a pity I could not use the green beans as ammo. I opened my mouth to protest.

"Guntram, before you start to rant, consider that University starts in September - and you should at least be able to maintain a minimum conversation level with the other students. Even if many subjects are in English, you still have to make acquaintances with your fellow students and teachers. You cannot spend the rest of your life speaking English with Friederich," he intoned with his best teacher/father/banker voice.

Even if he's right, and is open to the possibility of me having people my own age around (had he reconsidered the part when I said he lives in a Mausoleum?), I'm annoyed at how he unilaterally makes every decision for me.

"You could have asked *before* you made the arrangements, at least," I mumbled, unhappily by stressing the word.

"Monika made the arrangements. She says you would be glad to have the tutor. She also gave me a dossier about *Zürich Universität* Faculties and the main programs in Economics and Finance. You have to do a yearlong introductory course, then two years more for the BA and two additional years for the MA. She would be very pleased if you could study them next week, and discuss your decision with me next weekend. All your papers have been presented, and you are conditionally accepted. They did recognize your IB grades, but not your grades from the Argentinean University. You should be glad you don't have to pass the admission tests," I gaped like an idiot, unable to find my voice back.

"Guntram, you know it's for the best. You can ask the teacher what you don't understand and think peacefully without me interfering. If you need advice, you can also ask Ferdinand. Sometimes, you need a little push in the right direction."

A little push? This sounded more like a shove. "I see your point, but..."

"If you see my point, then don't argue," he interrupted me abruptly, and shot me a warning glare. I stood frozen. "Everything has been done on your behalf, to the best of your interests. You were ill in hospital, and are now recovering. You really don't need the hassle of running around the University's offices. You wanted to study Economics, and I accept it even though I think it's a huge mistake. You should be thinking of Art History or something like that, if you want security in your life. Your character just does not meet the minimum requirements of a banker or trader. Please don't misunderstand me, I'm very glad that your character does not. You are a natural-born optimist, an artist or even a healer."

"If you doubt my intelligence so much, why are you letting me go to the University at all?"

"I think you're very intelligent and talented, but for other things. Tell me: can you throw an old couple out of their home for not paying the mortgage?"

I wasn't able to suppress my sharp intake of breath at the horror of what he was suggesting.

"All right, let's not make it so dramatic. Can you lend money to a company, which has products you're aware will contaminate a whole population, if the return is more than twelve percent in a year?

"Not all bankers are so bad. Take the Graemen Bank or Unicef for example; they also need economists."

"They have good communication skills, but it's true. Gertrud needs some help in the Foundation, and we can use economists there. I'm only saying this, so you will realise the kind of people who will be surrounding you. Those who enter the field would kill for an internship in my bank and we are not like Mother Theresa. This is not the happy faculty you attended, believing love and peace will save the world. All the people here want to work, and to assume a position in society. Don't look so depressed. Your father would have told you all this."

I just sat there, looking into the depths of his deep ocean blue eyes and saw no deception there.

"Come *Maus*, don't stress yourself so much. I have no doubts that whatever you choose to study, you will finish with honours. But please don't ever think that you could work in my banks. I only want to save you from disappointments in your life. You're truly a rare breed."

"A lot of people are kind and caring. You are a pessimist."

"No, I'm a realistic. If I were a pessimist, I would have never spoken to you in Venice. You were too good to be true. I've only been around longer than you," he said, with a hint of sadness.

I left my chair to go to sit on his lap. He didn't protest, and let me put my arms around his neck and nuzzle his collarbone with my head in a soothing way. "I love you, even if you depress all the children in a circus," I said, while I kissed him on the temples.

"Would you consider what I said about the careers?" He pressed, like a dog with a bone.

"Yes, and you would have a decision by next Friday night," I let out a dry laugh. "Does this mean that, from now on, I would have to ask for an appointment every time I want to speak with you?"

"A forty-eight hour warning would be nice," he said, with a humorous glint in his eyes.

"Let's go to bed before Friederich comes back with dessert," I suggested this time, almost nibbling his ear.

"He has to be sure you take your medicines. We can go later and watch a movie or something."

"Yeah, something...," I trailed, kissing his neck seductively.

He gave a strong smack to my bottom. Hey, that's not sexy!

"Enough Kitten, doctor's orders. Nothing for the next two weeks, and then we will reconsider."

"That is absolutely unfair! How am I supposed to go through the next two weeks sleeping by your side and not getting anything? I'll move to another room!" This should do for a threat.

"I'm afraid the other room is in the process of redecoration. You need a studio for your things, and I don't want to send you to another part of the house."

"I could go to the library," I was utterly astonished.

"Nonsense, you need a place of your own and I need to save the family's Meissen collection from your outer space monsters."

Chapter 28

March 21st, 2002

In the past two weeks, I have settled into a kind of schedule. It has not been as bad or boring as before. I have started finally to feel more at home… at least I didn't feel like some kind of precious piece of furniture that nobody knew where to place (and I do not do well in showcases, mind you).

After our last dinner, Konrad stayed for three full days with me before leaving for China. Of course, he refrained from any sexual activities. I hate that doctor. Just a little couldn't hurt me much! But no, he's a pig-headed German, for whom orders are orders; and I should do well in remembering that. On the bright side, he has consented to cuddle in bed every night.

We spent the days walking around, going to a Museum in Zurich, discussing our relationship or in silent companionship. He would leave me alone for a few hours, because he had to check on his affairs, but that was fine with me: I was content to just be able to sit by him and draw.

On Sunday afternoon, he left after making me promise I'd behave. As if I would be able to do anything with my baby-sitters Friedrich, the dragon-in-charge, and Alexei, the infernal Russian. So I "behaved"; ate the food, went to bed early, took my medication and did not complain much.

On Monday, the teacher arrived. To my surprise, it's a she. A tall blonde, with striking blue eyes—before you get excited Diary, let me tell you that she is over forty and has two children, a musician for husband, and a cat. She has left all this behind in Argentina, while she works at Konrad's bank teaching Spanish until September. Her name is Anneliese, of German descent, but who has lived all her life in Buenos Aires. She is quite funny and nice and we got along immediately

German is difficult. I don't know how they manage to speak it! Verb placement seems simply irrational for me. It is either in the second position of the sentence, no matter what you say, or right at the end—so you have to hear the whole sentence before you understand what they want to say. Don't get me started on declinations. Well, maybe that explains why they are how they are. You have to be completely sure of what you want to say before starting to speak, and you have to wait for the other to finish before you can retaliate. The structure is fixed. And he wants me to go to a German speaking University? I'll be glad if I could tell if something is "der", "die" or "das".

I had classes from 9:30 to 12:30 every day, then she would have lunch with me. At 1:30, somebody from the bank would drive her back to Zurich. The rest of the day would be spent in doing the homework she left for next day. Alexei would take me out or to play with the dogs a little bit, since they had grown to a respectable size - Rotweillers, remember? Or I could read or draw a little. Once, Michael came to check everything, and it seemed he was satisfied because he didn't complain at all.

Very late Thursday night, Konrad returned. I was waiting for him at the library like a child, and almost jumped into his arms when I saw him. I was so happy to have him back.

"Missed me, *Maus*?" he asked me, tenderly, as he kissed me holding my face with his hands.

"A lot," I said, blushing deeply as I noticed Friedrich standing at the door. I quickly disentangled myself, but he held me in place.

"What is it?" He growled at the butler.

"When would his Excellency want the car tomorrow?"

"At ten would be fine." Friedrich disappeared leaving a tray with my night pills on the small table by the door.

"No chance that he will forget my medication," I groaned. "I have lessons tomorrow."

"I know. I would like to meet your teacher and see how you're faring."

"So this is an inspection visit. Here I am expecting some romance, and all you'd probably want now is to see my exercise book," I glowered.

"Now that you mention it…"

"No way! I'm an adult," I whined.

"The way you are now, precisely? Let's go to bed, dear."

Yeah, to bed and nothing more; I'm going to kill that doctor!

On Friday, he spoke with the teacher. It seemed she was happy with me, because at ten he was leaving for work relatively satisfied. I sat with her, and started to read today's piece.

"He's very much in love with you," she said to me. I blushed deeply. "He was asking me how you were doing with the classes, but he was more concerned that you were happy this week. You can see in his eyes he worships the floor you step on."

"Does it not disturb you? I mean, two men in love—after all you're married."

"Why should it be? Yes, I'm married with children, but you two have a sound relationship. It's endearing to see two people in love. Now, let's see your University brochures, so you have an idea of what they are offering."

On Saturday, Konrad decided to have our little discussion over my career choices. I couldn't decide between Management and Finance, or Economics with an emphasis on governance and politics.

"Management and Finance is not for you. Most of that is really learnt on the job. The best option for you would be Economics. I believe Ferdinand's daughter, Marie Amélie, will also be attending UZH although she will be in Banking and Finance. Your paths would not cross much."

"All right, then it's decided. I was expecting a bigger disagreement."

"Why should we have had one? Your choices were adequate and reasonable. You are a sensible young man, when the environment is right for you. When you're away from pernicious stimuli, you think clearly."

Was that a compliment? I wasn't sure. And what the hell are "pernicious stimuli"? "I think I don't understand. Are you telling me that I'm easily led by people and have no opinion on my own?"

"No. I only think that all these years of forced solitude in your early years have left you too vulnerable and open. You want to trust people, no matter how much they use or even abuse you. Do I need to remind you about Venice?"

"It's not necessary," I felt depressed that he had such an opinion of me: more or less a mindless doll that would do anything for a pat on the head.

"Guntram, look at me. I'm not thinking less of you because of this. I only

172

recognise that you're too vulnerable, and need protection until you grow thicker skin. You are totally selfless and this is not good for you, because most people will take as much as they can and not care if they hurt you in the process," he said with a hint of sadness. "I love you just the way you are."

"I love you too, even if you are bossy," I replied as I took refuge in his arms, burying my head in his chest.

"I'm a man with strong convictions," he intoned gravely, while cupping my head in his hands.

The worst part is not that he believes it, but that I can't be upset for too long with him even though he's a pig headed, stubborn mule that behaves like a feudal lord. He smiled softly at me, and again I felt myself drool over him. I kissed the palm of his hand.

"Let's take a walk before teatime."

On Monday, he was away to "only Europe" this time; just Frankfurt, Vienna and Milan "to visit Cousin Albert's bank". He would be back on Thursday, so on Friday he could go to the doctor's examination with me. (Honestly, Konrad, I can go alone, I'm not afraid of needles any more. But I didn't press the issue. If Konrad wants to play the knight in shining armour, defending me from a sixty year old doctor, let him be).

As he promised, he was back on Thursday. I had earlier been out with Friederich in Zurich to undergo all the tests needed for my visit to Van Horn. I didn't understand why he needed to get an electrocardiogram; perhaps doctors in Europe also skin private patients' wallets alive.

One of the butlers informed us that Konrad was waiting for me at his studio upstairs. I admit my heart quickened its pace at the news. I almost flew upstairs and had to stop in the middle, as I felt breathless. I have to exercise more it seems. I finished climbing the rest in a more composed manner.

Konrad was sitting behind his desk, writing. I approached him quickly.

"Why are you out of breath?"

"I ran up the stairs. I'm getting old," I laughed.

"You should not do it yet," he scolded me. "Your appointment with the doctor is tomorrow at three. He will see to it."

"I'm feeling perfectly fine. No headaches, double vision or pink elephants flying around."

"That is good to know, but I'm not the one you need to convince. Come, I have something for you and it's quite anxious to come out."

"Really? I can certainly help you," I purred. Maybe I would get lucky, finally.

"Yes, in the Library."

"Honestly Konrad, that isn't hot," I retorted sharply, taken aback by his choice of romantic ambience: Books and tapestries?!

"*Bitte?*" He looked at me, quizzically; then I think he realised what I was thinking. "What were you thinking?" He grinned, making me turn red and feel embarrassed.

"Nothing," I grunted silently, praying that he would not make any witty remarks.

He burst into laughter. "You have a devious mind, little one. It's a gift, and it's not happy in the box."

There in the Library, on the floor, was a big box covered with paper. The box was shaking a little bit. Konrad nudged me to open it.

Inside was a cage with a honey coloured, black-faced, small dog with big eyes—who was none too happy to be in the box.

"It's a pug and she's seven months old. In German we call them *Mops*. Do you like her?"

I took her out of the cage, completely astonished that she would roll like a ball in my arms. Are dogs not supposed to be a little more suspicious of strangers? "She's very cute. Are you really giving it to me?"

"Yes, the dog is yours. You need something to keep you company, apart from your duties in school. I didn't want a puppy to be trained, because that might prove stressful for you—not to mention Friederich's nerves if the dog does it on a rug. She's trained to go to a sand box. She's a house dog, which cannot be left outside for too long."

"Thank you so much. I don't know what to say. I thought you didn't like dogs." The pug had already nestled in my arms and was making happy sounds.

"I like dogs, but they need to stay outside the house. She can remain here but under certain conditions. She sleeps in the kitchen, and that is not open to negotiations; she does not come on top of the bed; she does not eat from our food, and that means that you're not supposed to feed her illegally under the table; and finally, she does not enter my office or bedroom if I'm there. Is that clear?"

"Yes, Konrad," hope I remember the Decalogue for a Well Mannered Dog. "How did you call it in German?"

"*Mops.*"

"Can you call a female dog Mopsi?"

"If she comes when you call her, I think yes."

We sat on the big leather sofa, with Mopsi on my lap (she likes to be petted a lot), as he asked me what I have been doing the past week. I told him about the lessons, my artwork, the doctor's tests and about the appointment I had tomorrow.

"Yes, I had to reschedule it to 3:00, because of some meetings. You would have your morning lessons; then at 12:30, you can drive to Zurich with your teacher, have lunch with me, and visit my offices. Ferdinand was asking me about you today."

I was petrified at the thought of seeing the doctor and all his entourage on their home ground at the same time; but, on the other hand, I was curious to see the bank.

"It would not be so bad, Guntram. You already know most of the most feared characters in the office; Monika, Ferdinand and Michael. The others are just employees."

"Not to mention you," I grinned deviously.

"Me? I'm one of the most loved of all," he retorted smugly, ruffling Mopsi's head in a way she liked at lot. I wonder if he would repeat the favour for me that evening.

* * *

The next morning, I had my German lesson. Then I ran to get changed, so I could share a car with my teacher. There was no way Friederich would allow me to go in a crazy blue sweater, like the one I wore in the morning. I had to go in a tweed jacket, cream shirt with matching tie and light brown trousers. (I swear one of these days I'm going to get a Nirvana T-Shirt or better—Marilyn Mason!). I said goodbye to Mopsi (she had slept peacefully during the whole lesson, lucky girl), and ran to the car.

The bank was located on Börsenstrasse near Bahnhoffstrasse, one of the most expensive streets here. It was not what I'd imagined. I mean, a bank typically has a public area where you have the clerks, ATM's and such things. Well, this did not look like that. It was an impressive five story building, built in the XIX century style with caryatids holding everything in the front, a huge metal door that opened and led to a big foyer with a receptionist, almost like an expensive hotel. My teacher disappeared after murmuring her goodbyes. I gathered my courage, and approached the brunette receptionist.

"Good morning. My name is Guntram de Lisle."

"Good morning, Sir. Somebody will escort you up in a minute."

In the next moment, another woman (this time blonde, tall, elegant and hot looking in her aristocratic way), appeared from a side door and asked me to follow her. We passed a corridor and entered the elevator, which took us to fourth floor. The waiting room was covered in *boisserie*, with elegant furniture in leather, oak and mahogany. There were two impressionists paintings on the walls. She discreetly knocked on one of the doors, and opened it for me. Then she smiled softly and vanished.

Monika's office was big and impressive. She rose from her chair to greet me, even as I asked her to remain seated.

"Dear, you look so well after those two weeks. The Duke is in a meeting for twenty more minutes, but you can wait for him in his office," she gave me two kisses on the cheeks.

"I'm glad to see you as well, Monika. I didn't have the opportunity to thank you for visiting me in the hospital."

"It was my pleasure. Oh, by the way, I have some papers for you to sign relating to the University. I'm so glad you chose Economics. I also have a major in that. You can always ask me anything you want."

I felt foolish for thinking that she was an ordinary secretary with good typing skills.

"Thank you, Monika. I hope I survive it. My German is still not so good."

"You have the advantage of being familiar with the curriculum. You only need to get used to the language. Marie Amélie will also be going with, and maybe she could help you with the translation while you help her with maths."

"It would be the one eyed man leading the blind," I smirked, while she fussed over some folders in her drawer.

"That would already be a great help for Marie Amélie," she mumbled. "Here it is. Sign here and here, please."

"What is this? I don't want to sell my soul to the devil without knowing the price." She musically laughed.

"This set of forms is for a trust fund established for your education. Everything will come out of this account, and its number has already been given to the

UHZ. There is a credit card you can use to pay for books and anything else you might need for your studies. There is also a normal credit card for other things. Your Swiss driver's license is also in this folder; but you're not supposed to use it until you get clearance from the doctor."

I looked at the forms for the trust fund, and was baffled when I saw all the zeros behind the five. Six to be precise. This should be a mistake.

"Monika, are you certain about this amount?"

"The Duke himself did it, but this money can only be used for your education. After you finish, the rest will be returned to his accounts."

"Well, either school here is very expensive or he expects a hyperinflation in the next five years."

"Better to be on the safe side, dear. Who knows, maybe you're a chronic student?" she joked.

"The Duke will kill me if I don't make it in five years," I mumbled, signing the papers. She removed the credit cards from the letters and handed them to me.

"All set then. I think the first books for this semester will arrive next week. You can start reviewing them with your teacher."

"I will. Thank you."

She led me to Konrad's office. Impressive is not strong enough of a word. It had big windows with velvet curtains, *boisserie* all over it and wooden floors. A massively huge desk was placed against the windows, and there were some chairs in front of it. There was also a small sitting area with dark brown leather couches, a private bathroom with everything, a dining room and a small bedroom. "In the past, the Duke used to stay and sleep here often," Monika informed me, as she finished the guided tour and placed me on the couch near the windows. Watching the street was entertaining.

Sometime later, Konrad and Ferdinand entered the room, chatting in German. (I understood three words!), I stood up when they entered. Konrad glanced quickly at me and said that he needed five more minutes to read something, while Ferdinand was nice enough to approach me to shake my hands.

"You look certainly much better. These two weeks, without any hassles, have been good to you."

"Thank you. I've not been seeing pink elephants or biting people any more. Monika told me your daughter will attend the same University as I."

"Yes, we were wondering if we should send her there instead back to her Grandmother in Güstrow. But since you're also attending the University, maybe you can teach some sense into her."

I was about to ask what he meant by that, when Konrad closed a folder quite violently and stood up.

"They're on different careers so they should not meet too much. Let's go for lunch. It's already 1:45. Ferdinand, I'm not retuning after the doctor's visit. Tell Monika to send those documents home this afternoon," he left the room quickly; I almost had to shout my farewells to Ferdinand, as I ran after Konrad, just in time to join him in the elevator.

"Are you upset about something?"

"Not with you; too much work and unproductive meetings. Now we'll go eat, and then go to the doctor's."

As soon as we emerged from the elevator, he spoke briefly to the lady in the hall.

"I hope you don't mind walking. The Königshalle is near and we can cross the bridge, so you can see the Zürichsee. The car will pick us up in an hour."

The Restaurant was old and aristocratic. Yes, I should know by now, that he would not eat at Pizza Hut. The rooms were warm and cosy, and the waiter promptly led us to a table in a secluded part of the room. On the wall, there was a copy of a Chagall. (Well, at least I think it was a copy).

Konrad ordered lunch, as soon as we arrived, without looking at the menu. I didn't complain, as I'm used to eating fish on Fridays, but I was not expecting him to do so. We were eating in peace, when a middle aged man approached the table and formally greeted Konrad. I almost rose, but the sharp look I got from Konrad, and the fact that he didn't move, made me stay frozen in my chair.

"My friend's name is Guntram de Lisle," he sharply answered the man when he asked about me. "He's staying with me," the man paled, and blurted out something in German and disappeared quickly.

"I'm sorry if I embarrassed you, Konrad. There's no need for you to bring me to such a place," I said softly. The last thing I needed was trouble from one of his banker friends.

"This is a small world and every one of us knows the tastes of the other. He's gone because he knows better than to interrupt me during a private conversation. If he wants to do business with me, he should ask for an appointment with Monika. These people from Goldman Sachs think they can burst into our lives just like that. Also, there's no need for you to stand up for them. They're not our equals."

We resumed eating, and were almost finished when a very old man (almost in his eighties), appeared leaning heavily on his cane. Konrad jumped to his feet instantly, and greeted the man in German very humbly, as he made a gesture to the waiter to bring another chair for him.

"*Mein Fürst*, may I present Guntram de Lisle to you?" He reverently asked him. I was already up and extended my hand to him. "Guntram, this is Gustav zu Löwenstein, one of my father's best friends and advisers."

"I'm *honoured* to meet you, *mein Fürst*," I said, bowing my head, as the man took a seat in front of me. He looked at me for a long moment, as if he were judging or gauging me. I held his penetrating gaze and he wisely smiled.

"He is very young Konrad, how old is he?"

"Nineteen, *mein Fürst*," he replied, sheepishly.

"He could be my grandchild! This is really robbing the cradle, my friend!"

"He's quite mature for his age."

"Yes, that might be true. He has the eyes of an ancient soul. I do hope that you live up to his expectations, Konrad. I do not think you could ever find somebody like him."

"Nothing more true, *mein Fürst*," he whispered.

"I'm glad you are staying with Konrad, young man. He can be stubborn as a mule, but that is a family trait. All Lintorffs have been known for it," I was mildly surprised as he patted my hand in a friendly way, almost like a grandfather.

"He's a man of strong convictions," I said with a smile. "I do hope not to disappoint him."

"I think you would not. Are you going to school?"

"I will start Economics this semester at the UHZ."

"I wish you the best of luck, young man. This can be a hard and unforgiving world; and Konrad has many enemies who will do anything to hurt him. They will try to get to him through you."

"Please Gustav, there's no need to frighten the boy with such stories," Konrad interrupted. "He just came out from the hospital due to an attack in Buenos Aires."

"I know. Next time, you should do your job better, Konrad. You should thank God that it was so clumsy and *amateur*," he chastised Konrad sternly, who lowered his gaze in shame. This was the first time I've seen Konrad do this. "You have been the best griffin we have had in decades, so you must be mindful of the dangers. They are ready to battle and will not stop at anything."

"I understand and thank you for your advice, *mein Fürst*. Come Guntram, you need to see your doctor," Konrad said, half rising from the chair, while bowing his head in respect.

I muttered my farewells and shook hands with the elder gentleman again. He smiled and told me to take care of Konrad, because Konrad needed someone who could love him without reservations in the difficult times ahead.

As soon as we were in the car, I asked Konrad what that had all been about. Konrad told me that the man was a little bit senile, but since he was a long-time advisor for his family and almost like a mentor for him, he had to listen to him every time.

"How many enemies do you have and why did he use the word 'battle'?"

"Banking in the international market is a permanent battlefield. That's all. Don't take things so literally. How has Mopsi been behaving so far? Has she already destroyed my socks?"

"Not quite. She was sleeping during my German lessons, and even snoring," I chuckled.

We arrived at the Clinic and went into the Doctor's examination room. I sat nervously in front of him, as he checked me thoroughly. Then he asked me to get dressed again and to go into his office.

When I entered his office, Konrad and the Doctor were already speaking in German. I sat next to Konrad.

"You are much better indeed, but you still need two more weeks of absolute rest. Your heart condition has improved, but we have to avoid any kind of stress."

"I'm afraid there's a mistake. I had a concussion—in the head," I clarified.

"Yes, neurologically you're fine and have no repercussions there. However, you went into cardiac arrest during the surgery. Hence, you must take things very lightly and not force yourself to do anything too strenuous. A young man's heart can recover very quickly; and since it was trauma induced, you should have no problems —if you take your medication and give it time. This means that you should engage in moderate exercise like walking, get lots of fresh air, eat healthily and abstain from sex or driving for the moment."

"Why hasn't anybody told me anything?"

"Guntram," Konrad said, as he held my hands gently. "I thought it was better not to worry you more. It was my decision, and I hoped I've not angered you because of it. Now that your heart condition has improved, the doctor and I have thought it best to let you know."

"We nearly lost you twice that week," the doctor chimed in softly. "Now, take it easy, please. The dangerous phase is past and you don't need to worry yourself with it any further. Please take your medication, follow my advice, and everything will be fine again in no time."

I stood up like a machine, still shocked by the facts. Konrad told me to wait outside in the car for him and I obeyed without thinking. I whispered my thanks to the doctor and left the room, feeling like I was walking on a cloud.

Goran was waiting for us next to the car. (Don't ask me where he had come from. I don't know. He can appear and disappear just like that.).

"Are you all right, Guntram? Was everything OK with the doctor?" he asked me, with real concern.

"Did you know I had a heart attack?"

"Yes, but you seemed to be recovering from it. We nearly lost you at that point."

"Why didn't anybody say something? It's my life after all."

"Because you were in a coma, and the Duke didn't want to make you more anxious. He even made me look for a dog, so you could relieve some of your stress. Animals can be very good for such things."

I was rendered speechless. Goran opened the door for me, and I entered Konrad's regular black armoured Mercedes limousine. Konrad's a fanatic for this Mercedes Guard collection and everything he normally uses belongs to them. I suppose he wants to support his own country's industry, not to mention the Porsches or the BMWs also used by the staff. Yes, I know I'm blabbering but it helps me to calm down.

Some minutes after, Konrad entered the car and sat beside me. Goran closed the door and went to sit with the driver, as Konrad activated the privacy shield between us and the driving area.

"Are you upset because I didn't tell you?"

"I'm still too shocked to be upset with you."

He took my hand and kissed my fingers, and I pulled away from the contact. "I couldn't lose you again. I feared that your knowledge of the heart attack would hinder your recovery. I'm sorry if I hurt you with my silence. I did it with the best intentions."

"You even got me a dog. Wonder if it had been summer, would you have put a dolphin in the swimming pool?" I trailed completely, indifferent to his talk.

"You are not making any sense, Kitten. Do you feel well?"

"I'm perfectly fine, as the doctored just confirmed."

"No need to be sarcastic. It's unbecoming for you."

"Since I met you, I have been involved in a drug case, beaten several times and even raped by you, been in a coma for a week, and suffered one or two heart attacks. I think you are 'unbecoming' for me. My previous life was boring and poor, but at least it was not killing me," I said, calmly, not caring at all if Konrad was going to explode. I was tired of his tantrums, and started to have a headache.

He didn't say anything, and I was glad for his silence. We arrived home and I didn't wait for the chauffeur to open the door. I just bolted out, and went straight to the kitchen to pick Mopsi up and went out again for a walk. Finally, I sat with Mopsi on my lap on a bench under some trees, caressing her head.

Suddenly she jumped out of my arms and ran to Konrad, who was approaching us. Great! Even the dog is on his side.

"Guntram, come home. It's too cold for you in your condition. If you want to yell at me, you can do it inside."

"It makes no sense to yell at you. It's useless. You'll find a way to twist my words, and then I will look like the bad guy who makes you suffer. The difference is that this time, there will be no make-up sex because I might have a heart attack, and dropping dead while fucking is also 'unbecoming'."

"Then I'll say nothing until you feel better and we can speak."

"It makes no sense to speak with you. You'll always have the upper hand. You're cleverer and more twisted than I will ever be. I can only wait until you tire of me and discard me. The worst part is how I'm going to survive without your love. Yes, even if you are a heartless selfish bastard, I'm in love with you and can't leave you even though it should be the best thing for me to do. Love can be more destructive than hate."

"I'm trying to change my ways. I didn't lie to you. I just kept the facts out, until you were in better shape," he defended himself, looking somewhat offended.

"Konrad, we both know very well that you will not change. You're too set in your ways."

"I really want your happiness even if you don't believe me. Come home with me. This is not good for you. I'm a man with many responsibilities and I make life altering decisions every day. I have learnt to live with this power and the best I can do is to carefully evaluate all my decisions, with the greater good in mind. When I look at you or when you smile at me in the mornings, I know that all the rubbish I have to cope with might account for something. Can you really blame me, and punish me, for willing to keep safe what I love most?"

"Konrad, you have to stop treating me like a child," I pleaded holding his hands but he disentangled from my grip and took my hands to kiss them. I pried them open violently away from him, and stuffed them in my pockets. "No, enough. Save me the customary tender moment, in which you hold me so I can feel protected in your arms," I said, dryly. He seemed to be taken aback. For a second more or less, he looked like he was planning the counter-attack. How long was it going to take? Two minutes? Three, if he felt trapped?

"All right Guntram. Do as you like. I'll take the dog back home. It's too cold for such a delicate animal," he replied seriously, picking up Mopsi. "Feel free to come to the house whenever you want," he went away.

I sat on that bench for a very long time. Until it was dark and much colder. He's a spoiled brat; a selfish child who, by some whim of fate, has taken a liking in me most probably because I look like his past lover—the one who really put him in his place. I wonder if he had been as nasty as described, because Konrad is not an angel. Anyhow, that is not my problem because he's not here to take my place and even if he were, I know I wouldn't let him have it.

Even if Konrad would agree to let me go back to my old life, I could not live without him. I realise that now and have to face it. On the days Konrad was away, I spent the hours counting the minutes between our appointed calls and secretly hoping that I would hear his footsteps in the corridor. I tried to tell myself that it was only the blinding flash of discovering sex with him, but the last two weeks without any made me realise that it was the cuddling after it, the soft kisses, the kind talk and his adoring eyes that I needed like a drug. I often felt I was doing that stupid, boring German homework, thinking it would please him and longing for a compliment from him.

"Je suis apprivoisé", said the fox to the Little Prince while it cried, because it would be left behind for the rose. I would not survive for too long without him, because he makes me feel alive and free.

It's getting colder by the minute. It's time to go home.

Chapter 29

"Are you all right?" Konrad asked me, looking concerned when I entered the house.

"Yes, everything is fine. I would like to check my e-mails if it's OK with you. I'll meet you later," I said softly, going directly to the stairs, not removing my coat.

"We dine at eight," he stated, intently looking into my eyes. I held his gaze.

"Can you please call me?"

"Certainly."

I climbed the stairs up and went into Konrad's room foyer. I still can't get used to the idea it's our bedroom. I went into the former guest room, now transformed into a small studio for me with an incredible desk and chair, two big closed bookshelves and a showcase with my Star Wars collection. It was funny to see the expression on Friederich's face when he saw it. More or less like the Romans seeing the Barbarians for the first time, a huge contrast to the almost rapt cry of happiness from Heindrik when he saw the Argentinean version from Top Toys, still in the original box. Yes, the Swedish is also a fan, and since he's 28 years old and the former baby of the pack, he can do it without suffering the scornful looks from the others. He even offered to lend me his copy of Episode 1 to make the wait for Episode 2 bearable.

I sat at my desk and saw that I still had half an hour before dinner. I could read my e-mails. It's funny how many people from the school who I was not aware, knew about my existence and wrote me to wish me well. Almost my whole class wrote, even Laucha (mouse) whom we never knew if he could do it because his only interest in life was horses and polo... playing *pato* also. I had no news from Federico and nobody mentioned him ever, so I preferred to close that chapter in my life.

I got an e-mail from Juan Dollenberg, my friend from school.

"Guntram, old thing. Hope you're getting better. This Easter I'm going to ski in Como at Luciana's cousin house. Yes, it's a full invasion of their property. I've noticed that I would be only 250 kms from Zurich and I wonder if I could visit you for the day just to check everything is still in place. In addition Luciana threatened me with killing me slowly if I don't do it and thank you for the Juan Ignacio's present. You have no idea how bossy women can be when they become mothers! Her secret plan also includes that I steal several paintings, drawings or whatever you have for a Russian, who likes your work and pays handsomely Luciana to redecorate his new elegant house in London.

My brother is still in Argentina working for the Duke, visiting Estancias and checking on cows. He will meet us in London by April when he gets a position in the office here. The baby is doing fine, and he's almost a month old. I have to play the responsible uncle and take care of him when she's out.

Best wishes, Juan."

A soft knock on the door made me jump a little when I was pondering what to answer him. Perhaps we could meet in Zurich. "Come in," I said expecting Friederich or one of the other butlers. It was Konrad.

"Are you busy?"

"No, not at all. Just looking at an e-mail from Juan, Pablo Dollenberg's brother," I clarified almost rising from the chair to be sat again under Konrad's palm weight over my shoulder.

"I remember him. His brother works with Landau in acquisitions and later he will go to the London office. They need someone in personnel. What does he tell?"

"He will be at Como for Easter and wants to know if we could meet in Zurich for a day."

"You should ask him to stay here for a few days. It would be good for you to have some young company. He could come for Easter Sunday. I always give a lunch after the Mass for the bank employees."

"I was not aware of that. Even so, it's in ten days!"

"He can come on Saturday and leave on Monday or Tuesday if he wants. On Friday, we have the Via Crucis, and it's only for the closest entourage. You can come to the Mass but have to go away afterwards since you are not part of the order."

"I never imagined that you took the Church seriously," I whispered utterly astonished. Konrad following the Catholic Church teachings?

"It's an important part of my life. I obey and defend their rules. The blood of Christ was shed for us and we have to defend his kingdom."

"We are not exactly following the rules, Konrad. When I was in Buenos Aires, I tried to go to confession, but I couldn't do it because I can't repent of our sin. Father Patricio told me I should mend my ways, but if I could not do it, I should not sully the Sacraments. I know it's wrong what we do and will not last. How can you go to Mass knowing you're almost rolling in sin?"

"We can't fight our natures Guntram. I love you and you should give more credit to the Church. It's more tolerant than you imagine and would not abandon you, even if you think so. A father never leaves his children. The Church even accepted that two men could celebrate a union contract, 'rites of twinning' were called if we believe Bowles until the XIII century. It was not a marriage or consecrated, but it was accepted."

"Yes, and in the XIV century they burned the Templars for heresy and being gay," I retorted.

"They were absolved of those crimes in 1308 by Pope Clement V according to the Chinon Manuscript, made public a year ago. It was the king of France, after the brotherhood's properties, the one who set the flames afire. Have any of my men ever treated you wrongly or contemptuously?"

"Never. However, they know better than to enter in a direct fight with you because they challenged your opinion."

"How I wish it were true, so I didn't have to hear Ferdinand's rants every day!" He laughed. "The only reason they don't question my choice of companion is because I support a traditional lifestyle and don't run around insulting the traditional concept of family. Furthermore, you have most of the virtues desired for a good mate. If you were a girl, I would have to spend the whole day fighting with them. They are happier with you here than when I was banging everything that moves."

He made me blush with his sentence's brutality and judging by his past performance, Friederich must have had a hard time cleaning after Konrad's messes.

"As I said you can attend the Mass on Friday, so all the others can meet you, but you have to leave after because we have to celebrate our meeting."

"I'm still not sure of what you say, but I do hope God will forgive me in the end," I sighed.

"God is more generous than men," he said simply, his words piercing directly my heart. Not realising, I have leant towards his face and softly kissed him in the lips. He not only returned the kiss and deepened it, forcing me to open my mouth for his tongue to enter. He pressed his body against me, trapping me against the back of the chair with his two hands on the armrests. I latched my hands from his neck pulling him more towards me, enjoying his scent and the softness of his lips.

He abruptly interrupted the kiss. "Guntram we have to stop before I throw you in the bed and do something more than kissing. The doctor totally forbids me to lay a finger on you for two weeks," he admitted looking utterly abashed.

"This is really unfair!" I whined like a child. "I do want to make love with you. I'm about to explode."

"Do you think I don't want it too? I will not risk you to be sick again. So let's have dinner and watch a film before going to sleep."

"Yeah, Bambi or Dumbo," I smirked still pissed with the world or better with the stupid doctor and this stupid German in my bed who does everything "by the book".

"You look adorable when you sulk."

* * *

March 29th 2002. Good Friday

I was almost sent away for the entire day, with Alexei as Chaperone. He's orthodox and got stuck with me; catholic but not a member of the Mighty Knights of the Iron Cross Order or whatever they call themselves nowadays. Honestly, I was glad I was shipped away in a nice Porsche Cayenne, which I can admire but not touch or much less drive The whole house was invaded early in the morning by black Mercedes, BMWs, Audis or other expensive brands alongside with a battalion of bodyguards. Nope, you would not see a Fiat or a Lada parking here.

I was surprised that of the thirty or forty guests... zero were women. Yes, these guys never heard the "equal opportunity employer" motto. They were very, very serious and aristocratic to no end. I saw briefly Ferdinand and Michael and somewhere Albert, Konrad's cousin speaking with the zu Löwenstein man. I was introduced to several of the younger members (in their mid-forties) and sat at the Mass beside Michael because Konrad was in the front of the family chapel with his older crones. I expected them to be arrogant and prissy to me but in fact they were distant in a kind way, looking curiously at me.

Since it's Good Friday any entertainment is out of the question, Alexei took me to Lucerne for lunch and to see the city. Yes, at 11:30 a.m., we were thrown out after the ceremony by Ferdinand. "Guntram, you can go now", he said.

I can take a hint. I looked around to say goodbye to Konrad, but he was immersed deeply in a conversation with four or five persons. I know better than to interrupt him or talk over a Crown Prince. Somebody touched my arm and it was the Russian.

"Ready to escape?" He chuckled as he led me to the car, a nice Porsche which he drives all by himself.

"More than ever. McDonald's?" Yes, I'm dying for that fine example or the Western decadence, and he also should be if it's true what they write on the Times; Russians sell their souls for jeans and burgers. I don't care if I'm still in a dark suit. I want to get out as soon as possible. Maybe I could pass for a Goth.

"It's Good Friday. You're not supposed to eat meat."

"I know. There's something called Fish Burger."

"OK, but no meat. I don't want troubles with the Duke and no fries also. Bad for the heart."

"All right Caesar Salad and fish burger it is," I sighed. It's better than nothing.

"Good boy. I'll get the double meat," he replied, snidely.

"Suit yourself. I'll get a big one on Saturday when Juan arrives, and I don't care about cholesterol or sodium levels."

"If I let you do it. You have to ask permission to Goran. Be nice and maybe I will accept to be your baby sitter for the rest of the year."

"You? No way; Heindrik or Goran."

"Goran has better things to do despite, he wanted the job. He's operations officer and Heindrik is too young for the job. So, the Duke chose me to take you to school."

"You have to be kidding," I said nervously. Am I supposed to go hand in hand with a Siberian Ape to School? What is he going to do, shoot the teacher if he yells at me?

"No, I'm serious. We're stuck together, boy. In a way I'm glad I have the chance to fix the mess from Buenos Aires. After all you were under my care."

"You didn't give me the concussion. Four or five poor devils did it."

"I should have seen the signs earlier after all I'm a trained officer from the Soviet Army," he told me visibly disturbed at what he considered his own fault.

"I thought you were in the KGB."

"That was later. Since we are going to be together, and I know all your backgrounds." (Yeah, I know; you read my file) "Maybe you should know a little more about me. I was born in Leningrad, St. Petersburg now, in 1967. I went to military school and in 1985 was sent to Afghanistan with the special forces. I remained there until February 1989 and was one of the last to leave. I was recruited by KGB in Afghanistan and worked for many years as an analyst for South Asia, specialized in counter-terrorism. The collapse of the URSS left us very weak and many in the military and secret service went into the weapons selling business. By 1995, I had enough of my country politics and decided to go away. It was not easy to resign, but finally I managed to do it, pulling favours and contacts. I moved to Berlin and there I met Michael, who offered me a job as bodyguard for the Duke. I took it and since then I have a much easier life than before."

I was startled. Did I have a guy sitting next to me, "specialized," In Taliban? Bring back the old KGB agent. Afghanistan was a living hell according to newspapers.

"How many languages do you speak?"

"Russian, German, English, Persian or Dari, Pashtun, Arab and a bit of Chinese, but not much," he shrugged as it would be the most normal thing in the world.

"Do you have a family in Russia?" I murmured completely overwhelmed.

"No, parents deceased many years ago and never had time to settle down and form a family. In my line of work, you're happy if you get an honest whore who doesn't sell you in the morning. Who knows, maybe now?" he dreamingly told me.

"Yes, I've seen many nice looking girls at the bank."

"I'm after the cook, Jean Jacques. I think you know him."

Second surprise of the day. He, gay? I would have never guessed. The cook I know is a small grey man, who doesn't speak and only cook. Unnoticeable. If you ask me his eyes' colour, or what he looks like I can't tell.

"You know, the way to a man's heart is through his stomach," he chuckled.

"Will you have no problems for that? I mean you work together."

"None. Ferdinand allowed me to ask him for a date before I did anything. All is very recent."

"Any luck?"

"A lot but these French men are hard to catch. Very independent for their own sake. He's not a lad any more and should settle down with me."

"Alexei Gregorevich you're starting to sound like your boss," I laughed.

"The Duke is an intelligent man. He liked what he saw and immediately took it before somebody else would come, or you'd start to look around. He's an excellent strategist."

"Yes, there was such a planning behind," I laughed bending over myself. "Go to San Marco and pick up the only one who was not moving because he was reading and cornered by doves! Honestly, it's not one of the most brave conquests I've heard of."

He only gave me a knowing smile, concentrating hardly on the driving. I felt my stomach flutter from nerves.

* * *

At seven, Alexei decided he had enough of Lucerne and put me in the car without asking. We drove in silence for almost an hour. When we arrived to the house, the cars amount had decreased, but there were still about ten of them. Excellent! The dinosaurs were still here. Well, tomorrow Juan comes and I would enjoy some young people time.

I said good night to Alexei, who, by the way, is quite a funny guy once you overcome your more than justifiable fear to have such a man beside you. He took me for a walk around the city and for the promised fish burger. He told me about his time in Afghanistan (the edited version, of course), his travels to Iran, Iraq and several African countries. Maybe and just maybe, it would not be so bad to have him around, and it's not like I have any other choice in the matter.

I avoided the main living room where all the super mighty men were shaping the world to their tastes and climbed upstairs after a quick expedition to the kitchen to fetch Mopsi. "The dog should not go in the bedroom," Friederich warned me. I went into my studio to play with her. She's such a nice dog.

"Don't wait up, Guntram. It might take very long until they're finished." Friederich told me as he entered in the room carrying a tray with dinner. "She was very nervous the whole day without you and with so many people in the house." Mopsi went to him, shaking her tail as he knelt down to pat her.

"Thank you, Friederich. Too many hassles today?" I said attacking dinner, which consisted of a soup and chicken with some greens. Back to hospital food, it seems.

"The usual but everything went fine. The Duke seemed pleased."

"Must be difficult to keep all these important men happy. I was surprised that none of them was nasty or scornful of me. Distant, yes."

"The *Fürst* zu Löwenstein spoke well of you, and if he accepts you, nobody here would challenge his opinion."

"But he only saw me for ten minutes! How can he have an opinion of me!" I protested, very shocked.

"More than enough time. He's an excellent character judge. Most of them are distant to you because they still don't know, which would be your place in the order, I mean, scheme of things," he corrected himself in no time.

"They should not worry. The Duke clearly said "stay out of my business" and I know better than to contradict him," I said, as a matter of fact. "The least I want in this life is to get in the middle of a banker's mud fight."

"I'm glad for that," he enigmatically said. "Don't feed the dog under the table. The Duke will not approve it," he scolded me, as if I were a small child.

"All right," I mumbled upset.

"To bed with you. Tomorrow, your friend arrives and you were already running around in Lucerne. The doctor said you have to take things easy. I'll take the dog downstairs if you want so."

"No need to. I'll do it in half an hour." This is too much mothering if you want to know. I'm not made of porcelain. I continued to eat in silence a bit upset.

"Alexei will take you tomorrow to the train station to pick up Mr. Dollenberg. You should be ready to leave at 10 a.m. The Duke wants to have lunch with you both at 1 p.m.," I had to self restrain a groan at the news. Good bye, Mc Donald's or any kind of burger. "He will be staying in the yellow guest room on the other wing of the castle." Well, you got a good one, Juan. "On Sunday the Mess is at 10 a.m. and the Easter Lunch is at 12:30 p.m. Mr. Von Kleist's children have been invited. The elder one is Karl Otto, 24, finished Banking and Finance at the UHZ and will go to Harvard for a MBA. The second one is Johannes, 22, studies Chemistry in Frankfurt and the younger one is Marie Amélie, 18 and she has just finished high school in Lausanne. Coffee time is at 4 p.m. I have placed you and your friend with them at the table."

I wonder if the Germans would be so happy like myself at being stuck with me for a whole day. Who knows, maybe we can all look for the hidden eggs in the 60 acres garden! Most probably they order them from Fabergé.

"Ms. Leyden sent today the plane ticket for Mr. Dollenberg's return on Monday evening to London. His brother will pick him up at Gatwick."

"Thank you, Friederich. I'll write to him about the planning," I said through gritted teeth.

The bossy butler went to the bedroom to organise who knows what as I was left with the dog, not hungry any more Well Guntram, think positive. Juan got a really good room, we have Monday to ourselves and the young Germans don't have to be a carbon copy of the father.

At ten, I hit the pillow, really tired. I hadn't realised the short trip had exhausted me so much. I could always walk like crazy, but today was too much for my taste. Perhaps that blasted doctor was right, and I needed to take things easy, for the moment.

At a very late hour, Konrad appeared and went into the bed, softly kissing me and telling me to sleep.

Chapter 30

March 31st, 2002 Easter Sunday

Saturday

Early in the morning, at eight to be precise, I woke up, got dressed and kissed Konrad goodbye because he was still sleeping, almost dead, in bed. Yeah, this happens if you party all night long with Dinosaurs!

I went to the kitchen to have breakfast and check on Mopsi. Who knows maybe I could convince Alexei to take her with us. I think the servants were a little shocked that I would be there. Friederich made me sit in the room reserved for the bodyguards, the former guards' hall to eat with them and not with the cleaning girls.

At 9:30 Alexei arrived but he went to the kitchen, and we know now what he was looking for in there. I told Friederich to leave Konrad sleeping, and he agreed with me. "The Duke had meetings up to four in the morning. It was a very stressful day."

The Russian drove me again to the train station where we waited for Juan at the platform. He looked exactly as I remembered from school. Tall, unruly dark hair, lanky with blue eyes. Always with a happy and carefree look but a real sharp man when things became serious. He was informally dressed and carrying a rucksack and his snowboard.

"Guntram! You are still alive!" Was his cheerful greeting.

"Yes, I'm still around. They sent me back from Heaven. It was crowded at the moment," I retorted as we started to walk down towards the car. He didn't let me help him with the bags.

"You are sure it was Heaven? You look well but different, old thing."

"You look almost respectable now that you're an uncle."

"Wait until you see the baby's photos. He's too cute to be my brother's son. He must take after the mother or uncle. Luciana and Pablo send their greetings and Maria, remember Martiniano's wife, the one who cooks? She sent you a big home made *dulce de leche* (caramel candy) glass. The custom's police almost seized it when they controlled us."

"I believe you. It's virtually impossible to smuggle food into Switzerland. You have to buy here all your groceries."

"I read the programme for the festivities. Good you told me in advance. I could steal a tie and a jacket from a distant cousin. The whole thing looks very serious."

"Wait and see, Juan. At least you'll get a decent meal now."

"That's good news. How's everything here for you?"

"I'm fine. Adjusting to the "rich and famous" lifestyle, which is not my case."

"I'm still shocked from what my brother told me."

"I understand if you don't approve my relationship with Konrad," I said softly feeling a hard constriction at my throat.

189

"*What? No*, it's not that. I'm very happy that motherfucker of Martiarena didn't get his way with you. I'm just surprised that the same old Guntram, who was always so quiet, defending his corner, threw everything away, moved to another country, started to live in sin with an older man and looks so glad about it," he defended himself as I felt very embarrassed with his description of my last exploits.

"My brother spoke very well of Lintorff. Even if he's imposing like my grandfather was, he's a true gentleman and Pablo thinks that you two are perfect for each other."

"We had our fights, Juan. It's not so easy to live with someone."

"Tell that to my brother and her formerly very pregnant wife! We all have ups and downs."

"And you, lover boy... Do you have a British girlfriend?"

"Nothing so far. The girls in the school are nice looking, but don't want a German Gaucho."

Alexei was waiting for us in the car, the monster Porsche again. He placed the bags in the back with ease, telling Juan to go to the front and I to the back seat. We drove in peace to the house, Juan pestering the Russian with questions about Moscow and St. Petersburg. I think he's planning his summer holiday there.

Friederich greeted and led us to the assigned room for Juan, another servant taking the bags. Yes, he has retired from such as menial thing and only pilots the house... with an iron fist.

"His Excellency will see you at lunch in the small dinning room. He's working at his private studio," he informed us gravely before leaving us alone. So Konrad is up and already messing around since he doesn't want us nearby. Well, somebody woke up cranky today if he sends Friederich to keep us at bay. Hope he's nicer in an hour.

"Wow, he's more impressive than the old headmaster at school. Remember him?"

"How could I forget him? He was always telling Fedérico off, and I got several times, parts of the heat," I sighed.

"Did you hear about his car accident?"

"No. When was it?" I was surprised as a pang of fear hit me in the stomach. "Was he hurt?"

"Not much. The idiot was into an illegal car race and hit full force a tree. The one at his side wasn't that lucky, got killed," he told me.

"I knew nothing about it. When was it?"

"More or less around beginning of March. One Saturday night, coming after nightclubbing with some other guys from school. Laucha told me that it was a miracle he survived."

"Was it so bad?" I was now horrified. Yes, I know Fedérico is an asshole to put it mildly, but he didn't deserve such bad luck.

"Imagine, driving at 130 km. on an avenue at 3 a.m. Another car had the green light and crossed his path and Fedérico made a turn to avoid it. Well, he had always good reflexes because he could go to the breaks to slow down and manoeuvre. Nevertheless, he couldn't avoid crashing against a tree. The one who died had not the seat belt on and was launched through the wind shield. Laucha was there, also racing and saw it. Fedérico got several ribs broken, one arm and a leg The other car vanished after the crash, and I don't blame the driver because he or she was not guilty."

"Do we know him, the dead one?" I was slowly processing everything. Could it be possible such a bad coincidence? No, it was an accident. Fefo always liked to drive fast but what was doing a car at 3 a.m. there and why didn't it stay?

"I don't know her name. Laucha told me it as a girl from the pub," he shrugged. "Really bad months February and March. First you and then him. The rest of the class is still alive. Anyway I don't know much about the whole mess because I was in London. Laucha told me the story briefly because he was just making a stop at Heathrow before flying to Dubai."

"Dubai? What is he doing there? Hunting camels?"

"No, playing polo for a Sheik or whatever, they're called there. Very rich guy who wants to have his own polo team and ordered one from Argentina, including the horses. Laucha has been professionally playing for the last two years and has a good handicap, so he got the job. He's making a lot of money, although he complains about the lack of booze and hot girls there. Can you imagine? The children of this man, our age more or less, come to Switzerland with a private jet if they want to have ice cream or chocolate. Sprüngli is the place in Zurich. Now you know where the rich and famous go, eh? Wanna give it a try?"

"It should be on Monday because tomorrow is big eggs hunting," I replied, mind absently, trying to keep my growing sense of concern at bay. Did I or did I not imagined all the things I heard in Buenos Aires? Was the concussion so big or not? Konrad's employees' CV's were not exactly fitting the Missionary Church, and he had already threatened "to settle the matter" but to go to the extend of direct attacking with the intention to kill was too much. And what happened with the five guys who attacked me?

"Hey, Earth to Guntram. Spacing away? Some things never change with you."

"I'm sorry. I was trying to process what you just told me. Poor Federico. I'm really sorry for him."

"You were not exactly on holidays. Did he call you or send an e-mail? Because I know for certain he knows. I told him myself when my brother broke the news to me, but he almost told me to fuck off."

"Yeah, we didn't depart on best terms. We had some troubles in Venice," I murmured not really willing to get into that particular mess again.

"I know the story. You, the great International Drugs Lord. Federico told the story to me like the pussy he is. Come on, Guntram, do you really think I believe it? It's hilarious. My God, you would take the cocaine for flour," he chuckled.

"I'm not so stupid. I know what it is," I retorted slightly pissed off that everybody believes I'm such an idiot. "Please, mind your language in front of Konrad. He's pretty old fashioned."

"All right, I'll put my best "grandfather present" behaviour on. Don't worry, I'll behave. After all he's my brother's supreme boss. Do you need some lessons for swearing in German?"

I laughed this time hard. "Not at the moment. I wouldn't know where to place the verb."

"OK, you miss it." He winked mischievously. "We eat at one, right? Because it's almost time and I have to get ready."

"Yes, I'm sorry. I'll see you downstairs."

"Leave me a map. Don't want to end in the dungeons."

"A clever architect should be able to find his way," I chuckled. Darn, I have missed the daft bantering from school days.

I went to Konrad's rooms to wash my hands and look for the noon pill before Friederich would come charging after me with the thing. Konrad's studio door was closed, and I know better than to enter into the Lion's den without invitation.

Downstairs I sat at one of the foyer chairs and was mildly surprised that Juan was now looking like a gentleman with a jacket and not any longer the rap boy from the train station.

"Hey posh boy. You were serious about changing your clothes," I said, playfully.

"You are one to talk! What are you wearing? Armani?"

"No idea at all," I confessed. Some English tailor made it. "Should we go to the dining room and wait there?"

"Lead the way."

We entered the room but didn't sit, waiting for Konrad. Juan was really interested in the house, asking for construction details and the alterations done to Friederich, who was more than happy to answer and even offered a guided tour later.

At 1:05, Konrad entered in the room, informally dressed.

"I'm sorry for my delay, Mr. Dollenberg. I hope your stay here has been pleasant so far," he said offering his hand to Juan.

"Thank you very much for your invitation, *mein Herzog*. Guntram and I were catching up with the gossip so far," he intoned, shaking hands with him and slightly bowing the head. Yeah, that's the way to go. Acknowledge the Alpha here.

"Good morning, Konrad. Juan told me Fedérico had a big car accident."

"I'm sorry to hear that Mr. Dollenberg. Is he all right?" he said looking completely surprised but not concerned.

"He's still in one piece but running at 130 km on a street is an accident waiting to happen." Juan said. "Beginning of March it was. He will make it through."

"That's good news. Shall we sit?" he said dismissing the matter as if it had no importance. Maybe I'm blowing all out of proportion, after all at such speed even a small stone can cause a disaster.

The conversation revolved around the house, Juan's studies and life in London, and I was peacefully eating until my good friend decided it was time to trap me.

"My sister in law works now for a famous interior decorator in Chelsea. She's redecorating the house in Kensington of a Russian who wants it in the "Pampa Style" and it seems she knows what it is. Guntram, Luciana told me very clearly not to return without some drawings from you."

"There's not much to show at the moment. I've been out of business for the last weeks."

"I'm afraid Luciana plans to put you to work and a recently mother woman can be very insistent. The thing is that this Russian saw one or two of your drawings of La Candelaria at the shop she used to work at. He fell in love, and I mean it, with them. He offered a lot of money for them but Pablo didn't want to sell them because they were our grandfather's. So he offered Luciana to work for him, but he would like to have something more from you—Pampas landscapes, animals, whatever you have."

Konrad was looking at him very interested, and I thought it was time to interfere.

"Juan I can give you what I've done so far so this Russian will leave Luciana alone. Even so, give them to him after she's paid."

"That would be fantastic. She offers to share 40/60 with you. He was so insistent that she framed," there he chuckled "parts of my art class sketching folder, the ones you made for me—the fruits, the animals we had to sketch that time we went to the Zoo and the ballerinas."

"Well I don't know if I can be part of an international Art scam," I laughed. "Even if the man is rich, don't over-do it. I'll give you whatever I have before it finishes in the trash can."

"Do you know his name, Mr. Dollenberg?" Konrad asked his gaze fixed on Juan.

"The Russian's name is Oblomov. He's into steel and oil. He just came to London. He's convinced that you're a mature artist, like eighty years old because of your classical technique."

I burst into laughter and Juan joined me. Me? Classical technique? Yeah, sure. "Honestly Juan, I don't know Luciana, but she should sell nothing from me to him. The poor man obviously knows nothing about painting."

"Or he knows a lot," Konrad said sternly. He knows certainly how to kill the mood. "I think exactly the same about Guntram's technique. I'm surprised that he even had a style at such an early age."

"Konrad, my only fan thinks I'm eighty. I'll look for something but you must promise not to charge him for the paintings."

"All right. Nevertheless, Luciana will charge him for the frames and share with you. She's already started to save money for the baby's university," Juan replied with a laugh.

"As I said many times, you should consider painting professionally. Rule number one in life: if someone wants to pay, don't deny him the pleasure to do so."

"But Konrad, with all due respect, I would be almost cheating him. I'm no artist at all," I explained to him.

"Don't underestimate Russians. He knows better and if he likes it, let him get it. I still don't understand why you have such a low opinion of your own work," he grunted.

"Guntram was always very shy. At school, he almost never spoke or got into the normal rabble behaviour. He remained in his corner, drawing, quiet, doing his work and nothing else. I think I never saw somebody so sad in my whole life. The only times when he looked "normal" were when he was with his pencil box. He was only going out of school when the class had a field trip because nobody was ever taking him out."

"Juan, I don't think this is the moment to discuss your opinion of my social life at school," I advised with a dark voice, upset, he would say such things here.

"It's true and you know it. This man has been after your paintings since seven months ago. He wanted to buy our house but Pablo didn't sell it because he didn't take the servants. He lacked the feudal touch," I threw a side glance to Konrad to see if he was upset by the remark, but he was visibly amused. "I even asked

Fedérico to tell you because after school you broke any contact with all of us. But you never replied to any of my e-mails or phone calls from my brother."

"He never told me," I whispered totally puzzled. Why would have Fedérico not passed the message along? He knew I was in need of extra money. I focused on my dish, wishing they could find someone else to pester.

"I believe most of Guntram's older drawings are stored somewhere here. You can pick something from there. Since his accident, he has not worked too much per doctor's orders. I remember a series of drawings from children and a dog which are very good. This is an opportunity he should not let pass." Konrad settled the matter just like that not even asking my opinion.

Fortunately, we had peace for the rest of the day, walking around and looking for the bloody drawings. It seemed Konrad ordered all my things to be moved here and the paintings were coming by private courier when I was in a coma. At 3:00, Konrad decided that I was tired (OK, true, but I'm old enough to know), and sent me to rest for an hour.

"Yes, you look tired. Don't worry. I will not tell all the horror stories I know from school," Juan said merrily.

Yes, clear. It's not you who're going to go to the pillory. On the other hand, I didn't want to have the classical babies' fight: "I don't want to go to bed".

At five, Friederich woke me up and informed me Konrad and Juan decided to go to Zurich to have coffee and dinner, and asked if I wanted to come along also. When I was leaving the room, he caught me and gave me the night pills in a small box. No, Friederich never forgets anything.

Konrad and Juan were speaking lively in German in the library, sitting on the sofas. Well, no problems so far.

"Come Guntram, let's go away before Friederich and Jean Jacques throw us out. They have to organise everything for tomorrow."

"Hi Juan. How many people have you invited, Konrad?"

"The usual, about 250 people with children and wives included. It's every year the same. I do hope this time we don't get the rabbits inside the house."

"Did you invite rabbits?" I asked innocently.

"They are for the children. Young people like them a lot and keep the smaller ones busy and not meddling with the adults. I cannot expect children to sit at a table for hours after behaving in the service. They're quite convenient," Konrad explained, quite entertained, as I sat by his side, with Juan placed in front of us.

"Normally the Mass is at 11:00, lunch at 1:00 in the gallery outside for the adults and in the garden for the children. I think this year, there are about forty of them. If it rains or snows then it's everybody inside. Buffet for grown up people in the dinning and ball rooms. Children in theory should be restricted to the old playroom, but they're everywhere. At 5:00 is coffee and at 7:00 guests should start to go home."

"Is is not too long for children? They have school tomorrow."

"No, tomorrow is a holiday too. Let's go now," he ordered mildly.

It was a strange evening. We drove in a limousine to Zurich and went to this confectionery Sprüngli for coffee and waited until nine before having dinner again at the Königshalle. It was more than obvious that those two had gotten along very well, speaking in hushed tones, exchanging meaningful glances and ignoring me most of the time. I didn't like it at all, but I kept my cool. Juan is not into men, but I wouldn't place my hands in the fire for Konrad. He can be quite persistent in his conquests and novelty is something he can't resist.

All right, I was fuming.

At midnight, we were back in the house and those two were a little drunk. Not to the point of being unable to walk but to the point the whole world is your friend. I'm not allowed to drink because of the bloody medications. At least I would be also happy and carefree! I said goodnight to both and went straightforward to bed as they started round number three with bourbon.

At 2 a.m., yes, 2 a.m., Konrad decided to join me in bed. How nice of him!

I sat on the bed, sending daggers with my eyes at him as he undid his clothes.

"Did you have a nice time?" I said in my sweetest tone.

"Very. Your friend is smart and funny, not to mention quite hot looking."

"It seems you have developed a new penchant for young virgin Argentineans, Konrad. Glad to know it," I said in a sarcastic voice.

He looked at me astonished for a full minute. Alcohol dulls your senses, doesn't it? Then he smiled like a child caught with the sweet jar. He got a pillow full in the face. This time he laughed at me.

"Are you jealous by any chance, Kitten?" He grinned like an idiot.

"No. About time, you found a replacement for me, so I can come back to my own country," I shoot back with an angry glare.

"Guntram, don't be ridiculous. I was only entertaining a guest. Come here Kitten, let me hold you if you felt displaced today," half naked he climbed into the bed trying to hold me.

"Get your filthy hands off!" I said loudly throwing a punch towards his face. He caught my fist in an iron grip without much effort before I even hit him. Guess he's not so drunk as I thought. That makes his offence more severe

"Be careful Guntram. I don't allow many people to hit me," he growled not so subtly threatening me. I don't care. "Let's go to sleep before we say more things we will regret later," he advised me in a stern and haughty voice. Fuck him!

"Yes, I know. Only Goran mops the floor with you."

In one fast and swift movement, he threw me against the pillows and placed himself on top of me, easily trapping my arms with his hands. I squirmed furiously but he launched himself to kiss me. It was a hungry and ravishing kiss, forcing me to open my mouth and devouring me, nothing like the soft and self-restrained kisses I've been getting since I was discharged from the hospital.

I went mad with desire, trying to match his burning lips. He abruptly stopped disentangling himself and going to the other side of the bed.

"Guntram, stop now. You're still not up to this."

"To Hell with the doctor. I want to feel you," I closed the space between us and put my arms around his neck as I knelt in front of him. "Please, I need you," I pleaded in a whiny voice, kissing him on the face softly as I felt the internal debate going through his head.

"I'm too drunk to restrain myself if you feel bad," he almost inaudibly said. I continued kissing him on the neck eliciting soft groans from him. I stopped and laid down against the pillows looking at him with my best puppy eyes.

"*Scheisse*, I'm not made of stone," he whispered before launching against me for the second time, delicately kissing and tasting me while he was unbuttoning my pyjamas.

"Come under the covers. It's cold," I murmured in his ear moving toward my side, so he would have space. He snuggled close to me, and I embraced him, both kissing each other hungrily. I didn't realise that he had pulled away my clothes until I felt his naked flesh positioning on top of me. I was so lost in his embrace that I lost contact with any other reality than his lips. I could feel my own erection hardening to the point of being painful, but I didn't care, too concentrated on his mouth.

"Always in a hurry, Lintorff?" I grinned between kisses trying to calm my ragged breathing.

"You have no idea how much I want this. Why do you think I was travelling the last weeks?" he confessed leaving me to get the lube from his bedside table. I jumped a bit and had to repress a stifle when I felt his fingers entering me.

"It was a long time without, my love," I reassured and urged him to continue under his alarmed look.

"Too long, Kitten," he replied kissing and sucking my nipples rolling his tongue just like he knows drives me mad.

He penetrated me in with one swift move, and again I had to stifle a cry of pain. I didn't want him to stop now, but he knew something was amiss and ceased all movements, waiting expectantly until I looked for his mouth with my lips, kissing and urging him to take me more deeply.

He started to pound inside me at a very slow pace, trying to cause the less possible pain or stress, giving me a long deprived pleasure. Nevertheless, we both were eager, and he sped up his pace meeting every thrust with my moans. I came too fast for my liking as he depleted himself into me.

I had to sit on the bed to catch my breath under control as I was nearly knocked down by a wave of dizziness and felt sick. Konrad was immediately holding me.

"Should I call for a doctor, Kitten?" he asked me, sounding very concerned.

"I'm not into threesomes," I joked trying to calm myself down with deep breaths, and it seemed it worked because my heartbeat was slowly returning to a normal one. After five minutes of him holding me and me panting like a marathon runner, I felt much better. "Could you give me a glass of water, please?"

He went to the bathroom and brought me a glass full of cold water. I drank it and felt much better.

"Maybe it's not a bad idea you look for a replacement. I'm not so sporty any longer."

"Guntram I will never let you go. It was a mistake to do this without the doctor's permission. It will take a few months until you're fully recovered. It's my fault. I should have never agreed to this, no matter how enticing you are."

I felt reassured by his words and caught him with my arms. "I'm all right, it's just I'm not used to this any longer. I will be fine. Just sleep beside me."

* * *

Easter Sunday

Early morning I was awakened by the pandemonium the house had turned

196

into. Konrad had already disappeared who knows where. I went to the window to see the army of servants placing tables and chairs. I stood there motionless, realising that it was real show time today. Lots of people, all Germans or Swiss and most probably coming to see what the Duke has placed in his bed this time.

I jumped in shock when Konrad softly kissed me on the neck. He almost gave me my second heart attack.

"Good morning. You have to get dressed if you want to grab breakfast. I was lucky enough to snatch something from the kitchen today. The cook is in a bad mood."

"I don't think I can eat now. Maybe later after Mass," I replied trying to disentangle myself from him.

"Are you nervous by any chance?"

"You would also be if you were the main dish today," I gulped.

"Nonsense. They are only employees; managers, brokers, traders, some secretaries. They are more afraid to upset you and get on my wrong side. The real sharks came on Friday, and they approved you."

"Anyway, I'm still nervous over so many people."

"You only have to shake hands with some of them and stay with me during the introductions. Then you're free to go with Ferdinand's children. Come, get yourself dressed in a morning suit and tie. It's already nine. Your friend is pacing around with Antonov."

* * *

Well, it was not so bad as I originally estimated. People started to arrive at 10:30 and wasted no time in greetings as they went directly to the chapel where Konrad was already speaking with the same Father from Friday. This time I was allowed to sit beside him during the ceremony on a bench separated from the rest. Honestly, I will never understand the protocol used in this place. Ferdinand and family sat just behind us and poor Juan was adopted by Michael.

At Konrad's insistence, I took communion and was not very happy with the fact that I haven't been to confession in a long time. Honestly, no matter what he would tell me, our love was not approved by the Church. At the end of the service the Father approached me and told me that he was glad for I was the duke's chosen companion. I just gaped at him while he was happily telling me that I should continue with my religious life as it was before and charity work, within the Church's frame, of course.

I had to remain by both men's side as they greeted all the attendants. Konrad knew most of them by heart and when he had a slip or a new face would show, Michael or Monika would tell him who they were. At quarter to one, the guests placed themselves without problems at the round tables in the courtyard. I was still stuck with Konrad, the priest, Monika, Michael and Ferdinand. It was a small surprise that I would have to sit beside the priest at the table. The children, who had been more or less running around, were sent to the tables prepared for them.

We had lunch and it was very long, including a short speech from Konrad, in German, in the middle. The food was excellent. Jean Jacques had overdone himself this time. I caught a glimpse of Juan sitting at a table with young people having a really good time there while I had to formally sit and not move much. Yes, exactly like those Sundays when I had to stay in school and have lunch at the Principal's house.

After a strange looking ice cake for dessert, that tasted great, Konrad quickly checked that more or less everybody had finished, stood up and said something in German, leaving the table, with the rest almost running to follow him.

"Come," Gertrud told me, Ferdinand's wife, again sitting with me. "It's time for the children to look for the eggs. The poor dears have been dying to do it since Friday."

In the garden, there was a pandemonium of small and not so small children destroying plants. Well, they were looking for the eggs and running after small brown rabbits. I don't think they will ever catch one. Many of the small devils ran on several occasions to Konrad to show what they had found, and he was nice to them, asking them where and how they got the eggs. He even picked up one or two of the smaller ones. I was… well shocked. I never thought he would like children or be as good with them as he was, judging by their happy faces.

A small girl came to him crying about something, and he picked her up and shushed her. "Come here and meet Guntram. He can draw a nice *Hase* (hare), for you," he said, handing the girl to me. "Ask for some paper to the children's entertainers. She only speaks German," he clarified for an astonished me, with a blonde girl in the arms, looking confidently I would draw her a rabbit.

"I had no idea you liked children," I whispered in his ear.

"I like them a lot. In my line of work, you don't see much of them, but I hope to get mine at some point with you at my side," he informed me. I think the wine has gotten to his head. Right, time to draw something because this little lady is suffocating me with her insistent tugging at my tie.

In less than two minutes I got many more orders beside that rabbit. An elephant, a rhino, a giraffe, several birds including penguins, and many children sitting around me while watching me draw. Fortunately, Juan saved me from hand cramps when he told them in German to go to watch the magician's show.

"Thanks, pal. I thought I would be chained there the whole day," I sighed, relieved.

"Yeah, you got a lot of small fans. Building up the market for your mature years?" he joked.

"I trust Luciana for that," I grinned. "What have you been doing so far? Any luck with the eggs?"

"None but the Easter Bunny brought something else for me. Come, let me introduce you to Marie Amélie von Kleist. Very beautiful lady," he said with his eyes shining and an idiot's grin.

"The lady might be incredible, but wait until you meet the father and his carbine."

"I know him. I'm already working on her brothers."

"Should you not get the lady first?"

"No, if you want to do things right. I'm glad you're already taken because she's a beauty, and I don't want any competition," he warned me seriously. All right Juan, good luck because I think Ferdinand will be worse than Konrad when it comes to his properties and daughters are every man's right eye.

Juan introduced me to the fair Marie Amélie, who, by the way, was very good looking and her brothers. Tall like me, blonde, blue eyes and perfect face, like a top model, soft voice and elegant movements. Juan, you have an incredible good taste. The brothers were not so impressive. I mean, the typical German look; brown hair and blue eyes, the elder, Karl Otto, was a carbon copy of his father in everything, working already in the bank and preparing to go in the summer to Harvard. The middle one, Johannes was still studying chemistry and looking like a frightened mouse, almost not speaking at all.

At some point the boys decided to go for a walk in the forest because they had enough of the dwarfs running around. Most of the adults had disappeared into the house or were sitting in the courtyard, while the little ones were entertained. I was feeling somewhat tired and excused myself from the walk and Marie Amélie also did it. I can understand her. Who wants to tread on pebbles with those high heel shoes?

"So, we are going to go together to school?" she fired dazzling me with her big eyes.

"Perhaps we take some subjects together, Miss von Kleist," I said, my mouth dry. "I'm in Economics and your father told me you would be in Banking and Finance."

"No need to be so formal. Everybody in the family calls me Nutte. The Duke always refers to me as such," she tweeted sweetly like a small robin. Yes, I can see why Juan is so besotted with her. I'm also.

"All my friends call me Guti. Guntram is very formal too."

"My father spoke a lot about you. It seems you have the Duke eating from your hand. I saw him watching you when you were playing with the children. Drooling would be a better word," she chuckled visibly entertained by her own witty sentence.

I didn't like her remark at all. Better switch subject because she's Ferdinand's daughter and Juan's wannabe sweetheart. "Children find amusing that one can draw animals."

She laughed now at me, without reserves. "Come on, Guti. Don't look so cross. After all I'm the family's official black sheep! Do you prefer to spend the rest of the day in the company of my two idiotic brothers? Where's your sense of humour?"

"I'm not comfortable with this conversation, madam," I said trying to look stern but her puppy eyes were getting the best of me.

"All right, I'll be good. I promise. It's just I want to know the man who caught Lintorff. You must have a lot of stamina to endure him. His horrible and short temper are legendary around here. I'm astonished you're so young," she said musically, her strong German accent made her voice sexy.

"I'm one year older than you," I replied suddenly appeased. Ever heard of the Pied Piper of Hamlin? I'm convinced now it was a woman.

"This is why it's so impressive. Lintorff is my godfather and I never remember him being nice to anybody and much less into a sound relationship. He's just a big bad ass, as the Americans say."

"He was nice to the children today. They like him and that's difficult to achieve. I saw him," I defended Konrad.

"Yes, he's nice to them until he considers them a threat to his power. All niceties are away, unless they bend to his will. Nothing moves around here without him knowing it."

"He has a lot of things on his mind. I know he can be imposing at times, but it's not his intention," I vaguely defended him again.

"I hope we'll be friends. Call me Nutte, really," she flashed me one of her smiles, and I gaped.

"All right Nutte, but you call me Guti, please."

"Good. Tell me something. Is your Argentinean friend interested in me?"

"He's very impressed by you. He's trying to make friends with your brothers to be accepted."

She laughed again. "Lord, in which century do you live in Argentina? I couldn't care less about my brothers' opinion! You yourself seem to be out of the XIX century! Maybe that's why you can cope with Lintorff."

"He's following the proper procedure for getting to know a young lady," I told her slightly upset at her haughty ways. "Your father is also quite old fashioned and would not appreciate him coming onto you."

"My father would be glad if he finds some decent idiot who wants to marry me!" She laughed, tears veiling her eyes. "Your friend is cute and I would like to know him more; pity he lives in London. I'll give you my messenger's number, so he can chat with me. Do you have a pencil?"

She wrote down her e-mail for Juan, and we spoke a little more this time about music and our schools. She had been in a boarding school in Lausanne and liked Green Day and System of a Down. Yeah, I can imagine Konrad's face if I play those in here. Sometime after two other girls came to us and started to speak about the party and the latest fashions, I decided to make myself scarce.

Since Juan was nowhere to be seen and the children were busy eating cakes and drinking chocolate, I decided to rejoin the older ones. Maybe I could get Goran or Alexei, who had been invited to the party also and had been sitting with two young women.

I entered the living room to find several groups of people softly speaking. In one corner Konrad, Ferdinand, some other guy looking like a banker and Michael were speaking in hushed tones. I guess he had enough of mixing with the serfs and wanted to mingle only with his kind. Yeah, Marie Amélie, Nutte, was right, he could be an arse sometimes and it was a wonder that he had decided to speak with me in Venice, a poor student with a backpack and a book. Konrad made me an imperceptible sign to come to them.

"Do you know Mr. Jenkins? He's the head of currencies trade at London," he introduced me.

"How do you do?" I said extending my hand to him.

"Pleased to meet you, sir," he said curtly after shaking hands. "If you would excuse me, my Duke, I would like to catch Landau before he goes away." Konrad just nodded, dismissing him. I was a bit taken aback.

We all stood there while the man quickly mixed himself in the crowd.

"Did you catch anything? I saw you very busy with the little devils," Michael smirked.

"Only a cramp in the hand," I smiled back at him.

"You have to practice more so next year we save one children's entertainer," Konrad joked.

"We had peace for almost a full hour thanks to you," Ferdinand added softly chuckling. "With little children you're grateful for every second they leave you alone."

"I met your daughter. She's very kind," I said to him.

"I hope Marie Amélie has not gotten you into trouble yet," was his sharp answer.

"Nutte? She's a nice girl." A strong silence surrounded us. Konrad and Ferdinand looking at me furiously, like raging bulls; Michael gaped like an idiot.

"What did you call my daughter?" Ferdinand growled low, advancing toward me. I noticed Michael placed himself discreetly between us.

"Have I pronounced it wrongly? Nutte. I'm sorry. My German is still very bad."

"You little slime. I'm going to…"

"Enough! It's Easter Sunday. Guntram, apologise immediately to Ferdinand. We will speak later about your behaviour," Konrad roared at me in a low tone, his voice loaded with fury.

"I don't understand. I apologise if it's unsuitable for me to use your daughter's nickname. She told me I should call her like that because all her friends do it and even the Duke calls her that," I intoned seriously eating my own fury at Konrad's public scold. This is not even from the XIX century. We are back in the Middle Ages!

Michael snorted finding my awkward moment very funny. Konrad dedicated him one of his killings looks.

"Nutte means whore in German. It's a word you don't use in public," Konrad slowly and seriously explained to me. I wanted to die in shame right there.

"I'm terribly sorry Mr. von Kleist if I used such a crude word for your daughter. I must have wrongly understood the name. It was most stupid of me. I never wanted to insult her," I apologized in a low voice, totally mortified. I don't want to clash with Ferdinand at all!

"Ferdinand, see to your daughter and tell her I will not tolerate this kind of behaviour in my house," Konrad barked to an enraged Ferdinand, who turned around to take his leave and kill his daughter for her childish prank.

"Please, Mr. von Kleist. It's likely my fault. I must have heard wrong. My teacher would tell you I'm not a very good student," I said in haste trying to catch him by the sleeve. After all, Marie Amélie was doing the typical joke for foreigners. How many times have we sent the English exchange student to the Spanish teacher with a horrible phrase? I should have been less naïve. Next time…

"Guntram, do not interfere. This is more than a stupid, childish joke made on you," Konrad warned me. "I will not have the Lausanne story repeated. Either she behaves according to her status, or she goes to Güstrow," he said this time to Ferdinand making him blush under his scolding.

"I will speak with my wife and her. Guntram, please excuse my daughter's behaviour," he said, leaving the group not even giving me time to answer.

Fortunately, the servants started to serve coffee and cakes. I could eat nothing at all and was very relieved when the people started to go away. I noticed the children were getting small baskets full of chocolate figures and presents.

Late at night, I had to hear the onslaught of Juan, telling wonderful things about Marie Amélie. Yeah, he had it bad.

Chapter 31

May 19th, 2002

It's been a long time since I've written anything. The winter melted into spring and I was allowed to go outside the house more and have been busy with the German lessons as the doctor gave me a clean bill of health for my brain. For the heart, it would need some more time, but by mid-April, he let me do more things. OK. Sex no more than three times per week, leaving one or two days for resting after it. Well, it's better than nothing and I was glad for it.

Our first times were completely shy as he were afraid I would break in the middle but nothing happened and we slowly recovered our previous loving status.

As Konrad predicted I started to feel less and less out of place and even accompanied him to some of his dinners at other bankers and industrials houses; once to the opera and twice to elegant charity parties. As Gertrud informed me, I was considered some sort "artistic character" who was not getting in the middle. Therefore, I was not dangerous to anybody and my age placed me more or less "in the kindergarten" so to speak. No need to be nasty to me since I had no further interests on their dealings and was well educated and polite (sic). Yes, Gertrud had a nice way to tell me that I was good flower vase happy to stay in its corner.

Despite our unsuccessful first meeting, Marie Amélie and I became good friends. Her careless way to treat everybody and funny nature was a sharp contrast to this house seriousness and made me feel young. Spending time with her was more or less like an escape for me when the meetings and Konrad's brooding became too much. I was really looking forward to starting school with her.

She, on the other hand, found Juan "very cute" and even went to visit him in London—the official story, going to shop for summer season. Unfortunately, it didn't work between them and she never spoke about him again. According to Konrad, "Dollenberg was clever enough as to put her out of the possible brides list." Needless to say we had a quarrel over his ill disposition toward her. "And you also should reconsider to have her on your friends list. Go to school with her, but do not trust her. She can only cause trouble," he even had the nerve to tell me. Konrad can be a real pig when people don't bend to his will and Marie Amélie, does not do it. Maybe this is the reason why I like her so much.

I started to take painting lessons with an old teacher, who had a studio in the *Altstadt*, relatively near the bank, once or twice per week in the afternoons. First, I was not happy at all because he was teaching all "good society ladies", but he was a nice guy who had no problems in destroying two drawings made more or less in a careless way.

"You don't need drawing classes. You need to find your own style and work from there," he scolded me and gave me a hideous blue mini plastic elephant from a Chinese shop to paint. "Make it look beautiful and I'll leave you alone," he grunted. Since March I'm working with this blue guy in pencil, water colours, wax crayons and even acrylic paints. I swear I'm starting to dream of that wretched thing!

Mopsi is doing well, always tagging along whenever it's possible. I even caught Konrad feeding her under the table once. Of course, he denied everything. I was feeling more and more in love and happy to be with him, despite he had to travel on several occasions.

My plan for today was passing by the University to pick up more text books for studying with Anneliese. German is not so horrible as was my first impression and more or less it shows some logic. The original plan was: lunch with Konrad at 1:30 in the bank—no chance of leaving the office; too many meetings, then I could go to school with Marie Amélie and at 5:00 it's my painting lesson. My Russian shadow will tag along. Sometimes Konrad is too much, I swear. What horrible danger can an eighteen-year-old girl, a University, a respectable coffee like Sprüngli, and a seventy year old teacher pose that I need to have a thirty-five years old, big bad Russian with me?

We had lunch with Ferdinand, Michael and two more managers in his dining room at the bank. I remained mute because they all were arguing in German. When we finished I tried to scurry away, but Konrad caught me and forced me sit in a corner in his office. "No need to run away. 3:30 it is more than a reasonable time to leave."

Fuck. I'm literally stuck! At least I had paper and pencil. I sent a brief SMS to Marie Amélie. "Can't meet you till 4:00. Sorry. Konrad bad mood."

"Fascist pig! I'll get your books. Meet me at Sprüngli. U'll see my new flat." Was her SMS. Konrad looked slightly irritated at me because of the phone's beep. Ferdinand was there, sitting in front of his desk, reading papers, deeply immersed in them.

"Ferdinand, may I visit your single daughter in her flat? She would like to show it to me," I asked him.

"Yes, no problem Guntram. Be careful not to fall on her trash," he absent mindedly answered.

"I thought you were going to the University with her. Why the sudden change?" Konrad barked. Great, now we have you venting your frustration at the Nasdaq on a girl.

"She will pick up my books and give them to me at her flat. She wants to show it to me. It's near Meister Ostermann's studio. I can walk there later," I explained slowly.

"Take Antonov with you."

"Konrad, he only goes to visit my daughter. Let the children be." Ferdinand mildly scolded him, looking through papers.

"Don't get into troubles Guntram," he seriously warned me, going back to his reports.

I met Marie Amélie at the door of the coffee shop but she didn't want to enter and we went directly to her apartment, with Alexei following us. She spoke about how she had been decorating it and how happy she was now that she would be free from her parents' vigilance. It was located in a XIX century building in the Altstadt.

"No fascist apes in here, Guntram. Get rid of him," she said loudly. Yes, Alexei must have heard by the way he was looking at her.

"Not sure he will go away. He's quite determined," I whispered.

"You Russian, go home. Come on boy. Hurry up!" She told Alexei snapping the fingers exactly like when you sent the dogs away. I turned red of embarrassment at such a rude way to dismiss him.

"Marie Amélie, there's no need to be rude to Mr. Antonov. He's following orders."

"Guti, he does not enter in my house," she warned me very seriously.

"Alexei, do you mind? It would be only ten minutes till I get the books," I pleaded the Russian, hoping he had not taken it very bad. I can already hear Konrad's rant when he complains to him.

"Ten minutes with Baba Jaga or I'll ask the Duke for further instructions," he mumbled looking truly pissed off.

We climbed the four floors up to her home. I arrived agitated but managed to conceal it. Three stores at full speed must be more challenging than one night of gentle sex.

She opened the door to a small flat with two guys sitting inside drinking whiskey.

"This is Marcus, my boyfriend and the other one is Peter," she told me pointing with her index finger at them.

"Hello. Look Marie Amélie you have company and I don't want to intrude. I'll get the books and another day you can show me the flat," I said not really willing to stay longer than necessary.

"Please Guntram, don't be so dense. Have a shot with us and then you can return to your boring life," she whined.

"You know I can't drink."

"All right, I'll give you a cola, grandpa," she teased me. "Your books are on that shelf. Help yourself."

"Thank you," I said sitting on the couch in the opposite direction of the two guys, who by the way I didn't like at all. One was looking like the regular hippie, Marcus (I doubt Ferdinand is going to be happy about him). The other looked like a member from the Hell's Angels and was devouring me with his eyes.

"Don't you think my friend Guntram is hot, Peter?" She asked the big guy as if it was the most normal thing to do. I blushed and took a long swig of the cola she had placed in front of me to hide my discomfort.

"Very. Like a sweet child," the guy said looking at me. All right. Time to go home.

I stood up to say good bye, but I was frozen to see that the other guy had just made four lines of white powder on the table and was offering Marie Amélie a small golden tube to sniff it.

"Come on, take one and you'll feel wonderful. It's on the house," the big guy said. "We could have a really good time together," he whispered seductively now grabbing me by the waist. I gave him a strong push and I suddenly felt my heart thundering, beating so fast that it hurt. The room moved around. I had to lean on the wall for support.

"No way—I had a heart attack two months ago. I'm out," I said, feeling worse with each passing second.

"Shit! Marie. You told me nothing! Get out of here. I don't want you dying in my flat! The man roared, pushing me to the door. "Go to a fucking hospital before you die, idiot!"

"Did you put something in the drink, asshole?" I yelled at him.

"Angel powder—increases your blood pressure to make you eager. Now get the fuck out and act like you never saw me," he said, this time pushing me out and almost making me fall down the stairs.

I still don't know how I made it to the street. Alexei was still there and caught me before I fell. The beating was so strong, mixed with a headache and my vision completely clouded.

"You have to take me to a hospital, now," I slurred to him. "There was something in the drink that makes my blood pressure high. I feel my heart like exploding," I complained almost clinging to his suit's lapels.

He said something loudly in Russian and took my pulse on my neck. "Yes, you're hypertensive. Calm down. So far you have no heart attack. Do you have your pills, the one with nifedipine?"

Kill me if I know.

"In my pocket there's a full assortment of them, identified."

"Good boy," he said as he fumbled with my jacket. He found the box and took one of a pink colour, gelatinous. He got a small Swiss Army knife out of his pocket and punctured it. "Open your mouth and put it under your tongue and slowly let it dissolve. This should control your blood pressure and give us some time to get to the hospital," he said, looking for his own mobile, dialling the numbers and speaking this time in Russian.

I did as he said and slowly my heart stopped pounding like crazy. Unable to stand any longer I had to sit on the street. In less than ten minutes, a black Mercedes with a furious Goran inside screeched its wheels in front of us. He jumped out of the car and only barked "which floor?" "Fourth," I said. "It's not her flat," he looked at me incensed.

"Take him to Hirschbaum, Alexei. Only speak with the Duke. Trust nobody," Goran shouted before disappearing into the building.

Alexei didn't waste time to dragging me into the car and drove me away to the Clinic. I was feeling slightly better with the pill. He didn't park the car and once more he nearly hauled me inside the E.R., where Dr. Van Horn was already waiting for me and placed me in a small separate evaluation room. I got a IV line, the heart monitor and a nurse getting blood out of me.

"What did you take?"

"The man said it was called Angel Dust. I don't know what it is," I said.

"It's a mild methamphetamine—very popular these days. Lethal if you have a heart condition. Why on earth did you take it?"

"I didn't know it was there!" I exploded. "I just took a sip of cola and this guy put it in without telling me. He wanted to get romantic and I didn't. He was frantic when I said I had a heart attack and told me to go to a hospital."

"That and your bodyguard saved your life, boy. Don't you know you shouldn't drink anything in discos?" He advised me as he was still checking my eyes with a flashlight and the EGC graphics.

"It was a friend's house! She didn't tell me she had such friends along! Do you think I like to have a heart attack every two months?" I yelled hysterically, breathing like a ragged bull.

"It's obvious that I will have to give you something to sedate you, young man."

"Don't you dare! I had enough of drugs for a lifetime!" I roared sitting on the table.

"Guntram, relax, the doctor only wants best for you," Alexei firmly said, pushing me down. "The blood pressure might be low again, but they have to look for further damage to your heart. Now be a good boy and let the doctor and nurses work," he continued to keep a firm hold on me, shushing me and speaking softly in Russian as I fought to keep the sleep away. Suddenly everything went black.

* * *

I painfully opened my eyes to a darkened room. It looked exactly like the one I stayed before during my previous adventure; elegantly furnished like a suite and with a view over the lake. I looked around, surprised to see the IV line still pumped into my arm and felt again the familiar uncomfortable pain of that thing you get in hospitals to force you to pee in a bag.

"Hey, welcome back to the land of the living," I heard someone's voice— Michael. "You were sleeping like twelve hours. You can't deny that you're a baby any longer," he joked visibly relieved that I was awake. "I'll get the Duke in no time. The nurse, Anke, threw him out an hour ago. He's pacing somewhere."

"He must be furious with me," I said with a croaked voice.

"He doesn't blame you or Alexei for what happened. It was a treacherous set up from Ferdinand's spawn. I'll call him now."

"It was not Marie Amélie's fault. That guy put the thing in the drink. She didn't know."

"Relax Guntram, let Goran do his job," he said leaving the room and softly closing the door behind him.

Konrad entered in the room with long strides, his face pale but his eyes darkened and more terrifying than ever. He sat at my bed, taking my hand into his.

"I'm afraid this is becoming a tradition for us," I tried to joke to lift the dark mood surrounding him.

"There is no excuse for what happened today. She will be punished this time."

"I don't blame her. It was her stupid friend."

"She deliberately put Alexei out of the game, took you to another flat which was not her own as informed, sold you to a petty drugs dealer for a tumble and almost killed you by nearly provoking another heart attack. If you're alive, it is because Alexei had the cold blood to counter effect the hypertension before it would have finished you off," he said coldly.

"How can you believe she would do something like that? She's your best friend daughter's! Ferdinand almost lives for you. Why would she do something like that? She has no reasons for that. She only wanted to introduce me her new boyfriend and they were in that flat. I don't think she would have organized a date with that guy. She knows perfectly I'm in love with you." I protested his crazy assumptions. Lord, he's so paranoid!

"That is not how I see the situation. You're too tired. We will not discuss this now."

"No, you will not accuse a poor girl of something she didn't do. You should be more concerned that she has a drug problem."

A big, unbelieving snort was his answer. I don't care. I continued. "I know you don't like her because she's more independent than any other person around you. But you're accusing her of something very serious, without giving her the chance to defend herself. If you are so sure, go to the police and let them investigate."

"Precisely because Ferdinand is my friend I don't want to involve the police. If I do, his whole family would be dragged through the mud. Do you want this? No? I'll deal with her as I see fit and her father agrees with me. She had been a big problem to all of us for some time."

"Konrad you were not there. I was. You have to believe me!" I pleaded becoming more and more agitated.

"You were busy having a heart attack. Forgive me if I don't consider you a reliable witness," he dismissed my words with a grin of contempt.

When I opened my mouth to shout something about his damned stubbornness, Anke, the nurse burst into the room.

"Upsetting my patient? I already told you the rules. Behave or I'll throw you out again," she told Konrad very sharply, as she came to me, shushing the big German away from the bed with a wave of her hand. She took a needle out and started to draw blood from me.

"It seems you can't live without me, dear. Again staying with me. But I must warn you, I've been married with children for the last twenty years," she said kindly, making me smile. "The doctor will see you in two hours and probably discharge you later in the morning. I'll send breakfast for you."

She pumped something more in the IV and rose to leave the room, throwing a warning glare at Konrad. That woman must have been a queen or something like that in a previous life. She closed the door softly and I was left again with the sulking German.

"See? It's not so serious if I'm released today," I said happy and relieved.

"Be quiet—I have to read this," he growled, looking for his papers in a briefcase and sitting on a leather couch.

Better to follow his advice and not move a finger because even if he's not upset at me; he looks very dangerous at the moment.

Sometime later, Doctor Van Horn entered in the room and after greeting us, he started to check on me.

"Well, you look better. I'll have to release you at noon. The drugs have flushed from your system, but there have been some slight damages to the previous condition," he cheerfully said.

"It was not so bad, doctor?" I inquired hoping he would support my side.

"No, it was really bad. It's a miracle you're alive this time. It's was real luck your bodyguard had medical training and knew how to react. Otherwise, you would not be here."

"This is why he was chosen for the position," Konrad intoned darkly, perched on his corner.

"Listen to me young man. It was most irresponsible from you to take this drug even in a small dose. You are still not twenty and your heart resembles the one of a sick man of seventy. This time was more serious because you were still in recovery. Maybe with a lot of care, we could get you back to your forties."

"I didn't know that thing was in it. It was a stupid joke on me."

"Joke? Criminal behaviour, I daresay, even if you were a healthy person," he said, now his eyes fixed on mine. "You are back to square one, so to speak, but this time your recovery would be more difficult than before because the original cardiac lesion is worsened. We will have to increase your medications, absolute repose for a month, not even walking much, strict diet, no excitement. You better obey me because I assure you there will be no third chance for you."

"I understand," I murmured really scared after his warning.

"On the bright side, you're young and don't have any other previous conditions that may hinder your recovery."

"Do you think I could go to school in September?"

"I can't say at this point. We will see when the time comes. At the moment go home and rest a lot. After two weeks, you will come for a re-evaluation and we will see if you can restart your German lessons. For now, the best is that you sleep, paint a little if you like it or read a book. No going out or partying. The nurse will give you a new medications list and my mobile number if you need to call me. If I were you I would buy a good book or a dog before having such friends."

"I'll follow your instructions, doctor," I mumbled, feeling completely small and losing all my earlier bravado.

"I will see to it, doctor. May I speak with you in private?" Konrad said, making a small sign with his head towards the door.

"Of course, *Herzog*. This way please." Both men left the room leaving me alone with my thoughts and fears.

It had been a very stupid prank and I would be paying the consequences for a long time. I should have gone away the minute I saw the two guys. Why didn't she tell me about them in advance? On the other hand, she's a good girl and wouldn't hurt me on purpose. She had nothing to gain by doing it. I'm afraid she thought she was making me a favour by inviting this stupid guy. After all she's always telling me to get somebody else besides Konrad because he's a fucking Nazi, absorbing all my energy and youth, not letting me move an inch without his permission. I should get a young boyfriend in the school to balance his dominating personality and fuck if I cheat on him, after all I'm young and he's old enough to be my father.

I've should have told her more strongly to mind her own business since I was very happy with Konrad, but again my weak character prevented me stopping her. In a way, I was guilty of the mess.

"Hi kid," Michael said with Goran and Alexei towering at his side.

"Hello," I replied, hesitantly.

"Alexei will take you home," Goran informed me, sternly.

"I must thank you Alexei Gregorevich. The doctor said you saved my life."

"Not at all. You belong to me now as they say. I saved your skin and I have to take care of you for ever," he smiled broadly. "It seems I've adopted you."

"You should not talk much," Goran advised me, this time using a softer voice. "We are glad you are back with us, little brother."

"Ugh!" Michael made a false gesture of disgust. "Even Goran is becoming sentimental. Let's get out of here before I proclaim my love for him," he whined, dramatically rising his eyes towards the roof.

"If you want to sleep without your tongue, you can do it," the Serb replied in a cold and well-mannered voice that was truly terrifying.

"That's more like it. The Goran we all know and love," Michael smirked, unshaken at the killing look from the other. "We have to run, but Alexei is your nanny from now onwards. To bed straight with you and don't get the dog in there."

"Where's the Duke?" I asked feeling somewhat nervous.

"Back in the office, with Ferdinand. Will see you this evening. Good bye, take care." Was Michael's curt reply before leaving the room with Goran in tow.

Anke came in later to remove all the bloody things and also gave me like six different boxes of medicines to carry home. "I gave your prescriptions to the big Russian out there. Take care now dear and I don't want to see you here ever again."

The drive home was in relative silence. I tried to fish some information out of Alexei, but he only grunted me to be quiet and not to worry since it wasn't my fault what had transpired yesterday. OK, KGB boys don't speak if they don't want.

At home, a Friederich in a full mother hen mode, wanted to put me in bed, but I held my ground saying I wanted to stay in the library with Mopsi till lunch time. We sort of compromised. I would eat and go to bed till teatime and then I could stay in the library with Mopsi reading or drawing until the Duke's arrival.

Chapter 32

May 20th, 2002

Yesterday night, Konrad came home at his usual time. I was in the library, drawing with Mopsi snoring at my feet. I'm surprised how much this dog can sleep. She will not die of a heart attack for sure. He kissed me tenderly on the forehead.

"You should follow the example of your dog and be resting," he chided me gently. Good, he was not so upset like in the morning.

"Staying in bed drives me crazy. I slept in the afternoon. How was your day?"

"The usual. We dine at eight thirty. If you don't mind, I'd like to work here a little. Today's meetings with lawyers made me fall behind schedule."

"I understand. I'll go to my studio," I answered whispering. It seemed he didn't want to talk.

"No, you two can stay. It's just I don't want to bother you with my papers."

"You never bother me, Konrad. Mopsi, on the other hand, snores quiet loudly," I smiled at him making room for him to sit at my side, but he refused and sat in front of the desk. I returned to my drawing of a big dog I saw a few days ago.

We had dinner together in silence, only interrupted once by a remark from Konrad to Friederich about the wine. I sat at my usual place at his right side, he at the head of the table. By dessert time I was more than distressed at his silence. Was he upset with me? Not probably since he had been nice just an hour ago. Did he blame Marie Amélie? Very likely, considering his reaction at my ill attempt at defending her. Had he took revenge on her? I really hoped that Ferdinand could have stopped him because I've had already several examples of his temper unleashed.

"Are you feeling well, Kitten? You look deadly pale. Do you want to retire early?"

Good sign. He calls me kitten. Let's try it. "About yesterday I believe it was a horrible confusion and honestly you should not blame Marie Amélie. I don't."

"Please, don't tell me what I should do," was his sharp answer. Excellent work Guntram. Now he's pissed off and on alert mode.

"I drank the cola, but it was not her apartment. There's no way she could have known it was contaminated."

"I will not discuss with you Goran's enquiry results. Everything is perfectly clear for me and Ferdinand. Even if you prefer to think that it was a stupid prank, she was perfectly aware that you're off limits. I still don't understand why was she taking you, deceiving all of us, to a drug dealer's flat—a convicted paedophile."

I lost all colours and felt very sick. "I thought she wanted to get me a new boyfriend. She doesn't approve of you for me," I said softly without realising that I've spoken out loud. Shit! I cursed myself, I've given him now more reasons to go against her.

"Then my decisions were correct," he said with an unwavering voice. I looked at him half expecting his fury, but there was none, only a blank stare.

"What did you do now?" I whispered painfully, not really feeling up to know. But some things attract you more than it's good for your own sake.

"Not as much as I would have wanted. She should be happy she preserved her life and didn't end up in jail. Her father's status saved her skin."

"I don't want that you hurt her. It was only a childish and stupid prank. I don't blame her even if I will have to cope with the consequences."

"I disowned her. She's cut off from my will, banished from all of my companies and it's forbidden that she contacts you. She will receive no allowance from her family and has to leave Zurich tomorrow. In three years, her family could receive her, but for me she's dead and will not move a finger for her any longer."

"Don't you realise this is a death sentence for her? She's an addict who needs help, not to be cast out to the streets!" I shouted rising from my chair, and immediately the dizziness made me grip the table and had to fight to keep my balance. "It's a death sentence what you're imposing on her!"

"Do you think she had so many scruples when it came to your own life?" He retorted not losing his calm.

"She's an eighteen-year-old girl! She knows nothing about working or living alone!"

"If I see correctly you started to work at that age and supported yourself relatively well."

"It's completely different. I'm a man!" I shouted back.

"Well, it's time for her to prove that women are equal to us as they claim. They have been complaining the whole century about us," he asserted without losing his temper.

"If something happens to her I will never forgive myself. Think on her family, on Ferdinand. I don't believe for a minute he agrees with you. He only does it in fear you would do something worse. He does not deserve it. You're punishing him and Gertrud," I pleaded, changing tactics because shouting was leading me nowhere.

"It's his fault for not controlling his children better," he said unperturbed.

"Please Konrad, I beg you. Reconsider your punishment."

"No. Sit down."

"At least let her have contact with the family, so they can help her. Send her to a detox clinic. We both know she will overdose in an alley or worse. Can you have this on your conscience? I can't," I crumbled in my chair, my eyes red and my breathing uncontrolled. "I swear I will never let her come near me. Do you think I like to be sick again? Deprived to feel your touch for who knows how long?"

He rose from his chair and knelt down beside me and took my hands into his bigger ones. "Don't think for a minute this is not hard for me too. Ferdinand and I have been together through a lot. He's like a brother to me, but I can't have such a snake nesting within the inner circle," he said in a very soft voice.

"Disown her from your circle then. Forbid her to be near you, but don't make a good man suffer. Please Konrad, do it for us," I pleaded, almost on the brink of tears.

"I can't deny you anything. Swear on your mother's grave you will never see her again. She's dangerous, not matter what you think."

"I swear I will never have contact with her."

He rose to his full height and shouted "Friederich!" The butler entered almost tripping with his own feet. "Call von Kleist and tell him to come here. Now."

"Immediately, your Excellency."

Konrad and I sat together in the library and he held me tightly making me feel safe in his arms. A soft knock on the door split us and Friederich announced Ferdinand. My throat felt suddenly dry. Konrad went to sit behind his desk.

Ferdinand was another man. His normally arrogant, military stance had been transformed into a slouched one, like an old man. Defeated. He had dark shadows under his eyes which were puffy and he looked haggard despite his clothes were as fine as always, not the proud wolf I was used to see. I felt very bad for him.

Without any preamble or even asking him to have a seat, Konrad charged in his usually overbearing way.

"Guntram pleaded your daughter's case von Kleist. I will shift slightly her punishment only because of the friendship we had in the past and at his insistence. Bear in mind next time she crosses me, I will treat her no different than any other of my enemies," he paused as if he still were debating with himself his decision. I held my breath. "The isolation period is lifted. I will let her have contact with your family and even support her within discretion .She will enter into a detox program. The rest of the punishment remains as it was. Dismissed."

"Thank you, my Duke. May I speak with Guntram, Sire?" he asked him, humbly as a wave of relief went through his body.

"Do not upset him," Konrad growled, still crossed to no end.

"Please Konrad, I would also like to speak with Ferdinand," I interfered softly, unwilling to ruin the peace achieved.

"All right," but he didn't move an inch. I sighed; all right, with an audience it is.

Ferdinand crossed the room toward me and knelt down in front of me, taking my right hand and kissing it in servitude. I was speechless and looked toward Konrad impassively sitting in his chair.

"I will always be indebted to you and never forget your generosity towards my family, my son. I plead my loyalty to you and I hope to compensate in the future all the wrongs we have caused you," he stated gravely.

"Ferdinand, you owe me nothing. You have always been very kind to me. Please tell Marie Amélie that I think this was a tragic accident," I replied, completely astonished and embarrassed to a certain point that such a proud man had humiliated himself in front of me.

"Do not tire Guntram, Ferdinand. I'll see you tomorrow at the office," Konrad said visibly appeased, but still not happy. The other man left the room without saying a single word more.

"Can you tell me what was all this?" I asked him when we were alone.

"He has finally recognized your place at my side. You have earned his loyalty. Your life comes before his. He should have done it long time ago," he said, resentment clearly lacing his voice.

"I didn't want this. I cannot live like this. What kind of insane world do you live in that men have to pledge their loyalties to you almost under coercion? You have just humiliated your best friend, treating him worse than a dog."

"This is the way we make things and our system has worked perfectly well for almost the last four centuries and still does. Each one of us is responsible for his own house and Ferdinand could not control his own. He's more than glad to have escaped with such a mild punishment. His house is still in one piece and his two sons can continue with us."

"You call this "mild punishment"? I was utterly shocked.

"Indeed."

"I can't understand you. Even Roman Emperors knew to be magnanimous from time to time. You even look upset at the fact you forgave, just a little, Ferdinand. You have no idea how much he defended you in Buenos Aires and how highly spoke about your ability to forgive and now you destroy his life without regrets."

"Playing with me was a serious offence, but nothing commensurable to attempt murder against a member of my family. I trust Goran in his conclusions. He has fully proved all his accusations. I had to restrain him from taking Justice into his hands on your behalf. He's completely loyal to you and I think he would defend you even from me. If she tries this at eighteen years old, she will be after me when she turns twenty. I'm protecting myself and all of us by doing it. Everybody understands my position and you should do the same and be more supportive of my decisions," he said, sounding a bit resentful at the end.

Goran likes me? This is new. However, Konrad has no right to ruin a girl's life. "You said it yourself. She's eighteen, hardly even out of adolescence! Do you really think she would be able to follow your every command like a robot? You dislike her very much and use this accident to turn her into a monster so you can get rid of her, with her family's wish if possible."

"Defend her as much as you want. My decision is taken and will not, be further altered," he dismissed me coldly with a shrug. Now, Konrad you have crossed the line.

"I'm the most damaged party in this whole mess and I have forgiven the alleged perpetrator. You, on the other hand, have blown the whole thing out of proportion and you are even looking for a conspiracy against you. You really need professional help."

"I will not argue furthermore because you're sick. You don't know her or her circumstance as well as I do. It's not my fault you have not been properly brought up for our world. Good night," he said like a prince and leaving me with the words hanging from my lips.

Ten minutes later, Friederich almost kicked me to bed "per direct orders of the Duke". Konrad had moved to one of the guests bedrooms.

Chapter 33

May 26th, 2002

Life is very boring at the moment. Not that I'm up to do much for the time being, but this forced calm bestowed upon me, is driving me crazy. I'm not even allowed to take the blasted German lessons. No, Guntram has to be nice: rest and sleep a lot (I'm an adult, not a baby who needs twelve hours sleep). "Eat your greens; don't move too much; read light things like a novel or a history book, draw a little bit and play with your dog (but don't pick her up because she's heavy! Yes, seven kilos. Why didn't you get me a Chihuahua?)"

The next morning after our fight...? Disagreement...? Exchange of opinions...?—I don't know what to call what transpired between us that night. Konrad decided to go away, taking Michael and Goran with him. He would call me every night to check how I was doing. First, I was distant and cold to him, but I slowly warmed up with the days. I'm still sore and disappointed, but not upset with him any longer.

One day, Gertrud came to visit me, but Alexei didn't let her see me. I faintly heard their discussion in German from the office next to the kitchen where Friederich and Jean Jacques were having their weekly meeting. I believe those two took pity on me and allowed me to spend some time with them. When the shouting reached us, both men continued with their talk as if it would be of no consequence. I was glad not to face her. Alexei joined us later.

"Would you not have problems for arguing with her?" I whispered to him, not willing to interrupt the heated ode to white truffles from Piedmont sung by the French Chef (he would kill me if I call him cook).

"I don't want troubles with Goran. Any member from the von Kleist family is forbidden to approach you with the exception of Ferdinand von Kleist. If she wants to speak with you, she should come with her husband."

I'm bored to the point of frustration. The bad thing is that I can't do much even if I want. I become easily tired. Must be all the pills I'm getting nowadays. I tried to get some information about Marie Amélie from Alexei, but the only thing I got was "the witch is away.

Güstrow. With any luck a bear will eat her."

Monika visited me twice, bringing well wishes notes from Konrad's friends. The Prince zu Löwenstein even wrote me a small letter in an elegant handwriting. Monika brought it one rainy afternoon and I asked her if she could stay with me for tea and she accepted.

"The *Fürst* is very fond of you," Monika told me. "He spent an hour with Ferdinand speaking about your health."

"Does he know what happened?"

"I don't know if Ferdinand told him. You should not be concerned any more about this woman. Since Lausanne she had it coming."

"What is this Lausanne thing everybody speaks about? I said visibly upset at being kept away.

"I'm not supposed to discuss it with you."

"Please do it Monika. Perhaps it will help me to understand why the Duke is so bent against her," I made my best puppy eyes. She's not the only one who can bat eyelashes. She heavily sighed.

"It's a nasty story. I know it from Michael who was there when it happened. There was this wedding from an associate, a lower member of the Löwenstein family. He had worked with us for several years taking care of the Frankfurt office and was two or three years younger than the Duke. I believe they also assisted to the same school. This man was about to marry a young economist from the Zurich offices and was completely in love of her. They decided to celebrate the marriage in a castle near Lausanne as she had been born there. It was sort of a miracle he would marry at all since he was forty and very unlucky with ladies," she stopped visibly disgusted for what was coming next.

"We don't know how it happened, but in the previous days to the wedding, Marie Amélie, who was seventeen at the time, lured the man into her bed and sent the video to the bride. She cancelled the wedding and resigned from the bank. She moved to France and never spoke with her fiancé again. She almost hit the Duke with the door on his face when he tried to intercede for his friend. Two months later, Karl Joseph was killed in a horrible car accident. Since the breakup, he drank heavily every day," she finished her voice almost trembling from emotion. I was speechless.

"Did you know him?"

"Yes. We were not friends, of course, but he was very close to Ferdinand and the Duke."

"Why did she do it? What interest could she have in a forty-year-old man?"

"I don't know. Perhaps and I'm only guessing here, she wanted to upset the Duke since he had introduced the young lady to Karl Joseph and was completely sure she was perfect for him."

"Why do they dislike each other so much?"

"The Duke can't stand the sight of her since that day, this is true, but before he was nice to her and even pampered her on many occasions. She was always a very strong willed child, a Lintorff trait used to say the Duke. Her father had a hard time trying to control her since high school. For some reason we don't understand, she likes to be a stone in their shoes."

"What she did on the wedding was very bad, but the Duke accuses her now of trying to hurt me."

"Nobody has any doubts about it," she retorted, her voice sharp, not the gentle tone she always uses. "We're all glad she's away. I can only hope she will think over her ways at the clinic. Maybe a dose of reality and working to support herself would help her to become a better person."

"I thought the Duke allowed Ferdinand to help her. To support her."

"It's Ferdinand who has decided to withdraw all financial support from her after she's clean. He will only help her to find a decent job. It's time she grows up, Guntram. He has frozen all her accounts and funds and will not give her a single Euro or Swiss Franc. She will be only allowed to live in a small flat her parents have in Berlin or Frankfurt. We have enough of spoiled young ladies in our society."

"He's hard on her."

"As a parent I support him. I had to play for years the ogre in order to balance my former husband's efforts to spoil my sons. It was not easy, but both of them are now good responsible young men, going to school or working. Perhaps in a few years they will thank me or not. I'm her mother, not her friend or 'pal'," she said sternly. "He was very successful with his two older sons, but he left Marie Amélie's education entirely up to her mother. I think he was afraid because he doesn't know much about women. Also her younger years were not easy because there was a lot of tension between Ferdinand and Gertrud and when parents fight, I know what I'm speaking about, one tends to bribe the children."

"I had no idea. They look fine together," I said puzzled.

"Everybody knows they tolerate each other, but live separates lives. It's very common in their entourage to solve these matters in such a way. They're both discreet in their dealings. Between you and me, I think he's having an affair with one of the secretaries from the third floor."

I was astonished. He? Of all people having an affair? I took a sip of my tea (yeah, coffee is forbidden and tea tastes like dirty water. I'm not turning into a lady). "It's incredible, Monika. They all look and think like if they were still in the Middle Ages."

"Even knights had their lady friends," she smiled, the mischief clear in her blue eyes. "I'm glad I got rid of the task of finding farewell presents for the Duke's one night stands. Don't feign you're surprised because you already knew he was quite naughty."

"Michael and Ferdinand implied those friends were, you know, professionals?"

"Those two can be real pigs!" Monika burst into laughter. "Prostitutes? No chance, dear—all people from society. You should have seen the queue for getting into his bed, hoping to achieve something. In a way, they might be called that because they were after his money or power. Despite the Duke and his men think more ahead of their times and understand perfectly well our society, almost never missing in their predictions for the economic future, they live under bygone standards."

"When I met him, he said something like taking me to eat to a hotel would be totally inappropriate. Do you know what he meant?" I inquired, deciding to know as much as possible from her boss since it was gossip time. She flashed me a bright smile.

"So it was as I thought. Love at first sight. Cupid must have used big ammo this time," she chuckled. "Only one night stands go to hotels. He was leaving clearly for Ferdinand that he was serious about you. The good thing about them is that they are perfectly clear in their symbols when they speak within their inner circle. They mean every word or gesture made. Did he walk you back to the hotel?"

"Yes, how do you know?" I whispered under her amused glare.

"He was telling the others he would protect you and that they were out of the game. Normally, one of his bodyguards would have had to get rid of the chosen fling. That was a declaration of intentions."

"He kissed my hands that night, but I think none of them was present."

"Did he? Oh, that means he respects and considers your status above him," she said this time seriously. Monika noticed the sun was going away and it had started to rain again. "I don't like driving under such conditions. I'd better go, dear."

"Thank you very much for your visit, Monika."

"I'll come by another day," she promised me with a big smile on her face. Monika kissed me on the cheek, like a mother, and went away.

I'm still processing all what she said, Diary. It's too much.

Marie Amélie is a nice girl, or at least that's what I thought. I admit she's quite careless and wilful; she's a lively person who despises all the conventions she is supposed to live under. I mean anybody would feel suffocated by this world and a free spirit like herself would do anything to rebel against the main enforcer; Konrad.

Why would she drag an old guy to her bed, only to destroy his wedding just to piss off Konrad? That makes no sense at all. She could have achieved the same with something less elaborated, like misbehaving in the ceremony or even paying somebody to make a scene.

Was Monika lying to me? It seemed unlikely, but everything is possible. Asking Konrad would be the best option. However, that was out of question as he obviously considered himself responsible for the mess, in a twisted way, as he had introduced the couple. He would deny everything, become enraged and tell me to mind my own business, if I was lucky at all. The whole story is too twisted to come from a sixteen-year-old. That girl is not Lucretia Borgia.

Perhaps what happened was a stupid and cruel joke gone very bad like with me. Maybe she knew what was inside of that bottle and thought I would get green or throw up. At school, we used to put salt in the drinks, preferably if the victim had to be at the teachers' table. If Marie Amélie and her friends had a line already in, everything seemed funny and clever.

On the other hand I can understand, but not justify, Konrad's strong reaction. He loves me and is very protective and repeating the hospital mambo must have pushed him to his limits, forcing him to react in his own paranoid way.

How could a man who is so bent on his old fashion ways decide after one or two hours of meeting me, in a public square and a Museum, that he wanted to spend the rest of his life with me? How could the others be so certain that our relationship would work at all?

Everything is so confusing here.

Chapter 34

June 2nd, 2002

Last night, or maybe today because it was very late when he came home, I woke up startled by a small noise in the bedroom. Konrad was sitting in the sofa placed by the window his eyes fixed on the bed. I sat trying to calm myself down because I was not expecting him at all and much less to enter so quietly.

"I'm sorry to disturb you. I'll go to another room," he said rising from the couch.

"No, please stay. I was surprised, that's all. What were you doing there?" All sleep was away from me as I sat in the bed.

"Watching you sleep and thinking," he said shyly like a child caught with the hand in the chocolate box.

"Come to the bed, you must be tired. When did you arrive?"

"Few hours ago."

"Remove your jacket and shoes or tomorrow you will hear it from Friederich," I said softly moving away from the center of the bed to leave room for him. He got rid of the things including his tie and laid down on his side, without touching me. I extended my left hand to caress his face and he closed the eyes like a cat, revelling in my touch.

"Why didn't you tell me about Lausanne?" I fired taking advantage of the fact he had all his defences down for once. He looked at me disoriented and then a flash of guilt passed through his eyes very fast. He tried to look away, disturbed. "Please, answer me," I pressed on.

"Marie Amélie was like a daughter to me. I thought to be quiet and give her another start with you; a clean one."

"Do you blame her for your friend's fate?"

"Not for that. We choose what we do and have to live with it. I was more disturbed that she was so determined to be on my way and fight her father and me so intensively. I didn't want to acknowledge that, at some point, I would have to place her on my enemies' side."

"I'm sorry for your loss," I kissed him on the forehead.

"I also made the mistake of not trusting my first impression of her. She's dangerous and like myself, will stop at nothing to get what she wants. For a moment, I thought, or let's better say, I wanted her to be like you, selfless and good hearted. I almost killed you with my gamble."

"Shh, it was not a gamble, Konrad. Why are you so afraid to like people and forgive them? If she was like a daughter to you, I don't blame you for wanting to give her another chance," I whispered pulling him close to me, his head against my chest. "Next time, I would like a warning before you do something. You should trust me more. I'm not a child or an idiot even if I'm not so clever as you."

"You have an intelligent mind, it's just you're so green," he said carefully choosing his words.

"If you don't tell me the things, how can I understand the reasons behind your actions? Do you realise how you make me feel every time you decree something like a king?"

He chuckled. "I'm also guilty of that. I cannot help it," I gave him a light punch in the biceps and he took my hand and softly kissed it. I returned the gesture doing the same and he pulled me against his body. We stayed like this for a long time.

"You were right about something else," I said half-jokingly. "Friederich is nastier than you when he reprehends you."

"I know," he answered, raising his eyebrows, looking very amused. "I gave you a fair notice. What was your offence?"

"Refusing to finish the greens," I said remembering a legendary scold that sent me back to my toddler times.

"Mayor crime. Should be glad you didn't get the spoon on the head like I did," he mumbled shrugging.

"Sorry?"

"Friederich has taken care of me since I was four. My father hired him as a tutor to replace the nannies and he had the old Jesuit school for dealing with children. You have to understand, he was born during wartime and there was no food, regardless your money. Rations cards for everybody. He was twenty-two when he came here, full of energy and convinced of the motto "to command, first you have to know how to obey."

"He has worked for you for the past forty years?" This is surprising.

"Almost. He was a seminarian in the Jesuit Order, but had to get a better job to support her mother and sisters. He lived in a monastery in Bavaria since he turned thirteen and was already a schoolteacher when I got him."

"I thought you had private teachers, not him."

"Yes, I had them, but he was the person ultimately responsible for me. I had to rewrite my homework several times till it was to his liking. Less than perfect was unacceptable. The strict boarding school I went to later was a holiday camp compared to his educational style. I think he stopped instructing me when my father, the Duke, passed away. He's like a father to me. Don't get on his wrong side, you will not like the consequences if you do. I know."

"I'll take your word for that. Anything else I should not do?"

"Hundreds of things, but he has softened over the years. And he does not plan to retire for a long time," he chuckled.

I smiled again at him and snuggled closer, closing my eyes to sleep.

Chapter 35

August 20th, 2002

The summer is almost over and I'm feeling better. I didn't do much, to be honest, and for the first two months, I didn't feel like doing anything, really. The doctor was right, not that I'm going to give him the pleasure of admitting he knew what he was saying. I felt exhausted after the smallest effort.

Having reached a sort of truce with Konrad helped me a lot. The tension between us disappeared and we started all over again, now that I could understand him a little better. His personality is very complex and once you think you can figure him out, he makes an unexpected turn and you're hanging in the air anew. Sometimes, he behaves like a child with me, others he's like the Prince from Machiavelli, cold, calculating and unforgiving, or he's like a father to me, despite his protests on the contrary. I will never get bored with him, that's clear.

We sort of established a routine. He would get up at 6, yes, at 6 a.m., would disappear to train with his bodyguards and not return until 7:30 when he would get ready for work. The rest of the day, I would have my German lessons in the morning and in the afternoons, I was free to do my homework, walk around, draw, read or take care of Mopsi. Alexei became my shadow and honestly he saved me from insanity for being more or less confined to the big house. At 7 p.m., Konrad would return and spend the rest of the evening with me, talking or watching a film together. We looked like an old couple, but he never complained or was mean to me. In that sense, I loved him more for the patience he was having and showing to me.

He travelled less than before and brought less papers home.

By July, the doctor authorized me to go once per week to painting lessons. No sex yet. I lost my temper with Meister Ostermann when he asked me what I've been doing with the bloody blue elephant. I threw it to the trash in front of him and shouted vulgarly I had enough of the thing and preferred to paint badly in my own way than suffering his "pseudo Zen wisdom" any longer.

The old man laughed at my face breaking the heavy silence made by the ladies who also studied with him. Not a moment I was particularly proud of.

"Finally you decided to say something on your own. Perhaps, I will get still something good out of you! Get paper and start to work."

"What do I do?" I said puzzled.

"How would I know? Do whatever you want. We will work on your techniques, but the rest of the journey is for you to travel alone."

I sat like an idiot in front of the easel for a long time while the others resumed their work. Finally, and not willing to waste more time, I started to copy a part of one of the windows of the building in front of us. He almost gave me the next heart attack when he crept behind me and said happily:

"Now it's much better. I can start to see something from you in the paint. Look here, you changed slightly the perspective and the proportions to adopt them to the point of view of the sparrow, who by the way, looks like it's coming from a revel."

"It was getting a dust bath on the street," I mused.

"This is exactly what you have to achieve. Give life to what you paint and make the person looking at it wonder. That's all. Let yourself go of making everything perfect. No need at all. I'll keep the elephant for you in case you return to your old habits."

"No if I get with a hammer to it," I promised seriously.

"Next week bring all what you have been doing this time. We will decide what to do next. Perhaps, it's time you start to really work with oil paints. It will force you to work slowly and meditate before doing anything," he said, doubtfully.

Since that day we got along. He criticized everything I did and I listening to everything he said because he was right... most of the time. Last week, he helped me to choose six paintings and drawings to send to Luciana for the Russian. At least, I will not feel so bad about cheating with my artwork. A well-known private curator chose them. Incognito, if not "you will have to set the price in more than several thousand". Konrad complained a lot when he saw the selection. He wanted to keep four of them.

Yesterday, I went to the doctor again and after some fighting he agreed that I could start the semester in mid-September at the University, but I should take it lightly. If I feel bad, should stop. Fortunately, my medications were reduced to four.

Strange as it might look, I miss Marie Amélie and her sparkling character. Had it not have been for my promise of never contacting her again, I would have answered her e-mails. I still don't know how she managed to write to me because if I see correctly it's completely forbidden to make contact with the outside world once you enter into these detox clinics, but she always was very clever to overcome difficulties. I do hope she does well nowadays. The last news I had was dated from a month ago and her father was not happy at my question of how she was faring. "She's in Geneve slightly progressing." Needless to say, Konrad does not allow me to speak with her mother. "She will only make terror to you," If somebody can explain me the meaning of that sentence, I would be very thankful because my stony German refuses to clarify.

Our imposed celibacy (big word, I know), or at least to me because for him I will not put my hands in the fire—on the other hand he has not given me any reason to be suspicious—changed our relationship making it deeper. The lack of hot, steamy sex (and how I miss it!), forced us to look for other ways to communicate and subtly we started to understand each other better and be more careful in our manners so we wouldn't hurt each other like we did in the past. We sort of fell into a routine of whispered confidences, friendly conversations and tender embraces.

Perhaps I understand him better than before. It's not so difficult to get along with him once you accept his character. He is a person who would really need to visit a shrink on a weekly basis and I believe he deeply knows it and has placed himself into an incredible set of rules to make his existence simpler. Between the boundaries he sets for all of us, you can move freely, but don't move a single thing out of place because he goes into panic and, with fear comes violence. He lowers his guard a little, but not much. Of course he would kill himself before admitting to other people he needs help, but maybe with years of a stable love he'll finally do it.

In a way, I would have never wanted his place in this world. He's like a big child with many responsibilities, the intelligence to overcome then but none of the skills of a mature personality to cope with them.

Konrad nearly broke my heart one night a few weeks ago when we were going to bed. His past week in the bank was a living nightmare with an inspection from the Internal Revenue Service looking for proofs of tax fraud from several clients. The investigators were in fact trying to find out evidence his banks were forging documents to help the customers to evade taxes. Even Konrad's own office had been searched thoroughly with a Court's order.

He spoke barely a word during the whole dinner almost not touching the food. He looked nervous, trapped and distressed. When I finished eating he just went to his studio and closed the door. I went to read in bed, waiting for him to come. My heart was pounding heavily. What else could I do? I'm no lawyer, no economist, just a student. I'm totally useless.

Very late he came in, put his pyjamas on silently and slid under the covers, laying close to me, without touching me. He turned his back to me and pulled the covers around him and said with a frail voice "Could you hold me tonight?"

"Always," was my answer as I snuggled against his back, my hand caressing his hair. This is my way to help him.

PART II

The Order

Chapter 1

December 19th, 2002

Tomorrow is the anniversary—if you can call it like that—of the previous Argentinian government's downfall. It's not that I miss the former President or that I like the new one but reading today's press, commemorating the mess, the deaths and the default forced me to stop for a while and start to ponder how it happened and how I did end up here.

As Corina, my good friend from the University, would say it was a bad conjunction of the planets, with Uranus destroying everything on its path. I don't believe that crap at all but I have to agree that it was collective madness what had befallen upon us all. For a moment everything looked like we were going to change and start anew, in a clean form but by July citizens were back at their houses, the poor people was still poor and the same blasted politicians were working hard to remain in their places.

The funny thing is, that even if I should feel upset or at least bother me, I don't care at all. My life in Argentina is dead and well buried. I don't think I could ever come back to live there—visiting friends, yes. I'm dying to go when the doctor allows me do it. My heart is in better shape nowadays, and I don't feel so tired all the time, but I still have to improve to get a clear bill of health.

Furthermore, my love should get holidays. Alas, his mind is at the World Economic Forum in Davos, due at the end of January. The only thing I know—because one of his men, Michael Dähler told me—is that he's leading a "group of friends" to increase investments in Brazil and Argentina. After a really bad 2002 (bad for people because his hedge funds and banks will show very nice figures, according to Ferdinand), the war in Afghanistan and the more than possible invasion of Iraq, all bankers will meet to "rebuild trust". The next bubble is on the way guys (that's sardonic).

Perhaps I should start to write a Diary again in this laptop. My original folder from the Cluny Museum finished long time ago, in March, and I used my old laptop, whenever I had free time. It's incredible how my life turned in one year. One day, I was in Paris purchasing it, and in a flash I was in Venice meeting Konrad and falling in love with him. Honestly, for me it was not love at first sight, and he behaved like a real asshole in the first date, but then, he was like a knight in shining armour, saving me from a real mess with the Italian police, dubious Argentinean friends, showing me a world of pleasure I never suspected could exist. Pity invincible knights have a bad temper, are possessive, obsessive, paranoid, bipolar, neurotic, calculating, but incredibly sexy, gentle, generous, intelligent, protective, funny with an absurd sense of humour, tender like children and reflexive.

Well, nobody is perfect, but for me, he is… if you rub him in the right way. Otherwise, Konrad can be your worst nightmare, and you'd wish to be dead.

However, I should not be unfair to him. For the last seven months, we have lived in a sort of permanent honeymoon, even if there were some highly disturbing personal events that should have set him into his "psycho mode". Nevertheless,

225

nothing happened to me, and he was relatively satisfied shouting the culprit and punishing them within reason and proportion. Maybe he's understanding finally the principle of proportional retaliation.

"You give me a peace of mind like I've never known before," he told me once.

We balance each other. On my own, I would be sitting still in my living room in Argentina, debating with myself if I should live with him, draw something or study. I need his "pushing in the right direction" (shoving would be a better description in many cases), and his love to feel free and part of something. Without me, he would be an empty shell of a man, hiding his fears under a mask of coldness, violence, super alpha macho, and living in the greatest desert for the soul.

I've just reread this and I ask myself the biggest question; when did I become so corny? Better don't tell me. I really don't want to know. Let's write down what I've been doing this semester in the school to update this thing.

By mid-September, I resumed school. Classes started at 8 a.m. and lasted up to 1 p.m. with some breaks and believe me, here you have to study hard to keep up with the pace or die under a mountain of textbooks. Very Swiss and exactly like the International Baccalaureate was; long programs and lots of extra work, but everything organized to the last detail. Better don't waste your time because it's very hard to recover what you missed.

The first month, I was quite lost as almost everything is taught in German. Yes, they speak English and French without problems because they're Swiss, but prefer you speak and present your papers in German. By twelve o'clock, I wanted to jump out of the window to escape the headache caused by a whole morning surrounded by teachers and classmates barking in that language. Well, they don't bark and are very polite, but after three hours of trying to pick what is being said, even the slightest hallo, is hard to understand. Per Monika's advice, I taped the lessons and would listen to them later in the library and take notes. In the mornings, I was glad if I could copy from the board.

I wasn't the only guy astray in the classroom, fortunately. There was also a girl, well a woman, from Argentina, Corina Fernández de van der Weyden. She had already a major in Political Science from a private university in Buenos Aires, but had recently married a Dutch, who was working at an insurance company here. At twenty-five, she was bored at home and decided to start another career to practice the language. "It was this, interior decorating classes or tennis and I hate those two. I will be here until the children come or graduate."

First, we didn't get along because she made a big face when I told her my former school's name, but necessity forced us to work together, especially in Maths for her and History for me. "You are a pretty normal guy for coming from the biggest concentration of rich spoiled idiots in Argentinean History. I thought you were different." Honestly, I was also a little bit apprehensive of young society ladies, no matter where they came from, but she was clever, funny and really wanted to study. We became a team.

Thank God Konrad decided that her friendship was "adequate" (sic, I swear), and Ferdinand "has a good opinion of the company the husband works for", leaving me alone. He even invited them for an informal lunch on a Saturday morning, which is very rare. If you ask me, I think he wanted to check on the husband to see if he would be able to "control his wife" so she doesn't jump on my bones in a crowded library one of these days. The man passed the test with honours, because later I knew that Konrad's own insurance company had offered him a good position with a better salary, but Van der Weyden refused. Clever guy, indeed.

By October, I was more or less adjusting to the classes and classmates. The ones from Banking and Finance were all like Charlie Sheen on Wall Street, but as I kept my relationship with Konrad secret, and Corina never said a thing, they didn't pay much attention to me. In Economics things were more distributed and you had every kind of people there, from the wannabe yuppie (majority) to the pure scientist and the idealist. I also got along with a guy from Denmark, Peter—impossible to pronounce his last name—Kjærgaard, a quiet Viking who would put us back to work when we were drifting too much. Intelligent as bordering on genius, he would speak no more than twenty words per day.

On the 19th, I turned twenty and my teenager years were officially over. Now I'm a responsible adult. Konrad wanted to give me a party but I refused because I knew nobody here and one night hanging with old CEO's and wives was more a torture than a party. Finally, he settled for inviting Michael plus unknown girlfriend for a dinner at home. Yeah, unknown girlfriend was Monika van der Leyden—big boss' secretary—to my utter surprise. Michael got her after trying for several years and enduring so many belittling remarks. He's tenacious and she looks like a real Empress. In my opinion, the wait was more than worth it.

You would ask why Ferdinand von Kleist, long time Konrad's friend and second in command, plus wife were not invited. Long and messy story. Despite Konrad had more or less overcame his fury towards Ferdinand because of her daughter's prank on me—mostly because Ferdinand was more stern in his punishment than him—July month's scandal proved too much for Konrad.

Shortly, Ferdinand sent the petition for divorce to his wife, Gertrud, to the bank, without a previous warning to Konrad. Big scandal in the morning, with her shouting and crying inside Konrad's office accusing him of being an accessory. They had had troubles for the last twenty years or so, but for the children's sake they had reached a non-belligerent status which looked like the Cold War. On top of the divorce, there was also a paternity suit for the last child, Marie Amélie.

At noon started the big fight between Konrad and Ferdinand, the first rabid at the insult towards his cousin who deserved some respect after almost twenty-six years of marriage, and the later furious for Konrad's meddling in a private matter. Monika told me, that Ferdinand finished the discussion with a "for twenty-five years I've endured this crazy Lintorff bitch and even fathered one of her bastards from who knows who." They had a violent quarrel and the poor Goran and Michael had to separate them, getting some of the blows in the process. You don't put the words crazy and Lintorff in the same sentence.

Ferdinand moved the next day with his lover, a young economist from the bank, and in the next week, he bought a villa in front of the Lake Zurich for her and his two sons, who also wanted to move with the father. I know he also presented his resignation, but the Administrative Council rejected it. Konrad, to his credit, refrained from voting and kept quiet the whole time while the council debated.

So silent he was that he didn't speak a word to Ferdinand until mid-November, and it was "von Kleist take care of that matter in London", much to

Michael's relief because he was overloaded with work, forced to replace Ferdinand in many things to avoid another clash between them. Maybe the Christmas spirit would soften him a little, and say something more to his childhood friend.

But even with such a huge fight and mess in the internal front, Konrad was always polite and loving to me, despite I could tell he was highly frustrated and enraged.

Beginning of December, there was a huge restructuring at the offices, and the whole Lintorff Foundation was moved out of the building to a much larger and elegant place and Gertrud got more manpower and resources for charity. The day she left, I went to the bank at five, there was a new, relaxed atmosphere in the upper floors. Konrad's dark mood also improved a lot and he stopped brooding so much.

I even got part of the heat. Not directly of course and in a much smaller dose than the people working at the bank. Every day after studying up to five in the library, Alexei would pick me up at the entrance and take me to the bank. Yeah, you argue with a big Russian with clear orders, and then with the basilisk sitting at his desk in Börsenstrasse. Anyway, I was supposed to sit quietly in his office or with Monika, working or reading my things, not making a sound until seven or eight when he would decide it was time to go home in his limo. This was the only time I could play a little bit with my dog, Mopsi.

Mornings, I would drive with Alexei and have some peace once we agreed he would let me one hundred metres from the Faculty. Honestly, you can't expect me to go to a public university in a huge van from Porsche. After some fighting he also agreed to change it for something less notorious... an Audi A4. What happened to the times when Russians drove Ladas?

In November, Konrad turned forty-five, and had a party in the castle, with important people around while I was wishing I could hide myself in a hole. The only good part was when we exchanged presents... in the bedroom. I think I got more out than him when we made love for the very first time in a long time.

It was so sweet, that I still shiver at the memory. I can't help to remember his eyes looking at me adoringly and shyly at the same time. His hands trembling at my shirt's buttons, his breathing ragged. Seeing the normally self-composed and haughty Konrad von Lintorff, *Herzog* von Wittstock behaving like a teenager in love breaks down all your defences and barriers.

We kissed deeply, our tongues battling for dominance, but soon I conceded defeat and let him roam throughout my mouth. It was his birthday after all. His kisses were more intoxicating for me than the bit of champagne I had at the party, and my head felt dizzy for a moment. He sensed me faltering and immediately stopped to my chagrin.

"Are you all right? If you want we can leave it for another day," he trailed and I silenced him with another kiss.

"It was just the emotion," I whispered in his ear having to go to my tiptoes to reach his head.

We fell on top of the bed feverishly tearing clothes like two animals. He was attacking my flesh with his kisses not giving me an inch to counter attack. "I'm desperate to feel you again," he conceded.

"I love you so much," I confessed almost melting in his arms.

"Can you come on top?" he pleaded.

"That's very romantic, you know," I smirked. "Besides, it's not such a good idea. I want you to enjoy it and you don't like that too much."

"I need to know that you're in control and can back up if you feel bad or not up to this. If I go on top of you, I fear I will not be able to control myself and might hurt you."

If he wanted this I could not deny him. Let's make it at least worthwhile. I took his erected member in my mouth, playing on the top with my tongue a little before engulfing it almost to the hilt. His surprised moans encouraged my sucking and my own excitement. When I felt the first drops of his cum I stopped and knelt at his side. The disappointment painted in his face was so blatant that I chuckled. He looked so cute, the expression of a kid denied of a candy.

"It's not over yet. We can do much more," I murmured while I laid down myself over the pillows offering me to him in a shameless way. He didn't waste time to jump on me and started to stretch me as my heart picked up the pace.

I was in bliss when he stopped, now leaving me like the child in front of the candy store.

"On top, young man," he half seriously ordered me. I complied inserting myself onto his hard shaft and going for the ride of a lifetime. We both came together in harmony and feeling totally complete and satisfied.

Since that night we resumed our activities in the bedroom. I don't know if he said something to my doctor because I didn't.

Corina told me a few days ago that it was logical we sort of got along. He was a Scorpio with ascendant in Capricorn and I a Libra but with much more in Pisces. He has the "magnetic character of Scorpio with the stubbornness of the goat, can be very dark, but completely honest to the people he loves. A love that lasts to the grave." I, on the other hand, was "from another galaxy like all Pisces, idealists to the point of being naïve, natural born artists, but need to be controlled if you don't want them to finish depressed and hurt. You are perfect for him because he doesn't feel threatened by you and loves your innocent nature. You need his clarity and determination to achieve anything." Nice way to call me a wimp. She likes these Astrology things a lot and I don't believe it but I had to admit I was surprised when she described his character quite accurately by only at looking his natal chart.

Chapter 2

December 23rd, 2002

Maybe it's a bad idea that I write a diary. Whenever I start to do it, somehow things become complicated or what was a perfectly normal day twists in a way I don't comprehend and without a warning.

Friday 20th was supposed to be a normal day. School finished and I was only going to pick up the ratings at about 4:00 and have a final coffee with Corina and Peter (yes, the man agreed to share a non-study moment with us!), before the Christmas break until February when the Spring semester will start.

First part of the day ran smoothly without problems. Konrad left early in the morning with his papers, bodyguards and cars, and I was left here to loaf. I played with Mopsi a lot, painted something, but not much, not inspired at all, had lunch, witnessed the huge 2003 Cooking Budget Quarrel between Jean Jacques, the French Chef on one corner and Friederich, the Austrian Butler and main Administrator on the other. Anything goes and no prisoners. I disappeared in the middle of it, because since I can't distinguish between Beluga, Osetra or Sevruga Caviar, I can't give an opinion and much less make a Solomonic decision. Perhaps Mopsi, who was following their heated argument with ears up, could give a more educated guess. Also the kitchen is full of knives, if you get my meaning.

Alexei drove me to the University and said he would pick me up at 5:15 sharp. I fetched up my ratings sheet, which was good, an average 5.3 over 6. My friends and I had coffee together and we said our goodbyes. I was out at 5:10.

I was waiting at the usual corner when somebody touched my shoulder. I turned around and there was Marie Amélie. I was shocked to see her. She looked very well.

"Hi," I said, hoping she would do the same and continue with her life.

"Hi Guntram," she replied sweetly, not moving a single inch from her place.

"I'm waiting for Alexei. Have to go to the bank," I said hurriedly, invoking one nasty Russian and a meaner German. OK, maybe I'm overreacting but our last encounter images were assaulting me.

"I wanted to speak with you. I'm terribly sorry for what happened. I swear I didn't know it. You know I like you."

"Don't worry about it. I never thought you were responsible. Are you OK now?" Stupid Guntram! You promised never to contact her again and here you're chit chatting, I chastised myself realising too late what I've done.

"I'm clean and working now, here in Zurich, at a coffee," she said with her big eyes. Wait, was she not living in Frankfurt per her father's orders?

"I thought you were in Frankfurt. Sorry Marie Amélie, I have to go," Yes, I have to flee before the Russian who loves you so much appears, makes a scene, and then runs to tell Konrad he was under the attack of a nineteen-year-old skinny girl.

"Since von Kleist divorced Mum I don't have to obey him any longer. I moved back with her. Please, Guti, don't go. I need a favour from you." Big tearful eyes.

"I promised Konrad not to speak with you ever again, I'm sorry," I mumbled, a little ashamed that I had to admit to her that I have to obey him.

"I know, Mum told me. You even interceded on my behalf. Thank you."

So? I was good to you, now beat it before I get into troubles because of you. I kept silent and looked the other way. My heart started to beat faster and nastier than before.

"I need money," she blurted out.

"Ask your father or your mother. I have none. Only $10,000 in a frozen Argentinean account."

"My father left my mother with nothing, only a lousy allowance of 12,000 Swiss francs."

Fuck! I would love one of those. I was making $1,300, and paid rent with that when I lived alone. Ferdinand even pays for the house maintenance and the service according to Monika. Gertrud has a good salary at the Foundation and large personal fortune. She's not exactly broken.

"That's a lot of money," I said firmly.

"I need €100,000. I want to go away from Europe and start anew. Lintorff will never leave me in peace or forgive me. "

Are you telling me that you need €100,000 in the middle of the street? Sure, I'll buy you a ticket for the Lotto and maybe you're luckier.

"I don't even have €10,000. I'm not making money in the moment. Honestly, I'm walking deficit nowadays," I smirked finding the situation absurd. "Ask Ferdinand. He will help you."

"You can get the money out of your trustee fund. We all have one for five millions. It's not much. It's just one year interests," she said desperately.

"It's not my money! It's Konrad's! He already pays for everything, and you want me to take more money out?"

"That is nothing for him, and it can mean a lot for me!" She jumped to my neck crying and kissing me heatedly, full on the lips. Not now!

The screech of a car stopping along with the coming out of a very pissed off Serb from that car instead of my nice, kind Russian bodyguard, was more than bad luck. It was the curse from a vengeful god. There was Goran Pavicevic. Had he seen the kiss? Most probably; he looked enraged.

"You. In the car. Now," he barked me, and I tried to disentangle from her but she didn't let me go.

"Lintorff let you out of your leash?" Marie Amélie said to my horror. Girl, you are speaking with a man who can hit his boss (during training) and lives to tell; the man who makes a former KGB boy, trained in Afghanistan recoil in fear.

"You were warned not to come near him," he darkly told her.

"And what are you going to do? Rape me and cut me into pieces like you did to Croat women and children?" I closed my eyes holding my breath. Goran pulled me violently by the sleeve and dragged me to the big black Mercedes almost throwing me on the passenger seat.

"Remember well my face because this is the last thing you'll see if you ever come near my little brother." Have I told you Diary that for some dark, unknown reason, Goran decided to adopt me as his baby brother since I had my first heart attack? It's unsettling to have him around, but he never said something out of place or much less did anything to me.

I slouched in the car seat, feeling sick. It was very likely he would tell Konrad I've broken a rule and all hell would get loose.

"You have up to 6:30 to tell his Excellency or I'll do it. Perhaps knowing it from you would lessen his fury," he warned me before entering in the private lift. I gulped and nodded.

Monika let me into his office. Konrad was busy reading and writing. He didn't lift his gaze from the papers, and I sat in one of the sofas by the window, looking for paper to draw in my backpack.

At 6:15 Goran walked in and pointedly looked at me while Konrad was checking the papers he had just brought in. OK, he's serious and Konrad is distracted maybe I can tell and get away with it.

"Today I saw Marie Amélie in school. She needs some money to leave Europe, and suggested I could give it to her. I refused," I slurred the words out.

He put his fine and noble pen down, making a deafening sound in the now silent room. No, he was not so distracted. When have I ever caught him unaware?

"Where did you meet her?" he said soft and courteously. Bad sign. Direct shouting is better.

"At the Faculty's entrance. I was waiting for the car," I said nervously. Yeah, Goran, there's something for you in this.

"How much?"

"One hundred thousand euros," I spat. "I told her I have no money."

"Why does she believe you could get her such an amount?" He asked me, dangerously throwing one of his predatory glances.

"I don't know. She said I could get it out of the account for the University but I said it's your money not mine. Goran saw it," I blurted out the last part almost incomprehensible. Goran stood motionless there and I wished for a minute he would keep to himself what he saw us doing. Well, she did it; not I.

"Is that all in their conversation, Goran?" He looked intensively at the bodyguard who didn't flinch a muscle in his face or diverted his gaze from Konrad. That's a real professional!

"I didn't hear it, Sire."

Thank you, I wanted to shout. I looked at him in gratitude for a fleeting moment, not even a second but Konrad caught me.

"Is that all what happened?" He knows or assumes which, in this case, is the same.

"She kissed me," I confessed totally embarrassed and looking guilty.

"With force. I saw that part. She jumped at his neck when Guntram looked the other way." Goran defended me with a soft voice. Now Konrad really looked into the Serb's eyes trying to tell if he was saying the truth and I felt insulted. Yes, I like to kiss the people who inadvertently almost sent me to the other side.

"I see," he finally said and switched to Russian with Goran. Great! Now he speaks Russian, like the bad boys from the Clockwork Orange.

Goran left the office in a rush. Now it's my turn to be told off.

"Konrad I didn't mean to disobey or disrespect you. I was distracted and shocked when I saw her. I didn't think fast enough—"

"Be quiet. I have still a lot of work to do."

I remained sitting in the sofa as the night became more and more dark. At some point, Monika entered and gave him a folder which he put on top of the pile at his right side. To read urgently it seems.

He finished his documents, and started to read the new folder. I kept quiet like a mouse, not fidgeting at all. It was almost 7:30 when he finished.

"Come over here, Guntram," he ordered in his no nonsense tone. I approached his desk feeling very small and with a big lump in my throat. "Your account for educational fees seems to be in order," I barely suppressed a sigh. "Your grades are fine although a 4.7 in History is not exactly thrilling but you compensate with all the others with 6."

"I did not understand all the questions in the final test," I defended myself.

"But your credit card is something else," he finished not even caring what I'd said. "Can you explain to me why in the last five months you spent 773 Swiss francs?"

"I have the bills at home. I don't remember exactly the amounts," I said gulping nervously, and starting to fidget like when I was at the Principals office.

"I'll refresh your memory. 47 francs, then 62 francs in stationary."

"Oil painting can be expensive," I meekly defended myself. And it was Meister Ostermann's idea to use it."

"Almost 535 francs in the University canteen."

"It's for the four months. Lunch time."

"Around 65 francs at a Museum's Restaurant."

"Corina and I ate there the day we went to Le Corbusier Museum. I didn't let her pay." I felt now really sick.

"There are other minor things but let's do not dwell. Just one thing. What is 35 Swiss francs for a watch?"

"My original watch went dead and changing the battery was more expensive than replacing it."

"Didn't I give you a perfectly good watch for your birthday?" Dangerous glint in his eyes.

"Yes, it's at home. In the third drawer of my desk. It's too good to take to the university," I whispered, now losing all colours and hopes to escape this one unscathed.

"Where are the expenses for clothes, mobile phone, books, eating out and such things young people normally do?"

"I don't have them. Friederich takes care of the clothes and he gets very upset if I complain it's too much, the books I lend them from the University library, and I eat there also. If it's too much I will cut down the expenses more."

"Would be interesting to see how you do it. For example we have an average of less than 7 francs in food per day. What the hell have you been eating?"

"Students menu. Half of it. The doctor doesn't allow me to eat most of the food there," I said, almost fainting under his scrutinizing glare.

"I can't believe my ears. You have been living with me for a year, and you still don't feel at home. You tread lightly over everything. You spent less than 800 francs in four months! Ferdinand's children used to get 2,000 per month only for pocket money! I saw that hideous thing you have the nerve to call a watch but I said nothing because I thought it was a souvenir from school days. You're going to throw it to the trash right now, and wear the one I gave you," he exploded in an enraged mix of fury and frustration at me.

"It's a Lange und Söhne! Even if it's a small one it's too much for school!" I was shocked. If I take it, I'll get all the yuppies from Banking and Finance on my throat, drowning me in flattery for the next five years!

"Leave the watch out of this!" he roared. "The problem here is your expenses or lack of them. Have I ever denied you anything that you insult me by refusing my support?" The half hidden pain in his voice hurt me. "Don't you trust me enough as to accept it without regrets?"

"I don't want to abuse you. You've been very generous to me, and I don't know how to repay you," I said almost dying with remorse and shame.

"What am I going to do with you? We are repeating the same conversation we had a year ago," he sighed looking truly tired. "Come here, *Maus*," he moved his big chair away and beckoned me to approach him. I did. He pulled me effortlessly toward his lap and I landed there, without grace and stifling a yelp. His left arm encircled my waist and he grasped firmly my chin with his right hand.

"I'm not telling you that you buy a Millet in the next auction, but you should spend some more. It almost drives me crazy to think you were eating for 7 francs per day. That's the price for a mineral water in a restaurant! How do you think I feel when I find out you're depriving yourself in such a way?"

"I'm sorry," I murmured now feeling really guilty. Honestly, I never thought that way.

"If it helps you as a directive, think on terms of 2,000 to 3,000 francs per month. Buy the books you want to read for example. If you don't have the time now, leave them for the holidays, and don't you ever come back with a watch from China."

"All right, next time is a Rolex President," I said softly, hoping humour would lift the dense haze over us.

"Please, not the watch from the rookie broker and the Latin American Dictator! It's so… snob!"

All right. Rolex is snob. Clear. I should have known.

I looked at him trying to see if he was joking but he was serious and coming to think, he has not a single Rolex in his collection. Let's change subject to a more important issue.

"Why did Marie Amélie think I could give her the money? She knows I have nothing, and would not go against your wishes."

"It was a set up. Find a subject where you would be uncomfortable and with a low guard so she could kiss you, and I would get the nice picture to make me explode and be away with you. She was counting on your silence to make you look guiltier," he explained as a matter of fact.

I was speechless. Why on earth would she be upset with me? I never blamed her for what happened. My head decided to cooperate by starting a migraine.

"By now, Goran and Michael must be betting on the arrival time of the photos. I'd put my money on Christmas day," he said, jokingly but stopped when he realised I've turned ash colour. "You don't look well," he observed.

"I have a headache," I mumbled burying my head in his shoulder.

"Go to the sofa and rest a little. Do you want a painkiller? We'll leave soon."

"No, thank you." I sat again in the incredibly comfortable sofas he has, and I think I dozed because I almost jumped when I heard Goran's voice saying. "Forgive me, my Duke, it's 8:30. We must hurry if we want to take off at 11:00."

"In a minute," was the sharp answer. "Guntram gather your things."

"Where are we going?" I can't think straight if I'm sleepy and hungry.

"It's a surprise."

Chapter 3

He's absolutely crazy… in a fantastic way.
I'm in Paris. Again.
Near Champs Elysée. Again
In the George V. I passed by last time I was here but now the doorman is nicer.

Empire Suite. The hostel was also nice although the cotton sheets were not Egyptian and I had no terrace overlooking the city skyline and the Eiffel Tower.

"I wanted to show you off a little, and since you are in much better shape than before, I thought that coming early this year to Paris, and later going to London for a few days, would be good for us. Who knows, maybe we could even go to pester my cousin Albert in Milan. I've taken holidays for fifteen days. This Monday we have to go to Mass in Nôtre Dame and then I have to lunch with some associates but then I'm free," he explained to me while dinning in his "small" Dassault jet (for short range trips).

Nearly dead we went to bed straight from the car. At 3 a.m. you can't ask me to be romantic, especially after a scold or nearly frightening me to death. I barely noticed the room and the big king size bed with canopy. I changed into my pyjamas and slid under the covers. One thought assaulted my mind. "Empire Suite"? As Emperor… as Napoleon? The decoration looks very in the Empire Style… Tomorrow you're so dead Konrad. I'll make fun out of you for the next years, was my last coherent thought before falling asleep.

A cold hand on my neck made me almost jump out of the bed. Clearly awaken, I threw a dirty look at the offender. Konrad. Who else can be a maniac to wake you up on a Saturday morning? If he wants to go out to play the tourist, he'd better call Goran or one of the other boys.

"If it's less than 9 a.m., I swear I'll kill you," I growled trying to be impressive. He snorted.

"Charming to the last," he chuckled. "It's already 10 a.m., and you have to take the medication or Friederich will take it out on me," he put in my right hand the two morning pills and in the left a glass with orange juice. Better obey because I also don't want to be resurrected by said butler only to shout at me for not taking the damn things.

"Thanks. I could get used to this."

"Come on, take your pills, and we can do something," he nudged me on the ribs. "I have almost filled the tub. Big enough for two," he said with a big grin, and his seductive voice. All right, time to pay for the wakeup call.

"I think I'll take a shower. It's faster and we don't want to miss the Louvre," I said with my best innocent voice.

He growled low as he threw the covers away, and picked me up in his arms as If I were a child, not caring at all at my protests, which were silenced with a devastating kiss. OK, teaching manners to the big German were postponed due a newer social commitment. I put my arms around his neck and kissed him back, hardly not realising where we (he) were going until I hit the marble counter top, loudly scattering the complimentary trash you always get at hotels.

Konrad didn't seem surprised by the noise as he was focused on munching my neck as he clumsily fumbled with my clothes. He lifted me with one hand to get my trousers off and threw them aside along with the top. He was desperate and without restrains, like in Florence. I was more than happy.

"I can't wait to make you mine. I'd have done it already in the office if I wouldn't have had so much work," he whispered in my ear, making me melt into his embrace. He took advantage of my momentary weakness to take my by the hips, and almost impaled me on his erection, moving at an incredible fast pace and without any kind of preparation. I shouted in pain, but he silenced my cry with a hard kiss on my mouth.

Even if it hurt a lot, I tried to relax and little by little I felt some pleasure as he changed the angle of his thrusts, pulling me closer to him, holding all my weight over his hips and legs. He came inside of me as he bit me on the shoulder blade while trying to kiss me. I was dizzy and not even realised when I have also ejaculated on his stomach.

"You are mine, Guntram. Say it," he intoned still hardly panting as he held me closer to his chest, not letting me go.

"I'm yours and you know it."

"I'm sorry if I was hard on you. The image of that bitch polluting you with her kiss drove me mad the whole night," he said now softly kissing my hands and face.

"Konrad I'm not a maiden in distress needing to be saved at every damn minute," really, amigo, this is a bit too much.

"I love you and I don't want that anything bad happens to you."

"I know, but you also have to trust me, don't treat me like a child. I can make my own decisions and fight my own battles. How can I grow up if you're every moment holding my hand?"

He frowned at me not happy at all. For a long time he remained quiet, thinking and looking into my eyes. Finally he exhaled a long sigh and said "All right, but I keep the right to intervene if I consider it necessary. *"Tu deviens responsable pour toujours de ce que tu as apprivoisé"*. [4]

I kissed him. Defeated.

* * *

Sunday

Finally, we didn't go to the Louvre on Saturday. After taking a bath, I was tired and sore and we went back to bed. Then it was lunch time and again it was cuddling time. At 3p.m., we thought we should really do something (as tourists, I mean), and we almost left the room, but he insisted on doing the other something for

---

[4]"You become responsible, forever, for what you have tamed" A. Saint Exupery. Le Petit Prince, chapter 21.

the second time in the day but slowly, and not so wildly like in the morning. At 4 p.m., it was almost dark and it made no sense to come out as it was so cold. At 5 p.m., it was totally dark, and perhaps there was something in TV. At 6 p.m., Goran phoned Konrad, and yes, all is in order. See you tomorrow. So it was room service again, and back to sleep hoping tomorrow would be a more productive day.

On Sunday, we didn't go to the Louvre but we left the room. Goran was granted holidays (under protest), until Tuesday morning when the Mass will take place. At my insistence, Konrad also forwent the car. It's Paris! If you are not in a hurry you walk it or take the Metro... Somehow, I can't imagine the descendant of the noble Teutonic Knights waiting in line.

We left the hotel very early in the morning and walked down the Avenue George V, crossed the river to the Quai d'Orsay bordering the Seine, and finally taking down the Blvd. St. Germain up to the Musée Cluny (Yes, I'm repetitive in my tastes but he likes history, so no problem), where we spent most of the morning, looking the collection. I was surprised that he knew so much about medieval imaginary and goldsmith.

By noon, he became restless. Yes, I've realised it's your feeding time. After discussing a little, he agreed to go to the Quartier Latin. Come on Konrad, the crazy artists from the XIX century moved away years ago, and the nasty, irreverent young people of May 68 are now working at La Défense! There's life beyond the Rue Saint-Honoré.

We entered into a small restaurant not too crowded and sat in a secluded corner. We ordered something small and we continued to speak about some of the things we saw at the Museum.

"I remember now you mentioned you had a flat in Paris, full with monkeys," I said casually as I recalled our last conversation in Buenos Aires when he told me how his family got their Meissen collection thanks to an entrepreneur grand grand mother and her courageous, free spirit at the Saxony Court.

"Yes, they are in the house at Avenue d' Iena," he replied curtly and a bit upset.

"Is it possible to see them? I never saw these things "live"."

"If you want to see them, we can arrange to visit the factory in Dresden when I fly to Berlin this year."

"Oh," I said disappointed and shocked that he didn't want to go to his own flat, no it's a big house.

"My mother lives there, and I prefer to avoid the place under all circumstances."

"Do you have a mother?" I was shocked. I thought his parents were six feet under, like mine. Well, he never said anything about them, and I certainly would remember something like "my mother lives in Paris."

"Like all of us," he answered back, truly crossed. I took a sip of my water, trying to digest the news. "I have not had much contact with her for the last thirty years and prefer it that way," was his explanation.

"Why?" I looked at him puzzled to no end. I would kill for a mother.

He said nothing, just played around with his food, not eating any more pondering if he should tell or not. I waited for an answer as I also played a little bit with the fish and beans. After a heavy silence that seemed to last for a long time,

Konrad drank some water, and spilled out the story.

"My older brother died in a hunting accident when he was thirteen-years-old. I was seven, and had to remain in the house when my father, Karl Maria, my brother, and some other hunters went out. It seems my brother took my father's weapon, and accidentally shot himself in the head while walking. My mother blamed my father, and wanted a divorce. My parents were fighting horribly for over a year till my father granted her the divorce under one condition: I would remain with him. She didn't think twice and moved to Paris. She got a nice sum for her services," he said, words almost screeching through his teeth, his gaze fixed on the remains scattered on his dish, his finger tracing imaginary lines on the tablecloth.

"I'm sorry for your loss. I was under the impression your mother lost a younger brother from you."

"She miscarried a child when she heard the news. I was left alone with my father, who never was the same man since that day, and with Friederich. When I was eighteen, I decided to cease all communications with her against my father's wishes. I think she didn't care much because a year after the divorce, she was living with another man, and later had two more children," he said as if they were of no importance. "The house where she lives belongs to me, since I inherited all my father's possessions but it's for her use till her death."

"Don't you even want to know your younger brothers or sisters?"

"Half siblings, and no."

"Can you not forgive her? It must be horrible for a mother to lose her son."

"And for my father it was not? He was called a murderer every night. Her duty was to support my father, not to run away from her obligations." His eyes bore holes into me, his breathing increased, and a dark, evil aura seemed to emanate from him. I started to fidget in my chair. "In my experience there are two types of women; the ones who have already betrayed you and those who soon will do it."

"I'm sorry I brought the subject up. I had no idea," I murmured with my head down. He was looking now infuriated at his mother's memory, and I wanted to calm him down before we had a fight in his need to vent out his frustration. This explains why he takes so hard refusal or abandonment. Did nobody realise that he was a child in need of help?

"*Mäuschen*, it's not your fault my family was so unstructured. It happens even to the best families," he explained resorting to his gentle tone of voice. "I still want children, but I need a kind hearted person at my side. I will not repeat my father's mistake," he firmly intoned, grabbing my hand.

"Konrad I can't have children with you. You know this?"

"Of course," he said mildly irritated. "I said I need a companion to have them. Don't look so shocked. I'm not planning to send you away in any case. I love you too much for that."

"No, you're planning on getting married, and I should become your part time lover," I said, bitterly.

"Me? A wife? Never in my life. They only cause trouble. Look at Ferdinand," he growled. "There are other ways for a man in my position to ensure the succession, but it's still too soon to speak about. You're very young at the moment to take such a responsibility."

"Konrad you're not making any sense now."

"In a few years you will understand."

Chapter 4

December 24th, 2002

It's late and Konrad has not yet returned. I know he is a big boy in more than one sense, but normally he calls me or sends a message with the bodyguards. It's 11:30 p.m. and I have no news from him since noon. A lunch can't last so long, and I don't think he can be upset with me since breakfast.

Early this morning, we went to Mass in Notre Dame. Funny, I was also there the previous year during my visit to Paris. Now, I remember it. On the left side, at the front of the reserved part for the church services, there was a battalion of men dressed in conservative business suits, all looking as if their solely purpose in this life was to restore Louis XXVIII to the French throne. Yes, that modern looking guys. Of course, the rest of the rabble like myself had to sit behind, hoping they would throw a bone at us, while the tourists continued to make their visits, circling around the altar and the sitting area.

"I think I saw you before Venice," I said during breakfast. Konrad was sitting in front of me, reading papers as usual, back to his old self big bad banker. He lifted his gaze and looked at me very seriously.

"Where?" He asked inquisitively, focusing all his attention on me.

"Here. Paris. Notre Dame. I was also in the Mass last year, on this day. The church was packed with a full army of suit dressed men. In the front rows," I replied shrugging. "Do you always come on this day?" Most probably. We're speaking of a man who takes always the same three cookies with his afternoon coffee, no milk, no sugar, with the same Meissen china set, ever present since his grandfather took over the bank's management.

"It's a *Dom*, Cathedral, Guntram," he corrected me mildly. "No I was not sitting there. My plane was delayed that day and I was late. I had to stand with the tourists until the end of the ceremony. So this year, I plan to arrive early. Finish your breakfast and don't stall," he ordered much stronger than necessary.

"I didn't see you," I intoned happily, and got an exasperated sigh from him for being interrupted again in his reading.

"You were supposed to be carefully listening to the homily, not checking the society pages," he scolded me rather sternly.

"I was!" I protested. So much for Christmas spirit in your case. I'm sick of being treated like the child who was caught eating chocolate in the middle of the preaching.

We didn't said a word as we rode in the car, went inside of the "cathedral", and I was allowed to sit next to him but my lateral view was blocked by Michael and Goran. Surely he thinks I'm going to wink at the nice looking Japanese tourist girls. I stood up as the ceremony started, still chewing my rage.

Once it was finished, most of the men surrounding me started to go out of the church. Outside they arranged themselves in small groups near the Charlemagne statue, on the opposite side of the square. Most of them were bankers and tycoons from industries. Konrad stood there with Michael on his right side, and Goran on the left. I was left to my own, and started to look around as the others spoke with the men approaching them. I didn't go away because being dragged back to my established place, was not on my mind. Heindrik was also there, making friends with the others bodyguards, and looking really bored. Poor guy!

I was distracted watching the tourists coming and going out, wondering when it would be time to leave. Some big black cars were already parking on one side. Not surprisingly some tourists took photos of the large line of coffins. I mean, not every day you see cars valued in more than several hundred thousand dollars waiting in line. It was almost noon, and the sun was encouraging the small sparrows to leave their branches and start looking for food on the street. It's incredible how fast they are, and nothing escapes their sharp eyes, jumping to get what they want.

"You may think you can rule the world but we are going to expose you! All your dammed plans!" A middle aged man shouted, surrounded by some other five or ten men, all dressed in workers attires. Excellent, the activists are here, I thought as I was dragged away by Heindrik, pulling me from my arm. My feet grew roots. No chance I'd miss the show!

All the men in suits looked at them, and resumed their talks as if they were of no importance while the bodyguards, not very discreetly, placed themselves forming a "defence line". Konrad's face was expressionless. If there was rage boiling inside him, it didn't come to the surface.

"All of you are worse than Illuminati. You want to destroy our democracy to make more money out of us!" The man now yelled directly at Konrad. Goran was in full killer mode. Konrad directed the man one of his cold looks, but said nothing. I got the final jerk from Heindrik, and understood his subtly message to go in the car with him.

The Swedish dragged me towards the black Mercedes while the other men started to slowly disband under the yelling of the workers. For Unionists they're very few and strange.

"Wait a minute Heindrik, you're almost breaking my arm!"

"Get in the car and don't speak. We go back to the hotel." This time he pushed me in. Are you not supposed to protect me without killing me in the process?

"Should we not wait for him?"

"No, the Duke goes in another car with Michael and Goran," he said making a gesture to the driver to start the car almost throwing me down with the acceleration.

"I don't want to go the hotel! I want to go around!"

"My orders are that in case of commotion you're to be taken to a safe place. In this case is the hotel."

"Commotion? Seven guys yelling at you? Commotion in my dictionary is two hundred angry people with torches." He huffed at me, the retarded civilian.

"You never know when things can get ugly. Anyway, knowing the place of meeting is bad enough."

"Secret place of meeting? You have to be kidding me. Last year, even I realised that the whole platoon of tycoons was out of place," I snorted. "Discretion is a word you all don't know."

When we reached the hotel, he took me directly to the suite, not even allowing me to go eating at the restaurant. I sat in the suite's spacious living room, literally fuming with him.

"Do you mind telling me to where the Duke and party have disappeared?"

"I don't know their meeting place. Ask Goran. Chateaubriand is fine for you?"

"Great. You have just saved me from seven old men to kill me of a second heart attack with red meat. I'm allowed to take it only once per week."

"Boiled chicken it is. No need to take it on me. I'm—"

"Just following orders," I smirked tiredly. "Do you have in the Army a banner with that phrase?"

"Navy," he corrected me in a haughty tone. "Look, don't be nasty to me because you're grounded till further instructions. I'm also stuck with you. Try to be nice."

"All right. Sorry. It's not your fault the boss is a control freak sometimes," I mumbled.

"Don't worry. It's horrible to be in a city like Paris, restricted to a room no matter how nice it is," he added sympathetically. "I'll order lunch, and then we can watch a movie if you want. I have the Original Trilogy in DVD; Star Wars, what else?"

"You are the true fan," I laughed. "Do you think they'd kick us out of the hotel if we order popcorn?"

"No if we say we want it in a silver bowl," he grinned.

We had a nice afternoon, watching the films and doing nothing else. At 7 p.m. he left the room to make some phone calls and didn't return till 9 p.m., when he informed me that I should not wait the Duke for dinner and go to bed.

I was a little disappointed. In Argentina, on 24th night you always meet with your family or friends. Even a lone wolf like myself, was always finding something to do. When I was in school, I would go to a teacher's family or even to my lawyer's house. Later, I spent one Christmas Eve in the shanty town I used to visit, helping with the cooking, and then staying with the children. The other one was in Paris, in the hostel's mini disco, where we met the two girls who got Fedérico into the biggest mess of his life and changed mine forever. I still feel sorry for them. They didn't deserve to end their lives floating in a Venetian canal only because they stole drugs from who knows who. Possibly, the guys who killed them had even recovered part of the shit, and sold it at good price. Not to mention that Konrad "compensated" them for the "loses" caused by Fedérico's adventure at trafficking.

Let's admit that Konrad also "compensated" himself in the mess of the bonds/local currencies, forcing the all-knowing Senator mother of Fedérico to make those transactions; about 535 million in returns before taxes, if my calculation was correct. OK, it was a "lesson to Argentinean politicians" but in the whole mess, he was clearly the one who profited the most. I wonder who was the biggest shark in the whole story.

But I still don't understand why Fedérico would be so stupid as to get into such a mess. Easy money? Sex? It still doesn't make any sense at all. If the girls were wannabe dealers, why risk everything with two idiotic tourists like ourselves? I bet there are hundreds of more qualified people to run around Europe with five kilos cocaine. How the police knew there were five kilos in total if the girls were dead before they found them? A snitch? Well, that guy should get a job in the secret service. Why was Fefo so bent in blaming me if he knew for certain the story will not hold? To win time over? To muddy the waters? Maybe the police lied to him in order to frame me, because they needed to find a culprit for the murders and Fefo couldn't have done it. Why if you have three kilos white powder at home, you put by yourself only 150 grams in the market? If you don't know what to do with it or don't have a distribution network, you pass it on, as Cucho, our local drug lord at the slums, told me once while explaining his job to me.

Did he truly believe that I was carrying the "package" or part of it? This whole mess was looking more and more shady and like a setup, like the Senator shouted. Perhaps the attack on me in Buenos Aires was not a simple mug but a vendetta as Konrad had been so bent to believe. The guys certainly knew who we were, and that was before the concussion, so I can be sure of it. Guilty conscience it is called.

With my thinking, I only got a headache the size of Paris. Too many questions with answers I'm not prepared to get.

"What are you doing still up, sitting in the dark?" Konrad's voice made me jump visibly from the sofa. I had to take a few deep breaths to calm myself down. He sat beside me and pulled me closer.

"I was waiting for you, worried you didn't come earlier. What time is it?"

"Around one in the morning. Didn't Holgersen tell you to go to bed?"

"Yes, he did. I lost track of time. Where were you?"

"In meetings and then out with Michael and Ferdinand. I picked up something for you by the Seine." On my lap there was a brown bag full of roasted chestnuts, exactly as I love them.

"Thank you. How did you know I like them?" I kissed him briefly as a sign of gratitude.

"I saw you looking at those things in the Quartier Latin," he chuckled. "One more look and I would have been jealous of the street vendor."

"You are impossible," I laughed, kissing him on the cheek. "You were with Ferdinand?"

"Yes, he came for the meetings, and then we discussed several private issues between us. Don't look so concerned. Michael was there to prevent us from killing each other. He's back in Zurich. All limbs attached."

"Have you made your peace with him?"

"We have explained our points of view. It's a first step toward real peace. I can't let go his offence toward my family, although Gertrud directly disregarded my orders, and brought the girl back to Zurich. But this is not a subject for Christmas, Kitten."

"Tomorrow is Christmas," I retorted.

"It's more than one in the morning, so technically it is. Will you not share?" He said pointing his finger to the bag, forgotten on my lap. I opened it and he took a chestnut, easily peeling the thing off; an ability I've never mastered, and usually ends in a mess of shells and mashed fruit. He smiled shyly and playfully at the same time making me also smile, my heart melting. He put the chestnut in my mouth, surprising me. I swallowed almost choking with my laughter and bent to kiss his fingers.

That was enough for him. He literally jumped on top of me to kiss me on the mouth, his tongue gently asking permission to enter. I let him, more and more excited at the perspective of some quality time together.

We kissed like there was no tomorrow, I was clinging to his neck, and pulling him toward me as he nudged me to lay down in the couch. I rearranged myself to allow him to position himself on top of me as he continued with his attack toward my neck, trailing kisses and softly licking the spots where he would place his kisses. I caressed his hair on the base of his head, making him purr like a big cat.

"Should we finish this in bed?" he whispered in my ear as he nibbled my earlobe. How can I make a decision if you're distracting me so much? Not fair!

He disentangled himself from my arms, and decidedly moved away to the bedroom. I sat on the couch a little bit crossed to be left behind. I stood up and started to remove my jersey and unbutton my shirt as I followed him.

"Well, someone is eager tonight," he chuckled.

"Says the one who's only wearing underwear? New world record for undressing?" I snorted, hungrily looking at him, biting my lower lips under his wolfish gaze.

"I just wanted to open my present," he falsely pouted making me laugh and throwing myself into his arms.

We fell like two children over the bed and resumed our earlier kisses. Our remaining clothes vanished in an instant and we lost a button or two. He moved on top of me grinning like a predator. I chuckled and he lowly growled as his lips started to suck my left nipple his tongue drawing circles around it, eliciting waves of pleasure through my back.

Without notice his head went down and took my member in his mouth, deeply gobbling me in one single movement. My hands grabbed the covers as a way to keep some anchor to reality for the pleasure was so intense that it made me feel lost. His ministrations were driving me mad, making me lose all coherence and chasing away my earlier disturbing musings.

I felt his fingers stretching me briefly but I was too eager to feel him inside me. "Please, don't tease," I moaned and he stopped. He knelt in front of me, lifting my lower part of the body and putting my legs over his shoulder and penetrating in one go me without much warning.

His body bent over mine, his weight supported by his arms carefully avoiding crushing me and his slow thrusts were a delicious torture. I knew he was restraining himself to prolong his own pleasure, but I was also desperately needing him. I arched my back trying to reach his lips and he bent lower capturing mine in a passionate kiss. When we parted his moves picked a faster pace up and we both reached our climax together.

He crumbled almost exhausted on top of me and I put my legs around his hips to keep him as close as possible. My hands caressed him with soothing movements from the head to his backside. We remained like that for a long time, until our breathing slowed down and I started to place butterfly kisses over his forehead and cheeks.

"I'm so incredibly fortunate to have you," he muttered in my ear. "You are my life."

"I love you too," I replied, puzzled at the powerful wave of shyness overtaking me.

"I have something for you," he also said, his voice a little shaky.

"I also. I'll go first."

"I spoke first. It's my turn," he taunted me.

"No chance. Most probably you have an Asian elephant hidden somewhere, and my present will look dull compared to your one," I said quickly. He laughed.

"Perhaps you're not so mistaken, but it's difficult to put an elephant in the plane," was his answer as he disentangled himself from my embrace.

"Turn around. I want to dress," I said.

"It's incredible that after a year living together, you become so shy after sex," he commented with an amused light shining in his eyes, not missing a single of my movements, while I was looking for my pyjama. Naughty boy.

"I have it hidden, and I don't want you to see where it is," was my lame excuse, turning red as he looked at my body more interested than before.

"If you're going to give it to me, why the secrecy?"

Impossible man I thought! However, I found my pyjama jacket and pants and put them on. Show is over! He groaned and closed his eyes. Good boy. I went to the dresser and looked in my suitcase where Friederich had placed the tube with the watercolour painting I've done for him for the last months and believe me, hiding something from Konrad it's not so easy. That old fox of a butler knew what it was, and had packed it along with the rest of the things.

When I went to the bedroom it was empty so I continued to the living room and found Konrad also dressed in pyjamas and his velvet *robe de chambre* eating my chestnuts, and sitting on the sofa, a leather folder on his side.

"I thought those were for me," I said half accusingly.

"I did share with you," he answered but he gave me another. "If this is going to be formal, I've dressed also."

I smiled and gave him the tube, praying he would like it.

He took the lid off and pulled out the big cardboard slowly and carefully unrolling it. He just stared at the landscape for a long time, his silence driving me more and more on the edge.

"It's…"

"The bridge over the small stream in Torcello, with the willow tree." Wow, he also has a photographic memory.

"Yes," I whispered. "If you don't like it there's no problem to throw it away," I added in haste.

"It's one of your best so far. I'm speechless. On one side the water and the plants reflected on it, look so peaceful and pure but on the other side, the leaves of the tree seem about to move provocatively, sensually, and you can almost feel the breeze. This is not the usual landscape," he slowly said.

"Well, you were not exactly a saint that day," I replied blushing at the memory of our first kiss.

"It's a very beautiful present. Thank you," he kissed me lovingly. "It will go to my office. Definitely."

"I'm glad you like it. But you have very good paintings there… not copies, precisely."

"It's decided. Ostermann can complain all what he wants. Now it's my turn," he said, handing me the folder.

Inside there was a property deed written in Spanish. I was puzzled.

"What is this?" I asked not really wanting to know.

"I hope it's the deed for the country house in Argentina, La Candelaria. I want you to have it. You liked the place so much."

"Konrad this is too much. It's a full *estancia*," I was shocked.

"Not all, only the house and gardens. The land was merged with the acres we bought from the neighbours, and now Dollenberg is planting soy like there is no tomorrow. My plants are your neighbours. If it's too big, you can always invite me."

Chapter 5

I'm still in shock. A house like that is too big to give as a present. He said that it's more for his sake of mind; that he needs to know that I have some security if something happens to him; that this is nothing to his finances, and it's only the house and not the land which by the way has increased its value by a twenty percent last year.

"Guntram it's not so much. You liked the place, and I do really want to give it to you. Please take it," he almost pleaded with me.

"This is bigger than the elephant," I said dubiously.

"Next year we stay at home, and you get one. It would keep the neighbours away," he replied seriously.

"You have no neighbours!" I said, laughing at his idea.

"Somebody has to cut the grass," he added mischievously as he kissed me. "In the next few days we'll go to London and you can sign the final papers. You "inherit" so to speak the foreman and wife."

So this is how I kept the monster for a house in Argentina. I have no idea of what to do with it.

By noon, Konrad decided to go for Christmas Lunch at the hotel's restaurant. I would have happily stayed in bed but he was adamant.

We sat by the windows in the luxurious restaurant, which was not only expensive, but also elegant in its decoration. We have just started when a tall, blonde, middle aged woman, over her sixties, with striking brown eyes, splendidly dressed approached our table and happily said,

"Konrad! You're outside your bank!" Konrad and I immediately rose as he made a discreet sign to the main waiter to set another chair at the table.

"My dear Tita. It's indeed a pleasure to see you radiant as ever," he said taking her hand and lightly kissing it. "Will you accompany us?"

"Nothing would please me more, dear, but I have to meet my daughter-in-law; just a drink with you and your friend."

"Forgive me. Tita, this is Guntram de Lisle originally from France, but closer to the Pampas. Sophie Marie Olsztyn is one of my dearest friends."

"How do you do, Madam?" I said shaking her hand briefly.

"And old friend, you can say it, Konrad," she joked. "Hello Guntram. No need to be formal with me," she sat at our table and Konrad softly ordered some champagne for her.

"Now it's time for catching up," she said with a musical voice. "What do you do, dear?"

"I study Economics in Zurich."

"He also studies with *Meister* Ostermann," Konrad added.

"With him? You must have a great talent if he accepted you. He hasn't taken a student in years, no matter how much money you offer him. He's one of the best experts for Early European and Impressionist Art, and has enlarged the collections of many museums."

"I'm afraid he has changed. There are several ladies studying with him."

She laughed. "Still with his idea to find a very rich widow to support him in his old age? The man must be over seventy! He should consider himself retired!"

"The last thing we lose is hope," Konrad smiled. "That he accepted Guntram after seeing his work was even a surprise for me, and reinforced my belief that I'm a good art critic."

"I must absolutely see your work. Perhaps, I could visit you, Konrad?"

"Whenever you want; my home is always open for you. Will you be attending the auction for the Pisarro this February?"

They talked for a while elaborating on the Arts Market, complaining about the "Russian Invasion", which had pushed the prices completely high at London, and happily chatting.

"I'm sorry Konrad, but I must leave you this instant if I want to meet my daughter-in-law on time. I'm very glad to have met you Guntram. Come to visit me in Geneva whenever you want. Konrad, you look better than ever."

We rose again as she prepared herself to leave us. She gave me a kiss on the cheek and Konrad didn't seem upset at all, only mildly amused at my embarrassment to be treated like a child.

"You should visit her house in Geneva. Antonov can take you there."

"She was only being nice. I don't think she really meant it. Besides she's your friend."

"Her late husband's private art collection is well worth the trip. Over two hundred pieces in that house alone; very eclectic, but one of the best in hands of private collectors. Now and then something is lent for an exhibition somewhere but normally not."

"More than two hundred pieces? This sounds like a Museum to me."

"Almost. Ostermann was one of the curators. Most of the pieces he acquired for the Modern Art collection have sky-rocketed. An impressive collection if you ask me. I will invite her by February. It would be good for you that she sees some of your things, and if she buys, you can consider yourself in the market."

"I don't know if that is a good idea. I never thought about professionally painting."

"Well you should. Even Ostermann agrees with my original assessment, and he's a well-respected expert. I admit, that for a moment I considered that my opinion could be biased by love, but it was not the case," he said, very proud of his criteria.

"I'm afraid you'll have a hard time when she laughs at me."

"Humour me," he replied dryly, setting the glass rather strongly on the table. I said nothing, too busy pretending to be eating with my eyes glued on the china's details. He let an exasperated sigh out. It's Christmas so let's don't start a fight.

At some point, I saw a hot, really hot looking brunette girl-woman enter the room. Tall, in the thirties or more, but youthfully dressed with a flashing short blue dress. She sat two tables away from us, and threw several obtrusive glances directly at Konrad. Somehow her face was familiar to me but in a younger version. He ignored her completely, concentrating also on his food.

I have it! She's the singer from that summer hit in 93 or 95. What was the name of it? Sexy beach? No. Sexy love? No. I can't remember, but it was huge success and her video was amazing. The song was on the radio every day while we were doing our homework. I'm eating in the same room with a Pop Star! Sexy Chick! That's right!

Don't remember her name at all. Wait! Was this the song's or the artist's name?

A waiter approached our table and placed a glass of milk in front of me. What? I didn't order it, and if this is your idea of a joke Konrad, I don't care if today's Christmas.

"With compliments from the lady over that table," the man said, with a mortified face.

From Sexy Chick? Somehow, I want to pluck some feathers now.

"Take it away," Konrad ordered just keeping his fury at bay.

"Merry Christmas, darling." Wow, Sexy Chick was here, as in front of our table and Stony German didn't look happy at all, and he was not getting up for the lady or making the minimum effort to get her a chair. "Don't stand up, darling. At your age, it can be challenging," she mocked him, saving me from the dilemma of standing up, directly disobeying Konrad or remain sitting and be rude.

Konrad just looked at her with contempt.

"I wonder if your son would like an autograph from me?" I saw the fire from Hell creep into Konrad's eyes for a second but he quickly hid it.

"Perhaps. It must be reassuring to know that the young generation still remembers you for your music and not for your other talents," he finally said with a humourless grin.

"I can only say, that I'm glad it didn't work between us, if the only thing you can get nowadays is a small little boy who can be impressed in bed. Must be almost like paedophilia. Or does he also fall asleep with your boring attempts?" Now, he looked at her with a murderous intention.

"Madam, your table is ready." A waiter said with the Floor Manager at his side, silencing the more than nasty retaliation from Konrad. Thank, God she turned around and went to her table.

"Your Grace, I must humbly apologize to you for this inconvenience," the Floor Manager recited in haste, looking more than contrite.

"It was just that. An inconvenience," Konrad responded dryly, dismissing the man with a sign of his head.

I returned to my eating barely concealing the urge to ask about this. Did he have an affair with her? Probably, but his way of treating her was mean, as if she were a cheap whore. Well, Guntram you can't complain at all. You knew he was not a saint and about his many, many adventures as he even admitted. So this part of his story is true. He had affairs with the jet set only. But why does it hurt so much? I looked at him, and he was also keeping his head down, ashamed, his fork playing with the leftovers.

"You should have not sent the glass of milk away so fast. It would have come handy now with the heartburn I have from that meat," I said half seriously. His piercing gaze was immediately fixed on my eyes as if to gauge my intentions.

"Cows here can't be compared with those from Argentina," he softly replied.

"European cows are difficult to tame and ride it seems," I chuckled under his relieved sigh. We both laughed. "Let's go away. This place is starting to look like the Ritz," I said, now imitating his accent.

"You have no idea how much," he laughed openly now.

I noticed Sexy Chick looking at me, inflamed. Girl you need something more than that. You don't play in my league.

Chapter 6

December 27th, 2002

We spent the whole day in the Louvre. At night we should catch the plane to London. The good thing of a private flight is that they will not charge me overweight in my luggage. I swear he forced me to buy all these art books at the Louvre bookshop, using my credit card. OK. He can't complain now about me spending little, and I have books to read for the next two years.

* * *

December 29th, 2002

Yesterday was my first contact with London... with a not at all happy Heindrik trailing behind me. Konrad had to spend the whole day at his bank's offices in the City. He certainly likes to catch people dancing on one foot because his visit was not announced at all.

He also has something like a Gothic style house, like those Englishmen loved so much in the Victorian Era at Melbury Road, relatively near the Victoria and Albert set of Museums. And relative is a key word here because it's not so near as it might look on the map but the walking around this town, with hurried people and colourful window shops, all similar houses and red buses sharpens your senses. The smells from the hundreds of small restaurants, the moist air, the frenzy main streets sharply contrast with the quiet of the interior ones.

No, I think it is the people. Even here, in an uptight place like Kensington, they all look very serious and stern, but if you take a closer look at the eyes they have that air of someone who discovered the intrinsic irony of life and lives accordingly.

I can't wait to see Piccadilly Circus or Portobello Road!

Around one, Heindrik had enough. He wanted to eat (and stop). "Would you stop for a minute? This is not a competition to know who lasts more," he grunted at me, catching me by the sleeve.

"The doctor said I should walk every day," I pointed out dutifully.

"You're not Mopsi."

"Come on, what's a little walking for an old experienced sailor like you?"

"Exactly. I'm a sailor. We sail, and this looks like a damn reconnaissance mission in the Peruvian Jungle," he growled low.

"You'll get fatter than Jabba the Hutt."

"He had a good life until some impudent blond disrupted his lifestyle, just like now." I laughed. OK. It's compromise time.

"We're at Brompton Road. If we walk down Knightsbridge, then Piccadilly, Regent St. and finally Oxford St. we'll be at the British Museum and in front you know what it is: Forbidden Planet," I said, showing him the map. He groaned in desperation.

"It's like five kilometres!"

"How many chances do you have to go to the comics' Mecca when you're in London? Episode II fresh, new merchandising. I'll tell the Duke it was my idea, and even that I forced you to come. We'll take a taxi for the way home," I bribed him.

"Well at least you're not asking for the Subway," he sounded half convinced.

"Please. Tomorrow I'll be at Dollenberg's house and will not trouble you much." Big puppy eyes. Not enough it seems. "I'll draw you a big poster with Darth Vader."

"Can you make it with Emperor Palpatine also?"

"Ewww. Pervert!"

"I thought Alexei had an easy life taking care of you!" he whined. "All right, but we eat first, and forget about Indian Food. With all those spices, and the walking I don't want to carry you to a hospital."

"Is Alexei in holidays? I haven't seen him for a while."

"He has returned to his old job so to speak."

"KGB?"

"No, travelling around Afghanistan. From now onwards, and till he comes back, you are my problem," he said dryly.

What the hell is he doing there? I pondered, but Heindrik didn't want to tell anything more, and quickly entered an Italian restaurant. I had to hurry after him if I wanted to eat also. When I finally caught up with him (this Swedish is tall and when he wants can be very fast), and sat at the table, he bombarded me with the question.

"Can you eat seafood? Probably not. Lots of sodium there. Pasta Carbonara?"

"It's OK. Why is Alexei in Afghanistan?" I pressed.

"Don't know. Ask the Duke," he answered, deeply immersed in his menu. "Do you want a *Focaccia*?"

"No. I would like an answer."

"You miss it," he shrugged. "OK, we go to Forbidden Planet. Should we enter the British Museum too?"

* * *

Konrad's house at Melbury Road was very big and built in Georgian style as I was later informed. Four stories high without counting the basement; red bricks and white windows, a small garden in the front, big trees, and a rear garden very beautiful with tall oaks. It was the family's old property as they had their coat of arms over the arches at the front door.

It was decorated also respecting the Georgian style, making it not so heavy as the Victorians liked later or baroque, with fantastic wooden floors and big windows giving a lot of light to the house. I liked this building a lot with their sparse, but incredible furniture, soft colours on the walls and big open rooms. I spent the rest of the afternoon looking at it.

Konrad returned in a relatively good mood from his offices here and we sat for dinner in the big dining room, with high ceilings and painted in cream colour adorned only with wallpaper.

"What's Alexei doing in Afghanistan? Is it not dangerous to send him there?" I asked him casually.

"Afghanistan? I hope not. I sent him to Karachi."

"Well, it's not exactly the safest place in the world."

"He's more than qualified to be there. He's checking some possible investments in the area. Oil pipelines. As I said before kitten; stay out of my business," he said very sternly.

"It's a war zone!" I protested.

"Your point is? Antonov has been in worse places before. He can't play your baby sitter forever. Goran needs him back in his position. Do not be concerned about him. He knows very well the area, the politics and the customs there. From now onward, Holgersen is your bodyguard. Obey him in everything," he said, leaving the matter for settled.

"Oil pipelines in Pakistan? To go where?" This is strange really. I thought the oil was in Iran, but I could be mistaken. The geography of that part of the world is not so clear for me.

"Turkmenistan and Uzbekistan," he said, nonchalantly.

"Afghanistan is in the middle! What is a banker like you doing there?"

"And what should I say? Yes, we finance a project for huge pipeline through said countries and while we're at it, we put down the Taliban regime, and pick some poppy seeds up for our directory meetings? No, better. I sent Alexei to organise the weapons trade in the area for the poor Taliban, and don't forget we are going to poison the whole local population by selling Coca Cola," he acidly said, raising his voice more and more, throwing, frustrated, his napkin on one side of the table.

"I didn't want to upset you. I was only concerned about Alexei. After all he saved my life," I mumbled, shocked and disorientated at his explosion.

"I'm sick of people immediately assuming that if you make business in a conflictive area you're a part of an international conspiracy or involved in shady activities."

"I didn't' mean to offend you," I murmured with my head down.

"If it's so important for you to know I'll tell you," he barked, still furious.

"It's not necessary," I hastily said. He's already in bad mood and likely looking for a fight. Sorry I'm not your punching bag tonight.

"I insist. An important oil company from America needs financing for some projects in the area. Before I put my funds' money in, I want to be certain that the risk is manageable. Alexei is very good for intelligence matters, and he knows people there who an oil expert sitting in London or New York has no chance at all to see in his life. For me, their prospecting is useless. Alexei can speak in their own language with the local warlords, exactly in the area planned for building the damned thing. I don't believe for a minute that Americans have total control of the country. The Soviets also said it, and look how their adventure ended. The important part of lending money is getting the capital back not only some interests for a few years. It's a considerable sum what the company wants to ask for."

"Konrad, I never thought you were doing something illegal. I'm just surprised that Alexei is there, after all he's just a bodyguard. Why are you so upset with me?"

"I'm sorry. A stupid journalist was grating to my nerves today."

"I thought you didn't give interviews."

"I don't. He was there, shouting like crazy at the entrance. It seems that now

I'm the head of the long forgotten Teutonic Order or the Templars, who makes money, finances worldwide weapons trade, drug trafficking and slavery only to destroy the Illuminati, horrible and bad Masons, who also by the way control the world leaders and plan to murder half of the human race to make their New World Order come true."

I laugh in disbelief. "Well let's admit that seeing all those bankers and tycoons together speaking, makes you immediately believe they're after something nasty. Is he the man from Paris?"

"Yes. Why these Americans don't read a history book before making accusations? There's a Teutonic Order nowadays, but they're peaceful old men living in Austria doing charity work. They had to flee from Germany during the war because the nacionalsocialists hated them for being catholic and not bending to Hitler. Himmler even stole their symbols for their obscene ceremonies. The original catholic order was extinguished when Grand Master Albert von Brandenburg converted into Lutheranism and secularized the Prussian territories. It was a long decline until Napoleon finished them off, and they had to run to Austria. You can even visit their museum near Stephansdom in Vienna. They declared bankruptcy in 2000 if I remember correctly."

"I always knew you were after something more than money," I half joked.

"What I still don't understand is how am I supposed to take over the world by destroying the Masons, making money in the process and installing the Pope as supreme leader as it was in the Middle Ages. I don't think His Holiness would be very pleased to have more problems on his desk, not counting the Muslims and the Jews opinions on the matter," he pondered, still very upset.

Yes, I can imagine the scene. You coming out of your car to find a middle aged man shouting that you're involved in drug trafficking or planning to destroy the democratic capitalist system. What a way to start the day. I hope the employees have survived your following wrath.

"Don't forget the Asians and Africans. You got it wrong. It's not world domination; only Europe. China is not ready for you," I said, returning my attention to my dish

"It's not my fault I come from a long line of bankers and aristocrats. I work like everybody else to make money, pay my taxes and give for charity," he said still incensed, leaving the cutlery aside, his appetite spoiled

"I know. You work like crazy, and it's almost a miracle you took this holiday," I said, trying to appease him. "Can you not call the police next time if he's insulting you? Twice in less than a week is too much."

"And get the whole press on me because I sent one of their precious members to prison for harassment? Not mentioning if they decide to publish his lies in a respectable newspaper. So far he only rants over the internet. No thanks."

"Perhaps if you were a little bit more open people would not wonder so much about you. After all, a still single billionaire with hair is news."

"Are you so bored my dear, that you need some competition in your life? I would get women coming from every country," he answered me, looking at the chandelier pending from the ceiling a deep frown marring his face.

"I see. Why did the *Fürst* zu Löwenstein call you griffin? I heard several people doing it too. It sounds so mysterious, like the rank of one of those secret societies."

"Ah, that's an old joke from several German noblemen to my family because our Coats of Arms has a griffin. This creature was known for keeping and protecting treasures. We are bankers since the XVII century. Always, the head of our family was called griffin, griffon or *gryphon* as a sign of respect, probably praying that we didn't lose their money," he laughed. "The inconvenience of being compared with a griffin is that they're also the symbol for monogamy. They only mate for life, and if one of them dies, the other remains alone for the rest of his life."

"With your nose you could pass for one," I said seriously, not really understanding what he meant by the last part of his small speech.

"Remember those words when you come to me for entertainment," he mumbled half offended.

I left my chair and went to kneel at his side. "Don't you want to relax with me after a hard day?" I whispered seductively.

"Maybe," I flashed a smile at him. "Promise me something Guntram," he said now deadly serious.

"What? I will do as Heindrik tells me to."

"Stay out of my business. There's nothing for you in there."

Chapter 7

This morning, I was supposed to see Pablo and Luciana Dollenberg along with Juan, old friends from Argentina, but at ten I got a phone call from Juan telling me that Luciana had to run to for an emergency at the house she was decorating and Pablo was at the office surviving an earthquake in the form of a well-known German. He, on the other hand, had to go to pick up some things at the construction site he works (the hard life of the Architecture student), and I would be a great guy if I could take care of baby Juan Ignacio till 5 p.m. because their baby sitter is back in France for the holidays.

Before I could refuse, as I have no idea about babies, Juan hung up and rang the bell. I know about children, but in the size when they go to the bathroom by themselves and speak. I hate mobile phones. I went downstairs to find my old buddy from school, carrying a blonde and very cute baby, dressed like the Michelin Man, a bag the size of the baby, a teddy bear and a giraffe.

"Hi Guti, nice to see you again. This is Juan Ignacio. Hey buddy, say hello to uncle Guntram," he started at full pace. "OK, here is your drill, as my sister-in-law told me this morning. He's changed and unless he makes something more than pi pi, don't put the hand inside. When he starts to cry, first, try with the dummy, if he throws it away, then mix one measure of the milk in this container with 150 ml of water already in the bottle and plug it in. He had lunch already. He stops when full, like refuelling a car." And I got the baby in the arms.

"I know nothing about babies," I stammered, looking at the giggling little thing. "This is not funny."

"You have nothing to do. Put him on top of a big rug. Nappies are up to twelve hours resistant. Let him crawl around. If he becomes tired and starts to cry and does not want bottle, then put him to sleep on a bed with some pillows around so he doesn't fall. He can sit, and looks for trouble permanently. Be mindful. You should have no problems. Look, I can do it."

"Juan this is too big," I started to protest.

"I'll be back at five with Luciana, and then she can fix what you have broken. Here is my phone number. Have fun!"

"You owe me big time for this."

"I'll make it up for you. I'll take you tomorrow to Tate's or the National Portrait Gallery."

"Not enough, Juan. All right, I'll do my best," I sighed.

"Thanks a lot Guti. You're the man. You saved my job. Bye."

Just like that I was left in the middle of a Georgian foyer with one baby, one teddy bear, one giraffe and a big bag full of unknown things. I swallowed hard as Juan Ignacio happily and rather strongly fisted my collar. Glad I'm not wearing a tie. Where do you put a baby in this house? Time to call the cavalry.

"Heindrik!" I shouted going directly to the kitchen.

All right, the glorious times of the Swedish Cavalry are over. King Gustav's Adolphus must be turning in his grave. Heindrik ran away at the sight of the baby. "No, I demand my charges are over a metre high," he said, and returned to his newspaper, totally ignoring me. Nope, not interested in raising the next Jedi Generation.

I went to the Drawing Room. It's full carpeted and with a lot of light. There are some big sofas and a piano. Have to take care of the two ferns; he could eat them. Artwork is high placed and there's no porcelain around. It's too cold to put the baby out in the garden. First question: If he goes on the floor, should I remove this kind of astronaut suit he's wearing? I think yes. Looks very warm in here. I put him down over the rug and immediately he crawled away on all fours, at an incredible speed. OK, he's fast, not a turtle.

After fondling with many buttons and zippers I got him out of his space suit. I was surprised how quick he was and how everything was interesting for him. His curiosity seemed to have no limits. At some point he wanted to be picked up and he snuggled against me as I showed him the room, the window and the furniture. These little guys smile and laugh a lot but they also pull your hair rather strongly.

Around one o'clock, he started to cry loudly. Don't panic, Guntram, you can control it. Dummy was not working, and he became more enraged when I put it in. Milk then. God, he has good lungs. To my relief he liked it, and drank it like there was no tomorrow and by the middle I had to use some force to get it out of his mouth to make him burp. He was happy to continue later, and fell asleep on my arms.

Problem number two. Even if he has done nothing so far, his nappy feels heavy. Should I change it? Is there a woman in this house who can help? No, the maids were away for the day. I placed the baby on top of the big sofas, surrounded by pillows (if he falls the mother kills me) and went to check again his bag. There was like a small mattress and several nappies. I gathered some courage. He's asleep so he would not move much.

I placed the mattress and the baby wipes on one side of a nice oak table, polished every day. Well, Konrad is not here to see this blasphemy. OK Time for the big operation. I placed him on the mattress, while he slept undisturbed and started to go through layers of clothes trying to remember the order they were set. Old nappy out, clean around (this guy really sleeps), new in. I closed with relative ease the clothes and put him back to sleep.

Problem number three. What to do with the old thing? Right, time to play the young lord because I don't want to leave him alone in the room, and I want to eat something too. I pushed the ring for the butler and big bird appeared almost immediately

"Take this away, please. Is it possible to make a sandwich for me? I don't want to leave the baby alone," I said.

"Immediately, sir," If he was disgusted, he hid it very well. Some minutes later, Heindrik and the butler entered in the room. The servant left a tray with my warm lunch. Broth and chicken with greens and something like a pudding for dessert. Hospital food. Again.

"Did you take your pills?"

"I see you got the full to do list from Alexei," I said dryly. "Don't wake up the baby."

"Did you?"

"No, I forgot it. I'll get them now," I replied slightly upset, rising and going for them to my room. When I came back, Heindrik was still there.

"You should not forget those pills. I don't want to take you to the hospital. I'm not qualified like Alexei."

"I'm not planning on dying on your shift."

"Good. Now don't get stressed over the child."

"Are you going to be a mother hen the whole time? I assumed you didn't get the position before because you were too careless and young."

"I'm ten years your senior, and if before you were under Alexei Gregorevich's care, it was because the Duke wanted someone with medical experience due to your illness. I'm perfectly able to fulfil this position. Now finish your eating and try to rest a little."

"Yes, Heindrik." From one overbearing Russian to a Swedish one. Life is unfair!

At four, the baby decided he had enough of nap time, and woke up giggling. He seems to be on a permanent good humour. I put him down in the floor, and started to play with him.

"Guntram, is there something you should tell me?" I was startled by Konrad's deep voice. He was standing at the door frame pointing to Juan Ignacio. I laughed as I rose from the floor picking the baby up.

"Juan Ignacio may I present you Konrad von Lintorff," I said gravely as the baby babbled something.

"He's very amusing," Konrad said, caressing his head softly. "Where did you get him?"

"Belongs to the Dollenberg's. Juan had to go to work, mother the same, father is under your iron fist and au pair girl is back in France. He stays with me until five o'clock, when the mother and Juan will pick him up."

"He looks quite happy with you," Konrad observed very seriously.

"Don't get jealous. You'll always be my first choice," I smiled.

"This is not what I meant. Children like you. I'll get dressed in something less formal as they should arrive soon. Tell Hanson we will be four for tea, and if the mother wants to refresh the baby she should get one of the rooms upstairs," Just like that, he left me alone again with a now wide awake baby who wanted to be entertained. I went with him to the kitchen to tell Hanson (I assumed he was the butler), what Konrad had said.

Juan and her sister-in-law, Luciana, arrived fortunately on time. Thank you! I gave the baby back to the mother, who was a nice looking blonde in her mid-twenties. I accompanied her to one of the guests rooms to change and clean him.

"Guntram, do you think I could get a tour around the house?" She asked me as she changed the baby quicker and more professionally than me. He was happy and chuckling at his mother.

"I'll ask Konrad when he's out of his studio. I see no problem. Do you like it?"

"This house was in my history textbooks; a fine example of Early Georgian period. The foyer is to die for, and the table I glimpsed on the room at the right is incredible," she explained to me hurriedly. "My Russian client was originally after this property, but Sotheby's people almost got the door on their faces when they suggested to buy it, and he was offering a lot of money; much more than the market value. Finally, he settled down also in Kensington, in a monster house."

"As you will see, money has not much meaning for him, it's all about power. Being "kicked out of his own house," Is unacceptable. The Russian had no chances at all. Is he your famous client who buys my stuff?"

"Yes, he's the one who likes so much your work."

"How did he find my paintings out? I never understood the story well."

"I was working in an internship at Christie's new offices in Buenos Aires. The Real Estate division was with us, and we all shared offices. He came around mid-2000, looking for a big country house in Patagonia, near Calafate. His name is Oblomov, and he saw one of the pictures from the house I had framed in my part of the office, and fell in love with it. He wanted to buy it right there, but I couldn't sell because it belonged to Pablo. Finally, and since my husband wanted to sell the house, we agreed that he could visit us at home. He liked the property, and almost bought it but Pablo didn't sell it to him because he didn't want to take the workers in. After insisting a lot, and really a lot, we agreed to sell him some of your discarded pieces and old drawings. During all 2001, I wanted to contact you but it was impossible. At some point he bought this house here, moved in and wanted to decorate it in the "Pampas Style" exactly like we had in Buenos Aires. He insisted to me several times to come to do it, and I came after the baby was born. Having more of your work for him, helped a lot. He likes almost everything you make, some not, of course, but the rest he likes it."

"I'm impressed. Hope he doesn't complain later about the quality," I smiled.

"The last six ones that you sent me around November were sold for £28.000 after taxes and expenses. I have a check for £16.800 for you."

"How much did you charge the poor man?"

"Market price. Pity you haven't done any exhibitions yet. The value would increase more," she said as a matter of fact, picking up the baby and bag easily, and going out.

Konrad and Juan were already chatting in the living room as we entered. Konrad and Luciana immediately got along, and he widely praised the baby. She started to serve the tea as the butler entered with a dish with something like a fruit purée for the baby.

"I hope it's to your liking. Must be horrible to seat in front of us and get nothing," Konrad said gently to her.

"Thank you so much Duke. He eats almost everything at every time," she chuckled as she sat Juan Ignacio on her lap, and expertly put the food in after getting him into a bib. He finished quite quickly, and started to crawl around the mother but didn't last more than ten minutes because he sat and yawned tiredly. Luciana picked him up and placed him in a sofa covering him with a small blanket from his bag, and he was fast and sound asleep.

"I wish I could do the same at some meetings," Konrad sighed, making us softly laugh.

"As I was telling Guntram, Duke, I have a check for him from his client, but he doesn't know what to do with it."

"Please call me Konrad, and believe me, I know what to do with a check," he said with a satisfied smile as he took the cup of tea from her hand.

"Luciana, please. My customer would also like to meet Guntram in person. His house is nearby and I could arrange the meeting as he's in London now."

"I'm afraid I will have to refuse, my dear Luciana. Guntram is still recovering from his last ordeal, and doesn't need more stress," his kind words contrasting with his stern face. Hello? I'm still here and it was supposed to be my call.

"It would be only a few minutes, Konrad. He's a very busy person, but he's completely in love with Guntram's paintings," she insisted bating an eyelash at us. I would go without problems, but unfortunately it's not up to me to decide, it seems.

"Oblomov is not from our circle, and I would prefer to keep Guntram away from his dealings. I don't like these new rich Russians at all. If he wants to meet him, he can come for the annual exhibition from Ostermann's pupils at Zurich. It's for charity. I'll tell my secretary to send the details to your husband." He's unaffected by women eyes. I, on the other hand, felt the necessity to be heard on the matter.

"Besides Luciana I'm not such a good seller as you. Probably, I would gape at him and say something like "how much did you pay? She robbed you!" I said laughing.

"I understand Guntram. If you're so determined to ruin my work for the last year, I can only keep you away, and concentrate on the other persons who want to buy from you. I sold also, at minor price, what he has rejected so far. "

"You are an excellent businesswoman, Luciana but please don't overdo it."

"Nonsense Guntram. You have your scales all wrong. A good designer's bag costs more than your paintings at the moment. The difference is that the bag loses half of its value the minute is out of the store, and your paintings keep it or increase if you become famous. If I would say "it costs a hundred pounds," I would ridicule myself. You paint, I sell," she informed me.

"I'm glad somebody else tells you how things are," Konrad triumph ally commented. Yes, I noticed you have already scored a goal, but your boasting should be your only prize for now, because in this moment I'm very focused on my cucumber sandwich (and here I was believing these things were a mythological creature from Oscar Wilde's plays teachers love to force upon you).

"Are you going to be in an exhibition?" Juan asked me, changing the subject for good.

"It's the first notice I have," I said chuckling.

"Exhibition is too much. Since ten years my foundation organises an art show for Meister Ostermann's students, and the works are auctioned among the poor people, like myself, who has to attend. I prefer to call it Ostermann's Spring Cleaning. You see, his students are the wives of highly placed people and he came with the idea of auctioning the pieces for charity. He cleans his studio, the ladies attending get their works photographed, and presented in a nice catalogue, and the husbands pay. My cousin Gertrud organises everything with him as he's one of the main Art consultants at the bank," Konrad explained. "He told me, he would like to include some of Guntram's works to see if we raise more money. Last year, it was a total disaster, only getting an average of 9,000 Swiss francs per piece. He hopes, that if Guntram gets good money, the husbands will have to pay more for the wives' things to balance the universe."

"Will it not be too much?" I asked him. "After all they're your friend's wives."

"And your fellow students," he stated firmly.

"It would be very good for you if start to be known in the high circles. I'm starting to regret the amount I asked on your behalf."

"Luciana, even 9,000 Swiss francs is a lot of money! Father Patricio's could feed 300 people for a month with that money," I protested, shocked.

"So this year try to get 30,000 francs Guntram, after all is for charity. Think; it's a three months food supply. Your colleagues in the studio will be more than happy if their artwork costs again more than a puppies' bag. Ask Gertrud what she's planning to do with the money. If it eases your conscience, you will see not a single cent of it."

Yes, he's right. But a little warning in advance would have been very nice.

Chapter 8

December 31th, 2002

Yesterday, Konrad ran to his office in Zurich. He promised he would be back tonight for the New Year's Eve, and totally refused that I accompany him. "No, you're in holidays and I have to work hard to settle this mess."

Here I am, at one in the morning, after the big fireworks writing in my laptop utterly bored. Alone. I gave up hope he would return at about 12. Happy New Year to myself!

I should not be so ungrateful. Heindrik did his best to cheer me up to nine, but then he vanished to an unknown destination, telling me to go to bed early, and try to sleep if the revelling people outside were not too noisy. Right, in Kensington.

I got several SMS at different times. First from Alexei with the typical "Happy New Year. Don't drink too much." Then Goran with a "Good 2003" His loquacity also extends to his writing skills. Michael and Monika called me, and we spoke for a while about nothing. Ferdinand also phoned me from Riga but it was more to check I haven't done anything improper the last two days.

Nothing from Konrad so far, and that gives me hope.

He's not in Zurich as Friederich told me this morning. No idea where he is and his excellency will contact me when he has time. He's a very busy man and have you been to the British Museum? The Elgin Marbles are truly worth a visit. Had Friederich not been such an old and kind man, I would have exploded to him but I had to mumble my fury in silence as he ranted on classical art.

It's half past one. I go to bed. Happy New Year to me.

* * *

January 5th, 2003

Not a single word from him. I'm about to explode in rage, and I swear it would not be a happy event. I'm not surprised he never married. No woman would cope with such a selfish, arrogant bastard who thinks he can disappear for a week without telling where he goes or what he does. Do it, and you'll meet her lawyers!

But I'm a guy and have to cope with it. And still pretend to be cool about this. What really infuriates me to no end is the phrase I got several times "the Duke will tell you at his convenience. Don't worry. Everything is under control," I've been on a roller-coaster of emotions and thoughts for the last week; from concern to fury and back to concern and so on.

Fuck him!

* * *

January 7th, 2003

Yesterday morning, Heindrik informed me that we were going to take the plane back to Zurich at 2:00. The Duke had the Dassault, and the other plane is currently busy. Oh, first notice I have about his whereabouts. 4,500 miles around the departure point... the whole world.

We took our flight and arrived at Zurich late in the afternoon, everything was dark and very cold. Heindrik came with me in the car and we remained silent the whole trip. At the house, Friederich was waiting for us with Mopsi. Seeing her lifted my sour spirit, but not much.

"She missed you, Guntram," the butler told me. "She was sad almost the whole time. Even Jean Jacques took pity on her, and prepared something special for her."

"I missed her also," I replied as I ruffled her ears in the way she likes so much. She playfully growled at me, and I scratched her belly. "I'll be in the library."

"The Duke will come at eight for dinner," he informed me. "You should get dressed." Excellent! I have to wear a tie. So much for my rebellion of a "no tie" day! I went upstairs picking up the dog, after throwing him an incensed glance.

Needless to say, I allowed Mopsi to sit on the bed while I dressed.

At eight o'clock, I was sitting at the dining table. Waiting as usual. Friederich took Mopsi away saying that it was her "bedtime" and feeding time. Do dogs have bedtimes?

At half past eight, I heard the familiar noise at the main door announcing Konrad's arrival. I didn't go. If he's late, he can come here. He's old enough to find his own dining room.

He entered in the room, wearing a normal businesses suit with Friederich trailing behind him. Without saying anything, he took his usual place at the head of the table. I said nothing, and took my napkin from the dish.

"I'm sorry for my lateness. My plane's departure was delayed at Malpensa."

"Must be a new world record. A whole week delay," I retorted bitterly using a cold tone of voice. "Where were you?"

"Around," he answered me, haughty like always, devoting all his attention to the soup that has just been served by Friederich.

"I see," I can also take care of my soup.

"Did you enjoy London?"

What? Does he want to start a civil talk I repressed the urge to pour my broth over his head. Sometimes being well mannered is a disadvantage. Normal people can release stress much easily... like those guys in Big Brother. Acid irony would have to do. "Very much before I was stood up for a whole week. Could you please answer the question?"

"I was with my cousin Albert. Malpensa is in Milan," he explained to the ignorant boy sitting next to him.

"I was not aware of that," I said, ironically. "Which one is the Airport for Around City?"

"Friederich, leave us," he said as the man literally ran away from the room. I looked at him enraged to no end.

"That you disappear for some time, making me sick with worry is one thing, but that you even take me for an imbecile, and lecture me at this moment is... too much!" I exploded.

"I was working the whole time. If you plan to make a jealousy scene, ask Goran and Alexei if I did something unfaithful to you."

"Don't use your old tactics of diverting attention with me! Where were you and what were you doing is the main question!" I said as I rose my voice.

"I don't have to give an explanation of my whereabouts to you. Some things became complicated and I had to set them in order before everything would escalate more," he said in a cold tone, not raising his voice.

"So much that you couldn't give me a phone call or an SMS?"

"I'm sorry if I worried you. My people told you to wait."

"What were you doing?" I said again this time slowly.

"As I said, setting things right. I don't like people meddling with my affairs, and much less trying to fool me. My presence was needed in order to terminate the problem once and for all. Now finish your soup. It's getting colder," he replied sharply, using his final voice to end discussions.

We continued to eat in silence. I was fuming. He can run around the world in his plane, and I have to sit, wait and eat my bloody consommé. I can think a lot of words to use to express my frustration, but unfortunately I don't know the equivalent in English or German.

Friederich entered timidly in the room to ask him if he could serve the meat. Konrad told him to do it while he slightly complained about the chosen wine not matching with the deer. I hope the alcohol gives you a headache! Good, point for Bambi! I looked at the chandelier to see the lights reflected on the crystals, de constructing themselves in hundreds of small rainbows, and I wondered how those elegant pear like shapes had been carved in the glass at the 1800. Konrad chided me with an "only fools or children gape at the ceiling Guntram." This is worse than a totalitarian state; you have to be quiet about everything, ask nothing and be happy about it!

Just when I was going to open my mouth to give him a piece of my mind in English, Spanish and German, my eyes met those of Friederich who shook his head negatively, making a gesture with the lips to keep me quiet. As nothing had happened, he withdrew our empty dishes and placed the dessert in front of us. Konrad resumed his eating in silence, his mind on another planet.

So absorbed he was that Friederich had to tell him twice, he had a phone call. He left the room without a word to go to his own studio.

"Guntram, don't be upset with him. He had a lot of setbacks this week." Friederich defended him softly. "He doesn't need the added pressure of a misunderstanding with you. He needs to have a clear mind now, and if he fights with you it would be too much for him."

"Do you realise that you're the first person in more than a week, that tells me he has problems? I'm no longer a child," I softly said, slightly hurt that even after a year of living together, he would still keep me aside from the most basic matters.

"Please, don't fight any more. Give him time to speak. He'll do it at some point. I know him since he was a child, and he would never betray your trust in him."

I rose from my chair, and went upstairs to find the door of his studio closed. So much for a talk tonight, I thought still upset with him for his way of treating me. I went to our bedroom, changed myself into my pyjamas and slid in bed to read one of the Art books I brought from Paris.

Konrad entered in the bedroom almost an hour later and also repeated the same ritual of sliding under the covers. He showed no intentions of speaking too.

After tossing in bed while he was engulfed reading his own papers from the bank I decided to start the counter attack this time on the personal flank.

"Don't you trust me enough as to answer a simple question like where were you?" I said, lacing my voice with pain.

He sighed. "Guntram you know I love you and this is why I keep you away from my dealings. I've told you countless times, that you're not qualified for this world. Besides, discretion towards my customers' business is a key factor in my profession."

"I was worried about you," I pressed.

"You should not. I'm more than capable to take care of myself. You must understand that on some occasions, I will have to go away for weeks and I can't take you with me because I would be only risking you. Come let me hold you a little."

"Risking me? In a bankers' meeting?" I asked puzzled.

"Some of the meetings take place in places where security is not so good, like an African country, for example. You would not like to be in Harare trapped for a whole week in a hotel room. Holgersen told me you almost exploded in Paris. "

"What were you doing in Harare?"

"I never was there! It's just an example!" He cried frustrated to no end. "I was travelling most of the time in Europe and Russia, if you need so much to know. Don't bother to ask more because secrecy is part of my business."

"Not very reassuring," I answered not happy at all.

"It's you who don't trust me with your incessant questioning!" he shouted at me, making me flinch. "Do you think I was on the fun run? Having the greatest time of my life with whores and liquor? Well, no. You have no idea how difficult it was this time to go through a web of lies and deceptions. Even Michael was bewildered. I was frustrated to no end, and not in the best mood. I didn't want to yell or explode at you. You're the only positive thing in my life, and I don't want to ruin it by directing my anger at you. I'm aware I have a difficult character to control."

"You could have sent a message. It only takes two minutes to type a SMS," I protested softly.

"Come here *Maus*, let me hold you," I doubted for a while, but he pulled me gently toward him and encircled me with his arms. He kissed me on the forehead as he delicately rocked me. I buried my head in his chest not so upset as before and let my anger dissolve in his embrace.

"Do you promise me not to do it again?" I said in a muffled and tiny voice.

"There will be times when I will have to go away. This can't be helped. I'll do my best to let you know where I am," he promised me with his nose buried in my hair.

I sighed and disentangled myself from his arms, turning my back to sleep. Konrad gathered all his papers putting them back into a folder and turning off his light. He snuggled his body against mine, but I wasn't at all in the mood to cuddle him as he most likely wanted. I remained motionless, slowly breathing while he softly petted the right side of my head.

"Don't be so crossed, Kitten. You know I have to work a lot. I'm sorry that our holiday didn't go as we planned," he whispered in my ear. "I hated completely to leave you alone but on the other hand, sending you back here seemed also unfair.

Holgersen told me you were finally going to the British Museum, the galleries and to the theatre. He says he has enough of culture for a full year!" he softly laughed.

"Anyhow, you could have called," I protested feeling my anger dissolving into his warm embrace.

"I kept a very orthodox schedule this week. When I was free it was very late to call you. Next time I'll write an e-mail if this helps you."

"But you had time to call Heindrik," I said resentful and frankly a bit jealous.

"No, I didn't call him. He has to present reports on you to Goran, and he updated me on your doings."

"Do you make him write about me?" I half shouted turning around to face him. What kind of lunatic makes this? Does Heindrik have to write if I look at the girls or boys? Control freak.

"It's part of his job. It's only your whereabouts and people you meet. They have to be careful because even the closest friends could pose a threat at some point."

"Konrad. I'm a jobless student! Who would be interested in me? You're spying on me to see if I have a lover hidden in the closet or in a bag!" I exploded furious with him this time.

"You live with me and are the closest person I have by far. It's more than logical than Goran is concerned about your environment. I'm not thinking you have a lover or being jealous. It's unfair to accuse me of that! I have many enemies who will gladly attack you to weaken me," he said haughtily.

"This is why you didn't allow me go to that Russian's house with Luciana?" Now he's more than his paranoid self.

"The name Oblomov does not exist among the list of wealthy Russians. He must be someone else. Despite it's something relatively normal to use an alias when dealing with outsiders to protect your privacy, I don't like the idea that you go to his house, on his own grounds. If he's a respectable businessman from Russia, he should introduce himself by his own name. And then, after Goran has checked him thoroughly, he can approach to you, if I think he's adequate."

"Are you planning on checking every person who comes to me? What about the university? Do I have to send a fax to Goran every time I want to study with someone?"

"No. The people from the University are all right. It's difficult to place a mole in there. Leaving its grounds with one of them is another thing."

"Konrad, do you hear yourself? Are you really thinking on checking on students? Or in one person who so far only bought some paintings from me, and always paid without complaints? Luciana has been working in his house for half a year!" I said incensed.

"What Dollenberg allows his wife to do is not my concern. If he wants to meet you, he should send you a letter, and we will see," he informed me. God! Is he quoting the Habsburg's Court Protocol?

"Nobody does this any more!" I cried in desperation. "Be glad he asked for a meeting and not my ICQ number to pester!"

"At my level things are done this way."

"How can he knows who are you if he doesn't know how old I am?"

"Are you telling me that a woman has not already spilled the whole story to him?" He laughed with contempt. "As far as I'm concerned it could be a very elaborate trap."

"He likes my paintings since mid 2000, and by that time you were not in my life! Are you jealous of him by any chance? Or is it that you really don't believe someone could like my things?"

"Guntram, you know perfectly well that I admire your work; you're acting in bad faith with that remark. I'm only being cautious like always. You're too naïve for your own sake," he said firmly.

"I apologise for what I said. It wasn't my intention to offend you," was my quiet reply. We have just finished one dispute and we're starting the next? Better I give him some ground. In his altered state we can end up very bad, regretting whatever we say or do. He looks more appeased after my apology.

"Kitten, I'm also sorry if I shouted you but you must understand that everything I do is on your behalf. You place too much trust in human nature."

"It's hard to understand your motivations if you never tell anything," was my murmured reply, looking for comfort again in his arms. He held me tightly for some minutes.

"If this man feels insulted because you refused his invitation, don't worry dear. There will be plenty of buyers once you're known. Ostermann is one of the best and most respected art critics, and he likes your work. Having you in this exhibition is his way to support you. Nobody expected you would be in it, after not even a year of studying under his tutelage, but he thinks you can present three of your pieces. If Dollenberg's wife wants to make business with your art, she must first understand you're not a penniless artist coping with and doing everything to make a sale."

"All right, I'll tell her to give him an invitation for the show. Why do we always fight?"

"I was not fighting with you. It was just a disagreement but the best always is the making up part," was his answer, whispering the words as he pushed me back to the mattress and slowly settled his weight over my body. He bent his head and first pecked on my lips, testing, checking the waters.

I laughed and returned his kisses with more urgent ones, tracing delicately his lower lip with my tongue. He growled in satisfaction and deepened his kiss, sucking the life out of me as he stuck his tongue inside of my mouth, roaming my insides and muffling my pleasure sounds.

"You can be very wanton my love"

"Takes one to know another. Shut up and do your part," I ordered him imitating what I call his imperial tone, putting my arms around his neck and pulling him closer as I rocked my pelvis against his one. My right leg went by itself over his backside as I arched my neck to allow him to kiss me better. He abandoned my lips to concentrate on my neck, softly, reverently kissing me and touching it with his tongue, flashing waves of pleasure through my body. His tongue and mouth travelled far upwards, up to my jaw and my ear, caressing it with the point of his noise, nibbling with his sharp teeth on my earlobe, not to the point of causing pain but to drive me almost mad with desire.

He disentangled himself from my arms to remove his pyjama jacket and trousers. I was more than interested in the show I was getting for free. I sat on the bed and started to unbutton my own jacket with trembling fingers, my eyes glued onto his, my lips suddenly dry. I wet my lips, softly biting my lower lip, drinking on the tension building up between us.

He jumped my bones tearing the trousers and devouring me with his kisses. I tried to pull him a little bit back. "Slow down, Konrad. I want to turn twenty-two if possible," I protested, squirming a little also. He froze for a minute, and then restarted to kiss me at a slower pace.

My hand grabbed his member and I started to pump it with slow and strong movements. He did the same for me making my heart go wild with its heartbeats, numbing my mind with a dense haze of desire. I looked at him, pleading him to take me.

I felt him penetrating me in one and determined push, not painful at all since he had taken care of stretching me first. His pace was fast and laced with determination but not brutal as he resumed his pumping on my member, driving me mad. His thrusts match with his jerking and we came together.

He covered my face with kisses as the rolled on the bed, taking me with him and making me lay on top of his body. I took a deep breath, trying to settle myself down.

"You could drive a saint crazy for you, kitten."

"Good you're not one," I chuckled, falling asleep on top of him.

Chapter 9

January 9ᵗʰ, 2003

Tomorrow morning Konrad has to go away. Destination; Shanghai and Hong Kong. Don't know when he would be able to return. I'm supposed to stay here and attend the painting classes with Meister Ostermann in the morning since I have nothing else to do. Well, I can think on other things to do, but as usual, the big German forgot to ask my opinion.

After our "making up night", we woke up in the morning, still holding each other like there was no tomorrow. But there was. We had breakfast together and then he disappeared to his office only to return at 11 p.m., going directly to bed.

Today, he offered me a ride to Zurich to my Art class. At first, I was surprised because it was not my usual time and I had made no further arrangements with my teacher but Monika had already done it yesterday.

Even if I wanted to smash his head against the window of his noble armoured limousine, I had to admit that I still have one month more of holidays before school restarts, and the perspective of staying at home all the time without him, is very boring.

Meister Ostermann's studio was relatively full of mature women. Seems it was granny time. He made me sit by a window with very good light. "Shows better when you screw it up," he informed me. I stayed there very happy, distracted with the dogs I was painting. Despite the foul smell of oil paints and turpentine, it's much better to paint with them. It gives you time to think, meditate, correct things and you have to plan in advance. I mean I still love watercolours, and you have to be very sure of what you're doing, having the mental image very clear in your mind before you can use them, but oil lets you explore better the figure.

"Out with you. It's one. I'm not going to feed you. Come back at 3 or 4. The small one on the left looks like a real pest." Ostermann took me out of my happy limbo. Was already so late?

"It was always barking and running after the horses. It was his natural right to make as much noise as possible."

"Try to keep tension reflected on his crouched position up to the forelegs. You concentrated too much in the head, chest and hind quarters. Has to look like a single unit."

"Yeah, you're right. I thought it was too much first but you're right."

"You'll balance with the other two on the sides. The one who looks asleep and the other chewing that thing and don't press too much the charcoal or you'll ruin it. It's just for sketching before painting. Go now, you'll work later."

Downstairs was Heindrik waiting for me with the car dressed in a dark blue suit.

"Hi. Burger?"

"You'd wish. Bank. Put on your tie."

I whined. I'm in holidays! I sighed as I looked for the thing in the depths of my coat pockets. I can't believe it's full regalia lunch! That explains why Friederich

269

made me dress with a "morning suit," Instead of letting me go with a jersey. My complaints about not being able to paint with a jacket on (maybe they could do it in the XIX century, but I can't), went into dead ears. The only grant he made was to allow me to take a light sweater with me.

I had to suppress another despair sigh when I saw Konrad's private dinning room in the bank was set for eight people. Great! With audience!

I stood there, resigned to endure a long and boring lunch. First, Michael and Ferdinand entered with with another four unknown men and nobody thought I should be introduced. I was sent to the middle of the table, on Michael and Ferdinand's side, as the last took one of the heads of the table.

They all started to speak in German about "containing the situation with the Russians". Michael began to elaborate on the theory of the rising powers always starting a war against the status quo and the need on using all available resources before they got more powerful. I was astonished to see the normally humorous man turn into a cold predator, speaking precisely like Ferdinand. Guess he's not the clown I thought. Well, he has a doctor's degree in Astrophysics, can't be a total idiot.

"Gentlemen, they were only testing our strength. Our response was correct, but they're counting on us to be self-indulgent and sleep. As I said we should concentrate on their legitimate dealings. That will clip their wings for a while as we reconstruct our position in the East," he said seriously.

"Michael, you could wait till I'm the room to start a war," Konrad said sternly as he entered in the room going directly to his place and sitting, making a slight gesture for us to also sit. Several waiters entered and served the dishes, leaving the room in haste.

"I apologise Sire, I didn't want to overstep." Michael looked truly contrite.

"We all are still upset for the Romanian issue, but we need first to reinforce our presence in the area," he said as I dedicated my interest to the food and kept silent. I don't like at all to be in their business meetings.

"Sire, I agree with Michael. We should not allow them to regroup. It's our territory after all," Ferdinand spoke from the other head of the table.

"An attack on their positions in roubles is the best option. All their incomes are in that coin. They're virtually trapped there," Michael suggested.

"Do you want another crash like the one in 1998 when the Russians couldn't afford to pay back 40 billions debt?"

"The situation now is very different from 1997 and world economy is recovering now," Ferdinand pointed. "I agree with Michael's view as everybody do in this room. We can't stop now."

"I see," he fiddled a little bit his food, completely lost in his thoughts. Nobody said anything or ate, waiting for a decision. Konrad took a sip of his wine and cleared his throat.

"I agree with you all, and you're perfectly aware that I have never let an offence go unpunished in my life, but we will let them believe we have fallen into their trap. No retaliation in the moment. Also, I don't want to fight with Antonov's former boss now in power. We both have the same loving character," he said causing a deafening laughter in the room. "Cohen, what is their position in commodities?"

"Focused around gold and oil; always bearish."

"From now onwards start to discreetly buy futures on both. If we can start a moderate bull market, with the Americans help with Iraq's most announced invasion, it would ease the Russian government problems. We need to have him on our side. Our opponent's movements in the direction of controlling the food market in Moscow already crossed him to no end. I want that he has no place to run in the end. Cohen, do it as quietly as possible. Take all the time you need, a year if necessary."

"Ferdinand, make Antonov return from wherever he is. The pipeline investment project is cancelled *sine die*. I will not divert resources on the idea that the Americans can control the Afghans, and our friend in Moscow could view it as a lack of trust on the Russian power from us. He's quite sensitive on the subject."

"Gentlemen. I don't want any provocation from us to them. Is that understood?" All of them nodded or said yes. "Michael, ask Goran to come with you to my office later. Also, I want you to outline several scenarios for a full scale retaliation within two years time frame."

"I would not expect they will stay quiet, gloating their so called victory. It was more a stalemate," Michael grunted, not pleased at all his, whatever was plan, had just been discarded.

"I am also not. For that I trust you and Goran to create a few diversions to keep Morozov busy. Nothing that they can link to us. I want upheavals in his own internal front," he sternly said. "Löwenstein, how's your father faring nowadays?"

"Much better Sire, thank you. He's already planning to escape my mother's watchful eye to go to the Königshalle's. He says the doctor's regime is killing him slowly," the man sitting in front of me replied.

"He's certainly on the way of recovery if he plans to go against his wife," Ferdinand laughed, giving the others the signal to start independent conversations. Michael devoted his attention to his partners and Konrad as I tried to understand what had been said, and why was I invited when I well could have been sent away with Heindrik.

After eating, all the men returned to their workplaces, and I was left alone with Konrad in his office.

"Come *Maus*, sit with me for a little while. I need to speak with you," he said going to the big leather couch by one of the windows. I approached warily, and sat beside him, waiting for what he had to say. He put his arm around my waist and pulled me closer as he grabbed my chin with his free hand.

"Guntram, as you must have understood by hearing our conversation today, our companies are under some stress from a rival Russian group. I have to admit they caught us unaware of their power, and hurt our business in East Europe. We had to retaliate in order to stop them, and in the moment we're even, but this war has only started."

"What did they do to you?"

"I'm afraid this is confidential information dear. I can only say that I had to take losses for several billions in order to save our investments in the newly privatized companies and public debt positions. I had to liquidate several profitable investments in other areas to obtain cash to counter effect their massive sales of bonds in Russia, Czech Republic and Poland. We managed to stop the bleeding, so to speak, and recovered a minimal fraction of the losses. My guess is that they wanted to force a pre-default scenario in those countries to drive plausible investors away, and keep the whole thing for them."

Not surprisingly he was in such a bad mood, not even talking to me.

"But Michael said it was a stalemate."

"I had to use all my influences to make them lose several profitable contracts for providing steel to several European and American companies. I had to extend some credit lines to those companies at a very convenient price for them, but not for me."

"I'm sorry for your troubles. I had not idea," I softly said, feeling like a real ass for being so mean at him in the last days.

"Never mind, dear. You had every right to be upset. What I want to tell you is that, from now onward, you will have to obey Heindrik in everything, and the security around you will be tightened. You can go to Meister Ostermann's studio every day if you want but no running around the city. You can return to the University but you should not leave its building without a bodyguard."

"Konrad, this is too much for an economical dispute. I'm not even part of your bank!"

"This man, Morozov is dangerous. When he lost the contract for providing the Georgian government, our main representative there died in a strange car accident. The local police investigates, but I don't want to take any unnecessary risks in your case. I was overconfident once, and almost lost you," he muttered, strangely affected.

Buenos Aires incident was still fresh in his memory.

"Please dear, humour me. Do as I say and don't complain. Most of these newly rich Russians have built their fortunes fast and on dubious methods. It's difficult to tell what is legitimate or not. After the collapse in 1991, many criminal organizations replaced the state, and made enormous amounts of money. The new leadership, is trying to reconstruct the state's power, but it will take time. I have every reason to believe his next move will not be financial. I have probed him that he can't beat me on this level of the game."

"What if he goes after you?" I asked fearfully.

"He will not. That would be suicidal for his organization. He lacks the logistics or power to survive a frontal attack against us. Even if I would be killed, others will take my place and revenge me. The consequences would be devastating for him and his associates."

"But you would be dead," I whispered in shock, trembling. He pulled me against his chest and hushed me.

"Nothing like that will happen. This is not the first time I have to face some nasty competition. I had to for the last twenty years; the only difference is I have you to worry about. I need your support in this."

"I'll do as you want and will not complain," I smiled weakly.

"Good boy. I'll have to go to Asia for some business. I don't know when I'll be back. Be good and work hard with Ostermann. Knowing that you're happy and safe is enough for me."

"What about you? Will you be careful?"

"Always. I'm not planning to let somebody rob me a life beside you. It took me a lot of pain to get you," he seriously said, cupping my head with his hands and kissing me. "Now go. I have to speak with Michael and Goran."

"Goodbye Konrad," I said giving him another kiss.

"We'll see us sooner than you think."

Chapter 10

January 22th, 2003

This afternoon I arrived to Davos, to the World Economic Forum. Not that the guys here are dying to hear my ideas, but I might have the chance to spend a few hours with Konrad as he has to attend several meetings tomorrow and the day after. It's a very small city, but the paradise for bankers and skiers. Pity I'm neither one of them. It's a place in the middle of a mountain region, very cold in the moment, minus 10°C! I'm freezing! And it's still not dark. Hope this hotel's walls hold the cold away.

I arrived with Heindrik, but he has vanished somewhere, I suppose to meet Goran or Alexei, leaving me in the hotel room with orders to stay put and wait. I will certainly not disobey him in this weather. Also there's the certain risk of meeting one of Konrad's friends on the streets and that he wants to chat. No, thank you.

I had a glimpse this morning of the abridged list of business leaders attending (Konrad is not mentioned there, not a big surprise), and this is without the world leaders' names, and since then I'm suffering from light-headedness. In theory you have the "public" (with journalists) talks and seminars and the closed meetings where nobody enters.

Fortunately, according to Heindrik, this year the "usual protesters" are not coming. It seems that cleaning the broken eggshells and yolk from your noble car, is a living nightmare, no to mention he had to throw to the trash one perfectly good coat after one girl spilled red paint over it (Well, it's not difficult to take you for a bear, if you want to know). They're in Rio, at the Social Forum, organized by the new Brazilian President. Anyway, the city is like a bunker, full of security people, private and public.

I haven't seen Konrad in long while. Since our last talk he vanished into thin air for three weeks. To his credit, this time he sent one or two e-mails and three phone calls.

I had a lot of time to myself. In the mornings, I would paint in the gallery on the other side of the Castle because it had a great light and the foul smell of the paints will not reach Jean Jacques or Friederich. As he said, sternly, when he saw for the first time the big canvas, I brought from my teacher's studio. "The Flemish gobellins of this house have survived since the XVIII century two world wars and your dog, but I don't think they'll survive those oil paints," I was sent to the upper floor in the newly built part of the house, reserved in the old times for the children or high servants, to work.

I think Heindrik was happy that I had decided to stay at home. This made his job much easier but he nearly gave another heart attack with his dammed habit of creeping on my back. I was there, painting, and in one moment out of nowhere, he was making me jump from the chair. And, no. It's not that I'm distracted, it's that he's soundless and thinks he should be my shadow. One of these days, I'll find him in the bathroom!

Otherwise, he's fine.

At 7 p.m., Heindrik returned to the hotel suite I'm supposed to share with

Konrad, and told me to come to dine with him, Alexei and Goran at the Restaurant here. The Duke was delayed in several meetings with other "hot shots" (a very abundant commodity here).

Alexei gave me a bear hug when he saw me, and murmured something like I was looking much better. Goran smiled, in his own patented chilling way, and that was it, his contribution to human talk for the evening.

Two hours later, I was sent to bed as they had to discuss tomorrow's agenda. Stomping on my pride, I said good night and returned to the room. If they were not so big and ill tempered, I would have given then a piece of my mind. Nobody sent me to bed since I was... ten, I think!

* * *

January 25th, 2003

Those days in Davos were strange. On the first night, Konrad finally arrived to the bedroom at one in the morning. I heard him coming in, trying to make the less possible noise while he undressed and slid into the bed, and embraced me lightly.

"Hi," I said shyly as I turned around to kiss him. He returned the kiss, hungrily and almost crushed my ribs with his hug.

"I didn't want to wake you up. It's late. Go back to sleep, Maus," he whispered.

"I missed you."

"I know. I also. We'll speak tomorrow. Now it's too late, and I need some sleep because I have a lot of work tomorrow," he said, kissing me on the forehead. OK, tomorrow morning at breakfast. "I needed to see you if only for a few hours and hold you," he mumbled looking lost and tired.

I kissed him on the cheek "Too much trouble?"

"Catching a swordfish is never easy."

"Are you all right?"

"Yes, don't worry. I have it on the hook, waiting for the final blow but first I'll have to wear it. Let's sleep dear and we'll speak later."

In the morning, I was hoping to find out what he had been doing, but he was immersed in his laptop and concentrating hard on his breakfast. I tried to catch his attention several times but it was useless. He would only grunt a "aha" or "yes" not caring at all. I mean, I asked him "can I keep the allowance for five millions after school?" and he said "yeah, yeah". Pity I didn't have a note pad and a pencil with me at that moment.

Ferdinand and Michael arrived and sat only giving me a brief greeting. The three of them started to discuss something in German and honestly I had enough of them and spaced out until Ferdinand put me down to earth.

"Hey, Guntram. I have one extra pass for you for the seminars. You can attend them. It's a golden opportunity."

"Why... Thank you. I'll go," I said puzzled.

"Do it. Take Heindrik with you and don't get into troubles, meaning *no press* at all. Enjoy it," he warned me with a soft pat on the head.

"We will be in meetings the whole day. Perhaps we could have lunch but don't count on it. Go to the conferences since you're not allowed to ski for the time being," Konrad half ordered me, picking up his papers, stuffing them into a briefcase, handing it to Michael and getting his coat in his hand.

Just like that they all disappeared. Heindrik, who was already informed that I had to be placed at the Forum's reception, was waiting for me. Rules: 1. Don't leave the premises without telling me. 2. Don't eat rubbish (you know very well what I mean), and 3. No speaking with the press. They're always looking for someone stupid enough (thank you Heindrik for the compliment), to talk about what is being said behind closed doors, and probably they know you share a room with the Duke. Beat me if I know that part, and how the hell would a journalist know who I'm...? Fuck; the tag I'm forced to wear with name and "Lintorff Privatbank" written so nobody has problems to identify the pond I come from.

The morning was uneventful, hearing some talks. Yunus, the banker for the poor people was there, explaining his experience in Bangladesh.

At 11, there was a coffee break and I decided to get one (Heindrik was not there to check I'm not drinking bloody tea, but I'd put some milk to cut the coffeeine down). There were other two guys from the bank, Petersen and Cohen busy with some other guys, so I stayed happily in my corner sipping my coffee.

A man in a normal suit, not tailored, approached and looked at me in a rather insistent way. Uncomfortably and impolite, if you ask me. I looked the other way ignoring him, but thinking that his face was somehow familiar.

"Are you with the Lintorff team?" he asked.

"Yes," I curtly replied not willing to engage me into a conversation with him.

"I'm Trevor Jones, Independent Times Magazine," he introduced himself extending his hand. I shook it not happily.

"Guntram de Lisle," I replied wondering why a journalist would waste his time with me, having the big guys from Goldman Sachs, Berkshire, Nomura, IBM or other top people just standing there.

"Where is the Duke now? After some poor country to exploit or doing some money laundry?" He asked irreverently, smiling smugly.

"Good day to you, Sir," I said. Great! I got the only cast at the party activist!

"Wait kid, you look very young, not even out of school. My sources tell me you're only his bed warmer. I have nothing against you. Wanna ask you something. I saw you in Paris," he said catching me by the arm.

"Remove your hand," I shot him a deadly glare and he put his hand away. "I have nothing to speak with you."

"Not even the Venice incident? I believe you don't know the whole story," he said with a disturbing certainty.

"I don't speak with the press, and if you want to bring the subject up, the police cleared me out as I was not guilty. Not even in the place at the time." Now, I'm pissed off.

"Come on. Don't be such a baby! Lintorff is a world class motherfucker and he tricked you! I can't believe you don't know it already!" he snorted in disbelief.

"Sir, leave me alone or I will call security," I growled. OK, it's not very masculine, but giving him a punch in the face doesn't look like something you do in this environment. If this idiot does not go away, then I'll do it!

Upset and with my heart hammering to a nasty point, I rejoined discreetly

Cohen, who was talking with people from Pemex, Mexicans are nice even if they're swimming in oil.

"Hi, Guntram," he said.

"Hi, could I sit with you? Don't know how to shake the press away."

"Came to the right place to learn," he chuckled.

So, I stuck with him and Petersen for the rest of the day. We even had lunch together in the cafeteria.

At night Konrad, Ferdinand and Michael returned, and I was mildly surprised they wanted to stay for dinner in the hotel. I was expecting them to go somewhere else with friends to carry on whatever they were doing. The dinner took place in the suite. We had two waiters to serve the food and after serving the main course they went away, leaving us alone.

"So, how was your day?" Ferdinand started the fire, asking me with a false lightly tone as he played with the duck's sauce on his dish.

"Fine. I saw Yunus. It's interesting what he says. His credit recovery is nearly a one hundred percent I replied, perfectly knowing they hated the concept of the "poor people's bank".

"Well, if you can't return one hundred dollars then you should not start a business. I would like to see him in a recessive context when all these micro enterprises crash," Michael said letting a dry laugh out.

"Perhaps they'll survive it better than you. The know more about survival strategy than many Economists," I said somewhat irritated at his superior tone. I want to see you feeding five children with less than two dollars per day in a big city.

"Guntram, 2.5 billion in credits over ten years is nothing for a bank. Good for selling newspapers," Konrad clarified for little idiot me.

"But for them it's a lot. Many of the women who used this money now have small companies and feed their children, or do you think that is better to throw some food around, and keep them in indigence? It eases our consciences not their real needs," I retorted slightly upset with him.

"Be careful Konrad, next time Guntram will start to shout the University belongs to the working class," Michael chuckled, making the others laugh.

"I think there are scholarships for that," I growled. Great, the masters of the universe laugh at us.

"Guntram, you know I like you a lot, but banking business is not the best place to find a selfless person," Ferdinand said softly. "Don't believe everything you hear there."

"You might prove more right than you think Ferdinand," I replied softly.

"Why? Something happened?" Michael pressed. Does he know? Looks like. Better spill the truth. They'll get it out from me at some point.

"There was a nasty journalist at the coffee break. I shook him off and spent the rest of the day with Cohen and Petersen."

"What did he say?" Konrad inquired, sounding almost sweetly. Almost.

"I don't think you want to hear it."

"Guntram, speak up." Bye bye sweetness.

"I already had to take one pill for the high blood pressure. Don't want to take the next because you lose your temper at me when I say it."

"Come, it can't be so bad," Ferdinand encouraged me.

My eyes went around the table, the three of them looking like hungry wolves. OK, if you want to hear it.

"For starters, I'm Konrad's new bed warmer, who is a motherfucker and exploits poor countries, does some money laundry on his free time, and to finish I'm some kind of drug dealer from Venice. He wanted to speak about you."

"When were you going to tell us?" Konrad said in his low and educated voice tone, the one he uses before the storm explodes on top of your head.

"What is to be said? I didn't speak with the man! I'm old enough as to take care of myself!" I said dryly.

"Guntram a journalist approaching and insulting you is a serious break in this place's security. I will have to speak with the responsible person. It doesn't look like the normal journalist who wants to know the hot stocks for next year," Michael said very seriously.

"He told me he was a journalist. Independent Times or something. Trevor Jones was the name and he had the official tag of an accredited journalist," I said a little bit more low tone than my normal voice.

"You are perfectly aware this a huge security break! Don't play the lamb with me!" Konrad roared at me.

"Excellent Konrad. Now you shout at me for something really out of my control because I'm not the one who checks the security. You have a mole or a bunch of them inside of your own bank. He was perfectly knowing who I was, what I do with you and the mess in Venice and the last part can only come from your people because my name was never mentioned in the newspapers or in the official investigation. Your people freely speak about your exploits in bed. Honestly, I'm surprised that I'm still not mentioned in the International Monetary Fund Working Papers. Fix your own security problems before you come to me shouting. Good night, gentlemen," I shouted enraged to no end as I stood and left the living room to my own bedroom. To my credit I didn't slam the door as I would have loved to do.

I could hear their muffled talk for a long time. At some point they all left.

Konrad returned the next morning as I was packing to go back home.

"Where are you going?" he asked softly, disarming my more than justified rage. I was expecting a confrontation between us.

"Home. To paint and wait for school. There's nothing for me in here," I replied firmly.

"I was hoping we could sort yesterday's problem out, kitten. I didn't mean to shout at you. You were right. I have a hole in my security. Michael will take care of that."

"Good. I'll see you at some point in Zurich."

He caught me by the waist and started to kiss me, softly licking the side of my neck and earlobe. "Please don't go. Stay with me for a while. This man will not bother you again. His credentials were removed. I need you with me. I'm under considerable stress these days."

"Konrad, I also apologise for shouting at dinner, but at the moment our tempers are short. The best is we split till we cool down. My health is not good enough as to endure another emotional roller coaster like before."

"All right. Go back to Zurich," he said and left the room without looking backward.

277

Chapter 11

March 2nd, 2003

After Davos, there was not much to tell. Really. Beginning of February, I started my second semester in the school, and macroeconomics, plus statistics and some accounting became my constant companions. Exactly as before, I got a full load of books to read, papers to write and homework to do. Luckily Corina was still with me, and we continue to study in the afternoons together.

Heindrik was also there. He would put me in the morning in the school and check (yes, check) that I would go inside (Yes, I skip classes once per week, smoke and do booze), and stayed there. Lord! He can be worse than Konrad... he was even asking for the bills at the cafeteria to check if I was eating properly! At five, he would haul me home to finish whatever I had left from school or paint till nine or ten, having dinner in the middle, and later being sent to bed by Friederich. At least, Mopsi was not ordering me around, always sleeping like a good girl.

Konrad was away during the whole February, only coming back for one weekend, and we were still somewhat both hurt from the last quarrel. He gave me a soft kiss when he arrived, a peck would be more exact, and went into his studio, closing the door. He didn't come down for lunch or tea, so I remained most of that Saturday painting in the other side of the house. I had finished the one with the dogs and was starting to retouch another with some children reading a book I've originally started back in November. Yes, I know. Children and dogs... next, I will be painting clowns and birds!

However, I was very busy, minding my own business, painting and concentrating especially on the little girl who was holding the book in her lap as her two younger brothers tried to read also over her shoulder. There was also a two year old sitting next to them but completely on his world like young babies do, checking on his hands. I've have seen then in a park in Buenos Aires and made some sketches at that time. Incredibly, the sketches made to Zurich in a folder along with other of my stuff that I thought lost in a trash container.

Somebody grabbed me from behind and I jumped at the touch ruining with the brush what I was detailing. Konrad.

"I'm sorry, didn't mean to startle you," he looked contrite but not much.

"It's OK. Can be erased," I curtly replied, looking for a rag to get as much as possible paint out.

"They are beautiful, so full of life and innocence. Who are they?"

"No idea, some little devils I saw in Buenos Aires, in the park in front of the Arts Museum, the pink one, remember?"

"Vaguely. Are they for the art show?"

"Yes, children and dogs always sell," I rose to my tiptoes to try to kiss him but he turned his face away,"Are you still cross at me? You know it was for the best that I left the city."

"I'm not upset. Disappointed would be a better term."

"In the morning I'm treated like an idiot, then a journalist insults me and rudely pokes around me, and then you shout me for 'not telling' as if I were a baby. Wait, you go away for a whole month, and still you're 'disappointed at me'".

"I'm disappointed that you didn't stay with me even if I asked you to do so."

Just what I was expecting. He thought I was abandoning him. "Konrad, I was not happy to go away. I wanted also to spend time with you, but we both were sore, tired and nasty. I could have only ended very bad for us. I don't want to ruin our relationship with incessant and pointless fights."

"I needed you," he said softly, whining a little bit. This time I put my arms around his waist and pulled him toward me, burying my face into his chest. I held him close and he didn't move. Again I rose to my tip toes and kissed him on the cheek, tenderly.

"I also," he sighed and returned my embrace. His kiss was more passionate than mine had been.

"Should we go to the bedroom?" I asked innocently.

"There's something more I want to speak with you," he said sternly. "Come to my office," Fuck. It's serious, and I can't think of any skeletons in my closet.

He asked me to sit in the chair in front of his desk and I did it, now really nervous. This was not his usual way of acting. Matters related to money or studies were normally discussed in the library. I tried to calm down and keep my cool.

"I would like to explain why this last incident worries me so much, and I do hope you understand."

"Konrad you can't control my every move. I shook the man off without problems, and I will never let him come near me again," I started.

"This is one of the things. That man was the one leading the protesters in Paris," I had to make a tremendous effort to suppress a surprised shout. "That he insults me, is part of the game. Many envy my position and there are many crazy persons around. But that he goes to you, who has no relation at all with my business, and hassles you, makes me think we are in front of a lunatic. I will increase the security around you. Don't bother to protest. It's already ordered, and it would be done in a discreet way so you're not disturbed in your daily occupations."

"But Konrad, Heindrik is more than able to do his job," I protested.

"He agreed and for the last two weeks you had them around you. Second issue and this is of a more personal nature. Your escape from Davos troubles me in the sense that you ran away at the slightest sign of problems between us."

"With our history together? Konrad, even you admit your own explosions!"

"I'm aware that I have a difficult character, but what I want to tell is that I need you by my side for good or bad. I want to take a big step in my life, but without you, I can't do it."

I felt ashamed at my own cowardice in Davos. In a way, I had defected him. "I'm sorry I let you down. I didn't see it that way then," I whispered.

"Shouting with you wasn't exactly the cleverest move from me. Anyway, what I want to say is that I'm forty-five years old and not getting younger. I can't delay any longer forming a family."

"Forming a family?" I repeated like a puzzled idiot.

"To produce offsprings. Children."

"Are you planning to adopt?" I asked again, more stupid sounding this time. I'm not! I'm only twenty! I almost died from nerves the day I had to take care of Juan

Ignacio, and he was a nice little fellow!

"No, no adoption at all. The children will not be recognized as *Geborene* by my peers. I want to have then with you," he said firmly.

What have you been smoking? We are both males from highly developed species, not flatworms!

"Konrad. The only way you can have children is with a woman. You need to get married and you don't want, unless you have changed your mind since Paris," I said, now fearing he had indeed done it and now he was going to end our relationship.

"No! I don't want to marry any of them! I was thinking more on a surrogate mother for the pregnancy, and educating the children by ourselves. In America there's a good legal framework that would protect me from future claims from the donors or the surrogate mother. I'm forty-five now and will be sixty-five when the children turn twenty, already too old to understand young people. I have trouble following you sometimes."

I was speechless—stunned to say the least. I'm still young and know nothing about children, and there he's telling me he wants to "order" several. Yes, I noticed he always referred to them in plural, not 'I want a child'."

"This is a huge step for me," I stammered, feeling dizzy. "What am I supposed to do with them? I know nothing about children!"

"I'm not planning to leave you alone in a nursery with them and a load of bottles and diapers. You'll get qualified help. Besides, you need to finish your studies, and you're four years away from your graduation still. I need you in the sense that you can provide me with a lot of mental stability and love for all of us. Children immediately like you. I'm afraid, I alone, would be too much for them; too stern. They need a gentle soul caring for them."

"Konrad, we are two men. What kind of family will we provide for them?"

"In my own experience, a stable one, without fighting and hatred, is more than enough. Children want stability and love," he said completely convinced. "I will appear in the papers as the father because the law here does not accept we both do it, but I will name you their legal tutor and guardian of the estate in case something would happen to me. For the practical life they would be as yours as mine."

"I'm twenty years old!" I protested trying to hold to something because his reasoning was sounding more and more appealing to me.

"I know. I was thinking more in March or April of 2004."

"That is in a year!"

"Enough time for you to get used to the idea."

"What if I don't want?"

"You want it. I saw it in your eyes when I mentioned the idea." True, but I won't give up without a fight.

"I don't feel up to the responsibility. I'm still too young."

"I also think you're young, and honestly I wanted to wait longer but the latest events forced me to make the decision now. Children will need my protection as long as I'm able to do it. These are turbulent times for us, Kitten. You love me too much to deny me my greatest wish."

"I don't know what to say," I whispered.

He left his chair and came to kneel in front of me, taking my both hands into his. "Please, Guntram."

And I couldn't refuse him any longer.

"How will you do it?"

"I have chosen three women for biological mothers and one surrogate. All are intelligent, educated and good looking. They have already accepted, and the children will be entirely mine. There is no chance they could take them away from us. The children will be born in the States, and come here after two weeks."

"Children?"

"Only three embryos can be implanted. I'm hopeful we get them all."

"Three?"

"Two nurses will help us. Not all of them survive the process."

"Konrad you know I can't deny you this. It's your right as man to have children, but I don't feel secure enough as to become a father or be responsible for a child. My own family life is practically nonexistent. My own father was only coming once per month to see me. Not much to learn from."

"Dear, there is no handbook for parenting. Most people learn on the way and we will always have the TV when they become too much."

"Don't you dare to poison the children with that rubbish!" I said incensed as he laughed at my reaction. We'll need several talks before I agree to anything if this is his idea of an education. What's next, candy and potato chips?

Chapter 12

March 12th, 2003

A few days ago Konrad announced that his travelling was finished for the time being and we should return to the old routine of me staying with him in the bank. I protested because I wanted to paint and had this art show (which in fact was his idea, not mine). He accepted to leave the office at six, and let me paint in peace until nine thirty at home.

He would move every evening in to the room I used to paint in, a former guest room with big windows looking over the court yard, with lots of natural light, a bed, bathroom and small desk and chair, now occupied by Konrad and his documents. To his credit, he kept quiet while I was working and I was happy to have him around. The last months had been pure hell for me, almost not sleeping and wondering where he was, if he was all right, feeling the empty space at my side of the bed as a permanent reminder of my own misery.

I have to study a lot at school; nothing new. Fortunately, Corina is still here and the Danish guy, Peter too. Now starts the first wave of mid term tests.

* * *

April 16th, 2003

D Day is back. Yes, Good Friday and all the Dinos will visit tomorrow. As usual, I can attend Mass and then disappear, this time with Heindrik. I really did promise to stay in my studio or painting upstairs without messing around but no. I have to go away…. Do they have an orgy when I'm out? It's not like I'm going to snoop their conversations or interrupt them. From 12:00 onward, I'll be officially a homeless person.

* * *

April 20th, 2003

It's Monday and I'm dead after the week end. On Friday was the Mass and all Konrad's friends arrived on time, with their big cars and bodyguards. I was up since seven in the morning and dressed in a dark suit at eight. I tried to ask Konrad to let me stay in my room (after all it's raining), but the only answer I got was "tell Heindrik to take you to a restaurant or to a hotel room if you feel bad. Zurich is big enough for you to find something to do."

When I descended, people were already sitting in the living room, library and standing in the corridors waiting to go to the Chapel at 10. The waiters were serving some hot drinks against the rainy and freezing weather; it was so cold that there was no snow. All of them, sitting together in one pack can look dangerous and intimidating. I stood hesitantly at the door frame, terribly abashed to enter in the spacious room. Fortunately the conversation didn't cease with my arrival. I noticed the *Fürst* zu Löwenstein making me a small gesture with his hand to approach him. He was surrounded by other three men and Konrad's cousin, Albert von Lintorff.

"Good morning, *mein Fürst,* Albert, gentlemen," I said gravely.

"You look much better Guntram. I hope you're recovering well," he replied shaking my hand and giving me a soft pat on the cheek. I noticed the other three had stood to attention when they saw me.

"Guntram will bury us all, *mein Fürst.*" Albert said, vigorously shaking my hand. "Do you know Fortingeray, Clemens and Hulsrøj? All associates."

I greeted them all, and was about to take my leave to say hello to Michael and Ferdinand when one of them, Fortingeray said.

"I hope this time Lintorff announces a full scale retaliation on this Russian. I'm not pleased with his actions so far. Russians don't understand any other language than a full scale war."

"My cousin has his reasons to act the way he does. I'm more than confident in his leading abilities," Albert retorted darkly.

"I hope he's not getting him softer," the man retorted making a not so discreet sign towards me. Albert blurted out a dry laugh.

"Soft? Konrad? You haven't been with us. The Russians paid in blood much more than they originally estimated, and he's not even finished with them." Albert intoned in a grave voice.

I was horrified at his statement. What was this all about? I looked at him, puzzled but a light cough from Löwenstein made me turn my head toward him.

"Guntram, do you think you could get me something cold to drink, like an orange juice?"

"Immediately, *mein Fürst.*" I went to the kitchen to ask for the juice, my head pounding with a headache. He told me this Morozov guy was brutal but "to pay in blood" could only have one meaning. I got the juice, and went back to the living room.

Löwenstein was sitting alone by the big couch, and I approached him. Albert and the other three were nowhere to be seen.

"Come and sit by me, child," he softly said as he left the glass on the small table beside him. "I can tell you're upset. Is it not true?"

"Yes Sire. What did Albert mean with "paid in blood"?"

"Konrad is the Griffin, and you already know that we had to counteract the attack on our positions in Central Europe by Morozov and his people. Our long time competitors felt that it was the right time to undermine our presence in those markets. You are not part of the game, therefore, you don't need to know what transpired in Georgia and Russia. No innocent blood was shed."

"But we are speaking of violent methods to do business!"

"They killed our associate in Georgia along his whole family. That couldn't be left unpunished. I know Konrad keeps you out of his affairs but you should know by now, that business disputes not always are settled in a negotiation table with lawyers around."

"Albert von Lintorff just implied Konrad had ordered the killing of people and don't lie to me because I've already had several proofs of his violent character," I said slowly and not rising my voice. His blue ice eyes were fixed on mine but I didn't downcast my eyes.

"Is there a place we can speak alone? The best would be if I introduce you to our world."

We went to my original studio in the tower and Löwenstein was interested in one of my early drawings framed and hung in the wall.

"Is it yours? No wonder Ostermann is so impressed," he said as he sat on the opposite side of my desk. "Come young man, I don't bite any longer. Sit," I did as he ordered me, full of dread, a suffocating knot pressing my throat.

"What happened in Georgia?"

"We should start our tale much earlier. You have noticed by now, the strong ties between many of the persons in the room below. Some of them are related by family, education, business or friendship, and those ties, in many cases, date from centuries ago. Since the XVIII century the Lintorffs have been a powerful house in Europe because they controlled most of the banks in Italy, and had a strong presence in the Hanseatic League. Instead of lending money to the Monarchies for their adventures in the New World or their warfare in Europe, they concentrated in lending it to the new born industries, travelling overseas companies, and building relationships reaching beyond the business world. Our order accumulated power and wealth over the years and we prospered.

"After World War II, Europe was in shambles, no matter on which side you were. Germany was utterly destroyed as well as France and Italy. Americans were looting everything they could, and the Russians doing the same in Central Europe. Konrad's grandfather faced enormous difficulties, trying to reconstruct our business. We had the capital in Switzerland, but our industries were destroyed. The only way to be back was if we combined our forces and we did it. We informally merged again our banks, industries, lands and know how in order to achieve contracts by the state and recover power."

"We operate as a big family in which the Griffin is the operative head of all of us, but he's nothing more than a *primus inter pares*; he as the decisional power, but he's voted every year in his post. Normally, the Griffin is the eldest son of the previous one but if he's not accepted by the rest of us, he should go away, and the next in line would be voted."

"You know about Morozov. Officially, he owns a big steel, oil and transport conglomerate in Russia. Off the record, he's head of one of the cartels in Moscow, mostly into weapons trade and some prostitution and drugs. He needed to clean his money and wanted to use our resources and contacts but Konrad threw him out and not very politely, I'm afraid. The Russian felt insulted and attacked our positions in Romania, making us lose several contracts in the soon to be privatization of the energetic sector. He heavily hurt us by forcing a pre default scenario in Central Europe. Konrad retaliated in his own way by making him lose his chance to control the pipelines in Georgia. Needless to say, our representative there was killed alongside his whole family."

"Konrad had now two fronts open at the same time. He had to contain the situation in Georgia and at the same time recover what we had lost in Romania. We can't afford to lose something like Petrom. As for the matter in Georgia, the Griffin decided to handle the whole intelligence we had on the heads of the Chechen Mafia to the Russian authorities, who were more than happy to deal with them since they control the black market for food and the transports that bring the goods into Moscow. Chechen mobsters are responsible for most of the inflationary process the Muscovites have suffered in the past years. The new government in Russia is unforgiving, to say the least, and organized a punishing raid around Grozny. Most of these mobsters were killed along with their families. Once the Russian Army is unleashed, you can't control it. Russians and Chechens hate each other since Stalin ordered the mobilization of the whole population to Siberia, back in the forties for allegedly collaborating with the Nazis; those who were able to come back hate the Russians with a suicidal passion."

"Morozov is less than contained or destroyed. He has only stopped for a year or two. Konrad knows it, and today we all hope he will outline his strategy for destroying this man. The problem is, that several of our associates believe he has not been strong enough; that a direct blown was necessary, not retaliating in a far away country, despite this would mean Morozov would lose an important part of his power in his own home country."

"He's responsible for the manslaughter of innocent people!" I was horrified that he could have done it.

"No. He just pointed his finger where the Russian Authorities should look. They would have done it anyway at some point. He only saved them time and resources. Guntram, this world is not a gentle one. This is not a war we looked for or even started. He has been our Griffin for the last twenty years, and one of the best so far. Without him, all of us would be still begging for a license or a contract. I hope he continues for another twenty years, despite the critics from some members like Fortingeray. He had to fight for his position since he took over his father's place when he was a little bit older than you."

"I know. He told me," I whispered.

"Our combined assets have increased ten-folded or more under him. This is why he kept his position. He sacrificed his personal life for it. Some of the associates feel that your presence may hinder his sharpness or strong character. I think not. You have been good for him, giving him more stability and confidence in himself. Remember when I told you he would need you more than ever? This is the time to prove your worth to him and us. I see in your eyes that you're shocked at his actions."

"How could I not be? He's responsible for the killing of people and fighting with a Russian mobster."

"We do not choose our enemies, only the methods to fight them."

"What if the others say they want more blood? Will he comply?"

"They can't make recommendations to the Griffin, only his advisers; Dähler, Kleist, Albert or I and some others in our role as past advisers. "

I was on the brink of tears. So this is why he kept me away, so he could do freely all what he wanted. I felt nauseated, and needed something to drink desperately.

"*Mein Fürst*, I'm not sure if I can continue a relationship with a man who causes pain on innocent people just to keep his banks accounts getting fatter."

"Child, do you really think you can walk away from us just like this? Even if Konrad would let you leave him, and I don't think he would ever do it, the others associates and enemies will go after you for what they think you might know. Konrad is no different from all the other men downstairs. Man is a wolf to man."

"I must attend the ceremony, *mein Fürst*," I mumbled, with the urgency of escaping, stronger as never before.

"Leave the Church out! I want to know what is your position in this!"

"My position? I have no position or saying in anything! You just told me that if I don't do whatever Konrad wants I'm dead!" I roared lifting from my seat.

"No, no, child. Nothing like that. Konrad would never hurt you. Even if you were at odds at each other, he would still do anything within his power to protect you. But he needs you at his side."

"How can I love him after I know his business methods are not legitimate? I'm sure now he tricked my friend from Argentina in order to get the money from them."

"No, this he did not. Your friend got all by himself in the trouble. Konrad only used his money, and contacts to get the lowlife after you away. I know he wants to start a family, but he needs you to achieve it. I know him since he was a small child, and he would never do anything wrong, unless he's provoked. This man has forced us to fight in his own terms. His father used to say, never get into a fight, but if you do, finish it."

"Why do you tell me this?"

"Because I need to be sure about you if I have to fight for Konrad today. Many want him out. They think that if Albert takes his place, it would be easier to overthrow the Lintorffs, and get all the power. I can sway the undecided ones to his side, but I don't want to do it, to find you making terror on him and thwarting everything. Tell me young man, will you be on my side or against me?"

"I'll never do anything to hurt him. I can't. But I can't also live with a man who does this."

"If you leave, you will kill him," he said with absolute certainty.

I know Konrad needs me to comfort and support him. Sometimes, I believe he loves me so much that in a way that he's hurting himself.

"Tell me, can a few moral principles prevent you from loving him? Is your love so weak? Love transcends good and bad times." I felt the tears veiling my eyes as he took my hand. "He's so excited with the idea of children, and I think they would be good for you too," he added dreamingly.

Yes, I'm also dying for the children. When I accepted to live with Konrad I knew I would have to let my dream of forming a family go and I did it. The coming of the babies was a terrifying source of happiness for me. I wanted them also, no matter if they were from Konrad only. I wanted them with every fibre in my body.

"It would be difficult to ignore what you have told me," I said slowly.

"I'm not asking you to do it. Think you'll play a great role in the education of the next Griffin. Perhaps you could even change our ways, or at least provide some comfort to those in need."

"Will you support Konrad?" I asked.

"Only if you do it too," he answered firmly.

"I will, so help me God," I said crossing myself.

"Then, we have an agreement, young man. I'll get those hungry hyenas out of his neck, and you will help with the next generation," he informed me, extending his right hand as to seal our deal. I shook it seriously.

We went downstairs to the Chapel to arrive in the middle of the service. We placed ourselves quietly in the back part. Konrad, as usual, was in the front with Ferdinand, Albert and other two very old men. Löwenstein almost pushed me to take communion. When I was returning from the altar, I looked at Konrad's direction to find his eyes fixed on me, wondering what had transpired between us. I just softly and briefly smiled at him, and his posture visibly relaxed.

At 11:30, I was looking for Heindrik to escape no matter where he wanted to go. Michael caught me by the arm and told me to go to Konrad's studio upstairs. I climbed upstairs with a heavy heart. He was already there.

"What did Löwenstein tell you? Albert said Fortingeray was nasty to you," he asked visibly nervous.

"Löwenstein only told me the story behind your latest deals. Don't worry. We are fine, my love. Don't waste your time with me now. You have many hyenas to put back in the fold," I said softly as a wave of relief washed him over.

"I love you."

"I also do, but don't let Fortingeray know because he already thinks I have softened you," I whispered as I kissed his cheek.

"Me? Soft? How little they know me," he smirked. "*Auf* with you, go with Heindrik. See you tonight."

"Yes, tonight at some point. Hopefully, before Sunday," I shrugged as he gave me a kiss on the forehead, and went away.

A few minutes later I heard a soft knock on the door. Heindrik.

"One minute, I change and go with you." Yeah last year, Alexei and I in dark suits at the McDonald's was looking like the MIB had taken over the city.

"No need to. This attire is good for the Eden. You're having lunch with Sophie Marie Olsztyn, old time friend from the Duke and really old. Bring your portfolio with some drawings and watercolours. She's in the city and wants to see your stuff."

Heindrik almost succeeded where Löwenstein with his talk and Konrad with his mood swings never did; almost gave me a heart attack with his driving skills. Normally, he's very conscious to the point of being a shy driver, but this time we were getting late, and the sailor decided the car was a rocket.

"Remind me to never drive with you again," I said as he left me in front of the hotel. He got out easily and threw the keys to the poor valet's face.

"You're in time. Don't complain," he shrugged. "I'll take you to the restaurant and when you're finished, call me and I'll pick you up. No wandering out of the hotel. Clear?"

"Crystal. Heindrik. What if she becomes too heavy? Can you rescue me?"

"Sorry, not in my job's description," he chuckled as he gave me my portfolio.

The maître led me to her table where she was sitting with another friend, also mature and elegant to no end.

"Madame Olsztyn. Thank you very much for your invitation," I said bowing my head and kissing her hand as she had offered it.

"Guntram, dear, please don't make me feel older than I am. Call me Tita. Everybody does it around here. This is my good friend, Elisabetta von Lintorff, Albert's mother."

"How do you do, Madam?" I said baffled, losing colours at meeting the other head of the Lintorffs. According to Konrad, she was something like the bee queen, with a big sting if you were on her wrong side.

"Hello, dear. You're exactly as my son described you. I'm sorry your health condition prevented us from meeting before."

"Sit with us dear," Tita chirped happily.

We spoke during the lunch a little bit about the weather, my studies and the upcoming exhibition. They told me about the Opera season, and that I should convince that "Neanderthal," I have for boyfriend (sic) to go more to the theatre and to parties because for the last ten years he was a sort of social hermit.

I was surprised that during lunch none of them mentioned the painting subject because officially it was the excuse for meeting us, not that I could do much as my portfolio was with my coat in the cloak room. When lunch was finished, I supposed I was going be sent away but they insisted to go to Elisabetta's suite so I could show them my work. "My nephew already warned me you would try to run away at the mention of watching your things, but you have no chance to outrun two women like us."

Her suite was very big, huge to tell the truth and had a fantastic view over the Zurich Lake. Pity it was raining, but in the summer it must be really nice. Both women went directly to seat in a large sofa with my portfolio, and started to look at them. Most of them were drawings in pencil, charcoal studies and some watercolours done during the last winter; nothing really good in my opinion.

For a long time the only sound in the room was the rustling of the papers as they examined together the things. At some point they would put one on the coffee table and look at it from a distance. Sometimes they would exchange meaningful glances with each other.

"Have you sold anything, dear?" Tita asked.

"Not really, only a few to a Russian living in England who likes my things; the wife of a friend's brother managed the sale," I explained feeling really small now. Great, they didn't like it, and want to know the idiot who bought from me so they have the whole story to tell.

"Somebody beat us, Elisabetta. These watercolours are magnificent. I'm not surprised Ostermann likes his work. It's a very complex drawing with a lot of technique behind, completely classical in its conception but fresh and modern at the same time. Very strange and bewitching, yes, that might be the word."

"Thank you. You're too kind. This is nothing, really," I said totally embarrassed at her praise.

They both laughed musically. "Yes, as all real artists, you're a hopeless case for sales," Elisabetta said. "How many paints are you going to present in May?"

"Only three."

"Pity. This auction will be a carnage. I'm already in love with this series of birds. Is it really pencil what you used? Elisabetta asked me.

"Watercolour pencils. With a wet brush you can uniform the colour and add details when dried. If you like them, you can keep them. I would be honoured."

"Guntram, I can't accept such a generous offer. This you should keep for selling or for a later exhibition. Your manager should start to look for a gallery for you."

"I have only been with Meister Ostermann for half a year. I need much more time and practice before I think about selling anything, and to be honest, my style is not very trendy in the moment. Perhaps I would have been luckier two hundred years ago."

"Yes, your technique is very classical but the product is fresh and free. You can feel yourself related to the object. It makes you wonder what it's or what is behind," Tita said.

"They are only birds who were eating the crumbs left from breakfast. I have no hidden message, really. I paint what I like or find interesting."

They both were silent and resumed their study of the paintings. The light was going away and I thought it was time to go home. I rose from my chair but they wanted to have tea with me.

"You can make us company a bit longer. My son Albert plans to stay at Konrad's house tonight. It's going to be a long meeting this year."

I stayed for tea with them. We talked for a long time about many things, and finally both accepted some drawings from me. After all, most of them would finish in the trash can at some point. I can't store everything!

A soft knock in the door announced Heindrik. He must be pretty bored the poor guy.

"Is it time?" I asked him.

"I only wanted to leave you your key, sir. The meeting will extend till very late. We return tomorrow morning, sir."

I must have looked dumbfounded because I could only gape at Heindrik.

"You can invite us for dinner dear. It's been a long time since someone in his twenties, not family, does it," Tita interfered, completely happy that I would stay longer, but I was becoming restless.

"Is everything all right, Holgersen?"

"Yes sir, just a delay. Good night."

* * *

Easter Sunday

It's very late and I'm dead from the day. Guess I'm still not up for such a thrill. Wonder if I could resist a nightclubbing session. After all, they were only children with balloons, chocolate eggs, bunnies, lunch with 150 people and so on.

On Saturday, Heindrik took me home at 11 a.m. He was looking more relaxed than before and I pondered the reason. I believe someone has been naughty on Friday night, but I said nothing and he drove me home without speaking. He had Madonna's latest CD, American Life. Where the hell did he get it? It's not supposed to be released until next Monday.

"I like her old hot, sexy style more. Too much thinking is not good for pop music."

"Buy something from Britney next time," I chuckled.

"Might do. I like silly blondes."

When we arrived, we faced the usual pandemonium of servants cleaning the house. It seemed they had quite a party here. I found Friederich looking contrite at the monstrous Dutch carpet from the living room being rolled by three men. It had a huge dark reddish-brown stain in the middle.

"What can I say? I didn't do it. Good morning Friederich," I said, moving quickly away as the men took it away.

"A real tragedy. That stain will never come out. By the evening they will bring another from Persia, nothing comparable. Should have put it in cold water immediately, but they were too busy to care. At least the wood is not too affected," he sighed.

"Where is the Duke? Still sleeping?"

"No, having breakfast with Lintorff, von Kleist and Dähler. In the small dinning room. You can go in there," he said, glum to no end. Time to disappear before I'm forced to attend the carpet's great burial.

The mood in the dinning room was no better. Only one word can describe it; hangover. Albert was not there. I was shocked they were having breakfast at almost 12:00. The three of them looked deranged and still tired.

"Good morning," I said softly, and was about to leave when Konrad told me to sit and have a tea. I got several appreciative grunts from the others as greeting. I sat next to Michael.

"Did you have a nice time with the girls?" He chuckled, getting a killer's look from Konrad. Well my love, hangovers are not your brightest moment.

"Very. They are very nice ladies. And you? Seems you can't hold your alcohol any longer," I joked.

"I can survive a full *Oktoberfest* evening, boy," he grunted. Well, your famous Bavarian sense of humour was also missing this morning. I kept quiet.

"Guntram I'm going to kill you," Albert shouted from the door making the other three almost jump, and look like they were going to strangle him. "My mother called me today at 7 a.m. to sing your praises. She didn't stop till 8! Why did you have to give her those damned birds? She's totally in love with them. Now, my beauty sleep is ruined."

"I doubt a hundred years could help in your case," Konrad chuckled, getting also a dirty look from Albert, who sat next to Ferdinand. A butler served him something like scrambled eggs for breakfast.

"Any news from the deceased?" he asked his cousin making me jump alarmed. "Black coffee, no milk."

"Rolled and away. The next generation will come this afternoon." was Konrad's dry answer. Ah, the carpet.

"Friederich was quite upset this morning about the rug," I said innocently. "Wine?"

"Minor loss. He'll get over it," Konrad growled. "Tita also called me at 11 to tell me how happy she was with the drawings you gave her. She has invited you again to her house. She will buy something from you at the auction, and I'm supposed to let her do it or suffer the consequences. The Russian will have very serious competition this time."

"I'm glad both ladies liked them. Was your meeting all right? You all look very tired."

"I'm still Griffin, and everybody is back in place for another year."

"Thank God. I don't want your job cousin. Fortingeray and the others had it coming. Loyalty is crucial in our world."

Chapter 13

April 23rd, 2003

I'm too nervous to paint tonight. I would destroy my work if I do it. What a shitty day. Yes, there's not other word for it: Shit.

It was a normal Tuesday. Without classes but Corina and Peter decided it was a good time for using the library in peace, and start with our papers for Macroeconomics. We worked the whole morning at a good pace and by 2:00, we had almost everything organized. It only needed now time to be written. I went for lunch to the cafeteria and almost got the door on my face. Germans, well Swiss, can't they be a little more understanding? It's only 5 minutes after 2 p.m. and you don't serve lunch any more? OK, tea and a salmon sandwich it is. No, I don't want cake at this hour. It's not coffee time despite your crazy timetable. There were people still having lunch!

I went back to the library to start my paper's writing on my laptop. Anyway I had to make time till five when I would be picked up by Heindrik. I was deeply immersed in my paper when I perceived somebody sitting on the chair in front of me.

"Hi, kid. Remember me?"

There was that idiotic reporter from Davos—Independent Fools or something. I closed my laptop and rose to go away.

"Don't go. I wanna talk with you," he said, grabbing my arm. I threw him a glance, and he removed his hand from my arm. Guess something from the boy's attitude finally stuck with me.

"I don't. Good day, sir."

"Look, I don't think you're involved in their dealings and you're a good person even. How a decent kid like you ended in the bed of a bastard like Lintorff is a mystery to me."

"Exactly. I'm no part of the banks. If you want an interview, call the public relations department," I suppose there must be one… somewhere in the structure.

"Yeah, I met them in Davos. One broken rib, otherwise I would have contacted you sooner," he snorted.

I stood there, frozen. "Come on kid. Talk to me for a while. Will you?" He asked me almost pleadingly. I sat again in my chair. "It's almost impossible to come near you. You have more bodyguards than the Prince of Wales. If you're not in that fortress, you're here with two or three monsters around. And the studio you go for painting is worse because I have there the added pressure of your old cronies' bodyguards. "

"Are you here to discuss my security details?" I said coldly, hiding the best I could, the fear running through me. Three bodyguards? I thought it was Heindrik only.

"Just stating the facts. Look, I've been investigating Lintorff's group for more than ten years, and they're dangerous and crazy motherfuckers; murderers who will stop at nothing to get their goals."

"Which are? World domination? No, no, wait. To re-establish the Catholic Church's power as it was in the Middle Ages," I said ironically putting a snug face.

"No. They only care about power, not money even. They want to control as much as they can. The Illuminati want to rule the world, this is true, but the Order wants to increase its power over the criminal world. You see bankers and tycoons on the front, but the real base of their power is in the fact they control the drugs, weapons and prostitution rings in Europe, part of Central Asia and Latin America. That kind of money finances their companies. They are too clever as not to enter in the States or fight with the Chinese or Japanese Mafia. But here, they rule, like they did for the last three centuries."

"I have no time to listen to your lies, sir."

"Sit down and tell me why Lintorff likes so much to keep everything secret. He never gives an interview or publicly appears. He has turned down all offers to enter into politics. His banker friends clean the money from almost every illegal operation in Europe and Latin America. His organization is clever enough as to be on top of the actual perpetrators, and offer them their services to clean their fortunes and protection from police. They put and get governments down in smaller countries. You have to be very nasty to make a Colombian drug lord recoil in terror when you only mention the words "the Order"."

"Good day to you sir. If you have proofs of your accusations you should go to the police."

"I can't boy! Most of the police belong to them! I need something final to publish about them. We have to expose them for what they're! Look, the mess in Venice was a set up. Those girls worked for a Russian drug lord, and he sent them to your friend in Paris with the drugs. I know this because a snitch in Paris told me. The local dealers complained to the police about the "invasion" of their territories, and somebody killed the girls so they would never tell who hired them. In a minute, your friend is in prison, and the logical step is that you're also arrested, but, by miracle the police only questions you just a little, and lets you go completely clean. What is really not clear for me is why Lintorff mounted such a charade to get you when he could have only seduced you. It makes no sense at all."

"It makes no sense at all, especially if you consider that I was more than happy with his wooing me. A snitch told you? Do you really think I would believe you?"

"I tried to speak with the Senator woman but she didn't want to do anything with me. Seeing the five guys she sent after you hanging in her own stables at her own country house, guts popped out and visibly tortured before death, made her rethink her revenge plans on Lintorff. Local police just got rid of the bodies and turned a blind eye. Her son was later involved in a car accident and almost killed."

"And you got all this from?"

"Can't tell my sources; they're reliable. Look kid, you can help us to stop this man."

"Us?"

"My organization. We fight against them and the Illuminati too. Their shady ways will destroy democracy and freedom. Under them, you only are free to change the channel on TV! Banks own up to your last breath!" he shouted.

Time to leave the fanatics. I gathered my things and packed then in the laptop portfolio. "You sleep with the guy, you can get information out of him! People talk in bed!" he yelled, making several students look at our direction.

Excellent. Now the whole university thinks I'm Mata Hari. Pity she was a woman and her own government shot her down. I went out not caring what he was shouting me now.

I left the building, my heart hammering and my sight a little bit clouded. I took a deep breath but it wasn't helping me. I started to walk towards the bank at full speed.

Not even a hundred metres from the building a black BMW stopped beside me with a very pissed off Heindrik inside. "Get in the car! How many times do I have to tell you don't leave the premises alone?" he barked at me as I was entering the car.

"Next time, do better your job and get the reporters out of the premises before they come at me," I answered back.

He cursed slowly in Swedish, I think. "To the bank with you. You look paler than normal." Yes, I feel like shit, dizzy, willing to throw up and my blasted heart almost deafening me with its beating.

He parked in his own particular style. In the middle of the street, making the other cars go to the breaks. No angry horns because it's forbidden here, but he got several angry shouts in German. Fortunately, one of the other bodyguards took the car away as Heindrik nearly dragged me, under the astonished look of the reception girl, toward the upper floor.

Monika stopped him in her unique way, totally ignoring him. "Guntram dear, I'm afraid the Duke is in a meeting now. Would you like to wait in my office?"

"No, we go to Mr. Pavicevic's," Heindrik grunted, dragging me again toward the elevator.

"Holgersen, will you please stop shaking Guntram like a rag doll? If you need to speak with Mr. Pavicevic you are old enough as to find his office by yourself," she said, her eyes sending daggers at him. If I would not have this horrible pressure in my throat, I would find the beaten puppy's look on Heindrik's face very funny.

"Yes, Ms. Leyden," he answered sheepishly, head bent down.

"Good, dismissed."

"Monika, do you think I could get some water? I don't feel good."

"Certainly. Sit down and I'll get you something," she said, looking at me concerned. In less than a minute she had a glass of water and I took the orange pill for the blood pressure, and I had to loosen the collar and stupid tie to breath better.

"Thanks a lot, Monika. I feel much better now." She looked at me with clear disbelief shown in her eyes, and went to speak on her phone.

A truly furious Goran entered, with Heindrik trailing behind. Only Michael was missing to make the party! Wrong. Here he comes.

"Tell us the situation," Goran growled at me.

"Guntram is not feeling well. I have already called the doctor, so you can keep your prodding for later," Monika said firmly. I love this woman.

"It will only take a second, Monika. Come Guntram, tell us what happened. Holgersen was not very clear," Michael interceded, shutting her up.

"The journalist from Davos was at the library in the University. He appeared out of nowhere and started to yell you all are part of some kind of Mafia, money laundering everything and banks owning people, Europe and Latin America. You also kill everybody who opposes you. But the best is, that Konrad hired two prostitutes to organize the whole mess in Venice, and then killed the girls so I would fall in love with him. I met those poor girls in Paris much before him!"

"This is outrageous, Michael. The Duke will not be pleased with you all when he hears that this man was again harassing Guntram and now he's on the brink of a heart attack!" she shouted at them.

"Monika, I'm not having a heart attack. I'm just nervous that this man can creep up on me like that. He knows better than I my own security measures, and you Goran, gut people alive in your free time. He was also shouting in the middle of the library that I should sleep with Konrad to get information out of him in order to save democracy and freedom. This person really needs a shrink!" I said in relative calm, starting to feel better.

"Goran, to my office," Michael said and they both disappeared just as the doctor entered in the room. Yes, there's a coronary unit here. Some days you need it, especially when trading becomes very harsh.

He checked me and the verdict was that since I have a previous heart condition, those were the symptoms of a stable angina; I should rest, take the medications as prescribed, and no trading for the next two days, but it was no heart attack, nor did I need to go to a hospital; just rest. When he left, I said to Monika

"I've just been promoted to trader. Do I get a Lamborghini now?"

"I hope you're not adopting Michael's sense of humour, dear," she said dryly. "You can go to the Duke's bedroom and rest there till he's free. I'll brief him."

Without much chance of doing anything else but to obey her, I went to the bedroom, crossing Konrad's office and closing the door. I hope he doesn't become upset I'm using his bed because after removing the jacket and shoes I felt very cold.

I slid under the covers, utterly tired, but I was unable to sleep. What if it was true what he had said about Fedérico's mother? I don't believe for a minute his version of what happened in Venice. I met the girls before Christmas, right? At a party. Even that American soldier couple thought they were after something. Konrad was in Paris at that time, even in Notre Dame, and even assuming this was the quickest case of falling in love in world history, he had no physical time to put on such a charade! Less than eight hours? Not to mention his jealousy might have exploded if one of he girls would have touched me in order to get my attention. After seeing him with his "pals," In Notre Dame, I doubt very much he would have had the time to drool over tourists and honestly, I was definitely a turn off with my old jacket and backpack. I still wonder what he saw in me in Venice.

Fedérico has no *estancia* in Buenos Aires or nearby. His family comes from the country's northwest side. They're into mining since the XVIII century as the poor Indians can testify. There's no chance Konrad or his people could have gone to their house at about 1,600 km within one the day; 3.200 km in total for the whole trip. Goran or the others gutting five people alive? Heindrik would have a nervous breakdown if his suit was sullied with splattered blood. And for a house in Buenos Aires, they live in a petit hotel downtown no stables at all there... garage yes, but no horses. Fedérico's car accident, Juan and Laucha, direct witness thought it was just that; very bad luck mixed with recklessness and foolishness.

But I still couldn't find my peace of mind about all the other things he said—the money laundering, the Mafia contacts and their obsessive goal to achieve power. His methods are brutal sometimes and bordering on illegitimate, but he wouldn't do something like that. If the reporter lied on the details, he could have done it on the big picture also.

Why would he do it with such intensity? I have nothing, and if he thinks this is a big conspiracy he should write a book or something, not get me in the middle.

"I confess this was one of my fantasies, but the context is not the one I had imagined," Konrad said, almost making me laugh with his serious tone while he sat on the border of the bed and caressed the side of my face.

"If this bed could speak," I trailed, smiling weakly. I was still feeling dizzy.

"Never here. Believe me," he said, now kissing me softly on the lips. "Besides, you need rest, according to the doctor."

"Yeah, I'm not so sporty any longer. I think I can drop the idea of going to a Metallica concert this summer."

"What did this man say this time?" Konrad asked with utter tiredness in his voice. I felt bad for him. Great, he has one problem more, and I just provided it.

"He says you're the head of a shadow organization that operates in Europe, part of Central Asia and Latin America but don't go into China, Japan or United States. You are the head of this organization that provides money laundering services for Mafia bosses, and they fear you. Even Colombians drug lords are terrified of you." He snorted a dry laugh.

"Yes, cancelling people's credit cards can produce that effect. What else?" he barked.

I laughed but he remained serious. "You hired two Russian prostitutes to lure Fedérico into smuggling drugs across Europe so I would fall in love with you, our big saviour. Pity the girls showed much earlier in my life up than you. Also, you killed the five men who attacked me and hung their bodies at Fedérico's mother's Estancia but that's 1,600 km. away from Buenos Aires, and our police covered it all. So you can travel 3,000 km., in less than one day and kidnap five persons, all at the same time."

"I'm impressed at my own abilities. Go on," he commented dryly.

"His sources are a snitch in Paris, somebody in Argentina and a Colombian drug lord, as if you'd find them on the yellow pages. This guy is obviously crazy, but why does he come after me? He could go after Ferdinand or Michael. They know more about you than I. He even had the nerve to tell me I should go to bed with you to make you speak about your plans for world domination, so I can save democracy and freedom from the bankers' tyranny."

"Is that all, Guntram?"

"I didn't take notes," I retorted obfuscated. He just glared at me. Now, I get your terror show. "He knows about my security entourage. Heindrik plus two other men I was not even aware of. Your house is a fortress and I'm kept there like a princess out of the fairy tales. Happy now?"

No, not really happy at all. He looked sombre; his eyes clouded as he mechanically stroke my hair.

"This man is becoming a nuisance. Approaching you twice is bad enough, but checking on your security is a real problem. I'll speak with Goran."

"Don't get him into trouble. He's just a very good *paparazzo*. I don't think he meant any harm to me. He's just a little crazy. Perhaps if you'd speak with him…"

"So what? If his brain has elaborated a delusion so complex, do you really think that one talk with me would change his mind?"

"The man said your bodyguards broke one of his ribs. Is that true?"

296

"If so, he should present charges against us. Of course none of the men did anything to him."

We remained silent for a long time.

"Why did you speak to me in Venice?"

"Pardon?"

"What made you speak to me in Venice?"

"You were the most adorable thing I had ever seen in my life. There, quietly reading your book, and unsuccessfully trying to frighten the doves. I was going for a meeting at the Correr Museum when I saw you sitting there, and I liked you. You know already, you remind me a lot of someone from my past. Physically at least, and for a minute it was like seeing a ghost. Perhaps, I wanted to make sure my mind wasn't playing tricks on me," he said, smiling softly at the memory.

"Is he dead?" I asked.

"For any purpose to me, yes. I cut all connections with him. Like when you leave a drug, you can't ever have it again."

"But I'm like him."

"No, you're not. I'm not sure you two look alike any longer. It was so long ago that maybe I idealised his beauty. Believe me. You're selfless even to a dangerous point. No self preservation instinct at all. I'm fortunate to have you," he said softly as I kissed him. "And mischievous. Nothing till your doctor sees you," he said going away from me as I groaned desperately.

"You could have told me I had three men tagging me."

"I told you your security would be increased. But they're not so useful if a simple journalist can beat them."

"A very persistent one."

"Indeed. Try to rest a little bit before we drive home. I have to speak with some more people."

"Don't blame Michael for this. Look at Lady Di. *Paparazzi* were always getting photos of her."

"Where is she now? A real shame; beautiful and intelligent woman. Goran should do his work better. Since Davos, Michael is no longer head of security. He has a lot in his mind to take care of everything."

* * *

I also got the heat from Goran. Yes, that same night. In the limousine back home. He's scary enough all by himself. He doesn't need to have Konrad backing him to be more impressive. But no, he had to give me the full drill in front of the boss, and then repeat it for Friederich's sake (and don't ask me why because the man takes care of the house, not me! It's not like that journalist is going to poison my food!).

So we were sitting in the car on the way back home-fortress from now onwards, Konrad on my side and Goran in front of us. No preambles.

"Guntram you will stay at home for the next week. No returning to the University. Since it's only the beginning of the second part of the semester, it should be no problem for you to study at the castle. Ask your friends there to inform you about the homework."

"This man makes a mess, and I have to stay at home?" I asked to deaf ears.

"Your mobile phone will be changed just in case and your laptop also. Make a list of the files you want to keep. The software people will look at it tomorrow. You will get also an e-mail account from the bank and can only use that one. Better security. Forget about all these things young people do; ICQ, messenger, chat and so on."

"What? I have nothing of value there, unless you want the Samuelson's handbook abstracts or my e-mails."

"They might be reading your things." I felt sick. "I don't need to emphasize to you that this man could be dangerous. In my opinion, religious and political fanatics are the worst kind. Till today, he regarded you like an asset he could gain for his crusade against the Duke, but now you're an enemy since you spilled everything to us. Twice. There's no mistake for him where your loyalties lie. You're a target now."

"What's next? Do I have to hold Heindrik's hand during the lectures?"

"Guntram!" That was Konrad. OK, it was nasty of me.

"I'm sorry Goran. But you're overdoing all this."

"No, I'm not. As for your daily schedule, once I have decided it's safe for you to return to school, it would be as follows: In the morning you drive with Heindrik and remain there only for the classes or lectures. When they're finished, you will come to the bank and stay there, studying with Monika or in the library on the second floor. If you don't like that option, you can drive home and stay here. You eat in the bank. You take nothing, and I mean nothing, in the school. No coffee, tea, cola or a sandwich."

"Good because I wouldn't know what to do if I want to use the rest room," I said ironically with a smug grin on my face.

"Only during the breaks when there are other students around. Never alone."

"It's an University. Not a prison's soap contest!"

"Guntram!" Konrad shouted me. Thanks, I know my own name. I looked at him, crossed that he was backing obviously this rubbish. What's next? Do I get a lunch box? I took a deep breath.

"This man got you twice. We don't know if he's a psycho or a professional killer testing our systems."

"Have you seen how fit he is? This guy could not even run after the bus!" I protested.

"It's my way, or goodbye to school for who knows how long," he barked. I looked for support at Konrad but no, he sided with the paranoiac Serb. "Your car will also be changed."

"No way I drive in one of those monsters!"

"There are smaller models, and armoured is fashionable in many countries," he retorted dryly. "You can still go to Ostermann's studio but Holgersen will remain with you in the room," I groaned and inwardly pitied Heindrik, now forced to take a painting class also. Yes, he can share the misery with me.

"Anything else?"

"Restrict your contacts in the University to the people you know from the previous term. Distrust anyone new who nicely comes to you. If you need to work with someone new, I want the full name before you do anything, even sitting together in the library."

"Konrad this is too much!" I exploded.

"Guntram, from now onward you're under Goran's responsibility in security matters. I'm afraid Michael and I have a soft spot for you and let you run free for too long. This is for the best till we have cleaned our own environment from leaks, and have found the traitors. I'm sorry that I have to place such a strict security net around you, but you must understand your heart condition doesn't allow you much stress. You heard the doctor today; clear symptoms of a stable angina. Dr. Van Horn will see you soon. "

If I see that wretched journalist again, I will be the one killing him!

Those two sadist pigs continued to speak in Russian considering the matter as settled. Guntram has to stay at home, obey, behave and not eat or go to the bathroom. Yes, like that. Unbelievable. I was furious and determined to tell my opinion to Konrad as soon as we would be alone and it wouldn't be pretty.

Goran was invited for dinner and, of course, they talked in Russian. For someone with a prince's education, Konrad you should know better than telling secrets in front of the others. The only thing I understood that night was when the Serb decided to tell everything to Friederich, and ask him a list of the workers and people visiting the residence for the last six months (postman included!). Surprisingly, the butler had it and only needed to print it.

After dinner, I was sent to bed (It's no more than 9 p.m.! I'm not a baby!) So here I'm writing, after making the bloody list and downloading into a memory stick most of my material.

Chapter 14

April 30th, 2003

I can't believe it. Goran was true to his word. More or less one week at home and I'll be released again... On May 5th, I can return to school. I'm so glad to come back. Just to shake Friederich off of my back! Forget about loafing with this Austrian teacher around. He would check that I started to study my lessons at nine (should be glad is one hour later than in school) and did it till 12:30. Nonstop. He even checked my German grammar (horrible, in his opinion, and I got several lessons to fix it). Fortunately, he left me in peace for Maths and Accounting. Eating with him and Heindrik (who by the way has a very good life nowadays. Does nothing and loafs around in the kitchen). Then back to study and don't delay it. At four, he would "release me" for tea, and then I was free to go out for a walk or paint. The only happy person here is Mopsi, because now she's with me the whole day. And Konrad had the nerve to tell me he's much "softer" now!

At least I could paint in peace till around eight when Konrad would come and this prevented me from being crazy. I have a deadline also, May 8^{th,} for delivering what I want (?) to send to the auction which will take place on May 23, Friday to be precise in a noble hotel with a private park. Exhibition or Show Art pending on how you want to call it from 22Nd till 25th when the happy buyers can take their purchases. Finally, I decided to give Ostermann three things; he should leave me alone minimum one year. The dogs, the children and the last one (out of ideas, really) which is a painting from one of his classes, five women sketching a nude female model we had at some point but she was so cold that I didn't feel to draw her and instead I started to make sketches of my colleagues. Finally the ones I decided to put in, with not so clear features, accepted to be there and I still wonder if I should not ask for their written approval.

According to Konrad if any of them complains—honestly none of them should do, because they look much better than in the flesh—she would sign her social death warrant. He was fascinated by the use of light in the painting and the chiaroscuro (Ostermann should clean his studio a little bit more at some point because this is the main reason behind it, but don't tell him because he's so happy with his evaluation). He said the model deceptively looked in the centre of the scene but the real living things are the women around her and even in shadows they get your attention and the movement is in they as they form a circle, symbol of perfection. The one on the left is the youngest one and she looks totally blushed at the naked girl (yeah, poor Marie, was a hard day for her), passing to all stages of age, with in the middle the mature ones, experienced, not impressed and secretly laughing at this or serious and finishing by the oldest one (Shit! I didn't realise. Claire will kill me when she sees it!), half turned around as if she's half out of this life (She's not that old, mind you).

"Did you paint all this in three months?" he asked, astonished.

"Well, almost five. Painting is not the problem. Deciding what to do is the mayor issue here. Once you get the hand with the technique, the rest is only work and fix what you screw up in the process."

"Can we reconsider it and I buy the one with the children? The one with the women is the best of them, but I like the other more."

"No. We had an agreement. If you push the prices high it wouldn't be fair. I'll paint you something else and you can keep all what I have done so far."

"I'll write you a check and you put the figure."

"No. Why do you want more trash at home? Konrad, you're not thinking clearly."

"I think a respected Art Critic also shares my opinion," he said royally. I sighed. I also like the children's paint, but come on, it's nothing out of the ordinary.

"All right. Since nobody would be so crazy as to pay for this, you can have the first bid and it's what the auctioneer says. However it's a total waste of money. By the way have you seen the catalogue's price?

"Gertrud's problem," he said as he escaped before I changed my mind. Damn! I should have told him no bribing the auctioneer or cutting the line! Now he thinks he has permission to do as he pleases. I hate his "selective hearing"!

Today I got the news that I can return to school! Not in the way I expected, but it's better than staying here.

This morning, Heindrik was looking like a child with a new toy. No, I'm not going to paint him. Back to business. He got the new car for me. Don't ask me from where it comes. At the entrance, there was a black Mercedes S Class 500 Armoured Sedan. A monster. Is this a smaller model? OK, it looks like another Mercedes, but this is too much.

"No way Heindrik. Couldn't you get one of these smaller cars that can be armoured?"

He looked at me in utter horror, and then his face showed a deep contempt for the foolish civilian he has to baby sit.

"Only Mercedes makes the full process by itself. The motor and the fuel tank are almost inaccessible; can't put a bomb on it. Everything is armoured, not a simple steel sheet and new windows. This car withstands a 44 Magnum repeatedly firing over the windshields, grenade shrapnel, gas, and can be driven with flat tires. I tried one of these babies with a Glock 9 in the Middle East, and believe me, it holds. It complies with B6-B7 safety standards; against terrorists. A true beauty."

"The word discretion does not exist in your vocabulary? This thing is an assault waiting to happen. It's too visible! Do you realise that with this thing the whole University will speak about? Not making new friends? Well, tell Goran that he can start to look at the whole Banking and Finance students' list, because all of them will want to be best pals with me. Why don't we put a small flag too?"

"The people who would like to attack you already know who you are and where you live. Let's just make it harder for them. Shall we?"

"Promise you will leave me at the door and disappear."

"I have to see you enter."

"Do you plan to park in double line?"

"No, the driver takes the car away. I have to ride at your side to protect you," I groaned at the news. Chauffeur, like the snots brats from here? He smugly smiled back. "Don't worry. I will not carry your books or open the door for you."

* * *

May 9th, 2003

Yesterday, all my paintings were sent to Meister Ostermann's studio for photographing and storing. He was very happy, and thinks he will get real money for them. Yeah, there's a naughty German who has the right for the first bid. If I know him, once he's rolling in the mud, it would be easier to get a wild boar out of there than him.

Driving to school is a nightmare. Monster car (I had nearly a third heart attack when I looked for the price in Google. It's like a good house! My old flat cost one third of it!), monster bodyguard (the nice Heindrik changes completely when working and looks quite dangerous), and chauffeur. He doesn't open the door, but he goes out first and makes a quick look around before knocking on the door so I can come out by myself. I'm not surprised activists throw eggs and paint bombs to these cars. I would do it without a second thought.

Corina, my friend from the University has been a great support. She didn't ask me anything and continued to sit with me at classes and offered her house for us to study, instead of the library. Goran has to think about it, but she and Peter are invited to use the bank's library with me. Peter speaks up to forty words now. He's not exactly shy like me; he's reserved and silent. He can be very impressive when he wants, as I found out when I failed to deliver my part for a joint paper. Just one killer look that would have made Goran feel jealous, and "tomorrow then," he's only nineteen, but some things you just carry in the blood. He accepted without problems to move to the bank for studying, while Corina was not happy at all, and preferred to avoid it. But Peter tagged along since the first day and seemed to be satisfied with the small but highly specialized library, full of reports and studies that there's no chance you can see in a public one.

We got the first inspection visit from Michael and it seemed we passed it, because he was going away relatively soon. On the next day, we got it from Konrad himself, rushing on his way to the airport.

"Good afternoon," he said and we both jumped to our feet like well oiled springs to greet him

"Konrad, may I introduce you Mr. Peter Kjærgaard?"

"Good afternoon, Griffin." Peter said and bowed his head in respect. I gaped not very elegantly.

"I trust your grandfather is in good health, Kjærgaard," he said kindly, not upset at all at the use of his "private rank (?)".

"Very well. Thank you, my Griffin. My father sends his regards to you."

"Thank you. Please extend mine to your family. Guntram, I'm going to New York. I will be back around the 16th."

It's not what I was expecting, but making a scene is totally out of question. I swear he will hear from me when he calls or is back. "Have a pleasant flight, Konrad," I replied softly, swallowing my own fury. One full week away and just like that I get notice!

"Thank you. Good bye," he answered and disappeared without a kiss (bad idea, I know, but I wanted it anyhow) or a hug (worse idea). Time to speak with the Danish who was again going through the pages of a handbook.

"How did you know you can call him like that?"

"My family has a small investment bank in Denmark. Medium size. Everybody around here knows Lintorff and his position. How else do you want me to call him and show our respect? He owns twenty-four percent of our shares after he saved us from bankruptcy in the big crash of 1996," he told me as if it were the most normal thing in the world.

"You never said anything about knowing him!" Well, I wasn't also saying out loud that I was living with him.

"You never asked. He lent money to my grandfather to buy a small bank in Gibraltar, and off shore business saved us. He was the only one in the whole community who wasn't cutting us into pieces for a better price. That, and the fact that he wasn't attacking us, stopped all the pressure against my family. My grandfather still controls the company. He was decent to us but we are nothing compared to him or will never be at his level," he explained with his eyes downcast as if he were ashamed of the bad business decisions from his elders. "Don't think I'm going to do you work," he warned me and I laughed.

"I wouldn't let you. You are worse than I for writing in German! We need Corina."

"Absolutely, and her ginger cookies too," he chuckled for the first time in more than half a year I know him. "Enough of distractions. We have to finish this."

* * *

May 24th, 2003

Yesterday was the exhibition. I still don't understand why Konrad is so furious. It's not like it was my fault. I did everything as I was supposed to do! He doesn't speak to me any longer!

On the 22nd from noon onward, the exhibition was opened to the public in the grand salon near the hotel's park. There were around eighty paintings from Ostermann's thirty students. Some presented one thing, others four, the limit being five pieces. To my utter relief, my things were placed on a corner almost at the exit to the park, away from the centre. Good.

I nearly bumped into Tita, Konrad's friend and Claire who were already in the salon chatting in front of my things, along with other four women I did not know. Not willing to intrude, I tried to sneak toward the entrance, but Tita saw me and happily shouted my name. I was caught, and like a beaten dog advanced toward them, hoping that Claire had not thought like Konrad that she was "the symbol of an accomplished life".

"Hello Tita. How are you? Hello Claire, I was going to see your work just now," I said sheepishly.

"I'm so impressed by this, Guntram," she replied softly, but seriously. Oh, oh. She's pissed off. I smiled feebly at her.

"I'm in a mess now dear," Tita sighed. "I wanted to buy this one, but Claire also wants it and she's a very good friend. I should go for the dogs, it seems. For the children there's so much competition. They are so lively."

"Do you like it Claire?" I asked her shyly.

"It's wonderful. I have many portraits of me looking like a Barbie doll or in a technicolor version but this is the first time I can see myself in. My husband is in love with it, and the others also want to have it."

"It's going to be knives and pistols at dawn dear," Tita laughed.

"More like bags and heels," Claire chuckled. "I'm not letting this Van Breda woman win on this."

"I'm so glad you like it. Do the others also?"

"Like? They love it! Even Ostermann says "it's good"!"

No chance I could escape from them any longer. They wanted tea and I was introduced to more women I can't remember. It seems it's not only the class but most of the high society from Zurich attending to the event. By sunset, I had a monster headache and only wanted to crawl under the table. I was very happy to see Heindrik standing at the door frame, giving me the perfect excuse to run away. I said good bye, after all tomorrow's school and had to suffer Heindrik's bantering all the way home. Yes, he calls me "party boy" now.

Yesterday after school, I went with Peter to study at the bank's library (where else?) and by five he went away as I was supposed to get dressed for the auction. Yes, it's penguin style! I went upstairs to be sent by Monika to change at Konrad's office. It was strangely unsettling for me to enter into his big office, completely alone as he comes back tonight from London for the event. I don't know, this place has bad karma if he's not here. It's like those places where you'd never sleep in. I dressed it as fast as possible and ran to Monika's office where she was still working.

"You look well. Come here, the hair is not properly done," she said after the inspection. "Now all settled."

"Can I stay with you?"

"No, go to Michael's office. He's ready by now. I have to change myself."

"You could not escape?"

"It's work I'm afraid. I have to distract Gertrud if she sees Ferdinand, and Michael has to hide Ferdinand's new girlfriend from her. If we fail, and both start to fight, you have to contain the Duke," she told me seriously.

"Could we not switch tasks?"

"No dear, you lost the voting." She dedicated me one of her flashing smiles.

"When did I vote?"

"This morning. Now go out. I don't want to be late and hear Michael complaining that he was delayed because of a woman."

We arrived at 7:30 and the room was already crowded. After greeting some of the people, mostly colleagues from the class and husbands, I escaped to the garden. It's not exactly "leaving the premises"; it's a private one and belongs to the hotel. I needed some peace and the freshness of the night was wonderful to sooth my nerves. To make it perfect I should have taken (stolen) a glass of champagne. Who knows, maybe I still have a chance when Konrad is busy with the auction, but I haven't seen him around so far.

The scent of a Russian cigarette spoiled my Nirvana moment; impossible to mistake them. I know the smell. Alexei used to have one now and then at night. Very strong, almost makes you puke unless you're used to it. I stood up and decided to go back.

I entered again and went again to see my things. Call me a romantic, but I wanted to say goodbye to them. Fortunately, nobody was there as the auction was about to start and I stood in front of then for a final look.

"These pictures are not worth of being here." A deep voice made me jump. I quickly looked to see a medium size man (well taller than me, but not a full head like Konrad), black hair with the darkest eyes I've seen. Mesmerizing, yes, that would be the word, well built and with hard features. Mid-forties I would say. He smirked at me in a derogatory way. "A blaze in this room would do a favour to mankind." Yes, strange accent, similar to Alexei's.

"Most of the people worked very hard. It's for charity, amateur painting," I replied upset.

"So I've heard. I wonder why a good artist like the one who made those three (mine!) would waste his time here. If he were not so eccentric, and refused any contact with the rest of the world, he would have saved me the annoyance of watching all this rubbish."

Sorry? Brain start to work because perhaps he's who I think he's? The Russian from London? I kept silent.

"A great classical technique hidden behind a deceitful simplicity. A common subject. Three dogs; the one in the centre destroying mind absently a blue elephant (Yeah, Mopsi the Destructor). Obviously from a good breed, the one on the left, small, declassed, dying to participate, secretly rabid because it's not invited and the one on the right, a big one, laying and dozing, but at the same time watching those two don't leave their assigned places. You can almost perceive the chest rising and falling. An interesting representation of our society."

"I only see three dogs playing."

"No need to be modest Guntram," he simply stated. I was petrified. He smiled in a predatory way making me feel very uncomfortable. "I have followed your work since 2000. It was quite shocking to find out finally that you're so young. How old are you?"

"Twenty-years-old," I mumbled. I want to die. He is *the* Russian. "Mr. Oblomov?" I asked extending my hand and praying he would take it and not be too upset because I'm a brat and not a reputed artist.

"Oblomov is one of my underlings. My name is Constantin Ivanovich Repin." He introduced himself taking my hand for a moment longer than necessary as he looked deeply into my eyes. I looked down, ashamed and embarrassed. "Your hands are small and delicate—an artist's."

"I must return with the others, sir. The auctioneer has just started." Was my lame excuse to disappear.

"There's no need. Your paintings are already sold under chapter 7. I bought them yesterday, and I would like to know the artist better. Come and dine with me."

"I'm afraid I can't, sir. I'm here with friends." No chance I'm leaving the premises with this man! He gives me the creeps like Konrad never did, not even during our worse fights.

"Lintorff is very protective of you. I'd also be if you were mine. The artist is far more beautiful than the pieces."

I gaped at the man, trying to discern his words. No, there was no hidden double meaning; time to run to Papa Goran or Michael. "Good night, sir. It's been… interesting to meet you," I chose the words carefully.

"Obedience and loyalty. Good traits also. We'll see each other again."

"Guntram! Come here!" Someone shouted me.

There was Ferdinand, standing like a god, looking at the Russian with a mixture of cold hatred and contempt. Shit, he heard us or he imagines something, and will run to tell Konrad. I'm so dead. I obeyed not looking at the man and avoiding flinching when I felt Ferdinand's big hand placed over my shoulders.

"Compliment Lintorff on his taste, von Kleist. He's worth every cent he paid in Venice," I could heard him saying at the distance as Ferdinand increased his pace towards the exit.

Ferdinand didn't answer him as he dragged me out of the hotel. "Should I not wait for Konrad?"

"No, you go home with Goran. Someone bought your things and everybody is upset. My former wife is more stupid than I thought."

"How could it be? It's an auction."

"Chapter 7 of the terms. If you make an offer fifty times the opening bid, you can get the things without going through the auction It was a clause put for the families who wanted to yield an object, but didn't want to lose it. The thing was exposed and the owner could make the offer before the auction and it was automatically accepted. Somebody paid 150,000 Swiss francs for your things."

"What? This guy Repin paid 150,000 for my crap? He's the Russian who buys my stuff. Oblomov is his secretary. No, underling he said," I blurted.

"Exactly. Now in the car and tell Goran whatever he has told you," he ordered me sternly. "Konrad will be furious when he arrives from London. To be publicly beaten on our own territory."

"Who's Repin?" I shouted before he closed the door of the car.

"Morozov's boss."

* * *

Goran was not cooperative at all. He only wanted to hear what the Russian had told me and nothing else. He didn't answer a single question from me. "Ask the Duke" was his motto.

When we arrived home, I was sent to bed. What? No dinner? I opened my mouth to complain but Goran's expression was enough to convince me of the benefits of fasting.

"I'll see my dog at the kitchen and then I'll go to bed," I said quickly.

"Do it."

In the kitchen, Mopsi was happily eating her dinner. Lucky girl! I bent down to pet her and in a minute Friederich was there.

"Did you have dinner?"

"Not really. Ferdinand put me out before I could grab anything."

"I'll tell the sous-chef to prepare something for you. Go to your room and stay there. The men have to discuss a lot. Have you taken your pills?"

What am I? A chicken? "No, I haven't," I answered dryly.

"Do it. The Duke will arrive at ten and have dinner with his people. Don't wait for him. You can take Mopsi with you. I'll get her out at eleven." Not only sent to bed, but I have now to stay nicely in the room. Who's brave enough as to defy Friederich with the brooding face he has at the moment?

Defeated, I went upstairs with Mopsi. I heard Konrad arriving and the voices of Michael and Ferdinand with him and perhaps Alexei. I wanted to go downstairs, but they quickly took their party to the library.

* * *

May 25th, 2003

Saturday morning Friederich was shaking me awaken. I sat on the bed, not totally up with my eyes half closed and I noticed two things. One; it was relatively late because of the sun's position over the window and; Two, Konrad's side was empty and unused. Had he slept somewhere else? Fuck! The mess with the Russian is not my fault! He couldn't be upset for it. I followed the instructions to the last word!

"Come on Guntram. You have to get up and be ready for breakfast. The others will be there soon," Friederich said as he laid out an informal outfit for the morning. Strange, no tie or jacket. Why were his eyes red?

I went to dinning room, the big one, where Goran and Alexei stood, also informally dressed. The Russian gave me a hug and started to ask how I was doing in school while the Serb looked more upset than normal. A few minutes later, Ferdinand, Michael and finally Konrad appeared and took their places at the table. If Ferdinand sits at his right side, it's business. Michael to the left. Yeah, business, no pleasure.

Two butlers served the coffee and disappeared. The ambiance was oppressive.

"Guntram, I want to hear your version before I make a decision." Konrad stated seriously with his blank stare, chilling my bones like never before. I threw a killing look at Ferdinand. Most probably he was already telling stories!

"This man, Retin is Oblomov, the one who bought all my paintings since 2000, the one who lives in London and Luciana works for. He also bought the oil paintings from yesterday," I slowly said. "No, Oblomov is an underling of him and Luciana works for him. That is what he said." I gulped.

"Is that all?" Dangerous edge in his voice. Lying is not a good idea but not telling the part of his courtship is worse, considering Ferdinand must have already spilled the whole story.

I took a deep breath and spilled the rest. "He said, and I quote, the artist is far more beautiful than the pieces and I would also be very protective of you if you were mine," I whispered, feeling sick to no end and losing all colours. Big heavy silence descended upon the table.

"Since when do you know him? Look me in the eyes, Guntram."

"Yesterday! I've never seen him in my life before. He buys my things through Luciana. You were there when Dollenberg told you he first tried to contact me in mid-2000, but Federico never gave me the messages he left for me."

"I'm trying to see how involved the Dollenbergs are in this elaborate charade," Konrad answered me, sternly.

"But you went to buy their house in Argentina! I didn't think they would recognize me! It was a coincidence! I'm sorry this Rubin ruined the auction, but I have nothing to do with his crazy buying. My work is not valued that much!"

"I visited the house at Landau's suggestion," Konrad replied surly, a deep frown marring his forehead.

"Sire, may I speak?" Alexei said from the other side of the table.

"Proceed."

"The name is Constantin Ivanovich Repin, Guntram. He's one of the biggest mysteries for the Russian intelligence nowadays. They assume he's the supreme leader of the Russian Mafia and responsible for most of the weapons trade since the fall of the Soviet Union. This man, Morozov, who has been so keen on making trouble for us, is just an underling. Oblomov truly exists, but he's only one of his fronts, and this is the man the Dollenberg woman knows. According to our sources, he's ruthless, a murderer and likes art a lot. Under different names, he has being buying a lot in London, Paris and New York, and perhaps he really likes your work since it's so classical. There's one registered trip of him to Argentina in 2000 and another in 2001 when he acquired several leisure properties. So I believe, she's telling us the truth about how he saw Guntram."

"He never saw me until yesterday!" I protested.

"He's like a chess player and his games can last for weeks. Russian mobsters are powerful and sophisticated to no end. They had to deal with the soviet state and Stalin, but they survived it and now they're more powerful than ever, with worldwide interests. I think he saw your piece in Buenos Aires, became interested in you and then decided to have you."

"Alexei, he never saw me till yesterday and Luciana never told him who I was! She told me he was convinced I was a grumpy old man painting!"

"If he has your name, he has the rest of your life, Guntram." Ferdinand said. "Intelligence on a simple, anonymous person like you is very cheap and easy to obtain. Maybe he was intrigued you were so young and upset that you never contacted him, no matter the money he had obviously offered to the Dollenbergs."

"That would explain the whole mess in Venice, Sire. It was always too much for my taste, even if Albanians were involved," Goran smirked. "This was revenge against that stupid Argentinian boy and a way to drag Guntram into his world, to make him disappear."

"I don't follow you Goran," I said quietly. This was too much. Another billionaire after me? Goran looked at Konrad as if he were asking for permission to speak and the other lightly nodded.

"I was in charge of the negotiations with the Albanians, as you know."

"Yes, you paid the compensation fee for their loses with the drugs."

"Not exactly. They had a contract from some Russians to kidnap you. They assumed it was a revenge for the lost material, so to speak. The idea was that once the police had detained this Argentinean boy, they would go after you and give you to the Russians and get a nice fee. Some very rich people like to have personal slaves for sex. I saw it a lot during the war; capturing young attractive girls or boys on the enemy's side and exchanging them for weapons. Most of them finish inside prostitution rings and if they die, it's not important. Others will come. But in the case of a high quality, top standard, with an education slave, like you, the organization needs to make the person disappear; an accident, troubles with police or drugs. Something that would discourage people to look for you."

"I noticed you already had a tag when I returned your backpack," Michael said.

"Let me finish. When you were questioned by the police, the news of two people smuggling five kilos of cocaine in Venice spread like fire. The Albanians told me the two French girls worked for the Russians, and they had stolen the drugs from them. The plan was that the police would release you, and then they will take you and give you to the Russians. Everybody would assume the Russians had "settled the score" with your death, and the lagoon is too wide to look for a tourist's body. When you said that you were with the Duke, the policeman in charge, Rossi, called us, against his superiors' wishes. He risked a lot and I'm convinced he saved your life by winning time for us to act, and not letting you out on the streets."

"This is why he made me do the sketches of the girls despite he already had the bodies," I whispered.

"Exactly. The lawyer did his part and I spoke with the Albanians offering a better contract. After all they don't want troubles with us in our own territory. Russians were only passing by. I always thought till now, that it was a personal revenge from the dealers for the lost drugs. But if this was a set up, in order to punish the Argentinean boy for not giving you to Repin when he wanted, it makes much more sense."

"Why would Rossi protect me?"

"He works for us. The Lintorff family is well known in Venice. After all, they're patrons of the main Museums," Michael explained.

"Repin is attacking me because he thinks I stole you from him. He had everything organised since you came to Europe. Punishing the brat who refused to cooperate, and certainly was looking like your lover, and getting you all for himself in one single move. He's good I have to admit," Konrad said. "Morozov's little war was only a test of my abilities. Repin and I never had trouble before. He does his things in his side and doesn't interfere with mine."

"Perhaps he wants to expand himself. If he knew all the time who I was, wouldn't it have been easier to approach me and try his luck?"

"Maybe he lacks confidence in his seducing skills," Konrad smirked, making the others laugh like hyenas. "No, he will not break a fragile peace with me. After all, he got rid of Morozov last week for attacking me without permission. If it comes to war, it will be a Pyrrhic victory for either of us," he mused.

"Konrad, with all due respect, it's very far fetched that a man who saw one drawing from me, maybe a picture, would spend so much money, time and effort just to get me. There are thousands of people in the world who are better than I. If he was so interested in me, he had a full year or more to act in Buenos Aires. I had no family or close friends."

"I also thought that," Alexei interfered. "But the trip from Buenos Aires to Moscow is thirty hours if they could get you in a direct flight, which is impossible. If you drug a person for so long you can cause severe brain damage, and the artist he likes so much could be lost; by ship is far more complicated."

I felt very dizzy and had to get a grip on the table. "I owe you an apology Konrad because I've always had my doubts that you had nothing to do with Fedérico's arrest. After all, you organised the move with the bonds."

"Only because that woman wanted to give you to the Albanians. I would have never risked you in a drugs case. These schemes only end badly," he whispered.

"What are the odds that this man and you were competing for me at the same time?" I asked in general.

"Not many. But an elephant can dance on top of a needle if you believe in Math," Michael replied softly. "That he has shown his interest in you, makes the game easier for us. Now we have the reason behind the dismissal of Morozov and his last attack."

"If we believe that his assassination was done in our favour and to punish his disobedience as Repin declared, and not just because Morozov wanted our help to depose Repin," Ferdinand retorted dryly.

"No, it's clear for me. Repin was furious because the Duke didn't give him the *Dachs* when he wanted, back in London. That woman should have handed Guntram over, even if she was unaware of her role in the whole play. I'm sure he encouraged Morozov to come to us so we would fall into a trap and he could start a real war against us. When Morozov started to lose so much money, contracts and men power, Repin backed off because he can't go against us if we retaliate with full force. Morozov's death was a sort of peace offering to calm us down and to restore relationships, Ferdinand," Michael said with a pensive air.

"He wants to force me to trade with him, but I will not give up my consort ever. With Morozov's killing, he shows the sheep we have for associates that he can be more powerful and determined than I. He expects that my peers will force me to deal with him or depose me. With yesterday's charade, he probes us that he can enter into our world, beating us with our own rules. After publicly buying Guntram's paintings, he has indicated to the associates what he wants from me."

"Konrad, Guntram is one of us and I'll give my life for his," Ferdinand stated.

"As all of us," Goran said with Alexei nodding immediately his agreement. Michael was less than happy, but he huffed his acceptance. "Never let the friendly fox get into your hen house."

Chapter 15

I'm back in the University and the security around me is tighter than ever. It's not just Heindrik, but his friends, Lars Amundsen (Swedish too, Army); Peter Jansen (Dutch, Army) and Jan Uwe Hartick (German, Army) around me, all the time. I can go to classes and then straight to the bank. My friend Peter can come sometimes, but I think this small army also grates his nerves. I don't blame him at all. Corina deserted us and I can understand her. Who wants to hang around with a guy that will not even take a sip of cola from the vending machine or stay for no more than two minutes speaking with you in the open?

Yes, I admit. I'm scared of this Repin man more than I am of death. Every night when I go to bed, my mind doesn't stop playing different scenarios of how my life could have turned out if it hadn't been for Konrad. After our encounter in the auction, I found inside my locker a package with a red ribbon, and I thought it was something from Konrad. I opened it and it was a book from Sargent's pictures of Venice with a letter attached to it.

"Words are not enough to express the immense joy your artwork gives me. It can only come from a beautiful soul like yours. No photos or films can do justice to your charm. I count the days until you belong to me."

"Heindrik, can you pick me up at the entrance? ... No. Now." Was all I could say over the phone as I threw the package and letter into my laptop's portfolio. Ten minutes later, he was at the entrance with the car. I almost ran inside.

"Better be good because if the Duke finds out you were skipping classes, we both are dead."

"Shut up and get me home or to the bank. Wherever," I said seriously. I think he was impressed by my tone and ordered the driver to go to the bank.

"Something wrong Guntram?" He asked concerned. I just handed him the package and he swore in Swedish after reading the note. "You have to speak with Goran." I nodded.

We went directly to the Serb's office in the third floor. It was discreet but elegant. He just looked at the paper.

"Where did you find it?"

"In my locker a few minutes ago. I don't use it much. The lock was not broken and I thought it was from the Duke. I have an extra copy of the key at home."

"I see. Don't worry. It's immaterial. I'll speak with his Excellency."

"I will not fight with you if you don't want me back in school," I whispered. Yes, I'm afraid of this Russian. He's much crazier than I thought and hiding behind a big nasty German like Konrad does not stop him.

"I don't think that would be necessary. You can go to our library downstairs for studying. I'll fetch you for lunch. Ask one of the secretaries to give you a tea or something. You look very pale."

So I remained in the library until 1:00 when he picked me up and left me at Konrad's office. He came in a few minutes after, alone and I almost threw myself into his arms. He held me for some time, caressing my back with soothing movements as I increased my hold on his waist.

"Come now, *Maus*," he said softly disentangling himself from me. "There's no need to be so nervous. It's a locker in a public place. Even a child can open it and leave a note."

"He implies he has photos and films of me! He's obsessed with me!"

"Indeed, but he doesn't mean any harm to you. If he would be upset with you because you are with me, he would have attacked you much earlier."

"No, he only wants to fuck me in the night and put me to paint during the day," I said now crossed with Konrad and his passivity.

"Guntram what do you want me to do? Do you want to drop school and live the rest of your life in fear of him? Anybody can go for this locker. Will you stop painting because he likes your drawings?"

"What if he attacks you instead of me?"

"He will not. If he didn't do it after Venice when I got you, and that was certainly his most enraged moment, he will not do it now. He has too much to lose. He's only adding pressure on you. Showing he likes you for your talent and not for your looks and all that romantic crap."

"How can you be so calm?"

"I'm not. I want to rip the bastard's throat for insinuating himself to you, but I have to keep my head cool in order to beat him. He's not the usual mobster resorting to violence to achieve his goals. He's a master chess player. Come now, let's have lunch here together and then you can go to Meister Ostermann's studio to work a little till six."

"I can't. Have to study. Finals this week," I replied mechanically. The least I want is to come near a brush! Look the shit they put me in!

He sighed and went to sit behind his desk.

* * *

June 19th, 2003

I can't believe it. I'm flying to Rome with Konrad. He's sitting in front of me under his load of papers and if we are lucky with the traffic, maybe we could get dinner at the hotel's restaurant.

Today, after going to school briefly in the afternoon to pick up the latest results (Everything 5 and 6 which is sort of a miracle), much better than the previous term, I went to the bank as usual to find myself trapped at Konrad's office when I wanted to go to the library.

"No, you can stay in the office with me. You don't have to study any longer. I have your grades here. Well done. Why don't you sit in the sofa by the window and draw a little bit? I found your pencil box hidden in a desk drawer," he said sweetly. No, I don't want to draw at all. In fact I haven't taken a pencil for a month or gone to Meister Ostermann's studio since that night.

"I have a book with me. I prefer to read," I said quickly fearing where he was leading me.

"About?" He asked nonchalantly, still pretending to be busy with his papers.

"Cash Flow Theory."

"Really? Impressive choice for a student who has just passed his tests, and is on holidays."

"Want to broaden the subject," Was my more than pathetic lie.

"I think I have something about Degas somewhere here—a catalogue."

"No thank you. I prefer my one," I said, inwardly praying he would drop the subject.

"Why are you not painting any longer? Nobody has seen you drawing you or doing anything remotely linked to art in over a month," he realised. Don't ask me how but he knows.

"I was busy studying."

"You have been evading Ostermann for the past month, and Friederich says you haven't opened an oil tube for a long time."

"Turpentine gives me headaches." That was bad, I know, but my brain is again on strike. It works badly under pressure.

"Strange you have developed such a sudden allergy. Why don't you try with watercolours or the pencils you like so much?"

"I was studying hard," I defended myself. "Besides you can't paint every day. Some inspiration is needed," I blurted out.

"Says the man who used to decorate my morning newspapers?"

"Honestly, I thought you were through with them!"

"Guntram not painting any longer will not make Repin go away." How do you know? Maybe he gets bored and finds somebody else to torture. "It will only hurt you, *Maus*."

"I'm on holidays of painting. Need some time to find inspiration." Yes, that's the right answer. Blame it on the artistic character.

"Your way of facing this problem it's very childish. What is going to be next? Are you planning to break your fingers with a door?"

"All right, you win. I'm not painting because it sunk me into this rubbish!" I shouted.

"Kitten, this will not help at all. Tell me, don't you miss drawing?"

"Every day, but I'm afraid of him. When I start, the images of him and the dead girls come to my mind. I can't shake them off. He's so determined to have his way with me. I lay every night imaging how my life would have turned if he would have got me first. I would be dead by now."

"You'll die on the inside if you stop painting. It makes no sense. Nothing will change if you do it. He knows already you're an artist. We both need a vacation and some time together. There is a huge Caravaggio's exhibition in Rome, at the Quirinale. We fly tonight and stay there until Sunday night. Tomorrow you can go to the Vatican Museums with Alexei while I meet some customers in Rome. On Saturday, we go to see Caravaggio and around the city. The hotel is in the centre, near the Spanish Steps. Can walk everywhere. If you don't start to paint again in Rome, I promise I'll get you a position in Accounting here."

"I have nothing with me."

"Friederich packed your things along with paper and your pencils."

* * *

June 23rd, 2003

I didn't see much of Rome when we arrived on Thursday night. Plane, car, hotel and very fast. I only got a glimpse of the Coliseum and the Forum and Trajan's Market lightened in the night. I was surprised that there were no so many cars and it wasn't that late; only 10 p.m.

This time it was the St. Regis the hotel who made me feel like the poor cousin from the countryside. I had to repress the urge to clean the shoes before entering the grand foyer with him and the two bodyguards I did not know. Immediately we went to the Suite Royal. Yes, Royal, where Alexei was waiting for us with another bodyguard and a secretary.

"Everything clean?"

"Yes, my Duke," Alexei answered very formally.

"I will see you all tomorrow at eight o'clock."

They all disappeared with the exception of the butler who started to unpack our luggage in the bedroom and the waiter in the private dinning room busy setting the table.

"You don't mind if we eat here tonight? I'm tired to go out, *Maus*."

"No, no. It's perfect," I tried to hide my disappointment; yes I wanted to go out, but tomorrow is fine also.

"Did you notice there's a piano in the living room? No wonder the Romans invented the word *luxus*."

"Don't complain so much because your former and very populist president was here too. The rooms were designed by the Aga Khan and this is why it's so flamboyant. I'd have preferred something smaller, but tomorrow I have meetings the whole day, it's more comfortable this one with dinning room, studio, living room and private entrance."

"Which President was here? I have two nationalities plus one more adopted," I laughed.

"Perón from Argentina. I met him briefly when my father was still alive. Very cunning fox. My father respected him a lot, and after two weeks in Argentina I also do it. How he could keep that party running is a mystery. He had the most extreme old guard from the right alongside with young pro Cuba guerilla boys. "

"You see, Peronist party is not a political party; it's a movement. "We Peronists are incorrigible," Perón used to say."

"Incorrigible in the sense of unruly, unalterable or delinquent?"

"You choose one," I laughed.

"Only one?" He joked. All right, his opinion of Argentineans has not improved so far.

"Do you have meetings tomorrow?"

"Let's have dinner. I want to go to bed," he curtly answered. OK, not speaking about business. We went to the dinning room and it was almost as big as his "small one". There was a table for ten services but set for two. "I've already ordered some meat for tonight," he informed me. The waiter served the dinner, opened the wine and vanished into the kitchen. Well, at least is not hospital food like the one I have to deal with all the time.

"I was thinking that tomorrow you can go with Alexei to the Vatican Museums and see St. Peter's in the afternoon. Then you can go around, and come back, let's say, at eight?"

"Am I kicked out for so long? Where's Holgersen?"

"At eight in the morning, *Maus*. I'll start my meetings at nine. Albert will come and the Museum opens at 8:30 and the rooms close at one. If the weather is fine you can walk around with Alexei. He enjoys more a cultural visit than Holgersen. In fact, he threatened with resigning if I forced him to make the Vatican Tour."

"I thought you wanted to see the city also," I sighed, a little bit disappointed.

"I know the city well. I lived here for a whole month in the summer when I was seventeen with Albert and Ferdinand, in a small flat in Trastevere. I was going to the History courses while they were fooling around. The apartment was a decadent pigsty. Girls every night because it was the 70s. I think in that month I slept on the street more than nine times. Never again in my life I'd share something with Albert. Ferdinand was no better than him. I'm not surprised the Italians consider Germans as a bunch of noisy potatoes eaters pigs, because those two made a fine example.

"From Albert I could imagine but from Ferdinand? Impossible."

"He was the worst of us. I will not tell the story of the two Swedish or Danish dolls he was alternating during that month. As it was too much hassle for him, he decided to put them together. I was not exactly a saint because I also had a few adventures, but at least I was having them out of the communal area, and never public sex to the point of the neighbours calling the police because of the disturbance."

"Not Ferdinand!" I laughed in total disbelief.

"I had to bail him out. My uncle signed the papers. I think it was the last time he ever made rubbish because later he entered into the Army, married Gertrud, had Karl Otto at a young age and it was over."

"He was complaining to me all the time about your bed jumping for the last years and he was worse than you! He's so serious and stern." I laughed really hard.

"At twenty, I still believed in finding a true love. When I was twenty-two or twenty-three, I fell in love like a total idiot with a man much older, working in one of our subsidiaries. Perhaps my father's death with all the added pressure of running two small banks and some minor companies, lacking support from the others, made me see things that were never there. I was not into men before, and after him I only had a few encounters with them, I preferred women mostly. Our relationship, a secret only Ferdinand, Albert and Friederich knew, lasted seven years. Now I realise it was very bad. I should have ended it much earlier but when you're in love you're blind and justify the unjustifiable."

"Why was it so bad?" I asked. "Tell me if you want."

"He was an accountant, a minor one, clever but not to the point of being brilliant—weak character. Most of his life he was always influenced by his father and brothers and did whatever they told him to. I think he started to date with me because his family saw it as an opportunity to socially climb. He was married to a beautiful and lovely woman and I felt very bad for her but love is selfish to no end."

"If you knew he was married, why did Friederich tell me he had betrayed you?"

"It was not betrayal in a romantic sense, more in an economical one. Over the years, I named his older brother head of the branch in Paris and the other one was in charge of the legal office. His father had a small company and got several credits from me. Nothing important. Despite I was Griffin for more than seven years, and had multiplied several times our combined capital, mostly by investing in technological development, newly born informatics, emerging countries debt, privatizations and all the derivatives you can imagine, many of the Order's members, would still not trust me because banking changed a lot in less than five years and they were still in the 60's. My only support was my uncle and Löwenstein. I added some spice to the boring banking business. Before the 80's it was very traditional and made almost no profits. If you think I work too much now, you should have seen me when I was thirty; fifteen hours a day."

"I named the brothers advisers, like Ferdinand and Michael, but they started to campaign behind my back to get me out. The oldest wanted my position because Albert was also very feeble in his job. Roger's task, that was his name, was to entertain me while those vipers started to stir the other associates with lies about my suitability for the position. I had returns one year for seventy percent and I was "unsuitable"!

"Fortunately, I named also Ferdinand as advisor but not associate because he was still too young and I didn't want to add more fuel to the fire. He never trusted those two and started to investigate them. First I didn't believe him but suddenly we started to lose contracts, make stupid accounting mistakes, foolish trading and in less than six months we took huge losses and lost markets. All contracts in many privatizations were falling for no reason and investors turned their backs on us. 1986 was a horrible year; from making a plus of sixty-four percent in 1985, I was only making a lousy three percent that year. That alone would have left me jobless."

"I was an idiot and believed that I was under a very bad luck strike, but Ferdinand started to investigate in secret with Löwenstein's support. Around the spring of 88, Ferdinand had his accusation ready... to present to the courts. Both brothers had been boycotting all my projects with other member's help; embezzlement, some criminal activities like money laundering and tax fraud to top it. But there was nothing that could link Roger to his brothers' deeds and this was killing me. Had he truly betrayed me like his brothers? Was he just a façade or was he the cleverest of them all? I was shocked and for two weeks I didn't react. Ferdinand literally kicked me into reaction. I confronted the brothers by threatening to go to the courts unless they resigned. Yes, I was weak, but I couldn't go against Roger. They threatened with making public my relationship with him."

"Before he disappeared from my life, Roger left me a letter in which he explained he never loved me; that it all was a scheme devised by his father and brothers. He couldn't stand the humiliation of being publicly accused of homosexuality since he was a married man with a child. I was devastated, but Ferdinand and Löwenstein took the matter in their hands and achieved what I couldn't do."

"I spent the rest of the year trying to fix the many holes we had, cleaning my own bank, assets and laying off associates. When I turned thirty-one, everything was again under control and making profit again, but I was dead on the inside. The only thing that kept me alive was to make more money and accumulate power. I took me two years to have intercourse with another human being and she was almost like a prostitute. Sex became only a way to release tensions, and from there comes the legend that I had so many bed partners. If you have so much money like I, people come to you and using them doesn't pose a problem."

"I never imagined it was so bad. You were so tender the first weeks with me and now," I whispered.

"You gave me my life back and asked nothing in return," he said kissing my hand.

"You were the first person who looked at me with love in his eyes, not even my father did it. I think he was nice and liked me but we never had a true connection," was my explanation as I returned the kiss, this time on his lips. When we split he cupped my face into his hands and intoned.

"Do you really think I would renounce you to another man or woman? Never. For more than twenty years I lived in Hell. Perhaps before also but I was too stubborn to realise."

Chapter 16

"*Auf mit dir*! It's seven!" The cheerful voice of Konrad, (who else?) woke me up. I groaned trying to bury myself deeper under the covers. No chance. He just stole my pillow and pulled the covers away.

"It's so early! I'm on holidays!" I whined. "You can't expect that after one night of hot sex I can walk straight and be out of bed at seven!"

"If you can complain so much, you're up. Hurry and you might get breakfast."

"Black and double," I muttered as I sat on the bed, still blinking. He was already dressed. I can't understand it. Last night he wanted two rounds with me; one almost immediately after dinner and the other at 3 a.m. Is this man related to the Batteries' Bunny or does he take these energizer drinks instead of water? The birds are still sleeping!

"Keep dreaming Guntram," he smirked.

"No chance since you already woke me up," I rebutted not happy at all with his wake up call. All right, I can kiss the bed goodbye. He laughed and went into the living room with his laptop. I washed and dressed myself informally because if I'm kicked out, then there's no need for suit and tie. I took a pullover also. I'm missing my backpack but I don't need it and honestly I haven't seen it in a long time. Probably it had succumbed in one of Friederich's pro elegant fashion raids.

Konrad was already sitting in the dinning room with his breakfast and computer, deeply engulfed into his e-mails. At his side was Albert, already dressed in a conservative suit like his cousin, eating scrambled eggs and bacon. I would give my life for something like that! Totally forbidden.

"Did you sleep well Guntram?" he asked solicitous. Strange.

"Very well, thank you," I replied sitting and suppressing a groan when the butler placed a cup of tea in front of me. I took a croissant but the man placed a bowl of cereal and another of fresh fruit aside. I dropped the full oozing butter croissant back on my dish and started with the flakes.

"I can't say the same. I had to be in one of the smaller suites. Horrible. Konrad, you could share a little more with your favourite cousin," he complained.

"Never again," he mumbled.

"Konrad told me about your housekeeping abilities, Albert," I snickered.

"Does he still complain about something that happened almost thirty years ago? Look cousin, that maid was hot and after being so nice to me, I couldn't ask her to do my laundry or the dishes. We were young."

"Perhaps, but an Eiffel Tower made of dirty dishes is simply disgusting. Guntram had his flat clean and the bed made."

"What was the point of making the bed if we were going to use it?"

Before Konrad could give him his opinion on the matter, Alexei entered the room, informally dressed and they both started to speak in Russian.

"I also hate when he does it," Albert whispered.

"Where did he learn Russian?"

"Private teacher since infancy along with English and French; useful for dealing with them. Italian he picked up during his holidays in Turin with me. When we were young, it was not so clear which side would win," he told me secretly. "Hurry up with your eating because at eight he will kick you out."

When Konrad and Alexei finished speaking, I guess the Russian got the update on my latest exploits and the "not to do" list for handling with such a dangerous criminal like myself. It's not like I'm going to spit in the Sistine Chapel or something!

"Guntram you can go now with Antonov," Konrad dismissed me using his most regal tone. Sometimes he can be a pig. I said goodbye to both Lintorffs and went out with Alexei.

"It's a fifty minutes walk to the Vatican. Can you make it or do you prefer the metro?"

"Wait, you're going give me another heart attack. Can I ride in the Metro?" I asked half seriously.

"Don't tell me you're a wimp like Heindrik."

"Does the boss know you're corrupting me by dragging me to a public transport?"

"I take care of you the way I see fit, and it is much easier to be inconspicuous in a public transport. Pity it's going to be full; rush hour."

"We walk then. "

"Good choice."

At about nine thirty, we were at the entrance and he nearly pushed me inside, eager to enter. Man, I want to see if you can pass the security control with the piece you must being carrying. Nothing, all clear. I was surprised because normally Konrad's bodyguards have weapons with them. Guess the jacket was because you were cold. While idiotic me was going straight to the long queue, Alexei went to speak with a guard, and the man disappeared only to return some five minutes later with an older person, over sixties and looking like a professor.

"Mr. Antonov? I'm Professor Baldesarri. Dr. Ostermann told me about your coming."

"Thank you very much for receiving us. This is Guntram de Lisle. He will be joining us."

"Then we should proceed. This way gentlemen. We will be going after the first wave of tourists."

At two, we were finally out of the Museums and Gardens (only looking a little bit around. I'm very tired), and my head was still spinning around from the Sistine Chapel and its vibrant colours. We walked alongside the big wall encircling the Vatican towards the street that leads to the entrance of St. Peter's Cathedral. The sunny and a little hot day, with the sun making the cobblestones shine almost to the point of hurting my eyes was increasing my fatigue, but I hid it from Alexei because I was more than happy when we started to walk down the street that leads you to the security controls before entering in the grand square in front of the church. It was full of people, small shops selling souvenirs and the air was heavy scented with these typical rosewood rosaries.

"Guntram, stop. You're on the brink of a collapse," Alexei said.

"I can continue."

"Yes, maybe, but it's more than your lunch time, it's hot and you've had nothing to drink since this morning. We eat and then go to the Cathedral. You can't run like crazy under the scorching sun. It's more than thirty degrees."

"I could eat. Pizza?"

"Not happy with your selection, but on the other hand, you haven't smelled a pizza since a long time. I'm in a demagogic mood today."

"Now that you mention it I haven't tasted one since Venice. Jean Jacques would kill me if I ask for one."

"No, he wouldn't. Give him a little bit more credit," he said as he turned back and started to walk the opposite direction. I followed quietly and was happy to get one.

We entered a very small restaurant with a family ambiance, full of Italians, no tourists. I was glad to be in a normal place, not in one of those uptight places I have to go with Konrad. Ten to one that here the dishes are round and the portions in a reasonable size and nothing comes with a mousse served aside.

"Well from now on, you're in charge. I don't speak a word of Italian and I want a *carpaccio* and a *pizza rusticana*," Alexei said to me as the waitress approached us. I did my best with my Argentinean Italian and she laughed at me, but brought what we had ordered.

"It's good," Alexei told me after the first bite.

"Couldn't agree more. Speaking of cooks, how's everything with Jean Jacques? When you were away, the man almost killed me with his borscht soup almost on a daily basis," I said attacking my own pizza.

"Fine. He agreed to settle down and make the relationship more permanent and serious. No more whoring around."

"Please, Alexei. He's like a little mouse. He spends the whole day in the kitchen. The only time I heard him shouting was when Friederich didn't let him buy a strange looking fish."

"Whoring around is how I met him," he said in a sullen voice.

"I don't believe it. You must be exaggerating."

"When I came here in 1996, I started as a normal bodyguard, like Amundsen or Holgersen are now. The Duke used to dine almost every night at the Königshalle, and I had to tag along. I was sent to the service area with the others and there I met Jean Jacques, chef of the German cuisine section. First, he was always speaking some nonsense to me, but later he would bring something to eat. One thing led to the other, as you know and beginning 97 we started to date."

"I thought you had to ask permission to Ferdinand a year ago," I said puzzled.

"To date as to fuck in the kitchen," he explained me as I blushed beyond red. Purple. "Anyway, we were one night, after my shift was finished, never during work, doing our thing when Jean Jacques' official boyfriend caught us. The owner of the Königshalle. I had no idea at all. Very bad for someone whose business is intelligence."

"That was really bad. Was the Duke very or totally upset with you?"

"Furious and nearly kicked me out. I got the speech of what kind of idiot shits where he eats. In other words, of course. Jean Jacques was fired, but almost immediately Friederich offered him to work for the Duke as chef in the Castle. At my insistence, he accepted when he wanted to go back to France. The Duke likes a lot how he cooks, and saw it as an opportunity to eat well at home. Until 2001, I refrained myself to initiate any contact with him, and then asked permission to Ferdinand. A scold from the Duke isn't something you forget easily. In the meantime, Jean Jacques had many adventures since he was only interested in me for a sexual relationship, nothing more."

"I had no idea. That was bad for you."

"I've been working hard this time. I want this to be something more than a night's sex with the hot bodyguard. If I become advisor like Michael or now Goran is, in a few years, I would have some more stability to offer him. At least, he stopped going to clubs. If he does it, he goes with me."

"I was not mistaken. You're exactly as your boss," I laughed, feeling happy for the big Russian.

"How are you? I haven't seen much from you since December."

"Well, you were in your big trip around somewhere," I trailed.

"Just visiting old friends," he told me with a smile but he changed the subject in the blink of an eye. "Speak up Guntram or should I try by other means?"

"No, thank you. I'll confess," I laughed. "Things are fine. OK, not at the beginning of the year when Konrad was disappearing without telling me where, but when he told me of this Morozov guy mess, they improved a lot. Very well at the moment, I could say. Excellent if it wouldn't be for this other crazy Russian. Sorry, I didn't mean to insult you. Bad phrasing"

"He's a crazy Russian. Don't worry, I don't feel insulted."

"His last note terrified me to be honest. I'm afraid of him. He could attack Konrad because of me. I never wanted this to happen, and I don't know what to do to stop it. In theory, I should speak with him and tell him to fuck off but I'm too afraid. Paralysed."

"It wouldn't help. Repin is too headstrong to give up, and if he has already being interested for three years he will not change his mind."

"What should I do?"

"Nothing. Leave it to the Duke."

"I can't. I got him into this mess."

"Repin started the mess," he pointed out. "He's one of the reasons I left Russia. Guys like him control everything, and you can't do a thing to stop them. The Duke allowed me to say this to you. When I came here, I had to leave the service because I was disgusted to no end with many of the deals we had to do. We were becoming worse than mercenaries, scavenging everything we could to make a living. I saw many things I didn't like, and one of them was Repin. I was twenty-six when I met him, in Kurdistan. I thought he was just another weapons dealer, like the ones who were visiting generals to buy material from us. We got along because he's an incredibly cultivated and sophisticated man and became lovers."

I gaped at him. Three years together?

"It lasted till 96 when I had enough, and left the country. It was never something deep or true love. I was like a sex toy for him and I learned a lot about arts with him. It was a huge discovery for me; the poor boy from San Petersburg, in the Army his whole life and then in the KGB. He was never brutal or nasty to me when we were together, despite he's a ruthless man who can horrify a person trained in Afghanistan like myself. Intelligent, cold, heartless to his enemies, he's generous to his lovers. Well, at least to the ones who he thinks will not betray or disappoint him. He let me out and even spoke with Lintorff to take me in. It was the only way, I wouldn't be killed by one of his underlings. He controls almost everything there, and his dealings in prostitution, weapons and drugs are worldwide extended. Al Capone was the bully in the kindergarten compared to him."

"You said you didn't know him," I said, fighting to control my breathing.

"I said he's a mystery for Russian Intelligence and he is. I'm not betraying the Duke or you. He knows everything I know, and that's more than I ever told my government. He knows where I came from. The Duke does not want the others to know it, yet. Repin will never hurt you. He likes you too much to damage you. He was always hooking up with art students or young artists in Moscow but they never lasted much because he was not seeing a true talent in them, and that frustrated him. I think he became interested in me because I was total brute to Arts but willing to learn. I never had exclusive rights to his bed or intended to have them. I can fully believe that he fell for your stuff. I like it a lot also; it's so vibrant and alive. You should not be afraid of him. If he knows you stopped painting for a whole month, he would be very sorry and might do something stupid to repair the damage."

"Will he not go away if I don't paint?"

"No. Probably he would kidnap you to explain to you how nice your art is, and you should return to it. If you don't comply with his order, then he would slowly torture and kill someone you like."

"If I screw it up? If I paint something hideous? Sad clowns and roses?" I tried, my breathing becoming more agitated than before.

"Bad idea. Two case scenarios; First, he repeats previous actions of killing someone you love. Second, he kills you for not being up to his expectations. I saw that several times. Frankly, I don't think you could do something bad even if you wanted. You're exactly the type of artist he likes. When he sent you the Sargent book, I knew there was no return for him. John Singer Sargent is one of his favourites painters, and many of your pieces resemble a lot to him because there's always something like a baroque, mathematical element in the figures' configuration, like Velázquez for example, another one he likes a lot and inspired Sargent. I tried to tell it to the Duke, but he didn't listen to me, and this is very important. It's not as if he was rubbing to him the fact that he paid for you in Venice. He was telling what you mean for him, and that he will stop at nothing."

"He's crazy. I don't know what to do," I said desperately. "Is there something you could tell me? Will he go against Konrad?"

"I can't tell. I don't know. The Duke is responsible for increasing most of his legitimate fortune. They worked together for years, but on the other hand, Repin cleaned after some of the Duke's messes so he doesn't feel indebted to him. Lintorff has many things he could use against him, and Repin has nothing on him. Logic would tell Repin would stay put. Unfortunately, we, Russians, have much hotter blood than Germans."

"How about a compromise with him? Something like he can have all what I paint and leaves me alone."

"It would not hold in time. What you have in your favour is that he wants you to come to him. Willingly. I don't know how long he will wait for you to decide."

"I can't live the rest of my life hiding behind Konrad," I whispered.

"No, you can't. Return to your life. Paint and study as before. Maybe something will come up, and change the situation but in this moment, we all are at an impasse. I can try to speak with him, to reason but I'm not sure it will help. Come, eat your food. You have lost weight and look haggard."

"That's because of last night activities," I said tiredly. "I don't know if I could do this. I can't ignore him. I'm afraid most of the time."

"This is what he wants; to be on your mind always; for good or bad. That you think on him before you think on the Duke. To become ever present. You should not let your fear rule your life. Try to be as you were before. Paint something; go to the University; make Heindrik's life hard, he's a lazy guy," he suggested to me softly, and I couldn't help to laugh a little bit at his last sentence.

"If you say it's hopeless to deal with him or wait till he gets bored, I'll try to return to my normal life."

"Now you're speaking. I'll even buy a dessert and take you to St. Peter's. You need sun glasses also. You walk like a blind mole under the sun."

"Do you think it would look too bad if we steal some paper napkins? I have only a 4B pencil with me."

"Better not. That waitress looks quite territorial."

We paid and I left the napkins in peace. I know from experience how very annoying is to reorganize a full box of napkins.

We went back to St Peter's and I was totally in love with the building. It's strange. From outside it looks huge, monstrous but when you enter is small and disturbingly cosy, yes, that would be the word. You only realize how big it is when you start to walk and it never ends. Only when you're at the centre and look up, you really see how tall the vault is.

But I was rendered speechless when I saw the Pietá. I just stood there, motionless, petrified and in awe of such beauty. Was it made of stone? It looks so incorporeal; lightness and movement at the same time. You can get lost in the folds of the Virgin's clothes or can feel the veins within her body or the contained tension of her sorrow contrasting with the languid posture of Jesus' body. I saw true beauty.

"Impressive. Michelangelo was only twenty-four when he finished it. Either you have or you don't. Simple as that," Alexei said standing next to me.

"I should have stolen those napkins," I muttered cursing myself for being an idiot and not bringing paper along. It's not like I can use the pencil on the floor here.

"Guntram, we're in a Church! He replied falsely shocked. I threw him a dirty look. "I have a notepad with me. Knew you couldn't resist it, boy," he laughed producing a small hard cover note pad, white pages, exactly like those who are so good for drawing standing, from his jacket.

"You know me better than myself. Thanks a lot."

"Lots of experience in breaking hunger strikers," he chuckled and went to sit in one of the wooden pews.

At first, I was a little bit "rusty" so to speak with my drawing skills but after three or four failed sketches I recovered the old pace. I don't know how long I was there, but I think I made more than eight sketches of different parts and views of the statue. I was now concentrating on the Virgin's face when I felt a little push on my back.

"Sorry." A small man apologized, dressed like a priest with the Jesuit order emblem on his right lapel. "I was clumsy but I couldn't help to look at your drawing. Nobody does it any longer."

In less than a second, Alexei had discreetly and silently placed himself beside the man, and was looking at him intently. Come on, he's just an old priest.

"I'm sorry. I didn't know it was forbidden."

"It's not. Just nobody does it any more unless you come with an art class. To copy directly from the piece. My name is Enrico D'Annunzio. I work here, at the Treasure."

"How do you do? Guntram de Lisle," I said shaking his hand. Alexei stood there but the man didn't seem impressed.

"May I look? Thank you," he said as he removed the pad from my hands and started to turn the first pages quickly but stopped on the last ones. "Yes, the first ones are not good at all, as if you were still testing the material, but then it becomes much better and around the last two you capture the spirit of the sculpture. Where do you study?"

"I don't study Arts. It's just a hobby," I muttered.

"Then I'll correct the first ones so you can see what you have to achieve in future. Pencil please," I lost my pencil, too stunned to say anything. Now I know from where Friederich gets his dominating ways.

"You, the bodyguard, hold this," Alexei got full in the chest the portfolio the man was carrying, as he started with the second sketch. "Here, long traces, don't hesitate. Look well at the thing first, memorize it and then draw it. Don't make like many who test on the paper to find the proper line. Better, don't look at what you're drawing and only focus on the object, letting the hand follow your command. It's your brain who does it, not the hand," he could work very fast, and in less than an instant he had completely changed the original rubbish. "I don't understand why you do so bad at the beginning and then it's very well done."

"I didn't paint for a month," I said.

"Wrong thing to do. Drawing is like a sport. Have to practise every day. You should reconsider studying. If you don't want to make it a major, you can always find a private teacher. Come to my office and I will give you a list."

"I live in Zurich."

"There, let me think... there are several acceptable ones. There's one, horrible temper, but very good. Pity he doesn't take students."

"*Meister* Ostermann? I study with him."

"You're in good hands, but never show him the first ones. He will destroy them and make you eat the pieces," he chuckled.

"I know and I would be back to drawing something hideous," I softly said, letting a sigh out.

"Are you the one who painted the dogs and his classroom? Ostermann sent me this year his catalogue. If we weren't friends for so long, I would have thought he hates me."

"Yes, I did them," I gulped. Time to hear the critic from a real expert, not some ladies with tea cups.

"Good. Promising. Can achieve much more if you would work harder. The concept behind is good, the use of light and space are also well done but there's still a lot of potential hidden. Don't be lazy young man. How long will you be here?"

"Until Sunday night." Alexei will kill me for revealing top secret information.

"Pity. Here's my card. There's an e-mail address. Send me pictures of your work. I would like to see examples of your progress. We always need good artists here. Good afternoon." He left in haste before I could even say good bye. I put the card in my folder.

"Hey bodyguard! Do you understand what happened?" I said jokingly.

"These youngster, nowadays. Next, you would be calling me Aliosha," he huffed, not really offended. "Wait till I tell the Duke a cardinal, who allegedly works in the Treasure of St. Peter's, liked your work... and that you're lazy in your painting and studies," he smugly grinned. I looked at him horrified. Guess I will have to be nice for the rest of the trip if I want him to leave that particular piece of information out of the report. I really don't want to be chained to an easel! "Card please, have to check with Goran."

It was my turn to huff as I handed the piece of paper with the Pope's seal out. "We walk to the hotel? I'm kind of hungry and in theory there should be "complimentary cakes at tea time" according to the brochure."

"Not surprised. It's almost six. Good I'm a man who likes to meditate, but next time I have to baby sit you in a Museum, I'll bring a cushion along."

We walked slowly back, making a small detour to watch the Castel Sant' Angelo from the outside and then cross the river. I liked a lot the fact there were so many big trees along the river and in the city. I really like the building but I wanted to go home.

Then we returned to the original plan but he wanted to get me sun glasses (It's getting darker, you know?), and we had to stop to buy them at a posh place.

"Happy? Now I have the look of the professional killer," I said a little bit upset.

"You? Never. You're born for such things. Either you have it or not," he chuckled.

Of course, we had to make another detour to watch the Trevi Fountain. I was so tired that all the sirens and tritons could drop dead or be canned like tuna fish. This Russian took very seriously that we were not supposed to return till 8 p.m.!

"No! I'm not going to see a bloody crypt made of bones," I said when he suggested we should go to the Capucines Chapel in Barberini square. "Besides, it must be closed at this hour."

"OK. Tomorrow."

"I want to go back to the hotel. Look, I'll go to the bedroom and be quiet. Better, I'll go to your's, so I'm not interfering with anybody," I whined, lacing my voice with some pleading tones, sounding like a five-year-old.

He took pity on me because he resumed his walk in the direction direction of the hotel, and we were there in less than ten minutes. We entered through the special door reserved for his suite, and he briefly spoke with one of the security guards before taking the lift to the room.

At the entrance, there were another four big bodyguards. Guess the meetings aren't over yet. I said nothing, and went straight to the bedroom, closing the door, leaving Alexei behind. He can make friends there. I was dead. Truly. I thought in taking a shower before dinner because it's more than eight and I can forget about tea time now. I heard a soft knock on the door and there was Alexei. "Afternoon suit, Guntram. Sorry kid. It's not over yet," he told me sympathetically. Great! Dinner and a show!

I left the notepad on the desk, and went to shower and change. I felt much better after it but still sore, with some back pain. I'm getting older. The twenties are not so kind, it seems! Tonight, I would go to sleep without detours was my firm belief. I sat again at the desk, and started to draw mind absently what I remembered from St. Peter's square. I'm too tired to try to understand the Italian TV.

Konrad entered the room in a good mood. Whatever he was doing today was had good results. He lightly kissed me, and peered at the picture I was doing, but didn't show much interest. He went to shower and change clothes. I continued to finish my stuff.

"At nine comes Monsignor Gandini for dinner. It's an honour he visits us. Albert will be there also." Konrad told me as he was looking for a tie in his closet.

"Gandini, like the lawyer in Venice?"

"Uncle." Guess we're all family now, I couldn't help to think.

"I think I never saw so many priests together in my life as today. A full sortiment of crows." Yes, I'm nasty when tired.

"Guntram!" He scolded me. Mildly. Not impressive enough Konrad.

"One of them was even looking at my drawings. He gave me his card, but Alexei has it now. He works in the Treasury of the Cathedral. He was called like the Italian poet... D'Annunzio. He knows Ostermann too."

"I'm not surprised. If he's Enrico D'Annunzio, he's a well known Renaissance Art historian. I have several of his books. Did he say anything to you?"

"Ostermann is fine as a teacher. I draw well but could do much better. I should be not so lazy and practise more and the lazy part he said, because I was doing nothing for a month. Should send pictures of what I'm doing, and they need good artists here," I said nonchalantly as I was concentrating again on the paper, now working on the details. Damn. I need a sharpener and I don't have one. Perhaps there's one in the big pencil box. "Oh, by the last drawings, I was finally catching the spirit of the thing."

"And "the thing" was...?" he trailed off.

"The Pietá," I replied now in another world, focusing on the columns. I heard him letting out a long sigh.

"You're hopeless, Guntram. A world reference in Arts tells you that you're able to catch the spirit of a masterpiece and you tell it like it's nothing."

"I'm telling it so we don't get Alexei coming with stories later. Saving you time. By the way, did you know he was good friends with Repin?"

"Don't change the subject," I looked at him. Crossed. "Yes, I did," he admitted.

"When were you going to tell? Or you were not going to tell at all?"

"Whatever happened between those two was almost ten years ago, and it wasn't much than some sport under the sheets. Repin sent Alexei to me because it was the only way he could leave the service, and I think he also wanted to get rid of him in a friendly way. Antonov is completely loyal to us."

"How can you be so sure? I like Alexei and he saved my life once but this Repin is crazy as hell."

"Because Repin nearly killed Alexei by torturing him, trying to find a leak in his organization. Alexei was not guilty and Repin felt something akin to remorse, so sent him to me when he could have well ended everything with a shot in the head. If you're thinking he might betray us in order to return to Repin's good graces, you're mistaken. He hates the man with every fibre of his being, because his family was killed during his "investigation". Never say a word of what I've told you. The others don't know. Not even Ferdinand. Alexei is one of my best assets for the area, and I don't want the others ruining his career with old women tales."

"I'll say nothing," I whispered, turning green and willing to throw up. "Why did he say nothing to me?"

"Because he doesn't want to worry you with this man's activities. Perhaps, he also doesn't want to remember. Took him six months to be back in shape. He was more dead than alive when I got him."

"It's horrible. Alexei was his lover!"

"Guntram, not all people are like you. Being a lover doesn't make you immune to treason. In fact, normally lovers are the ones who give the final blow to people like us. Alexei had nothing to do with the situation at Repin's lair, but he couldn't be sure. He's surrounded by bigger sharks than I. Any sign of weakness serves as an excuse to attack him," he thoughtfully said, his gaze lost in the air.

I felt a pang of fear running through me, as the flashback of the meeting when he told me about Repin and his cold way of saying "let's hear your version before I make any decision"; perhaps that would have explained why Friederich was so sad in the morning and Goran upset. Was he thinking I was part of an elaborated scheme, devised to betray him and he had considered eliminating me? After all, Konrad and Repin are very similar.

"Why did you keep him?" I whispered when I wanted to ask why he had kept me alive. His paranoia has no limits and I know that when he feels threatened his violence has no restrains.

"Alexei? Because he's excellent in what he does. Nobody can enter where he can go. Sometimes, I believe he could convince Bin Laden to let him marry one of his daughters, if he would be interested. He's a natural born diplomat and soldier. Repin's loss was my gain, because nobody knows him like Alexei. You know what they say; keep your friends close but your enemies much closer."

"Alexei says Repin will not go away or give up on me. The book he sent represents the way he sees me and what he likes about me. "

"It's possible, but it doesn't change the fact that there are hundreds of books about Sargent, and he chose one with Venetian landscapes. He's telling me he considers I stole you from him and wants you back," he closed the distance between us and crouched beside my chair and dragged me toward the floor with him, embracing me to the point of almost suffocating me. "I will never give up on you. You are mine," he said with deadly seriousness.

Chapter 17

June 25th, 2003

The dinner went well and the Monsignor was kind and polite to me. He was more than happy to get three nice checks from Konrad; one with the auction results (I guess Gertrud lost the chance to use that money for the Foundation after the fiasco); another one mirroring former amount plus the 150,000 from Repin and a third one with the Russian's money with explicit orders of spending it on a Church's project in Argentina.

"I'm afraid this year the bank clerks will have to work more." Konrad said as I was utterly astonished. The total amount was something like my educational fund. Not that I mind. I prefer a hundred times that he gives his money to something useful instead of throwing it on a fancy watch.

"My Duke, we're grateful for your generosity, considering what you already give to us."

"You should thank Guntram. He set the standards so high this year that we had to pay more, but we will survive it," Albert laughed.

"Thank you very much young man. God will reward your actions."

"It's nothing Monsignor. The people who gave the money deserve the credit," I said very embarrassed to be the centre of attention, my eyes fixed on the fish. That was my contribution to the dinner's talk because then they started to speak about the Vatican's internal politics, and I simply lost track.

At 12, we went to bed and I fell asleep while Konrad was elaborating something about the Sistine Chapel. Tomorrow morning you can speak about arts.

* * *

Saturday

More relaxed day—in theory. I was still processing what had happened yesterday, and nervous around Konrad and Alexei. They both came for the Caravaggio's exhibition, but the Russian disappeared the minute we entered in the Quirinale.

"Where's Alexei?" I asked.

"He's not my nanny. The man is visiting the place like we do. Let him be," was his answer, a bit upset at me.

We went around the exhibition, and it was truly large and impressive. I'm moved by his painting. This man truly makes his creations alive, not like me. My things (and I'm being generous with myself), are completely corny. Yes, corny and priggish. He goes to the extreme with the figure he paints; he abuses it, but the result is wonderful. Full of life and human at the same time. The man from the Vatican was right; my use of space and light is adequate but nothing like Caravaggio's. I would need years or maybe a lifetime to get closer to his little finger.

I was very quiet during lunch in a small restaurant nearby the Museum while

Konrad was speaking about the Roman Forum and the Trajan Market but he abruptly stopped.

"Am I boring you?" he asked getting me out of my musings.

"No, not at all. Sorry. I was distracted."

"Are you still thinking on Repin?" he barked. "Honestly, when I saw you drawing again yesterday, I thought you have overcome this problem."

"Huh? No! Why do you bring this up? I was thinking that I could never reach, not even remotely, a level of painting like Caravaggio's. That man was right. I need years of practice and even then everything I do, would still look as coming from a prude who can relatively draw well but nothing else. "

"Nobody's asking you to paint like Caravaggio or anybody else. You have to find your own style."

"Me? A style? Did you take a good look at what I presented? Dogs, children and tea drinking ladies? What's next? Pottery and flowers? Better don't answer," I said dryly.

"I don't think you're a prude. You have an innocent look on things. Caravaggio's life was not exactly an example of innocence and his end was very violent. I don't know why is suddenly a problem for you not to be in the middle of a constant mess? Your nature is peaceful. Honestly, I can't imagine you going to every tavern, well pub nowadays, starting a fight and drinking to death. Do you want to start to experience with drugs to see if you "achieve a deeper look"? Just do what you like, and if somebody likes it, good and if not, it's their loss, not yours," he said with more than obvious annoyance.

"Konrad, I paint because I like it and makes me feel alive, not because I'm good at it."

"Are you going to tell me that Fra Angelico is a prude? Or Johann Sebastian Bach? He lived his whole life with his wife, several children and never got into trouble. Why nowadays everything has to be dark and depressing to be considered as real art? Cynical? Either people behave like selfish children with a golden credit card or they fall in the most absolute depression, thinking there's nothing good left and let emptiness rule their lives. They only look for entertainment and instant retribution, positive or negative, it doesn't matter any longer. What a lemmings' society we live in!" he exploded without shouting. I was speechless, as usual.

"Paint because you like it, if nothing else. It's true you need more practice, and really much more, but it's not for the reasons you believe. You have no problems with the technical aspect. You don't work more because you're afraid of seeing what's inside of you, and don't come up with the excuse of Repin harassing you, because we both know it's not the truth. I don't deny it's much better than before, but you haven't even started to push your own limits. From the dogs to the women's picture there's certainly an evolution, and in less than six months! You're infuriating with your... passivity."

"You're a banker, not an arts critics. I don't remember ever asking you to turn me into an artist! It was never my original idea of life!" I said hotly.

"No, of course. You will cut your hands before you face your fears. Self discovery is not a nice trip. I know. Perhaps you need six months in the Accounting Department, and then you will really see how is the life you think is appropriate for you."

Fuck, no! I thought but said nothing. Only glared at him. "I even don't know what to do next with that white canvas at home."

"For once in your life, don't think and rationalize everything. Just feel and let your true emotions go into that canvas, not a representation of them. There's nothing wrong with your vision of the world."

"How can I have a vision of the world if I live in a house like yours and I'm surrounded by bodyguards the whole day? If I look for a model, it would be a woman with more money in her purse than most mortals would ever see in their lives."

"Then tell me, why a man like Dollenberg's grandfather, who survived the defeat of a war, was left with nothing, only with his intelligence and had to start from zero again, liked your painting even after his memory was dead? Why a man like Repin, who has seen and inflicted more misery on human beings that you can imagine, likes it too? Guntram, perhaps you don't realise it yet, but beauty goes beyond a few cannons imposed by a certain society or age. It's timeless and ageless. Maybe we are only vessels of much higher truths or principles."

"I don't know," I muttered, now more lost than ever before.

"Don't look any more at the previous masterpieces. Start you to look around and see what you like. Make sketches from people. Whatever has to come out will come out when the time is right. Let me see again the Guntram who painted the stream and the willow tree in Torcello, and the children reading a book."

"Maybe the greatest freedom comes when you disentangle yourself from everything and everybody," I said softly, carefully choosing the words.

"This is not what you were really thinking."

"No. It was more in the lines of fuck you all, but you don't allow me to swear," I said sweetly.

"Swearing within discretion is acceptable," he intoned as if it was the eleventh commandment. I smiled at him. "Come, now it's my turn and I want to see the Roman Forum, the Trajan Forum and the Palatine."

All that in one go? What are we going to do tomorrow?

Ah, I see.

Chapter 18

July 14th, 2003

I haven't done much this month so far. It can be described in two words; reading and painting.

Not the holidays of a twenty-year-old year old guy, I know, but I was not feeling up to much and there was nothing else to do. Really. Konrad would leave for his office (I swear this man suffers if he hears the word holidays), early in the morning, dragging me along to Meister Östermann's studio and I should stay there; working and trying to redeem myself after the big scold I got from my teacher after I returned from Rome.

1. I'm lazy (does everybody love to use that word with me?), and there are no excuses for not working at all after the auction mess. He does not care. 2. If there's an idiot who pays so much, then there'll be a second too. 3. Somebody has to support him in his old age, and from now onward he's my manager and we share 50/50 (Isn't that abusive?). 4. D'Annunzio called him to say what a waste of talent I am. He should be more stern with me. 5. Art is ten percent inspiration and ninety percent work so he should not waste more of his precious time trying to explain the obvious to a recalcitrant (sic) brat like myself. 6. Sit. Work. Be quiet.

Heindrik found the lecture very funny, and was glowing with satisfaction. Wait till I suggest the ladies here they can use you as model. Oops, sorry for the oil stain on your pricey Italian shoes. Shaking a brush can do this. Don't stand so close, please.

"Shit, Guntram," he said louder than necessary. Well it's just a shoe.

"Sorry."

"Isn't that the von Kleist girl you're painting? Wait till the Duke sees it. You like to dance on top of your grave, boy," he said, after watching carefully the sketches I had made during the past week at home.

"Good. It looks like the real thing," I replied already in my own private world. "Her face is perfectly symmetric, almost like a Madonna; the virgin not the singer."

"Well, she behaves like the singer and not like our Lady. Do you realise you'll be in troubles with his Excellency?"

"I promised not to speak with her. Nothing about painting. I like her features a lot. What should I do? Paint you dressed like a sailor? If he doesn't like it, he should turn a blind eye, like I do for him. I'll paint the hair light brown. Now move to the right because you're blocking the light" He complied, still looking at me with a mixture of concern and fear. Boy, if I make rubbish it's not your fault. I love her delicate frame and hands, and she would look well, sitting in front of a table, holding her head with the left hand.

I'm working in the moment with her portrait. Don't know what I will do with it, but it's truly nice to paint it. It's not like I can hang it here. I started also other two paints. One with a landscape from around here that will finish in the trash can because it looks horrible, and another with glasses and fruits just to practice transparencies but

331

will follow the other to the trash. I could never be a professional on this because I don't want to work on what I don't have an interest of feel related to it. Can you imagine if someone asks for a portrait and I say "sorry, you're boring to paint"?

I need to go out of here and start to look around or I'll start to sketch the cleaning ladies and Friederich will kill me for harassing the staff.

I'm sick of being here. Trapped. Time to go out. I can't live from old sketches and studies!

Time to prepare the battlefield. I think the landscape would be perfect. Maybe I should add some Heidi looking girls... and a few ducks and young calves.

* * *

July 20th, 2003

"Hello *Maus*. Did you have a nice day?" Konrad said cheerfully last night when he came home and entered my studio. All right, lets see if I can do some major hunting.

I pretended to cover quickly what I was painting with a rag, and went to kiss him sweetly, rising on my tiptoes to reach his face. He kissed me back, hungrily, holding me against his body and for a second, just a second, I felt my resolution faltering. I disentangled from his arms and playfully smiled at him.

"You're certainly happy tonight, Kitten," he observed.

"Yes. Shall we dine now?"

"In half an hour. What have you being doing?"

"Nothing special. Just finishing something. You were right in Rome." Yes, that's the Navy's way; screw it and blame the superior. Thank you Heindrik for an invaluable lesson. "I should paint according to my circumstance and if people don't like, it's their problem. Not mine," I answered sweetly and shyly smiling.

"May I see it?"

"It's not finished, yet." Good, boy. Straight where I want you.

"Just a look. I will not criticise." Curiosity killed the cat... and the banker.

"All right. But it's something small. Just a landscape from around here. I was working on it the whole week." I replied as I discovered the painting...

My New Art School; Return to Kitsch. Two mountains, one lake, glistening reflections made with silver paint, three girls dressed like Heidi (Have I not overdone it with this reference to the Three Graces?), two ducks from Argentina (couldn't get a local one for posing) and a young, light brown calf looking at us... It has such thoughtful eyes!

I remained motionless in front of the tableau, looking at it in pure ecstasy. Konrad also looked at it... in utter horror but he hid his shock very fast. Not enough, poker face.

"Do you like it?" I asked in a light tone. "It's the lake nearby and it looked like a such a peaceful place that I couldn't help to paint it. It's different to everything I've done before," I finished proudly.

"It's different. No question about it." Good, he can't stop looking at it! Yes, those details in the far away tree in pinks and reds would hypnotize anybody. He's slowly breathing as his eyes are glued to the cow's eyes.

"You were absolutely right, my love. I have to let go of all this crap and paint what I feel inside. There's already too much gloom in the world." Now, he was looking deeply into my eyes for a sign of deception. I held his gaze (Goran's school) and grinned like an idiot.

"Normally, you are more subtle with the use of light," he trailed.

"You don't like it? I thought I was finding my true self." Big puppy eyes. Maybe the last sentence was too much; let's try to fix it. "Perhaps you're right, and it's too much. I'm only drawing from memory, and it certainly looks very brightly."

"Like 100 kWh lamp. But it's all right. Fits to the general idea."

"No, you're right. Sketching very fast from what you see from the car is not good enough," I sighed. "But I'm not allowed to go much out with this crazy Russian around."

"Guntram you know you can go wherever you want."

"Yes, but it only causes troubles to Heindrik and the others. Better not." Now or never.

"Guntram you can't hide here for ever. You should go out a little more and draw, like when you did the children's picture. Take Holgersen and a pad with you."

"Things might improve. I have not much left from before, and certainly starting to work outside would help me a lot. I'm not very much into painting fruits and flowers." I said doubtfully. OK, Konrad you can really stop looking at the cow/calf. It will not be frightened and go away!

"Yes, do that. I'll send Antonov up and you can tell him where you want to go, and he'll speak with Holgersen," he said with his commanding voice. He gave me a peck on the forehead and disappeared as fast as he could. Well, I know what you get this year for Christmas if you're nasty to me.

Coming to think, there's something bewitching in that cow. It's impossible to pry your eyes away from hers.

"Fuck! Guntram! What the hell is that?" Alexei shouted, visibly shocked.

"A pagan goddess. Behold the Cow."

"Did you get a contract with the Chinese Restaurant to make next year's calendar?"

"There's a man who sees opportunity in the crisis," I laughed. "You have to tell Heindrik he has to drive me around?"

"Sure. I'll put him to work," he said deeply satisfied. "What are you going to do with this?"

"I don't know. Trash container?"

"Don't you dare. Give it to me."

"Alexei, I want to be friends with you. But take it if you want it."

"Go downstairs. The Duke is waiting for you, and hitting on the cognac before dinner. Guess I would also need a drink after this," he laughed.

Konrad must be at his usual spot in the library. I knocked the door and entered as I heard his dry "come in". Guess he's not so happy about the cow or the fact that he has just given me permission to run around with a bodyguard. I'm still afraid from the Russian, but he wasn't exactly telling the bodyguards to drive around or getting them out of my neck. Time to face the tiger, was my thought before I went to sit in front of him. Let him have his personal space by the couch, only shared with the almost empty cognac glass in his hand.

"Come Kitten. Sit by me. I don't bite, yet," he said with his light and cheerfully false tone. All right, he wants a confrontation. Bad loser! I obeyed and I settled next to him, letting him encircle me with his arms. He pulled me closer, and started to kiss me and stroke my hair softly. He sighed and forced a little bit my head to rest over his chest while he played with my hair strands

Not at all what I was expecting. I closed my eyes, satisfied.

"You should not be so jealous dear. It was a long time ago and I didn't speak with her in Paris. It's all in the past and never meant anything," he intoned very softly.

"I don't understand. Something to confess Konrad?" I replied starting to feel my anger boil.

"There was truly no reason to paint that awful cow in the front. My affair with that singer in Paris only lasted one night, but you know how American women are. A little sport, and they think you must marry or give them a pension. I thought you understood this and forgave me. "

What the hell? Sexy Chick again?

"There is no reason at all for you to feel threatened by her. It's just a stupid woman who can't take a no for an answer. I don't even remember her name." He continued slowly and almost sounding pained.

Now I'm not only lost but clueless also. From where came that from? Has he been doing something nasty lately, and now he was covering it with that old rubbish? Was he thinking I've being doing something and wanted to force a confession with his "gentle method"? Was something funny in the cognac? Yeah, that's the way to play along.

"Konrad do you feel well? This is not making much sense to me," I replied softly.

"That hideous painting upstairs. The cow looks like her, not to mention those three women dancing like in her video. I still haven't found out the meaning of the ducks or the mountains. Must be something from Argentinian lore."

"NOOO. It's just a painting with no hidden meaning.!" I protested.

"Guntram, you don't fool me. This is not your usual style. You're punishing me for something." Konrad said looking contrite and sad, his big eyes making my heart sink with remorse for causing him pain.

"No, no, no. It's just a stupid picture I was going to throw away. I thought you would hate it and let me go around more, not only to *Meister* Ostermann's studio," I said hurriedly, taking his hands into mine. "I never had a second intention or wanted to be so rude as to rub your past at your face."

I'm a total IDIOT. I confessed in less than five minutes!

"Just what I was expecting," he said, his composure regained. He let go of my hands and adopting again his normal king's posture. "Next time, tell me what you want, directly."

"All right. Sorry. But you would have said no. Don't deny it!" I said frustrated. He reversed the tables… again.

"All right, Guntram, what's this time?"

"I'm sick of being trapped here. I want to go out. On my own," I buffed.

"You know this is not possible in the moment. The only thing I can do for you is to let you walk around the city with Holgersen or some other member of his team.

"I'm not a criminal and yet I feel like a prisoner! I can't live my whole life trapped because some crazy mobster likes art! It's driving me crazy. Soon I will start to copy pictures from the internet! If you say there's no danger, I should believe it."

"I'm glad you finally understood what I said in Rome. Took you almost a month," he retorted dryly.

"You are the first one to admit Repin is dangerous," I retaliated upset at being discovered and now ridiculed.

"Yes, but I continue with my life anyway. Next August, I will send you for two weeks to Argentina. To the country house. You need some holidays, and I would be travelling most of the month, so it makes no sense to keep you here. Brooding. You can leave, and I will pick you up after the 15th. Monika will make the arrangements."

"Are you letting me go to Argentina?" I asked hoping my ears were not deceiving me.

"Yes. In August. To the *estancia*, Guntram. No running around the city without me. Holgersen and his people will go with you. You can ask your friends to visit you there, if you want. There's enough space in the house."

"I'm overwhelmed. I don't know what to say."

"Go, enjoy your time there, paint something better than what it's upstairs."

"After the last time I was there, I thought you would never let me return..."

"Why do you think I gave you the house? The security has been increased, the land around it belongs to me. Should be safe enough. By mid August, I'll join you and we can spend a week in the city together."

I jumped to his neck and started to kiss him. Passionately and he was not shy also. "Let's go to the bedroom," I mumbled as he was softly biting me in the neck. He didn't answered and continued to trace long lines with his tongue on my neck. My moans were becoming louder as my erection grew bigger.

He pushed me on my back against the couch without interrupting his kisses. I put my arms around his neck and drew his body on top of me, arching my neck so he could have a better access to my lips.

He stopped. "Bedroom it is," he stood up and pulled me up by the hand, exerting a little jerk. We climbed the stairs, still holding our hands and went directly to the bedroom. He left me at the door and went to the bed, removing and throwing his jacket and tie on the way, and sat on the border. Shoes also were discarded.

"Wait till Friederich sees what you have done with it," I grinned with an evil smile.

"Come here, Kitten. Don't stall," he whispered seductively as he removed his belt also and easily unbuttoned the collar. I advanced towards the bed and stood near, within his arms reach. Hesitantly, waiting for him to make the first move.

"Are you going to put on a show?" He asked

"You're shameless," I said falsely shocked, removing my jacket and tossing it aside. Guess tomorrow Friederich will shout both of us. He grabbed me by the arm and made me stand between his legs. His large hand started to travel along my back and I relaxed under his touch, closing my eyes, enjoying the electricity running through my body.

His hands started to open the buttons of my shirt and Konrad easily slid it down and kissing my stomach almost making me chuckle with his feathery touches. I placed my hands over his shoulders and purred like a cat when he he started to undo my belt and trousers. His strokes on my penis were strong and slow driving me mad with desire. I bent my head to kiss him and he used my momentum to make us both fall on the bed.

I disentangled myself from my trousers and and started to fumble with his ones. "Eager tonight my love?" He chuckled as I continued with what I was doing, not even bothering to answer his taunt. I was so absorbed in his kisses that I didn't realise when he turned me and placed himself on top of me. We resumed our kisses hotly than before, his hand pumping my member faster and faster. I tried to control myself but I spilled my seed in his hand.

I had no yet recovered my normal breathing when he inserted himself into me. His thrusts set into a firm pace and I entangled my legs over his hips trying to match his movements. I could feel him reaching his climax.

We both were exhausted. I placed his head over my chest and started to caress it slowly, soothing his earlier tension, that was still present on his shoulders. In a flash, I realised we were going to revisit again the mess we had the first time I went back home.

"Konrad?"

"We go eating in a minute."

"It's not that. It's about Buenos Aires."

"Don't tell me you're afraid," he lifted his head from my body and sat on the bed. "Everything has been taken care of and there should be no problems. Just stay away from the soy beans."

"I'm thinking more on what happened between us last time. I don't want to have another fight like that one. It was very bad."

"Guntram, circumstances have changed since then. You had a very bad year, and need some time with your own people. Your friends from school can visit you, that neighbour friend you had."

"Last time you behaved like a psycho before I took the plane," I said seriously. No chance I'll let you beat the bush around this time.

"This is why I'm going to pick you up in two or three weeks. Holgersen will stay with you in the house," he replied sweetly.

Some things never change. Ever. Still a control freak!

Why do you want me so much off-stage?

Chapter 19

August 3ʳᵈ, 2003. Sunday

It's been five days since I arrived to Buenos Aires. Well not to the city; the countryside house. I haven't seen the city so far. On July 29ᵗʰ Heindrik and I took the plane. First class, and he was more than happy to be pampered. Growing a soft side, pal? Wait till Goran or Alexei realise it. He was most of the time engulfed in his copies of Jane's Navy International and Jane's Intelligence Review magazines. From where he got them, I don't know.

"Can I look, please?"

"This is for mature audiences only. Read The Economist or watch a film," he growled from his seat, across mine.

"I'm surprised that you're able to read. I just want to make sure it's not only pictures," I teased.

"Surprised I'm not only a hot blond? Guntram, don't pester me. I have left twelve hours of peace till we get to the mess."

"Heindrik. I'm not planning to run around downtown. Only going on Friday to a meeting with friends. Star Wars Fan Club, you know?"

"Forget it. You go to the *hacienda* and stay there. Those are my orders, and the others are already waiting there," he smirked.

"Are you telling me you will forgo of a Star Wars meeting?"

"Can't have everything in this life, boy. How is the Plaza Hotel? Do you know it?"

"Yes, I was going every weekend for tea," I replied seriously. He looked at me hopeful. "It's one of the most expensive hotels there! In front of Plaza San Martin, near Florida Street, where all of you were shopping last time. Why do you think I know it?" I shouted now frustrated. He can be a real snob sometimes!

"Good, because the other one was not so nice—very modern. Can't blame Monika with less than two days notice, and the Alvear?"

"Are you doing Monika's work now? I don't know also."

"Too bad. I'll have to tell her that you don't know. Any preferences?"

"I don't know. I was in the Alvear for a fifteen-year-old birthday party from a friend's sister and it was very elegant and Parisian looking."

"Good. I'll tell Monika that one, and if the Duke hates it, it's your fault. The other was grating to his nerves and does not want to come back ever... and we also not, if you get my meaning. A pissed off Duke is bad for business."

"Do you know when he will join us?"

"No idea. We have to take you to the countryside and let you run free there... within reason of course."

Damn! I have the Swedish for baby sitter and he doesn't want to take risks or anything. I will be glad if I can go to the garden at all.

"How many are 'we'?"

"You know us all. Me plus Lars Amundsen and Peter Jansen. They're already there, checking everything. Can't trust the locals enough according to Pavicevic."

Excellent. Two grumpy Swedish and a grouchy Dutch without counting the Argentineans.

We arrived early in the morning. Very early, like 7 a.m., and after brief exchange of opinions with the local authorities over Heindrik's new laptop—too new; perhaps we want to sell it here without paying taxes—I had to speak with my best local accent and explain how idiotic these gringos can be and bring such expensive things here, and that in Europe people change laptops almost every six months. Look if he doesn't have it when we leave, you charge him the taxes. They took me for his translator and let us go.

Outside a man was waiting for us. Hermann Mayer, new office head here. He would take us to the house with his car. I greeted him, but was surprised that Landau was not there any longer.

"Mr. Landau had an accident early July while skiing in the south. I'm his replacement, sir. We all are still very shocked with his death."

"I wasn't aware. This is horrible. How did it happen?"

"I'm not sure of the details. He hit a pillar full force. It was a difficult slope, and the weather was very bad that day. He never recovered from the coma," he softly replied.

I was silent for the rest of the ride, looking through the window.

* * *

The house had changed a lot. First, it's not pink any more but beige, like the original was. Martiniano, the original foreman, and his wife were still there, but most of the old staff decided to quit or went into a very generous retirement during the last year. The decoration was altered. It was now much more austere but the furniture was more expensive than before—we have the real thing now, not something similar—aristocratic and elegant. Nothing for clumsy tourists who can spill orange juice over the Damask fabrics. This was the real colonial style with mahogany, good carpets and draperies.

According to Maria, most of the people went away because of the hassle provoked by construction workers changing pipes, windows, electricity installations and so on. Even her nice kitchen was altered and she got a kitchen safety standards handbook. Later came the new "house manager" who was truly nasty to them. This former five stars hotel staff manager, uptight nose, had changed all the house rules to very strict standards; new linen made of a horrible cotton, impossible to iron, new maids (two) and butlers (two more); new priceless china. The house was used by the Duke's employees working downtown (not the principal rooms reserved for him and me, which were off limits) for working meetings. Everything must be always perfect and in pristine condition as these Germans were much stricter than the old *Herr* Dollenberg.

Security was also changed, and nobody could come unannounced like in the old times. Now that we were here, there were security guards around, cameras and endless checks and protocols to follow.

Most of the old bedrooms for tourists were dismantled, and were turned into offices, studio or guests rooms. The interior decorator who was in charge of everything, was nasty to Miss Luciana work, and nearly was throwing everything to the trash container or giving it to the workers as if the pieces were rubbish. To make the insult final, the new manager hired a cook who was coming when they had visitors, and she had been discharged from cooking duties when visitors were in the house.

The only thing making them staying was that Martiniano was very happy with his work, directing the new lands; the whole 5,000 acres, which is a lot either for Argentinean and European standards.

The reform was more than a new paint job. If this is Konrad's idea of a "minor change," I really don't want to know what a major one is. Important question; should I call him or not? Who knows what he's doing now... or where he is because he deposited me (literally) in the airport and disappeared to his own plane. Should I call Monika? No, better not. SMS it is. "May I call you?"

Almost immediately my phone beeped. "No" At least he knows I want to speak. I'll go for a walk.

At the exit I was stopped by Amundsen, the other Swedish. "Excuse me sir, Mr. Holgersen would like to have a word with you," he said courteously.

"All right. Tell him I'll meet him by the lake." Move your legs Heindrik, you're far away from Alexei or Goran's status. They can make me run.

I took my coat as it's very cold now with the sun hiding behind some clouds and walked to the pond/lake. The mean male swan was still there, like always, and immediately looked at me defiantly. No chance you can kick him out. This guy has ruled this pond since 1995. I sat in one of the new iron benches; very comfortable with the cushions and started to look around.

"Well, now I have you also giving orders. Don't get too used to it. I'm still in charge of you till the Duke comes here," Heindrik told me visibly upset.

"Oops. Sorry, Heindrik. Did I rub you in the wrong direction? You look quite flushed with the walking exercise," I taunted him.

"Look. I'm not in the mood for your bantering. I don't understand a word those stupid natives say. The local security hardly can say a word in English and are totally unprofessional. Who hired these idiots? I'm most certainly complaining to Goran."

"Hey. Sit down with me and try to relax. We're in holidays. In a few hours we'll get a real barbecue. Nothing like fancy Europeans eat," I chuckled.

"Might improve the day. Did our worst enemy make the security arrangements in here? Maybe would have to work harder than ever if he wants to survive the Duke's fury when he finds out what a rubbish this is."

"Just a few minutes ago, Maria was complaining about your strict security net and weapons around. Nothing moves without telling."

"Well it's wrongly made; stupid endless rules and wrong location for the cameras, for example; hundreds of dark spots with the motion detectors. The guards can't even mount a FAL—that is rifle produced here, nothing fancy—without a handbook. Amundsen and Hartick can't believe they were hired at all."

"Sorry. I didn't know you had so much trouble. Is there something I can do?" Yeah, sure.

"No. I'll speak with Goran and he will make the decision. In the meantime, here's your drill: 1. Don't leave the premises and by that I mean house and garden, only the lake area. No running around the hundred acres till I give you clearance. 2.

339

Mobile phone always with you and on. 3. When it's dark, inside of the house, Guntram. 4. Amundsen or Hartick will be with you every time you want to go out," he listed.

"Heindrik! This is too much. We are in the middle of nowhere! Are the soy beans going to attack us?"

"For my peace of mind?" He told me with a smug grin.

"The Duke says 'humour me'. More impressive," I retorted truly crossed. What's next? He tucks me in bed and gives me a good night kiss? No, that no. Konrad would kill him.

"Good to know. Now, you go inside. I have to speak with Goran," he said while pulling me by the arm, and almost dragging me in.

At night, I was tired and still cross with him. After lunch, Amundsen took me for a walk along with Mopsi (yes, she arrived yesterday), and let me draw in peace around the gardens till tea time when he put us both inside the house.

Heindrik was waiting for me for tea at the living room. He nearly drew his gun out when Maria brought me a *mate* and served it.[5]

"Heindrik put that thing down. It's nothing. It's like tea," I explained to him tiredly. Grudgingly he obeyed.

"This blond is more idiotic than the others. He should be careful I don't put some *ombú* leaves in his tea." Maria said in Spanish staring at him hard. "All the same crazy guys."

"Maria don't get yourself into trouble. Let them be. He didn't mean to be disrespectful to you. He doesn't know our traditions," I explained to her in Spanish.

"This Duke of yours is no better. Look how he changed everything. He destroyed the peace of this place. We never had guns in this house before."

"Maria, he has a lot of money and has to protect himself."

"Then his money must not be cleanly earned. People with a clear conscience don't need weapons around. He can't be good for you, Guntram."

"Maria don't say such things. You'll only get into trouble with him. He's very kind to me. Last time I was here we got mugged and I nearly didn't live to tell the story."

"He should have taken you to a hospital here, not dragging you out of the country. Mr. Dollenberg told me what happened. It's his fault you are so sick nowadays. You were a healthy and vibrant child, and look at you now."

"I don't want to argue with you. The Duke always has my best interests on his mind," I said now pissed off with the old woman's meddling.

"He's not good for you. He has the cold eyes of a killer. He's a perverted old man."

"Maria, please! Enough. You only saw him once in your life to pass such a harsh judgement on him. He's your boss now," I scolded her, losing my temper. I don't care if she's my elder. She turned around and left the room very upset. Excellent! I will get now the super laxative *ombú* leaves in my tea!

"What did the witch say? Why are you so upset? "Heindrik fired rather hotly.

"Nothing," I silenced him. I can be nasty too. I learned from the best.

---

[5] *Argentina's national beverage (in addition to being popular elsewhere in South America), yerba mate is a sort of tea, similar in appearance to green tea. Yerba means 'herb' and mate refers to the actual drink and the vessel in which it is traditionally served.*

I spent the rest of the day drawing in the living room with Heindrik working on who knows what on his computer. True, he was quiet, and the only sound in the room, was Mopsi's light snoring. We had dinner and went to bed. Mopsi can share a room with me, because nobody told me to send her to the kitchen here.

The main bedroom was now almost like a suite with a small living room, bathroom, and sleeping area with a king size bed in a classical style and a French chimney, all decorated with good woods and some golden fabrics. I should know the decorator's name; really good work.

I was soundly sleeping when the mobile phone woke me up. Half asleep, I answered it as Mopsi barked her disagreement at being awoken… at 2 a.m.

"Hello dear. Are you all right?"

"Konrad, you called me. I'm happy to hear you. Be quiet Mopsi. Sorry," I mumbled, trying to chase the sleepiness away.

"Not even two days out and the dog is already in my bed. Tell it to enjoy it because it will be evicted sooner than it thinks. What time is there?"

"She's not in the bed; in a basket, near the chimney. She doesn't like to be disturbed. It's very late here."

"I'm sorry. I'll call you later."

"No, no. It's OK. Who knows when I catch you again? Where are you?"

"On the plane to London. Do you like the house?"

"It's a fantastic job. In a way it reminds me your place at London. It's sober but at the same time luxurious—very elegant. Who did it?"

"Someone who has experience with *estancias*. Don't remember the name at the moment. She renovated another one in the north of the country which belonged to a XIX century President. I'm glad you like it. I asked to keep it as simple as possible and looking like the house in London. You liked so much the style."

"I'm in love with it. It's not Georgian but it's very classical, and somehow it matches with the countryside. All the brickwork disappeared."

"The hostel ambiance is gone? Good. It was too much for my taste. I believe she will meet us in the house, and later we'll see her downtown. I would like to buy some Argentinian paints, and I need her help to know where to hang the pictures"

"Completely away; pity the original staff is also away and the remaining ones are not very happy too."

"You know kitten I set minimal standards for the staff. If they can't comply, they should go. Most of them have been relocated in other places."

"I know, but somehow Heindrik is upset with the place's security. He must have exploded to Goran by now."

"This will be fixed tomorrow. Don't worry. Obey Heindrik."

"I miss you. When will you come?"

"I also. I don't know exactly. So far everything is running fine but you never know. Enjoy it as much as you can."

"You've been wonderful to me. I love you."

"I also. Be good and don't make terror to Heindrik. He has many things to fix in the next days. I have to return to work now. I'll see you soon."

Not at all what I was expecting. Is it not customary to engage in a phone sex talk with your lover if you find out that said person is in bed? Probably not, if you're on a plane, going to London before the market opens.

August 16th , 2003

It's Saturday night and I'm not going out like I should do if I were a normal, nondescript young man. But I'm not. At least I'm downtown Buenos Aires, in one of the most chic areas. Hotel Alvear as Fedérico's mother's maiden name; family of hers. But the place now belongs to an international holding, and it was named after the street where it is. Strangely, Konrad was not upset by the fact that he has to sleep in a room with her name embroidered on the cushions over the bed. Or perhaps it doesn't bother him at all to play in that particular bed. Better don't ask. Probably I wouldn't like the answer.

Yesterday, Friday, I was like always drawing in the park, near the lake. After almost two weeks in the country side, I was a bored to no end. I spent most of the time either, walking, riding horses, sleeping and making sketches of the landscape, animals, plants, some people, crops, house, hen house, etc., etc., etc. All right. I'm a city boy. I need some action, and to see other people than Heindrik, his two friends, the foreman and his wife and the service staff, polite and discreet. Maria decided to start a campaign against Konrad and his "perverted attentions" toward me. She was driving me to the edge, and my politeness was one tiny step from being over.

The figure of a tall woman approaching us (Lars was with me), surprised me. She waved her hand at us and Lars was not impressed or changed into his "psycho mode" as he almost had done once Maria broke the "security distance" (sic) to me.

"Are you Guntram by any chance?" She said with a delicate voice. "Glad to meet you. I'm Malú Arriola de Blaquier. The decorator."

"Hello. I'm pleased to meet you. I'm sorry I didn't recognize you before. I was not expecting you at all."

"Well, it's supposed to be a surprise. You haven't changed much, Guntram. Don't you remember me? I'm Coco's Blaquier aunt. You were going together to school. We met at his birthday party several times."

Now I remember her but with black or brown hair. With women is impossible to tell. She was dressed informally but very elegantly. Jeans and tweed jacket under an alpaca shawl with matching hat. Not surprise the house looks elegant and sober at the same time. She married the sugar tycoon of this country.

"I'm sorry again. I'm always so clueless. Yes, I remember you Malú. What a fantastic job you did on the house. It's unrecognisable. By the way, how is Coco? (Coco is an alias; Coriolano Cosme Blaquier, yeah worse luck with names than mine), I haven't seen him in a long time."

"He sends his regards. He's studying law now. You're supposed to call him when you're in Buenos Aires and arrange to go for a drink with him and some others from school. I have passed the message."

"Thank you. Would you like to go inside? It's cold here. But you know better than I this place."

"Oh yes. It was a never ending work. Horrible, but I'm happy it's finished. I would like to ask the Duke his permission to publish some pictures in a magazine. The things you can do when you have unlimited budget, and clear orders from the customer. Do you know I was at his house at Kensington? Incredible. To die for. After he bought this house, he called me, around November and asked to refurnish it anew. He got my number through Ernesto, the one who owns that building company in

Puerto Madero and personally asked me to do it, as he had seen pictures of my work in Córdoba."

We reached the house as she was speaking, not letting me say anything, but I was glad for it because I honestly had no idea what to tell her. When we entered, she stopped for a minute and I could ask her if she wanted coffee. "It would spoil my appetite; a light cola please."

"As I was saying. I met him in London at his office, around February, only half an hour. This man has a crazy schedule. Jorge, my husband, should not complain at all because he loafs the whole day in his office or in the club. However, I went to his house later, returned here, took photos, spoke with the architect in charge of the renovation, and we agreed on covering those hideous bricks—it's so the eighties—and went back to Paris to buy the fabrics and show him the preliminary sketches. He liked them a lot, and even told me to go to Venice to buy other fabrics there. Have you seen his house there? He let me use it for a week. A lady like me should avoid hotels. Wonderful. Those Mary Cassat hanging in the living room are superb and the rest of the art collection is exquisite."

How Konrad can fight a war with a Russian, run his business, and still check on drapes it's beyond me. I can't.

"If I were not married I would be hitting on him, Guntram" (Good luck girl), I forced a smile. "He's elegant, cultivated, really good looking, old fashioned in an adorable way. Imagine, he never let me stay in a hotel in Europe, only in Paris, and it was the George V, because ladies travelling alone should not be in such places. I've had the funniest year so far. I think my husband is jealous of him. What are you doing now?"

"I study Economics in Zurich. Not much in the moment," I answered, still not really knowing what to understand from her previous remark. Does she know I'm Konrad's boyfriend?

"Yes, he told me. I believe you also paint."

"Sometimes. Nothing extraordinary. It's a hobby." When do they serve lunch in this place? I want to escape. She looked at me puzzled.

"He spoke very well of your work and he should know considering his art collection. I thought he was sponsoring you."

Sponsoring? Perhaps. Let's say he copes with my rubbish and hasn't complained about Ostermann's bill every month (I'm sure he charges him. That old man never loses a dime). Loving support would be a better description.

"He takes care of the University's fees. I live with him. Together," I said in a low voice, some red creeping to my cheeks. The idea finally dawned inside of her head. She coughed lightly. Yes, it did.

"Would you show me some of your drawings? Coco told me you were always drawing in school," she recomposed herself in no time.

Thank God, Heindrik burst in the room in his shy Viking way. He announced we should eat and then go around the house. I was a little surprised but said nothing. We had lunch all together and Heindrik led the conversation asking about Argentinean history. He had a relatively good idea about it and not the usual commonplace. Perhaps, he could read a book after all.

At three, it started to rain, and we had to return to the living room from the garden, where she resumed her big refurnish saga. I was more or less spacing out at her description of the Venetian velvets and how she couldn't resist them and bought almost the whole store, and shipped everything here. That explains why the curtains and bed covers are such nice brocades.

Through the window, I saw two big black vans stopping in front of the house. Heindrik escaped at full speed from the living room (lucky guy), as she carried on with the story. I looked again, and to my utter surprise, I saw Konrad coming out from one of the vans with Mayer and one bodyguard. I wanted to jump at his neck, and my heart was so happy to see him! Lord, I truly missed him this time!

I heard the distant noise produced by greetings from Heindrik and the rest of staff at the main door. Knowing Carlos, the butler and new manager here, people must have been set in line to welcome him. I tried to cool down my anxiety, but it was hopeless. I heard also the happy howl from Mopsi at seeing him.

"I think the Duke has arrived," I interrupted her careless chat.

"Yes. Strange. He was supposed to meet us for lunch."

The door opened and there was Konrad, informally dressed with courderoy trousers, shirt, jersey and a conservative plaid jacket, Mopsi running between his legs. I stood up but remained in my place despite I wanted to hug him. I flashed him a big smile. He advanced towards us, and kissed Malú's hand.

"Mrs. Arriola Blaquier I'm terrible sorry I'm so late. We bumped into a workers blockade, and it was impossible to evade them for almost three hours."

"I'm glad to see you again, Duke. Guntram and I were speaking so much that I lost track of time. Did you take the highway after 11?"

"Yes. I was delayed after a meeting at my office in Puerto Madero, and we took this big avenue that leads to the highway, but its entrance was blocked by demonstrators. All lines. Nobody passes no matter what, even the ambulances. The police were just looking and taking care nobody would complain to these people. Incredible."

"Friday. Unemployed people protest in front of the Welfare Ministry. They start where you were stopped, and by two they move to the Ministry, to have everything finished by five."

"Is there a schedule too?" he asked astonished.

"I'm afraid so," she answered sweetly.

"Hello, Konrad," I whispered extending formally my hand, and he took it, pulling me into a light embrace and patted the side of my face briefly but lovingly.

"Hello Guntram," he replied returning his attention to her. "I hope you Madam can reverse today's luck for me. Since I arrived, I've been spaced into the Twilight Zone. Do you mind if I order tea at four? I haven't eaten since this morning in the plane at around 5 a.m."

"Please do it. It sounds as if you were in an adventure."

"It would be something to tell to the younger generations," he chuckled as he sat in front of her, beside me. "I arrived on time today from New York, at 6 a.m. with some people from my banks. First stop. Migration Office. It was closed. Opens at 6:30" he said. "Our watches must be wrong because they opened at 6:40. As we were the only ones standing there, a man decided to come to check our passports. He didn't speak English and we didn't have any translators with us. So he went to fetch a colleague. I was surprised because with private flights things are done much faster and privately."

His tale was interrupted by the butler's arrival with the tea tray… with cake and sandwiches. Someone was really hungry it seems. To his credit, he waited for her to start.

"At 7:10, a woman with some knowledge of English, came to us as we noticed that a commercial flight was also arriving. She opened her service window—slowly—and she beckoned us to come near."

"Form 452!" she shouted at me. I had no idea what it was and there was not a single paper around to be filled. "Excuse me, I don't understand," I told her. "You have to fill out the Form 452 to enter this country. Didn't they gave you one at the airline?" "It was a private flight," I answered and she made an ugly face at me. She looked in her drawers and got some papers out. We distributed and filled them out."

"The room was starting to be crowded with the other flight's passengers, but she was in no hurry to work, and nobody was coming to help her. She took my passport and written form and tore down the paper, raising her eyes towards the sky. "Full name as shown in passport. Do it again. That goes for all of you" She cried to everybody," he stopped to eat part of his sandwich while we were barely containing our laughter. Someone had just met one of our finest products; The Public Servant. This could be really funny.

"I wrote my full name: Konrad Maria Ulrich von Lintorff Sachsen Löwenstein, and gave it back to her. She read it and said "Seven words! You don't have a name, do you? If you shorten it, you'd get a lot of free time in your life."

We couldn't help to burst into laughter this time. Malú was on the brink of tears. Konrad laughed but not really amused.

"She continued to read the paper. "Do you have money?" she asked me. "I beg you pardon?" "Cash, credit card, health insurance. If you are going to stay for a week here you need to show me a minimum of $1,500 cash or a credit card. Your hotel voucher too."

Malú was now coughing from the laughter and I was trying to regain my composure.

"I could have exploded there, but I tried to keep calm. "I assure you I have enough money with me and I don't carry hotel vouchers with me. My name is enough. The person who's waiting for us should have everything" "Look, we don't want any illegals here. Are you Swiss?" "Yes" "Show me a credit card. It's mandatory," I had to pull my wallet out and show her my credit cards. By now the passengers' line was very long. "OK. Here it's wrong. You wrote "banker" as profession. It's "bank employee". Don't worry I'll fix it." Fortunately, she stamped my passport and let me go. She repeated the same questioning for all my staff with minor changes," he sighed.

"It wasn't personal," I chuckled.

"It doesn't finish there. We were done at 8 a.m., and we had to run with the car to the office in Puerto Madero because our meeting was at 9:30. We barely avoided the traffic jam. Fortunately, I was already dressed for the meeting, and had some time left to be briefed by Mayer. It was a working breakfast with some local bankers who want to associate with us. Their business proposal was not bad but I wanted to hear it from the CEO's. The one who was speaking started to repeat what I have read so far, and that infuriates me. I wanted to clarify some aspects over their financial health, since they want to represent us in Latin America. I only asked if they had finished implementing Basel II protocols and if they could explain how their ratios were for Tier 1 and Tier 2; something simple. Also, the part for their general provisions description was muddy. "He took there a deep calming breath.

"Answer: "If you want one more point over the profits, just say it." I could not believe my ears. What a pathetic waste of my time. I finished the meeting there. When they were away, one of the secretaries was so nervous that she poured a full cup of coffee over me. Back to the hotel to change."

"It was one of those days when it's better to stay in bed." Malú added, lacing her voice with sympathy.

"It gets better and better. I went to the hotel. No problems. Changed myself and took the car with Mayer. I was still hopeful I would be here in time for lunch, but we were stopped by the blockade. I couldn't believe that only a hundred people were stopping all of us. Isn't there a law against it?"

"Several, but the best is if you read in the morning newspapers the cronogram for demonstrations, and avoid those areas." Malú explained as if it were one of those life facts you just know.

"Incredible," he muttered. Argentina's stocks had just lost another quarter. "However, I can't deny that they are natural born entrepreneurs. During the three hours we were stopped—no chance you can drive backward—several wanted to clean the wind shields, sell watches and perfumes imitations, different kinds of food, some beggars came and something akin to circus artists made a performance. I tried to work, but it was impossible with that horribly loud music and drums. Finally, one of our local security guards reached an agreement with the organizing committee, and I paid the revolutionary tax. They take pesos, dollars, euros and I suppose credit cards will be accepted soon," he said letting a dry laugh out. "I was even called an oligarch as Mayer explained me."

"You got the full welcome committee today," I said softly making my best effort to keep my hilarity under control. His German core must be shocked to no end. Konrad, you should not complain so much because I know several protest chants from my school time here, and you wouldn't like to hear them. Many start with the word "oligarch" and all your ancestry is mentioned. Davos protesters are nothing compared to our own bards.

"Indeed. But Mrs. Arriola Blaquier you must show me the house. What I've seen so far meets my expectations."

"I'm so excited to show you the house. It was such a rewarding work. Shall we go?"

"Yes, of course," he answered, rising from his chair as she had already done it. Poor Konrad, you've just lost your chance to eat another sandwich! Today it's not your luckiest day. "Guntram pack your things together. We're leaving when we are finished here."

I had to suppress the urge, no the need to smash the new china service on his head. Why can't he tell me things in advance? Just a warning beforehand. His *fait accompli* policy is... too much! I counted inwardly up to ten... and then to twenty before I answered grinding my teeth "Yes, of course."

They went away for their tour, and I stormed to the library to pick up most of my papers. Inside were Heindrik and Mayer, sitting around the table and having coffee like real men, not tea.

"I'm sorry. It's just a minute. I have to gather my stuff together. The Duke wants to return to Buenos Aires."

"Carlos the butler already packed your things except the drawings here. No need to hurry. Sit with us for a while," Heindrik said nonchalantly.

"Tough day?" I asked Mayer trying to start a conversation.

"You have no idea and it's far from finished."

"Did he even get a cup of coffee on top of him?"

"My mistake. He asked me about Landau's accident and I was telling the details, when Sofía—my secretary—entered with a tray and tried to serve the coffee but her hand was trembling so much that she spilled a full cup on his right sleeve and started to weep."

"It was an accident. He can't be upset with her."

"She was Landau's girlfriend," he explained to me as Heindrik winced sympathetically. "The Duke tried to calm her down but she went mad with grief. Hysterical. I should have been quiet. Later, we ran into this demonstration and I thought 'I lost my job'. We got all types of insults from those lefty people. Good he doesn't understand Spanish. Please, never teach him. We had to bribe them, if not, we would be still there. Now we have to return to the hotel, and he has a dinner with same local bankers from the morning plus congressmen. I hope they fix this morning's fiasco. I checked their proposal several times before submitting it to the Duke, and it was OK, but this gross man answered him back. One would expect that the owner of one of the leading banks here and this government's favourite banker would be more sophisticated but he was coarse. A real yokel."

"If it's any consolation to you the Duke despises Argentineans. He will not place all the blame on you." I said softly.

"We all know that. The only reason we are here is because he believes in this country's farming potential and nothing more. Every project for real estate development, industry, tourism we presented was rejected in less than twenty-four hours. On the other hand, he likes Brazilians a lot. We will move these headquarters to Sao Paulo in no time. I was mainly responsible for that area till Landau's accident and I had to move here to reorganize everything. My family is still there because the real money is in Brazil."

"But their new president is from the left, a workers party," I said dumbfounded.

"Yes but the core policy remains as it was since the seventies. Brazilians are very nationalists and don't take any rubbish. They earned the Duke's respect. It has nothing to do with political divisions. He looks for stability and accountability in a government. If you want to know my personal opinion about today's meeting, Argentineans have no chance to get a contract with us. The Uruguayans will get it for Spanish speaking countries, because they were sounder in their presentation yesterday in New York. They have much less capital, but really knew about offshore banking business. Their legal framework resembles the Swiss one."

"Guntram, cows are not as hot as you might believe. Eventually, you weary of so much meat," Heindrik told me speaking for the first time with true seriousness to me. Is there a second intention? I don't know. Who knows? Maybe Konrad finally grew tired of me, and now looks for the perfect excuse to get rid of me. That would explain why he sent me here for holidays. I stood up and gathered my papers in a folder.

"I have to organize myself gentlemen. See you later."

In a way, it fits. One night stands used to get a nice present from Monika. If your services lasted longer than a year, then a house would be more than appropriate. It's just a matter of scales, as he would say. Perhaps fighting with Repin had taken its toll on him. Business is business.

The next surprise I got was that I should ride with Heindrik and Mayer as Konrad would ride with Malú (still called Mrs. Arrieta de Blaquier), and the bodyguard. One of them will take her car home as he didn't want to let a lady drive alone in the dark. He will escort her to her house, and would go to the hotel. He agreed to meet her on Monday to visit this Arts dealer's shop.

I was mute the whole trip, trying to guess what was hiding in the shadows cast by the approaching night.

The hotel was impressive as usual. No doubt it would "meet his standards". The suite had a hall, a living room, a small dinning room (only eight people), master bedroom and a smaller one both with separate bathrooms. The assigned butler started to unpack my bag in the small bedroom. That was a clear message, I thought as I was going to sit in the living room with today's sketches. Drawing helps to keep the mind absent.

At around nine, Konrad entered in the room in a total hurry. He kissed me briefly on the forehead, and went into the master bedroom and later emerged completely changed into cocktail attire.

"Don't wait for me up. I have a dinner with the natives. See you tomorrow," he informed me almost dashing to the door.

Seems I have to eat alone, I didn't want to do it here so I called Heindrik to see if I could go outside.

"Yes, Guntram. Of course… when pigs fly. You? Alone at night in Buenos Aires? Right. The hit on your head was bigger than the doctor estimated. I'll dine with you in the suite." So we had dinner together. He was not happy at all. Don't worry I'll turn myself in early so you can go out looking for adventures, like all sailors do.

I went to bed and almost immediately fell asleep. At some point during the night, somebody shook me not too gently.

"What are you doing here? This is not your place," Konrad said slightly irked.

"I thought you didn't want me in your bed. My clothes are here," I replied tiredly. "You went out without me, and you want to get rid of the Argentinean bankers Mayer told me."

"The butler made a mistake and I have to sleep alone? For two weeks I'm sleeping very badly without you," he said upset now and sounding like a five year old without his cuddling toy.

"I'm not a damn teddy bear, Konrad. If you want to get rid of me because you're ashamed of our relationship, please do it once and for all."

He gaped and looked dumbfounded. "Have you been drinking behind my back? This is unfair. I always take you with me to the parties in Zurich, and there are people I care about. Here was a stupid meeting with congressmen. I wanted to save you the embarrassment of meeting that stupid Alvear cow. She was part of the committee."

Now I was dumbfounded. Fefo's mother in the same room with him? They hate each other with a passion. Politics make very strange bed partners. "What were you doing with her?" I shouted.

"Nothing. Business. It's over. For appearances sake, I had to give them a second chance but they blew it up. Again."

"I don't understand."

"I have almost made up my mind on a matter but I would like your opinion first. Would it be too bad for you if I back totally off from Argentina's projects in three years? I don't want to have a fight with you over this," he stated seriously.

"Since when do you consult your business projects with me? If you want to say something else, do it," I fought back.

"Since you love to make terror and complain about all the poor widows and orphans a bad banker like myself can make with his decisions," he retorted, escalating the fight one step more. Now, he makes fun of my political beliefs.

"Someone is upset because some poor but fearless devils told him the truth about his business?"

"You have three minutes to move to my bed, and you'd better be there if you don't want me to drag you there," he warned me as he rose from my bed and stormed to the other room.

Damn if I go! Damn if I put up with his crap! I jumped out of bed and went to the living room where he was hitting on the brandy.

"Go to bed Guntram. We will discuss this tomorrow," he said without looking at me.

"Which one?" I said defiantly.

"You have your orders."

Is this how you see me really? Like one of your bloody slaves? I turned around, went to the master bedroom and slid under the covers. Much later and several glasses after, I'm sure, Konrad came in and undressed himself leaving the clothes in a crumbled pile on the floor. He positioned on the other side of the bed with his back turned to me. I did the same.

* * *

Saturday 16th, 2003

I woke up with the sun very brightly shinning on top of our heads. Konrad's body was entwined with mine, and I tried to disentangle myself but it was impossible. His hold became more suffocating than before. Guess I was the chosen teddy bear.

"Konrad, please, move aside," I pleaded but he only growled as answer. "It's very late and I want to get up," I pressed. Nothing happened. I elbowed him in the ribs. He jumped like a spring and his right hand was immediately firmly clutching my throat trying to suffocate me. He released me in no time when he saw it was me.

"Damn, Guntram! What is the matter with you today?" he shouted.

"Do you always strangle your bed partners? You're crazy!" I coughed trying to regain my breath.

"Are you all right Kitten? I'm sorry. You know better than doing this to me," he said, embarrassed and worried. He tried to inspect my neck but I gave him a light shove. "Please don't be upset. I didn't mean it."

"No, of course not. You never mean anything. Shit just lands on your desk."

"I thought I was drunk, but you're still as crazy as you were yesterday. I flew twelve hours to meet you. Suffered seven stupid men, lost a whole working morning and a hundred of lefty activists just to be with you, but you are looking for a fight since we entered this hotel. If you don't like the house, just say it."

"The house is perfect. It's you who is the problem."

"Not again one of your jealousy displays!" he whined. "Should I show you my schedule so you believe me I was doing nothing bad for the past two weeks?"

"Please, Konrad. You want to finish our relationship and you don't have the courage to tell it to my face!" I roared hysterical.

"What? From where did you get that stupid idea?"

"Clear. I should have seen it earlier. I get a nice house for Christmas and now it's refurnished. It's a fantastic and generous farewell present," I said ironically.

"I changed the decoration because it looked like a cheap hotel for teenagers. You can't expect me to sleep in there. I totally refuse."

"You don't want to break up?"

"NO!"

"Why were you asking yesterday about backing off from Argentina?

"Because I don't want a fight with you! I'm very disappointed with this country's idiosyncrasy and I want out as soon as we make some profit. I intend to keep only the house—well it's yours—for holidays. You already complained on behalf of the lazy staff in that house not being happy with me, when in fact they went away by themselves."

I was ashamed at my own behaviour. He didn't want to break up and here I was starting a fight when he was generous enough as to let me come here. I kept my eyes glued to the sheets, ashamed, not able to look into his eyes any more. He cupped my face into his hands and forced me to lock my gaze with his.

"I never meant to insult you by not taking you to that dinner. I wanted to save you an awkward moment," he kissed me softly on the lips.

"I'm sorry Konrad. I'm a total idiot. I don't know why I thought that," I mumbled. Well, maybe two weeks of constantly being told I'm nothing more than a perverted old man's toy could have influenced me a little. Maria can be very persistent but I'll tell nothing to him. It would only cause her trouble.

"Is there something in the water or a bug in the air *Maus*? Why every time you come here, you get such crazy ideas? Last time you visited Buenos Aires, you were nice to me for a week and then, out of the blue everything changed, and we almost destroyed everything we have," he whined increasing my sense of guilt.

"I don't know," I whispered again burying my head in his chest, the buttons of his pyjama hurting me a little. He increased his hold over me.

"I'm starting to believe there's something here. Really. I've been in problematic places, dealt with difficult governments, but nothing like this before. It's collective madness, I think. Yesterday, no more than fifty persons were keeping hostage for hours several hundred people going to work, and the police was taking care that none of us would disturb their illegal activities. That Senator woman was telling the others that her son was going to school with my protégé, and you two were best friends and should meet again," I snorted in disbelief.

"I'm not so crazy as to do that," I rebuffed that idea. This can't be true. She despises me since day one and the whole Venetian mambo made her hate me more. I have a reminder of her actions every morning in the form of assorted colourful pills. "Please, let's go home now," I said in a tiny voice.

"Guntram, not everything is so bad. We will leave in five or six days. You can still meet your friends from school. Many of them sent letters to you in the past, and you still exchange e-mails with them. There's that priest you helped a lot. You should make an appointment with him. You have this neighbour of yours, and I'm grateful with him for feeding you all these years," he listed. Konrad grateful to George? Well that's an opportunity the man should not let escape. "Come now *Maus*," he comforted me.

"You forgot to mention the Star Wars Fan Club."

"Are you planning to bring another piece of junk home? You go there with Holgersen," I laughed. Still not appreciating true art it seems. "Let's have brunch, shall we?"

"Why are you not jumping my bones?" This is not his normal behaviour. Here is the part when we make love like crazy.

"Because if we start we're going to do it till sunset. Tonight, I'll make you mine," he said kissing me fiercely, his tongue caressing my lips, asking for entrance. I let him enter and roam playfully with my mouth. He was so focused on doing it that he didn't realise when I almost forced him to lie down over the bed. I topped him without interrupting the kiss. No chance you escape now, Konrad. I have you where I want.

My victory was short. All of the sudden he moved and I lost my balance. In less than a second he was on top of me, trapping my body with his and holding firmly my hands against the mattress with his ones. "*Strolch*! (Rascal) You will not get it this time. Out of this bed. Now!" he said his tone between stern and playful.

"I can't. You're on top of me," I clarified mustering all the dignity I could.

He let a dry laugh out and again repeated Strolch as he released me. Don't get used to the word because I don't like it. He went for a shower and I looked at my watch. 12:30! Have we slept so long? I abandoned the bed, and went to the other bedroom to change myself.

After I dressed and asked the butler to serve directly brunch (Sorry Konrad, no attacks on our cattle till the evening), I went to the dinning room, and found him already sitting there, reading the *Argentinisches Tageblatt*, a small local newspaper written in German.

"Where did you get it?" I asked, taking my usual place at his right.

"Not so bad. I want to know how some of us can survive in here without losing their sanity," he answered, his eyes not leaving the newspaper. He was reading an article on the local social organizations and cooperatives established after the new government expropriated closed and abandoned factories to give them to the former employees. Not the kind of news you break to a banker in the morning.

"Do you take holidays at some point in your life?" The butler and two other more servants entered and started to serve us coffee and setting the table.

"I declined an invitation to meet the leader of the majority. *Nur Kaffee bitte.*" Konrad they speak only English or Spanish here I wanted to tell him.

"*Jawohl, mein Herzog.*"

Great. He not only got the newspaper but the German speaking butler! Do you still dare to complain about us? I heard him telling the man to move my things into his bedroom

"I took the liberty to call your former teacher, Anneliese. She agreed to meet us with her family at five for tea. Here. During weekdays she has to work. I have a working meeting with Mayer in half an hour. You can go out with Holgersen, and come back around four. "

I knew it! He had some hidden reason to go out of bed! Here I was thinking he wanted to play the tourist with me! Well, we'll see tonight if I want to play with you at all! I smiled at him sweetly, and sighed. He looked at me suspicious. "If it's all right for you," he added.

"It's perfect. I'll go with Heindrik for a walk if it's suitable for you."

"Very well. It would be a very dull meeting. We have to wrap some investments up. He's willing to return to Sao Paulo as soon as possible."

"So everything is decided?" I asked puzzled. He asked my opinion not even half an hour ago.

"Yes. This is not safe at all. I will set a time frame of three years to sell the acquired fields, discreetly. Cows and soy beans are not my style. I prefer finances and industry."

"What about Dollenberg? Will you fire him?"

"No. He's loyal to us and has fixed the issue of his wife working for Repin. He can keep his position in London or perhaps will go to Sao Paulo with Mayer."

"Konrad, you can't blame him for what happened with Repin! He even refused to sell my things to him!"

"I don't do it and this is why he's still with us," he replied now busy with the set of mini chautebriands the butler had just set in front of him. That guy is back on his good graces again. Another servant placed a third dish set at his left side. "I asked Mayer to join us at his convenience."

I only let you twenty minutes alone, and you have already organized my life for the day, a business meeting, got a German-Argentinean newspaper, ordered my things to be moved, changed what I ordered for brunch and most probably something else I'll find out soon. I concentrated on my tea and salmon sandwiches.

A few moments later, Mayer entered in the room, informally attired with a laptop and a briefcase full of papers which he placed over a chair. He respectfully greeted Konrad and me. Both men started to speak in German and I had to make an effort to follow then as they did it so fast. Finally, I gave up. Heindrik also joined us but he remained standing at the door. I asked Konrad to be excused and went away with him.

The Swedish had with him a Buenos Aires Guide with him. "If I have to walk you better know where."

"Heindrik I lived in this city for fifteen years. Believe me; I know which bus we have to take."

"Bus?" He looked at me as if I had grown a horn on the head.

"Or subway."

"Keep dreaming," he smirked. "It's car. Small Mercedes," he intoned with satisfaction written all over his face.

"That is very dangerous, Heindrik. You know small thieves here immediately follow you if you have a nice car," I said, putting my best lamb face.

"A little of sport is good," he snorted. "Mercedes around the city or walking in Recoleta for two and a half hours. You choose."

"Walking and I would like to go to a book shop. I would like to buy some books in Spanish. You can carry them back." OK, the last part came a in a cheery voice.

"Guntram. I'm an officer from the Swedish Royal Navy, not a damn slave. You carry your things. If you can walk like you want to do, you can help," he said to me very seriously standing to his full height in the middle of the hotel's lobby and looking intimidating. Our local pick pocketers will think twice with him around.

"It was just a joke, Heindrik. I'm sorry if I insulted you," I said meekly.

"That's better. There's a shopping centre nearby. I can take you there to a book store."

"I would like to go to the one I used to work," I suggested. "It's really big and belongs to the Duke."

"I know. All right. We take Callao Avenue up to Santa Feii."

"Did you study the map yesterday? It's pronounced Santa Feee"

"Only the routes to the places you might want to go. I do my job thoroughly."

We walked up the avenue framed by the big trees and elegant shops, and a big feeling of home sickness engulfed me. I've missed it. The multicolours arrange of buses, the black and yellow taxis, the crazy car drivers expressing their frustration at the traditional traffic jam of a Saturday noon. Heindrik was strangely relaxed walking by me, not running like always and even looking at the shop windows and checking the girls very interested... and the girls looking at him also. Yes, Vikings here are a huge success because they're exotic! I noticed one really good looking girl, mid-twenties smiling softly and shyly, exactly like all Argentinean women do when they're interested.

"Careful Heindrik or before you know, you'll get introduced to her mother, and in less than a month to the Priest."

"My single man days are numbered since I visited this country. I know. All the women here are like this?"

"How? They're nice looking, yes. Local legend says it's the mix of different European types, but you should see the Colombians. They're beautiful and sexy. Be careful here. The ones you're looking here are from good families, and you will not be the first foreigner who ends up in jail for disturbing them. You see, girls here show a lot but do little, unless they're sure you're serious with them. In a disco, you'll see them dressed like European women do when looking for a night's adventure but if you touch or say something out of place, you're dead."

"Good to know. Thanks. Perhaps one of them will produce the next Holgersen," I couldn't help to laugh at his seriousness. "There's even a Swedish speaking Church here originally built for sailors," he pondered... You have it bad, man! Already thinking to pick up girls in a Church? Don't you know girls there are for marrying?

"You look much more relaxed in the city than in the Estancia. It should be the opposite. Here is the danger, not there," I pointed out changing the subject before he asked me to get girls' phone numbers.

"No, here is easier to work. There, I had more trouble."

"Why? There was nothing around. Only the staff."

"Too many security holes purposely done. Bad staff. Many bugs planted. I'm glad we're out. By the way, your dog is on its way to Zurich with Hartick."

"Sorry? Bugs planted?"

"Listening devices. Everything is cleaned now. I'm not surprised the Duke didn't want to stay there as planned. Somehow somebody was there before us. There was even a video camera on your bedroom Guntram. Amateurs job. We removed it on the first night."

"You think it was Repin?" I felt very sick and willing to throw up right there, on the street.

"No, too clumsy. Looks more like the locals trying to catch a billionaire to blackmail. All the staff with the exception of the butler, will be changed."

"Even Maria and Martiniano? Why not the other one? He's new."

"He was chosen by Mayer and checked by Goran. He's good. The others are out from Monday onward. I tell you this so it doesn't come as a surprise, and you start to fight with the Duke. It was my decision, backed by Goran and approved by the Duke. Now you can shout at me for doing my job."

"Where are they going to go? They're old."

"Retirement and don't worry about them. We have everything under control."

We continued to walk in silence up to the book store, and I was surprised it had not changed so much. Everything was still as I remembered, the bookshelves in place but the restaurant part was more professional and the waiters better qualified than us. I started to look for some literature in Spanish as Heindrik decided to show his attentions to a nice looking brunette who was looking at him with adoration in her eyes from the "Travels: Europe" section.

"Go. Call if you need assistance," I chuckled.

"I can manage on my own," he replied before going in for the kill. Good luck, you'll need it.

I was engulfed flipping through the pages of a recent history book explaining the crisis of 2001 and the new emerging social groups when somebody pulled my jacket.

"I can't believe it. Guti! I thought you were in Europe."

"Juanjo? Hi." A former school acquittance. We were in the same class but he went home every day.

"When did you arrive? It's incredible to see you here. What have you been up to?" he asked speaking fast as ever.

"I live in Zurich and study Economics there," I noticed Heindrik placing near us, but not intruding.

"Yeah, I've heard. I'm in Civil Engineering. Survived the first year; second is hard. You should see the rest of the guys. Some of us meet on Saturdays for a beer if girlfriends allow it, of course. Do you know Juan Martin will marry next December?"

"I don't know if I could. I'm only for a few days…" I trailed off.

"Give me your mobile number. You will not call me if I give you mine. Where are you staying? At Fedérico's house?"

I lost my colour. "No, no. At a hotel," I got a pencil from my jacket (Friederich would kill me if he sees I put one in the pocket), and wrote the number down.

"Thanks. Funny you're in a hotel. Fedérico was always speaking very well of you. He's working now at the Congress and in Law School. He's a respectable and serious guy after his accident. You wouldn't recognize him at all."

"I'm glad for him," I said dryly. "Call me and we'll see."

"See you later. Bye."

"Friend of yours?" Heindrik asked.

"Yes, from school. Juan Martín Brown, like the Argentinean Admiral. Very close friend to Fedérico Martiarena Alvear, the one from Venice. Wants all of us to meet. Do you need more information?"

"Sometimes you can be a true brat," he whined.

"Why do you need to know if I'm not going to go? Do you really think I want to meet all my formers colleagues from school? I never had a relationship with them, and I don't plan to start one via Skype."

"Would not be a bad idea to have some allies. You depend too much on the Duke's support. I'm not saying that you can't support yourself because you're more than able to do it, but your life revolves around him. You never know when he could change his mind."

"Heindrik what's your problem with the Duke and me? Yesterday you were almost implying he was going to throw me out," I said now upset with him.

"I didn't say that. Just be aware he's a rich man that considers you his property, and acts in consequence. Your only friend in Zurich is a Danish, whose family almost owe their asses to the Duke. The Dollenbergs are in disgrace, and I would be very surprised if you see them ever again. Us? No way. The women in your painting class? They do what their husbands say, and you know which side they'll choose. I'm only saying Guntram that you might need some friends, in case things become nasty with him. He's obsessive when it comes to you. Let me give you an advice. Always have an escape plan ready. Nobody is good and nice for ever."

"Is there something you want to tell me? Normally all of you tell me to obey and don't bother you."

"Guntram you're a nice kid; too green if you want to know. A small fish in a shark's pond. Of all the reasons for being with the Duke you have the worst: you're in love. He has slowly built a net around you to keep you isolated; golden prison. I'm concerned about what will happen to you if he gets tired or if you want to get away from him. Don't let him become the centre of your life. Come, let's go because you have to be back at the hotel at four thirty for your meeting at five. Did you pay?"

"Not yet," I answered with my mouth dry, going on autopilot to the cash desk. The girl there started to count, and I waited there. Calm appearance on the outside but a nervous meltdown on the inside.

"One hundred eighty-six pesos, sir," she said kindly, and stupid me realised I was carrying only Francs or euros with me!

"Pay with credit card," Heindrik said with a tired voice. "You see now my point Guntram? In theory, you're not supposed to be out of Switzerland or running around without us," he smirked. I gave her my credit card and French ID card and there were no problems. I signed the receipt and we went out. Heindrik gave me a hand with the second bag.

We walked in silence for about 500 metres back to the hotel, the traffic had considered slowed down at this hour.

"What should I do?" I asked him. "Maybe I should get a job."

"Guntram I don't want to take care of you inside of a McDonald's. My suits would be destroyed with that greasy stench, not to mention my reputation."

"You're right. We are unbalanced. I will never be like him."

"Why don't you sell your paintings? Many of the women there would like to buy. Ostermann would be more than happy to make an extra franc."

"I don't sell. It's not good enough."

"Guntram even before the stupid mess with the Russian, those women wanted to buy. Are you going to pile up everything till you die or throw it to the trash container? Sell them, and start to build your own account in a commercial bank separated from the others you have; something of your own."

"I don't know. He would be furious, and shout something like his own companies are better or that I don't trust his judgement."

"Tell him you want to keep track of what you make with your things, and don't mix it with the rest."

"It could work out but I don't know."

"First sell something before you worry about the bookkeeping."

"Yes, you're right. Ostermann will have to work a lot before he sees a dime."

"Guntram, don't tell the Duke I suggested this. He reacts badly when someone interferes with his relationship with you. I could lose my job."

"Most probably, he will kick you out," I affirmed

"Toss me into oblivion," he retorted half seriously.

"Your ashes scattered in the lake."

"No… he prefers evisceration," he said to me so gravely that I couldn't help to laugh as we were reaching the hotel.

Upstairs the mood was not so good. Konrad, Mayer and a young woman, Sofía Verohen, had taken over the dinning room table and transformed it into a meeting table. There were many papers scattered around, three laptops, empty coffee cups. Heindrik was clever enough as to disappear the minute he left me at the door. I greeted them and was introduced to the secretary-legal advisor.

"Guntram, could you please excuse me with your friends? I would like to finish this today as Ms. Verohen was so kind as to come on a Saturday. I'll be at the restaurant in about an hour. Start without me," Konrad said before returning to his work and not paying attention to me any more.

Guess I have my orders now.

I went for a bloody tie and a grey tweed jacket. I had to hurry if I wanted to be downstairs at five. I dashed to the door and they were deep into their things and didn't realise I was leaving.

Fortunately, I arrived before Anneliese and family. I decided to wait for her at the lobby. She was very punctual as usual, dragging her husband behind, Lucas, but no children (away in a camping site with the school). I excused Konrad and we went to the restaurant. She was nice and lively as ever. She was working as translator for Konrad's company here (not a big surprise there), and for a school. After coming back from Zurich she was teaching some Spanish to the German employees here, but from February onward classes were stopped, and she was only translating documents. We spoke about my school, my health, her children and her husband's musical career as a classical pianist (lots of offers to play, no money to pay).

Konrad arrived one hour later, excused himself, and was very nice to them, speaking about music with the husband, and asking Anneliese about her children. They spoke about the socio-political situation in Argentina, and how things were more or less returning to normal. At seven, we were elegantly kicked out by the maître. Konrad offered to go out for a drink but the husband had to go to work in an elegant restaurant as pianist, and his shift started at eight. She invited me to go to her house next Tuesday for lunch as Konrad would be busy the whole day at his office.

When they left, I returned to the suite with Konrad hoping to get some long awaited quality time together.

He sat in front of his computer to check his e-mails.

I jumped his bones devouring him with kisses and closing his laptop with a firm slap. I clung like a drowning man to his mouth, relishing his taste, smell and familiar body, all so well known but missed so much. He interrupted our kisses and looked at me as I was panting with desire.

"Bedroom," he growled. Now you're speaking Konrad. It took you twenty-nine hours.

We made love like two animals; fast and unrestrained. Not even getting all the clothes off; just what you need to do it. We were desperate. I fell asleep after my climax so tired I was after. I think he tucked me in because when I woke up with the touch of his cold fingers I had the bed cover wrapped around me and my shirt still on.

"I have to go out tonight, *Maus*," he whispered in my ear, softly and seductively.

"But you're in holidays! When are you going to spend more than ten minutes with me?"

"I promise tomorrow and Monday we will be together," he kissed me delicately on the lips and I melted. "Please don't be upset with me. I have to do this. Why don't you go downstairs and eat something with Amundsen? The Restaurant seems to be good here. Or you can ask him to take you somewhere you want."

"All right." I sighed; from one Swedish to the next. But I could really go for a pizza place I know and it's not posh. Lars is the kind of guy who would not complain about sitting with workers. "When do you come back?"

"Late *Maus*," he replied slightly, looking guilty.

"Where are you going?"

"A dinner with some politicians and bankers."

"Again? I thought you had enough of them."

"I'm withdrawing from the country but there's a chance the president pays back part of the defaulted bonds and they're looking for someone who can connect them."

"Excuse me Konrad but asking you to do this is like letting the fox in the hen house as Goran would say."

"There are many ways to earn respect, *Maus*," he stated shrugging. Well that would explain why Fefo's mother was so nice to him last night.

"Be careful. I'm afraid they will betray you. They're not to be trusted," I whispered.

"I know. I will not be involved directly. I have no interests in this. I would only make the connections. Not a single cent from the banks or the funds," he told me very seriously his eyes fixed on mine, making me shudder unwillingly. He realised it and smiled trying to calm me down. He bent down over me and kissed me deeply. I put my arms around his neck and returned his kiss. "I missed you so much, Kitten."

"I also missed you my love," I breathed into his mouth and smiled turning red.

"You're adorable. See you later. Don't drive Amundsen too mad."

I stayed in bed for half an hour longer. It was almost ten when I was ready to go out but I was too tired to make the whole trip to the pizza house. Honestly, room service was an interesting concept to try. However it's Saturday night on my own! No CEO's or bankers to visit or uptight parties to go to. If Konrad would have been a little gentler with his lovemaking technique I would be out but he was a needy brute. Let's admit it; I'm sore and tired. Maybe, I could convince him to come with me another day... we have a whole week still.

Yes. There's a pig sitting on the moon too.

I called Lars (Amundsen), to tell him I was going to eat something at the Hotel Restaurant. "No chance", he told me "All full. Order something, we eat together and then we can have a drink at the Lobby Bar."

So that was the plan and here I'm writing on my laptop after Lars has disappeared with a hot looking blond (I had to promise to go to bed as soon as I finish this and not leaving the hotel, like a good boy). I got a non alcoholic cocktail. Shit! Who's the sadist who invented this? It tastes good but it's not the same. It's a bloody fruit juice!

"Hello Guntram. Nice to see you again."

Chapter 20

"Hello Federico," I replied in a cold voice, after I recovered from the shock of seeing him standing there like nothing ever happened between us.

"My mother told me you'd be here in this hotel. I wanted to speak with you, alone. Do you want to go out for a coffee?"

"No. Thank you. Good night," I stood up and gathered my laptop. He caught me softly by the arm. Nothing comparable to the grips I get from my loving bodyguards.

"Please, stay. We need to speak. For old time sake," he pleaded me.

"For old times sake you could have saved me one drug trafficking accusation. You almost ruined my life in Venice."

"I was an asshole and my whole life would not be enough time to apologize to you. I never wanted Lintorff to get you."

"Lintorff saved your ass. Pity your mother thought otherwise and I have to suffer the consequences."

"Please Guntram. Let's sit down and speak. There are many things I have to tell you and I don't know if I ever would have the courage again."

I debated with myself if I should stay here with him, but it was the safest place of all. I resumed my seat and made a gesture for Federico to sit. I remained silent as the waiter came running to see what he wanted.

"Whiskey, and you Guntram?"

"Merlot, please."

The waiter returned with our drinks, and placed them in front of us. We were looking at each other intently—gauging us, studying us—I remained silent. He came to me. He should make the first move.

"I'm terribly sorry for what happened last March. My mother was an idiot to organize this and to fight directly with Lintorff. She knows now that he had nothing to do with the drugs as she believed. The money yes, he did."

"Good. I'll pass your apology to Konrad," I said almost rising from my chair.

"Wait. We have to clear up what transpired in Venice. Please, listen to me. Our lives are endangered. There's this man I must tell you about. He's behind all this."

I suppressed the urge to shout him, 'idiot I know already. All is your bloody fault'. "I'm listening."

He took a long sip of his whiskey. "It's not easy to say this. When we finished school, I was partying a lot and one night I met a guy in a disco. He was much older than us and very rich. He had a lot of pretty girls around and good stuff. Our party got along with his own. He was from Russia, and was buying properties in the South. He's like an Art Collector, and has many companies. His name was Oblomov."

"One day he saw one of your sketches and told me he wanted to meet you, but I refused as I didn't like him, and I believed you were not gay. He offered me money several times to arrange a dinner with you at his place in the Kavannagh building. Last time it was $250,000."

"Why didn't you give him my number? I could have sold him some paintings and this would have been the end. He was buying from me a lot last year through the Dollenbergs, and they said they told you. I needed the money."

"Guntram that dinner was not eating and going home. It was eating and fucking you even if you didn't want to. He was obsessed with you, calling you 'his angel', and pressing me to give you to him. He had photos and videos of you! He was going to watch you work at that book store whenever he was here!

"When we were to Europe I met those girls, and I swear it was nothing more than sex. When I arrived to Venice with them, he was there waiting for you. He was furious you were with Lintorff. The Russian knew him, and wanted you away from him. He threatened me with jail as we were having lots of cocaine around, but never the five kilos the police thought or the three they found. It was no more than 250 grams. He told me I should give you to him or pay with my life. I couldn't do it. This is why I fought with you that day hoping you would go away from Venice or stay with Lintorff, who looked like a rich guy."

"Wouldn't have been simpler to tell me the truth?"

"Would you have believed me that this guy was after you?"

"No. Why didn't you introduce us? I would have disappointed him sooner than you think."

"I didn't want to lose you. You were the best thing in my life."

I took a deep breath of air, and then a long sip or wine trying to calm my nerves down. I looked again into his eyes and held his gaze. "I was in love with you since I met you, but I didn't want to acknowledge it. You never realised it, so I buried my feelings for you. I couldn't stand the idea of this guy or Lintorff touching you and look now. You're his favourite toy and you hate me." His voice was almost inaudible, tears of rage or frustration came to his eyes.

"I never imagined you had such feelings for me. You were like a brother to me—nothing else. This whole thing hurt me much more than you think," I spoke slowly, old wounds reopening in my chest. Had he been brave enough to tell me, our lives would have turned out so differently.

"I wanted to die when Dollenberg told me about your attack. I wanted to kill my mother but in a way I got punished, and it was well deserved. I wish it would have killed me."

"I don't believe Konrad had anything to do with your car accident," I hurriedly said.

"He did not. It was Oblomov's doing. He blamed me for my mother's actions against you. Lintorff's vendetta was against our assets, one mini devaluation of the peso, and dealing with the guys who touched you. The whole political class turned against my mother when he nullified every deal he made that week. Everybody is terrified of him, after what happened to these poor devils! It was horrible! He's like Oblomov, but more elegant."

"The man's name is not Oblomov. It's Constantin Repin, head of the Russian Mafia. Oblomov is just one of his underlings. He introduced himself to me in Zurich, a few months ago. In May. He will not bother you again because you're useless now. He fights directly with Konrad now," I said bitterly.

"Let's get the fuck out of here, Guntram. Let them kill each other. This has nothing to do with us."

"Go where?" I snorted. "Even if my health would allow it, Konrad would destroy you and Repin probably too. But the main issue is that I don't want to go away and much less with you. I love Konrad and he loves me. You can inform Repin. Good bye."

Chapter 21

August 17th, 2003

Konrad was away as I discovered this morning. Montevideo. Will be back Monday at noon; so much for a Sunday of love together. The day is over and I'm a total wreck.

As if my meeting with that asshole was not enough stress, Konrad didn't come back at all from his dinner. After tossing in bed like crazy, I fell asleep till next morning. His side of the bed was untouched. Had he gone to the other bedroom? I stood up and went to check but he wasn't there.

Heindrik was in the living room, sprawled on a couch, dressed in a dark suit and reading some reports, looking quite professional.

"Do you know where the Duke is?" I inquired of him.

"I took him to the airport this morning, very early, like six. Montevideo for meetings; tomorrow noon, he will be back. He says I should take you around if you want. First, eat your breakfast and I'll change from yesterday's clothes."

"Didn't you go to bed?"

"No. Boss' party was up to 4 a.m. and then he decided to catch that blasted plane. He's away with Mayer, Horowitz and Verohen, the hot girl. We all had to run. You're supposed to stay in this hotel, and visit one of your friends. Blaquier. He has a party/barbecue, that decorator woman told to the Duke and you're invited. We have to be there at 1:00."

I groaned at the news. I didn't want to go!

I had my breakfast downstairs since it was no more than ten, and this thing with the butler around drives me crazy. Heindrik joined me later and the poor guy looked really tired. He was alone with me. Lars was away with Konrad as well as the other bodyguards. I took pity on him, and decided to be nice and go to that wretched party so he could relax a little. After all, the house where it is, is in San Isidro, near the gullies over the river. House is not the proper word. Better say Northern French Style Mansion with ten acre garden looking over a small private beach in front of the river. I was there for Coco's birthdays once or twice. The gardens were incredible and I could make the sacrifice of putting up with some former classmates and their not discreet prodding at my life... and sexuality because by now, I'm sure everybody knows.

"Heindrik, are you up as to drive to San Isidro? You look like you could sleep."

"I won't drive. Chauffeur. It would be good for you to see other people. Remember what I told you?"

"Yes. All right, we go. Get into something casual. They will think you're the undertaker."

"How funny you are."

At 12:00, he was ready, looking like the perfect society child. Sometimes, I believe his posh poses are for real. We took the car and we almost had a fight when I realised he was carrying a weapon. Glock. His favourite.

"Heindrik there's no need to kill the cow when we get there. It's already done."

"Never know. Let me do my job. Will you?"

"Why do you need an automatic weapon at a party?"

"Why do you carry a pencil and a notepad in your coat pocket?"

I snarled at him, and decided to look through the window. We arrived at the house on time and it was already filled with people. Not young, but mostly middle aged. Far away, I saw Malú speaking with some guests, and decided to go and say hello.

"Hello Guntram. And you brought your Swedish friend. I'm afraid you will have to help me with his last name," she said happily after introducing me to her friends.

"Lieutenant Heindrik Holgersen Wallenberg Madam, at your service."

"Is it Wallenberg like the oil company owners?" One of the men there asked, disdainfully eyeing him.

"Belongs to my grandfather," he replied shortly, making the others gape at him.

What? Heindrik comes with a silver spoon? Well, platinum in this case. Now, I understand why he is like he is sometimes. What is he doing baby sitting me when he could be doing something much better? I'll have to ask him, some time. I asked Malú if she knew where Coco was, and she sent me to the other side of the garden where "all the young people are". Poor Heindrik was caught by her, and she started to speak about how nice the fjords are, the cruise she took in 1998, etc. etc.

The young people area was a concentration of Polo Ralph Lauren True Believers... There were some of Lacoste also, but not many. I gathered some courage. Come on! They're just people your own age and you have been sitting at the same table with bankers and old European Nobility. It's just, Coco, Juan Martín, Pocholo, that one I don't remember who he is, and four nice looking girls.

"Hi Guti, you got my message! Don't you turn your phone ever on?" Coco shouted waving a hand.

"Hi Coco. Thanks for your invitation." He embraced me and patted my back with some force, exactly as he was doing in school.

"Don't mention it. My Aunt Malú speaks non stop about the Duke's house. You look much better now. Sorry you got caught in this barbecue for my father's birthday but there was no other chance to see you again."

I was introduced to the girls, all cousins of his, who were more than interested to see how I was living in Zurich, the fashions there, if I ski (yeah, with a heart condition), if I have seen some rich and famous around (not really. I'm not in Gstaad or Zermatt. I was in Davos but there are not hot guys there). The boys asked me how was school, the soccer teams (Swiss are world famous for that!), the watches (there you might be luckier) and chocolates. Finally, they got to the touchy subject we all know you want to speak about but you don't dare to ask. The girls giggled a little bit and decided to go away since it was becoming too cold for them.

"My aunt told me you live with this man. Is it true?" Coco fired bluntly.

"Yes, I live with Konrad von Lintorff. He's my boyfriend," I said firmly. Better they understand once and for all. Konrad would be furious to be called "boyfriend". He always refers to me as "consort" or companion.

Heavy silence as if they were processing the information.

"You don't look like one," Juan Martín whispered.

"How should I look?" I asked him, looking directly into his eyes. He looked down, ashamed. "Yes, I live in a far away country with a man who's older than me and I love him. How can this be a problem for you?"

"No, no, it's not what I mean," Juan Martin replied. "I know you since forever, and you don't look at all as the Guntram we all knew. Before you were shy and almost not answering, and now you look like a real prince, and hold your ground."

"My aunt was surprised that you could talk with her for so long, and that you even put her in her place when she started to hit on Lintorff. I mean, you're living with a disgustingly rich man, and before we all considered you like a silly boy; a real loser," Coco added to the previous explanation.

"I met him in Venice and we fell in love. Is that such a problem?"

"How is it?" The one I did not know asked.

"Sorry?"

"With the age difference; he could be your father according to my mother," (He's Malú's son, I remembered).

"Fine. I don't feel there is one."

"Is it serious?"

"I suppose."

"Don't you miss girls? Get one, now and then? You know what I mean." That was Coco.

"No, it would be like cheating! I love him too much to do that."

"Have you been to Geneva? I heard you can buy very nice watches there for half the price. That one you have is nice."

So that was the entire quiz. Perhaps Corina was right. I come from the highest concentration of idiots in Argentinean history.

Around two, the gardens were full of people, and I managed to get rid of my classmates and cousins. I saw far away, poor Heindrik, now caught by two women on their thirties. Not every day you see the grandchild of a Swedish oil tycoon, single and around thirty-three. I started to have a headache. Maybe championing Konrad's love was too much for my nerves. I decided to go away from the buffet area towards the big willow trees that were over the gully's brink. Nice place with some benches to sit.

I needed some time alone even if it was so cold. I removed my gloves and pulled the jersey over my fingers as I got my pencil and notebook out of the coat. I saw a small rufous colour bird jumping around. A *hornero*. It's been years since I saw one of them. It must have been looking for fresh mud to make his nest. I started to draw it and the trees around it. I felt somebody sitting beside me but I was too busy with my things to realise.

"Lintorff's main problem while handling you is not competition from humans but from pencils," that somebody laughed, freezing the blood in my veins. "Hello Guntram. We meet again as I told you we would."

Constantin Ivanovich Repin was there. I just looked at him in disbelief.

"I got your message, angel," he said softly smiling, his eyes fixed on mine.

I tried to stand up and go away, but he was faster than me and caught me by the hand before I could even stand. "Shh, angel. Don't be afraid. I will never hurt you. You don't want my men to take care of your bodyguard. It seems Lintorff has been telling you stories about me."

"Please, let go of my hand. There's nothing for us to speak about," I struggled but he didn't let me go, exerting more pressure to my left wrist. It will be bruised tomorrow. I stopped my escape attempts, and he released me.

"Yes there is. You're always very shy. Let me see what you've been doing," he said, prying my sketch book from my freezing hands. I was petrified as he went through the pages, looking at him, like an idiot. How was he here? At the other side of the world?

"It's much better than before. More free."

"Please Mr. Repin, let me go. You can keep the drawings if you want."

"Why are you so afraid of me now? Before you had no problems with my admiration for your work"

"This situation is very uncomfortable."

"Is it my line of work, angel?"

"Don't call me that."

"How should I do it then?"

"Don't. I'm sorry if you misunderstood my actions at some point, but I've never been interested in your affections. I'm in a sound relationship with another person. I don't like the way you come onto me and I don't like you seeming to spy on me." Fuck! I've just told a Russian mobster to piss off!

He laughed at answer. "You still owe me one dinner, angel. Come, dine with me tonight at my place, and we will set things as they should have been before Lintorff's meddling."

"I will never go to your place!" I shouted. "How did you enter here?"

"I'm one of Blaquier's best clients. It's logical they invite me to his birthday. That his son invited you was an added bonus. Getting rid of Lintorff yesterday was more complex. Tonight at nine is fine? I'll send the car for you."

"No!"

"Either you come, and can bring your bodyguard along—I swear I will do nothing to you—or I'll go to your room on my own, and believe me, nothing will stop me from taking you there to myself," he affirmed his eyes so fixated on mine that I felt very sick. "I only want to speak with you angel. Nothing else."

"I don't want to go. Alexei told me who you are," I slurred.

"Do you really think I would hurt you after spending almost three years of my life looking for the best way to approach you? Do you think I'm so simple that one dinner and a rape would be enough to quench my thirst for you? No. I want you at my side, willingly, and I want to see true love in your eyes when you look at me. All the things Lintorff stole from me."

"Do you think I will go willingly your house?"

"Tonight at nine. Be ready. Tell Lintorff to reconsider my offer."

"If you want to speak, you come to me. My hotel's restaurant and my bodyguard stays with me," I said seriously. He seemed to ponder for a minute.

"All right. Keep Lintorff away. I don't want him ruining things between us."

"I'll inform him of our meeting. He's my companion, and I will not deceive him."

"As you wish. Would be interesting to see what he likes more; you or his banks. From New York to here it's an eleven hour flight," he said with enormous satisfaction. "Don't try to use the time to flee the country. You will never reach the airport and your men will be killed needlessly."

He rose from the bench and left me there. I also did the same but in the opposite direction, looking for Heindrik. I found him talking with some older men and I excused us briefly. We walked away toward a secluded place.

"Big rubbish Heindrik. Repin is here."

"I know. Many Russians around. Will do nothing to you. Too many people."

"I beg to differ. He just ordered me to have dinner with him tonight, and if I refuse or try to escape, you're dead."

"These Russians are always charming," he huffed. "Did you speak with the Duke?"

"Not yet. What is he doing in New York? You said Montevideo."

"He's there. Not in New York. Idiot Repin bought it. Goran is fixing the New York issue in his own peculiar way," he sauntered. "Call the Duke and ask for instructions."

I took my phone out and dialled Konrad's number. The Swedish was not impressed at all and I was on the brink of collapse. It rang only twice till I got the usual "One minute." Great! He's busy and I have interrupted him.

"Hello Kitten. I'm sorry I was not able to say goodbye to you yesterday," he said cheerfully. It sounded so misplaced for me.

"Konrad, Repin was at the party you sent me. He wants to meet me at the Hotel's restaurant tonight because he thinks you're in New York. He says he will kill Heindrik if I try to go to the airport."

"I see. Don't worry. Stay in that party until Heindrik arranges a flight for you from the small airport downtown to Montevideo. You can come back with me to Zurich tomorrow in the afternoon."

"I don't want to risk Heindrik's life!"

"Give him some more credit. He's perfectly aware of the risks. Act normally, and let him work. Now let me speak with him, kitten. I'll see you tonight."

Frustrated and furious I handed the phone to Heindrik with a "The boss wants you," Heindrik went away with phone speaking in German with him. Those two and Repin are crazy to no end! I started to pace around trying to cool down.

"All set. We leave at five from here directly to the hotel. We stop at the 'Jorgeie Newbery' Airport, the small one from here and we take a plane to Montevideo at 6:35. Unfortunately, there's no business class available. We will have to be with the smelly mob. Excruciating."

"Are you mad? Repin will kill you. He said it. Besides, I don't have my passport with me."

"I have your passport, and your laptop plus some clothes in a small bag. The chauffeur picked then up hours ago. It would be like a romantic getaway with me Guntram, so stay close to me, and do everything I tell you. It's gonna be fun!"

"You're truly nuts! Are you planning on fooling a Russian mobster?"

"Miss the opportunity to rub it at Alexei's face for the next, let's say, twenty years? Forget it boy!"

"You're totally crazy Heindrik," I protested this time, feebly.

"Where is your sense of adventure? It will be fun. Go around a little, but don't say goodbye to anybody. Look normal."

It was horrible to engage in a shallow conversation with most of my former classmates. I was calming down when I didn't see Repin anywhere around. Perhaps he's gone and his friends also. Five minutes to five, Heindrik told me he needed to speak with me.

We walked toward the entrance door at a quick pace and in no time our car was there. Heindrik nearly pushed me inside the Mercedes. Our driver broke all the traffic rules this country has and some more. Heindrik was unimpressed. I wanted to throw up. A normal fifty minute drive was done in less than twenty-five. He left us in front of the passenger's entrance and Heindrik pulled me out of the car. I grabbed my laptop bag in the last second.

With long strides, and I almost running, he went to the help desk of the airline company to pick up the tickets. She said that there had been a mistake, and I almost died there. She only had business class available for that flight and the price was very expensive. Heindrik almost jumped for happiness, and took the tickets. No need to check in as we only had the laptops and a small bag with us.

I could have killed Heindrik when he wanted to go for fifteen lousy minutes to the VIP's room. I almost shouted at him, and he agreed to continue to the gate... with one stop to look at the saddlery in the free shop. "What? Do you have any idea how much it costs in Copenhagen? My youngest sister wants one for her mare. Relax. The fun is over."

He complained to the stewardess that the champagne was local and they didn't have Dom Perignon, not even Moët Chandon. Fortunately, it was only a forty-five minute flight.

My relief when we landed in Carrasco Airport, Montevideo was so visible that he said "I wasn't aware you were afraid of flying."

We got out and I was going to the exit with him behind when his phone beeped. He spoke briefly, and said to me "Change of plans. We fly to Zurich tonight."

"Konrad told me we were going to the city," I protested.

"No. One chauffeur will drive us to the plane, and we'll take off at eleven. The Duke still has some more meetings here."

We arrived at the plane without problems but Konrad was nowhere to be seen. I suppressed a frustrated sigh, and went to sit on one of the couches and started to write in my laptop. Heindrik did the same but before he ordered Marie, the stewardess, coffee and tea. He drank his own black coffee, and went away to the front part of the plane.

I still doubt which one of them I would like to kill first. Repin for being a crazy stalker with a lot of money on his hands or Konrad for being a crazy, irresponsible man for sending me to this stupid party, probably knowing Repin would be there because he's not in New York as the other believed, and had an "escape plan" perfectly designed in case Repin would appear. The last one, but no less guilty was Heindrik.

What happened in New York that Repin considered enough reason to make Konrad move his noble bottom there? Why was Goran fixing the mess in his "own peculiar way"? He knows less than I about finances.

My phone started to ring. I fished out of my jacket, not even looking who it was.

"Konrad, if you think it's funny for me to run after planes, and from a Russian. Well... (there I swallowed a lot of words in Spanish, German and English)...

It's not!" I barked.

"So I'm not the only one annoyed at Lintorff tonight. I'm glad you arrived safe to Uruguay, angel."

I lost colour and my soul went to my feet. "Mr. Repin. You threatened my bodyguard's life."

"Call me Constantin. I allow it. I can't deny Lintorff hasn't lost his touch, but I thought him cleverer than trying to fool me like a child. I hoped we could fix this problem peacefully, but he has declared war on me. Could you please tell him that my offer is withdrawn my angel?" he told me softly, his voice sending shrives down my spine."

"Mr. Repin... Constantin. Please, there's no need that we are at odds with each other. You frighten me, but I think we could talk this over."

"I'm not upset with you angel. I take your offer of another talk, but next time we see each other, I will not be so lenient with you. I will remove the cloud Lintorff has placed before your eyes. By the way, should I send your drawing book to Zurich?" His voice tone was gentle.

"No. Keep it," I replied hoping a peace offering would appease the Mongol.

"This is very generous. Thank you. Your style is very fresh and delicate when you work with charcoals. Somehow it reminds me of Bronzino a lot."

"He was one of the reasons I came to Europe. There was an exhibition of him in Florence at the time. I can't be compared with him. I learned how to draw copying from a book about him at the school library. Much later, I started to copy others, always using charcoal or chalks because they were easy to get. Pencils came much later when I was eleven or twelve. Watercolours and some tempera came later. At fifteen. Keeping eggs in a boarding school is not so easy. The other students used them for cocktails. Finally, I gave up with using the original technique and went for the ready made who looks more like a gouache," I told him, speaking very fast. Guntram, besides an idiot, you're crazy. Telling your "art history" to a maniac! Shit. My tongue is totally disengaged from my brain.

"Which painters did you like to copy?"

"First it was Bronzino but then Perugino, Albertinelli and some Raffaello, but not much. I wanted only to achieve their graphic quality nothing else. Later I turned into Gothic with Giotto, Daddi, Cavallini, Cimabue, Gentile da Fabriano and Fra Angelico because of the gentle beauty of the faces and equilibrium. I started to understand the use of light when I was fifteen or sixteen, not before with the Flemish painters. I could imitate it, but I did not really know how to reproduce it by myself. From Vasari and Michelangelo I liked their geometric perfection, and finally Leonardo was to admire, but not to copy; too big for me."

"You never took lessons or something?"

"Just what was at the curriculum. I copied hundreds of things before I ever draw something from nature. Maybe that's why I don't have a style, and only paint what I like; not very professional. My main discovery was in Europe when I saw the paintings by themselves. They were alive, and no photo can capture that."

"I was not wrong when I said you had a classical technique. You learned from the classics, and later you started to paint on your own."

"My first customers were the children from the slums. I used to make reading cards for them. In a way I should be grateful for the money you paid for my oil paints. It was sent to Argentina. To be honest, I think it wasn't worth it. You paid too much, even if it was for charity."

"I enjoy them very much. They're at Moscow. Why are you working with oil now when tempera would be more your style?"

"I don't know. To try it. Ostermann told me to work with it and it helps me to think before I do anything, and I can correct much better than with watercolours or tempera. I believe he wants me to paint what I feel, and get some confidence that I will not ruin the thing if I don't take care so much about technique. He says I think too much and restrain myself," I explained. When did we start to speak buddy/buddy?

"Guntram, who are you speaking with?" Heindrik shouted from the door.

"Someone from the party." Not a total lie. Don't want to start a long explanation why I was speaking for over twenty minutes with Repin.

"Cut it off because the Duke is here," he ordered me, and went away to shake his tail to the master.

"Was it so difficult Guntram? To speak with me?" Repin asked me when I returned to my mobile.

"No, but I can't do it again. Good bye."

"If my presence disturbs you, perhaps I could phone you."

"It's not a good idea. I have to go. Sorry."

"Just talking. Perhaps Lintorff and I wouldn't fight so much over you. I can't promise we'll keep our corners, but I could try." Repin tempted me. Could those two stop fighting? It's worthy of giving it a try.

"All right, but don't call me angel. It's creepy. Don't overdo it too. Bye." I hung up as I heard Konrad approaching.

Have I just agreed to speak again with a Mafia boss who just has threatened to start a "war" with my love? I'm beyond normal crazy. Lunatic. Moron. Konrad will kill me when he finds out. I realised it was the first time I spoke so much about me. Normally, I listen to the others judging me. Odd.

"Hello *Maus*," Konrad greeted me as he kissed me briefly and tenderly on the lips. I returned his kiss shyly.

"Hi, you're back." I smiled feeling a little guilty, when there's no reason at all. It was just a friendly talk! 'Yeah, he only wants talking to you' my inner voice said again. 'Next time you two will discuss the use of colour in Giotto. He's Konrad's enemy! Brother you're in so much trouble!'

"We will take off in no time," Konrad said

"I'll be glad to be back at home. I have had enough adventures for a year."

"We go to London for a week. I hope this time we can see the city together."

"But Repin lives there! I don't want to meet him!"

"Your big plan again is to avoid London at all costs? Really Guntram you should control your fears and not let them rule your life," he scolded me, annoyed.

"By the way he sends you a message: You should reconsider his offer. Could you explain what he meant by that?"

"Are those his words?"

"More or less. I'm sure he mentioned the word "offer" and consider it. You didn't answer me."

"Nothing. Issues between us."

"Issues that put me in the middle of your own private fight."

"Kitten, it's something between us. He wants something dear to me, offering in exchange something that could benefit my customers. Anyway, it's illogical to make a deal with him. He's a criminal. How can I trust his word? Once he gets you, he will attack me again, but for some other reasons. This we have to solve by ourselves."

"Should I not speak with him on neutral ground? Perhaps we could reach an understanding," I suggested.

"I can imagine it, Guntram. You go and tell him right in his face that you're in love with me, and he should disappear. Excellent idea. I haven't thought about it. Perhaps Alexei could give you some advice as how to negotiate with him when he's torturing you just because you didn't obey him," was his sarcastic reply.

Well I've just done it, more or less, and he wasn't upset and didn't explode. He laughed in my face, true. In fact he was very civil and polite in his later talk, letting me speak, and not giving me a lecture about what should I do or not do. What am I thinking? He's a killer! By definition they're neither polite nor kind! You almost have a heart attack when he sent you a book! I'm insane. There's no other explanation.

"He was very certain that you have fled to New York. Why? Is something wrong?" I asked.

"I took a commercial flight to Montevideo to pick up our jet. No chance I would let it in Buenos Aires. One of our employees there decided to negotiate with the D.A. his more than certain paedophilia charges by giving a list of our American customers evading taxes. It would have been a disaster if he would have succeed in his deal. The situation is contained. I'm sure Repin gave the D.A. the videos from this man's activities in his brothels. You can make a lot of money with children in such places," he said, this time with a tired voice and sneering.

I felt very sick.

"Guntram stay away from Repin's world. He will tire, eventually, or the costs of crossing me would be too much to pursue with this game. Give me time."

Chapter 22

August 29th, 2003

Still in London. I don't complain at all. I like the city a lot. Konrad took several days off after the New York mess (don't know how it ended, but he's satisfied, and his customers' asses, plus Sacrosanct Swiss Banking Secrecy are safe from American D. A.s) We went to the National Gallery, to some *marchands* (his suppliers, of course), to the Covent Garden once, walking around the city (much to Heindrik's chagrin but he didn't complain to his boss, and stoically endured it). It was like the planned vacation in Buenos Aires but here.

As the weather was fine (not much rain) I started to sketch at a park near the house (with Heindrik trailing behind), going back to charcoals (Friederich will kill me when he sees the stain in one of the jackets), and some strange pencils I saw in a store here. Graphitint. It's like graphite but if you wet it becomes like watercolours but with a more dense quality. I also found a "diplomatic solution" for the tempera. Ready made egg base. Not the best, but at least I'll survive Jean Jacques fury if he finds in *his* refrigerator a container with a mixture of egg yolk, turpentine and oil.

Somebody didn't call me at all and I'm glad. Honestly, I don't know how I would react. Konrad is right. He's the devil and evil comes in many disguises. He can look civil and nice, but he has no problems to have a brothel with children. I still don't know who is worse, the solicitor or the provider. Both should be boiled.

No. I should not speak with him ever again. It's a problem to big for me. If I'm returning to my old materials is because I feel more comfortable with them and it made no sense to buy oil paints when I have many perfectly good tubes at home. Nothing to do with his suggestion of using tempera... that's for children.

Shit! Children again! I can't get rid of the image of a Thai girl I saw in a documentary some time ago. Shit, he bought my portrait of the children reading! New decoration for his clubs!

I want to throw up.

* * *

September 5th, 2003

Konrad went away on business again. Our holiday was longer than expected. Almost three weeks together and no more than three or four hours going to the office or locking himself in his studio. That's spoiling me. I could get used to it.

But reality says I have to return to Zurich on the 12th to prepare for School, and submit myself to Ostermann's big shouting when he realises I didn't touch a single oil tube since August. Pencils, graphitints, charcoal, temperas on paper, some watercolours. He can't complain I didn't work; six field sketch pads of eighty sheets 9x12, plus two other more of 5x7 (one is lost, pity), and five charcoal pads of thirty-two sheets and several watercolours. The Amazonian Jungle lost several trees with me. Certainly I have bulk—quality, I'm not so sure.

371

September 7th, 2003

It was a good day until tonight at nine. I spent the whole day drawing in the park with Lars, who had a book with him. No problems at all. We returned home and I bought another sketch pad. I had dinner alone and went to bed early with Mopsi—in the basket. She knows she has to go away the minute Konrad is back—to read a book about classical mythology in Renaissance Art I purchased here.

My mobile beeped and disaster started. Why don't I look at ID callers ever?

"Hello?"

"Good evening Guntram"

Oh God, it's him. I swallowed hard and sat on the bed, throwing my book aside. "Mr. Repin it's not a good idea we talk. Good bye."

"I've seen temperamental artists before, but you are the first real case of multiple personalities," Repin chuckled, amused at my reaction.

"Please, don't call me ever again, sir," I said firmly.

"At least, you're well mannered. Normally, they shout and hurl things. Very vulgar."

"I don't want any kind of association with someone who encourages the misuse of children," I hung up and turned off the phone. Tomorrow, I will speak with Goran. Going first to Konrad might prove counterproductive.

* * *

September 8th, 2003

Everything was normal till five o'clock. After lunch, I went with Lars to Holland Park and I was busy drawing some trees totally away from whatever that wasn't the trees or the paper.

"Hello angel. It's time we have our long due conversation."

I was stunned and I never expected him to be here. With five of his goons who look more threatening than Konrad security people ever did. Two of them were holding Lars tightly and the other three made like a circle around me. Not that I would run far away as I was sitting on the grass with the sketch pad on top of my crossed legs and pencils scattered around. I gathered some courage to look up at Repin, standing there against the sun. My heart started to hammer like crazy at seeing him his men holding Lars. The Russian extended his hand to me as if he wanted to help me stand.

"Gather your things and we go," he ordered me, his dark eyes fixated on mine. I set my pencils in order in the two small boxes along with the pad. Slowly, I put everything inside the backpack I use when I'm field sketching. He didn't tell me off for my slowness, and waited with the spider's patience for me to be done. He extended his hand again and I looked at Lars for guidance. He briefly nodded at me and I took Repin's hand more fearful than ever.

One of his bodyguards pried my backpack from my hands. I didn't protest since I had bigger problems than a lost bag.

"My house is across the street, at Ilchester Place." Shit, that is like 300 metres from Konrad's house! "We'll have tea together and the I'll take you to Lintorff's place when we are finished," I took two steps away from him and the three guards closed in. "My men will take care of your escort until we have sorted out our differences. I will not be lenient with you like in the past. Now, move if you want your bodyguard returned in one piece."

I looked again at Lars but he wasn't looking at me. "All right. I will follow you," I said.

Too fast we travelled the road to his house. It was a mansion, like Konrad's but not so imposing. It was similar to one of these cottages decorated with red bricks, located in front of the park with a big garden around it, huge trees looming over the building. However, the size of this one must be bigger than ours.

One of his men opened the gate for us and we passed through the garden which was beautiful and very quiet. We entered into the foyer which was very classical.

"Would you like to have tea in the drawing room or in the garden?" He asked solicitously. I was surprised. How could he be polite again after almost dragging me by the arm—not painfully or anything—and he can be brutal because I had bruises on my left wrist for almost a week after he crushed it at the party?

"Garden if it's not inconvenient for you." Perhaps it would help me to evade the suffocating ambiance of this place.

"No problem at all," he answered and gave a series of orders in Russian to the butler there. This is the part when he asks poison for me. "This way please," he said to me starting to march toward a door, a corridor and finally the backyard where there was a table already set for tea and a butler setting the samovar and a maid some dishes with pastries.

"Please, sit down," he ordered again and I complied not willing to enrage him further. Without asking me, the maid served me a cup and put one sugar cube and no milk, exactly how I take it. That's spooky and scary. She repeated the operation for Repin but with a spoon of honey for him. Both servants made a slight bow before scurrying away.

"Is it so hard to sit in my garden and have tea with me? It's not poisoned," he said in a gentle tone contrasting the sharp tone he had been using with me before. Perhaps he was saving face in front of his underlings after being stood up in Buenos Aires.

"Where's my bodyguard?"

"Having tea with my men. I'll keep my word and your man would be returned in one piece which is more than Lintorff did with the one who left you the present in Zurich."

"I don't understand," I said turning pale as a sheet of paper.

"Just issues between us. Sometimes Lintorff and I have our disagreements. Did you like the book Guntram?"

"I never read it. I turned everything in that package to Konrad," I said firmly.

"Either you have two personalities or something happened in the middle. Not even a month ago you allowed me to call you and even spoke friendly to me. Could you explain it?"

"I have no interest in anything you may want from me or in any kind of association with you, sir."

"Constantin," he corrected me using again his sharp tone. "Why is that?"

373

"Your business repels me. The Duke told me one of his men was visiting your whore houses in New York. A paedophile. How you can do this to children and sleep at night is beyond me. It's disgusting."

"Ah, Lintorff is still sore about the Goldenberg issue," he chuckled to my utter horror. "Yes, his trader was visiting one of my associates' establishments quite frequently. I admit, I passed the photos and videos of his activities to the D.A. just to retaliate for what happened with my man in Zurich. That the man wanted to make a deal with the authorities was not my doing. But I believe Lintorff has taken care of the matter as Goldenberg is nowhere to be found. Pavicevic is very good at his job. I also don't like or approve these activities, and they're no part of my ventures, but this is a free market, and I can't force my business partners to change their livelihoods. Think this way; there's one trader and one paedophile less in this world."

"Do you freely admit you're aware of this and do nothing? That is far more disgusting."

"Lintorff is not less guilty than I because he knew for years of this man's inclinations, although he was making fantastic profits for one of his hedge funds. He did nothing till his precious customers' faced some problems from the IRS. Guntram, everybody who works for him is double or triple checked. You'd be surprise how "normal" some things are in the financial world. Lintorff tells you one fifth of what he knows."

I felt sick. Truly. Was Konrad aware of that and did nothing? Had this man just suggested he had killed two men? One for breaking into my locker and the other for selling his clients? I took a sip of my tea.

"You're not very aware of his ventures also. The Order is more discreet than me and had more time to disengage from low criminal activities and most of their deals are legitimate. Several centuries of existence gives you respect. Besides overthrowing governments, shaking markets or helping people like myself to organize our wealth, you will not catch them in something as low as prostitution or drugs. But make no mistake; nobody fools with then or with the Griffin. Crossing his path is suicidal. They are the top predators. By the way, where's this Fortingeray man? I heard he wanted to rise against Lintorff, but nobody has seen him since Easter. Even the family is reluctant to look for him."

I just gaped at him now, horrified and not truly believing what he had said. Not possible. Konrad's banks are Switzerland based. Hundreds of controls every year. The companies he owns are industries with long traditions; his hedge funds operate in the best markets. He works side by side with governments, not from small countries precisely.

"I don't remember where I read it, but it was something like the biggest accomplishment of evil was convincing mankind to deny its existence," Repin said softly. "It's ironic. Konrad and I are fighting over an issue not related at all with our empires; before we had a sound business relationship based on mutual respect."

"I can't believe you," I whispered trying to control my nerves and breathing.

"The world is more shadowy than you believe Guntram. Maybe that's the reason I like your Art; full of life and light. In a way, Lintorff and I are at a stalemate, like in the Cold War. I have enough power to destroy many of his underlings and profit from it. Alas, he's powerful enough as to destroy me with all the information he has about me. Pity he will fall along with me because he's responsible for most of my profits' legitimation. He has more power in his hands than I will ever have, but he has to account for his deeds to the Order every year, while I have absolute and unlimited reign over my assets. My only chance to hurt him is if he's deposed, but even in that case, his personal fortune would be more than enough as to back a vendetta against me."

"He's an honourable person. Not a Mafioso," I muttered this time as I was trying to understand what he had told me.

"I don't deny he has honour. He always backs up his word. I respect him. I hope you understand the situation you have placed us both."

"I? I did nothing! One day I was reading a book in Venice and the next in the middle of a police investigation with several Albanians trying to kill me or sell me as your bed slave!" I lost my temper and shouted him.

"I see now that this approach was not the best. I should have done like Lintorff. He was cleverer than I. You see, I had already tried it several times, but you never noticed me or believed I could be interested in you."

"I never saw you till the auction or knew you wanted to buy my stupid drawings!" I protested vehemently.

He laughed at me. "Guntram we met on two occasions before, and even spoke. I feel hurt that you don't even remember it. First time was at Federico Martiarena mother's birthday in March 2001. I spoke to you in French, but you fled. You were so nervous, staring at the floor, to be approached by an adult. The only thing you said was 'I've never been in Russia. Excuse me', when I asked you your name. The second time, I offered you a lift with my car, one rainy night from the university, and you almost hit my head with your handbook. It only proves that you are not from this planet. Most people would at least take a look when they're introduced to a millionaire or see a big car."

"I don't remember you at all. Anyway it's not the normal way to approach people."

"A party given by your best friend's mother is not? Offering a ride to a boy standing at 11 on the street, soaking wet, and coughing like you were in the last stages of consumption?"

"This is how you pick up street whores! Perhaps it's normal for you!"

"I told you my name and the Alvear's so you wouldn't distrust me, but you were so incensed to be mistaken by one of those street prostitutes that you didn't listen to me. You're a lousy waiter too. You never come when called and send the other stupid girl over."

"Verónica needed to get as many tips as possible. Single men always give more than women. We agreed she will take care of such cases," I murmured. Now I think I remember him: the tall foreign guy who came several times and left hefty tips.

"Then in Paris I tried to engage you in a conversation once as you were Argentinean and your country had just exploded, but you were busy, running at full speed through the city, driving my men crazy trying to catch up with you. It was infuriating! The girls you didn't look at them, and went to bed so you could go in the morning to do some more walking. I was the laughing stock of my men. Behaving like a stupid teenager or a pathetic old man trying to get your attention. At forty! By Venice, I was decided to take you no matter what."

"Perhaps this will show you that I was never interested in you."

"You didn't notice me. Then Lintorff showed up and stole you from me. That boy is responsible for that. He was supposed to bring you to me, and he gave you to him!"

"Fedérico knew very well your ways. He was a good friend, and you set him up with the drugs."

"He took $250,000 cash for his services for bringing you to Europe." He retorted upset to no end. I was speechless. Fedérico told me he tried to get rid of me to save me from Repin!

"Do you really think that kidnapping and raping me would have made me fall in love? What exactly was your plan? Fucking me and then making me paint it? Or perhaps feeding me with so many drugs that I couldn't tell right from wrong?"

"I lost my patience for the first time in many years. I was desperate and furious when Lintorff stole you in less than five minutes. I had dedicated you almost a year!"

"He stole nothing because I was never was yours or his. I'm an independent person," I said softly. I could understand his rage and frustration but never justify his acts. "Constantin Ivanovich, even if we would have met the normal way and if we would have fell in love, I would have never accepted your lifestyle. You deal with other humans' misery. I saw the drugs you sell destroying all chances poor people had to get out of the slums; ten-year-old children selling themselves to perverts for another fix. The violence and degradation it brings along. Let's don't mention your other deals." I took his hand. "I'm really sorry for the sorrow I caused you. Unwillingly, but this has to stop. Now."

"Incredible. You can live with Lintorff who's twice as much worse than I am, and you reject me because not all my businesses are legitimate. I would have never involved you in my organization like Lintorff did. You would have been always separate."

"I'm part of no organization! Konrad has no illegitimate business!" I shouted back.

"Being the Griffin's Consort is not being involved? Good to know. Being the main cause for a hidden war between Konrad and I is not being involved? Maybe you never pulled the trigger, but you made someone else do it," he smirked. "Perhaps this defence would hold in a court room, but not in front of your conscience. Tell Lintorff to reconsider my offer and perhaps, we could settle this matter peacefully, and save a bloodbath for both parties."

"And your offer is…"

"He allows you to live with me for six months. I will give him collateral, of course. Otherwise, it is total war, like with Morozov," he stated.

He's crazy. No. Both are crazy as Hell. I took a deep breath. "Let me understand this. Konrad gives you the right of raping me for six months, because there's no way I would let you touch me, and you don't start to shoot decent people down?"

"Guntram, you know I will never hurt or force you. I only want to have the opportunity to know you. The chance Lintorff robbed me. What he does with you is unnatural and frankly disgusting," he intoned looking truly revolted as he took a sip of his tea to cast away some imaginary bad taste from his mouth.

"It's the same thing you want to do with me. Alexei told me you're not going to sit and look how I paint," I smirked this time. Hypocrite!

He let a long sigh out as an answer and started to drink his tea, deeply thoughtful. "Will you not accept to have contact with me at least?"

"No! I'm here because you threatened my bodyguard!"

"By now he must be drinking vodka with my men. There's no reason to fight for them. This is why this conflict is so absurd. Nobody wins anything and we all can lose a lot. The Order and my people never had trouble before. This is why I sent Alexei to Konrad. The one protecting you today is good friends with Ivan Ivanovich. Konrad knows it, and is perfectly aware I will not hurt you in any way. The problem is that for some reason, you're very afraid of me, and nearly had a heart attack when you got my present."

"Not being afraid of the head of the Russian Mafia? Of a stalker? The man who killed a whole family because of a lost contract? The same who wanted to kidnap me? The same who almost killed my best friend?" I said in disbelief.

"The same who had tried almost everything to get to know you. The one who doesn't criticize your Art or your ways. The one who has been in love with you for the last three years. You react too strongly to my approaches, and this is Lintorff's fault because he has poisoned you against me. I never lied about my activities or denied them like Lintorff. Ask him about his business and see what he tells."

"He does not allow me to meddle with his affairs. Just understand I love him. Not you. Please don't start a war for something it's not worthy. I'm sure you could find someone better. There are hundred of artists in the world. I'm not even one," I said, frustrated with his stubbornness

"Guntram what happens now goes beyond you and me. Lintorff has ridiculed me twice in a year."

Excellent, really mature. Fucking me, literally, will restore your pride and place in crooks high society. I had a headache, and he was busy eating cookies.

"It's getting late. I would like to go now," I said.

"Yes, of course. Speak with Lintorff about my offer. You could come before the semester starts, and stay at Lintorff's house if you don't feel comfortable at my home. I'll walk you to your place now. Amundsen must be gone by now and telling to Pavicevic."

What the Fuck? I go home now.

I rose from my chair and he did the same. Without giving me the time to react he said "You truly have no idea how beautiful you are. I beg you; give me the chance to win your love."

I was speechless, and in a way felt sorry for the man. Despite he looks terrifying (no, he is) he seems to be so enticed by me, that I feel responsible for it. I never meant to play with his feelings. A true pity because if he were not a murderer, he could get anybody he wanted. He looks fine, strong, intelligent, educated and masculine. He's not dashing like Konrad, but he's not bad to look at. His misplaced devotion towards me is somewhat touching.

"If you don't want to come here or that I visit you, then let me call you. Once per week," he pleaded.

"Konrad will kill me. He's very jealous, and will never believe you only want to speak about Renaissance Art," I whispered my resolution not so strong as before. Damn, he's a bad person! Guntram you're totally insane. Say no!

"He doesn't want a confrontation with me. Let me speak with him and he will allow it."

"No, he will kill me at the mention of your name. Maybe he will really do when he finds out I was here. I must go now." I already had proof of Konrad's jealousy fits in Venice... and how he can punish you if you try to leave him, like that night in Buenos Aires so long ago, but still fresh in my memory.

He cupped my face with his hands and looked into my eyes. I was too surprised to push him away. Now that I remember, nobody has touched me in a long time (except the pulls I get from the bodyguards when they want me to move), but Konrad. "Was he ever violent with you, little one?" I turned my eyes away from his dark ones.

"It was rough at the beginning. I tried to leave him the first time I returned to Buenos Aires because of his beatings, but he caught me in less than two weeks. I don't even want to remember the punishment. But since I was in the hospital, he has done nothing to me. He has been caring and tender with me since I learned my place at his side," I confessed ashamed and wondering why on earth I told him.

He closed his eyes as if he were trying to diminish the impact of the news. He opened them again showing a glance full of pain and sympathy, like nobody ever gave me before. Not even Ferdinand.

"I had no idea Guntram. You can't return to him. If his temper is unleashed, I fear you would be seriously hurt."

"I love him and he loves me," I murmured. "He will do nothing to me," I said not truly convinced.

"For a twenty-year-old, you have almost no friends in the University or outside. You are always surrounded by his people. You never go to any place that isn't his office, the school or this teacher's studio. None of my men ever saw you in a cinema, a shopping centre or even eating out if he's not there. I've should have seen the signs much earlier," he said this time closing the distance between us more and starting to caress my cheek with the back of his hand.

"Thanks to you I can't speak with other people. Too afraid they're your agents," I complained.

"You will stay with me in this house. Don't protest. I will have none of it. Lintorff can come and pick you up whenever he feels like. We will speak about this. Ask your butler to send whatever you might need," he ordered me.

"You can't ask this. I want to go home now!" I shouted now infuriated and dashing to the door... to find it blocked by a monster of a man. He only made a gesture to return to my place. "Constantin Ivanovich, let me go back, and Konrad will not go against you. You are the first person to say you don't want a fight."

"No, he will retaliate fully on you. I've seen what he does to traitors, and he will think you're one the moment he finds out you spoke with me without telling him. Don't want to risk it. Let him come and face one of his own size. Ivan Ivanovich will show you to your room," he said leaving me alone with a monster, bigger than Alexei, looking at me intently. I stood there, frozen, like the pussy I am.

"Come boy. I'll show you to your room," his accent was thicker than Alexei's and Constantin's. "Call your bodyguard and tell him what you need. Now."

Russians are naturally born bossy guys, no matter where they come from. Exactly like Alexei, but he says please. I fished my mobile phone from the depths of my jacket pocket. I took a long breath and quickly dialled Heindrik's number. No way I will try Konrad first. I prefer the Swedish direct shouting. It's not as if it's totally my fault I'm here.

"Guntram you are late. You're supposed to be here at 7 p.m. Give me Lars."

"I can't. He's not with me. I'm at Mr Repin's house." Better be polite as I have the monster here.

"What? Are you drunk boy?" I had to put the phone away from my ear with his deafening cry. The Russian raised an eyebrow sympathetically and whistled softly.

"It wasn't exactly my choice. Mr. Repin insisted. Really. I don't know where Lars is. I haven't seen him since I got here. Repin's wants me to stay with him and ask for my things. He says he will speak with the Duke. I need my medications, you know. Tell him I'll try to call him later."

"Don't do a thing. Let us do everything. I'll speak with his Excellency. Don't cross Repin under any circumstance, do you understand me? Your life depends on it. Are you all right?"

"Yes, he has been very polite and civil so far."

The mountain moved toward me and pulled the mobile away from my hands. When I was going to protest energetically, he raised his hand making a gesture to silence me. "This is Oblomov. Bring his medications, clothes for a week, his laptop and a book, if he can read…. Look in the yellow pages," he hung up and put my mobile phone into his own pocket. "You'll get it back when the boss says so. Don't cause trouble to us or you'll regret it. Move. Upstairs," he barked for my exclusive benefit.

How on earth Luciana Dollenberg took him for an Art collector or a millionaire? I threw him a disdainful glare and with all the dignity I could muster and went inside the house.

Chapter 23

It's so late and there's no chance I can sleep even if I try it. I have already typed today's events, when I was sent to what is supposed to be my bedroom. I have my laptop, but no internet. I can't complain at all of this prison. It's big, with several windows with a garden view, bullet proof glass, a big bed with dark red damask cover, a desk with two chairs, a French marble fireplace, also marble bathroom and some pictures. One was pastel of a nude woman looking like someone from Renoir's School did it. Yes, that must be. Nobody is so crazy as to let a Renoir drawing in a guest room. There was another which was a delicious Pisarro and an incredible, it has to be, reproduction of a melancholic blue grey landscape from Monet.

Must be excellent quality reproductions because they all look almost real and alive. But such things are only in museums. Over the chimney there was a collection of five small animals, a crow, a pig, a horse, a frog and a buffalo.

"It's Bowenite with ruby eyes and the crow is obsidian. All Fabergé's. Made around 1900," the deep voice of Oblomov startled me. I didn't realise he had entered in the room accompanied by a butler who carried a suitcase and my laptop's briefcase.

"Unpack your things and see if there's something missing. Dinner's at nine. Wear a suit and tie, boy. Mr. Repin is very formal and has enough of alley cats posing as artists."

Why does everybody immediately assume I'm a donkey when it comes to society conventions? True, I space a lot, especially during stressful situations, but it doesn't mean I don't know how to behave. Lord, they took care about that in the school. I could be as crazy as a cuckoo, but I should always know what to say, what to wear and when to shut up.

I couldn't get out of my mind all Repin's accusations against Konrad. More or less what that lunatic journalist had said, but with more data. Why was Repin calling him "Konrad" sometimes? Had they been friends before? Didn't Alexei tell me that Konrad was responsible for the increase of his "legitimate" wealth (money laundering?)? Was it true that he ordered the dismissal of Repin's man? I have no proof of that; only a gangster's word.

Fortingeray. The carpet. No, it can't be. There were about fifty people in that room, all of them from respectable companies and banks! For some reason, I was sent away for the night when normally Konrad would never allow me to go alone to a hotel. The previous year, they had also a meeting till very late and I went to bed as usual. That stain was too big to be the result of a spilled glass. It was more like four or five bottles together. Wine stains are red or bordeaux and you can get them out with a special cleaner. We did it all the time at the Restaurant. Dried blood is something else and it's never really cleaned as to pass a luminol test.

No. It's crazy. Nobody in his right mind would kill in front of fifty witnesses. Fortingeray was only complaining about me! He didn't deserve such a punishment. Konrad told me he had faced the opposition from his associates before. No. "Lack of support" he had said, which doesn't mean direct opposition. Löwenstein said it had been almost like an upheaval against Konrad for being "soft" with Morozov.

I went to the bathroom to wash my face and get ready for dinner. Being late is a way of pissing people off. I placed my hands on the sink for support and felt so utterly tired. Konrad could not be like Repin. He's caring and gentle with me, sometimes smothering me. He told me once he was only nice with me, but to the rest of the world he was unforgiving and hard. With me, he can "lower his guard". By the way everybody runs in the bank, whenever he speaks and how he treated Ferdinand with her daughter's prank on me, it's true. All the bankers that I've seen approaching him, always do it with a mix of respect and fear and they're not employees. Many of them have almost as much money as him.

I went back to the bedroom and opened the suitcase. On autopilot, I started to unpack and chose a granite suit and a white shirt, as it's formal, and a blue tie. I dressed myself and was ready at five to nine.

I truly need Konrad to survive this.

The door was not locked and I was surprised. Yes, Guntram and you can walk out of here. It's just a trick to give you a false sense of security. I advanced through the corridor to the stairs and Oblomov was waiting for me. He checked on me. Thoroughly. Asshole!

"Follow me," he grunted.

I was led to the living room and left there. He has a real collection of impressionists hanging from his walls. Konrad's collection is different. You find stunning things from the XVI century onwards, lots of religious art of fantastic quality and some impressionists, but not in the "private areas". "Modern things" are in the bank or scattered around his other houses. In his private studio there's a small Rembrandt and a Ghirlandaio. Nothing post war. If he buys modern, it is as an investment. Last thing he bought was a Judith by Cranach in New York for almost a million… and a Brueghel the young for more than two million… to top it with four drawings from Tiepolo, now in his house in Venice; back to the origins so to speak. Nothing from the XIX century onward.

Repin's is different. More vibrant and modern. He has also two paintings from Picasso, something that Konrad would never hang in his house (kept stored in a special vault, which is a pity). I also saw a Max Ernst, a Miró and a Kandinsky on the corridor. This pastel looks like a Degas or a Renoir. A beautiful forest. Incredible how the artist achieved the grandiose air of trees. Almost no traces at all. Everything is suggested by his use of the shadows.

"It's a Degas. I acquired it last December. Do you like it?"

"It's very beautiful. He suggests more than he draws. You fill in the brackets with your mind. It's so simple but so complex at the same time. How could he do it?" I said in awe forgetting who my interlocutor was.

"Art is not a representation of reality, only an interpretation."

"Your collection is magnificent Constantin Ivanovich."

"Thank you. Would you like to go around the house and see more or to the dinning room?"

"As you prefer, sir," I replied shortly. Let him choose. It's his house and rule number one when dealing with these people (and Konrad too) is, always acknowledge the Alpha.

"You're my guest," he taunted me and I had to make a supreme effort not to shout at him or directly give him a well deserved punch in the face. I counted to ten before answering.

"Dinner then." Does he think I'm going to go for a tour with him? Why does he look amused at my answer?

His dinning room was... eclectic. Modern. I can see Luciana's style, but with a real budget. Old elements mixed with modern distribution and more free. Not like at Konrad's, where if the living room is baroque, everything is from that period (I think all the pieces come also from the same area)... like in a Museum. Repin indicated to me where I should sit. In front of him as he was not taking the table's head. We started to eat in silence until I refused the wine.

"Believe me, it's not laced with anything."

"I can't drink. Alcohol mixes bad with my medications and increases my blood pressure."

"Why do you take so many?"

Strange question. "I went into cardiac arrest twice during a coma due to a head injury and later my condition worsened with a misunderstanding with my medications, and finally I developed a stable angina. My doctor says that I have a previous heart condition that went unnoticed till they had to operate on me. Nobody thinks that a nineteen-year-old might be sick. I should avoid being under too much stress."

"Misunderstanding with your medications?"

"Somebody wanted to play a joke on me and put a methamphetamine in my drink, not even three months after the original heart attacks. Wasn't much, but I had to lay low for a long time."

"What happened in Buenos Aires? Between you and Lintorff. You said you wanted to leave him."

"Nothing," I started to play with my food.

"Tell me."

"I don't want to remember it. Please. You already know too much."

"Why did you want to leave?" He pressed, this time his voice was menacingly veiled.

"I was nervous and everything was too much for me. I wasn't used to living like he does, and all the important people around him were overwhelming. I missed my country, and I was afraid of the change and the intensity of his affections. He was smothering... and I felt trapped. He can be very stern, and doesn't allow any kind of deceit or play. You have always to remember your place." I said not even realising what I've done until the last word escaped from my lips.

"When was the first time he was violent to you?" he asked me, this time with a gentle tone.

"In Venice. He hit me because Fedérico made him believe he was my lover. He accused me of being a whore after his money. I can understand him now. It hadn't been easy for him with all that money. People always want to take advantage of him. I got several slaps more for not well behaved or being disrespectful. But that was a long time ago; more than a year already."

"What happened in Buenos Aires when you returned?"

"I... was afraid of his violent character and mood swings. I believed that I was in love with him, but when I was there, I thought it was just an infatuation. I feared he would kill me if I did something wrong, because he reacted very strongly to any kind of challenge. I ended us two or three days before my return date. But he came after me. He bought my flat and the book store I used to work, and kicked me out from both. He made some threats over some people I cared a lot for."

"That's not enough to make you so afraid. You were almost hyperventilating when I said you should stay here, and it was not because of me, but of Lintorff. Did he rape you?" He asked casually. I looked at him in horror remembering that night so long ago. I turned my face away quickly trying to hide the pain, shame and terror.

"I see. Standard procedure. I was right in making you stay with me. Stop playing with your food and eat."

"Your man said it would be a whole week," I said starting to eat mechanically even if I wanted to throw up.

"In principle. Lintorff and I must reach an agreement over you."

"I'm not a piece of furniture you can move at will," my tongue said before I could stop it. Shit! I have defied him directly.

"I will not turn a blind eye on this. Hurting you is unacceptable. It's like beating a child. Look, I only asked you to eat and you did it without questioning or daring to disobey. A normal teenager would shout or tell me to mind my own business."

Repin as the new Defender of morality and decency? I'm in another dimension. "You are not exactly an example of peace and love in the world," I said through gritted teeth.

"Do you think I have no morals? I'm perfectly aware who I am, but abusing your lover is evil, especially if he is like you are. Lintorff keeps you in a cage, abuses you all the time, and you still say you love him? I've never seen such a conditioning in a person. It's a miracle you can still paint."

"Don't you dare to speak about Konrad like that! We had a rough start. That's all. So far he has been loving, caring and generous to me, coping with my sickness and supporting me, despite the fact my painting is trash."

"Why are you so afraid that he finds out we were speaking before? You didn't tell him I phoned you and you gave me permission to do it again?"

"Because I betrayed him by talking with his worst enemy. I'm a complete idiot!"

"Doesn't love forgive everything?"

I didn't answer his taunt. I had enough of his playing. Now I see why Konrad hates people playing with your feelings so much.

We remained in silence, I playing again with the meat, till Oblomov, the monster, entered the room with a phone in his hand, and spoke something in Russian with Repin.

"Excuse me. Business," he said curtly and left me… with Oblomov. Big Monster sat at the table and started to look at me. Suit yourself!

"Do you have any idea of the mess we are in?"

"I? It's not my fault if your boss behaves like a small child who lost his candy. I didn't kidnap myself here or ring his bell."

Monster chuckled. "That's true also. I don't remember Lintorff so furious since that man tried to overthrown him in 88 or 89. Boss should be glad if he survives it in one piece. All because of you."

"Do you really think I was after your boss? I told him twice already I'm not interested and I'm in love with the Duke. He doesn't listen."

"Boss is a resourceful man. How's Alexei Gregorevich? I haven't seen him in a long time."

I was speechless. Is it a veiled threat or real care? No. Threat. "He's doing fine. Happy with work and personal life."

"I'm glad. Clever and loyal kid. Pity his family was so stupid. Was a good thing to have him around. Boss really liked him, and he was refreshing compared to those crazy artists he fucks. Was he not your bodyguard for a while?"

"When I was sick; he saved my life."

"Boss would be glad to hear it. I have the utmost respect for him. Too bad his uncle betrayed us. Aliosha was always a good kid."

"So good that your people tortured him to the point of death."

"This business is like that. Boss tried to make it up by sending him to Lintorff. I'm really glad he has good job and is happy. Does he have a boyfriend now?"

"Yes. He wants to get a promotion to offer him more stability. He's truly in love with him."

"Lucky bastard. He tried to talk boss out of his fixation on you, but no luck. He speaks very well of you and that's already a lot. He likes you. That Mr. Repin decided to keep you longer is unexpected and could cause problems."

Repin entered back in the room and said something to Oblomov in Russian. Both men laughed.

"Lintorff is upset but wants to negotiate. We will meet in five days."

Why not before? Shit Konrad. I want out. "Negotiate?" I said.

"The terms of your return. If he makes a move in the meantime, everything is cancelled and I'll keep you. Isn't he worthy of the trouble, Ivan Ivanovich?"

"Don't know. I like girls. With the exception of Aliosha, he's the best quality we had around in a long time. Even his paintings are good. Made some money out of one I sold recently." Excuse me? Did you buy anything from me?

"I would have bought it," Repin protested.

"Wanted to see if he was as good as you say boss. I paid $3,000 to that woman and got it out for $4,700."

"You had one of my paintings and were able to sell it? With profit?" I asked puzzled.

"Not sharing with you," he immediately answered as Repin laughed. "I bought it in Buenos Aires when Boss and I were there. The decorator woman offered it to me. Group of ballerinas. Very beautiful girls. Ethereal. Had it for almost a year till I had enough of the other men laughing at me for paying so much. It was either selling or shooting somebody down."

The butler entered and removed our dishes and brought the desert. Oblomov also got one.

"May I call Konrad, Constantin Ivanovich? He must be sick with worry about me. Just to tell him I'm fine. Please," I asked.

"No. He should trust in my word. Is your room fine?"

"It's fine, thank you. Mr. Repin, keeping me here will not change my ideas. You will only enrage the Duke. Whatever happens between us is our problem."

"Not if he kills you in one of his outbursts or gives you to his hounds for behaving like a whore. That's the punishment for repeated infidelity. First offence is punished with rape. That's the Order's way," Repin said in an emotionless voice, terrifying me more as Konrad's last words that night had been "next time you behave like a slut, I'll give you to my men for their entertainment."

"I don't know what you expect to achieve. He will not give up and I will not give in to you. Do you think I want to spend six months of my life with you, in the hypothetical case Konrad would accept your offer? This is insane."

"At least, there's someone who tells you the facts to your face, boss. Good." Oblomov chuckled as Repin took my hand and kissed it. I jerked it away, making Oblomov now laugh openly. "Good luck boss. He's a wildcat. Only saints and children speak with the truth."

* * *

September 10th, 2003

Two full days here and still three more till those two start "to negotiate". What is to negotiate? Obviously there's no money involved because both are as rich as you can be. Power? NO. I have nothing or represent anything. Love? Not sure at all. Konrad loves me, but Repin is more into this mess because he believes my German insulted and robed him of something. Pride would be a better description in his case.

I have to suffer him almost the whole day with his puppy eyes. I should have thrown that book right into his thick head. Doesn't he have some business to run? After all he owns several companies. Steel, oil and transport if I'm not mistaken. No. "I have people that do it for me. Not my thing. I studied Engineering and Chemistry at the Moscow University."

No. He sits by me and looks at me. "How I draw". With a pencil, idiot! Wants to see "the creative process". In the moment, I'm feeling very Rembrandt and we could recreate "Dr. Tulp's Anatomy Lesson" and guess who could be the main model? It's very difficult to concentrate with him around, not to mention when he smokes that hideous Russian Tobacco. I don't understand how Alexei can do it too.

I refuse to speak with him. He talks and I let him do it. He will not engage me in another conversation. Everything I said could and will be used against me. I planned to ignore him. It worked till he decided to kiss me, when I was busy copying one of his Monet's. He succeeded and I turned red with fury. Without thinking, I punched him hard in the stomach almost breaking my knuckles against it. Does he carry a bulletproof vest inside of his own house? Oblomov and he just laughed, finding my reaction terribly funny.

"Next time be more attentive or I'll drag you to my bed. Go to the kitchen and get some ice for the hand."

I went to the kitchen and asked for the bloody ice under the snickering looks from his goons, and barely contained laughs at seeing me. When I was going away with my right hand wrapped with a cold pack, one of the apes blocked my way extending his arm over the door frame. The other men immediately went serious and one of them shouted something in Russian. The Ape just smirked at me and slurred something like "wanna play pretty boy?"

"Let me pass."

"Big blue eyes of a child, full lips, perfect and soft features. Lintorff is a sadistic monster, but we can't deny he has great taste in his mounts. Exactly what I like when I'll fuck you, pretty boy," he whispered seductively and tried to touch my face. I dropped the ice pack and pushed him away, but he used my momentum to catch me by the wrists and forcibly pushed me against the wall. "You like it hard? I also."

His body pressed me against the wall as I went into full panic, squirming against him and trying to kick him hard. The Ape started to lick my neck and kiss it or better say biting. I revolved now like crazy, but he was very strong, heavy, like a stone. "One good fuck and you'll be a good bitch. Boss should have done it long time ago." I closed my eyes in disgust as he renewed his licking on my face. The others did nothing to stop it.

Suddenly, the suffocating weight was violently pulled away from me. I opened my eyes to see Repin beating that man. Furiously. Efficiently. Bloody. Not a single sound was coming out of him. Oblomov dragged me out of the kitchen and continued to haul me upstairs towards my bedroom. He shoved me in.

"Are you all right?" he asked.

"No... I mean, yes. You have to stop it. He's going to kill that man!" I shouted.

"How we fix our problems is not your concern. Did he hurt you?"

"No, I'm fine."

"It's all your fault. The men are nervous because you're here and the Griffin wants blood. They have been expecting boss to fuck you and be over. Now, stay here. Don't move. I have to do the cleaning now."

I sat on the bed. I just lost it. I started first to sob and then openly cry.

I cried in fear of Repin, for disappointment at Konrad's true activities, for knowing that there would be no turning back for me any longer and that from now onward I was a toy for both of them, for all the horror I was living in.

"Shh, don't cry angel. My men understood that you're special to me. None of them will ever bother you again. Please, don't cry," Constantin voice started to sooth me along with his soft petting of my hair. I felt his body bending over my back and holding me dear. Not sexually. It was more like when you hold a frightened child. I rose and threw myself into his arms, still crying.

"I will not negotiate with Lintorff. I will give you back to him. I can't see you suffering because of me. I love you too much for that," I could feel he was really pained, and I disentangled myself from his embrace. I looked at him with red eyes, not truly understanding what he had said.

"Angel, if I keep you against your will, I will kill all the good within you. I can't do that. I must let you go and hope that some day you will come back to me. Please, stop crying."

"Can I go home?"

"Yes."

I did then the most stupid thing in my life. I put my arms around his neck and kissed him in gratitude on the forehead.

He kissed me back. On the lips. I was so stunned that I let him do it. He started with a soft peck, chaste, soft, delicate, tasting me, his tongue softly caressing my lower lip as his hands encircled my waist and pulled me closer and I didn't protest. I slightly opened my mouth to breath and his tongue was immediately inside of me, tasting me. I closed my eyes and enjoyed the pleasure of his ministrations. He was the second person ever to kiss me so intimately, and I was curious to see how it was.

His kiss was not possessive or passionate like Konrad's. It was more delicate, reverent, as if he would be asking permission to continue. The kiss from an equal. Of a lover willing to discover what you want to do and not to take all. I kissed him back. This time deeply.

Without realising, he made me lay against the pillows and he placed his body on top of mine. I moved my hips to let him better place his manhood over mine as my hands roamed his back. Without interrupting his kisses and letting me shove my tongue inside of his mouth to savour the faint minty taste of his cigarettes, his hand went down and cupped my bottom to have better access to me. Our pelvis started to rub with each other in no time our erections met. Without even getting the clothes off he started to pound on me and I arched my neck to let him now roam it with his mouth.

We rocked each other till we both climaxed together, he groaning in my ear.

I felt so much at peace after it. Relieving tension through sex, oldest thing in men's history. It wasn't like with Konrad at all. With him is incredible and we both love it but with Repin wasn't unpleasant at all. It felt... the right thing to do at that moment. He was tenderly kissing me over my closed eyelids. I tiredly caressed the side of his face, not willing to open my eyes. I didn't want to accept the fact that I've just been unfaithful to Konrad with his enemy.

"You're so sweet my angel," he said in awe as the wave of guilt hit me with full force. He moved away from me but stayed on my side.

"What have I done?" I wanted to weep like never before.

"Shhh. We did it. I should have not taken advantage of your weakened state, but I couldn't help it. I love you too much to let this opportunity pass," he whispered, looking directly into my eyes. "But you belong to another. I know it now," he said sadly.

"I'm sorry. I never wanted to hurt you."

"Was Lintorff your first experience?"

"Yes and you the second," I whispered, blushing. Well, technically it's not completely done, but on the other hand we were not just shaking hands. Lord, how could I do this to Konrad? He has every right to kill me. I buried my head in my hands.

"Guntram we did nothing, just kissing. We both were stressed and it didn't mean anything for you. You reacted mechanically to my touch. For you, it was like kissing a friend. You can stay here if you want or if you are afraid of him. I will not let you down."

"No! I should go back to him and if he punishes me, it's his right to do it."

"He has no right to beat you or cause any harm to you," he replied completely convinced of his words. "I will not back off from my word. I will give you back to him in three days, but if you want to stay, I will accept you and cherish you."

"I can't stay. I can't live with you knowing what you do, even if you're not the person I thought you were. How will I ever look at Konrad's face knowing what I know? He does the same," I mumbled now desperate.

"Do you want my help to go away from him? I can make you disappear. To go somewhere he will never find you," he offered pulling me again into his arms.

Would it be possible to start anew? Without Konrad? No. I can't leave him. I love him despite all the shit he puts me through. It would kill him if I leave him.

"No, thank you. It's very generous but I can't endanger you furthermore," I whispered.

"I only want you to be happy. Without me if necessary."

He broke my heart. The poor man was in love with me, and I couldn't return his love at all. Friendship at best, but this would be pernicious for him. "I can't accept your offer. I have done enough to hurt Konrad for a lifetime. I could never be more than friends with you but this will hurt you more."

"I hope Lintorff realises what a treasure he has," he said as he hugged me, placing my head close to his heart.

We remained like that for a long time.

Chapter 24

September 13th, 2003

Tomorrow, I'll go home if Konrad wants to have me, that is. Guilt is gobbling me. No matter what Constantin says, I know I sinned with him. That is my own doing. I didn't stop him and went all the way with it. I will have to tell and face the consequences.

The last three days were strange. Odd. After our affair, we both fell into a terrible shyness. I would try to hide it by plunging into my drawing and he by hiding in his own office. He would creep in on me at the most unexpected times. Several times, I almost jumped to the roof, when I found him standing beside me and looking at me as he couldn't believe I existed.

"Why did you like my first drawing? I asked him once, during dinner.

"Oblomov and I went to this Real Estate company. I didn't want to be known, and he was playing boss for a while. Should not do it often. He might like the job," he chuckled. "Anyway. He had enough of looking at photo houses and left the desk and started to walk around while I continued with the folders. He went to the next office, where he saw a landscape, pencil and ink made, and was transfixed. Yes, there's not other word. I was curious and went after him and I also liked it a lot. It had such a serene beauty. Without asking me, Oblomov wanted to buy it for himself, but the woman said no because it belonged to her husband. He offered up to ten thousand dollars, but no success. She offered to ask her husband or to find out if you had something else to sell. She told us you were just out of school, and I believed it was beginner's luck that you could achieve something so good at only fifteen years old. I thought she was making fun of us, the idiotic new rich Russians."

"Several days after, she called us and said that her husband didn't want to sell. Oblomov was also now bitten by curiosity and wanted to see the place you have painted and offered to buy the house they had for sale. I was almost dragged there because he was very insistent, making me lose a full day's work just to see some paintings from a brat. I mean, nobody who is fifteen can do something like that."

"I think you exaggerate. It was just a landscape."

"Let me finish. We went to the house and Oblomov liked it and wanted to buy it for himself. The Dollenbergs had found some more works from you and had then into a folder. Chronologically ordered. Oblomov liked several and offered to buy two or three. The ballerinas he told you about, a landscape and some children. I had to wait till he finished choosing what he liked, because I was still playing employee of the month," he growled and I laughed. Somehow I can't imagine Konrad and Ferdinand on the same situation. "When I got the folder, I was stunned. It was not beginner's luck at all. All of them were good and they looked as coming from someone with sound academics behind, not from a teenager. I asked them if this was a joke because this was the work of a seasoned artist."

I burst into laughter. "Sorry. Please go on."

"Anyway I said to Oblomov to buy the rest for $5,000. I ordered him to make a full investigation on you. Everything they said was true. You really were eighteen, and working as a waiter. I fell in love the first time I saw your picture in a report. You were not only physically beautiful, with classical features, but you had the kindest regard I've ever seen. I always preferred men to women, and had many more than I can count, but with you, it was like seeing everything for the first time. A week after reading the report, I took enough courage as to go and see if you were real."

"I spent a whole morning looking at you. You were even better in the flesh than in photos. Even if you hadn't been the artist I liked so much, you alone were worthy the effort of trying to get you." I blushed deeply. "Either you don't work much or it was a very slow morning because I saw you sketching something on a paper napkin and leaving it on the counter. I took it and it was the same hand that had drawn the other pieces. Since that moment, I needed to have you, no matter the costs or the consequences."

"Next day, I came back but you were not even noticing me. I left a good tip to that stupid girl, hoping she would tell and you would come when called. Don't go into the catering business. You're a really bad waiter. Being polite to the customers is not enough. They want their orders fulfilled."

"As this technique wasn't working at all and I had to go back to my business, I ordered a full investigation on your environment. Friends, school, work. There should be a way to get to you. I learned everything about you. Four months later, I started to work on the Alvears. We both met at that god-damned party and nothing. Then in October, I tried to pick you up with the same result. Nothing. This is when I offered the money to Martiarena Alvear for bringing you here. I pressed the Dollenbergs into selling me something more or establishing contact between us, but they didn't have any clues where you could be. It was so frustrating!"

"I had no idea. Honestly, I never saw you," I whispered feeling very guilty.

"It's part of your character. How can you live in another galaxy, and still make such beautiful and deep things is inexplicable. I could have killed Lintorff for taking you so easily. Oblomov said you were a little whore, worthless of my time and I tried to believe it for some time. A month. I found out that Lintorff wanted to establish an operational base in Buenos Aires and I bribed the man he had there, Landau, into showing him the Dollenbergs' house. I was hoping they would make contact with you again and I would have a way to reach you. Lintorff had placed a very strong security net around you. You were always with him or in his house in Zurich. Never alone. It worked and I got many of your things over 2002, but all my efforts to know you were fruitless."

"Around Christmas, Luciana told me you wanted to meet me but Konrad didn't allow it. He said Oblomov was a ghost, that there was no rich man in Russia with such a name, that it was somebody else and he should introduce himself with his own name. You should have written an introductory letter to him. He can be that old fashioned."

"He doesn't know Oblomov? Hypocrite! They know each other for more than ten years! Oblomov convinced him to take Alexei!"

"This Morozov business truly scared me. Why did you do it?"

"That was really Morozov trying to overthrown me. To his credit Konrad didn't help him. He kept his word to me. They both started to fight like crazy. Lintorff is like a bulldog. Once he bites something, he doesn't loosen his jaws. The whole thing went out of scale when he had the domestic front rebelling against him. There he made me personally responsible for that. I had to eliminate Morozov to pacify him."

I was overwhelmed and remained silent for a long time. Konrad not only knew Repin, but they had some sort of "gentlemen's agreement," in their business. Some kind of non-aggression pact. It was more than some money laundering and free advice on stocks what was between them.

"Guntram, promise me that you will count on me if he becomes nasty to you. If we can't be lovers, let's be good friends."

"I don't know if it would be good for you. I would like it, but it's not a good idea. We should split our ways now."

"I can survive it and I would like to see your art now and then. Have a talk. That's all."

"It would be good to have a friend," I admitted my voice full of doubt. "But you two are enemies."

"I realise now that I can't get you romantically involved with me. I have no further claims on this issue with Lintorff. If he wants peace, we should achieve it. "

* * *

September 14ᵗʰ , 2003

Konrad is gone. Furious.

He's right, but I should be also furious with him. He has been lying to me for almost the last two years. If it's a matter of trust, then we both have issues and reasons to hate each other.

At noon, I saw from the window of the living room the familiar shape of one big Mercedes limo and another black sedan. I left what I was drawing and dashed to window to look at him. My heart was jumping with happiness to see him. A big ape rushed from the other car to open the door for him and there he was. Impressive as ever... wearing a blank expression in his face. Goran came out of the car, behind him.

"Guntram go upstairs with Oblomov. Lintorff came with Pavicevic. Not a peaceful sign." Constantin ordered me softly. "Go, now. Whatever happens between us is our business. Not yours."

I gave him a light hug and kissed him on the cheek without saying anything. I do hope he finds someone who can love him. He gave up on me for my happiness sake. Not many would do it.

Three hours later, the butler came in and told me to go downstairs. Konrad and Constantin were standing in the foyer. Both had stern faces, not looking at each other.

"Come Guntram. We go home. Now," Konrad said with his temper barely in check.

I advanced towards him very afraid.

"Lintorff! Remember what I've told you. One word out of place and I will act," strangely, Konrad forced himself to calm down and just looked at Constantin with real hate in his eyes. "Good bye Guntram. It's been a real pleasure to have you here," he said extending his hand toward me.

"Good bye, Mr. Repin," I said shaking his hand briefly.

"I'll send your drawings to Zurich."

"No. You can keep them, sir."

"Thank you."

I turned around to Konrad, and he just started to walk toward the exit with me running after him. One of his men opened the car's door and he entered with elegance. I did not, but managed to be inside before the engine started. I sat next to Goran, who was more serious than his normal grouchy look.

"Hello Guntram. It's good to see you again," Goran greeted me. Konrad just looked at him, deadly, but he wasn't moved at all.

"Hello Goran. It's also good to see you," I whispered.

I noticed we were not driving to the house but direction to the highway. I wanted to ask where we were going, but Konrad's enraged face was enough incentive to make yourself small and disappear, dunking in the leather seats.

"Are you all right?" Goran inquired. Yes, the first person to ask about me, because Konrad didn't even say "Hello" to me. I looked at him and saw real concern in his eyes.

"Yes. Repin kept his word. Didn't do anything to me," I whispered.

"Good."

"Where are we going?"

"Home. Zurich. Or have you already forgotten where you live?" Konrad barked at me. I kept quiet for the rest of the trip to the airport.

He had the Dassault ready for us. Without waiting for the driver to open his door, he got out of the limo and went in a straight line toward the plane's stairwell. I stood, full of hesitation, by the car till Goran softly touched my elbow.

"What happened in there? Why is he so furious?"

"Furious? He's a good natured kitten now. Should have seen him last week." Goran smirked. "As for your question. I don't know. Repin kicked me out. It was the two of them alone for three hours."

"Did he ask for something?" Giving me up didn't mean Constantin would give up to gain something in exchange. I'm so stupid!

"I don't know. Now move. He's waiting."

The ambiance was no better inside the aircraft cabin. Konrad was perched on his usual seat, reading papers. He didn't bother to pry his eyes from the documents as I sat in front of him. Goran went to sit on the farthest corner of the plane. I waited for him to make the first move.

And I waited. We took off. The stewardess served us some coffee and mineral water and vanished. I waited for forty minutes more and nothing. Well asshole, if you think you can pull the silent treatment you gave Ferdinand, I assure you it's not the case. All right, I kissed the guy. It was wrong and I'm really sorry for it, but you made me believe you were a law abiding citizen.

"I'm also glad to see you again Konrad."

"I have to work," he grunted for an answer.

"Just tell me this. Did you two reach an agreement? I don't like to be in the middle of your private war. It's not good for any of us."

"What does it mean to you if I go to war? It's my privilege to decide so."

"He's a honourable man—yes, honourable despite he's a Mafia boss—who had the misfortune of falling in love with the wrong person. He understood it and gave up on me."

"It's the first notice I have from Repin being a nice man," he retorted sarcastically, giving me a disdainful look as if I were the village's idiot.

"Exactly as you are," was my sweet reply. He half rose from his chair and crossed my face with a hard slap. Not a punch, but painful nevertheless. Goran was immediately up with clear intention to murder Konrad.

I rose my hand to the offended cheek. "Considering your work on Landau and Fortingeray, I should be grateful it was only that." Konrad looked at me and a flash of terror went through his eyes. Very fast. "Yes Constantin told me about your joint ventures in the past, present, and who knows, future if you two arranged a visitation schedule."

"He's Constantin now?" A dangerous and sarcastic edge laced his voice.

"Yes. Before all your midwives come with stories, I'll tell you. I kissed him three days ago. On the lips. Nothing else. That, convinced him I was not interested at all."

He launched at me and this time gave me a punch in the plexus. I bent down holding my mid-section trying to lessen the pain and recover my normal breathing. Goran was there in no time separating us and even gave him a punch in the face. They both shouted enraged at each other in Russian.

"Do you want to kill him? It's not his fault! He just saved your House by stopping this war!" Goran roared getting ready for a bigger fight "Whatever happened is between them. We all have enough of this bloodshed my Duke!"

Konrad gave him a big punch in the face. "Respect your Griffin!" Goran didn't retaliate and bowed his head in submission, like a serf in the Middle Ages.

"I obey and follow my Griffin," he said humbly falling on his knees. I couldn't believe it, and I looked at them both, gaping. Konrad extended his right hand to him and Goran kissed it, like you do with a king or the Pope. "My life is devoted to him."

Konrad withdrew his hand from Goran's, and readjusted his jacket, looking at me as he sat in his chair. Goran went away, with the stewardess, I imagine.

"I suppose all French men have a little whore in themselves," he commented, his voice full of contempt. That hurt me more than any of his punches. "Get out of my sight."

I sat where Goran had been sitting before for the rest of the flight. Looking through the window and wondering if I haven't done the second biggest mistake of my life by not accepting Constantin's offer.

I realised something else. I was not afraid of Konrad any more. Constantin had cured me of that when he showed me the game and the real person Konrad was. The uncertainty was what terrified me most, but it was away, leaving only sadness behind.

We rode with his car back home. Goran was left behind with an imperial gesture from Konrad. We didn't look at each other the whole trip. It was almost seven when we arrived to the Castle. It seemed somewhat strange to be back. I was away for a month but it felt like a lifetime. Visiting Argentina is never a good idea for me.

Friederich was waiting for us at the entrance, and I was very happy to see him. I had to repress the urge to run toward him and give him a totally inappropriate hug. I stood in front of him, and weakly smiled. He immediately looked at Konrad, his dark mood more sombre than before. Finding out you're a murderer wasn't exactly the highest point in my life.

"When will his Excellency have dinner?" Friederich asked breaking the heavy silence as we entered inside the house.

"I'm going back to Zurich. I'll sup there," was his sullen reply. He turned around and left us. I saw him through the window going to his car and catching the poor driver completely unaware. He didn't wait for him to open the door and entered by himself into the limo. The car started and left the house.

"May I see my dog? She must miss me," I whispered feeling worse than before.

"Certainly Guntram. She's in the kitchen. I'll bring her to your room."

Konrad's room was exactly as I left it, I noticed as I removed my jacket and shoes. I was too tired to care about formalities. In my studio, someone had piled up all my sketch books and individual paints from the last month. I sat at my desk and started to go through the big watercolours made back in the *estancia*. Most of them were landscapes, some studies of people working and children playing. There was a portrait of a young woman holding her baby both looking at each other lovingly. I wanted to make it later with oil paints. I noticed several spots on the image as if someone would have shaken a brush against it.

No. Those were tears. Konrad's, as he's the only one who has access to my stuff. I felt a horrible pang of guilt and I wanted to cry again, but I refrained to do it as I heard the light and fast Mopsi's footsteps on the corridor and her scratching over the door. I opened it, nearly tripping over her, jumping and placing her paws on my trousers. I bent down to pet her and she was more than glad to see me.

Friederich came in after her, bringing a tray with tea and some toast. "You might be hungry. The men told me neither of you had lunch today."

"Thank you, Friederich."

"What happened?"

"Honestly I don't know. He and Repin locked themselves in the library for three hours. Repin gave up any claims on me and told me he wouldn't start a fight with Konrad, but I don't know if it's true."

"That is very good news indeed. Why is he so upset?"

"I told him I kissed Repin once. He exploded in the plane. Pavicevic prevented him from beating me. I still don't know why I did it. One of his men tried to abuse me in the kitchen and was becoming violent when Repin caught him. He started to beat the man and Oblomov took me away. He said that everything was my fault and that I would start a bloodbath between the Order (there Friederich flinched), and Repin's organization. I know what the Order is now. Repin told me everything. I started to cry like crazy. Repin found me and told me he would give me back to Konrad because he couldn't stand the idea of hurting me. He said he loved me so much that he preferred living without me than making me suffer. I jumped to his neck and kissed him in gratitude. He kissed me back, this time for real and I let him do it. After the kiss he said that we could never be more than friends. That it was clear for him that I was in love with Konrad."

"I see. He might be upset, but not to the point of hitting you. No, it's something else."

"He said I had a little whore in me, like all French do," I said bitterly.

"Did Repin say something to him? How did he greet you when he saw you?"

394

"He only said "come Guntram" very sternly. I was taken aback and Repin told him something like 'one word out of place and I'll act'. Do you understand this?"

"Repin has something big against him, and will use it if he deems it necessary. Not good at all. I'll have your dinner ready in half an hour, and then you can go to bed. You must be tired. Did you take your pills?"

"Repin wants to make friends with me. What should I do?"

"The Duke was very concerned when he took you away. I think he played all possible scenarios through his head. We didn't know what he would do to you. The police found Amundsen's body in a lake near Edinburgh. They are Mafia and Repin is a cold hearted killer."

"He told me he had sent Lars home! He said he was friends with Oblomov!"

"Now you know the meaning of the word 'friend' for them. Be very careful with him. He has only taken two steps backward, but he has not given you up. If that were the case, he would have immediately returned you to us, never asked your friendship or threatened the Duke if he is ever mean to you. Repin is very clever, and more twisted than the Duke will ever be. He's only trying to win your trust and affection."

Chapter 25

September 24th, 2003

Konrad still hasn't returned, given a call, or answered any SMS. He just doesn't talk to me.

A few days ago, I went back to school. Heindrik continues to be my bodyguard despite it's not needed any longer. After all, we're in peace with Repin. I think Constantin is right. Heindrik's work now is jailer as he has to take care I don't move an inch from my assigned place in this world because there's no real threat to me any longer.

I went back to the studio with most of my work for the summer and immediately I had all the women crowding me, and looking at the things. Meister Ostermann had to shoo them away, so he could evaluate my work. The Van Breda woman wanted to buy one of the watercolours, and immediately another wanted the same also. Like children, they all wanted to buy and started to "fight" jokingly around them, causing a ruckus.

"Ladies. It's impossible with you," Ostermann scolded them. "We're not at a Bloomingdale's sale, please." All the women laughed happily. "If Guntram agrees, I can select a few of his works. The good ones, not those when he's wasting paper in an effort to make me believe he works dutifully," the ladies laughed much louder as I turned red. "We can make an auction with them; students only, let's say next week. The winter is nearby and I need to increase my nuts stocks. I'm an old man," he joked.

I had to agree with his crazy idea as the women were truly happy about it. Ostermann selected around fifteen watercolours and graphitints and was upset I didn't want to give the "mother and child" because it was ruined with those stains. Not really, I think it belongs to Konrad for some unexplainable reason. Yesterday, they had their party/auction and I stayed in my corner, painting because their shouting was too much for my nerves. Ostermann should have not given them champagne with their tea.

"Here Guntram. Was not bad at all." Ostermann got me out of my rapt as I was working on Marie Amélie's portrait, detailing the hair. "She looks also nice, but take care of the table better. The roughness of the wood is still not completely achieved. You can do it better," he said extending me a gross envelope.

I opened it and saw a lot of money inside. "What is this?"

"Your part of the sale. I take only cash. 22,452 francs. The one with the cow was a real frenzy. Didn't know you had it in you. Almost 10,000 francs. Go, your man is about to fall asleep on his feet."

"That cow was to throw in the trash!" I exclaimed shocked. Didn't Alexei keep it or throw it?

"Are you crazy? I would have bought it had I not been the auctioneer! You're normally so serious. It was a most welcomed surprise to see it. It's wonderfully hideous!"

I have the money in my backpack and I don't know what to do with it. Maybe I should do what Heindrik's suggested; open my own bank account. In an institution separate from his own.

I need to speak with him. It's 9 p.m. Maybe he has some free time now, unless he's at a business dinner or meeting the locals wherever he is. It would be logical, wouldn't be? I cheated on him and now we can consider the cheating season officially open. I took my mobile phone and wrote for the hundredth time; "May I speak with you?" It took him half an hour to write back "NO".

We're communicating, right?

I don't know what the fuck I'm still doing here. It's almost ten days since the fight. If he wants to break up and hasn't the courage to do it face-to-face, he should send a message with Monika. Perhaps I should do it. I can't return to Buenos Aires. There's nothing for me there. Perhaps I should go somewhere else in Europe or the States. I could get a job and start again. I'm almost twenty-two and used to work—should not be difficult. It's very clear that he will not forgive me. My mobile phone rang, and I dashed to answer it without looking at its screen.

"Konrad?"

"Not what I was expecting, but I should be used by now to this"

"I'm sorry, Constantin. I was expecting him."

"I wanted to see how you fare. Is everything all right?"

"Constantin it's a bad idea we speak. As a matter of fact, Konrad does not speak to me because I kissed you. Sorry." What on earth makes me always trust this man and speak with him like with an old pal?

"You told him? Guntram, honesty is virtue everybody desires in a relationship, but avoid at all costs. Frankly, it was a stupid move, dear."

"It would be worse if he finds out by somebody else. He's very upset. Furious. Doesn't speak to me. I don't think he will ever forgive me. This time I screw it up badly."

"If you want to go somewhere to think about it, you can use one of my houses. Just tell me and somebody will pick you up."

"That would be an even worse idea. No, thank you. We have to fix this by ourselves. If you come in the middle he would be more than furious with you."

"It's true, but it's nothing I haven't seen before. Take care, and don't hesitate to call me if this becomes too much."

"I will. Thank you. Good bye."

"Until then, Guntram. I will call you again. I'm concerned about you."

I checked again my phone but there were no lost calls. The "NO," is real.

＊ ＊ ＊

October 1st, 2003

He hasn't called me yet or shown any signs of life. I have enough. I've tried to resume my life with the school, and doing some painting, but it's useless. It's driving me mad. Not even a message through Monika, Ferdinand or Friederich. Nothing. *Nichts. Nada.*

Constantin called me twice and we mostly spoke about my drawings and going to an auction at Christie's. He found very funny the auction and the mess with cow's kitsch portrait. He said Konrad had been more than incensed when he saw my paint of the reading children in his library. The dogs are at his office in San Petersburg and the women in Moscow. He lifted my spirit a lot.

I can't continue like this. I'm going away tomorrow. If he doesn't have what it takes to break up, I'll save him the problem. I'll go to Geneva first and from there where the train takes me. I don't know. Must be somewhere in France because I have to ask for a new passport. Mine is in the safe box, and I don't know the code, and Konrad will not speak to me. I can get a new one relatively easily if I go to the police station and denounce the loss.

I tried again to call him, but not even a "NO" as answer. I have enough money left from the auction to survive a few months till I find a job. About $20,000 cash. The best is if I leave him an e-mail or a letter. No, e-mail is better because the letter could be lost and Konrad might worry. I snorted at my own imbecility. Worry? He doesn't pick the phone up, asshole! I can be truly stupid.

Anyway. E-mail is better.

"Dear Konrad"

Guntram you are an Asshole. Yes, with uppercase! You don't write "dear" when you're sending someone to Hell. Write a simple note... and not too many words because maybe he will not read it up to the end.

"I'm sorry it didn't work between us. I never meant to hurt you with my actions. But I can't live like this. I go away this time for good. You will never forgive me, and even if you would do it, I can't live with you, knowing what I know now. You can't stand the sight of me and this is your house. It's logical I leave. If you need my signature to close any accounts, please tell Monika to contact me and I'll give her an address to send the papers. All the other documents are on your desk. Farewell. Guntram"

That should do. I'll send it from the University before evading Heindrik. We'll see who's better. You with your Seals Training or I with lots of experience in running away from teachers or policemen in the slums.

I gathered all the papers I had from the University and Bank along with the house deed and credit cards. I don't know why I put the mother and child portrait there also. I took the backpack I use for my painting stuff and placed my laptop inside, the money, my family's photo album, pills for a month and some underwear and two shirts. I don't need more, and frankly going around with Henry Poole's bespoken jackets is noticeable if you are around hostels.

* * *

October 3rd, 2003

I still have it in me. Almost two years of pampering haven't destroyed my ability to evade the authorities... well Heindrik and his boys. Yesterday morning, I went to the University as always and let the Swedish do the whole thing he wants to do. Went to the first class and at 9:34 I was out of the classroom and in front of the University entrance waiting for 9:38, the moment the bus to the train station stops. I had to run to catch it but I did it.

I bought a ticket to Geneva and I was on the train. My mobile rang furiously. I answered it.

"Where the fuck are you?" Sweet Heindrik yelled on the phone.

"In a train," I replied.

"I imagine, you idiot. Get your ass down on the next station, and wait for us there. If the Duke doesn't kill you, I'll do it myself, little prick!"

"I thought Swedish Royal Navy Officers had better manners. I'll send you a postcard." I hung up. Yeah, Heindrik must be pretty mad at me and Konrad, he can fuck himself.

Well, it's also goodbye to you GPS phone. In Geneva. I wrote down Constantin, Goran and Ferdinand's numbers. I turned it off.

In Geneva, I bought a ticket to Avignon. Paris brings me too many memories, and Avignon looks like a nice place to think a little before going somewhere else. Perhaps Spain or the North of France. I looked at the departure timetable, and I saw there was a train on platform 6 leaving for Munich in thirteen minutes. Phone, perhaps you catch the leftovers from Oktoberfest. I turned it on, and saw twelve missed calls.

As I was quickly walking there—this coat is very warm—I checked from whom the calls were from. Seven from Heindrik—must have a lot to tell me—two from Goran—not good. He must be very pissed off. Probably Konrad blames him, and that's bad because Goran is a decent fellow, two from Ferdinand, and one from Konrad. Wow, I was impressed. He knows how to dial a phone. For a split second I thought of returning his call, after all sending an e-mail to your lover of two years, isn't very polite. What should we say to each other? He would curse me five generations backward, and tell me to come home… to what? To sit and wait for him to forgive me? To wait for him to beat me for my gruesome infidelity? Fuck you!

The phone started to ring again. Speak of the devil—Konrad. I answered as I entered in the train.

"Everything is on top of your desk," I said dryly.

"Guntram come home. We can speak about this, Kitten. You understood all wrong," he asked me in a soft voice. Kitten? Well this one has some claws and in the moment is like a wildcat or a rabid badger.

"The time for speaking is over. I'm through with getting the door in my face. Good bye!"

"Guntram it's not safe for you. You have a heart condition! Tell me where you are, and I'll send somebody for you," he sounded as he were pleading. I smirked at my own idea. He? Pleading? No chance.

"I'm losing my train." I hung up. It's almost the truth! Phone has a date with a big jug of beer. I put it on silent mode and left it in one of the seats pockets.

I still had an hour before my train was leaving. I went to the McDonald's. It's about three hours journey to Avignon and TGV prices kill you. As I was eating, I remembered a little detail in the whole story. Constantin's threat. Maybe I should do a last favour to the Order. Yes. I don't want to have in my conscience the outcome of a fight between those two. I should call the Russian ASAP meaning, after I finish this.

I looked for a paid phone and dialled his number. Somebody answered almost immediately in Russian.

"It's Guntram de Lisle. May I speak with him, please?"

"Hello Guntram. This is a surprise."

"Hello. Is it a good moment to speak?"

"With you it's always good. Is everything all right?"

"Yes and no. I left Konrad by my own will. I had enough of this situation. I only wanted to let you know that there was no violence or shouts. It's just over. Don't blame him for this."

"Did he let you go?" he asked, incredulous.

"I took a train to Geneva, and in twenty minutes I'll take another one."

"Don't do that. It's dangerous for you. He will find you if you stay in Europe. Tell me where you are, and someone will get you to a safe place till you decide what you want to do."

"No, thank you. This I have to do on my own. Goodbye Constantin," I hung up and this time went to my own platform.

It was dark when I arrived to Avignon, and I took the bus from the station to downtown. It left me in front of the wall, and I started to walk around, looking for a place to stay. Finally, I found a small hotel for €35 the night. The woman was looking insistently at my clothes. I guess women know better about clothes than us, because she asked several times if I wanted to stay with them or preferred to go to the Grand Hotel nearby. I paid her for three nights.

The place is not bad. It's small and austere, but it's clean and I'm so dead that anything would do now. The bed squeaks when you move and the tap on the sink looses water, but I don't care. I want to sleep and sleep.

* * *

Today I woke up very late, like twelve. I was more tired than I thought. It's Friday and I should hurry if I want to ask for a new passport. I dressed and went out of the hotel to the police station.

I explained to the very young and nice policewoman that I was living in Zurich (I have the residence) and I've lost my passport during my holidays in France. She said that it was no problem to get me a new one, but it wouldn't be ready till Wednesday or Thursday because it should come by post from Paris. I filled out the forms as she asked me a lot about Zurich and if it was nice to live there. Was she flirting with me or just being nice? I don't know, but at the moment I have my mind elsewhere.

It was already late to visit the Castle so I wandered around the city and bought a small sketch pad. I had the graphitints with me. I ate a *panini* and took some notes over the Castle from outside. As it was becoming colder and darker I went back to the hotel.

The old lady in charge of the reception asked me if I was going to dine in the hotel because there was only onion soup and *ris de veau á la financière*. No complaints on my side. I can eat it. I asked her if I could stay in the living room because the light was much better than in the room and she agreed. I stayed there detailing better one view of the castle using only brown colour.

"It's nice and looks like the original. Dinner is served," she said some time later.

The dinning room was also the hotel's bar, deserted at this time, and it comprised of several small tables that had been put together to form a large one. It was so like in the forties. The hotel served dinner only once per day. No restaurant at all. At the table there were four more men, two of them travelling salesmen (do they still exist? It seems so), one a truck driver and a bank manager visiting small companies—normal people. All French speaking. One of them found very funny, that although I was making some grammar mistakes, my accent was good. I guess I've taken it from my father.

Hearing the men's conversation was soothing for my nerves. I mean, it was a normal talk. Wives, children, work, how to make the money last till the 28th. Nothing like what I could hear in a dinner with Konrad and his friends.

I've been writing here in my room, and probably I'll go to bed soon. In a way I'm more relaxed than the previous month but the sadness is overwhelming. I realise now that I will never see him again, and how much I need him holding me. But it's over. I screwed it up. I was so confused and lost that I trusted Repin, and that was a mistake. I would love to undo what I did, but it's impossible. I have to live with it and without Konrad.

I still can't really understand all what Repin told me about Konrad. A part of me doesn't want to believe it. It can't be true. He's a good person. He has a horrible temper but he never was mean to me. Violent, yes. The last year he was the kindest person I've ever met. I hurt him deeply but he also did it to me with his silence about his activities.

On the other hand, how do you say it? "I had a meeting with my staff, and then with a Drug Lord who wants to invest" or "Yes, Landau was a mole and had to be put to sleep." There were so many signs and I ignored them. For that I'm responsible. That old fox, zu Löwenstein, made the things look perfectly legal, and I bought it because I wanted to. Because I love him and couldn't bear the idea he was not perfect.

I go to sleep now. There's nothing to do now. It's over.

* * *

October 7th, 2003

Still in Avignon waiting for my papers. They should arrive tomorrow. I think I'll go to Toulouse or Bordeaux. Both are big cities, and finding a job should not be a problem.

I try hard to forget Konrad, but it's impossible. I attempted to copy some buildings, but it was useless. Everything is mechanically done and his face keeps appearing in front of me. I found myself yesterday sketching the contours of his face. Shit! Then I started to copy a bloody griffin from the Gothic palace. I nearly jumped on top of man who looked very similar to Konrad. Yes Guntram, as if you EVER saw him wearing jeans, snickers and a fluo jogging top.

I have to get a grip on myself.

Chapter 26

October 17th, 2003

It's a very bad idea to write a diary. I know it now. I should have never keep this stupid writing, but it always helped me to cope with the stress of the day's events. All this is too big for me. Two years ago, I was a nameless waiter, attending a small university, and thinking I could make a difference in other people's lives. But all went to Hell the minute I came to Europe. How right was my father to send me away. This place can only bring misery despite its shiny and glamorous cover.

I'm back. Zurich. Not by my free will. Living again with Konrad.

Morning October 9th, I got my new passport and decided to take the train to Paris and Brest. I had all my things together and I went to the bus stop when my path was blocked by nobody else than Goran. I was stunned as my heart started to hammer like crazy.

"Easy Guntram. It's just me. You know me. I wouldn't hurt you," he softly spoke, advancing like a wolf toward me. "Come here, little brother. You must return home. This is not safe for you," he continued his hand going to the pocket of his big trench coat.

I panicked at his gesture and turned around to flee but two dark haired men in suits blocked my way. "Relax boy, don't make it harder than necessary," one of them said to me. I looked for another way of escaping but Goran was already literally on my back

"Guntram there's no need to do it the hard way. You can come with us, willingly, and save all of us a lot of trouble. The Duke wants to see you. He's concerned about you," he told me in a soft and calm voice.

"No, I'm not coming back to him!" I shouted, turning around to face him. Stupid move because now I had my back to the other two.

"Hard way it is," he told the other goons, dejectedly.

Before I could understand what he meant with that sentence, I felt one of the monsters holding a smelly rag against my face with a very strong grip. I fought against the man, but I started to see big black points till I knew nothing more. Goran caught me before I hit the ground.

At some point, I woke up, and I think now, that I was in a plane because the seats looked very much like those, but it was not Konrad's. Goran was immediately by my side, and said softly. "Not yet little brother. You have to sleep a little longer. We'll be home soon," I felt a prick on my left arm, and the world started to turn around, and I had to close my eyes not to throw up.

The next time it took me very long to open the eyes. My whole body ached even if I was lying on something very soft, and well tucked by the covers. I had a strange metallic taste in my mouth, and was so thirsty. As if I would have been walking on the desert. I opened my eyes and realised that I was in Konrad's bed, dressed in my own pyjamas, sleeping on my side.

I pulled the covers aside, and tried to stand up, but I was still very dizzy. I had to grasp the bedpost to avoid falling hard. Stumbling, I went to the bathroom. After drinking some water, I felt much better, and went to look for some shoes. My slippers were exactly where they were supposed to be. I went to the door expecting to find it closed but it was open. I went to the common area and noticed that Konrad's studio had the light on. I took a deep breath and knocked on the door.

"Come in," I heard Konrad's deep voice.

I entered the room, still needing to have contact with the wall. I looked at him and realised to my utter horror that he was reading the contents of my laptop. My diary. I closed my eyes to hide the sudden need to cry at this. He had been going through it at his own will. Now he knew everything. I never felt so humiliated by someone.

"Go back to bed. It's cold for you. I'll join you later," he said without looking at me. I stood there motionless gaping at him with a horrified look on my face. He's an obsessed monster, exactly like Constantin said. I wanted to die right there.

"Are you hungry?" I shook my head. "Go to bed now. You need to rest."

"You read my diary," I stammered.

"Yes, twice. I needed to clarify what has been going through your head in the last months, what you've been doing and the depth of your entanglement with Repin. Your diary was the easiest, and less painful method for you. Go back to bed. You are in no shape to argue," he said this time giving me his blank stare. The one which tells you'd better obey.

And I did it. I retraced my steps, and went to bed, tired and dizzy, but unable to sleep. Sometime later, he came into the bedroom, and violently took his jacket and tie off, throwing them over a chair. I looked at him, and he held my regard for a long time as I felt his fury creep into his eyes, becoming more and more real.

"You read my diary," I repeated, unable to stand the tension any longer. He put his watch rather strongly on a small desk and advanced toward me as I flinched on the bed. He crossed my face with a strong slap, much harder than the one he gave me on the plane. I fell to one side of the bed and started to sob.

"You did more than kissing with that piece of shit. You spoke with him on several occasions. The only thing preventing me from killing you now is, that you refused him twice even if it meant your freedom, and that you truly love me. In that regard, you never lied to me. We are in peace now," he shouted heatedly.

He finished undressing and put on his own pyjamas. He got into the bed and I curled on the farthest possible corner. He caught me by the waist and jerked me toward him, his arm trapping and suffocating me. I squirmed but the strong, warning squeeze I got, forced me to remain still.

"Didn't you want to be held? That's the last you wrote. Be quiet and sleep. We'll talk tomorrow," he ordered me in a lower voice.

I stayed there, unmoving and trying to control the growing fear inside of my heart.

* * *

The next morning, he was still there in bed with me, holding me within his grasp, deeply asleep. I tried to separate myself from his body, just an inch, and that was enough to wake him up. He let me go and I turned around to see his head propped on his hand, watching me like the predator he is. I turned my eyes down.

"Get showered and dressed. Meet me in the living room," he said curtly. For a second I though in defying him, but I knew it was useless. He always has the upper hand.

I rejoined him half an hour later in the small living room where the table was already set for breakfast. He was reading something on his computer, this time. As I was standing at the door like an idiot, Friederich entered and smiled softly to me.

"Good morning Mr. de Lisle. Are you feeling better?"

"Yes, thank you Friederich," I replied completely shocked with the man's casual voice but secretly happy that somebody was nice to me.

"Sit down Guntram. Don't stall like always." Not everybody was nice. I did it after Konrad barked at me. The butler served the coffee and tea and I got a dish with this *Bauernfrühstück*, with less bacon than the normal one. "You had nothing yesterday, child," Friederich whispered into my ear.

I felt very alone and lost when the old man left the room. I started slowly to eat because I was not hungry, but, on the other hand, I didn't want to enrage Konrad any more. I know already what he's capable to do to the people who cross him. Even Russian mobsters think twice before "crossing the Griffin's path". He just drank his black coffee, and I felt his eyes boring holes into my skull as I ate with my head down.

"Running away like this was extremely dangerous and stupid. Did you really believe that you could escape from me? Foolish boy. I can find you no matter where you hide. It's just a matter of time."

"You were not interested in me any more. I saved you the trouble to kick me out," I defended myself.

"I'm still interested, as you say, in you. You're the Griffin's Consort as you're aware now. Your place is at my side. Whatever issue we have between us, is to be solved in private. This was one of the first rules I set for you. You cheated on me by letting yourself be entangled in Repin's cobweb. That is enough for a severe punishment. If I did not speak with you for some weeks, it was because I needed time to calm myself down before I would decide an appropriate punishment for you."

"Running away was stupid. Your acts could have been mistaken for a betrayal, and that would have been your death sentence. If I would have not executed you, then the associates would have done it. Nobody leaves the Order. You belong to it and to me. I appreciate you called Repin off my back in order to avoid further conflicts."

I looked at him in horror. Executed as in death sentence?

"It's very fortunate for you that you like to chronicle so much. It has saved you a great deal of pain as we were looking for the truth. Frankly, none of the interrogators would have believed your version, because your naiveté is impossible to understand. But all the entries in your journal have been done at the time the computer shows. So far, the other associates haven't found out that you were missing for six days. The official story is that you were visiting old friends in the south of France, and travelling like a student."

Interrogators? I felt very sick now. "Is it true what Repin said about you?" I almost cried out.

"Yes. Essentially. I'm the Griffin, and I was brought up for this since I was seven years old. My entire life has been devoted to my family and to the Order we helped to restore in the XVII century. I am what I am and it can't be changed. I've always kept you away from my business because you were not properly educated to be one of us. You have nothing to do with us, and your role is only as a personal companion for me, therefore I'm responsible for your acts. You are a part of my house and line now. You're allowed to live and pursue an artistic career if you want as long as you follow my commands."

"This is insane. I never knew what kind of monster you were!"

"The *Fürst* zu Löwenstein explained to you what was expected from you, and you agreed. You were informed of our activities in Russia, and you accepted them. You have given him your word to support me and help me raise my children. You will abide your promises to us."

"Why do you want to keep me at your side? I don't want to stay with you! I was unfaithful."

"Kissing and speaking with Repin is a serious affront but not enough as to call it an infidelity. There are some mitigating circumstances like the fact that you didn't initiate it, were under considerable stress, and bought his scene with the bodyguard assaulting you so he could be the man who saved you from a rape, one of your biggest fears, if I'm correct. Also you never said anything about my activities to Repin, and constantly declared him your love for me."

"I never lied when I said I loved you," I muttered sadly.

"I'm certain of that now and this is why I'll give you another opportunity if you want it. Bear in mind, that outside these walls there's no possible life for you."

"I don't understand you," I said desperately. "You're so convinced that you love me or at least desire me, but you have just threatened me with killing me if I don't do what you want."

"Welcome to the adult world where love is not picking daisies and singing birds," he mocked me dryly. "You have the opportunity of living with me and fulfilling all your dreams. Would you reject all that only because you judge me with a middle class mentality? We are rulers, therefore we are above such laws, made for ordinary people. My responsibility lies on the fact that all my decisions must be carefully evaluated before making them. Would you tell that Karl Otto, Barbarrossa or Claudius were murderers? No. They were leaders. When I was invested Griffin, a huge responsibility was placed upon me. I don't even own the title. It belongs to my line and my children. I'm not a criminal like Repin. I don't exploit children and women nor sell drugs or weapons."

"No, your customers do it. You and your associates profit from it."

"Do you really think that if the Order were to disappear from this earth, all its problems will end? No more drugs, no more gangsters, no more prostitution? I'm afraid not. We can control these criminals, and many times I have had to stop these people from doing more damage than necessary. They fear and obey us. Where we live is relatively safe, compared with other places in the world. Go to Russia or to America where the likes of Repin rule. We helped in this continent's reconstruction. How many times have you witnessed my companies taking risks in order to save people's jobs or lending money to others who should have been destroyed according to free market rules? Do you know how much money we have invested in East Germany or Central Europe? The Soviets left them in shambles."

"You are no ruler, just a businessman with more money and power than anybody else. Nobody elected you."

He laughed. "We elect the people you happily vote later Guntram. If I were a simple businessman, things would be much different. For example, if I were only looking for profit, there would be hundreds of new designer drugs around. Young people love them, they're cheap to produce, and the dealers would be more than happy making enormous profits and in need of our advice. But no, I don't allow them. There's a limit to what they can do."

"You even make it sound as honourable," I smirked. He didn't like my remark and fulminated me with one of his looks.

"Albert and Ferdinand were right. We should have informed you after I had decided to keep you. Unfortunately, your poor health condition prevented us from doing it. Now that you know it, you must reach a decision. Stay with me and accept your place and duties or you'll be eliminated. I promise your passing will be as painless as possible."

"You're a monster. How could I ever loved you?" I whispered.

"I can give you twenty-four hours to make your decision. On Friday, is zu Löwenstein's wedding anniversary and we are both invited. Either you come or you don't at all," he said with his blank expression. "Guntram, you don't have to be a part of our activities. I never wanted you to be. You have placed me in a very difficult position. I love you with all my soul, and I need you at my side more than ever, but your running away and repeated contacts with our enemy, almost label you as a traitor. Repin knowingly condemned you by telling you about our ventures. We can't let you go away now. What he did was a clear move against me. He's perfectly aware what your death would mean to me."

"How would you do it?" What morbid fascination made me ask it? I don't know. I was on the brink of tears.

"A strong sedative and poison. I'll do it myself as nobody has the right to touch you. In a few months I'll follow you. There are things that need to be arranged beforehand. I can't live without you and I don't want to do it."

He was serious about it, like I've never seen him before. His hand reached mine and took it, taking it to his lips and softly kissing it. "There's no life for me without you. When Repin took you I was plunged into desperation. Those six days without you, thinking all the things he could have done to you, imaging he could kill you, not knowing if I would ever see you again, were pure hell. I hate the fact that he found the perfect word to describe you: Angel. You are the light in my darkness. God sent you to me. There's no other reason I got you. You are the only good thing I've ever had."

"Can't you just let me go? I'll never tell anything. I don't want also to hurt you. I can't."

"I can't let you go. Your existence would be miserable, and your death horrible. All the others would go against you, and I could not protect you because I would be dead. We are together in this. Think in all the wonderful things we could do together; the children we want," he took my face with his hands. "You can give so much to the world, not only with your art. In a few years, you could take Gertrud's position in the Foundation and make a real difference with the resources it has. Don't destroy everything."

"I don't know if I could love you knowing what I know," I whispered feeling the temptation to give up stronger than ever.

"I haven't changed. I'm the same man. Maybe you need time to discover me again."

"The man you are is not the problem. It's what you do. What you stand for." My resolution was faltering more and more.

"We will not go away Guntram. I'm the best choice in the moment. Löwenstein told you that you'll play a great role in the next Griffin's education. Perhaps you could change our ways, but I can't promise you anything, but my endless love."

"I don't know what to do. If I stay, I will be accepting all this and causing a war with Repin. I don't want it either. I went away because I thought you hated me, and also because Repin threatened you."

"Leave Repin out of this. He's my sole concern. Do you still love me?" He asked me desperately, his eyes full of sorrow like a child fearing to be rejected.

"Yes," I replied without thinking twice or blinking.

"Stay with me. Please," I nodded my accord and half rose from my chair to kneel in front of him, burying my head in his lap seeking comfort and refuge. He briefly said "No, no, you don't do that, you're my consort," and pulled me up forcing me to sit on his lap.

I laid my head this time on his shoulder and put my arms around his neck. His arms encircled my waist with a strong and vicious grip pulling me closer to his body, almost suffocating me. He moved his head backward changing the angle so his lips reached mine and kissed me deeply, ravaging my mouth as I tried to match his passion. The need for air made us split and I was gasping raggedly when he smiled to me. Soft and lovingly; with adoration. I couldn't refrain myself to replicate. He kissed me again but this time briefly. "I swear I'll dedicate my life to making you happy, Guntram."

I didn't know what to answer so I just nodded again. "I will love and respect you."

"No one should come between us ever," he said firmly.

"No. I've learned my lesson. It's you and I."

"For the moment. When the children arrive, it'll be over. They get in the middle always, and you can't say a thing about it," he chuckled nervously, to my astonishment.

* * *

We spent the rest of the morning together. First, sitting in the library, he reading his papers, but checking on me almost every five minutes to see if I was still there, pretending to read a book. He even allowed Mopsi to be in the same room with him, and sleep curled on top of the sofa, next to me.

We had lunch together and he informed me that tomorrow we should go to the Löwenstein's Fifty-years Wedding Anniversary as he was also related to them. I should be relaxed and stick to the story that I was in France with some friends from Argentina. My new security arrangements would be discussed today with Goran—I shuddered remembering his role in my kidnapping, and how cool and calmed he had been about it—and him. "Goran is very good at what he does", Repin told me once.

Yes, I had proof. How did he find me? He and Heindrik should have been furious with me.

At three, the Serb came and our meeting took place in the library. Konrad let him do the talking all by himself. He didn't waste his time with reproaches or shouting at me, and I was grateful for that. Konrad's morning talk had been more than enough.

"Not telling us your exact location was a huge breach in our security procedures, Guntram. From now onward, we will have to be more careful with you. Heindrik's team has been relieved from its duties. You're directly under my responsibility. Of course, I can't take care of you personally as I have many duties to fulfil. Two of my best men will do it, and they will respond to me. Personally."

"What happened with Heindrik?" I asked. I never wanted him to lose his job or his people. Guilt was hitting me again with full power.

"He's transferred to another section. Amundsen's death was enough proof of his incompetence, not to mention being fooled by an untrained boy like you," he said firmly.

"Goran you're not fair with him. Amundsen's dismissal was Repin's doing. Not his. You were not there like I was. He intended to kill him all the time as retaliation for whatever happened with his own man here, the one from the book. He fooled me with his promise of releasing him. Heindrik risked his life for me in Buenos Aires. I know more about evading authorities than you imagine."

"Only one bodyguard with you? That's irresponsible and a huge break in the procedures. He claims that Amundsen wrote that morning that Oblomov's people were away from London. Repin doesn't like to leave loose ends, it seems. This will be a good reminder for our own men. We're dealing with scum, Guntram. Holgersen is still with us. Explain the last part. Now."

"When I was working in the slums, I met our local drug lord. He was very paranoid, but he liked me and told me about his business, and how to evade the police." Better be honest with Goran.

"Pity he didn't explain you about not using your own name in front of the police. Asking for the new passport gave you away. The rest was very nicely done," he huffed upset, making me more afraid than before. Do they have access to official databases? This is government's only stuff.

"Milan Mihailovic and Ratko Bregovic will be your bodyguards. You met them in Avignon," I was now terrified. Those two were not bodyguards, they were trained assassins! "You will continue with your normal life, going to school, the same specifications as before still apply and to Ostermann's. Repin's move in London was bold, but effective, and we can't allow it twice. Your phone conversations with people outside our circle will be listened to, and recorded, and perhaps your personal files now and then will be checked. The Duke has still to make a decision on the matter." I lost my colours.

"No Goran. It would not be necessary for the moment." Konrad intervened softly.

"So you're warned. Every talk with someone other than the Duke, Mr. von Kleist, Dr. Dähler or myself would be listened, and if something is amiss it would be reported to me."

My mind was frantic trying to know if this was possible or a bluff. Do they have that technology? Don't you need a judge to authorise this? Yes, Guntram. They will ask a judge his opinion. Idiot! Does it make any sense to protest?

"You have no right to do this Goran," I grunted half furious.

"It's for your protection. You're almost labelled as a traitor within the inner circle. You have to prove your loyalty to us. His Excellency has gone through a lot of trouble to cover your own stupidity. Next time you want to do something like this, ask the professionals first," Goran retorted without flinching.

"Guntram, it is as Goran says; for your protection. You place too much trust in human nature; all this problem arose because you believed Repin's obfuscations." That was Konrad's turn.

I kept quiet. What else could I say? I have no privacy left and have to obey them if I don't want a bullet in my head. No, some cyanide in my tea.

"As I was saying, this whole mess remains between us and Mr. Von Kleist and Dr. Dähler. Holgersen and Hartick will keep their mouths shut as they don't want further problems, and are glad with this new opportunity they get. The official story is you got this invitation from friends and went to the South of France for a week. Is it clear?"

"How many?"

"Sorry?"

"How many friends did I meet there?" I asked tiredly.

"Two. Don't make it too complicated. You can fill in the details. Would be better if you make it up and not us. Keep it as close to the truth as you can."

"Good." Goran, really. I know how to lie. I've been doing it to myself and other people all my life.

"Mihailovic and Bregovic are to be trusted. We are brothers in arms, if you are familiar with the concept. We were together in Krajina during the war. Do exactly as they tell you. Repin's men are afraid of them like they're of me. If they're around you, they will prefer to defy the Russian before us."

"Repin said that you're very good at what you do," I muttered truly sick. I googled once Krajina, and that was one of the places where the Serbs tried to settle the score with the Bosnians and Croats (well, with all Muslims or non-Serbs). The largest cleansing episode of the whole war from both sides, and the biggest black market of all. That area was always conflictive "The Border"... against the Ottoman Empire, and a few crazy Serbs contained one of the biggest armies in world history for several centuries. Almost like Taliban.

"Milan and Ratko will take service on Monday. Any questions?"

"No. Thank you," I replied, the last part coming automatically out. This is now a real prison. There's no way I could ever escape those two. Konrad says all this is for my protection, but this is his punishment for betraying him. He will never trust me again.

"Guntram, go upstairs. You look tired. Goran and I need to speak." Konrad's voice took me out of my dark reverie. I obeyed and rose to my feet, ready to leave. Goran also rose and extended his right hand. Was this his way of asking forgiveness for what he had done or just sealing a deal? I didn't know. I shook his hand, because after all, he's following orders from Konrad or the others. Knowing his background, I'm perfectly aware he could have beaten me to a pulp, and then said that "I tried to evade them" but he was gentle with me all the time, and even fought against his boss in my behalf.

"We all must make sacrifices in order to keep things running, little brother. Do your part and we will do ours."

"I will follow your men commands." He just nodded his acknowledgement and let go of my hand. I left the library, letting them to their own devices.

I spent the rest of the day in my studio with Mopsi. I think she realised what was going on because she spent the whole time sitting on my lap softly whimpering. I was in shock, not really knowing what to do. I had agreed to live under Konrad's terms and he will make sure that I'll follow them. I felt like an empty shell. Crying was useless because it would solve nothing or allow me to escape. Going to Repin was a worse idea—suicidal and homicidal.

A soft knock on my door made me jump. Mopsi was immediately at the door scratching it. I chided her and said "come in," It's not really necessary to knock any longer. I have no private space left. Everything I say, write, see or read would be "reported". I'm a traitor now.

Friederich entered with a tray with tea and cookies. I wasn't really hungry or willing to speak with anybody, but, on the other hand, I didn't want to be alone any longer. Anyone would do.

"Please stay with me, Friederich. Only for a while," I asked him when he was about to leave.

"You have spoken with the Duke, I see," I nodded unable to speak again. He sighed as he sat on the chair across my desk. "You're in a difficult position now. I don't believe for a minute you had any desire to harm or betray him. You should have talked to me much earlier. Nobody knows his Excellency better than I. It's very hard for him to speak about all what he knows or feels. The incident with Repin pushed his endurance like never before. Not even when we had the problem with his former "lover" (deep disgust at the use of that word). That Russian is a criminal of the worse kind. He's educated and highly sophisticated. His movements are unpredictable. Konrad was completely taken by surprise when he kidnapped you. He never expected a move like this. Kissing Repin woke many ghosts from his past up. I believe he went away so he could chase them away by himself. He blames himself for your actions, and reading your diary, and finding it so full of love toward him, destroyed all his balance."

"Did you also read my diary?

"No. Only the Duke. He blames himself because he knows it was his fault you were in such a vulnerable position. You were absolutely unaware and this spider told you in the most possible shocking way and the little charade he organized for your benefit, almost forced you to do it. During the month he was away, he would call me once per day to see how you were doing."

"Why didn't he answer my calls?"

"He couldn't. He was ashamed for what happened on the plane; for not fulfilling his promise to protect you; for not telling you what the Order was about."

"How could you stay knowing this? You educated him. He says you're like a father to him."

"I did a good job if I compare him with his ancestors. He reserves violence always as the last resort, and it's never meaningless. You're unfair if you judge him like a normal person. He didn't choose to take this place in the world. He inherited it, and did his best to make it better for the next generations. He can't afford the luxury of being soft-hearted outside these walls."

"Konrad's life was always very hard. First, his mother never liked him because he was much better than his older brother. Konrad did everything a child could do to please a parent, but he overshadowed his brother in the process. Karl Maria was a nice creature, but not as intelligent as he is; weak and unfit to become Griffin. His father decided to pass the title on to Konrad after his sixth birthday, when he was already showing his character. The Duchess hated the younger brother for it. Konrad, on the other hand, adored his brother, and remained mute for a whole year after his death. He did nothing else than working harder than before and be silent while his parents fought. The former Duke divorced finally to avoid any further damages on his surviving son. Her own mother blamed the child for causing his brother's death with his will to do everything perfect."

"But he was only a child! Konrad only told me his mother made his father's life a living hell and blamed him for his brother's death."

"Never mention the Duchess, Guntram. He supports her and her lifestyle, only because she was consort of the previous Griffin, and his father never took the title away from her. Later, he fell in love with this man and his constant infidelities left a deep wound in him."

"But Konrad knew he was married with a child!"

"That was not the problem. The wife was someone from our circle, and he respected her a lot. It was the many others his lover had. He knows he can't place all the blame on you, but his memories of a bitter time pushed him to react how he did. He went away in fear he could hurt you. When you ran away, you placed yourself in enormous danger. What if Repin would have gotten to you? It was the perfect opportunity for him to catch you. What if the other associates thought you were betraying us and took the matter into their hands? What if you were a real traitor like the other one? That idea is what was killing him more than your kiss with that lowlife."

"Friederich I swore I would never do anything knowingly that could hurt him. I wasn't thinking straight when I did it, and I told him so he wouldn't find out by somebody else. I accepted his punishment and, never denied him the right to do so, but he never answered me. I thought he hated me, despised me, and wanted me out. I thought this would end Repin's interest in me. I never went to him or asked for his help. Repin said I was responsible for many of the deaths on both sides."

"Whatever happened was Repin's doing, not yours. Anyway, you have to prove your loyalty to the others now. To the *Fürst* zu Löwenstein and the older advisers, to Dähler, to von Kleist (I closed my eyes in pain at the mention of his name), and he's the most enraged with you. He has been looking for evidence of your betrayal to Konrad, of your involvement with Repin, but he found nothing. Fortunately, the Duke convinced him to stop before he would have taken the matter into his hands. Pavicevic and I were the only ones at your side."

"What should I do now?"

"Nothing. Act as before. You have nothing to fear. Konrad believes your innocence and love. Don't force things. Do as he tells you because he knows all of them better than you."

"I never wanted to fight with Ferdinand. I respect him too much."

"He's enraged because he thinks we were going all over what we went with this man. When he sees there's nothing to fear, he will be the same as before. You saved his daughter's life without asking anything in return."

"I don't know if I can go on like this. Everything was taken away from me."

"You're stronger than you think. There's no coming back for any of us. Old things are away, so new ones will come. Do it for him, Guntram. He needs you more than ever now."

I nodded my accord but I couldn't think anything more to say. I was perplexed, scared, shocked and astonished. "The Duke will return at eight for dinner. Be ready."

When Konrad returned I was already expecting him at the small dinning room. We ate trying to ignore the deafening silence. I tasted nothing, too busy keeping grief and remorse at bay. In the middle of the dinner his hand reached the back of mine and caressed it before giving it a light squeeze. I looked into his eyes, and he shyly smiled and said almost inaudible "I'm glad to have you back."

* * *

Going to the Löwensteins' party was a real test for my nerves. In the car, Konrad informed me that Michael would be there also as Monika's fiancée. She was niece on the *Fürstin's* side. Third daughter of Löwenstein's wife's sister, married with van der Leyden a rich industrial from the Netherlands ages ago. Ferdinand would stay away in order to avoid a confrontation with Gertrud who was a Lintorff therefore relative in direct line with the *Fürst*. I have to get a family tree soon. They're all cousins!

It was a black tie event and I had to wear a dinner suit. I was so nervous that tieing that stupid bow took me almost fifteen minutes. The Löwensteins had a villa in the outskirts of the city. Ruschlikon. The Fürstin was nice to me as always, and also Monika and many of the people there. Konrad was near me till some of the men wanted to speak with him in private, and he was away in no time.

The wolves in the form of Michael, Löwenstein's second son, Jürgen something, and the old *Fürst* circled me. After the exchange of the polite niceties we are supposed to do, Michael went for the killing.

"How was the South of France?"

"Fine. I was around Avignon; very beautiful place."

"For almost seven days? That must be pretty boring," Jürgen commented in that peculiar voice you use when you don't believe a thing.

"Some friends from Argentina came by, and they were staying in the camping site nearby the city. They called me the night before I went away. It was unplanned. My health didn't allow me to go with them, so I had to remain in a small hotel. We stayed in Avignon, and travelled the Provence for four days." Yes I can see the shock on your faces quickly hidden. Camping sites… uggghhhh. "They went away to Paris or Brussels, and I remained two more days, sketching."

"In the middle of the school period?"

"I admit *mein Fürst*, I escaped my obligations. After a full week enjoying the Russian's hospitality I needed some time to relax but from Monday onward I'll start to work again," I answered, sweetly.

"What transpired there?" Michael grunted, grating my nerves. Without

Goran at your side, you lose a lot of your charm and Jürgen zu Löwenstein is a kitten compared to the Serb and his friends.

"Nothing you should enquire about. I have already informed the Griffin, and he accepts my explanation. I did my best to contain the situation given my limited resources. It should give you some extra time to carry on whatever the Griffin has ordered you to do," I said with my coldest and derogative voice, like when you speak to the serfs.

"Do you think it's true?"

"I don't know what you refer to. The Duke spoke with him alone for three hours. I can only tell you that he "gave any further claims up on the subject. We should achieve peace if Lintorff allows it." Those were his words. I don't know if they were true."

"Was he honest to you?"

"I would like to believe him, but Winston Churchill once said, we may forget Russia, but Russia won't quit us."

"We should be glad you like painting, and didn't choose Law School, child." The *Fürst* chuckled visibly entertained by our exchange. "Who were those friends?"

"Are you doubting my word, *mein Fürst*?" I growled. Direct attack is better.

"No, of course not. I assumed you came from a good school, and wondered which kind of parents will leave their children to be in such a place," he said looking a little shaken by my answer and reaction. So pissing off the Griffin's Consort is bad? Good to know.

"It's very traditional to do it like that. The parents pay the ticket, the children manage the best as they can. It's like an initiatory journey. After all, when Argentineans come to Europe, they like to stay for a long time, like myself," I laughed, and the others had to join me, not happy at all. "But my friends were from the University. Economics." There you have like 2,000 students in the introductory course alone for that career. Pity we share subjects with people from other faculties, so it would be around 5,000 students only in that building. It's not well organized like in Switzerland, you know.

"Is there no school in Argentina now?"

"In theory yes. They started again in August, but public university is free, and if you lose one semester nothing happens. You can recover it the next period, and maybe that's why about sixty percent of the students take much longer than necessary to finish their studies." All of them looked at me horrified at that waste of resources. "Coming to Europe is one of their biggest adventures. They can be here without visa for forty-five days. The other adventure, but for the independent minded students, is trekking around Latin America following the Che Guevara's Diary." Yes, now they look frankly disgusted. Time for the final blow. "I was thinking myself to go to Bolivia and Peru during the austral summer. Machu Picchu must be breathtaking, and the indigenous communities are willing to take people in to experience their lifestyle, and learn their teachings."

Now I had their attentions fully focused on me, staring at me with a mix of disgust and horror. "Perhaps Venezuela too, President Chávez is changing the country into a classless society, and Bolivar's dream for Latin America might become a reality," I trailed, dreamingly.

"Konrad will have to speak with you more about politics in the region, child." Was zu Löwenstein's dry remark, looking frankly disgusted at Chávez' name mention. "I understand he's going away from Argentina. Is it true?"

"I wouldn't know, *mein Fürst*. He doesn't allow me to pry in his business," I replied sweetly.

"Father, did you hear the story of the Buenos Aires Airport? It's quite funny, indeed," I heard Jürgen asking and I knew I had passed the test.

Chapter 27

December 15th, 2003

University is almost over for this term. One more test and no more books till February. I haven't written much later. In fact, nothing at all. I'm afraid Konrad reads everything again. I have enough with people checking on my phone calls and schedule.

I went back to school and had to study very hard to recover the lost weeks. Peter was very helpful and didn't complain when he had to explain many things several times. My mind was elsewhere most of the time. Konrad is solicitous as always, but I'm disengaged of everything and everybody. I react mechanically to every stimuli. "Read those chapters for tomorrow" and I do it, without complaining or discussing. "Give me a kiss" and I do it, feeling completely numb. In a way, it's like when I was a child and my father had just passed away. "Be ready at nine." and I am, polished like a wedding cake doll.

Konrad, of course, has realised everything, but has said nothing so far. He only looks at me with a guilty expression dangling from his eyes. After his fourth attempt to make me enjoy the sex, he gave up. I'm just not in the mood, and don't want it at all. If he wants to do something, I would oblige him, but nothing more. I'm just so tired. I don't deny he did his best to calm me down. For my birthday he took me for a weekend to a big house he has in the French Riviera. The estate was very nice, clinging from a cliff over the deepest blue sea I ever saw, but I was not interested at all. He suggested going to a Casino, and I just said, "yes, why don't you go? I'm not good at Math". His birthday present was a delicious paint from Fernando Fader, a German-Argentinean impressionist I admire a lot. It's not that I'm not grateful it's that I'm not interested any more.

On my birthday's night, he tried to make a romantic dinner, but my comment at seeing the candles was "do we have a power failure?"

It's not that I don't love him any more. I still do.

But I can't shake from my head all what I know. Every time he says "I'm flying to…," I shudder thinking on the poor souls he will visit.

I got a note from Repin. In my locker's, as usual. It just said "I can help you. C." I handed it to Milan when he was picking me up at noon. "Good boy. We already knew it was there. Goran will be pleased you gave it to us." The day forwent exactly as it was supposed to be. I had lunch with Goran in the bank and the other men, and later went to study in the library, waiting for my time to go to Meister Ostermann's studio. Nobody ever mentioned the letter again. I try to avoid Konrad and the others as much as I can.

Only painting is when I feel free again. Nobody can enter there. It's just me. I'm not even paying much attention to Meister Ostermann's criticisms. I do what I please. By November, I had finished Marie Amélie portrait and I got several offers from the ladies to buy it, but I didn't want to sell it. I gave it to Gertrud, Ferdinand's wife and mother of the model. She was completely astonished to get it and thanked me profusely. Konrad was furious with me and I got a big scold from him that same night.

"I promised not to speak with the daughter. You said nothing about the mother," was my defence and I didn't care much about his rage.

Perhaps this was the reason why I gave Konrad that painting for his birthday in November. Was this a way to make peace with him? I don't know. I just felt it was the right thing to do at that time. I took the watercolour he liked so much of the aboriginal mother and her child I did in Argentina and redid it this time with oil paintings. Not much remained from the original, that is true. Only the faces, the posture, the rest was changed. I included a background with trees. According to Ostermann's it was "a haunting Madonna. Classical but provocative at the same time. I should send pictures of her to D'Annunzio." You can do whatever you want. I don't care at all.

I'm currently working on two landscapes from Argentina and perhaps will do something with what I have from the older sketches. I was thinking on a still life composition. A nice table I saw around here and on top a flower vase with some lilies, orchids and a silver urn reflecting the room. Perhaps one of those cashmere scarves, silk and half peeled lemon. I don't know. I've just got Ostermann's warning about the upcoming cleaning auction in May. This time, you can't blame me for the rubbish accumulated in your studio. I put away all my trash already. I don't feel very inspired in the moment.

Konrad liked the painting a lot, and was even showing it to some of his noble friends, the ones who came for the birthday's dinner. About thirty people in the dinning room. I asked Friederich to place me near Monika van der Leyden and not near him. After some consultation with Konrad, I got my wish and was placed between Monika and a young girl. Since it was his birthday I thought he would like to have sex in the night. I put my best face and will and it wasn't that bad. He got his release, and that what was important that night. Nothing else.

We still share the same bed, and every time he's here, he kisses me and wants to hold me, but I feel dead on the inside. Well, technically I'm a walking corpse. Keep the Griffin happy or die. Perhaps he gets tired soon and this all is over.

Would be good.

* * *

December 23rd , 2003
Vienna

Honestly, I would have preferred to stay in Zurich, but no. Konrad has several meetings here... from January 3rd onward, and decided to come earlier to pass the holidays here, dragging me along and Friederich, extremely happy to be back in his home country. The man disappeared the minute the plane landed. I know he has a room reserved somewhere in this hotel, but I haven't seen him since yesterday.

My school grades were not exactly thrilling, but I passed. A 4.7 over six possible points. I don't complain. It's OK under the circumstances. I only want to sleep tonight and this suite fortunately has two bedrooms.

* * *

December 26th, 2003

It was a strange Christmas. As I've never seen these Christmas markets before, Friederich took me to one in the morning of the 24th. It was funny to see all the wooden decorations and the people very busy around buying. Vienna is like Paris, but full of Austrians. There's music everywhere and fantastic buildings. It seems he also misses his own country as he was running like a child to see all the things. The waiters immediately realised he was Austrian too and spoke to him in their dialect (couldn't get a single word out of it), when we had lunch at 12:00 and the "*Kaffee*" at 3:00.

We returned to the Grand Hotel, looming over the Ringstrasse. I asked Friederich why the Duke didn't go to the Sacher as this would have been the most logical choice. "No! That hotel was built for the Aristocracy children to bring the choir girls and artists from the Opera. This is no place for you!" "Friederich, the Habsburgs are out of office since 1919!" I laughed. "The intended use remains as his Excellency could testify," he said with more dignity than a Chamberlain. I had to suppress a laugh with a lot of effort.

We split at the Hotel's foyer as Milan came to tell him something and both were away. It was a most welcomed surprise that the Serbs didn't tag along as usual. Milan and Ratko are discreet and polite to me, but it is very hard to have them around, snooping with the excuse they do it "to protect me". Despite their smaller frame (in size) than Heindrik's and his guys, they're more terrifying with their penetrating glares and dark silences. Goran is a talkative guy compared to those two.

I went into the elevator almost giggling, and the serious look I got from the other guests almost made me sick trying to hold the laughter. Totally inappropriate behaviour!

At the door entrance was Heindrik. I stopped dead in my tracks.

"Hello Guntram. Nice to see you again."

"You're back? I'm so sorry from what happened. I never thought this could be a problem for you."

"I was never away. I was working directly for his Excellency in Mihailovic's place. It's not so relaxing as taking care of you, but it's good."

"I'm glad. Goran was so upset with you and me."

"With you? Never. He's still impressed that you evaded us for a whole week. Finally, Dr. Dähler interfered and Goran knew where to look. You can be quite sneaky, kid. And I was thinking you were a little idiot. You can go in. Meeting is over," he said not really upset with me. Is he so sport? I don't think so. He was always shouting if I moved an inch or didn't obey him. I entered in the room as he opened the door, half expecting he would back stab me.

Konrad was sitting in front of the fireplace, reading a book. Strange, normally he's with documents. "Hello *Maus*. Did you enjoy your day out with Friederich?"

"Yes, thank you," I replied softly. "He can be quite energetic as a tourist." I had again to suppress my stupid grin at remembering Friederich's haughty tone at the other hotel.

"He's a local. Not a tourist. He knows almost every corner of this city. You look in a good mood today, *Maus*."

"And its history too," I said trying to regain my composure. "He said the

Sacher Hotel was only for the choir girls from the Opera."

"Indeed," he said sounding like one of those evident truths in life... like don't eat fruits without washing them first. I couldn't hold the laughter any more. He looked at me, puzzled, as I was laughing and trying to control myself. I had to sit down in one of the chairs, not beside him. Finally, I could stop it.

"It's been a long time since I heard you laughing, *Maus*," he said looking at me. "I thought I would never see it again," he whispered this time, more to himself than for my benefit.

"Just something Friederich said," I answered. Perhaps he's right. I don't remember laughing in a long time. Just a few polite smiles at parties but nothing more.

"Never took Friederich for a comedian. What did he say?" he asked looking directly into my eyes. I looked away unable to stand it and becoming serious again.

"Nothing important," I shrugged.

"Guntram, I don't know what else to do with you," he said dejectedly. "I've tried everything I can to make you happy again, but it seems nothing is enough. You sit by me but never next to me. You sleep in the same bed but you never touch me. You barely accept my touch, and it always looks as if you are gritting your teeth to endure it. You have no idea how I miss what we had before, how I miss you."

"That person is dead and you know it. You killed me with your threats and your dealings."

"Guntram I never threatened you. I only explained to you the consequences of your acts."

"Oh yes, you never threatened me Konrad. Stay with me or be killed. Your phone calls are registered. You have two killers as bodyguards. You read my personal files when I've never done anything like that to you. And do you want me to be happy beside you?" I said heatedly.

"I had to do it. Soon the men will trust you again. Ferdinand already does. Michael is still weary. Löwenstein has nothing against you, and in a way, he's grateful for the time you got for us. Mihailovic and Bregovic are a necessary inconvenience for the time being. Goran wants to keep Repin's men as far as possible. Once you know them, you will see they're not so bad."

"Excellent, I can go to bed now with Ferdinand and the *Fürst*," I answered bitterly. Perhaps our long due fight was coming now. He had the decency of flinching at my sentence, and looked somewhat shaken.

"Can't you not forgive me? I've done it with you. I was sincere when I said we were in peace. I understood you were under a terrible situation and forgave you. Can't you not do the same for me? Do you think I liked to keep everything away from you? Or being forced to invade your privacy? It was the only way I could find at the time," he sounded almost pleading his case.

"You could have asked and trusted my word! But no, you needed proof that I didn't fuck around with a Russian or sell him your precious Order! How do you think I would do it? I know almost nothing about your ventures, and much less about your associates! Don't take me for an idiot. This has nothing to do with your position as Griffin. it's your bloody paranoia and jealousy. I'm nothing more than one of your possessions!"

"You know perfectly well that's not the truth!" he answered raising his voice. "I love you more than my own life!"

I snickered at his answer. "You love me so much that you lied to me for two years!"

"I only kept some information to myself. It has been disclosed now."

"Just only that you're a Mafia Boss"

"I'm no such thing!" he roared deeply offended.

"Yes, you lead Caritas Internationalis," I smirked. "This is the moment when you hit me, and I kneel down asking for your forgiveness. Isn't that what you wanted all this time?"

He came at me very fast and crossed my face with a strong slap. I rose from my chair, and gave him a strong push and without realising what I was doing, I punched his face, breaking his lower lip. I was horrified that I'd done it and gasped as I looked fascinated at the small trail of blood coming from the corner of his mouth.

Konrad jumped on top of me and easily knocked me down, he landing on top of me. Without effort he grabbed both my wrists and started to kiss me passionately, like we haven't done in a long time. I squirmed and tried to kick him, but his body was heavier than mine and I couldn't move at all. He was unimpressed by me and continued to kiss me forcibly in a way that somehow made me remember our first kiss. Perhaps, it was feeling again the metallic taste of his blood in the kiss. I don't know.

I kissed him back. Hungrily like the first time. He let go of my wrists when he felt that I was reacting to his kisses, and I put them around his neck pulling him against my body. I closed my eyes to revel in all the forgotten sensations; his smell, the soft touches of his tongue inside my mouth, the softness of his lips against mine, his soft locks tangling in my hands. We remained kissing like that for a long time.

I'm insane. There's no other explanation. Love is madness.

Finally, I let him go and he sat on the floor next to me as I rose from my lying position, and laid my head over his shoulder still panting from the emotions going through me.

"I never wanted this position, Guntram. I'm trapped too. We have to survive this the best as we can," he whispered dejectedly. He put his hand over my head and caressed it. "I wanted to be a historian, but my family forced me to take over my father's place," he sighed, heavily and muttered. "I need your love, please, forgive me."

"You need ice for your mouth. Goran will never believe that I did it," I said softly taking his hand and kissing it. "I'm sorry for the punch. I didn't know what I was doing. I was too furious with you." He turned around to look at me and I smiled shyly for the first time in months. "I think we both should forgive and trust each other more."

He pulled me against his chest and I muttered "should we start all over again, Konrad?"

"Yes, my love." His kiss this time was soft and delicate, nothing wild like before.

"Konrad, using an ice pack is not a sign of weakness," I said half seriously, noticing his wound getting worse. "Goran will force to dress me like Hannibal Lecter. He already thinks I bite people as a sport."

"He's still impressed that you could evade him for so long and disappeared in front of Holgersen's eyes. He has been one of my best bodyguards for years," he confessed softly. "Michael does not believe that you don't have a previous military training."

"Me? He's crazier than I thought. I have no chances in a direct fight with any of you. If I punched you now, it was because I caught you by surprise. I got my Rambo training working as a waiter in a book store and in the University," I laughed dryly. "Tell him to run a check again on me! Maybe he finds where I left the pencil box I lost in the third grade," I retorted truly upset with that idiot.

Konrad kissed me on the temple. "You can't blame him for doing his job. Give him time to overcome this situation."

"I'll ask Heindrik for the ice pack," I said, disengaging me from his arms. The Swedish looked at me suspiciously when I asked him to go for the bloody thing. Yes, there's ice in the room, but for the champagne, and no bag to put it in. "You look fine…" he trailed.

"It's not for me. Go for it. Will you?" I answered almost losing my patience with him and closing the door on his face.

"You have quite a temper yourself, *Maus*." Konrad observed half seriously.

"Me? I wouldn't last two hours in a fight."

"No… You told several times to one of the most feared mobsters in the world to piss off," he said with a hint of pride in his voice.

"Konrad, let's don't start another fight because we both know that I will say that he's a man who had the misfortune of falling in love with the wrong person, and you will tell me that he's a cold hearted killer who hangs people from his house windows."

"All right. No more fighting, Guntram. I have enough for one night," he said, touching the swollen lip. Ice will not really help now.

"Don't be a sissy. You had much worse from Goran, and who knows from whom else."

I heard a soft knock and this time it was Milan with the gel pack. Do they have meetings or what? I muttered a "thank you", and the Serb asked "is everything fine?" "Of course. It's not for me!" I answered truly upset this time, closing the door almost in his face.

I went to apply the pack on Konrad's face as he had already washed the blood away in the bathroom. I felt very bad when I saw the results of my actions on his face. He took the ice pack and applied it.

"Shouldn't you lie down for a while? It looks really bad," I said feeling very guilty.

"This is nothing Guntram. I had it much worse than this. Don't worry," he said and went to sit at his original place in the big couch. I went there and also sat beside him holding his free hand until the thing became warm.

"I think we should go out kitten. I'm getting hungry."

"Konrad, even if it's not swollen any longer, you have a nasty cut on the lip. Should we not order something?"

"I would like to walk around the city, just to St. Stephan's. It's been years since the last time I saw it at Christmas time."

"All right. I hope Goran doesn't shoot me for attacking you. Does it hurt?"

"Guntram, I'm fine. Get your coat and we go."

Outside was Goran waiting for us. Yes, Milan and Heindrik can't keep a secret for more than ten minutes. He said nothing to us and we also not. He offered to come with us, but Konrad dismissed him and the others till the 28th in the morning, when they would leave for Linz. He will only keep around the "normal security people" whatever that means for the time being.

Alone, I think, we started to walk down Kärtner Street toward the Cathedral. There were still some Christmas trees sellers but not so many as in the morning. Strangely, the Germans and Austrians like to decorate their trees on the 24th or even in the night, not before.

"Konrad, were you not supposed to be in Notre Dame today?"

"No, we changed. We all go to Linz this year. It's more private. Journalists are a pest. I have a property in front of the Danube, it's a lovely place. Do you want to come or stay here with Alexei Antonov?"

"The idea of getting there, and being kicked out later is not appealing. Can I go to Salzburg? I always wanted to go there," I said not really believing I would get Alexei back.

"I think that could be arranged. I'll go on the 27th and be back on the 29th. Antonov will have to take care of you. I need all Goran's men at the moment."

"Does Alexei become my bodyguard again?" I asked hopefully.

"Only for a week or less. He has many things to do, but I don't want him in Linz. It could be counterproductive for him," he mumbled. "He stays with you from the 27th till Silvester. Don't drive him mad."

I wanted to ask what was in Linz to keep Alexei away, but I know better by now. "Do you want to go to the Cathedral?" I asked switching the conversation.

"If you don't mind. I would like to pay my respects to our Lady."

When we arrived to the Cathedral Konrad turned to the right and went to a small altar with a Byzantine style figure of Maria. He lit one of the candles as I remained behind, leaving him some privacy. He crossed himself three times and went to the kneelers. He stayed there for almost forty minutes, praying, I think, unmoving and not really connected to this world. I will never truly understand him. How can he be and do what he does, and then show such a deep devotion to our Mother? I also knelt down and prayed her for a way for us both out of this madness.

He touched briefly my shoulder to indicate me to go out. The Church was already packed with people coming for a late Mass. I stood up and went outside as he didn't want to stay for the service.

I was surprised when he wanted to eat at a very small place in a side street, nothing elegant or fancy like what he normally goes. "I used to come here with Friederich when I was a child. It's good." The people on the streets had diminished a lot as it was already more than nine o'clock and truly cold. Dinner was simple, but very nicely done. We almost didn't speak both very focused on our dishes engulfed in a shy silence.

"Do you want to go to the Sacher for a cake?" he asked.

"Is it appropriate for me?" I asked half seriously, biting myself hard in order to contain the laughter. He seemed to ponder for a while.

"Yes, I think so. You're with me and we're only going to the coffee, not inside the hotel," he announced, finally.

"Konrad, those hot girls must be six feet under!" I laughed now.

"Some things never change. Others unfortunately do." Was his sombre answer.

* * *

Christmas Day

What do you give to a man who has several billions assets? Another painting, similar to the one he "lost," in that far wretched auction almost a year ago. This time are two children playing with a big dog. I saw them in a park in England. Boy and girl and a huge beige animal, but the setting is inside a nursery. Don't ask me why I did it.

"It's almost ethereal. I don't know what to say, Guntram."

"You can frame it. Merry Christmas."

"There's something I want to give you, but it would be better if I show you something first. Let's go outside."

We left the hotel and he walked briskly, with me running after him. Strangely, he took a leather folder with some papers with him. He went to the Schillerpark, which is relatively near the hotel, and sat on a bench. Very odd as it was a cold morning, deserted as most people would be at home having breakfast, which we didn't.

I sat at his side, and he handed me the leather folder. "Open it," he said. Inside there were some strange pictures, very blurry and dark, nothing distinguishable, like an ultra sound picture.

"Those are Klaus Maria and Karl Maria. They're not very photogenic. They hate the press, like myself," he informed me in a gentle way. I could have dropped dead the moment I realised those dark spots were his babies. "Guntram, you can breathe again."

Good thing I was sitting when dizziness hit me full force. I looked again at the papers not really believing my eyes.

"My reaction was the same when I saw them for the first time. Almost drowned a full bottle of Napoleon's. There was nothing else in that hotel," he continued taking my hand and squeezing it. "They're boys and will be born beginning of April. Are you all right, Maus?"

All right? I was in shock, idiot! I took a deep breath and my eyes were glued to the pictures again.

"Guntram, I told you we were expecting them around April or May next year."

"You never brought the subject up so I thought you have dropped it," I stammered feeling my heart hammering like crazy.

"We agreed to have them almost a year ago. If things became complicated later, it was not my fault. The children were already on their way. Are you not happy?" he asked, this time fearfully.

"I don't know what to say. If things were different, I would be thrilled to have them with us, but I can't forget which world we are bringing them in."

"This is why I wanted to speak with you outside. I can't trust the security in that hotel. Here is safer," he paused to take a deep breath. "Klaus and Karl will not be Griffins. I've reached that decision over the last months."

"But your whole family has been! You yesterday said yourself you can't

422

leave it also."

"I can't leave my post, but I can choose my successor, and he will be none of my children. The Order has changed a lot since I took office. We are richer than ever and greed has fallen upon us. From this point, it can only go downward. I've realised it over the last months with the actions of several associates and with what you wrote in your diary about your conversation with Löwenstein. Nothing of what we stood for originally is left. We were supposed to support our Church and protect it from whatever danger fell upon it, particularly against Masons. After our defeat in the Thirty Years War, several of us, decided to keep our faith and allegiance to the Church in secret, even to its princes, so we wouldn't stain its name if we failed and were discovered."

"I made the huge mistake of increasing our combined wealth to incredible heights, and now the only thing that matters is to obtain more and more power. Nobody cares a thing about loyalty and honour. They follow me because I can make more money for them and keep the seedy parts of the Order at bay. They would have given you to Repin without blinking if that would have meant more money. I don't want my children to have their lives ruined like my own was. I never knew a moment of true happiness till I met you. For forty-four years I lived for them, never for myself. How do they repay me now? They are pressuring me to make Repin a member!"

"What? He's your enemy!"

"He's my enemy, not the Order's. He has approached several members, and offered a full access to Russian and Central Asia markets, not to mention his ventures in America, in exchange for becoming a full member and associate. He wants to be fully legitimate, who knows, maybe even founding a line for himself and his children."

"Children? He said he didn't like women!"

"So? He has four in Russia. Married to the same wife for twenty years. Olga Fedorovna has a lot of patience with him or gets a good compensation for her troubles," he huffed.

"They will force me to accept him this year in Linz and I will do it. My private wealth is more than enough as to keep me in power. My ancestors never had something like this before, although they were rich and powerful. I intend to keep only the banks, some of the industries and the hedge funds. The rest would be passed on. If Repin enters, he will be Albert's responsibility, not mine. As my interests collide with the Order's best, I will transfer the title to him. His eldest son was already invested as the future Griffin years ago."

"Will your associates not attack you?"

"They know better than that. Any move against me or my line would be suicidal for them. If I go down, they come with me. Guntram, not even Ferdinand knows about my decision or plans for this meeting. It has to look as a surprise for them. It will need years to be done, but I swear to you, that our children will not inherit this poisoned job."

"Having Repin here is very dangerous, Konrad. He will destroy everything you have built. What if he goes against your own people, Ferdinand or Goran?"

"He will not. He knows better."

"Yes, he knows better, like kidnapping me against all logic."

"That was a bold move from him. Unexpected and unwelcomed, but let me do my part. I will get Repin out of our lives and teach a lesson to the Order."

"Do you promise me the children will not be a part of the Order?"

"There's no Order any more, Guntram. I see it now. I swear they will not partake of that decadent organization. Pray our Lady that she grants me the will and the strength to fulfil my oath."

I kissed him on the lips, not caring if we were seen or not. Just briefly.

"Give me your hand, *Maus*. I can't marry you as I would like, but I want you to have this ring as a symbol of my fidelity and love for you," he said pulling a small box out of his coat's pocket. Inside there was a very old looking gold seal. It was a Griffin's intaglio in a deep red Cornelian.

"It's my family's original seal. It represents the Griffin, and the tree of life. It's Sassanian on its origin, but the motive is Sumerian. We have it since the XIII century. It was a gift from Pope Innocence IV for our services in the Teutonic Order. You should pass it to the eldest son when he marries," he explained to me as he took my left hand and slid the heavy seal on the ring finger. "For a new beginning, my love."

Chapter 28

Contrary to all expectations, Konrad is still Griffin. Albert didn't want the job for anything in this world, and the others backed off from accepting Repin into the Order. They were too afraid it would be a manoeuvre, designed to look for traitors. Fortingeray's fate was still fresh in their memories. It was decreed that Albert's eldest son, Armin, would become the next Griffin in order to avoid the problems of a very young Griffin in case of Konrad's death. More than twenty-five years difference between generations was too dangerous. The boy is about my age, twenty years old, and he will start to work directly under Konrad's orders and live with us. I'm so happy about the last part! Another Lintorff around!

Poor Armin should be ready to take over in twenty years or less!

Konrad's babies, if they are born, were put out of the succession line, and will only inherit his personal fortune and titles. The Lintorffs are still in power but the "lines" have been changed.

Armin is a nice guy. Very serious; a huge contrast with his father. In a way he makes me think on a younger Konrad. He's the eldest of five brother's and sisters. I suppose that taking care of that pack of rabid siblings makes you mature quickly. He's tall, a little lanky with dark hair and green eyes and like his father, a real ladies' man if I were to judge for the many looks he sent (and got) to (from) the girls the day we had a coffee together in Zurich. I don't know how, but we both are stuck together for this term in the University. He moved in four days ago and was sent to the room where Juan was staying before.

He was not even here twenty-four hours, when he had to run after Konrad to work in the bank, and stayed there till the "uncle" decided it was time to go home. He's Michael's "new slave" and it "should give him some stamina before really working under me." (Konrad's dixit).

Poor guy. He just was informed that he not only has to cope with me (not a real problem he said, you're a decent fellow), but he has to share bodyguards with me: Milan and Ratko as the main responsible persons for us. Goran's idea. He doesn't want to risk both the Griffin's Successor and Consort.

I'm busy in the moment with Friederich and the children's nursery decoration. Fuck, I'm so nervous and I had no idea of what to do.

I'm not qualified to be a parent!

I couldn't decide the colour of the babies' room and I'm supposed to be an artist. Yeah, big help!

It's brown and beige. How original! Konrad decided to hire a decorator, and leave a wall free if I want to paint something. Yes, sure! I'm into frescoes now.

* * *

January 24th , 2004

Not much to tell at the moment. Still in holidays, only painting everyday at Ostermann's studio, and at home a series of watercolours about children's tales. They will be framed, and hung high so there's no poisoning risk.

Armin is still around and surviving Michael—who can be very nasty as a boss. Guess the story of the Navy officers going to check the decks with white gloves on is true. Armin has to run permanently up and down the bank, looking for non-existent data (and then being told off for being an ignorant fool who blindly runs after the first thing), reading and memorizing reports or just listening to their rants. Ferdinand is no better, and treats him like shit, sending him for coffee, to pick up the newspapers and even walk his dog once. Konrad contributes by forcing him to work out with him and Goran four times a week.

At least, they let him in peace on Saturdays nights when he can disappear. He invited me once to go out with him, but I had a cold, and wanted to stay home, not to mention the ugly face Konrad made at me when Armin suggested it. That guy must be dying to start school. At least, they will let him in peace till 5 p.m. I think I never heard him calling Konrad "uncle": he's the "Duke", "his Excellency" or the "Griffin". They don't let him speak if he's not spoken to first (I can say more than him in a meeting), no drinking, no smoking, no loafing and always obeying his superiors. In a way, it's worse than the Army.

"Guntram, I don't know how you put up with the Duke," he told me once.

It would be five years more like this until he gets the opportunity to attend one of their meetings and perhaps then, he would get some responsibilities within the Order.

"Do you really want to do this?" I asked him.

"All my life. If I succeed, I will be Griffin. That only is worthy of everything."

Two days later, he got a slap from Konrad to the point of making his nose bleed for answering in a disrespectful tone to him. Armin said nothing and bent his head, mumbling an apology. He was sent out of the room.

"Are you planning to do that to the children?" I shouted enraged to him.

"No. They're not going to be Griffins, but learn by now that I will not tolerate any disrespect or rebellious thoughts from them."

"You hit your own nephew! He's just twenty years old!"

"So? You are also, and got much worse than him. Do you think the people he will deal in the future with, will wait for his convenience? He has to be stronger, and being able to endure much more than a simple corrective. This is nothing compared to what Repin could do to him."

* * *

February 16th , 2004

Since two weeks I'm back in school, studying now with Peter and Armin. We are together at classes and later we work in the bank's library. Well, Peter and me because Armin has to run under Michael's temper (whims).

I saw Marie Amélie in the university several times, but she didn't speak to me, and I did the same. I'm still coming out from a lot of shit to start the next trouble.

March 27th. 2004

In a few weeks, the children will be born. I'm very excited even if I know they will not come here till they're two weeks old. Too young for flying. Everything is ready, from the bed linens to the babies' clothes. Three trained nurses will take care of them at the beginning. First, I was upset, that Konrad was already planning to give them to other people, but my bloody doctor forbade me to run after the children. My heart is much better, but babies can be exhausting, and I have no experience at all. I can help all what I want, but the sleepless nights are reserved for professionals.

Konrad is very happy to have them. He has already chosen the names; Klaus Maria, for the eldest and Karl Maria for the second one, like his brother. He has already selected the kindergarten too!

But, on the other hand, he's apprehensive. Becoming a father nerves? Nooo, nothing so noble. He's afraid to be displaced in my affections when the babies get here. "Those little ones are cute and they want it all," he mumbled one night after some "quality time together". It seems I will have three babies at home now.

* * *

March 29th , 2004

The babies are here! Two weeks earlier than expected. Konrad was gone this morning to America to meet them, finish the paperwork, and bring them here in two weeks if their health allows it.

I was left behind. "Too many meetings and things to-do". He only took two of the nurses with him, and the other was left here to get everything ready. He promised to send pictures (well the nurses will do it; Marie and Ulrike).

This year, the Order's meeting is postponed to May, but the Sunday Easter Lunch for the employees remains. "The children like it so much that I couldn't cancel it. Don't let the rabbits inside the house, Guntram."

Translation: I have to chair the whole mess with the help of Albert von Lintorff, representing the family and Ferdinand for the bank. Shit!

Armin told me he has a girlfriend, a girl from the first class of Banking and Finance. Good family too. He doesn't want to tell the name, and I don't pry in his business. He sees her every weekend when Konrad and the others leave him alone. Dark brown hair and wonderful blue eyes… a real tigress in bed. Exactly what he likes. Please, don't tell me more about your business! We're not brothers! He says I don't know what I'm missing… right. I have my own jealous, possessive tiger in bed. I know the type, boy.

* * *

April 13th, 2004

Konrad will kill me when he returns. Hopefully, he'll do it after I see those beautiful babies. I've never seen something so small and pretty and it's only two days more till they're here.

Honestly it wasn't my fault. Maybe I should have asked more. It's all Armin's fault and that witch helped a lot!

On April 11th, Easter Sunday, Armin deserted from his duties as next Griffin. Yeah, coping with 250 people and put your best face to greet them all. Fortunately, everything went well, and Ferdinand and Albert didn't let me do much of a mess. Most of the time, I had to speak with CEO's and their wives, showing the babies' pictures in my mobile phone. They're so cute and very photogenic, no matter what their father says! Monika is absolutely in love with Klaus and Karl, "If I were not retired, I would like to order more", she said making Michael terribly nervous.

Armin didn't come back at night, and his father was furious; like I've never seen him before—very similar in his rage to Konrad's outbursts. Albert decided to stay with us, and kill his son in the morning. When I went to bed I called him on his mobile phone.

"Armin, your father will kill you, not to mention the Duke when he finds out you were not here!" I said hurriedly when he picked it up.

"Not on the phone, Guntram. See me tomorrow at the coffee shop near the university. I need to talk to you. You're the only one who can help us."

"Help? Shit! Armin what have you done?"

"Tomorrow at 10 sharp." Yes, it's in the family. All love to order people around. I'll tell Milan not to get comfortable because tomorrow we have to go to Zurich. Why do I have to be with the Serb all the time and Armin not? That's unfair!

My mobile started to ring again. Konrad. Shit again!

"Hello dear, how are you?"

"Hello Konrad. I'm fine. How are the babies?"

"Eating and sleeping as usual. They don't do much else. Klaus has quite a temper, but Karl is quieter. You'll see them soon. Did the nurses send you the photos?"

"Yes, thank you very much. They look so nice. All the women here were dying for them. When they grow up, they should have no problems in finding a wife."

"Everything went all right today?" That was his casual, but with an edge voice.

"Yes. All happy and your furniture is safe from the rabbits. The babies can destroy them by themselves," I chuckled. "Albert will stay tonight. He's tired to drive back to the hotel," I added, hurriedly.

"All right, keep him away from my wine cellar. Is everything fine, Guntram? You sound strange."

He knows! How does he do it, I don't know. "I'm tired from today. Lots of people coming. You know I don't like this," I replied very softly. "When do you arrive? I'm dying to see the babies."

"The landing is planned at 9 in the morning. We will be home around 11. I took the rest of the week off," was his mildly stern answer. He knows, and when he's back he will do whatever he can to find out what was amiss. He should have been school principal, not banker.

On Monday, a very unhappy Milan drove me to the coffee shop. It was supposed to be his "non official" free day and the guy had planned to loaf the whole day around the garden. Evading Albert was not easy, as he suspected his son and I were into some murky business. Last night, I had to endure a full interrogation process like the Spanish Inquisition, without the tortures. Honestly, I don't know anything about Armin's extracurricular activities! I could only say he has a girlfriend from the school, and don't know her. He never told me a thing—well, things you can tell to a father because how to make a standing 69 without getting cramps is not on the list.

I escaped from Albert using the kitchen door, under the astonished looks from the cleaning ladies. Friederich will shout at me tonight. Milan had the car already there, and was looking at me, suspiciously.

"You don't know by any chance where the young Lintorff is?"

"I'm going to meet him in the coffee. Perhaps he comes back with us. He's twenty-one now!" Yeah, and I will be twenty-two next October. Why do I have this sense of déjà vu? I'm not qualified to chaperon anybody! Hope his shit is not too big.

"Mr. Pavicevic and his father will have a word with him later. Stay out of whatever he has done, Guntram. You'd been doing so well lately," Milan warned me

The coffee shop was almost empty, and I choose a table near the windows. Very sunny, and I ordered a coffee. I needed one.

I should have gone directly for the scotch.

Hanging from Armin's arm was Marie Amélie von Kleist, in a more classy brunette version. Not platinum blonde any more. I rose from my chair out of habit.

"Hi, Guntram, meet my fiancée. Marie Amélie," Armin said as she smiled to me.

"Miss von Kleist and I know each other," I said sternly. *Fuck*!

"Guti, don't be so formal. Armin's my boyfriend," she said with that incredibly seductive voice she has.

"Guntram, I know her for years, she's like a cousin to me and we want to marry. You have to speak with the Duke."

"What? No way. When your father hears this, he will explode, and I don't want to be in the middle. I had enough from this bitch before!" OK. It was not polite, but people should understand why I'm so nervous around her. Konrad will certainly kill me for this.

"You don't talk of my future wife like this, faggot!" Armin roared.

"Do you know she's banished from us, twerp?" I shouted back, getting everybody's attention. "It's forbidden to speak to her. Only her direct family," I explained in a lower voice.

"She's pregnant from me."

I had to sit. "Idiot," I muttered. "The Duke will never allow you to marry her and much less become Griffin now."

"This is why we need you Guntram. You're the only person who can make him change his opinion. This baby is a blessing and we want to have it. I never wanted to hurt you and it wasn't my fault what happened. Peter put the thing in the drink when I was out of the house," she pleaded me. "I don't want to raise this baby alone!" Now, her big blue eyes were veiled with tears.

"Marie, you never told me you had troubles with the Duke, only that von Kleist disinherited you because he's not your biological father." Armin said now shocked.

"Well, the Duke hates her with all his soul. You see, she tried to kill me once. Accidentally, of course, but it doesn't change the fact you don't give amphetamines to someone with a heart condition! You got her pregnant?" I shouted again.

"Yes and I will fulfil my duty toward her," he intoned solemnly.

"I'm telling your father, and he should decide what to do. No, I'm telling Ferdinand he's becoming a grandfather."

"Guntram, don't do that. They will kill my baby!" She was almost crying.

"They're Catholics, they will not touch it. I don't know what your problem with me is because I was always kind to you, but I will not be dragged into your machinations once more. Good morning." I stormed out of the dammed place, leaving some money over the bar's counter.

Milan was outside, waiting with the car. "We go to the bank, now."

"Nobody is there today. Holiday."

"Mr. von Kleist's house then." I started to feel bad, gagging and short of breath. I had to open more the collar so I wouldn't feel suffocated. My pulse was very fast and that was not a good sign. Stable angina it's called. I fished the bloody pills from my pocket and took one.

"Goran will kill me slowly if something happens to you. Do you need to go to a doctor?"

"No, just to von Kleist. I'll be fine, Milan."

"What happened? This is more than meeting the young Lintorff."

"I can't tell you, and promise me you'll say nothing to Goran till I speak with von Kleist or Albert von Lintorff. It's their call."

Milan just grunted his agreement, still looking at me suspiciously.

Cecilia, Ferdinand's new wife/girlfriend was shocked to see me, but she let me pass, got me a glass of water, and went to fetch her husband/boyfriend. Ferdinand rushed in his elegant living room.

"Is something wrong Guntram? You are very pale."

"Hello Ferdinand. There is only one way to say this: Your daughter will make you a grandfather very soon."

"I have no daughter," he said, seriously and fulminating me with his eyes.

"The next Griffin is the father." I was unimpressed by his display. Now, it's your problem. He lost all colours, and had to sit in one of the chairs. "Albert knows nothing but we should tell him before the Duke finds it out."

"How?"

"The usual way I suppose," I shrugged, and Ferdinand looked at me really pissed off. "Ah, how they met? I don't know. Armin never told me a thing. Only that they were dating for the last month or more. He thinks I can speak with Konrad and convince him to let him marry her, and have the child. Marie Amélie is afraid Konrad will attack the baby."

"The child will not be touched. It's a Lintorff. All right, Guntram. You did well in telling me. I'll speak with Albert now and we we'll decide what to tell Konrad. You have to be completely quiet about this. Is that understood, child?"

"I don't want to be in the middle of this. I will not speak on behalf of Marie Amélie or Armin as they want. Konrad would be furious with me if I disobey him once more. I'm still walking on a cliff thanks to all of you."

"You will not be involved? You were not so afraid to help her once. There's a small life at stake here!" He said with deep disgust lacing his voice. For someone who does not recognize his daughter, you react strongly to my refusal. Well, Guntram is more selfish now. "Keep your mouth shut. Don't ruin Konrad's day tomorrow. He's very happy bringing his children home. Good day."

"Good bye Ferdinand. Next time you want to involve me in one of your daughter's mess, warn me in advance."

I was going out when my mobile phone rang again. Goran. Milan is a gossip boy, no doubt.

"What was it?" he barked at me.

"Nothing. Just speaking with Ferdinand."

"That woman is bad. Milan told me you had to take your pills."

"I take hundreds of pills per day! Cut it off! I've done nothing wrong."

I have to speak with Friederich. He knows better, and will not sell me or use me like Albert or Ferdinand. Who knows if the baby is true. For some reason they want me out, and sending the good, naive, stupid Guntram to Konrad to plead for that bitch's case is a very good way to make Konrad kill me in one of his outbursts. Why?

Friederich thought it was indeed a move from Ferdinand and Albert in order to cover the mess and look for a scape goat (I'm not the one who was on the horizontal Olympic games!) I should stay out, and speak with the Duke as soon as possible. The more I delay, the worse.

Why every time a joyful moment, like the babies' arrival tomorrow, is ruined by this fucking Order?

* * *

April 14th, 2004

Yesterday, I fought with Armin. He decided to grace me with his opinion about my cowardice for not risking my neck to save his and Marie's Amelie's one. He burst into my studio, uninvited and started to call me names. Pussy and faggot (second time). It was too much. I rose my voice and told him to beat it before I would kick his ass out.

"What pussy cat? Are you going to call my uncle to defend you? Take it up your ass! Faggot."

Third time. Enough is enough. I launched myself against him, giving him a punch. I think he was surprised, and taken aback. I waited for him to recover, and we started to really fight on the floor. Goran has taught you nothing, sissy, because you were under me in no time, and I was really hitting him on the face, when Friederich pulled from me like crazy, but he couldn't separate us. He had to call Milan.

He also got one punch. I didn't mean it. Really. I apologized immediately to him, but he was quite amused by the fact I could fight "like a real man. Look what you did to the brat". Friederich ran to get some ice for Armin and his nose. I had a small cut on the lip, and still wanted to beat the asshole some more.

"Well, it seems you don't need me any more boy. Don't tell the Duke or I'll be jobless!" he chuckled very amused. "Where did you learn to fight like that?"

"Slums, or do you think some parents will send their children to school if you don't show some strength?" I grunted. "I'm sick that all of you think I'm a sissy."

"You are! And a coward!"

"Shut the fuck up or I'll show you what I can do with a rusted razor blade."

"Shut up Lintorff. Do you want more? Guntram has shown you he's more than able to fulfil his promises." Milan interfered jerking him from the arm, and literally threw him out of the room. "Always wanted to say that sentence," he sauntered, truly happy this time. "Why did you hit the brat like that?"

"Issues between us," I growled.

"His Excellency will be most upset when he sees his nose. It's almost broken, and those bruises will take several days to heal. Do you really know how to use a knife or do you need some lessons from me?"

"I know enough, but I'm not going to start to butcher people! I have no chances with any of you! This was beginner's luck, and he's an idiot who can't plan an attack or repel one. I'll explain myself to his Excellency, Milan."

"Good, get some ice too."

* * *

On the morning of the 14th, Konrad and his babies (well ours) arrived, and I nearly broke my neck flying down the stairs. I had to catch my breath under Friederich's stern gaze (He's very upset about last night's fight. He says I'm much cleverer than boxing with Armin).

Konrad was coming out of his limo and the two nurses were carrying the car seats with the babies. I had to repress myself from running to the babies as all the staff was there and remembered that I'm supposed to greet the father first.

"Welcome back Konrad," I said respectfully and smiling softly. He looked at me suspiciously the moment he saw I had the cut on the lip.

"Hello Guntram. Come, meet Klaus Maria and Karl Maria."

They were sleeping still, and they were more beautiful than anything I've ever seen in my life. Still wrinkled in an adorable way with a mop of dark blond hair and well covered against the cold morning.

"I think the children should go to the nursery now," he said. "When they're awakened you can see them better. Perhaps even try your luck with a bottle. They need some rest after the flight."

The two nurses almost ran to carry out his order. I was disappointed as I wanted to kiss the babies, but I know better than making a scene. Friederich formally greeted Konrad, and they both went inside, directly to the library.

"Where's the *Strolch*?" he asked, casually.

"Young Lintorff is gone with his father. They will come this afternoon to meet the princes," Friederich announced formally.

"Thank you Friederich. Lunch at 12:30. See the nurses have everything they need." The butler went away closing the door almost soundlessly. I gulped hard. I have to spill it out or it would be much worse.

"Come *Maus*, you're very formal today. Do you think you can give me a kiss or your broken lip will prevent it?"

"No, of course not. I just hit a door in the night," I said going to kiss him and hiding my wince at the contact of our lips. No need to put Armin in more shit than he already is.

"And the door's name is...?" He asked going to sit behind his desk. Now we pass to the formal enquiry phase.

"Nothing happened really. It's finished. There's something I must tell you before you find it out by yourself."

432

"Yes, Goran informed me about your fight with Armin and the results. You're full of surprises Guntram," he said with his cold and polite voice, the one reserved for those rare occasions when shit truly surrounds you.

"I didn't want to hit him so badly. I was enraged, and his training is lousy if he can't shake me off."

"Enough! Why were you two fighting?"

I took a deep breath. "Marie Amélie von Kleist is pregnant, and it seems Armin is the father. They wanted me to intercede for them but I refused. Armin ca lled me a coward and a faggot, and I lost my temper. I hit him last night. I will apologise as soon as I see him," I said very fast and truly afraid of him as his eyes took a darker shade.

"What were you supposed to do?"

"Convince you to let him marry her—for the baby's sake. She thinks the baby will be killed, and I really don't want that. Ferdinand was upset with me for not helping, but Friederich told me not to meddle."

"Helping? As usual, Friederich is the only sensible person here. Go out. I'll see you at lunch."

"Armin didn't know about your punishment. He was shocked when I told him."

"Out. Now," he growled.

I went to the nursery to see the babies better. There's nothing else I can do. The place was fully decorated almost a month ago with soft brown colours and beige. Not many teddy bears but some plush animals that look almost alive. All toys should be kept in cupboards, nothing thrown out. They have independent cribs and changers. The babies will live in the old nursery, on the second floor, with big windows and a view over the courtyard and the cherry tree. In the moment they will only use the playroom and bedroom. There's an adjoining room, free, for when they will have to study. The nurses have one bedroom for the night here, and private rooms in the service area. My studio is on the other side of the corridor, and I can check on them as much as I want.

Lissette was there, taking care of the clothes, and preparing something at the same time. "Mr. de Lisle" she greeted me, politely.

"Is it convenient to see the children now?"

"Yes, they sleep now, but soon will be hungry. You could help me then. Normally Klaus, the eldest is the first to cry, but Karl will join him soon."

I approached the cribs, and started to look at the "eldest", Klaus Maria. He was sleeping peacefully with a frown in the head. I think he's going to be hungry soon. Maybe he realises everything has changed around him. The other one, Karl Maria slept soundly, his features were more relaxed. I moved just an inch and the wooden floor cracked and Klaus decided he had enough and started to yell at full force.

Shit! Juan Ignacio was nothing compared to this one, and he's only fifteen days old!

"Take him a little in your arms while I prepare his bottle. He has zero patience. Let's pray Karl sleeps longer." Yeah, I know from where this comes. I lifted him from his crib, very carefully holding the head, and shushed him as I pulled him against my heart. "You'll get something soon. Hello baby," I said not really expecting him to stop. Bottle is bottle.

He stopped crying, and looked at me. Are they not supposed to be unable to do that?

"Incredible. He stopped. Nobody could do that before. Only with the bottle or the dummy," she said astonished. "This one has a very strong character. A little devil, sir. Karl is very sweet and peaceful baby on the other hand."

"He's just a baby! They have no characters!" I said as I looked in the eyes of the small one nestling in my arms, ready to sleep some more. She handed me the bottle and told me to sit in the sofa and start to give it to him.

"If Karl wakes up, I'll take care of him, sir," she said, as I started to give him his bottle. Strangely he didn't close the eyes like all babies do, and kept looking at me the whole time. When his brother started to make some soft sounds, cooing like babies do, and I turned my attention to him, Klaus made a gesture of discomfort, puckering, exactly like Konrad does when he's mildly upset about something, but can't complain. I rocked him, and he was appeased. Yes, it runs in the family.

He was not so happy to be returned to Lisette as I went to see Karl. He was very busy chewing his dummy and looked at me directly in the eyes for a brief moment before losing all interest in me. I took him around the room as the nurse finished changing Klaus, and putting him back in the crib. She immediately gave me the second bottle, and I repeated the same ritual.

A light cough from the door made me look and there was Friederich.

"It's lunch time. The Duke waits for you."

Oh no, he hates to wait. I returned the baby to the nurse, and went away, only stopping to wash my hands and straighten the tie.

Konrad was already sitting and not happy at all. I excused myself briefly and sat at his right. Friederich started to serve the soup.

"I was in the nursery. Your children are truly beautiful, Konrad. You must be proud of them."

"Our children Guntram. Ours," he grunted.

"Yes, ours. I'm sorry. Klaus is very nice and looks a lot like you. Karl, on the other hand, is very sweet. He waited till his brother finished before asking for his bottle. How can they be so different and have already characters?"

"Different donors. All children are different, even twins. Klaus has a real temper. You will see it soon."

"He can cry out loud, but he stopped when I carried him. Maybe he only wanted to be picked up. Can I take them out to the garden today?

"I can't see why you need asking my permission. They're yours also. Take them out, but see that they're warmly dressed. In fact, it would be good if you and the children go away this afternoon at around four. They need fresh air and I need to discuss with Ferdinand and Albert," he said dryly.

"As you say Konrad. Thank you," I muttered casting my eyes down.

"*Maus,* I'm not upset with you at all. This is between me and them," he said this time more gently than before.

"Don't go against the baby, please." He looked at me enraged.

"I have my beliefs! Of course I will not touch the baby, but hear me well, if this idiot wants to marry her, he's out of the succession! That viper always tried to catch a Griffin. First, it was me when she was sixteen, but no chance. This is why she hates you so much. Later she was after Karl zu Löwenstein, who was mentioned as possible successor, and now she caught that little imbecile, Armin! She will never be a Consort or give birth to a Griffin if I have something to say in the matter!

I looked at him astonished. Marie Amélie wanted to have something with him? Well a wedding ring for sure. Shit! I'm a total idiot.

It was never an accident. It was a vendetta in the best Lintorff way.

Chapter 29

As announced, at four, Albert arrived almost dragging his son plus Gertrud and Ferdinand—not speaking with each other. I made myself scarce with the babies and one of the nurses, Ulrike.

The children were both awake and in a good mood. According to Ulrike that was the moment to make them tired, and hopefully they will have their bottles and sleep from eight to one or two in the morning. The general idea is that they start to learn the difference between day and night, and don't eat so much in the night. We took them to the forest, and walked around till we sat for a long time with them on the arms. Klaus wanted to be with me all the time, while for Karl it was the same, no matter who was taking care of him.

"You should have been in New York with us Mr. de Lisle. Our lives would have been more easy," she chuckled, strangely puzzled that Klaus was so nice to me. The poor guy had already made a name for himself. He's just a baby!

"Call me Guntram, please."

"I can't, sir. The Duke tolerates no familiarity at all and we were warned against it. I'm sorry."

Around six, it was getting colder and I told her to return. Also it was their bathing time. When we entered, I saw Armin miserably sitting on the foyer as the adults were deciding his fate inside the library. I excused myself from the nurse and asked him if he wanted to meet the children. He was relatively nice to them and soon they were away. I can understand if he feels nervous around babies.

"Armin, I'm sorry for what happened yesterday. I just went mad with it," I said extending my right hand and he shook it.

"Guntram you have no idea how much shit I'm into. Without your help, the Duke will do whatever he wants to us. Nobody here would go against him. They're too afraid of him."

"He promised me not to touch the baby. You should not worry about that."

"What about me? I will be out. Permanently. All my life I wanted this honour," he said burying his face in his hands, messing his hair.

I felt sorry for the guy even if I noticed he didn't apologise to me. However, he got the worst part of the fight and he's a high society brat, like many I know. Perhaps Konrad and the others are right in treating him worse than trash till he humbles himself more. How was it? "To command you have to obey first"?

"I can't side with Marie Amélie. She almost killed me last time I met her. Konrad forbade me any contact with her. Didn't you know it?"

"I didn't know she was cast out. After all, aunt Gertrud called me and told me she was coming back to the University, and if I could help her to feel welcomed after the cure in Geneva. I've been always attracted towards her. Since I was 12, but she never paid attention to me till this year. I'm a total jerk. She was after my position. She even tried to be in the Duke's bed once. My father almost killed me when he found out that I asked you to intercede for us. Gertrud suggested it, and I bought it."

"Look, I also screwed it up last year. Badly, and I'm in a sort of probation. I can't get into more troubles. If I'm alive is because Konrad supported me," I whispered feeling glad that it wasn't Ferdinand's idea. I guess I will have to apologise to him tomorrow. The fact that Gertrud was against me and trying to get rid of me, was very unsettling. After all, she sold the bloody paintings to Repin, and there the real mess started. She could have always refused to make the transaction or raise the opening bid to a crazy price, and nobody would have been upset as Konrad would have gladly paid it. But she didn't say a word to him until everything was consummated. Didn't he give the same amount as the total paid?

"Father told me you and the Duke had real trouble last year. What was it?"

"You'll find out when you're a real part of the Order. I can't say more. It's for your protection." I sighed. Excellent. I'm speaking now like one of them! Soon, I will be saying something like "the thing about that thing in Nice, but the second thing not the first thing".

"Wow. You speak like the Griffin's Consort truly, and you hit like one of them too. Sorry, won't happen again. You're no faggot. I see it now."

"Do well in remembering it," I said imitating Konrad's accent, and he chuckled. "Really. I have a heart condition that doesn't allow me to do much in the moment or be under too much stress, but before I wasn't sewing and singing by a window. I worked hard to make a living, and was around people from the lowest spheres. You have to punch hard when a drugged father wants to take his child to sell her for another fix. I will never be like Konrad or the others, but I'm not a sissy."

"Honestly, Guntram, you are frail, look very young and weak if we compare you with the Duke."

"Well, some of us come in small size."

"Dr. Dähler is right. He calls you Dachs (Badger) when the Griffin is not around. They're fearless and short tempered. Do you know that the African ones can eat a cobra, and recover from the poison intake?"

"Yes, he did it the first time he saw me. I thought it was only a joke," I said bitterly. Another reference to my biting habits! I'm a peaceful guy! Compared to Konrad, I'm in the kindergarten! Without mentioning I'm afraid of all of them, because I really know what they're capable of, not like this boy. I think, he believes life is like the playstation, and the ones who die, really don't do it. Psychiatrists would have a field day with this family.

"Friends?" he asked me, offering his right hand.

"As long as you don't touch my pencil box again," I replied shaking it.

We remained there for a long time, not speaking and waiting for Konrad to pass his judgement upon us.

Very late, like at nine, Friederich came in and told us to both go to the library. If I'm present it means Konrad would do nothing against Armin. I knocked on the heavy wooden door, the memory of doing the same in Venice many years ago, flashing through my mind. Funny the things you remember.

We entered and Konrad was sitting at his usual place behind the desk. The others were nowhere to be seen.

"Sit down Guntram," I did it in one of the chairs on one side of the desk wondering why Armin wasn't allowed to do the same. "You have done well this time by speaking with Ferdinand, and not letting yourself be tangled by my cousin Gertrud's power games. I understand many more things now. I have fired her from her position at the Foundation, and Ferdinand's fiancée will take over her place from

Monday onward till you finish your studies, and can do it in three years," he said, with his no nonsense voice. I gulped. Me? Running that monster foundation? He's crazy, but this was not the most appropriate moment to speak.

"I'm not sure if I would be able to do it. I have almost no experience," I protested slightly, more for my sake than expecting a real result.

"Dr. Cecilia Riganti will tell you what to do. She was Gertrud's right hand till this other incident. Elisabetta von Lintorff will also guide you. I'm pleased you have finally learned to live under our codes."

"I'll try to do my best, Konrad," I mumbled with my eyes glued to the carpet, waiting for the worst now that he had finished with me, and his attention was fully directed at Armin.

"As for you, I'm highly displeased with your behaviour; unworthy of a future Griffin. You are perfectly aware of the rules against breeding outside the established line. No bastards under any circumstance. All consorts and wives must be approved by the council. You knowingly deceived us all, by not informing of your engagement with this woman. I will not interfere with the decision you make now, but be aware that this child will not be accepted by your father or I. If you decide to father the child, you're out of the succession, and the next in line will take your place."

"I can sympathize with your position due to your young age, and I'm willing to let you continue with us for five more years. If you prove your worth to us, respect the rules, your elders, and avoid any contact with this woman, you will be considered again a suitable candidate for succeeding me."

Armin only bowed his head, accepting his fate. I couldn't stand this unfairness to the unborn baby. Konrad was knowingly depriving him from her father! I coughed getting their attention.

"With all due respect, Griffin." Konrad looked at me, shocked that I have used his title for the first time. "The child carries Lintorff's blood and should be treated accordingly."

"If the mother decides to carry it to full term, she will be provided for. Gertrud's personal fortune is worth several millions. If the Consort is not happy with my decision," I flinched a bit at hearing his use of "my title", not nice at all, "I can offer an educational fund for the child."

"It's not about the money Konrad, it's about a small child growing without his or her father. I've been there, and it's not good at all," I whispered losing my colour.

"Guntram this is not your choice. It's Armin's. If he wants to be a Griffin, he has to learn to make very difficult decisions on a daily basis. I hope Armin is clever enough as to realise this was a move against his line in order to destroy them or rule along with them. My responsibility is to preserve the Order and internal fighting and betrayal is deadly for us. Dismissed, both of you."

* * *

April 23rd , 2004

The babies will soon be a month old—on the 29th to be precise. I'm totally in love with them. I spend as much time as I can with them and more or less I have mastered the challenging Nappies Changing Art. How can they move so much and kick? Mopsi is also delighted to have them around and is very protective of both, sneaking to sleep under their cribs. I hope her good disposition lasts when they start to pull her ears.

I go in the mornings to the school and come back at five to stay with them. Konrad can take his own limo back home and it's better this way. I'm still sore with how he managed the mess with Marie Amélie's baby.

I should be furious with him, but every time I see him carrying his children or kissing them, my heart melts. He was even singing some German lullabies to them (when the nurses are nowhere to be seen, of course). I never imagined he could be so tender to the three of us. I already caught him several times looking at me with adoration in his eyes while I was cradling Karl or Klaus.

Armin decided to stay with us, and suffer five years of pure Hell. By the way they treat him, I had an easy life after Repin's episode. He told me she didn't want to carry on with the pregnancy, and I was very sad for it. According to Armin I shouldn't be concerned because that would have been a disaster waiting to happen.

Chapter 30

March 29th, 2005

Today is Klaus and Karl's birthday. I still can't believe they have been with us for a full year. They're amazing now that they crawl and try to stand using everything as my wrinkled (and dirty) trousers can testify. Klaus is like a carbon copy of his father physically and mentally. He has big blue eyes and a mop of unruly brown hair and is very big for his age. He's strong willed (OK, he has a lousy temper when crossed), but if you explain your reasons for not letting him touch the plugs, he accepts the ban and never does it again. He can't possibly understand what is being said because he can't speak, but he likes to have the explanation and maybe he thinks it's due to his royal persona. Like a tribute. Klaus always does the things first and later comes his brother. He's permanently running after me and likes to play with me.

Karl is more sensible than his brother. If you tell him off, he becomes completely depressed and cries. He's shy while Klaus comes immediately to investigate who are you and what you do. Karl loves to be held and that you play with him. He has a sweet nature, and the nurses like to spoil him a lot. I can understand them; he looks like the Gerber Baby from the glass jars with his blonde hair and ice blue eyes.

Karl likes if you show him a book or if you draw for him whereas Klaus loves to see people working. He's utterly fascinated with the gardeners or cleaning girls. You will never find Karl doing something inappropriate or placing himself in a dangerous situation like his brother (e.g. going downstairs by himself).

But don't think Karl is weak. Hell, no. He's sweet and loving, but stubborn as his brother or more as Konrad found out a few weeks ago. Both babies were having a hard time eating their food (both hate boiled fish; they preferred it oven cooked), and the initial hunger was over. Klaus was more or less accepting it, and just protesting for his pride's sake. Karl, just closed the mouth and this was it. He will not open it. I was going to give up with him and let him starve till tea time so he would learn to eat next time, but Konrad entered in the nursery and decided to interfere.

One single and low growl directed at Klaus was enough as to make him finish the fish. Karl was not impressed at all and refused to open his mouth even if Konrad put a spoonful before him. The baby looked at him defiantly and kept it closed.

"Karl. I have no patience for this," he said, pushing the spoon a little. Konrad got a full fury look from the baby. Wrong move, Konrad, you have to respect their spaces. Both are quite jealous of it. He might be sweet, but somehow he knows he's supposed to be respected. Flattery and playing with him might help more. "Come on," he urged Karl.

He would have none of it. Karl just pressed the lips more and threw him an incensed look. Konrad pressed again with the spoon. Baby took a handful of purée, and hurled it towards Konrad's suit with an incredible good aim.

I rose from my chair, afraid Konrad would react in the way he normally does, but he remained calm, looking at the baby directly in the eyes.

"So you want it the hard way. We'll stay here till you finish this fish. It's time you learn what discipline is," he said chilling my bones. Klaus looked alarmed at me. "Take Klaus out if he's finished, Guntram."

"Konrad, the child didn't mean it. He's just a baby. Let him starve a few hours, and he will learn," I said hurriedly.

"Guntram, he has to learn his place. It's not about the eating any more. He should respect his father."

Konrad just remained sitting in front of Karl looking at him and forcing him to remain in his high chair till he ate the fish. He didn't care or even flinched when the baby started to cry or hurled something else at him. He just waited for him to tire and give up... after almost three hours. Karl finally ate the fish, and Klaus was very shocked at his father's behaviour. I think they have never seen him like that before.

So far, we never had trouble with the boiled fish again.

Konrad is not always with the children as he has to travel as much as before, but he spends all the time he can with them. He "oversees" their education and has set many rules for what he considers a "proper" one. The children can't have many toys and the electronic ones are forbidden. Only wooden or some plush animals, and they have to share them. I was surprised one day when they wanted to have a cookie from him and he took one, and broke it in two equal parts giving one to each child. "If they want more, I can give them another one, but they should learn to share their things."

I have to refrain myself from speaking German with them as my grammar and accent are not so good. I can teach them Spanish (but a correct one, not this "dialect" you speak in Argentina) or English. So the poor things have to fight with three languages at the same time.

Their day is scheduled to the last minute; sleeping, playing time, strolling, eating and bathing.

Anything from Disney or Japanese toons are banned from this house. Honestly, I don't know why. He just said that they were "very vulgar in their conception and if we can avoid them till kindergarten, it would be very good. Destroy the children's aesthetic taste". Toys should be educational, meaning they can get a full kitchen set, tools or even a mop, but nothing from the "Baby Einstein" factory.

Konrad is very nice to them and they love him, crawling at full speed towards him when they see him. He's stern (really) but strangely they adore him. He doesn't tolerate any nonsense from them and has a firm hand to discipline them.

"They will have a lot in their lives since a very early age. They should learn to obey. If not, they will become monsters. I've seen it happening many times to other people. Klaus and Karl will get enough kisses and hugs from you. It's in their best interest that I keep them in line."

But don't think he doesn't spoil them in his own peculiar way. We had a huge fight when I learnt he wanted to give them a small pony (2) for their birthdays. No way! They're only one year old and can't even walk! Not to mention their backs will be ruined. The horse, after they turn four or five years old. They will not even realise it's their birthday today!

Finally, we agreed on a plush horse and we would reconsider the real horses in two years. He ordered them from Kösen (always buying German stuff!) with everything (saddle and blanket) and two because "asking them to share the horse might prove very challenging". They also got an account, but I don't think they will appreciate it at the moment. Anyway, they can't touch the money till they turn twenty-one.

In the horses' box there was a life size Badger. You're so funny, Konrad! Pity I can't still fully appreciate your German sense of humour. "I couldn't resist it. Michael is damn right," he said that same night when I was asking what to do with the blasted thing. "You can put it with your space dolls. After all, you still keep your childhood toys," he chuckled.

"Action figures!" I roared, deeply offended.

The badger sits in my studio in one of the shelves, and my Star Wars Collection is boxed again, till the world learns to appreciate it. We will see if you find it so funny when I start to collect something expensive like Japanese Ceramics or Porcelain. Who am I kidding? He would love it.

My painting is not so abundant as before. I have no time or energy left after the children play with me, or I feed them. I know we have the nurses, and they do a fantastic job, but I love to do it. I paint after eight or when I go to Meister Ostermann's twice per week. Elisabetta has already threatened with a slow and painful death if I don't produce something more than "one miserable paint". She said "I might not be a Lintorff by birth, but remember we, the Battistini were mentioned by Dante in the Third Circle of Hell."

Better I start to paint on the weekends, the lady is quite bossy and she's now in Gertrud's former place. Last year, she "*only*" rose 1.3 million, and thanks to my paintings, it was not so bad. Guntram, start to work, and produce something good. I'll work my way with Tita and Van Breda. If my nephew complains again about this Russian collector, then he will hear it from me." Good luck, Elisabetta because Konrad will shoot the "Russian collector" if he sees him around.

I tried to tell her "quality before quantity", and she called me "lazy lad". Yes, better start to do something before she teams up with Ostermann, and they devise something horrible to do to me. My teacher is still upset because I didn't sell the "Madonna" Konrad got as birthday present in 2004 to D'Annunzio. Yes, as if I could ask him to give me back his own present! Not even for the Vatican!

I think I could make four different things, but I can't guarantee the quality.

Repin sent me two letters, but I didn't open them. I just gave them to Konrad. In January, I saw him briefly at the Davos Conference—he has many legitimate businesses and was invited too. Konrad was in one of his "private sessions", and I was with Armin, going to the public lectures. He came to us during a break.

"Hello Guntram. You look much better than before," he said, not even looking at Armin.

"Hello Constantin. This is Armin von Lintorff."

"Yes, I imagine. Go with your father, boy," he said giving him a cold stare. Armin opened his mouth to protest, but I interfered to save his skin. I think he doesn't know who Repin is.

"Please, Armin. See if the Duke needs anything," he went away after giving me his patented fury look. I waited till he left the room. "It seems you don't like the Lintorff's at all," I commented.

"I have no problems with them as long as they remain in their territory. "

"It's a bad idea that we speak. The Duke will be most upset with me. Good bye," I said formally.

"Have I ever hurt you, Guntram? Let's have a coffee, shall we? You know I don't take rejection well."

"In front of the whole Order? Do you want to put a bullet in my head?"

"We're at peace now. My candidacy will be presented this year. It's customary to reject it the first time."

My mind went blank, and he took the chance for dragging me to one of the tables in the cafeteria. I sat like an automata, and was not even realising when one of his men (aides now), placed a tea in front of me.

"How are you, Guntram? Are you all right? I haven't seen much of your work lately," he asked, solicitously, making me feel bad for him. Still in love? I thought he had overcome it.

"I'm fine, Constantin. I don't paint much lately. I have no free time left with the University and the children. They occupy most of my day," I answered hoping it would give him an idea.

"How is it with them? Do you like them?"

"I love them as if they were mine. Well, in fact, they almost are. I was appointed their legal tutor and Guardian of the Estate if anything happens, but I should not worry about that since you two are peaceful now. Should I?"

He laughed and took a sip of his coffee before answering. "No problems between us at the moment. I have to admit Lintorff is very clever. More than I originally estimated. His move with the children is the work of a genius. Two in one go. He ensures the succession and keeps you beside him forever, chained to the children."

"He speaks about having children since I met him, much before you decided to enter in our lives," I fired somewhat hotly, but not losing my temper.

"Tell me one thing. Why didn't he let you father one of them? Normally, gay couples don't want to know who's the father and they share the baby," he asked, hurting me with his question.

"There are legal and dynastic issues at hand. The children should be recognized as Lintorffs."

"Why? If it's true that his line is out of the succession, there should be no problems at all to have your own ones under his name or yours. He's free to do whatever he wants with his money. The blood only matters for the Order," he shrugged, casually.

"It was decided much before he would name Armin as successor, and his line would be in charge in the future. Be nice to him if you want to join it so much. You might have to take orders from him one day," I used my best formal tone with him.

"From that brat? We'll see if he ever gets the job. Lintorff has still to invest him. He has only been appointed, Guntram," he laughed this time openly, making me shudder. "However, these are ugly things to speak with you. I only wanted to see how you were faring. I never got an answer to my letters."

"I never read them. I gave them to Konrad. Unopened. You see, thanks to you, I was nearly executed for treason. Next time you kidnap me, please, shoot me before you return me." Yes, I'm still sore for that.

"That kiss was worthy, angel. Truly. Escaping from Lintorff like that was very daft, Guntram. Anyway, catching you, took them longer than expected. I won over €500 betting against my men when they will find you in Avignon," he chuckled.

"You have earned Oblomov's respect, angel."

"Did you know where I was?" I think I turned ash colour.

"Of course. You told me yourself. "My train leaves in twenty minutes". You called from Geneva. It was just a matter of finding a train schedule. I doubted between Avignon and Rennes, but the first city has an old charm that would appeal to you. My men protected you since the second day. One can never know how Lintorff can react when crossed."

"You said nothing to me..."

"Would you have listened to me? No, you clearly told me to leave you alone. You needed some time to yourself. It was a pity Pavicevic himself intervened, scaring my men away. But if he was there, Lintorff wouldn't dare to hurt you much. According to Aliosha, he sees in you the brother he lost in Croatia many years ago."

"Does Alexei speak with you?"

"Not really. I had to press him to talk to me. Only by swearing on my mother's grave, I wanted to help you if Lintorff became violent. He's not in good terms with me since 95 or 96."

I was surprised he didn't rat me out. Perhaps, and just perhaps, he has more honour than I credited him.

"Anyway, the only thing I was saying in the letters was that I enjoy very much your painting with the girl at the table. Are you planning to present something for the Lintorff Foundation Auction this year? I would like to buy."

"Konrad will shoot you down if you go there. He's still cross about your move two years ago."

"Of course, I will not go by myself. Somebody else will bid for me. Perhaps someone close. We're almost family now." He said with a satisfied grin plastered on his face.

"You're very certain you would be admitted, and that is still to be decided. I will not presume as to give advice to a man like you, but do you think this is wise? I have already told you I have no further interest in you than a mere friendship, if at all. I will not leave Konrad for anybody. I love him too much and with the children, I do more now. All his dirty secrets came out of the closet, and he has nothing more to hide. My love for him forced me to accept the Order. Please, give up on me. This obsession you have for me will only make you very miserable. You're an intelligent and handsome man. You could get anyone you want."

"Lintorff has not fully cleaned his closet yet. All right, Guntram, we'll see each other at the auction."

He went away with his three aides (goons really, they should take some etiquette lessons if they want to sit next to Ferdinand or Michael). I felt totally defeated and utterly tired.

Armin was in no time sitting in front of me. "What the fuck was that?"

"Watch your language. Remember your position," I growled before I realised what I'd done. Where did that come from? Shit, now I'm starting to sound like Konrad. I'm only one year older than him! Nevertheless, it worked. He looked humbled, waiting for an answer. "Ask your uncle after I speak about this with him."

Konrad was furious to find out: 1. Repin "still wants to fuck around with me". 2. "I'll make Gertrud pay for selling your paint to him". 3. "No chance he will be one of us." 4. I can't believe how foolish you can be. Why did you tell him where you were? He could have killed you just to weaken me!"

* * *

April 9th , 2005

Last night, Konrad returned from travelling for a full week abroad. I think he was in Russia, but I'm not sure. He arrived very late when the babies and myself were in bed. I was not expecting him for several days more and he looked utterly defeated as he sat on the bed. I was immediately putting my arms around his neck and kissing him.

"Is something wrong, my love?"

"The Order accepted Repin ten days ago, without consulting me, and after our meeting. I was forced to fly to St. Petersburg to coordinate our new joint ventures."

"Can't you kick him out?"

"It was a unanimous decision. The whole Council voted against my recommendation. Even zu Löwenstein. I can't go against all of them. Repin bribed some of them or blackmailed others. I don't care. Idiots! Now that he's in, there would be no way to stop him from taking it over. I was even told that we should "modernize", and forget our original rules and objectives. These rules saved us many more times than I can remember. Repin is already planning on eliminating several of the councillors because "they're no apt to be where they are. Look Konrad, they sold for less than thirty silver coins their best Griffin!" He had the nerve to tell me. All of them are touched by greed and complacency."

"You knew this would happen sooner or later. You told it to me in Vienna. Will you resign?"

"I would love to, but I can't. If I do it now, Armin will have no chances at all. I still don't know if there would be a Griffin's title left for him, but this is the least I can do for my ancestors."

"I'm terribly sorry you have all these problems because of me, Konrad. Your life was more or less in order till you met me." I was sorry for him. After all, this bloody organization was his life.

"Guntram, this is not because of you, dear. Repin's line has been against the Order for many decades."

"Line? Since when did mobsters have lines? He's just a criminal!"

"He's a criminal like many of his ancestors, but it doesn't prevent him to descend from old Russian nobility. His family left the country after 1905 Revolution and established themselves in France. His mother was an Arseniev. His great-grandfather was a councillor for Nicholas II and her wife was a lady in waiting to the Empress. They blame the Order for not helping the Romanov during the Revolution. The Arseniev were powerful and clever enough as to move to Paris, where they continued to rule till 1917. They lost all their lands in Russia. The Order should have contributed more with the White Army, but my Great Grandfather decided to put his money on the communist side so the Russians will fall back from the War. He made also many businesses with the Reds during their industrialization process. This Arseniev woman married Repin, who was a senior officer in the KGB, almost ruling by himself the Caucasus area. By the 70's, his family returned to Odessa where they profited from smuggling Western products into Russia. With the fall of the Soviet Union, the cash he inherited from his mother's side and the contacts from his father, he bought the main industries, and organised many of the criminal bands."

"I don't care if he cleans the Order a little. It will teach them right. I never wanted him with us because he only plays for himself. He's using us for something else, bigger. Repin will destroy us all in the process. Now that he's an associate, I can't do a thing against him, unless he deliberately attacks us, which he will never do till it's time to give us the final blow. That you crossed his path was an unfortunate coincidence."

Chapter 31

June 2nd , 2005

The bloody auction was yesterday. Under pressure, I presented four paintings, and all of them were sold. I pleaded Konrad not to participate in this charade because it was useless to fight openly with Repin, now that he's the Order's favourite child. He agreed and behaved like a gentleman even congratulating the same person who bought two of them for a crazy price. At least, Tita could buy one, and the last one went to a known banker from Frankfurt.

Konrad told me he had to meet with Repin already twice. I swear next Easter, I will leave the house one week before the holidays and return a full week after. If they meet for Christmas, I'm not going, no matter what Konrad says, pleads, offers, threatens or bribes.

I wish it were already August and I could take the children somewhere for the summer. I will not go to Argentina. Somewhere here. They're getting bigger and bigger with each passing day. Klaus said "papa" to Konrad… and then to the nurses, Friederich, me… and Mopsi. Karl decided to go for a more useful word: *Wasser* which he uses whenever he wants some.

* * *

July 17th , 2005

Two days ago, I arrived with the children to Sylt. It's a very small island in the north of Germany but the house is very beautiful. It used to be the holiday place for the Lintorffs in the XIX and XX century, and they still keep part of the original private beach. It's a desertic place, and I'm still surprised how soft the sand and how blue the sea are. The children are completely happy about rolling on the sand but they look the sea from a safe distance. Even Klaus. The haunting loneliness of the place appeals me a lot.

The villa is built in the traditional Island style and has eight bedrooms. I admit there's not much to do around here and if you want to go to a restaurant, you have to drive twenty minutes, but on the other hand, you can sit on the beach in absolute peace and relax. The wind might be an inconvenience when drawing but it's no more than two toddlers trying to eat your pencils and drink your ink. I love the place and still don't understand why Armin said I was crazy for coming here. "*Majo* ('Boy', he's learning some Spanish for his own holidays in Ibiza… should I tell him they prefer Catalá there?), you're utterly crazy. There's nothing, but old aristocrats, people with money and one good restaurant. It's like the Königshalle, but with sand and wind. Why don't you come with me and some friends to Ibiza? Lots of alcohol and women!" Yes, Armin, I can imagine myself there. I can't drink and for the girls, didn't you notice I share the bed with your 'uncle'?

So far we haven't done much with the boys. They crawl and play with the sand in the beach while I draw them or read a book. Konrad has to work in London, but he promised to be here around the 20th. I already miss him.

* * *

July 23rd, 2005

I was with Ulrike trying to feed Klaus as he was probing to be a real challenge today. With many, many blandishments I was able to put half of his purée in, but he was still making faces at the chicken. I was so focused on trying to put a small piece of it inside of him that I didn't hear Konrad creeping behind my back. He nearly made me jump of the chair when his covered my eyes with his big hands. Both babies found my shock very funny, and they started to laugh.

"Do you need help with Klaus? He asked me after giving me a mind blowing kiss. Ulrike discreetly disappeared only nodding at him.

"No, thank you, he's slowly eating. Karl would like to carry on. The doctor says we shouldn't force them to eat. We have to let them do it at their own pace."

"I'm not so sure about that. They should learn discipline."

"They're only a year old, still trying to stand up without holding," I protested somewhat feebly.

Konrad kissed Klaus and Karl and took Ulrike's place and started to feed Karl much faster than I, and the baby was delighted to have his father around. They finished fast and Konrad took the Karl outside, after cleaning his mouth. It took me some time to finish with Klaus as he had decided it was time to make funny faces at me to get as much attention from me as possible. I supposed he was jealous that his brother got their father all to himself.

Finally, he finished his dish, and I released him from his high chair, after getting him cleaned. "We'll see what your father and your brother are doing," I whispered as I took him in my arms. I got a happy pull in my hair as answer.

Karl and Konrad were very busy in the beach as the baby was piling sand. Konrad had removed his jacket, vest and tie, leaving them on the sand. Klaus was immediately interested in them and started to move the fabrics around. His Italian silk tie was immediately inside his mouth and he bit it with a lot of enthusiasm.

"Don't you want to save your things, Konrad? I'll take care of them while you change your clothes."

"Don't worry, it's only a tie. I'm coming directly from a meeting in the morning in Berlin."

A rapt cry of happiness from Klaus as he found his father's mobile phone attracted Karl, who in no time caught the blackberry. "No, that thing not, little man. That toy is only for grown ups." Konrad said, recovering it from the baby's fingers. I rescued the phone before it would finish on the sand or in the bucket full of salty water they had.

"Konrad really, you should change. Next, they will be trading euros against pounds," I giggled.

"No problem as long as they get a good price," he laughed as Karl fumbled more with the jacket and took his noble fountain pen out. "All right, these gentlemen have convinced me," he said as he gathered his things, under the unhappy look of the babies.

448

Sometime later, he returned, changed into a casual polo shirt and trousers. We spend one hour more playing with the children on the beach, till they started to become nasty as their nap time was long past due. I took them inside the house and gave them to the nanny Ulrike. They should sleep up to five.

I went outside again and I looked for Konrad. He had left the sand and was sitting in one of the big closed chairs facing the sea, watching at it. I sat beside him and he put his arm around my shoulders, pulling me against his chest, kissing me softly on the forehead. I returned his tender gesture, kissing his fingers. I felt him tightening his embrace. I opened my mouth to say that I was happy to see him again, but he only shushed me delicately. "Shhh, Guntram, enjoy the peace."

We stayed for a long time, just holding each other and looking at the sea and hearing the seagulls croaking. I was overwhelmed by my love for him. I felt completely in peace with myself and for the first time in my life, I had a family.

Chapter 32

December 19ᵗʰ, 2005

Yesterday, I had to go to one of Konrad's charity parties in Paris. I was surprised that we had to attend since he hates to go to such things, and keeps his appearances to a minimum. But this one was organized by Aunt Elisabetta von Lintorff and we both knew better than to miss it. I was not happy to leave the children in Zurich, not even for a night, but at the last moment I let Konrad convince me to take the plane with him.

The party was to celebrate the fifty years of a Non Governmental Organization for children living in war zones. Elizabetta is one of their past presidents, and I'm sure she got a check from Konrad as birthday present. The place was absolutely full as they had invited all the organizations, donors, press, etc. who had worked with them. Walking through was an impossible task. Forget about getting to the buffet table.

In order to avoid being crushed by the elegant mob I took refuge behind Konrad who was clever enough as to find a good corner and defend it. No chance he would start to mingle with people. If you wanted to speak with him, you should come and since it was no business or an art auction, he had no interest to speak with anybody. Several were brave enough as to approach us, but his stern face kept the rest at bay.

I noticed a man in his sixties looking at me several times, and I smiled back at him, thinking he was one of Konrad's business acquittance also trapped like us. He understood that it was an invitation to come to me. Excellent, I have to speak with somebody when departure time is only 10 minutes away!

"Good evening. My name is Nicholas Lefebvre. I'm sorry to importunate you, but you remind me so much to a person I met in the past."

What? Is he using that old pick up line in front of Konrad? By the way, he was already looking at the man like a lion to a gazelle.

"I'm afraid, I don't know you, sir," I replied praying he would take the hint and beat it.

"No, no. That person is dead. He was a lawyer working with me in a long deceased foundation offering legal assistance to political refugees, immigrants and poor people. Your features are so similar to his when I met him in May 68. It's like seeing a ghost. Perhaps this legend about doppelgänger is true," he explained.

"I was born in 1982, Mr…"

"Lefebvre. Nicholas. Your grace?"

"De Lisle."

"Are you related to Jerôme de Lisle, the lawyer?" He asked me, sounding genuinely surprised.

"He was my father," I said losing the colour in my face. Konrad was immediately behind me.

"Yes! You must be his son. Gustav!" he cried in ecstasy.

"Guntram."

450

"Yes, I remember now. Guntram. Your father named you after the Merovingian king to ease the tensions with your grandfather, but it was hopeless. The *Vicomte* never accepted his lifestyle. He was the black sheep of the family! A real pity he was so sick in the end and took that decision. You look so much like him. He was never the same man, after Cécile passed away."

"My father was sick?" I asked utterly astonished. Nobody ever told me a thing.

"Yes, pancreas cancer. Spread like fire. One of the worse kinds. Nothing stops it and the pain is horrible in the last stages. I would have done the same. Are you feeling all right?"

"Mr. Lefebvre, I think is time for us to go. Good night," Konrad said starting to pull from my arm.

"I never knew my father was sick. He left no suicide note or said anything to me," I whispered, feeling very dizzy.

"You didn't know? I recommended the lawyer in Argentina who took care of your trustee fund. Your father and I worked for several years in that foundation. He was an idealist and a hell of a lawyer!"

"My father worked in a bank."

"I don't think this is the appropriate place to discuss such things. If you want, we can make an appointment for later. I'll give you my card." Konrad interrupted us, hurriedly.

"It was pro bono. They were not paying us at all," he answered me, totally ignoring Konrad "He started in Credit Auvergne, in the legal office there. His family put him to work before he would start to throw cobblestones at De Gaulle or Pompidou again. That small bank belonged to your family, if I see correct, but it was dismantled in the 90's. It's incredible. You're exactly like him at this age. Even the gestures! Why don't we run away from here, and you tell me about you. My firm already left the present and they don't need me any more."

"Yes, that would be nice," I replied before Konrad would say no, and ranted about security. Let's choose a neutral place. "Would you like to have something with us at the hotel's lobby. It's not far away from here."

"Say which one, and I'll tell my chauffeur to pick me up there."

"Crillon," I answered as I felt Konrad becoming more upset than ever. I don't care if we fight later. This is the first person I met in my whole life who knew my father and could say something to me!

Konrad was furious when we arrived at the lobby. I was going to go to the Restaurant, but he grunted something like we have a living room upstairs. The man was telling us that he was an associate in a legal firm specialized in international commercial law based in Brussels. He gave his card to Konrad who was looking at him distrustingly. We entered and sat on the couches, and I ordered some coffee.

"This is such a coincidence! Unbelievable," the lawyer re started his happy chit chat.

"Indeed," Konrad growled still unhappy.

"Are you German?"

"Yes. Konrad von Lintorff."

The man was not impressed at all, and dismissed Konrad as if he were of no consequence. "The hair and the eyes colour are from Cécile. She was such a lovely woman. An artist without much luck, but her work was very nice and refreshing. She was giving me one of her paints for my marriage. I still have it in Brussels. The wife is gone with part of my money."

"My mother was an artist?" I said puzzled. I knew almost nothing about her. Only her name: Cécile Dubois.

"Not a professional. She used to paint and that is how your father met her in 1975 or 1977. I don't remember. It was summer and she was much younger than him, eight or ten years. I remember now. It was 1975 because your father was joking during her pregnancy that it would help him to overcome the "Seventh Year Itch", like the comedy. When he married her in 1975, it was the family's scandal because she was an Art Student in Paris, without family or money. Jerôme told me once that they wanted to marry him with some rich German woman, but he hated the idea, and after school he was in bad terms with them."

"I never met my family. It was only me and my father."

"Not surprised to hear it. His whole family died within months before his suicide. The father, brothers and families. No, no. Only one brother and family. The other went away to… South Africa, I think. Jerôme didn't like his family at all, and I believe this is why he looked for a lawyer to take care of you. How is Martínez Estrada? Did he learn French finally? I defended him when the French government wanted to send him back to Argentina on terrorism charges. He was just an activist escaping from the Military Junta. I got him to be a political refugee, and later a French citizen despite he couldn't say *bonjour* to save his life!" he laughed remembering.

Yes, that is true. Luciano never spoke anything else than Spanish, and this is why he never was able to communicate with my father. He told me there was another French lawyer who explained him what was required of him.

"He's very fluent in several languages," I said testing him.

"Luciano? Impossible! Spanish and nothing else. He even taught me to swear in the local dialect, very funny. He was in Montoneros, but in a lower rank. Compañero Chano was his *nom de guerre*." Also true. He told me about his time as a refugee in Paris and how he came back in 1985.

"Why do you say my father was the black sheep of the family?"

"Did I? It's ironic boy. His family was old nobility from Poitiers, had a small bank in then Auvergne, and some lands in Poitiers. His father worked in a bank here in Paris; a private one. Very strict man and Jerôme was the rebel of the family. He was the middle child. I met him in May 68 when he was studying Law at La Sorbonne; a total rebel. Casting stones in the middle of the mess, several times in jail for street fighting with the CRS. The family disowned him after the third time they had to bail him out that June, afraid they would lose their contacts with the establishment here. Stupid people! It was the national sport at the time!"

"My father was an activist?"

"Activist is a word too big. He was in the middle of the mess like all of us. He was in no party or believed in anything. He was a total hippie and idealist. He had no money to buy food, but was giving the little he had to homeless people. He was one of the best lawyers I ever saw. Impossible to catch in the Courts. Creative to no end. When you were finished exposing an idea, he had already rebutted it. He also specialized in tax law and finances. He hated with passion the banking system, saying they were the true rulers of the world, and the only way to finish with them was to undermine their power from within the system. He graduated with honours at twenty-three years old. The family made enormous pressure on him to put him to work along with his father. He hated it completely, and was working with us every time he could. We still believed in changing the world. He had a strained, but polite relationship with his family."

"Everything changed when he married. Your mother was below their expectations, so to speak. I would have killed to have a woman like her! Sadly, she had a heart condition and couldn't work much, so he had to work more at the family's bank branch in Paris to make ends meet as he had bought a small flat for his wife. And boy, this is how all rebels finish their careers; with a mortgage," he chuckled.

"Did he have no support from his family?"

"He could have had, but he was too stubborn to accept it. "You sell your soul if you take something from them" he used to say. I never met his brothers or father. He told me once "Why do you want to ruin a perfectly good day by meeting them?" We used to gather with some other people from the *fac* at cafés but when I got a job as junior partner in Brussels in 1979 in this big law firm, I moved and lost contact. I met him again in 1982, after his wife passed away and he was another man—defeated and utterly sad. A real pity. He only lived for his work and to support his child."

"You never saw him again?"

"Now and then. Mostly we wrote to each other or talked over the phone. Consulting cases of mine. That is the strange part. He was always very reserved about his job or clients. By mid 1988, he came unannounced to my office in Brussels, and asked me to look for a trustful lawyer to be appointed your tutor in case of his dead. I recommended Luciano, thinking that he was too paranoid. I didn't know he was already sick. These things are very bad, kill you in less than five years with treatment. One of the partners in the firm had it too. I saw him again in Brussels by December 1988, and he was very sick then. He told me the doctors were not giving him no more than a few months. He set all his affairs in order, and went to Argentina to meet the lawyer I recommended. Later, in the Spring of 1989, I read in the press about the his father and brother's deaths', along with the Credit Auvergne bankruptcy scandal. I tried to contact him to see how he was faring, but it was impossible. He had just disappeared like his other brother. Both accused of fraud and justice fugitives."

"Honestly I never believed it. He was too decent to do something like this. It made no sense. He was not interested in money. He had a very good paying job as a bank's legal office head, and that's every lawyer's wet dream. All the money he earned was put into your accounts. He was still living in a small two bedrooms flat in Montmartre! He didn't have a car! Taking the metro always. On August 4th, the police asked me to collaborate in the inquiry regarding his suicide. He had even made the arrangements for his own funeral, and it was only me and my wife there."

"I was informed of his death one week after and never knew anything about uncles or my grandfather," I whispered.

"Chano decided to keep it away. You didn't know them. They never cared about you and rejection hurts children a lot. You can ask for the police report if you want. There is everything explained. I can help you with the forms. I'll give you my card and you can call me whenever you want."

"Perhaps. I don't know. I was under the impression he never loved me much. He was very kind to me when he was around, but he was always away."

"He put up with his family and job only to give you a better life. He worked his way to his grave. With his death he saved the capital he had put together for you, not to mention that it was in another country, supporting a minor. No judge could have touched, it in the unlikely case they would have found it because it was never registered. Only Chano knew about it. Not even I. Chano joked several times that it was the only time in his life he was near a Swiss bank's account. He was a good hearted man, but with a Machiavellian intelligence."

"How can you be so sure he wasn't involved in the fraud?" Konrad asked softly, visibly pale.

"It wasn't his way. If at twenty you give your sandwich to a *clochard* what makes you think you would be different at forty? No, he was a selfless person. You should have seen his eyes sparkling when he spoke about Guntram the last time I saw him. He was a fantastic lawyer; never lost a case or a negotiation in his life. A real shark. My firm offered him countless times a job as Senior Partner, but he refused. He stayed in that place because of his father and brothers. Do you really think he would have been caught with something so stupid like bank fraud in a third rate institution, when he was head of legal affairs of a Swiss private bank? No. It's not logical, and Jerôme had a Cartesian mind. There was something keeping him there."

"Do you remember the name of this bank?" Konrad inquired.

"Let me see… it was dissolved in the 90's… just a second… Services Financiers Méditeranée. Geneva based."

"Do you know them Konrad?"

"Guntram in the 90's, there were about 550 small private banks operating in Switzerland alone!" he snorted letting a dry laugh out and shaking negatively his head. "In the last decade the number decreased to 350. Some of them are just for bookkeeping or belong to private families, and they're just a few million in a hedge fund. Many are just postal addresses. This is a very traditional business whose future depends on innovation, therefore changes and merges are very common. In Bahamas there are more than 400 authorised banks, but less than 200 have offices, and many of them are only a desk. I could try to locate them, but the best is if you ask your own lawyer."

"My lawyer told me he never knew where my father worked. He only gave me a box with his personal belongings like letters and photos from the family. Perhaps it would be still possible to track the origin of the money in my trustee fund."

"No chance Guntram. Swiss Banking Secrecy laws. There is no time limit. It can only be lifted in case of drugs, weapons trade or terrorism now. The law allows it also for divorces and inheritance claims, but it's almost impossible to get something out. Besides, your inheritance is already settled. Perhaps the Argentinean records are already destroyed as well." Mr. Lefebvre explained to me. "The best you can do is read the police report over your father's death. It will not be easy, and I'm afraid you will achieve nothing. He had not many friends. It was strange. He liked to help people a lot but never made any kind of friendships. After Cécile's death he stopped visiting most of our friends from the school. At his funeral, it was only me and my former wife."

Chapter 33

December 27th, 2005

I've decided to call this French lawyer, my father's friend, and ask him if he could help me to look for the police report about my father's death. I'll do it after the holidays are over. I know it won't be nice and I don't want to ruin Konrad's days off.

I would like to know more about my father. Alas, I have to ask "permission" from Konrad. After the man left our suite in Paris, he shouted at me like crazy for almost going "blindly after an unknown man. You're worse than a child. What if I had not been there, and it would have been a trap? I will make a full investigation on him before you ever go near him."

However, this man's story was true. I found him in an old photo with my parents and three other people, sitting outside a café in Montmartre. Behind it was written "Cécile, Jerôme, Silvie, Nicholas et Louis, 7 Julliet 1979". Chano, I mean, Dr. Martínez Estrada, my lawyer, also confirmed the story. He was very surprised that I've met "Nico". He only spoke with my father in Argentina because when "Nico" helped him with his case, in 1977, my father was only sporadically going to this place. He used to take more cases about people being evicted or with with troubles with banks, nothing related to politics. Besides, my father never made the slightest effort to learn Spanish.

"Guntram, do you think I would have taken such a responsibility as a child is, if I haven't known at least the person who recommended me your father? Nico saved my life, and he told me that your father helped me a lot to present my case. I would have been meatballs if the French Government would have returned me. When your father came to my office, he had to bring a translator along. He only signed the papers, and informed me of his accounts. He ordered me very clearly to be quiet about your family's death in France. I never saw him again."

I don't know why Konrad looked so shocked when Goran confirmed that Lefebvre and my father worked together in that law firm for poor people from 1972 to 1984 for free. They both also worked in a NGO for political refugees. The NGO is long dead, since 1988. It's not so rare to help people, Konrad. Lefebvre is Senior Partner in a law firm in Brussels and works there since 1983. He's one of those several thousand euros per hour lawyer, divorced and without children.

During May 68, he and my father were arrested four times. I know from where comes my dislike for police officers.

Not everybody is trying to fool you Konrad.

* * *

December 28th, 2005

Konrad exploded when I told him about my idea to know more about my father's death.

"What do you want to know? He was very sick and killed himself to avoid a slow and painful death! End of story!"

"Why all my family died before him? Why was he accused of bank fraud if he was such a good person? I don't understand a thing, and it seems I have a living relative. An uncle, no less! You have no idea how hard is to grow without anybody around you!" I shouted back at him.

"And what exactly do you want to do? Ask for the files of a case closed over sixteen years ago? The only thing you will find are the photos of your father's body, and it won't be a pretty sight! He jumped from a building! Have you ever seen a dead body in your life Guntram?"

I never thought of it that way. I gulped and lost my colour. He continued. "Normally, the head is the first part that hits the ground. It literally explodes when it touches the ground. Do you want this to be your last image of your father? Remember the man who used to play with you or the man in the photos you have."

"I want to know what happened. All my life I asked myself about it. I didn't even know he loved me, like this lawyer said. I didn't even know how my mother was or that she was an artist! What happened in that bank? Where do I come from? Why my father never told me my Grandfather was a *Vicomte* and his family name dated from the XV century, but their origins were much older? Where is my uncle and why did never contact me?"

"Guntram, such things are not in a police report. If you want, I could hire someone to investigate more about your father, but don't ruin your life by looking at something you don't want to see. Most probably the title is lost with the land."

"I don't want the title! I only want to understand what happened."

"*Maus*, let me check thoroughly this man Lefebvre again. I don't believe in coincidences. If he's a real person, you can speak with him again, but don't ask for those papers. It will only hurt you. Do you want to read your father's medical reports? To see how much pain he was in?"

"No," I whispered.

"I'll ask Goran to look for somebody to investigate your family's history. The bankruptcy's story should have been in the newspapers. It will not be nice to read it, and the press can be truly hurtful."

"I see. Could you do this for me, Konrad?"

"Yes, my love."

* * *

January 23rd, 2006

Konrad kept his word, and hired a private investigator in France. The man searched in the local newspapers, and found some information about the Crédit Auvergne's bankruptcy but nothing about the other bank, the one my father was working for. No society was ever registered under the name "Services Financiers Méditeranée", in France or in Switzerland. Lefebvre swears that was the name, and even gave me a card with my father's name on it, and this bank's address in the Ave. Kleber, in Paris. That's not the place for a bank.

The Crédit Auvergne's bankruptcy was the typical story. Local bank, heavily relying on the local politicians, farmers and industrials, with more debts than capital and no way they can come out of it. My grandfather, Louis de Lisle and his two sons, Pascal de Lisle and Jerôme, started to grant themselves credits for millions of francs when the things started to go really bad for the institution, robbing the clients' money. According to the press, they all made a suicide pact before going to jail. The money just vanished into thin air, and many people were ruined; most of them farmers, retired people, veterans and shopkeepers. All my family assets were liquidated by the Justice to make some payments to the clients, but they only recovered twelve percent of their deposits. I felt very disappointed at my father's deeds.

"Darling, I'm so sorry you had to hear such bad things about your father." Konrad comforted me after the private investigator left his office.

"You were right that is not what I wanted to hear. I don't know why Lefebvre said he didn't believe it for a minute. There was an official investigation and they all were found guilty, except my uncle Roger."

"Guntram, I've seen this many times before. Come, sit down with me. I think you need a hug."

I circled his desk and sat like a small child on his lap, putting my arms around his neck, and burying my face on his shoulder. "I'm the son of a crook," I said dejectedly.

"Shhh, don't say that love. It's not true," Konrad told me, caressing my head lovingly. "That lawyer couldn't be so wrong, and perhaps your father was an honourable man. Didn't you tell me that he was defending embargoed people without charging a cent? Look what a fine son he sired. I will always be indebted to him for giving you to me."

"Such things you say. I love you." We remained holding each other for a long time. Sadness engulfing me slowly and determinately.

"I'm sorry I spent your money on this."

"Shhh, don't mention it. It was nothing. Guntram, your father is dead and can't defend himself. Don't judge him, and remember him as the man who used to play horses with you. His friends never believed those accusations. Lefebvre described him exactly as you are, well without mutiny against the police officers. Do you really think that such a man would have stolen money from retired people? Whatever happened is in the past, and you can't change it. Think on the future, on our sons, not in an old story."

"Yes, you're right, but I can't help to think about my uncle Roger. Where is he now? Why did he never care about me?"

"Lefebvre said your father and your uncles had a very bad relationship, and you lived abroad all your life. Why should he care about you?"

"Yes, you're right. In my family's photo album there are a lot of photos of my mother's side family; the old aunts who rose her, of her and my father, friends of them, several from my grandmother. There are only two photos from my grandfather and his sons when they were small children. My father didn't appreciate them much."

"Do you want that the investigator looks for your uncle? I don't know if this would be possible. Perhaps he changed his name when he moved to South Africa. Was it not there where he went, according to Lefebvre?"

"No, let it. I don't think he will receive me with open arms." I smiled weakly. "You're right. It's all in the past, and I don't feel it like mine," I sighed.

"That's right my love. You are part of my family now, and have to go to all the family gatherings. Aunt Elisabetta was telling me the other day that she's thinking in going for a few days to Lisbon, well Sintra, and she needs someone named Guntram to accompany her. You and the children could go there for four or five days. I have to go to China for a few days also."

*　*　*

February 3rd, 2006
Sintra

Elisabetta has a fantastic villa here, like a French Style Mansion. It's a little bit far away from the town and in the middle of the forest one on the Kings of Portugal planted on the XIX century. I don't remember his name, only that he was brother of the same who married the Queen Victoria... Someone from the Sachsen Coburg House from Germany. The whole area is a national park, Cascais.

It's not so cold as in Zurich and more sunny even if it's February. Klaus and Karl are very happy with the place, and I have trouble keeping them away from the fountain. They love to play with water! Their favourite game is to bathe Mopsi by filling their sand buckets with water and pouring them over her. Fortunately, she has learnt her lesson well, and runs away when she sees them coming.

I'm completely in love with Sintra. It's a very small town, with a huge, strange looking castle with two big towers, which were kitchen ovens in the centre of it, big trees on every street, houses decorated with tiles of every colour, pottery stores and small streets full of life. It reminds me in a way to an Italian city, but the Portuguese are less noisy. The silence around the place is incredible. They all speak very softly, and the language sounds very musical even if I don't understand a word of it.

*　*　*

February 5th, 2006

Yesterday, Elisabetta decided to go to Lisbon for the day. She wanted to "buy new linens, and there's nothing like the Portuguese lace work." First notice I have. I was supposed to tag along with her, but Klaus woke up in the morning running a little fever, and I decided to stay at home with him.

In the afternoon, I decided to go with the car to Sintra to have a coffee and some peace. Both children were completely excited, and I was dead after playing with them. I love them but I also need some time off. I took one of the small cars, and left the security guard at home, because nothing can happen in this small town, and I only intended to be out for two hours.

I drove to the town and parked near the castle. It was too late to visit it. I saw a small café in front of it, and decided to go inside for a cappuccino and some peace. Perhaps draw a little.

The waitress brought me what I ordered, and I just sat enjoying the silence, only interrupted by the crackling fire in the chimney. The place was empty, and I took my sketchpad out, and started to draw what I remembered from the other castle on top to the mountain.

"It looks like the original one. Do you sell?" A tall and informally dressed woman asked me. She looked like a tourist. American by her accent.

"Thank you. No, I don't sell them. I'm not a professional artist," I replied, while she sat uninvited at my table. What happened to the times when ladies behaved as such?

"You don't need to. You look pretty well loaded," she stated as she extend her hand. "Linda Harris."

"It's just a hobby, Ms. Harris," I said coldly, not shaking her hand, but bowing my head.

"Wow, you're a hard nut to crack," she laughed. "Won't you invite me something? Always thought European aristocrats were very well mannered," she snorted this time.

"I'm not an aristocrat, madam. If you'd excuse me."

"Are you not the grandchild of Louis Philippe Alphonse de Lisle, *Vicomte* de Marignac?" She asked "Don't you live with Konrad Maria Ulrich von Lintorff Sachsen Löwenstein, *Herzog* von Wittstock?"

"Madam is very well informed. Good evening," I said and rose to leave the place.

"Come on, I'm much better looking than Trevor Jones from the Independent Times. I don't want to talk about Lintorff or his banks. I would like to speak about your family."

"I don't speak with the press."

"Don't you feel curious about your father's death? Trevor and I worked like crazy on it. The Order did an incredible job to cover everything about the de Lisles. There's not even a stone left in what was the *château* they had near Poitiers," she said nonchalantly. "Buy me a coffee, and I'll tell you something about it."

I took my seat again. Was this another elaborated ruse? 'Guntram what are you thinking? They're against the Order, therefore they're enemies! Get the fuck out,' my brain told me. Alas, my heart decided to stay.

"What would you like to drink?" I asked her. She laughed.

"Coffee would be fine. It's almost impossible to speak with you or come near you. Where are your goons today? Didn't you pay them, and they're on strike?"

I gave her a cold stare. She coughed and dropped her act of "cocky outgoing girl". "Your own family told us about the Order, sixteen years ago. Roger de Lisle was our main informer till his death two years ago. Car accident, like always. Trevor thought you would help us, but it seems you didn't want to."

"As I said to your friend, if he has something, he should go to the authorities," I told her automatically, completely shocked by the news my uncle was dead, and I didn't have the slightest idea. Was he an informant? Of what? "I don't believe for a minute you knew my family. It's a very stupid and hurtful lie."

"Well boy, we were shocked that you, of all people, would be on a permanent basis in Lintorff's bed. I suppose he has a clear idea of what he likes. You look very much like Roger. Almost like a twin. Funny because your father was a brunette with green eyes. You take only your features after your dad."

"I don't understand a word."

"Easy. Look at this picture, and tell me what you see," she said, putting out of her handbag a photo, and giving it to me.

It was a picture of four men in evening suits. One of them was my father, exactly as I remembered him, looking totally unimpressed and bored, another man, looking very similar to me, but in a more elegant and sophisticated version with his blue eyes and dark brown hair, and a two other men. One of them was a younger version of Ferdinand and the other was none other than Konrad himself.

Time stopped as I tried to understand what my eyes were seeing. Konrad knew my father? And Ferdinand too? They were sitting at a table in a party or something like that. No, it's a trick, like those you can make with Photoshop.

"It's a photo of my father," I said with a trembling voice.

"With your uncle Roger, Lintorff and von Kleist. Roger gave Trevor this photo the minute he found out that you were living with Lintorff. He could have never approached you because he would have been killed on sight. He and his family. They're now living in Brazil, I think. Trevor tried to speak with you, but diplomacy was never his strongest feature. Roger only told us that his family was part of the Order, and tried to go against the Lintorffs, but they failed and everybody with the exception of him and you, were murdered.

I sighed very relieved. "Do you know how ridiculous it sounds? The Lintorffs massacred my whole family, and then Konrad decided I'm the best option to put in his bed?"

"I know it sounds bizarre. You don't have to believe me. Ask Marianne von Liechtenstein, Lintorff's mother. She will tell you the truth. That woman is very brave, and will do whatever in her power to destroy that evil organization. She lives in Paris. Call her. She wants to tell the truth only to you. I'll leave you her number and mine, if you want to talk afterwards."

"Don't bother. It's another elaborated charade from your newspaper. Get a life!" I shouted at her, leaving the place and going directly to my car. I threw a €20 note on the counter on my way out.

On the wind shield, there was a small note with the phone numbers. I made a ball with the piece of paper, and threw it into a trash can. No need to sully a nice town despite the lousy visitors it has.

I drove home at full speed the sinewy road. It was dark when I arrived and went directly to my bed. I was too nervous to go to the children.

Fuck those journalists! Fuck the Order! My family had nothing to do with them! We had only a second, no, third rate bank in the Auvergne! Nothing that could be considered "suitable" for "membership". Konrad and the others would have never spoken to one of us. Sitting in the same table? Never! That photo was an hoax to make me fall, and talk about the Order.

Konrad would have told me if he knew my father or Ferdinand for that matter.

Didn't Konrad tell me that his former lover's name was Roger? I'm sure. I wrote it down in my diary. He always said we looked alike, as my uncle and I do.

No way! Konrad helped me to get information about my family, and defended my father even, and his former lover was more or less the devil in disguise. *No*, his brothers and father did it. They were scheming and plotting against Konrad behind his back. This Roger was a sexy puppet on their hands. Konrad wasn't lying when he spoke well about my father. I can tell when he does it.

Anyway, it's just a coincidence. Roger is a common name. If he would have been called Guntram or Lothar, the story would have been different.

Why the hell did Konrad say that he was grateful to my father "because he gave you to me"? I can't shake the idea off that it was more than a common place said to appease me. It's an absurd phrase. The way my family died looks very much to the Order's "modus operandi" as Repin would describe it.

No. It's too crazy. Guntram, you're buying their poison. Those guys are fanatics. Some of them believe that the Illuminati are an alien race of lizards, like those on "V" or that they want to exterminate two thirds of the whole human race. Nothing would prevent them from glueing heads on a photo and come up with that lie.

I will say nothing about this. Tomorrow, I will take the children and return to Zurich.

Chapter 34

February 8th, 2006

This morning, I was working the whole day, trying to catch up what I missed in school the previous week. I stayed in the Library, enjoying the peace and quiet of the place as everybody were in the classrooms. I couldn't shake an uneasiness feeling off since that woman approached me in Sintra. She seemed so sure my father's death wasn't a suicide.

He was very sick, two different people told me that, and Chano had a copy of his medical file from the insurance company. He really had cancer and was declared terminal.

Why would she name Konrad's mother, and what could she know? Konrad hates her guts. He didn't invite her to the children's baptism, although she's the grandmother! He never mentioned her ever again since that time in Paris. If she needs something, she speaks with Monika. She's a society lady in Paris, Marianne von Liechtenstein Faubourg, living with her second husband and children. I saw a picture of her in a posh magazine, at a VIPs room in Gatwick. It was taken at the Red Cross Ball. Friederich, who was with me that day, made me throw it away before Konrad would see it. "The Duke would be furious if he sees it. Those were very bad times for him." Why on earth would she want to speak with me, if true?

I closed my laptop and went to one of the PC stations. I wanted to do some research, and I didn't want it to be registered in my own computer. The probation period might have been lifted, but one can never be sure.

I googled my family's bank name and there it was. Several old press articles about the bankruptcy, many stories of the people ruined by us, the chronicles about the "suicidal pact". Shit! My cousins were seven, ten and twelve years old when they died! What kind of parents would do that only to avoid jail and bankruptcy? I had to close my eyes when I saw the first picture of the burned down house, and take a pill.

Konrad is right, there's nothing for me in here. If I would have been my father, and lived through all this, I would have jumped from that window too.

Still it doesn't make sense that a man, who spent eight years of his life, working pro bono for poor people, cheated or squeezed by banks, would steal millions from the same kind of people to give them to a family he despised.

* * *

March 19th, 2006

In ten days, it will be Karl and Klaus second birthday. I'm so happy and proud of them. Since they can walk alone, they're a constant source of mischief. No way they stay where you put them. They only last a few seconds!

Konrad and I had a huge fight over the birthday presents again. Konrad insisted with the bloody pony story! Again! Doesn't he ever give up?

"If you want one, get one for yourself!" I shouted at him finally. "No way I'll let you buy one till the babies turn five or six!"

"I'm their father and I know what is good for them."

"Good, don't come crying to me when the horse kicks one of your sons or if the doctor shouts at you because their backs are bent from horse riding! Can you not buy them something normal like a ball or a car?"

"All right, if you're so against my idea, I'll wait till next year," he said with a lot of dignity.

"Thank you. If you want, I can take care of the present. They're still too small to realise it's their birthday. You are the first person to say they have too much. I'll look for something small. Klaus likes wooden tools and Karl wants to have a grocery shop."

"Keep Klaus and his hammer away from the porcelain and Karl should keep his distance from my check book."

I laughed and replied, "You can always lend him some money to start his own business."

"If the business plan is good, perhaps," he said seriously.

I suspect that if the children ever ask for some extra money besides their established allowance, he will charge them interest without mentioning that he will force them to show him their bookkeeping.

* * *

March 22nd, 2006

After the University, I went to a toy store in Zurich to get what the children wanted, or at least, I think they like. I left Heindrik outside the store with the car.

"Sure you don't want to come in? You might find something you like," I asked him half seriously.

"A leash and a muzzle for you; I'll buy them at the pet store," he answered dryly.

"Do you really think you'd be able to hold the leash?" I fired back, slightly pissed off.

"Just go in, and don't take a full year to buy something."

"You're my favourite bodyguard," I snorted. This man can't take a joke.

"Exactly. Be nice or I'll complain to Goran."

"And I'll make you baby sit me and the twins in a children's place. Imagine a full afternoon, surrounded by screaming toddlers and bored mums. Toddlers are absolutely careless when they get an ice cream."

"You can be scarier than the Duke," he answered laughing. "Only the birthday presents, Guntram. I know you're fond of plush animals. I saw a badger in your studio," he gloated with infinite satisfaction.

I had to laugh. Inside the store a nice girl helped me with the things: one wooden stand with groceries in a very big size so they wouldn't eat them and a work bench with tools. They also got other toys to fulfil the order; one kitchen as they both want to have but they will have to share it along with the customary pots for it. Konrad can rant all what he wants about gender stereotypes later.

When I was paying and telling the saleswoman where to send the things, a nice looking girl dressed in a business suit addressed me.

"Mr. de Lisle? My name is Claudia Ellenberg. I'm Marianne von Liechtenstein's personal assistant. She asked me to give you this letter," she said curtly, putting an envelope in my hand and quickly going away. I was so surprised that without thinking I put it in my pocket, and went outside.

When I was at home, I went to my studio to open the letter.

"Dear Mr. de Lisle,

I need to speak urgently with you about a serious matter concerning my son and his relationship with you. Please contact me at this number, and we will arrange a meeting.

Marianne von Liechtenstein Faubourg"

Perhaps the woman wants to meet her grandchildren. Maybe I should give her a call, but after the birthday party. I can already imagine the explosion when I tell my love that his mother wants to meet Klaus and Karl. After all, it's her right as grandmother.

* * *

April 14th, 2006

This afternoon I phoned Konrad's mother. It's not that I didn't have the courage to do it, it's just that I had other things to do, like the birthday party, the bloody Order's meeting (I took the children to Geneva to Tita's house and she was delighted to have them, and returned on Saturday evening), the Easter Sunday Show, and hundreds of small things, like catching the brown rabbit smuggled and hidden in my closet. I wonder who could have done it?

I dialled her number, and a very cold voice answered it in French.

"My name is de Lisle. May I speak with the Princess, please?

"This is her. Good afternoon Mr. de Lisle. You took your time to answer my letter," she scolded me with a voice very similar to Konrad's.

"I apologise for my delay, Princess. I lost track of time. What can I do for you?" I replied not happy at all. She wants me to get in the middle of their war, at her side, and treats me like a dog?

"Can you come to Montreux for a meeting?"

"Madame I can't promise anything without knowing your intentions. I'm not sure if I could be of any help regarding your relationship with your son."

"With Konrad? I have no relationship, and I don't want to have one. He's a Lintorff," she said sounding like the iceberg that hit the Titanic.

"I'm afraid I'm lost now, Princess. You wrote it was about him."

"No, I wrote it was about your relationship with Konrad von Lintorff. It's about your father, Jerôme de Lisle. His mother, your grandmother, was a good friend of mine. Can you meet me in Montreux next Tuesday?"

"I'm not so sure if I can travel there."

"Tuesday at 12:00, Hotel de la Paix. My secretary will be waiting for you. Good day, sir," she hung up on me.

Well, bossing people around comes from her side, not doubt. Do I go or not? Will be difficult to shake Heindrik off once again. He's more alert now. Still doesn't trust me.

No, the best is if I take him with me.

Chapter 35

April 16th, 2006

It's not so easy to evade Konrad, but I think I did it. As almost five years of relationship have taught me, the best moment for asking for things, is after a particularly hot, steamy round of sex. He's tired and lowers his guard just a little. I cuddled against his chest and put my arms around his waist, nudging it with my face.

"Guntram, stop rubbing me as if you were a cat. You want something. Spill it."

"Only advise," I said falsely shocked. He pushed me away and looked at me, waiting for me to start. "Remember my art teacher, the one from the last year of school?"

"No."

"Yes, you should; the one who gave us the "Shopping at Christie's Introductory Course".

"Do you want something from Christie's?"

"No!" I said now frustrated. "She wrote me that she will be in Montreux next week, and wants to meet me to see how I am and etc."

"And etc.? What kind of sentence is that? You spend too much time with Armin. Soon it will be impossible to understand you."

"She wants to see my work, personally. I always send her a catalogue every year. She says she would like to buy something from me, but I'm not so sure about going. It's on a school day. A Tuesday!"

"And your student's honour forbids you to skip school," he mocked me. "Guntram go and return on the evening."

"Perhaps. I could take the train."

"No, you take Milan and Heindrik and your car. Where would you meet her?"

"Hotel de la Paix, at twelve o'clock. I'm sure she will buy nothing from me."

He sighed. "Guntram you will sell nothing. I know it. Probably the woman will return home with drawings worth several thousand francs for free. You're a disaster for sales."

"If I sell anything, should I tell Ostermann? Maybe he gets jealous. He's my manager after all."

"Last auction you told Tita not to pay more than 4,000 francs for your work, and the piece she loved so much was sold for 53,000. Ostermann gets an average of 12,000 for your oils."

"All right, I will take only watercolours or pencil drawings! It was not my fault people were in the mood to give! I'll put one of my paints on eBay and see if I get more than fifty dollars!"

"No more than ten pieces. Someone has to watch over your own interests," he said with a weary voice.

"Yes Konrad. As you say," I answered him sweetly.

* * *

April 24th, 2006

My life is in shambles. I can't still believe it, but he didn't deny it. Konrad admitted everything. In cold blood, and even told me I can't leave the Order never as I'm the chosen Consort and his children's tutor. The best thing he can do for the moment is to let me go "for a few days to Ferdinand's house to calm yourself down".

I hate that son of a bitch. I will never let him come near me again. I feel so dirty.

On April 20th, I attended my meeting with Marianne von Liechtenstein. She was already waiting for me at the hotel lobby, and ordered me to go to the hotel's restaurant as I refused to go to her suite. I still believed it could be a trap, and better to have some witnesses around. I noticed that Milan sat at a table far away.

"I see the Order still keeps a watchful eye on the Consort," she told me disdainfully. "Even if I don't approve of you for the position, you have my sympathy. I was also in your place and wore the same ring you wear now."

She was a tall and elegant woman. Mid-seventies I would say, and very nice bone structure with the most striking ice blue eyes, like Konrad's. Her voice was authoritative, and she spoke with mechanical precision.

"Madam, I'm not sure if I could intercede on your behalf in front of the Duke."

She chortled, humourlessly, freezing my blood in my veins. "I see he has fully trained you. Exactly like his father. Are you supposed to call him also your Grace at home?"

"If you don't approve of my relationship and you dislike me, why did you send for me?" I asked now losing my patience with that haughty woman.

"I don't intend to restart any kind of relationship with Konrad. It was an enormous satisfaction for me the day he decided to end any kind of contact between us. Rest assured, that I have no interest also in those two abominations he has for sons. That mockery of nature, created in an effort to look like a normal man."

"Good day, madam," I said, half rising from the chair.

"Sit. We'll go to business before your man jumps at me with his weapon. Is he from Krajina?"

"Yes."

"Like always. Blood thirsty hounds. One of them is always head of operations. The Lintorffs' like to breed them since several centuries."

"You said you knew my grandmother and wanted to speak about my father."

"You look very much like Roger de Lisle; almost a copy of your uncle. He was a truly despicable man, like all the de Lisles. Your father, on the other hand, was a good person; must have taken after her mother, Sigrid zu Guttenberg Sachsen. I still don't understand what she saw in the viscount to marry him and move to that forgotten place. She died completely alone of a cancer in 1965. Her husband wasn't even there, too busy shaking his tail to Hermann von Lintorff."

"In 1997, your uncle approached me in Capetown where I was on holidays. He said that he had met Konrad many years ago, and I told him that I didn't want to have any contact with him. But this person was aware of our bad relationship as they both had been lovers from 1981 to 1989, if I see correct. That Lintorff's son was homosexual didn't interest me at all, and I sent him away. If he wanted to blackmail me, he was wasting his time. I would not give a cent for Konrad."

"Why do you hate him so much? It was his father the one who changed the succession, madam," I said softly.

"This is what he told you? I see. Konrad actively sought to replace his brother since the day he was born. He would do everything to outshine his brother, Karl Maria. No matter how many times I pleaded him to stop it, he continued and continued. Karl Maria was never a strong or a very clever child. He had the most sweet nature you could ever wish, while Konrad was already wilful, impudent and very intelligent. His father adored him, and cast his eldest son away. In a way Konrad is much more responsible for his death than his own father."

"Konrad loved his brother. One of his children was named after him. He was silent for a full year, facing your cries and accusations of murdering. He was seven years old. As a mother you're a failure. It was a hunting accident," I retorted now furious.

"My son got a shot in the head so he would be out of the succession. His own father did it as he was considered "unworthy" of becoming Griffin. All of them did it because Konrad had exactly all the characteristics they were looking for in an heir. If he would have done what I asked from him, my husband would have passed the title to Hermann's line, and that would have been all. But no, he kept working harder and harder to displace Karl Maria. At seven, he could speak properly four languages, read and understand mathematics like a ten year old. He used to make his homework several times till it was perfect."

"As a parent, I should have been very proud to have a son like him."

"I was not. He was the cause his father nearly abandoned Karl, and finally killed him."

"I'm terribly sorry for your loss, but it was an accident. A horrible accident. Konrad was only seven year old! All children love to please their parents at that age," I tried to reason with her but she would have none of it.

"I hated him since he was born. I never wanted to have him. His father forced me to sire him as Karl Maria was "deficient" and "faulty". I gave him to the nannies since he was two days old, but he would still keep following me like a puppy all over the house. Pathetic creature!"

I couldn't believe my ears. This woman really carried him for nine months? Konrad had every reason to hate her if she made his life such a living hell. The person who hates you the most is your mother, and accuses of killing your brother at seven!

"I have no time to hear your rants Princess. All this should have been discussed with your husband and not with your child."

"You must be really in love to justify everything he does. Good. It serves my purposes. Do you want to know about your father's death or not? I know the story from Roger de Lisle himself, and I can prove every word I say."

"I'm listening to you, Madam," I said through clinched teeth.

"In 2003, Roger de Lisle came to me again and told me about this group of journalists fighting the Order. They're not many or have any real power, but they're persistent, and the only ones who had done something against them in decades. I knew about the de Lisles and several other members uprising in 1989, and I was surprised that he was spared because Konrad, as usual, had shown no mercy at all. This time, I was willing to hear him, and he said that he needed my help to get his nephew out of the Order."

I gaped at her for some minutes. It felt as if the air had been sucked from the room. "Are you telling me that my uncle and Konrad's lover were the same person?" I asked horrified as I understood finally.

"Yes, Roger told me of his adventure with Konrad, and how like the pathetic creep he is, fell in love with him. He would have done anything for Roger. Unfortunately, Konrad discovered the conspiracy, and stopped it before they would have succeeded. Roger spoke about Konrad's new lover, a small boy, not even twenty and not very bright. The boy was appointed Consort, like I once was; a true insult to me, a mockery of my own rank. I asked around, and it was true. Guntram de Lisle, his own nephew was Konrad's latest flame. Konrad was almost eating from the hand of a silly little boy, a sick and weak thing. His father must be turning in his grave! His superior Alpha Male child in love of a pathetic weakling like you!" She laughed cruelly.

"I don't believe a word," I whispered, turning green.

"No, you don't have to believe me. Read this. Roger gave me some of Konrad's letters to him, photos," she said triumphantly.

My hands shook terribly when I opened the leather folder she had placed over the table. There were several photos of my uncle and Konrad. Some of them had been taken in the Sylt house, and others in elegant rooms, like hotels.

"My son used to have a permanent suite at the Ritz where he would meet Roger. But the letters are better than his photos," she was practically glowing in her triumph.

I drew my attention to the folded papers and I opened them. It was his unmistakable perfect handwriting. There were like twelve letters, notes better, as they were very short. I took one randomly.

"My love, can we meet tonight? My body and soul longs for you. K"

"How can you be so mean to me? Have I done something to offend you? You asked me to come to Paris, and I waited and waited for you. I went to the bank at midnight, and only Jerôme was working there. He said you left with one of the traders. You're a whore. K"

I had to close my eyes, but I couldn't escape the reality.

"Everything stays in the family, it seems. How does it feel to be sodomized by your own political uncle? Do you call him daddy in bed?" she gloated.

"Shut up," I growled looking directly into her soulless eyes.

"But we are getting to the best part, dear. Konrad ordered the execution of your whole family for treason, even your father. According to Roger, Jerôme, in an attempt to save your life, sold you to Konrad like a replacement for him. A vulnerable orphan, unloved, who would fall for the first person who would pet him just a little. Konrad could have, in a few years, what he desired the most, but this time with someone easy to control and bend to his will. A life size doll; very convenient."

I started to breathe raggedly as I felt a strong and acute pain in my chest. I disentangled the tie, futily trying to grasp for air, but it was useless. My vision was getting clouded and breathing was becoming more and more difficult.

"It's almost like under the Roman Emperors. You go to bed with your father's executioner," was her final blow.

"Call a doctor please. I have a heart condition," I whispered feeling worse and worse.

"That you would die now, is an added bonus. Tell Konrad that we're even now. I finally destroyed his life like he destroyed my son's," she said as she rose and left the room, not even looking behind.

Milan came almost running to see what was going on. "Guntram, what is it? Do you feel bad?"

"I think… I'm having a heart attack. Get a doctor, please."

Milan roared for a doctor, and to my luck there was one who came running, and forced me to lie on the floor. He checked me and my pills, but he discarded them, asking for his own medical bag and an ambulance. He injected me with something.

"Easy lad, this should make you feel better. It's only an acute episode of angor. I have controlled your blood pressure, and now I will give you a small sedative just to relax you. Don't speak now. Is anyone we can call?"

"I'm his bodyguard." Milan said.

"Good, do you have his medical record? It certainly would help he doctors in ER."

"In the car. I'll ask for it."

I was starting to feel more and more tired, and almost missed the two other doctors rushing in the restaurant, and starting to prod me as the doctor spoke with them very fast in French. I had to close my eyes for a minute because my head weighed like a ton.

I woke up in a hospital room; very small, a cubicle. Heindrik was sitting on the chair next to the bed.

"Shit Guntram. You're going to make heart attacks a contagious decease. How are you feeling?"

"Where am I? Where's the folder?" I whispered, feeling very weak and dizzy.

"In Saint Pierre. The doctors say it wasn't very bad, that they caught you on the brink. What did that woman do to you? I saw her leaving the hotel as if she was chased by the devil."

"The folder, do you have it?"

"I have your paintings, and Milan grabbed another folder, but he says that's for Goran and not for you."

"Good. What time is it?"

"Almost six. The Duke is coming back from the Netherlands tonight. He will land in Geneva. Can you tell me what happened?"

"That woman was his mother. She showed me pictures and letters from the Duke. Horrible ones. Please Heindrik, don't let him in the room with me. Make something up, but keep him away from me."

"Do you realise it would be like trying to stop a tornado?"

"I beg you, Heindrik, help me with this."

"I'll do my best, but I can't promise you anything. The doctors said I can take you home, if you feel up to it. I'll drive you to the hotel."

"Not there please, take me to Geneva. It's nearby. Can you help me to go out?"

"I'll call a nurse first. Goran is already here."

"Let me speak with him before you call the doctors. It's very important."

He seemed to doubt for a minute but finally nodded with his head. In no time, Goran entered in the room and took my hand.

"Little brother, how are you feeling?"

"Do you have that folder?" He nodded. "You saw what was inside?" He shrugged dejectedly. "That man was Roger de Lisle, my uncle. I didn't know it till she told me. He was the Duke's previous," I paused, "lover." He lost his colours for the first time in five years. "Please Goran, keep him away from me. If I see him, I don't know what might happen."

"Who was that woman?" he growled.

"Marianne von Liechtenstein, his mother. She hates him, and wishes I drop dead to ruin Konrad's life completely. She's a lunatic because she thinks her seven year son killed his own brother. Konrad was not even there when it happened."

"Damn! I'll keep the Duke at bay, little brother. Do not worry."

"Can you take me to Geneva? I don't want to stay here. Please."

"Yes, no problem if the doctor allows it. We have a place to stay there."

"Don't put us together, please."

"I'll make the arrangements. Rest now," he ordered me, leaving me alone again.

Sometime later, Heindrik returned with the doctor, and he released me with a serious warning for next time, and several magical pills.

Heindrik escorted me out where there was already a black Mercedes waiting for us at the door. Hartick was the driver. "Where is Milan?" I asked as I entered the car.

"He's gone to Geneva with Goran. I don't know, they both were speaking in their language. Left in a hurry. Relax now, it's an hour driving from here."

I think I dozed because Heindrik's mobile phone beeping made me jump. "I have to take you to the Hotel d'Angleterre. The Duke will stay in Beau Rivage. Why Goran did that? Both are small things. He should have tried the Kempinsky. His Excellency will be furious, but at least I will not have to face him."

"It's OK for me."

"Guntram, if I have to stick my neck out for you could you give me an explanation?

"No. I spoke with Goran already. Let him make the decisions. I can't." I replied, closing my eyes again.

The Swede woke me up again when we arrived to the Hotel, located in front of the lake. I got out of the car and followed him meekly to the reception where Goran was waiting for us.

"Take Guntram to the Executive Suite. You stay with him till further notice. I will go to the Airport to receive the Duke."

"Thank you Goran," I said very softly. He only nodded, and went away, after throwing the keys at Heindrik's face.

"Charming as ever," he commented dryly. "All right, you have the good one, and I have the next one to you. I hope you don't plan on throwing a pyjama party, Guntram."

"Please, I would like to go to the room," he looked at me, alarmed. Yes, normally I go along with his bantering, but not today. We went in silence to the elevator and to our rooms. I didn't take a look at it and went directly for the bed, sitting on it and starting to remove my shoes.

"Don't you want to eat something?" He asked and I shook my head.

"I just want to sleep, Heindrik. You dine without me," I said and started to remove my jacket. He left the room closing the door behind him. I took off the rest of my clothes, went to the bathroom, and slid deeply under the covers, pulling them around me.

I started to sob and then to cry, muffling the sounds with the covers. He killed my whole family and then fucked me for four years just because I look like my uncle. He took me away from everything I knew, and twisted me into what he considered "the perfect companion", "the perfect doll" who would satisfy him in bed and take care of his children.

He killed my papa who never hurt a soul. I'm sure he's responsible for the Crédit Auvergne's fraud. He ruined my father's reputation. He made my life a living hell for so many years! I always thought my father didn't love me enough as to stay with me, but he took him away from me!

He violated everything I had, my body, my thoughts, my decency, my love and my honour.

He knew it all the time, and rubbed it on my face. "You remind me to someone from my past." Ferdinand and Friederich knew it too because they were there when this all happened, and said nothing at all. Probably, they were happy to get a bed warmer for their boss who would not give them more troubles and could be easily controlled.

I want to go away, but they will never let me go. They will sacrifice me like a horse with a broken leg. I'm useless now.

I feel a profound disgust at myself.

I hate him.

* * *

Next morning, Heindrik told me he had orders to bring me home despite my protests. I was still too tired to protest, and only nodded my agreement. I finished dressing, and I was very shocked when I saw my face in the bathroom mirror. It was gaunt, pale, with dark lines under my eyes and dead. The man there was not the Guntram I used to know. He was somebody else, a much older person. I was not yet twenty-four and I felt like sixty-four.

I didn't know how I would face everything from now onward. I should be furious, rabid, full of hatred.

But I feel nothing; only an overwhelming sorrow over my father's death. I don't care if they kill me. I only know that I despise Konrad von Lintorff.

"Are you all right, Guntram?" Heindrik asked me for the tenth time that morning. He was having breakfast, and I was playing with the tea cup. "Eat something, will you? We have to go back in an hour and it's a three hour drive."

"I'm not hungry."

"The Duke and Goran had a huge argument last night; in Russian. Goran didn't let the Duke enter in your room. He drew a gun on him, and when Goran does it, you'd better start to pray because he's like the sharks when they smell blood. Thank God, the Duke pulled back, because I wouldn't like to fight with Goran and Milan. No chance against them. Those two invented the art of people evisceration."

"Do you mind if we stay for a while on one of the benches in front of the lake? I need some time to think, please; just an hour before we drive back to Zurich."

"No problem. I don't want to go back also. The Duke is enraged, but Goran is not his main source of anger. Have you done something bad, boy?"

"Nothing Heindrik. I did nothing. He did. You were right about all the things you told me in Buenos Aires. You're a good friend. It's a pity I didn't open my eyes sooner. I feel so tired."

"You look like shit. Perhaps some fresh air will make you look alive. Come, eat something because I hate that they charge me fifty francs for nothing. The croissants are good, and forget about cholesterol."

Much later, I sat alone on a bench in front of the lake. A few tourists were passing by over the esplanade, but my gaze was fixed on the glistening waters and boats. I couldn't think on anything to do, to make any kind of decision. I was too overwhelmed by everything. The only thing I could think about was "He killed my papa."

My mobile started to ring and when I saw it was Konrad. I stood up and smashed it against the balustrade, breaking into several pieces. Shit!

I picked up the broken pieces, and without looking I threw them into a trash can.

"Sir, It's forbidden to throw electronic waste in the organic trashcan." A local police officer woman informed me in French. Excellent. I fuck with a Mafia boss, and I now accused of ecological terrorism.

"I'm very sorry. I didn't realise," I mumbled.

"Very well, Sir. It will be 135 francs. Full name for the fine."

I opened my mouth to shout at the stupid bitch, standing in front of me what she could do with her ticket when I realised that it made no sense at all. I let a dry laugh out, and she looked at me as if I were crazy. I gave her my ID and paid the fine without complaints.

"Are you all right, Sir?" She asked after finishing the papers.

I really considered my answer and suddenly the world was not as ugly as I was believing. "Yes, I'm fine. My life is totally ruined but I'm fine. I feel free, detached from everything."

"*Alors, vous êtes un ètranger dans la vie.*" She told me in French and she was right. I was an outsider to life; an alien. I have no feelings left. All is in the past. Love. Passion. Fear. Lintorff was the centre of my universe, and this big star exploded leaving a big black hole behind, sucking away everything I had. I have nothing left, but I've never felt so free and alive in my whole life.

"It's true, Madam. Thank you and good bye."

"Good bye, Sir. Good luck."

Chapter 36

Late in the afternoon, we arrived to his house. Friederich was there to receive me, and immediately asked me how I was feeling and if I needed something.

"No, thank you. Please ask the nurse to take care of the children today. I don't feel up to it," I said coldly.

"Guntram, child, what transpired in Montreux? The Duke has said nothing. He came home this morning and went to the bank."

"I met Marianne von Lintorff. She gave me another version of the Duke's past love life. My uncle Roger was an important part of his life, and his Excellency decided to stick to my family. She mentioned something about him killing my whole family too. I will wait for his Grace in the library," I said emotionless, as Friederich eyes were wide open with horror. "Don't concern yourself. I already had my nervous breakdown. Unfortunately, I didn't make it to a heart attack as would have been the Duchess' desire."

Not even waiting for an answer, I went to the library, and waited for him to come back. Friederich entered once to leave a tray with the tea and sandwiches, but I didn't touch it. Later, he came again to switch on the lights.

"Guntram, this can't be good for you. You haven't eaten anything today. Please, have something."

"I'm not hungry. Thank you. Please leave."

"Guntram, I'm very concerned about you. Your health…"

"If you were concerned about me, you should have prevented your protégé to commit incest with the son of the man he murdered. Or does the Griffin have a special permission from the Church to do it?"

He left the room, leaving me again alone. When it was dark, I heard the cars stopping outside. I took a deep breath, but I didn't go to him. I waited alone in the room.

His familiar footsteps resounded in the hall, but this time I felt no joy to hear them. He was not alone. Probably Friederich and Ferdinand. The door was opened to reveal Lintorff, and the other two plus Goran behind.

Lintorff came to me and knelt in front of me, taking my head into his hands. I let him do it and just looked at him with deep contempt. He immediately put his offending hands away.

"Are you feeling better? We were very concerned," he asked.

"Your mother sends you a message, Lintorff. She says you two are even now, as she has destroyed your life like you destroyed your brother's." He flinched and closed his eyes with evident pain.

"Whatever she has told you, it's not like that," he started.

"I would like to have this discussion in private, Duke. It's the least you can do. Send your men away."

All of them stormed out of the room before they were told.

"Guntram, I never wanted you to find it out like this. Whatever happened with Roger was years ago, and I never wanted to hurt you. You're the most important thing in my life; more important than my own children."

"You killed my whole family and my father. You fucked your political nephew. Was this some sort of extra punishment from the Order to the rebellious de Lisle family?" I growled. "Murdering, incest, sodomy. Something more to add to the list?"

"It was never incest! You're not blood related to me! I could have never married Roger or even wanted to! Your father gave you to me! He would have never forced his son to commit such a sin. He loved you deeply!" He shouted incensed.

"My father gave me to you?" I asked incredulously. He couldn't be so cynical.

"In exchange for your uncle's life and yours. I can prove it. He freely gave you to me, and I took you in."

"So, you admit killing my whole family, and ruining our reputation?" I was not truly believing my ears, but he had just said it, as if it were nothing.

"They were executed, yes, but not by my hand. My uncle Hermann and zu Löwenstein took the matter into their hands as I could not do it. Your family betrayed the Order, and made public many secret documents. You know the punishment for high treason. Many lines fell that year. I am responsible for many associates executions done later, but not for your bloodline. The fire in Poitiers was our traditional punishment method and I have never used it. Fire purifies the sins."

"You killed three children, and only God knows how many more!"

"I wanted to spare the children, but the Council decided to set an example. I couldn't do a thing. When your father came to me, I didn't know he was so sick, he asked me for two things, your life and to choose his own death. He offered you, so you would take Roger's place in the future, and I took his gift because I didn't want to kill a child! I never had any sexual thoughts about you! I considered briefly to adopt you, as I knew I would never have children of my own, but you would have never been recognized as a Lintorff, so I let you live your life in Argentina. I never had any kind of contact with you before I saw you for the first time in Notre Dame. I didn't know how you looked like!"

"You saw me in Paris?" I asked incredulous.

"Yes, in Notre Dame during the Mass. It was like seeing an angel sent by God. He placed you in my life, in his own house. I swear I never looked for you. I didn't know who you were until you told your name to the Director of the Army Museum. It was too late for me, because I was in love with you, and couldn't let you go. You were the image of purity at the Louvre, looking at everything in awe. I followed you to Venice, telling myself that you were exactly like Roger, but you had a very sweet and caring nature, the opposite of him. I thought it was an elaborate hoax, designed to trap me again, but the story of you working for the poor people, your job as a waiter, the university, all was true. I never forced you to do anything, and took some time before we consummated our love. You also fell in love with me, immediately."

"And does it make your crimes less horrible? You're a monster. Your mother called you a pathetic creep and how right she was! You killed my father! Murderer!"

"No! I didn't kill your father. He jumped out of that window by his own will!" He shouted back angrily. I flinched in pain as he denied once more his crime.

"It's as if you just pushed him though! How did you threaten him? To burn down his son to purify his sins against the Order? To torture him to death? To make him witness how you killed his brother?" I jumped from the couch, and started to hit him on the chest, but he didn't move, accepting my onslaught. I hit him several times, starting to cry like a baby.

"I never wanted to hurt you Guntram, and this is why I never told you a thing. Ferdinand and Friederich knew it, and they both supported my decision," he said putting his arms around me and embracing me.

I stopped. "Get your hands off, Lintorff. I would rather touch a snake than you," I said coldly.

He looked at me transfixed. "I'm leaving, and I don't care if that means my death. You killed me already. You can be proud of yourself. My "line" is finished."

"Guntram you can't go away. You know it. You have a place with us. You're my Consort. My beloved."

"I was nothing but your whore, and I'm through with you. Move aside."

"Guntram, you're not thinking clearly. I understand you feel upset at me, but you can't leave. Where would you go? Who would protect you? When your father gave you to me, I swore to him to protect you and cherish you. I've always treated you with the utmost respect and consideration! Roger was never my Consort as you are!"

"I don't believe a thing of what you're saying. My father offered his own son to a blood thirsty monster like you? No! He was a good man whose reputation you destroyed along with his life."

"He had no life left! He would have been dead within the next two months! He sacrificed himself for you and that piece of shit of Roger! Don't ruin his sacrifice!"

"You're a liar!"

"Your father gave me a letter for you before he left this house. He wanted me to give it to you in case it would have been necessary," he stated strangely calm, and I had to sit again on the couch. With morbid fascination, I looked at him going to the safe box hidden behind some false books. He opened it, and took a folder from there. He came toward me and placed it in my hands.

Full of dread, I opened it and inside there was a sealed envelope addressed to my name. I broke the seal, and took a two page handwritten letter out. The paper was starting to become yellow.

"What is this?"I asked disoriented, not willing to know.

"Jerôme had it ready when he came here. I don't know its contents. It was addressed to you," he replied very softly, going to sit behind his own desk, burying the head between his hands, in a desperate gesture.

I cleaned my eyes with the sleeve of my jacket, and took several deep breaths before starting to read.

Paris, July 15th, 1989

My dearest Son,

In my life there were only two loves; You and your mother. God in his infinite wisdom took her from me at childbirth. I never blamed you for that. She had a serious heart condition since she was young, and doctors always forbid her to have children. When we found out that you were coming we were happier than ever. We were counting the days for your birth, and our faith allowed us to place our trust in a happy ending.

Her high blood pressure thwarted our lives. The doctors said they had to operate to save the baby, and she only asked them how long would it take. Her last words to me were "My love, think that in two hours we will have the baby with us."

When I saw you for the first time my life changed forever. You were a divine gift, and I always regarded you this way. I would have done everything in my hand to protect you from any harm.

My life has not been spotless. My family's greed has been the cause of our line's downfall. My father thought we could depose the Lintorffs from their place as Griffins. We tried, and we failed. Now we must pay with our lives, wealth, and position.

Konrad von Lintorff was appointed Griffin in March 1980, after his father's death. He was so young and inexperienced, that most of the lines thought he could be easily overthrown. Our line was a minor one, not rich or powerful at all, only servants to the principal lines. My father believed that an association with the major lines would result in our promotion to the upper scales of the Order. My younger brother Roger would be the means to achieve it. I was discarded because I was too old for the task. The new Duke was ten years younger than me, but Roger was only five years older, and much more ambitious than I. Your uncle is clever, handsome and attractive. He married above my family's expectations with a young member of the Löwenstein family, and has a daughter with her. Perhaps that would be his safeguard to avoid Lintorff's righteous anger.

Our plan was simple. Too simple. Roger would use Lintorff's adoration toward him to move us up inside the Order. No matter how he looks now, the Duke was a weak and insecure man. He fell in love with my brother in no time, and gladly accepted any kind of condition my brother set, in order to gain his attentions. First, Roger demanded only small favours that cemented our economical position. My father and brother Pascal reached the rank of Associates and Advisers within the next two years of Konrad and Roger's relationship. I was only head of the legal office in Paris and was never awarded a rank in the Order.

By 1985, my father decided to move to the next phase. To destroy all what Lintorff had achieved in his five years as Griffin. To everybody's surprise, he had been successful, and that year the Order's legal profits were near ninety-one percent. The middle size Associates started to accept him, and those lines with some opportunities of inheriting his position, became restless because their chances of finishing the Lintorffs diminished with each passing day.

My father, Pascal, Roger and I, along with several others whose names I will not tell to preserve their lives, started to secretly undermine every deal we could. At the end of the year, our profits fell to sixty percent which was still good, and Lintorff never suspected something was amiss. He was so in love that he saw the world through Roger's eyes.

I was afraid to where it would all lead us. To betray the Order or the Griffin is the most abominable crime. The punishment is to be erased from this earth. I wanted to protect you in case we would fail, so I sent you to Argentina, a neutral territory as the Order had no interests there. I couldn't bear the thought of losing you like I lost your mother. My own private Hell was to send you away, and leave you behind every month to return to Paris. You inherited your mother's sweet and caring nature, and I wanted to keep you away from the Order, my own brothers, and father.

We almost succeed, but my father miscalculated Ferdinand von Kleist's devotion toward the Lintorff family. His own line was saved after the war by the Lintorffs, and he always felt indebted to them. Along with Gustav zu Löwenstein and Hermann von Lintorff, Konrad's uncle, he discovered everything. In April 1988, Konrad terminated any contact with Roger, and we lost our positions and wealth. I'm convinced that his vendetta would have stopped there, but my father and brothers leaked all the information they had about the Order to a group fighting against the Illuminati.

That was our death sentence. Löwenstein was our executioner because Konrad couldn't bring himself to do it, and he had to restore his own power. My father and Pascal's whole direct family died in a fire at our Estate in Poitiers. The press said it was a suicidal pact as we had lost everything. No one was spared: my father, my brother, my sister-in-law, and my three nieces.

My brother Roger placed all the blame on us, and said he was forced to take a role in the plan in order to save himself. I'm convinced Lintorff believed his lies because Roger and his family disappeared, and I'm sure Löwenstein would not go against his own bloodline.

I'm next, but I'll receive death with joy. It's a liberating feeling. My only fear is that something will happen to you. A small, poor orphan child is vulnerable. Our laws decree your demise to avoid a future bloodbath within the Order. The only way to stop Konrad's vendetta is to offer him something he desires so much, that he will overlook my faults and grant me one last wish. You.

Lintorff's love for my brother is as big as my own was for your mother. I would sell my soul to the Devil for a second chance to be with her.

Guntram, you look so much like Roger at your age. If you ever read this letter, it means I succeed in my pact with Lintorff. Don't hate me. It's the only way to save your life. If he thinks he could regain what he lost in a few years, he will grant me the gift of your life and a clean passing. I pray to God he loves, cherishes and protects you from all evil.

There's the chance that he accepts my offer, but is never interested in you or finds another love. Many things could happen in ten years. Don't hate him or blame him for my fate. I don't do it. I blame myself and my family.

You were a better son than I a father. May the Lord protect you,

Jerôme de Lisle

I didn't know when I started to cry, silently, during the reading. My father had loved me, and that monster robbed him from me. That bloody Order forced him to stay till the end, and he had to send me away to save me from them. He was forced to return me to their hands so he could save my life. They're monsters.

"I go now," I said.

"I will not allow it! You have obligations to fulfil! You belong to me!"

"I belong to nobody! My father didn't have the right to do this!"

"Your father was brought up to be one of us. He understood our codes, and respected them till his last breath. You were given as collateral, a guarantee to prevent further bloodshed. Therefore, you're mine as long as you're treated with gentleness. No one here will dispute my rights over you!"

"I will not stay a single minute more with you! The times of the serfs and masters are finished since a long time!" I roared furious.

"I will give you a few days so you can soothe your nerves. You can go to Ferdinand's house and think it over. Your children also need you," he said, not rising his voice and strangely calm.

"Don't put Klaus and Karl in the middle of your shit, Lintorff!"

"You gave us your word to take care of them, and you will fulfil your oath," he shouted me this time enraged, placing himself in front of the door as I rose from the sofa, clutching my father's letter with my hand.

I advanced toward him, and spat at him on his face. He looked at me, furious, but only cleaned his face with the back of his hand. Without prying my eyes from his, I removed the griffin's ring from my left hand and threw it to the floor. "I'm not your Consort any longer," I said in a voice I've never heard in me before. "Move aside."

He let me pass, and I opened the door. Ferdinand, Friederich and Goran were waiting there, all looking alarmed.

"You can go for four days to Ferdinand's house. Then, you will resume your duties toward the children," he said with a stern voice.

I turned around, and I looked at him with all the hatred I could muster. "I do hope you rot in Hell," I said coldly.

Chapter 37

April 25th, 2006

I've been staying at Ferdinand's house for a few days; three to be precise. His wife, Cecilia, was very understanding, like only women can be, and left me alone. She came several times to check if I was all right or if I had taken my pills. She never asked a thing or tried to pry, like the others. I slept a lot. Most of the time, as I've never been so tired in my life.

Perhaps, I didn't want to think.

I should hate him, but I'm too tired to do it. I only want to be left alone in a dark corner.

But they will not let me be.

Ferdinand came this morning to my bedroom, and informed me that we will meet this evening with Lintorff.

"Boy, you have to put yourself together. It's not how you think it was. I was also there, and I knew your father or believed to know him. He was a very reserved man. Silent. He only spoke in the meetings when asked. He was a fantastic lawyer. Only now we found out that he was working pro bono in that NGO. He was so cold to everybody. He had no affairs and was the opposite to his brothers. He never had a good relation with Konrad; he was polite, but you could literally feel the wall he had placed between him and the rest of us. First, we thought it was because your father disapproved of Konrad's entanglement with Roger, but now, after reading his letter, we understand many things more. He was never comfortable with his family's deception nor being a member of the Order."

"You were the one who discovered everything," I said dejectedly. He's the one who pointed his finger to him, releasing the wolves. He's as guilty as Lintorff, but I need his support to save my life.

"Not really. I had my suspicions, but somebody put me on the track. I don't know who it was. Your father took the blame in front of Konrad for many of your relatives doings. He chose to believe him as he was so in love with Roger, but I knew Jerôme better. It was not his style, alas nobody ever wanted to listen to me."

"Was my father the one who told you?"

"I don't know, honestly. Perhaps he had enough of his family or realised that Konrad was not the worst option as Griffin. Maybe he knew the other traitors were real animals without scruples. Perhaps he wanted to unleash a full scale war inside the Order so we would destroy ourselves. He was a very intelligent man who understood us well and believed in a greater good. If he would have been on our side, everything would have turned out so differently. With him, we could have achieved the Order's original goals. I swear Guntram, Konrad had nothing to do with his dismissal. Konrad destroyed the bank and industries from your family, this is true, but the ones who decided to go one step further were the older members when your grandfather exposed us to a group of fanatics."

"I can't believe you Ferdinand."

"I understand. We must find a way for you two to solve your differences.

You have a position and responsibilities. Konrad can't let you go because of the reasons you already know."

"At this point a bullet in the head is not so unappealing," I mumbled my eyes fixed on the wall.

"Perhaps it would be a good solution for you, but what about the children? Those two babies adore you. I've seen them become completely happy when they see you. Konrad needs you to give him emotional stability. Do you want to leave Klaus and Karl alone with him, unstable, and turning their lives into a pure hell, as his own childhood was?"

"He loves the children. He will do nothing against them."

"Yes, but he doesn't know how to show it. Probably he will disappear and leave them alone with a nanny till they turn fifteen and become useful for the Order. I know him since we was nine years old. Even if his mother was not living with him any longer, she made his life a living hell over the phone or when he had to spend the summers with her. She always blamed him for his brother's death."

"She told me the old Duke killed his own son to put Konrad on his place as Griffin."

"Guntram, Karl Maria could have never been a Griffin. Look carefully at his photos, and you will notice that he had a cognitive retard, like Forest Gump. Konrad told me that his brother was very kind and loving to him, and he adored Karl Maria. His death was a very huge shock for him. His mother was like Medea, and his father, well, only saw in him a good heir, but never a son."

"I think he never loved Roger, not in the way as he loves you. It was more a magnetic and animal passion what they had, and Konrad disguised it as true love. He was desperate to find someone close to him. Loneliness can drive a person mad. There's a place, in every man's soul, that no friend can reach, only a lover, and he longed for the chance to close that emptiness."

"I don't love him any more. I don't hate him either. I feel nothing for him, and I would like to never see him again."

"You know this is not possible."

"Once you promised me to help me to escape," I reminded him of the promise made so time ago in Buenos Aires. He was my only hope to go away, and start anew.

"I promised to help you if he was ever violent to you, and he has not been. We have to find a solution for this situation," he answered, destroying also my faith in him.

"I will only have contact with the children. He's dead to me."

"I understand. I will see what I can do," he sighed, leaving me alone with my thoughts.

* * *

April 26ᵗʰ, 2006

The meeting took place yesterday, at 8:00 p.m., at Lintorff's office in the bank. At 5:30 p.m., Goran picked me up with his car at Ferdinand's house, and we drove engulfed in an eerie silence.

"Heindrik told me you risked your job for me, Goran. I'm indebted to you. Thank you," I said softly.

"That Swedish speaks too much," he grunted, uncomfortable at my gratitude. "All this is very bad, little brother. I don't know what to think about it. The Duke swears he had nothing to do with the execution, and I believe him. My predecessor confirmed it, but to have taken you under lies and deceptions is something I can't tolerate."

"You know the ones who did it?" I asked horrified.

"Yes, but as I said once, don't live for the dead ones. Think on the living. The main issue here is if you want to continue or not. I can't help you to go away for the moment. Your health is very bad, you wouldn't last two months alone."

"I can take care of myself."

"Under normal circumstances yes, but this would be a real manhunt. You have to remain here. I will do everything in my power to protect you, but you must promise me to accept the rules they will impose on you."

"Do you know something I should know?"

He took his time to answer me. "The Duke wants to keep you at his side. He will not let you go away. You will remain with him, taking care of the children. He will respect you, but you must forget about starting a new life with somebody else, or fooling around like young people do. That would make him explode, and his jealousy can be very violent. For everybody's sake, your behaviour should be impeccable, spotless, little brother."

"I see," I said feeling more and more desperate and depressed.

"You are stronger than you think. You will survive this."

The top floor at the bank was almost deserted. Only Monika and Michael were still around. She looked at me with hundreds of questions in her eyes, but I said nothing. Ferdinand came out of Lintorff's office.

"Come Guntram, we all should speak. Monika, no interruptions, and give me the papers I asked this morning, please. His Excellency says you can go now."

Ferdinand took the folder she handed him, and I followed him to the devil's den. Lintorff was standing at the window, looking toward the street, his back to the door. I stood in the middle of the room, not caring if Ferdinand nudged me, slightly, to come near the huge mahogany desk.

"Please Guntram, Ferdinand, do sit down," Lintorff invited us. Ferdinand took his usual place at the right side in front of him, and I the left one. We waited for some minutes till he turned around and sat in his big chair. "I trust your health is better now, Guntram."

"Yes Duke. The change of air has been good for me," I replied coldly, looking him in the eyes. He had the decency to cast his gaze down.

"We need to solve this in a civilized manner, gentlemen. I do hope we reach an understanding today. As you are aware, Guntram, you play an important role in our society. I'm afraid his Excellency can't grant your wish of resigning from your duties." Ferdinand said, carefully choosing his words.

"The former Consort lost her title, and now lives an independent life from the Order," I pointed out.

"That is because she's a Liechtenstein and you are a de Lisle. There are other issues at stake, like the fact you were given to the Griffin by your father to atone for his crimes against me. Your family's history of treason is not forgotten," Konrad retorted very seriously.

"Interesting point gentlemen. I, who have never spoken a word of all the things I've heard here, am accused of treason. This woman supplies information to this magazine at her own will. Yes, gentlemen, the first one to approach me with a note from her was a journalist from theirs, Linda Harris," I said, not caring if I was sending the witch to the fire. She wished me dead and destroyed my soul.

Both looked at each other for a second, alarm clear on their faces. "According to the Princess, my late uncle Roger worked with them for the last ten years, and now she does it. She wants to destroy your precious society, and she still has access to people in the Order, as she easily found out that I was appointed the Griffin's consort. As usual, you're looking for leaks where there are none, missing the biggest cracks in your structure."

"I'm willing to offer you a temporary cease of cohabitation, Guntram. In return, you will watch over the children. They have grown very fond of you, and miss your presence."

"I have no interest in living under the same roof with my father's murderer."

"I had nothing to do with that. You read the letter. You can move to the rooms in the nursery area, if you want to."

"I want to live in a separate place. I will come every morning to take care of them."

"No. I will not allow this. You will live under my care and protection, as I swore to your late father. Living away from me is a huge risk. You will continue with your education. I insist on this," he said with his cold and regal voice.

"Regarding your new status, Guntram" Ferdinand intervened before I could tell him what he could do with his protection and oaths. "His Excellency has decided to keep you as the children's tutor. You will be given a monthly allowance of 4,000 francs, and you will continue to assist to the University. Your educational fund remains as it is. Also, the Duke will cover all your medical expenses."

"I don't want any of your money. It's filthy. I will look for a way to support myself."

"Nonsense! When would you spend time with our children?"

"Your children. They were never mine. I love them as if they were, but they're not."

"As you say. The condition I set, is that we will never fight ever in front of them. I don't want their lives ruined like mine was."

"You can't ask me to feign what is not there any longer! I will not quarrel with you, but I will not show any love for you; only the respect due to an employer, Duke."

"Guntram, this is not reasonable." Ferdinand whined. "You're not a servant! You're a part of Konrad's family! What's next? Do you want to eat in the kitchen with the cleaning ladies, and use the rear door?"

"Certainly, I will not dine with the Duke! I don't consider myself part of his family. I used to have one!" I retorted starting to lose my temper.

"Ferdinand, let him be. Guntram is still upset with the news. He can stay in the nursery with the children, and eat with them or with me if he wants. You will come home with me this evening, and I will have no further discussions with you. It's unfortunate you were informed in such a tactless way by a woman who wants nothing more than my own downfall and your death for taking her title over, the same she lost because of her own wickedness."

"I still haven't heard you once apologizing for my family's fate," I said more to myself than to him, still unable to believe that he didn't consider himself guilty of anything. He was only sorry to have been caught!

"There is nothing to apologise for. They played the game and lost. All of them knew what was at stake. I only regret the pain that I caused you, by not informing you before of my relationship with this man. I have always treated you with respect, care and consideration. I have never been unfaithful to you or let my love falter, despite the many trials we had to endured together. I named you my Consort as a proof of my love and fidelity, something I never did with Roger. You will keep your title and that is final."

"You can't demand what doesn't exist any longer. I'm only staying because of my love for your children. However, because of the affections we shared in the past, I will treat you with the respect and courtesy due to their father, but I'm not your Consort any longer."

"In this case we have an agreement. Gather your things. We drive home in an hour."

"As you wish, Sire," I replied softly, fighting the tears threatening to come to my eyes. Did they come from fury, despair or hate? I don't know. I rose from my seat and went to the door. I opened it, and left the room, closing it behind me. I had to lie down against the heavy wooden frame, feeling exhausted, my breathing coming out raggedly.

"Shit, Konrad, this is very bad. Let the boy go away for Christ's sake! He blames you for his father's death! You're going to destroy him!" I heard Ferdinand's voice pleading.

"He agreed to stay. I can still win his love back. The last thing we lose is hope. Now, I think it's time I teach a lesson to my dear mother and the Masons who encouraged her latest adventure against me. Perhaps it's time for some people to understand the concept behind these infamous Collateralized Debt Obligations."

"Never liked them myself. It could be huge. Many have them," Ferdinand chuckled.

"It must be huge. Exemplary."

PART III

The Griffin

Chapter 1

May 25th, 2006

It's been some time since I've written anything. I didn't have the feeling for it. I was, and I still am, very tired, sick of all. I curse the day I accepted to return to Lintorff's house. I know I didn't really have any other option, but I should have never accepted this "arrangement" as he calls it. For me is a slow torture. I have to see the bastard on a daily basis, and keep my cool in front of Karl and Klaus.

I think the children have realised that something is amiss. They're two years old, and they have noticed that his father is not all the time on top of Guntram, kissing and softly petting him like he used to do. Not any longer. I hope they soon forget how things were before, and continue with their lives. When Lintorff comes into the playroom, I normally find an excuse to disappear from there, till he decides to go back to whatever he's plotting at the moment. I completely hate that he loves so much to creep in on us in the playroom. I'm one second sitting with the babies on the floor, making a pile with wooden cubes, the children looking at it happily and when I lift my gaze, he's there, looking at us with an anxious and melancholic expression. His mother was right. He's a pathetic creature if he thinks, believes, waits, that I will ever come back to his bed.

As promised, we don't fight or clash. I ignore him and keep my exchanges with him to the minimum. If I need something, Friederich has to ask him. I trust that if we both keep our tempers under control, the children will soon get used to the idea that I'm their tutor and he's their father, and there's nothing more than a professional relationship between us. They're too small, they will forget soon.

I wanted to move to the room I use for painting, away from the noble furniture and carpets, but Friederich didn't want to hear about it. The second floor of the castle, where the nursery is, had still one room free, and I was installed there. The night shift nurse, Lissette, was sent away to the servant's area and she got an intercom. "It's totally inappropriate that she's near you." Friederich huffed, still upset with the new arrangements.

As if I would creep during the night into her room for some sex! However, my new bedroom with the adjoining studio for my paints, is comfortable, and next to the children's. I can hear them if some problem arises in the night, but they sleep like bears in winter.

Most of the time, I clash with Friederich, who is not happy at all that I have broken up with his adored boss. What did he expect? That I would cry a little, smash something expensive and forgive him? He has told me over a hundred times that it was never incest—we can't deny he knows about ecclesiastical law, but that's not the question here—that my father died by his own hand; that it was unavoidable as he was so sick; that the Duke truly loves and can't live without me; that my father's letter is very clear on all this.

Friederich nearly kicked me out from the kitchen the morning after I returned from Ferdinand's house. I woke up early, and went there to have breakfast with the rest of the staff. Heindrik, Milan and Ratko were there too.

"Guntram, this is no place for you. Go to the dining room if you want to have breakfast. You're a member of the Lintorff family. His Excellency will join you later, after his training." The butler scolded me with all the dignity he could muster.

"No, leave it. I'll go back with the children," I said dryly. Fuck if I sit with him ever again!

"Hey Guntram, no need to be upset. You can eat with us. You had nothing since yesterday morning," Heindrik interfered putting his "Heir to the Wallenberg Oil Empire" face. He might not be a Lintorff, but he's not a "worker". That shut all protests up.

"Thank you Heindrik. I'm not hungry any longer," I said, leaving the kitchen. I went back to the children's bedroom where they were still sound asleep. I woke them up and started to dress them. They were surprised that I was doing it, but they were happy and didn't give me any troubles. Ulrike, the morning nurse, was very shocked to see me doing it.

One of the butlers entered the room with the children's breakfast tray, so they would take it at their small table in the playroom. They will be allowed to eat with the grown ups when they turn six. Soon after, Friederich came in, also with a tray with my own breakfast.

"The Duke allows you to take your meals with the children for the time being, but you will not mingle with the staff. There is where I draw the line."

"I leave for the University very early in the morning. I drive at seven with Armin, I can't wake the children up at that hour."

"You will take your meals with the young Lintorff in the small dining room. If his Excellency decides to accompany you, you will remain in the room, and behave accordingly to your education and status," he informed me very formally. I threw him a dirty look, but he continued before I could say what was on my mind. "His Excellency relieves you, for the time being, from your social duties in this house," he finished, totally and obviously upset at this last part.

"That means I don't have to attend to his dinners and meetings?" I asked, full of hope.

"Yes, after you dine with the children, you can remain in your rooms or join the rest of the family. As your health is in bad shape, you're excused from attending on formal occasions. Young Lintorff will take your place."

Poor Armin, his Playstation days are over! He will have to endure tedious dinners with dinosaurs, be quiet or only say something stupid about the weather or an art exhibition, and listen to the Masters of the Universe shape the financial world to their wishes! But he wants to become Griffin. He should be glad to be there.

He was less than happy with the new "arrangement" as he told me, that same evening, when he returned from the bank with Lintorff.

"Guntram, can you not make it up with my uncle? He just said I have to dress like a penguin and be downstairs at eight! I'm still twenty-two years old! He has two decrepit crones from the European Central Bank and one guy from some steel company plus their witches!" Armin whined.

"I started at nineteen and lived to tell," I said dryly. I know it wasn't nice of me, that it's not his fault what happened or the motherfucker he has for uncle, but the name Lintorff just grates my nerves.

"Look, you two can work it out. Be sensible, he will forgive you anything.

Just ask for it. He practically eats from your hand," he switched tactics to pleading instead of pouting.

"The thing is, Armin, that I don't want to forgive him. He's dead to me."

I returned to school the next morning I came back here, as usual driving with Armin and Milan or Ratko. I suppose that I'm on probation again as Heindrik asked Goran to return to the Duke's service alone. He says that he doesn't want to be responsible for me if we both are "at odds". Nice euphemism! He had enough to do it once. So I got the hounds from Hell to "protect me" from whatever.

I really don't understand why do I need them. We are not related any more, and there's no risk that Repin or any of the associates would attack me. I'm out. The journalists or fanatics can't tell me anything more about the bastard, and honestly, nothing would surprise me any more. I will not speak with them or side with them. I'm not a traitor, and I will not leave Karl and Klaus without their father even if he's the worst kind of trash. I was there. I know what is to be alone, depending on other people's good will to spend a Christmas with some other humans or get a nice word or if somebody remembers it's your birthday.

No, Milan and Ratko have to be sure that I don't escape or rat them out. Also, there's the possibility, as Goran told me, that they're there "to prevent" me from engaging myself in any kind of "inappropriate" contact with another student, like getting a girlfriend.

As if I had any romantic intentions in my mind! Fucking out of spite has never been my thing! I only did it with Lintorff, and I'm so disgusted at him, at myself, that it will take some time before I even look to another person, and most likely it would be a woman.

The second fight was when we finished the lessons, and I wanted to come home to the twins, and study there.

"No chance. You come to the bank, as usual," Ratko barked at me, as Armin quickly entered the armoured Mercedes I still have to ride in. "Goran has not given me further instructions."

"I'm not setting a foot in there and much less eating with the b—Duke," I retorted hotly.

"You. Bank. Speak Goran," he said as if I were a retarded. I entered the car, and he slammed the door behind me.

Without saying a word, I went directly to Goran's office. "No chance I'm sharing the same room with Lintorff! I want to return home after school or remain in the library. There's not reason for me to be here."

"Guntram don't make my life miserable. You are perfectly aware of the security issues involved. You're the companion of a very rich person. I don't want to have to split the team by sending you home every day at noon. Come here, eat with me and the boys, you're more than welcome, and go home, like always at five with the *Strolch,* (the Rascal, better known as Armin)." "You need to study somewhere, and at the castle, the children can make an incredible noise. Stay in the library like always," he said, perfectly calm.

"We are nothing any longer. It's over and you know why!"

"The Duke will not bother you, I can promise you this. Besides, he's always in his office or travelling."

"He wants to control my every move!" I shouted back angrily.

"He wants to protect you from any harm. I'm sure of it. He loves and cherishes you."

"Are you on his side now?"

"I'm taking no sides. Couples should fix their problems by themselves. Third parties abound. I only said what he did was wrong. He should have told you the truth much earlier, and bear with the consequences. If you forgive him or not, it's your decision. I agree with his Excellency that you need protection, and his children spend their time with you on a permanent basis. They're targets too. So, your security arrangements will remain as they were before this problem arose."

I have to lunch with the Serbs and sometimes Armin, when he can escape his uncle or Michael, or when Ferdinand or Monika grant his leave.

I continued to study as before, hard and not stopping. It helps me not to think. If I do it, I will turn mad. Next September, I will be on my last year for the MA. I should start now to prepare the thesis. I want to finish it as soon as possible. I wonder if it would be possible for me to get a job in Zurich not related to Konrad or his friends. Presumably not. In theory, I should help Elisabetta at the foundation, but I can't do it. I want out. Cecilia should do it or some of the other Lintorffs, like Albert's wife or his eldest daughter, who's now nineteen years old and studies Literature in Paris.

I have to get a job or something to support myself. It kills my soul to eat his food or be dressed, "like a life size doll" by his tailors. This should stop. I don't care if Friederich shouts something about "being inappropriate to wear servant's clothes" or something like that. I have to bite my tongue every time he says something is "inappropriate". Fucking your "political nephew" and killing his whole family was appropriate?

Perhaps Ostermann could help me to sell something else for a reasonable price. I have several things that could go away. I have many drawings, if he could help me to choose something good, maybe we could sell it. There's always eBay.

Heindrik was right. I should sell part of my work. It's only collecting dust, and I could use the money. I'll open a separate account from the ones he made under my name. I want to have nothing to do with them.

* * *

May 28th, 2006

Yesterday after school, I spoke with Ostermann about selling outside the bloody charity auction. I can't withdraw from it now, no matter how much I want it, because the catalogue is printed, and he has already several people interested in three of my pieces. They will be auctioned on June 4th The only condition I set is that Lintorff is not allowed to bid for them. If he does, I swear I'll throw paint all over them!

He thinks we should wait till Autumn to offer anything as people will spend money now, and we should not "tire" the buyer. However, he spoke a few days ago with Coco van Breda, and she wanted to offer me a job for her publishing company. She has a small one, specialized in Art Books and Cards, and, honestly, it sells nothing. Her husband pays the bills from the company because it's a way to keep his wife entertained, and honestly, cheaper than letting her loose in the Paris Fashion Week, the Milan Fashion Week, the New York Fashion Week... or the Mobutu Fashion Week.

Not even waiting for my refusal because I can't publish a book, and much less expect that somebody buys it, he phoned her. It took Coco less than twenty minutes to show herself at the studio.

"Guntram darling, *Meister* Ostermann tells me you need a job. Well, I have the perfect one for you. Of course, I could not give you a big money advance as my company is a little cash strained at the moment," she started.

"I have nothing worthy of publishing Coco."

"Yes, you do! Look how much money you get for a paint! Over ten thousand dollars!"

Yes, people pay because I am/was the Griffin's consort. It's a relatively cheap bribe to the boss.

"I remember that some time ago you were here, illustrating some children's stories, and, frankly, the drawings were exquisite. We all loved them. They were so delicate, detailed and sophisticated that most of us wanted to have one for our own children, and some of their grandchildren." That part came rather loudly, aimed at some ladies in here. "Anyway," she resumed her speech, after getting several angry glares from five women, pretending to paint. "I thought we could make a small edition of children's classical stories, the ones you don't have to pay copyrights, like Cinderella, the Three Bears or Snow White. You can work on them during the summer, and have it ready, let's say around November, so we can distribute them for the Christmas campaign."

"I'm not sure," I trailed.

"Nonsense boy, the ones I saw were good, almost like Arthur Rackham's. Yours are not so twisted like the Victorians, but they have the same ethereal grace," Ostermann said to me.

"Do you really think any child will like it? Rackham lived over a century ago! It's nothing like nowadays!" I protested.

"I don't care about the children. The parents control the wallets, and if they like them, or better, if the grandmothers like them, the brats get them, and we make a sale." Coco ended the discussion.

"And we could sell later the original plates, if the the book sells well, of course," Ostermann suggested.

"The plates will belong to the company as we publish it. We will have the copyrights over them."

"Then you will have to pay them each one of them as if they were Guntram's normal work," Ostermann sweetly retorted. "A watercolour from him ranges between the 3,000 to 5,000 francs. Let's say he makes five stories with ten drawings each, then it would make around 150,000 francs, valuing them at the minimum, of course."

"Ostermann, no illustrator gets such amount of money! We are not printing mangas!" She protested loudly. I was shocked that he came up with that after she had been so nice as to offer me a job!

"Guntram is not "an illustrator", he's a young artist whose work increases its value every year," I was on the brink of a heart attack! He was now fighting with her!

"All right, he can keep the copyrights over his work, but I will give him no

491

money advance. We will share the profits. I will give him a twenty-five percent of them."

"Only twenty-five percent of the profits? Please, Coco, I thought you liked him. Either you give him a fifteen percent of the sales or a forty percent of the profits. You choose."

"I'll give him thirty percent. I'm risking my capital here!"

"Make it thirty-five percent"

"All right, but don't deplete Guntram with your commission," she huffed.

"I have to live also. The lad and I have a deal. And I will oversee the quality of the materials you use for the books."

"All right. Do you want to write the preface, too?" she asked, completely upset at his last request.

"I think a professional writer would do. Thank you," he answered sweetly. I gaped at both. "I was thinking over the last two weeks what you told me, Coco, and we should go for something exclusive, nothing mass marketed. We should centre on heroines. Since Guntram is so good in adopting the styles of bygone eras, each story should be placed on a different century. Everybody knows them, we need to be unique in our style"

"This might work very well," she said. Don't I have a word in all this? After all, I'm the guy who has to paint it.

"How about Cinderella, Little Red Riding Hood, the little Mermaid, the Three Bears and The sleeping Beauty?" He suggested

"Could work, *Meister* Ostermann. The French court, perhaps Louis XIV for Cinderella, the social climber."

"Exactly, Louis XIV had an extensive collection of lovers. I remember the story of Morphee, the Greek girl he ordered after seeing a painting of her."

"The Sleeping Beauty. She has to come from the Renaissance," Coco trailed.

"Certainly, and from Germany. We Germans love forests. The little Mermaid should touch land in Venice, in the XIX century, in the middle of the pre-Raphaelite school."

Excuse me? I have no idea of what you two are speaking about. And the Three Bears what? Do they have a Hotel/Spa in Switzerland? Better be quiet and listen to those two.

"The Red Riding Hood is more complicated; could be placed anywhere."

"The black Death. I'm thinking in Brueghel," Ostermann suggested.

"It's a book for children. I'm not drawing bodies scattered all over the woods!" I protested.

"All right. We will think about it later. You have three stories to start to work. I'll send you the texts tomorrow, Guntram. I want some results by early July.

* * *

June 2nd, 2006

Last week, I had some much needed peace. Lintorff went away on business, and I had only to fight with children not wanting to go to bed or Friederich buffing about something like I refused to see the tailor (I want nothing), didn't eat in the dining room with Armin or made some "menial tasks" like taking the children's dirty clothes to the laundry room. I only studied for my tests and my assignments with Peter. Armin was, as usual, copying from us. He has a lot to do, coping with Michael's temper.

The children were in bed as it was almost nine, and I was reading a book about Louis XIV court I got from the University's library. For the Cinderella girl story, remember? I was at my desk taking notes, meaning, starting to draw the characters faces and copying the women clothes; three different layers of skirts plus corset? Impossible.

Lintorff burst into my room, completely furious, still dressed in a business suit. I rose from my desk.

"How dare you? I leave you not even for a month to your own devises, and you start to behave like a shameless brat!" he roared.

"Do not raise your voice, sir. The children are sleeping. If you have any complaints about me, we shall discuss them downstairs," I growled. He turned around, leaving the room in a whirlwind. I closed my eyes. It took him one month to explode. I gathered my courage, and followed him toward his studio, only to remember that I will not set a foot in his private rooms ever again. Friederich had to make my moving because I refused to enter in there. I went to the library, downstairs. He can shout there much better.

Thirty minutes later, he entered the room, more enraged than before. Of course, he hates waiting. He went directly to his place, the huge chair behind the monstrous desk and sat. Well, is official scolding, I thought.

"Monika has told me that you have asked her for your social security papers to give them to Van Breda Publishing Co. I clearly said, you don't need to look for other employment, and much less, go around begging for charity!"

"I have only agreed to illustrate several children's stories for a book Coco van Breda wants to publish this Christmas. I have to support myself, and I can do this on my free time, when the children sleep," I replied calmly, not even looking at him.

"You have a fixed income every month! You don't need other's people money! It's an insult to me that you beg for money from some lower member of our circle!"

"I'm not a beggar! I work and sell my paints. Did his Excellency not press me several times to do it professionally? I will receive a percentage on the profits, if we make any at all. *Meister* Ostermann also thinks on selling the plates later, if the book is successful. I will sell many of my paintings upstairs. It makes no sense to keep them."

"I forbid you to work outside this house," he said through gritted teeth.

"I will paint inside of this house, if that is your wish, Sire," I replied now pissed off. "I will not take a single cent from you for taking care of your children. That is an insult to me; that you consider that money can buy my affection for them."

"I don't want that we repeat the seven francs lunch story again! Friederich already informed me you refused to be fitted."

"There's no need to, and you can't force me to do it. I will sell my pieces, if somebody wants to have them."

"You are under my care and protection. You will accept my generosity, and will not complain any longer."

"I will pursue my artistic career the way I see fit, Sire. If you don't like it, you'll have my resignation on your desk. I'm not a child who needs to be told what to do, and we have no kind of relationship any longer. I have done nothing indecent."

"You told Elisabetta to ban me from the auction! How dare you! You're also nobody to tell me what I can do!" he howled, this time truly enraged.

"Bid if you want so much to look ridiculous. Don't you think your mother has already spread the story about our breakup to the whole European Nobility and Bourgeoisie? You will look pathetic," I stressed the last word your mum taught me, "when you bid like a lovesick puppy for the lost whore's drawings. I'm saving you from a social ridicule, Duke."

"Get out," he grunted.

"What about van Breda's offer? Do I have your blessing, Sire? I said, sarcastically.

"You have my permission for selling your paintings, but Ostermann should consult first with me about the client. Dismissed."

That last sentence hurt a bit. I suppose it's because I'm not used to hear him speaking to me like he does to the servants. I should better get used to it, because I will be hearing that for a long time.

Chapter 2

June 20th, 2006

I went to the University to pick up my grades. It wasn't so bad as I feared; an average of 5.5 points out of 6. A broken heart is good for the studies, as it was the only thing I did over the last month. My paintings were sold at the auction and Repin bought one for 43,000. I'm glad he did it because it was one of my best so far, a young couple sitting at an open café. Lintorff found an excuse to avoid the place, and I didn't go as I had to study for my tests. Ostermann told me the whole story, still upset at the Russian who had the nerve to call him a "mercenary" for no letting me to truly explore my limits. "As if one of those brutes could tell something about Art!" He also told me that D'Annunzio has a friend, a newly appointed Cardinal who needs a portrait for the Cardinals' Gallery at the Vatican. He's from Italy, and liked a lot my style when he saw one Madonna and the portrait of father Patricio with some of the children he helps. I should travel to Rome for a weekend to meet the man, and make the first sketches.

I have to ask permission to the monster. I'll speak with Friederich, still unhappy with my "impossible and childish behaviour", kicking me out of the kitchen every time he sees me around. I'm postponing a more than probable huge fight when I announce that I want to disappear for a whole weekend, leaving the children behind.

Today, Armin and I shared the car in the morning, he, still upset at several mistakes he realised he had made in his final statistics test, and I not caring at all. We got our grades, and he decided to go for a coffee with some guys from Banking and Finance, already flattering him over his "uncle". No, they don't know who the uncle really is, but owning a bank is already a very good introductory card. I excused myself, and went to the library to make time till lunch when we both have to go to the bank.

The place was empty as most of the students were away on holidays. I sat in one of the banks near the big windows to have good light, and put out my big sketch pad and started to work in the composition of one of the illustrations for the Sleeping Beauty, using graphitints. I think they would kill me if I put some watercolours over this table. Pencils and a wet brush is not so obtrusive.

"It's not what you usually paint. Do you have a creativity crisis?" I heard a deep voice rumbling.

"Hello Constantin. This is also not your usual environment," I answered also noticing Oblomov taking the chair in front of me. His boss sat next to me, blocking the exit of course. Some habits die hard.

"Hello, Sable. Is it for your children?" Oblomov asked with real curiosity, prying the paper from my hands. So much for your manners!

"It's for a children's book. The Sleeping Beauty. This is a draft for the part when all fall asleep. What did you call me?"

"Sable. Fits you better than *Dachs*. Sables are aristocratic and rare creatures, horribly difficult to catch, short tempered. I had one when I was a child. Got several bites from it," he explained.

"I see. Constantin, are we going to have trouble now?" I asked him.

Constantin said something in Russian and Oblomov dashed out. Boss is boss.

"No, why? I was around in Zurich, and decided to pay you a visit as your guards are away for the morning," he shrugged sounding almost innocent.

"Do you really think this is a good idea? Lintorff is still upset with your "meddling with me," in Davos. I like to see you, but I could be in a lot of trouble, and honestly, this is not the best moment to add more to the list."

"You were not at the auction," he pointed out.

"Thank you for buying the painting. I think, it was the best I had that year," I answered hurriedly, changing topics.

"And you're working on a book."

"Why is it so strange that I work? I'm not a kept boy!"

"My logical question should be now; is everything all right between Lintorff and you, dear?

"This is none of your business!" I exploded.

"So, it's true. That you left him, but he forced you to live with him for his children's sake."

"Mobsters also chit chat," I said to him seriously and royally pissed off.

"Like everybody else, but we prefer the expression "intelligence made on the adversary". The cause is not so clear, but it must have been a big one so you needed to be admitted at a hospital in Montreux. Rumour has that you caught Lintorff on an adventure, but I don't really believe it."

"Constantin, leave it. It's none of your business. I will not go away with you. I will stay with the children."

"How did you find out about your family's fate? Who told you?"

"You knew it?" I shouted.

"Of course, your father's name was on the list of people disposed after the 1989 upheaval against Lintorff. I was very busy with my own affairs at that time, but the whole story reached us. Quite impressive, I might say. Löwenstein and his friends had the old school. The punishment designed to warn the others. I always wondered why Roger de Lisle was spared, till I saw his photo a few years ago. You two look similar, like cousins. Did those two have something going on?"

"My uncle was his lover for almost seven years," I confessed, feeling very sick and ashamed.

"I see. I was imagining something like that, but couldn't really believe it. That might explain why Lintorff almost threw himself at you in Venice, and kept you on a very short leash since that day. Who told you?"

"His mother. She hates him."

"What a family!" Constantin chortled. "Do you really want to stay?"

"I have no other choice. I love the children and I'm a member of the Order. I can't leave it walking on my feet," I said dejectedly

"Guntram, is there anything I can do for you?"

"No, thank you Constantin. I don't want any more trouble between you and him. This has to stop."

"As you wish, angel. Whatever you need, call me. If he gets violent with you, you should go away. He's not stable, and you don't want to know what he's capable of when he feels threatened. Instead of the Boogeyman, we have Lintorff to frighten the newbies."

"I thought it was Pavicevic."

"No, he's all right. Lintorff follows his ancestor's traditions when dealing with Russians. The Teutonic Order was a living nightmare for all of us."

* * *

June 28th, 2006

I can't postpone it any more I have to speak with Friederich. This morning, I got a letter from the Cardinal himself, inviting me to go to Rome on July 7th, to start to work this weekend. I can't say no, and the thing is exactly done "in the proper way". Written letter, with Vatican stamp on it, very politely formulated, but it leaves no doubts that you have to move your bottom there.

* * *

July 9th, 2006

I'm back from Rome. That fucking German invited himself! He even checked on a man from the Church! I want to kill him.

On June 29th, I took the courage to show the letter to Friederich, who was more than happy that I've got "a commission from the Vatican itself". Of course he would speak with his Excellency about letting me fly to Rome alone to start with the portrait. It was a great opportunity for me, and I should not be concerned about a thing.

Idiot! Never trust a Jesuit, no matter if he was not really ordered. They're all the same.

On July 6th, Lintorff called me to his office in the library. It was very late and I had given up all hope to go.

"Friederich has informed me about Cardinal Righi Molinari's request. I will accept that you do it as it's an activity proposed by the Church. However, I will not allow you to charge for your work. It will be a donation from my family to the Church."

"Sire, you can't ask this from me. It's my work. May I remind you that the Cardinal himself set the price? I accepted all his conditions without complaints," I answered, starting to get annoyed.

"My family has never taken a cent from the Church, and much less a Griffin did it. The Order was created to protect the Church from all its enemies, and we will not divert resources from it. This portrait will be a gift. I'm very pleased that you have been chosen for it. It shows that your work is improving."

"I'm no part of your family or related to the Order," I growled. "Besides, *Meister* Ostermann will not accept it after he negotiated the price."

"I have already given Ostermann his part from the sale. I will pay your share, if you're so money needed," he said disdainfully.

"You have no right to interfere. I was only communicating you my leave for a weekend."

"It's under my conditions or you stay at home, de Lisle," he said very

497

sharply.

All right, I accepted the whole shit because I wanted some free time out of this fucking prison. I don't care if I have to sleep under a bridge as long as it's away from Zurich.

"It will be an honour to paint his Eminence's portrait," I replied, nearly destroying my jaw muscles as I was gritting my teeth.

"Good. Dismissed," he said nonchalantly and returning to his papers.

Armin ran away at the mention of the word "Vatican". "No chance I'd go. You got yourself in the mess. I have a date with a cutie, and you want me to spend a whole weekend looking at you drawing an uptight old man? No way!"

On the 7th, in the afternoon, I said goodbye to the children, who were not happy that I would go away and not play with them that afternoon. They still don't understand the concept of time. Ratko had the car ready and drove me to the bank.

"I need to go to the Airport."

"You fly with Duke. Move, boy," he said nearly pushing me out of the car. Fuck!

I had no other option than going to Monika's office. Excellent! Not because of her as she's very kind to me, but her office is next to the bastard's. As usual, she greeted me and started to speak about the University and the upcoming holidays. She already knew my reason to go to Rome.

"Here is your schedule. Tomorrow at 10:00 you will meet his Eminence, and have lunch with him. You have to return to the Castle at five for tea with Carolina von Lintorff. She's in the city with her mother-in-law because they will deliver the money from the auction to Monsignor Gandini. At eight you have dinner with all of them, his Excellency and the Cardinal. The Duke invited him personally."

"At the Castle? Monika please, don't tell me you put us together in the same hotel."

"Hotel? No dear, you go with the Duke to San Capistrano. It's a family residence built around 1350 in the Lazio, thirty minutes away from Rome. There are ten bedrooms, and you will have separate rooms."

"I had no idea he had a house in Rome."

"He has two. One is a small villa near Villa Borghese, but he said that if he opens that house, he will get half of Rome's society banging on his door tomorrow. He wants to have his peace. So he will go to San Capistrano. You will love it. It's like a fairy tale castle, perfectly preserved. You should not miss the art collection there. It's one of the best in the hands of private collectors. Several pieces are priceless: Cimabue, Rafaelle, Bronzino, Daddi, Titian and many others. Mostly focused on religious art, this is why the Cardinal is so keen to visit the Duke."

I can't say that I was surprised. He loves to hide things, like an art collection, a castle, a house, relationships with the Church at the highest level, murdering your family, etc. I smiled back at her, and went to sit in the sofa in the foyer, even if she told me to go to the Duke's office as "he's in a meeting till 5:30."

I busied myself with my sketch pad working on the Sleeping Beauty. I have to present something by mid-July or Coco van Breda will make my existence miserable.

"Hurry up, de Lisle. I haven't the whole day for you."

As if anybody asked you to come. I even had my own ticket! Shit! I stood up and followed him, not happy at all, in case somebody didn't realise it. I was going to go to the second car parked behind his one, but Ratko stopped me, and sent me to the limo, where he was already sitting, looking at his bloody papers. I sat at the farthest corner from him.

I was looking out of the window when I felt his gaze upon me. I looked at him and there he was, studying me instead of reading his things. I gave him a cold stare, and returned to my window.

"Your grades in the school were very good. Your best so far."

"Thank you, Sire," I replied, not even looking at him.

"I have invited Cardinal D'Annunzio too. He wants to ask for several pieces from my collection for a joint exhibition. Cardinal Righi accepted to pose in the house tomorrow afternoon, after lunch. You will work better in there."

It's incredible how pathetic he can be. Not only he does not let me charge for my own work, he will not paint a single line of the portrait, but he has to control the whole process. Is he afraid that I bang a sixty something Cardinal? Her mother might be a real bitch, but Lord, she knew him. Creep is a word that fits him perfectly. I can't go to the Cardinal's flat in the Vatican; He has to come to a far away Castle, no matter how nice it might be, to get his stupid portrait done. Is he afraid that I'll burst into St. Peter's crying "Sanctuary! Sanctuary!" like in the Middle Ages? Perhaps, that might work. All of them still live under those crazy codes.

"I suggest your mood tomorrow is better than what we all had to suffer during the last months. Friederich is tired of being your private courier. If you need to say something to me, ask for an appointment, and we will see."

"I find quite bizarre that the Duke himself will bother to take care of his children's tutor during a work visit to a Cardinal."

"I'm overseeing your behaviour as it has proven to be quite unsuitable during the last weeks."

I didn't give him the satisfaction of starting a fight by throwing the insult he was expecting after his last demeaning remark. "As the Duke wishes," I could feel he was really upset at my answer.

In the plane, I sat in the corner, as usual, surprised that it was only us and one stewardess, no bodyguards at all. I worked on the story for almost an hour, in blessed silence, only caring about my own business.

"As I said earlier, your grades this semester were very good," he interrupted me. I just gave him a blank stare. He looked mildly crossed that I was not answering his praises. As if I would care!

"I have decided to send the children to a day care centre from September onward."

"May I ask why, Sire?" I said totally shocked at his move.

"They're old enough to start to relate with other children, and they can't depend on you for the rest of their lives. They will go in the morning and return for lunch. It will be the same school they will attend next year. I will let one of the nannies go. We will keep Lisette for the menial tasks with them, but it's time they start to learn to fend for themselves."

"I understand."

"You can start with your thesis next term, and present it next July, as you have so much free time in your hands that you need to find an occupation elsewhere."

There's the reason. He's still pissed off that I got a "job" outside the Order, one that he can't control. Put me to study more and clean after the children so I don't do something "stupid" like being independent.

"As you wish, Sire," I replied unimpressed and returning to my own drawing.

After one hour driving, we arrived at his Castle. As Monika said, it was truly an impressive building, keeping the original style, never altered. It was located on top of a hill, dominating the valleys. The cars entered into a big courtyard, much larger than the one in Zurich, and the staff was already formed to receive him. As usual, I tried to remain in a second plane as I followed one of the cleaning ladies towards my room. Only the paintings in that corridor on the second floor, were absolutely fantastic. I think I saw something looking very similar to Gentile da Fabriano, but I can't be sure, I'm not Ostermann. I understand now why he has a job with Lintorff.

"Dinner at ten, sir," she said as she disappeared, leaving me in an spacious room. I have to eat with the bastard, and show "a good behaviour". I had to lay down in bed for some minutes because all this was proving to much for my nerves. Honestly, I didn't understand what he was after.

Ten minutes to ten, I descended the stairs, looking for a servant to tell me where to go. As Juan would have said, I needed a map not to end in the dungeons. I found the main butler at the entrance of the living room, a huge monster thing of more than a hundred squared meters. He informed me that tonight the Duke would use his private quarters on the second floor as it was only us.

How charming!

The private area for the Duke was on the second floor, on the other side where I was staying. The butler left me in a small room with a big chimney, the dinning table, some chairs, small square windows looking over the mountains. I saw a portrait of a gentleman dressed as a Prussian general from the XVIII century. It was not exactly a fantastic painting but you could see the family air there. Speak about endogamy!

"Friederich Maria von Lintorff. He was acting for Griffin for over fifteen years; one on the main supporters of the Hohenzollern dynasty. Albert and Gertrud come from his line. Shall we?"

We sat at the table with the usual distribution. I was decided to keep silent and avoid to engage to his many provocations. If he wants so much to fight, why didn't he stay at home, in Zurich? The salad went away without problems as he decided to inform me about the castle's history, and I spaced out as it's my trademark. The mess started by the bloody fish course.

"Last week, Dr. Van Horn spoke with me about your health. He's concerned about your very high cortisol levels. Stress is not good for a heart patient. He says you should find a way to release stress or he will give you something for it."

"I'm under considerable stress. I will see what I can do," I said now starting to become enraged. Am I now responsible for my own stress? Of course, he's a poor soul, always forced to act.

"As you're on holidays, I will send you with the children to Argentina in August for three weeks. To the countryside house, the city might prove too much for them yet. I think the children will like the landscape," he announced to me. "You will take Goran's men with you."

"I'm not willing to return to Argentina, and much less to be placed in a remote area, surrounded by your security staff. I prefer to remain in Zurich for that matter."

"My decision is made. You'll leave on July 25th and I will join you on August 14th. I'm sure Karl and Klaus will like the place."

"Then I will go to Buenos Aires or return to Zurich while you enjoy your holidays there."

"I can allow you to go two or three days to the city so you can visit your friends there. But you will return with us on the plane."

"His Excellency should understand that the Master and Serfs times are over," I retorted now truly upset at the snotty bastard.

"Your working conditions have improved a lot, considering how they were till the XIX century."

"You have no right to order me to go to another country. I refuse to have such a responsibility!" I nearly shouted. Did he imply what I think? I'm not his bloody serf!

"Well, stay at home. Do as you like. I was under the impression you would be delighted to have three weeks on your own in your adopted country. We'll go together to Sylt," he shrugged, and I nearly collapsed. Three weeks with him on a fucking island, full of Germans and seagulls? The house is "small", no place to run.

"I will go."

"Good. Regarding tomorrow, his Eminence will come at 2 p.m., and you can work with him till dinner at 8:30, if it's convenient for him. Do not tire him, Guntram. You're excused from the meetings with Gandini and D'Annunzio, but you will be there for dinner. We will return on Sunday at 4 p.m. Is that understood?"

"Yes, Sire."

"Is there anything you want to ask?" he asked when he realised I was fidgeting again with the fish.

"May I go on Sunday morning to St. Peter's? I will be back at 2." Like a toddler, asking permission to go out... to a Church!

"Unusual request, but I'll allow it. One of the men will accompany you." Fortunately, he didn't press the issue. Yes, I wanted to go to see the *Pietá* again. You can laugh all you want.

"May I retire, sir? I'm tired from the flight," I had enough from the bastard, and no dessert was worthy of all this.

"You haven't finished your dinner," he pointed out. Do you really want to know why I have high cortisol levels? I can't go if I don't finish my dish. Excellent! I gripped the fork to the point it was painful, but it relaxed me.

He forced me to remain with him at the small living room he had while he worked. I sat on one of the sofas, near the light, to continue with my drawings, ignoring him. I think it was more than one in the morning, when he lightly touched my face, stroking it, waking me up.

"Go to bed, Guntram. I'll see you tomorrow at breakfast," he said soft and kindly.

I piled up my things and dashed out of the room, going to the safety of my own bedroom. Shit! The bastard was touching me.

Saturday morning, at 9, I had again another sample of his "eat with me or starve" new policy. I remained silent the whole time, and he didn't disturb me. After breakfast, I was left to my own to look at his art collection.

It was impressive. There's a good reason why D'Annunzio is so keen on coming to visit him and asked to see it. There were many incredible things, all what I've loved when I was a child, and the bastard never bothered to tell me he had it! I hated the fact that I could only see it for a few hours! He had more or less the whole list of Middle Ages and Renaissance painters made by Vassari. There were around forty pieces, all of them worthy of the Accademia in Florence. How did they get them? Is this what he calls a "small collection scavenged from ancestors"?

In one of the corridors, were three drawings from Bronzino. Two were studies for a portrait and a beautiful Madonna. I don't know for how long I was looking at her.

"There you are, sir. The Duke awaits for lunch," the butler almost scolded me, quickly leading me towards his private dining room, while I tried to fix my tie and jacket and hid the pencil and pad in my pocket.

I entered the room almost out of breath, and he was already sitting at the table, looking totally pissed off.

"You're fourteen minutes late, de Lisle."

"I'm sorry, sir. I lost track of time looking at your art collection," I mumbled like a little sheep. Shit! Did I just apologise to the bastard?

"Sit down," he ordered me with his same commanding voice he uses with the traders. "Did you enjoy it? he asked softy. Yes, he has multiple personalities, there's no other explanation.

"Pardon me?"

"The collection, de Lisle," he said slightly annoyed. Oh yes, he doesn't like to repeat himself.

"It's very well balanced, your Excellency. A pity I didn't see it before," I said, again focusing on my food and not looking at him at any moment.

"D'Annunzio wants to ask several of the pieces on loan for the Vatican Museii, like the Fabriano, the Lippi, and many others. I still have my doubts. Those are irreplaceable pieces if lost or stolen."

"Dr. Ostermann is a better judge in those matters," I said very quietly. "The Fabriano is worthy to be in a Museum, not in a private collection," I whispered.

"I admit it is a clever move from D'Annunzio to make you paint this portrait in order to get to my soft side, but it will not work."

"You have no "soft side", sir. Perhaps you can show something akin to friendliness," I retorted. If it's "hurting time", I can also play. He seemed taken aback for a second. Guess he was not expecting that I would hold my ground.

"Have you ever done something like this before, de Lisle? Do you think you can do it?" he smirked.

"Unfortunately, there's always a first time for everything. I will get by, sir. That you have offered yourself to pay for the portrait lifts an enormous weight from my shoulders as I doubted my technique was good enough. But, as his Excellency said many times in the past, he's a good art critic, and knows where to place his money," I answered with my sweetest voice, kicking the ball towards his side of the field, as strongly as I could.

"I'm glad you're confident in your skills. After all, your only commission so far, is a children's book and they're not very demanding judges," he returned the ball to my side of the field, effortlessly.

"Mme. van der Loo asked me to paint her portrait too. I haven't made up my mind yet." That must have hurt. She's the wife of very important banker from the Netherlands. His husband bought for her one of the paints in the previous auction, and she was fascinated by it. She called Ostermann several times, but I was not really sure, now I want to do it. "She saw part of my work in London, at Repin's house. She specially liked that old first piece, the one with the children reading. I think she offered to buy it, but Repin didn't sell it."

Now, he looked crossed. Furious. That was one of his favourites pieces and Repin "stole it" from him like he had "stolen" me from the Russian in Venice. Those two are like two children, competing to see who gets more. I'm convinced they don't care shit about me, it's only about showing the other "his place". Lintorff had to think for a full minute the answer. Most probably he was already planning how to screw it up.

"It's good news, indeed. Portrait painter is one step over comic illustrator," he replied finally.

"Comics books have a strong influence of hiperrealism. I would love to be at the level of Chuck Close, Richard Estes or Jean Olivier Hucleux."

"Did Ostermann place you there? Strange. I was placing you nearer to the Pre-Raphaelite School, but with different topics, more modern and adequate to our times. You could never be a hiperrealist because, even if you have the photographic quality required, there are slight changes in the perspective, use of light, volume and composition that give your paintings some originality, but I could be mistaken, and your work be worthless. I'm not so bent to it as before."

Not his best, but it hurt me nevertheless. I didn't reply as ignoring him, drives the bastard crazy. I should have taken some lessons from your mother. Also, the motherfucker knows about Art more than he normally shows. Ostermann and his friends were placing me into that category after heatedly discussing it for several months.

We finished eating and he left me alone. I went to the gallery in the second floor to look at the Bronzino drawings and take some notes, on them. It's a real pity I will never see them again, because Lintorff never comes to this house.

"Hello Guntram," Cardinal D'Annunzio greeted me. He was dressed as a normal priest. I knelt down and kissed the ring.

"Your Eminence," he patted me on the head and shook my hand.

"Let me see what you have been doing," he started to go through the pages. "It's good, not bad, but much darker and intense than before."

"I've grown older, your Eminence."

"Like all of us," he chuckled. "I have a difficult customer for you downstairs. For over seven years I've been after him to get his portrait done. He does not want to do it. He accepted you only because he saw your paintings, and considered that there was something spiritual in them, specially in the way you paint children. He thinks this is a waste of time and money. He will not pose. Be glad if he gives you a photo. He's now with the Duke. God enlightened him, and Lintorff started to tell about how much money you have already collected for charity and your work in Argentina. I think he's already softening him. Go get your things and we will see."

"I have everything I need. I will only meet him and perhaps make some sketches of him and discuss what he wants to do. Only charcoal. I work faster with it, but I should better go for a bigger sketch pad, would look more professional," I mumbled.

"Bring the folder I asked Ostermann to do," he ordered.

Yes, the folder-box. Why does he want to see my old watercolours, some unmounted oils and drawings, is beyond me. All of them look very appropriate for showing to a priest. Nothing scandalous... well, my style is very prudish. I went for the box and the things.

The three of them were already sitting in the "drawing room", really good light. Cardinal Righi was a man bordering the seventies, not looking happy at all. Later I learnt that he had always been in the Missionary Church, related to the Third World Movement Priests, and didn't like to be in Rome.

"Come over here Guntram. Give me the box, and we will leave you to work. Righi, this is the artist I spoke about," D'Annunzio said as he took the box from my hands and, exactly as he had done with Alexei, gave it to Lintorff to carry. I had to make an effort to keep myself from laughing at his barely concealed annoyed face.

Righi and I were left alone; time to look "professional". "If your Eminence would be so kind as to tell me if he has some ideas about the portrait..."

"I don't know. You're the artist."

"I see. Is there something you would like to include in the portrait, like a Rosary, a prayer book or a special set?"

"As simple as possible."

"I see. Where was his Eminence living before coming to Rome?"

"Working in Honduras, El Salvador and Guatemala, mostly on the more difficult areas."

"I used to help in a poor area too, but now I have to settle with painting and getting money for them. The Duke would never allow me to go again to a place like that. I really feel useless now."

"Were you really working in a slum?" he asked me, sounding very dubious.

"Of course. From fifteen to nineteen years old, then it was over. I used to help with teaching the children, and in a way they were my first customers, and so far the best I had. I used to make reading cards for them or illustrate stories," I explained as the man visibly relaxed. "My health wouldn't allow me to do it now, but I really miss it."

"I know it's hard. I was not really believing D'Annunzio when he told me about you, but I was surprised that your paint of that priest and the children reflected so accurately the misery and at the same time, the deep happiness of some of these children. Some of them show the deep sorrow of growing up too fast."

"I draw all of them from memory. They're real children. I tried to send the original paint to Father Patricio but he said that I was encouraging his vanity. So, it was privately sold at the end of 2005, and he got the money from the sale. He was more than happy to use it to rebuilt and enlarge the school."

He became more peaceful, if that could be the correct term, and started to speak about himself, that he had met even Bishop Romero and many others. I started to sketch his body, face, some details of the hands. "Should I not pose?" he asked.

"Would you hold it? No. Don't worry I'm used to working with children and animals. I look first, make the image on my mind and then check if it's accurate," he looked at me, surprised. "Oh, it sounded very bad. I'm sorry. I didn't mean to be disrespectful, your Eminence."

He laughed. "Men of my age enter in a second infancy, but I was expecting to delay it for a few years more. Do you want to see the photos?"

"Yes, it would be good if you give me a photo for working later."

"Here is the official one and this is my personal photo album. D'Annunzio forced me to bring it and show it to you. "

"Thank you," I said taking the photo and the album, full of pictures from his missionary times and some others priests. "I will not keep it, but I would like if you explain to me some of the photos. Perhaps we could include some of it in the portrait."

"Are you not supposed to do it following some cannons?"

"Yes, and I will do the dull thing, but I'm interested in other aspects of your life. Everything shows finally," I said returning to work, now looking at the album.

"Guntram, you're impossible, dear." Elisabetta said, startling me. I didn't see her coming as I was working on the album. "It's more than five, have you offered something to his Eminence? I had to rescue him by myself from your clutches. You should also come, we're having tea in the living room."

"I'm sorry. I didn't realise it. Could I not stay here? I would like to finish with this as I have to return the photos to him."

"Darling you know Konrad will not be happy. He sent me to fetch you. Come, drink your tea, eat something, and then you can escape to work again. It shouldn't take more than half an hour."

"Honestly, I don't want to go."

"Guntram, I'm aware that my nephew really did it this time if he was unfaithful to you. Lord knows, I had to put a lot with my late husband. All Lintorffs are the same; completely idiotic creatures when it comes to their desires. Konrad is one of the most evolved specimens of his family. You should try to forgive him, for your children's sake," she said very sweetly, trying to convince me.

"I can't. It's much more than that," I replied very quietly. She kissed me on the forehead.

"All right dear. You're the best thing that ever happened to my stupid nephew. If you need some place to meditate, you can always come to my house in Zollikon," she said, softly smiling to me.

"Thank you Elisabetta. You're very kind."

"Now move," she ordered returning to her usual dominating ways. After all, she had to deal with her sons and Lintorff in addition. "Wash your hands. You're full of charcoal. I thought I would never have to say that again," she laughed and I echoed her.

When I entered the living room, I went directly to greet Carolina and Gandini, and had my tea with them, as Lintorff, Righi and D'Annunzio were arguing over something and I didn't pay attention to them. After finishing, I asked the women to be excused, and returned to my work in the drawing room.

Sometime later, a butler asked me to go to the dinning room, and I complied, leaving my things there. I sat at the farthest corner in the big table, near D'Annunzio who asked me about the portrait the whole evening. Finally, I agreed to show him what I'd just done. He was also interested on several things, he had seen in my folder.

"Could you convince the Duke to lend you the paints you wanted?"

"Impossible man! He does not want, no matter what I say. For the last two years, I've been trying to convince him, even offering to pay the insurance, but he still refuses. He wants to protect his privacy, and something like this will put him in the spotlight. He's not exactly a shy person, but he can't stand any kind of public appearance," he complained to me.

"It's truly a pity. I've seen magnificent pieces upstairs. People should be able to enjoy them."

"He doesn't even let them be photographed, not even if you only write "private collection," in the credits. Perhaps you could convince him."

"I? I'm only his sons' tutor. Nothing else. He will not listen to me. You should try with Ostermann. He gets away with many things."

"I've offered to buy two of your pieces, but he refused my money. He offered to pay for them and donate them to the Church if I think they're valuable. I refused, of course."

"His family respects the Church enormously. He will never take money from you or let me do it. Take whatever you like, your Eminence. It's an honour and a great opportunity for me to say I've almost sold something to the Vatican," I advised him, smiling weakly.

"This is most generous from you."

"After dinner, you can take the two you liked. Ostermann will complain a lot. You might have to send him one of your books," I smiled this time wider, quickly recovering from my relapse at hearing that Lintorff considered that he could do whatever he wanted with my own work.

"I will send him the new one, if he doesn't come first to my office to strangle me for accepting your offer," he chuckled.

"He's a very good manager. If it were for me, I would be sitting on a square making portraits for twenty euros No, I would be working as a waiter, and painting on napkins. He has just got a contract for me to illustrate some children's stories."

"Yes, I've heard his Excellency ranting about it. This can't be so bad. I'm under the impression he wanted me to press you into not doing it in exchange for a loan of two pieces from his collection."

"He fears the book will interfere with my duties towards his sons."

"He's concerned this might prove to be too much for your health. He said that two months ago you were admitted in a hospital in Montreux. He will send you and the children to a country house for a month this summer."

"I'm afraid so. I've just been exiled. I will work there." It was hard to keep a smile there. I looked around and my eyes meet those of Lintorff, staring at me from the table's head. I immediately returned to my dish, avoiding making any kind of eye contact with him. I said nothing for the rest of the evening.

After eating, we all returned to the living room, and I was allowed to finish what I have started, mostly because D'Annunzio insisted on seeing me work. I still don't understand what people find so fascinating about one guy with a piece of paper, some charcoal pencils, chalk and an eraser. At eleven, they all decided to call it for the night.

I went to my bedroom and put my pyjamas, sitting on my bed to continue drawing.

I've must have dreamed it because next morning I woke up in my bed, tucked in, my sketch pad and pencils away from the bed, on the table. I didn't remember to have put them there or leaving them in order. Normally, I throw them in a messy heap. I think I dreamed it. He wouldn't dare to do it. At some point during the night he came to my room when I was sleeping over my sketch pad, took the things away from me, forcing me lay down on the bed, tucking me in. "Guntram, this can't be good for you.", he whispered, caressing my face softly. I turned around to escape his hand.

Sunday morning, one of the maids woke me up telling me that I had to hurry as the Duke was driving away to Rome in forty minutes. I had to hurry to shower, dress and put all my things together. I was hoping that he was going to Rome to do whatever he needed to do there, and leave me to my own in St. Peters with one of the bodyguards.

I was wrong.

It was either driving with Lintorff to St. Peter's or staying here till one of the men would have time to drive me to the Airport.

"I'm going to the 10:30 Mass also. It makes no sense to distract resources with two cars."

I wanted to shout that I didn't plan to go to Mass, but it would have been useless. Last time we were here, he also went to the same service... in Latin. Darn! Refusing to go to Mass will result in a full hour preaching by him, later to be repeated by his spiritual director, *Pater* Bruno in Zurich when he comes for Mass next Sunday. No, thanks. I want my peace also.

I had no other choice than to take the passenger's side on a "discreet" black BMW, without the bodyguards. That was strange. We said nothing during the drive. He left the car in Piazza della Rovere and we walked in silence to the Basilica. We passed the security controls without problems and had to make the small queue in front of the entrance, where, like always, the security people were rejecting the men wearing shorts (we're in the middle of July!), and women not well covered.

The Mass took place at the Altar of the Chair and in Latin. He can follow it much better than I, because his religious education comes from before the Council Vatican II. I tried to go somewhere else, but the look I got from him froze the blood in my veins, and I decided to stay next to him.

The worst part was when we got to the Kiss of Peace. It was a brief handshake, but my hand was burning for the rest of the service. We both took communion together.

"May I go to see the Pietá? It will only take some minutes, your Excellency," I asked him after the ceremony ended. He nodded his approval.

"I will go outside, to the square. Meet me there. I have to make some phone calls," Lintorff said just like that, emotionless and leaving me there, in the middle of the central corridor as he went away. He's big and tall enough as to make a group of tourists move aside to let him pass. I think he could make the Swiss Guards jump to attention.

I took some time to admire the sculpture, memorizing every detail. I had no time to make a sketch or several as it would have been my desire, but at least I could take a look at it. After half an hour, I knew it was time to go away.

I was partly blinded by the sun glaring against the stones. I had to put my sunglasses on, and looked around for him. I saw him in the shadows, near one of the portals, completely engulfed in his Blackberry. For a second, I was surprised that he wasn't guarding the entrance like a pit bull. Then I thought, 'he's distracted, it's now or never. Probably he would think something like "The Lord gives, the Lord takes", if you go away. You have your passport with you. Could go to an airport and take a plane somewhere.'

'And you will never see Klaus and Karl again.'

I approached him, slowly. Before I could say a thing he lifted his head, and asked, "Are you hungry?"

"No, thank you. If you want to go to the airport..."

"Good. We go to Sant' Angelo. Alexei told me you were never inside," he cut me, putting away his gizmo. I looked at him in disbelief. Does he think I want to play tourist with him of all people? No way. When I opened my mouth to tell him what he could do with that big Castle, he was already briskly walking toward the exit direction Via della Concilliazione.

We walked for ten minutes, I trailing like a caboose behind. Now, I understand the hard life of Heindrik, always running after his boss, and the many others I don't know their names. Asshole!

I arrived almost out of breath to the entrance of the Castle.

"Did you take your medications this morning?"

"It's the race done in mid-July, under the Roman sun," I answered darkly. No reaction at all.

"Should I go with you or do you prefer to be alone?"

"As the Duke wishes," I said coldly. Get the hint, asshole.

"I'll meet you inside in ten minutes. I have to make some arrangements before. Start you. It's too hot for you out here."

I didn't answer him, too busy controlling my temper at how things backfired at me. Again. Like in Venice. Not only once, but twice. I had forgotten his "selective hearing" problem. No, he has no hearing problem, he does whatever pleases him whenever it suits him.

He left me alone for almost forty minutes. I could visit the palace in peace, at my own pace. Whoever was giving him a hard morning, thank you very much. He rejoined me at the top of the castle, where there's a terrace and you can see the river and part of the city.

"Italy is always beautiful no matter the circumstances you are in. I always used to come to Venice to think or to Rome, much before I met you," he said very softly, his gaze lost in the line of houses across the Arno. I said nothing. "Let's go for lunch."

"Should we not go back for the car?"

"One of the men has it now. There's a place near the Palazzo Altemps. Riccardo will pick us up there at 2:30." He explained in a cold voice again resorting to the master and servant treatment again. I had to run to catch him on the stairs. True, this time he didn't run as much as before.

The restaurant was small, not one of the posh places he normally goes. It was on a very small street, almost like an alley. I was not hungry at all, and the prospective of sitting with him on neutral grounds was not appealing at all. Most probably, he would engage in a conversation I didn't want to have. The waiter left the food over the table and it became the centre of my universe as I didn't want to lift my gaze from the tablecloth to find his eyes looking at me, studying me.

"Did you mean it? During the Mass," he asked abruptly.

"I don't understand," I said briefly, directing my attention now to the salt and pepper shakers.

"You accepted to shake hands with me during the Kiss of Peace."

"It's customary to do it. It means nothing."

"Yes, it does. You were in the Lord's house. You could have shaken hands with the other people and ignore me or refuse my hand."

"It was unplanned." He fixed his eyes on me. "It didn't mean that we are friends again. Nevermore. I have no feelings for you in any sense."

"I don't believe it," he stated.

"Believe what you want. I don't hate you as I should for what you did to my father and my family. It would be very easy for me to deny the four years I spent by your side, and dwell in hatred for you, but it's stupid. Goran was right. To hate you will only devour my soul, and poison the children's life. I could take revenge on you, telling all what I know to your enemies, but I will never leave your sons without their father, suffering the same childhood I had."

"Guntram I swear on my sons heads that I had nothing to do with your father's or family's death. When he came to me to offer your life to me, I was going to let him go, not accepting the deal. He should have disappeared like Roger did, but he begged me to take you as a proof of his repentance toward the Order. It was the only way the others would have left you alone. I never knew he was so sick. If I accepted his offer, and swore to protect you, it was because I didn't want to have the blood of a seven year old on my hands. I never demanded his suicide. I thought he was bluffing! I was after the others; the real associates who planned all this, not a simple clerk, no matter how clever he was. They were trying to kill me and all my allies, like Ferdinand or Albert. Do you think that removing a Griffin is just accepting his resignation? It's a full scale war, and it can end very bad for the civilians."

"I can't believe you. I've seen you acting when you are furious. Your fury is cold and calculating. There's nothing left to chance."

"Do you have any idea what is to find out that the person you loved the most in this life wants and plots your death?"

"Do you know what it is to be told that you're alone in this world?"

"You're not alone any more. I'm here and I love you exactly as the first day I saw you. We have a family together now. We built it overcoming hundreds of pitfalls. Please, Guntram, forgive me, and let's start again," he said taking my hand over the table.

I didn't remove it as I was deeply lost in my thinking.

"Perhaps we could go to Paris, as it was where you saw me for the first time," I started to speak very slowly as his eyes lit with hope, squeezing my hand harder. "We could go to Père Lachaisse and romp over my father's grave. It's so nice this time of the year for tourism and romance, but this time would be more Gothic than before. My family's vault in Poitiers could be more challenging as the maid has not dusted it for sometime," I finished looking at him with all the hate and contempt I had in me.

He withdraw his hand very fast as if he had been burnt. "Is there anything I can do to atone for?"

"Leave me alone. Ignore that I exist. I will do the same for you," I said through gritted teeth.

"You really don't mean that. You need me in your life."

"No. I needed you in my life when I loved you. You mean nothing to me now. If you are really sorry for what you did to me, let me continue my life as I see fit. Do not interfere any longer in my affairs, like you did this weekend. I don't want you near me. I don't want your support or protection. Everything between us is dead and well buried."

"You know that is not possible," he said flatly. "You will not leave my house."

"I will continue to be the children's tutor and nothing else. Find yourself someone else to warm your bed. I had enough of you. You should have no problems at all."

"All right, if you want to play the servant, I will treat you as such," he almost spat, resentfully, like a small child who lost his candy.

"I ask nothing else from his Excellency."

Chapter 3

December 14th, 2006

Another term finished and with good grades too; 5.6 points. I was very surprised because I was not working too much on it. I can't do everything. I have to take care of the children when they're back from the school, paint in the night, after nine, when they're in bed. I finished Cardinal Righi's and van der Loo's wife portraits. Both were widely praised and even got two more orders which I had to decline. I was too busy painting for the book, and by sheer luck I finished by mid-November. I also want some time to myself, to study, to work on the thesis and to paint what I like.

I have the book in my hands, and I still can't believe it. It was so nicely printed with good paper. I believe Ostermann really pushed her limits. The price is somewhat expensive but I can't say a thing. She knows better (thirty-nine CHF or thirty euros) for a forty page hard cover book. Coco was absolutely fascinated by the illustrations, and printed a first edition of 5,000 copies. We are going to have a lot of toilet paper. It's too much, but she thinks she will sell about seventy percent of them, and it was a matter of costs 3,500 is more or less the same price than 5,000, and the rest can be put for sale after the festivities. I'll keep ten copies: two for Karl and Klaus for Christmas, two for Corina's twins, one for Juan Ignacio Dollenberg, one for my former neighbour George (Jorge) in Argentina and another two for Tita's grandchildren. She was very nice as to buy two of my paintings, and sent two of her friends to buy more.

The book has been distributed in book stores in Germany, Switzerland and Austria.

But the big surprise of the year came from Michael Dähler himself. Alexei told me he plans to marry Monika next April, and the Duke offered the Castle for the ceremony and reception. Ferdinand calls now Michael "Mr. Van der Leyden," in his face, much to his annoyance. I'm very glad for both of them. I got the invitation from Monika a week ago. I don't know what I'm going to give them as wedding present. A painting would be too much, as it would look as if I'm trying to get rid of my trash. Besides, Michael doesn't like art so much. He's more into electronics, gadgets and weapons.

Ostermann was able to sell part of my paints through a gallery in Geneva (6). After the *marchand*, my manager who takes fifty percent over the profits and our friends from the tax office, I made 19,000 francs plus the other 4,000 I got from Mme. Van der Loo. It reassures me to have some money on my own in the bank. My previous 21,000 and this; 41,000 after expenses. Lintorff would laugh at such amount.

Repin offered to buy one Madonna I painted after Rome which is very beautiful—I don't know from where she came from—but I couldn't sell her. She's special. He offered as much as €35,000, but I refused and told him the truth; I liked her and couldn't part with it. "Now you understand my feelings for your paintings," he said and left me in peace.

Constantin and I became something akin to friends. Friends don't love each other like what he would like, but we can't say we're at odds or that we ignore each other. Frankly, besides Alexei and Goran, he's the only one who has the guts to overlook Lintorff's orders of casting me out from the "inner circle"; I'm now in the evolutionary scale, one step on top of the cleaning lady, but one below the rookie trader. I think he has even forbidden Armin to speak with me as we don't work together in school any more after the lessons, I pick up the children from the day care centre and drive home with them to have lunch, study and play with them the best that I can. Milan now has to deal "with three children more, fortunately they behave, unlike the oldest one." The other one pissed off with me is Friederich.

Anyway, Constantin writes to me and I do the same. It's the less conspicuous way to do it. All in the open, so I'm not accused of treason again. We write mostly about art, my university, my work, his opinions, politics and things like that. It helps me to make me feel that I still live in a world of adults and I'm not always surrounded by children.

Alexei had much more stomach that I would have credited him. He ignored his boss when he ordered him to cease all contacts with me. "My Duke, with all due respect, my free time is that. Free time and I will employ it as I see fit," he said to him, according to Goran. Sometimes, I go out with him and his boyfriend Jean Jacques to a movie or to dine with them (Jean Jacques cooks, no chance he will let "enter in his kitchen (Was this not Alexei's flat?), a brute who used to live from ravioli's cans and didn't know how to use a microwave". In a way it's strange to see how a real mature relationship works. Alexei may dream all what he wants to be like the bastard, but Jean Jacques does whatever he wants. He's independent. They fight sometimes, but Alexei always stops when things become too heated. They're perfect for each other.

Lintorff is away most of the time. He travels for weeks, and then comes home to see the children for a week or two. Fortunately, he does not pamper them for catching up the lost time. He writes to them almost every night, and I read his letters to them. First, the children did not understand well what that piece of paper was, but now they realise it's from papa and they're very happy. Sometimes, he phones them, if the hour is appropriate. When he's around, he plays with them in a loving manner, and listen to their stories very attentively. In that way, he's a wonderful father.

He treats me like the rest of his servants; aloof, cold, and demanding results. I have to present reports on the children's doings twice per week. If they were sick, what they did in school, what they read, what they did at home. He wants fully detailed descriptions, and he reads them, because many times when he speaks with the children he asks for things I've written about. He calls me "de Lisle" and I "Sire", "your Excellency" or "Duke". He makes me leave the room when he comes to see the children. If I see him with the boys, it's only because they're outside playing in the garden.

* * *

December 21ˢᵗ, 2006

Today, Friederich told me that my presence will not be requested during Christmas. Translation; get a life for the holidays Guntram. The Duke will take the children to Rome, and stay there until January 7ᵗʰ. He will take Lissette with him. The children were most upset with this. They were expecting to get Guntram full time for them as there's no school for any of us.

What should I do? It's more or less holidays… for three weeks. Lintorff's very wrong if he thinks I'm going to remain in Zurich to freeze my ass. I've just turned twenty-four!

I'll go to Paris and from there to the north. Perhaps Lille and Brugges to paint. Yes, that would be good. I'm sick of hearing German the whole day.

* * *

December 23rd, 2006

Huge Christmas fight with Goran as Lintorff is gone with his boys to the house near Villa Borghese. He took Friederich with him, very upset that "his Excellency is planning several dinners and gatherings with friends. That's hardly appropriate for the young princes!"

Goran came to the house like a whirlwind, furious that I wanted to go on holidays. "Do you have any idea of the logistics involved in the little tour you planned?" he shouted.

"Which logistics? I'll book a hotel room, the train tickets and that's all. I have a hotel for Paris for the first five days. From there I will see."

"I will have to move like four bodyguards to keep up with you! Do you even have his Excellency's permission?"

"For what? He's in Rome with his sons for three weeks. What am I supposed to do? Sit here and knit? No, wait. I have to sit and paint a flower vase. It's inside," I said sarcastically.

"Little brother, what did I tell you about your behaviour? It must be spotless. The minute you set one foot out of this house with someone else than me or Alexei, his jealousy will drive him mad. Save us all from such a mess. You, alone in Brugges? No way. He will drag you back home, and shoot me in the head for letting you do something so stupid. You're the Griffin's Consort!"

"I? It's finished since April! Didn't you realise he treats me like shit?" I shouted now.

"You treat him worse than garbage. I've seen it. The Arctic is warmer than you. Your indifference is slowly killing him, but he still can't let you go. Do you know he started again to date whores every time he's out of the house?"

"Buy him a box of condoms!" I roared out of my polite lamb persona. No, I'm not jealous. He can fuck whoever he wants for what I care.

"Look how you react! You're jumping at this. Why don't you stop all this?"

"Am I jealous? Your boss was already jumping on every European bed before I came here! So do your job and don't take it on me if it's not so easy as before. You're the only one who knows the truth besides Ferdinand and Friederich! You can't ask me that! How would you feel if you were in my place?"

"Guntram, this has to stop at some point. You don't have to be in the bank with him the whole day!"

"I'm sorry if I didn't let your boss fuck me last night so your life would be easier," I retorted. "But, you see, he was like that much before he picked me up from a Venetian square. So it's not as if your boss has changed, you knew him."

513

"He's still deeply in love of you, and suffers for it. It must be a real torture to have what you love with all your heart, reject you every day."

I was in another dimension. Goran Pavicevic, our own beloved Serbian Killer, playing Cupid.

"I thought you said, third parties abound in a couple. What's it gonna be? Do I have your permission to go or should I do it on my own? I already outran you once," I said defiantly. He didn't like it at all.

"I'll consult with his Excellency," he replied getting his mobile phone out of his pocket. He dialled a number and he started to speak in Russian. I went to sit on the couch, very upset with him. Goran spoke for a long time. Almost fifteen minutes.

"All right Guntram. You can go for almost two weeks to the house in London. This is the best I can do for you. Take it or leave it. You can go after the 28th and stay till the 6th. I have some security staff there who can protect you. Milan can go with you."

"I don't want to go to London!"

"London or Zurich. It's your decision, and I will double the watch on you so you don't come to stupid ideas," he said very seriously.

"All right. London it is. You two are a bunch of paranoid lunatics!"

"I'm not paranoid. I forewarned you. He will not let you run around Europe without security. You're still very important to him, and if something might happen to you, he would be devastated. We had already the London Experience with Repin in 2003."

"He does it so I don't fuck around, like he does," I answered back. "For a moment, I thought he was letting me go as he treats me like trash, that he was getting bored, that I would be kicked out the moment the children would go to school, but no, he's still the same obsessive compulsive psycho. He will never let me rebuild my life," I said now desperately.

"Little brother, he will kill whoever comes near you, and he will do it with his own hands."

* * *

December 29th, 2006
London

I'm here, at his house. I arrived yesterday with Milan, who's happy to be here. Like a child. He was never "for holidays," in London and he wants to play the tourist. Today, he was dragging me all over the city to see it. He wants to go to the Covent Garden and somehow he got tickets. He also would like to visit the National Portrait Gallery… and he brought along a tourist guide that he was reading on the plane.

Coco called me a few days before Christmas to tell me all the books were sold out and that she was going to make another edition for the Magi Feast, but this time only 3,500 copies as she didn't want to risk the nice figures she has having. I let her do it.

I will not call the Dollenberg's or Juan. With all the heat I have on me, it's better to keep them away. I imagine Lintorff is quite pissed off at my "controlled escapade" from Zurich, and he's looking for an excuse to retaliate.

I called Goran to apologise for my rude behaviour, and he was kind enough as to say "Don't worry, I understand this is very hard for you. Enjoy your holidays, little brother."

* * *

January 3rd, 2007

I still don't believe it. This afternoon I was with Milan at Harrods, buying two of these teddy bears dressed like the Buckingham Palace Guards, but in the good quality version, when I met Oblomov.

"Hello Sable. Madame wants to see you. She's having tea at the restaurant with her daughter, Sofia Constantinovna," he said, with his air of being totally bored of this life. He grunted to Milan as "hello" and the other did likewise. Don't they hate each other?

"Madame as Mr. Repin's wife? Do you think that's a good idea?"

"Madame knows about you since 2001. She was almost glad that boss would consider to stop having affairs with crazy artists and settle down with you, but Lintorff screwed it up. She wants to speak with you. Mihailovic, do you want to have a drink? This is nothing for us."

"Sure," he shrugged.

"Good," Oblomov replied, taking me by the arm, and almost dragging me to the fourth floor to the Georgian Restaurant. As revenge, I gave the bears to the gorillas.

She was a middle aged woman, mid-forties, perhaps fifties, elegant with brown eyes and hair. Not what I would be expecting from a Mafia boss wife, you know, the cheap skinny brainless blonde. She had her daughter sitting with her, a young girl around fifteen or seventeen with the father's black raven hair, but the features from the mother.

"How do you do Mr. De Lisle? My husband speaks only good things about you. I admire your work a lot."

"Thank you very much Madam. I'm at your service," I said kissing her hand. The daughter giggled a bit. "How do you do Miss Repin?"

"You can call me Olga Ivanovna, Mr. de Lisle. Please, do sit down with us."

"Thank you," I said very embarrassed and not really knowing what to do.

"Ask him mummy," the girl pressed her mother. I lost my colours if she was going to ask about "that".

"My daughter has no manners, sir," she laughed. "To be sixteen again. I would like to commission a portrait from her for my husband. It will be a surprise for our 25th wedding anniversary. I know he plans to give me a house in Paris, and I would like to give him something very special. Sofia is his only daughter—we have three boys more too—and she's his father's eyes. I thought you could paint her. We will need to have it ready for mid-May 2007. Will it be sufficient time?"

"I don't know if this would be the best idea…" I trailed.

"Please, do it. Papa has so many of your pieces. He even gave me one for my birthday. The dogs, as I love them. I have a pug," the young one said.

"Miss Repin, honestly, I don't know when I could make the sketches from you. I reside in Zurich, and most of the time I'm in the school or taking care of my two pupils."

"Sofia, let me speak with Mr. de Lisle alone, dear." The girl disappeared.

"Madam, this must not be comfortable for you. I'll go away."

"Nonsense Guntram. I've been married to Constantin for almost twenty-five years, and I know him since he was fourteen years old. Do you think I don't know his tastes?" I lost my colours. "He's been quite besotted with you for a very long time, and now that I see you in person, I can understand him very well. Constantin and I are very good friends, really. Ours was an arranged marriage, and he has been an excellent father to his children, and a good and generous husband to me. We both know what the other likes. We had our children, but we don't share a bedroom since ten years ago," she explained me with a gentle voice.

"Madame Repin, Olga Ivanovna, there are many reasons for me not to do it."

"Please Guntram, I beg you to do it. You and Lintorff have no relationship for almost a year. Constantin told me about his infidelity, and I'm sorry for you. My husband adores your work and her daughter. Please, if he can't have you, let him have something from you that will give him an enormous joy."

"Does your daughter know who's going to paint her?"

"She knows her father admires you and her mother too. That's enough."

"I'm afraid that even if I would accept your commission, I would not have the time to do it. I live in Zurich, and this is my last semester in school. I have to present my thesis by the end of the summer…"

"My daughter will go to Zurich at your convenience. Please Guntram, do it as a very special favour. There are no problems in the moment between Constantin and Lintorff. Both work together, and the Duke has since been at my house in St. Petersburg twice."

"I could make some sketches of her in the two days I still have here, and present you a plan on the 6th, before I come back to Switzerland." Goran will kill me for this. "But I must insist that my bodyguard and you are present when I do it. Your daughter is under-age, and Lintorff is still very difficult to deal with."

"I agree with your conditions. Shall we start tomorrow? Would you come to our house? It's near where you are staying. My daughter will be very happy."

"Tomorrow at ten?"

"Of course, and you must stay for lunch with us. I insist," she said, offering me her hand.

"Thank you Madam," I said kissing it and leaving the table.

It's official, I'm insane and have a death wish. Lintorff will kill me when he finds out I'm going to paint his worst nightmare's daughter, and I don't give a damn. The girl looks nice, and Constantin is a good friend of mine. Honestly, I would have jumped out of a window had it not been for him, Alexei and Goran. I only hope I can do a good work. I will inform Goran about tomorrow's activities. I don't want to get Milan into trouble.

Wondering still where the other Serb could be—I hardly doubt Oblomov could do something to him and Milan had no problems to see him—I dialled Goran's number.

"Hello Guntram. Everything all right?"

"Yes, I hope. I lost Milan, he's with Oblomov, but this is not why I called you. I have agreed to paint Repin's daughter at her mother's bid. We start tomorrow at his house in London. Milan and she would be present while I make the preliminary sketches."

"You're going to make heart attacks a contagious disease, no doubt," he sighed. "Can you please tell me how am I supposed to inform this to the Duke?"

"Don't tell. I will do it when we return to Zurich. It's my own mess. I'm only informing you, in case you need to make further alterations in the security or if you think I should not do it."

"There's no danger at all for you. Repin would never mix his wife in our dealings. He's like you and the Duke for such matters. Tell Milan to call me. Bye."

* * *

January 6th, 2007

Sofia Constantinovna is a sweet girl; nothing like the father. She told me she wants to be a fashion designer and study at St. Martins in the Fields, here in London. We got along almost immediately, as I started to work with her. She was thinking it would be like this Titanic scene, but I'm no Leonardo di Caprio and we spent most of the morning chatting in the living room with her mother. After lunch I started to make the sketches.

"You work so fast. It's incredible," she said in awe. "I can't draw that fast and accurately."

"It's like a sport, you have to practice every day."

"No, no matter how much you practice, the talent can't be replaced." Olga Ivanova said. "There's not a single stroke out of place. I studied Art in the Moscow University and even had several exhibitions, but I never mastered the technique like you do. My husband told me you studied all by yourself."

"I used to copy a lot, that is true, and read all the books about art in the school library," I shrugged.

"How do you decide what to paint?" Sofia asked.

"Honestly, I don't," I laughed. "I make many sketches about things and then one day, without previous warning, I know how to combine them. I make a preliminary sketch with tempera or watercolours and then I transfer to the canvas. From there is a free ride. Things may change when I'm painting it. For the book, I made many more plates than necessary. Ostermann finally helped me to choose what to use."

"That book is divine. I ordered several copies for my friends' children. It was almost impossible to get them. You should make another edition. I thought I would never see my husband reading a children's book!" Olga laughed. "You still have to send me your conditions, Guntram."

"*Meister* Ostermann is my manager. I have no idea of what to do. I don't even know how he estimates the prices, but don't trust him, he overcharges."

"I'll keep that in mind," she laughed.

By the next afternoon, I had already two charcoals with her face and one bigger with pencils. I was still not happy with them even if both women were enrapture by them. Sofia threw herself on the bed of the room we were using to work and started to look at them, like a young girl. This was what I was looking for. The sun was making her dark hair shine and the light blue evening dress she was wearing was a nice contrast against her pale skin.

I decided what it would be. She was laying over her stomach in this bed, holding a small mirror showing her face, the sun literally bathing her. If she wants we can include her pug on the floor or bed. I started to work, after the mother accepted the idea. After all, is her under-age daughter in a bed.

"Such ideas you have Guntram! You will not make it pornographic at all!" Olga laughed when she saw this morning the preliminary drawing, made on tempera. "My daughter looks like a princess from a fairy tale. It's very beautiful."

Sofia was happy with it and wanted to include her pug at the feet of the bed.

I want to paint it no matter who the sitter was or to whom it will be sold.

At six, Milan and I took the plane back to Zurich. Tomorrow, I will see the children and I have missed them a lot.

* * *

January 8th, 2007

Yesterday evening, Karl and Klaus arrived home. They both almost jumped out of the car the minute they were released from their seats. Lissette looked very, very tired. I had to crouch on the floor as they both wanted to jump on my neck, crying out loud my name. Their father didn't even look at me, going straight inside of the house; so much for communication; time to ask for an "appointment".

"Friederich, could you please tell the Duke I would like to speak with him at his convenience?" I said hurriedly before the man would run after his employer.

"Certainly Guntram."

I managed to bathe the children, dress them in their pyjamas and make them eat their dinners. I told Lissette to rest because she had enough of them. "Two little devils, Mr. De Lisle. I don't know how you control them so well. Even their father was running away after the fourth night. They can cry a lot. Look at them now, so formal and correct, sitting in their places and eating in peace. I had to fight with them nonstop the whole day."

"Lissette, you're very tired. Why don't you rest, and take the day off tomorrow? I can take care of them. We read now a story and they will sleep soon."

"Good luck, sir. You will need it."

Around ten, Friederich came to my room to announce to me that the Duke would see me while he dined.

I put back on the bloody tie and the jacket I had removed for painting. I washed my hands and went to the small dining room, knocked on the door and entered. He was sitting as usual at the table's head, with Dieter—one of the butlers—behind him.

"You wished to see me de Lisle. Speak," he said, not even offering a seat to me. All right, standing it will be.

"I wanted to inform his Excellency about a commission I've accepted from a member of the Order."

"Thank you, Dieter," he said and the butler ran away, closing the door behind him. I was not invited to sit or anything. He just gave me one of his blank stares. I took a deep breath.

"Mrs. Olga Ivanovna Repin asked me to paint her daughter's portrait for her 25th Wedding Anniversary. I have accepted and I wanted to inform you before you found out through other people. We had already made the preliminary art concept, and she has approved it."

"I don't allow it. Dismissed," was his reply, completely ignoring me again.

"May I ask the Duke's reasons?"

"You have to take care of the children. You have no need of money as you have a generous salary. If I accepted this book venture, it was because there was nothing wrong with it. It's something for children, but this is something else. Work and study here. You will resign your commission tomorrow."

"I will not, your Excellency.

His fist smashed the table, making me wince at the noise. "Remember your place and to whom you're speaking to!" He roared, now truly furious.

"I clearly said that I would pursue my artistic career the way that I see it fit," I growled back.

"You're a snake if you think you can paint one of my worse enemies' daughter! Shameless slut! Exactly like your uncle!" He shouted again, this time rising from his chair, and advancing toward me.

"Knowing you as I do now, perhaps my uncle was right to do it. You squeeze people till they bend to your will. You smother people. It's a miracle I can still paint. I can understand him perfectly well. You reaped what you sowed," I said slowly and firmly, not caring at all if he would explode.

He did. He took me by the neck and started to squeeze it to the point of really suffocating me. I tried to fight him back, but he was very strong. He lifted me from the neck to smash me against the wall and I knocked one porcelain figure to the floor to make noise otherwise I believe he would have killed me.

Friederich burst in the room and shouted something to him and he released me immediately. I fell in a boneless heap to the floor, trying to gasp for air. Friederich ran toward me and helped me to sit, checking if I was still in one piece. It was so sudden that I didn't have time to realise what was going on. I was expecting him to shout with me or even given me a slap, but this was a brutal onslaught, exactly like Goran predicted he would react in case I would "betray him" with another. Did he think that I was going horizontal with Repin's wife? He can't be so crazy.

"What did you tell him, child?" Friederich asked me as he tried to calm me down stroking my hair.

"I only want to paint Repin's daughter portrait. The mother asked for it," I said, feeling a horrible pain while speaking.

"Did you really say that to him?"

"He said I was a whore like my uncle and I told him that my uncle was right to cheat on him because he's a control freak. He got what he deserved. There he exploded."

"Guntram, this was the most stupid thing you've done in your life. Never mention Roger in this house! How many times do I have to tell you this? As for Repin's girl's portrait, it's impossible what you're asking from him! What is going to be next? That you want to move in with this Russian?"

"You know this is not true! I have no feelings for him! I will paint that wretched thing because I like the girl and the mother really wants to give it to him. So far, after I broke up with this murderous bastard, he has been the only friend I have. All of you disappeared as though I had the plague. No, I lie, Alexei and Goran, were loyal to me. The rest sided with your boss."

"You're not thinking clearly my boy. I'll take you to your room, and I will speak with Konrad regarding this. Do not interfere and stay in your bedroom. I'll get some ice for your neck. It will be very bruised tomorrow morning."

This morning, I woke up still feeling a lot of pain in the neck and it was already turning a deep blue colour. I wore a turtle neck sweater because no tie could possible cover this. I didn't want to scare the children. I took care of them in the morning and had lunch with them, but my mind was elsewhere.

"Guntram, bird! not dog!" Klaus whined. I realised I'd drawn a dog instead of the bird he had asked of me. They take very poorly when you don't understand what they say.

"I'm sorry Klaus. I'll make you a nice sparrow now," I said to a very pouting boy as I restarted the drawing with Karl playing somewhere else.

"Mr. de Lisle. I'll take care of the children now. Friederich told me that the Duke wants to see you in the library," Lissette interrupted us sometime later.

I thanked her, washed my hands from the paint and went to the library. I knocked on the wooden door and I heard his voice dryly saying "come in". Not a good sign, I thought. Inside, I was surprised to see Friederich sitting in front of his desk, completely serious. I advanced up to the middle of the room and stood there, waiting to get permission to come closer.

"Come over here Guntram. Do sit down." Friederich said with a gentle tone.

I took the chair next to him as I felt Lintorff's eyes completely fixed on me, and his cold aura of anger radiating from his every pore. I couldn't stand to look into his eyes for more than a split second, as they were truly terrifying.

"You knowingly defied my orders," Lintorff barked. "Men have perished for much less than that."

"Please Konrad, let me deal with this. Guntram is under my command now." Friederich cut his tirade in a stern voice and much to my shock, Lintorff's backed away. "Who approached you with this commission?"

"Olga Ivanovna Repin," I answered quietly. "I worked for two days at her house in London."

"Yes, that is what Goran told us. He only let you do it to avoid further problems. Milan says nothing inappropriate transpired there." Friederich supported me. "The main problem is, that you should have never accepted it. You have no need to do it, therefore it can only be understood as a clear challenge to the Duke's orders," Friederich continued.

"Which orders?" I asked perplexed.

"You're perfectly aware who the Repins are. They're not like us and will never be. You belong to the Lintorff family, whether you like it or not. I see only two solutions from this dead end you have placed yourself. One is that you call Ms. Repin and refuse the commission," Friederich explained me with an oddly gentle voice.

"I don't want to resign. I would like to paint that concept, not to mention that

I consider Repin as a friend."

"Or you can paint it, give it to her, without charge of course, his Excellency will never let you take a single cent from that criminal, and end any kind of friendship you might have with him in the future. The Duke will accept this as compensation for your insolence toward him," Friederich finished.

"What if I refuse to all this? You can't tell me what to do!"

"I'm not telling you what to do, as you say. I'm only outlining the best and most efficient solutions for this situation," Friederich said with an emotionless voice.

"Could you please enlighten me with the less suitable options?"

"Guntram, you're perfectly aware of the costs of crossing the Griffin's path. Do I need to remind you of your family's fate? Perhaps this time it will not be directed against you personally, but over the people who entangled you with their machinations. It's your decision child. I would suggest the second option so we are clear for the future."

"You have no right to choose my friends!" I barked not too loud.

"It's for your protection. Repin might be a member now, but he's not one of us. One day the costs of crossing his Excellency will exceed the benefits he might think to obtain, and he will cast you to the wolves without a second thought," Friederich told me with a cold voice.

"I can't stop to paint it now. I like it and I need to do it," I said. "I will finish it and give it to Ms. Repin without getting money from her. I only request to end any kind of contact with Repin after June. I will give you my word, Friederich."

"Your word has not much value. I had it when you went to Buenos Aires and then when you took my family's ring." Lintorff intervened letting all the poison he had built up flow freely. "You will swear on your father's memory that you will never have any kind of contact with this man."

"Konrad! We will come to your manners later." Friederich growled, making the bastard flinch and look down, ashamed of his own explosion.

"I will do it as you will, Duke. I swear on my father's grave that I will have no further contact with Constantin after June," I said very slowly.

"Good. Dismissed," he barked.

I stood up, ready to leave the room, but Friederich said "We are not finished. Konrad, your turn," I gaped at the butler, well former tutor is more appropriate, astonished to no end that he will tell the mighty *Herzog* von Wittstock what to do.

"I apologise for my behaviour last night. It was most inconsiderate of me to physically attack you. I regret my actions toward you. It will not happen again," he said taking a deep breath and looking me in my eyes.

"It was tactless from me to report it in such a crude way, but I don't regret my actions. I accept your apologies, Sire. I'm sorry for bringing up your past so vulgarly," I said with all the coldness I could muster.

"Very well, we all have explained all our points of view. Guntram, you may return to your duties." Friederich intoned, and I knew better than to cross him. If he can put Lintorff in his place, well, you have to admit that the man is much more than meets the eye. I bowed my head to both of them and left the room, closing the door as quietly as possible.

Chapter 4

March 29th, 2007

Karl and Klaus turned three. Time flies as they say. I'm so proud of them. OK, not when we had to go to the "let's leave the nappies behind" phase, but Lissette somehow survived. That woman is candidate for sainthood. They had a small party in the garden with some of the friends from the day care centre. They had four ponies for the day only, with people to take care of the children. I did my best to remain in the background, and it worked as most of the invited mothers were after the big prize; Lintorff. Still single, two children the age of your own, loaded and good with them. A real catch, at first glance, of course.

I couldn't get the children to bed till 10 p.m.! They were so excited with the presents, the friends, the cake, the horses and a long etc. I was dead on my feet from having to coordinate all this mess. Fortunately, Jean Jacques helped me a lot with the logistics. You can say in a minute, he's a real professional... with a lot of temper when it comes to shouting at providers.

At eleven, Friederich told me that the Duke wanted to see me in private. Shit! I'm tired, totally out of my working hours, and he wants to speak!

I went to the library and stood in front of him as he was very busy reading and signing papers.

"Ah, you're here de Lisle. I want you to take the children to Venice from the 5th to the 7th. You should return around the afternoon as on Sunday is the bank's lunch. Go around the city with them," he ordered me not even lifting his gaze from the blasted documents.

"Yes, Sire."

"Good, dismissed."

I truly hate that word. Nobody is more happy to leave the room than me; there's really no need to send me away like the dogs. He's nicer to Mopsi than to me. That we tolerate each other, doesn't mean you can be rude.

At least, I will not have to attend to the Dinos' Meeting.

Fuck! The freak wants me away so I don't cross my path with Constantin! What is he expecting me to do? That I drag the Russian into the Confessional and get dirty? Better don't try to understand his mind... it's way too convoluted.

The bright point is that his daughter's portrait is finished and I'm truly happy with it. I will send it to Ms. Repin next week. I told her to donate the money for the portrait to a charity in Argentina; Father Patricio's school. He said I can't accept money from him, but he said nothing about other people taking it. If this continues, Father Patricio will soon build a University! I'm very glad the money is used for something useful, and I will not insult her as was Lintorff's original idea. I will not work for free! There's a slim line between good and idiot.

* * *

April 23rd, 2007

On Saturday 21st, Monika and Michael's wedding took place. A civil celebration as her previous marriage was not dissolved by the Church. I know the guys went for a wild bachelor party the night before according to Alexei. Michael invited me, but I didn't go as, honestly, I would look like an idiot in a classy whorehouse. Albert and Lintorff, along with Ferdinand, went; another reason to make myself scarce.

Honestly, I didn't want to meet the bastard on a social occasion, much less in a strip club or wherever they went.

Monika was looking radiant in her wedding dress, knee long, adorned with some lace and in a champagne colour. Michael had to wear a two button morning coat and was not really looking comfortable about it. I'm sure he would have preferred his old Navy uniform, but Monika didn't let him wear it as he's out since more than ten years. Under Friederich's pressure, I had to wear a morning suit tuxedo, with the only concession of letting me use the stroller variant (semi formal). In grey with light blue waistcoat matching the bloody striped tie.

Getting the children inside of their suits was very challenging, and I still don't understand why the father insisted they should wear waistcoats and ties! The poor dears looked truly nice, but they hated it. I never thought they will cope with them till the end of the banquet. Then, I took them away to the nursery because they had enough of being kissed, patted and pinched on the cheeks... It's a hard work to be cute! Lintorff as usual looked incredible in that morning coat. Some people just know how to wear these things.

It was a short ceremony in front of a judge at noon. After pronouncing the vows, there was a small reception, where the one hundred guests greeted the newly weds and I did my best to keep Karl and Klaus away from the bride with their dirty hands (yes, in no time they got them in the earth). Fortunately, several women decided to take the children to pamper them, and I had some peace.

"Hey Guntram, lost the children already?" Alexei greeted me, winking.

"No, traded them for a little peace and some champagne. How are you?"

"Dying to check on the kitchen," he whispered.

"Jean Jacques will kill you if you ruin his lunch. Since three days ago, it's impossible to speak with him. He even shouted with Friederich."

"I know. He's upset at everything. Where are you sitting for the eating?"

"With the children, Ferdinand and Monika's sons. It's an all guys table. If something goes wrong, my table would be the usual suspect. I'll get the children away right after the cake. I hope it's good because I've promised it's something out of this world, and they should be very nice to get a piece of it," I explained, hearing him chuckling at the last part.

"And people say you're immune to corruption!"

"Deal with toddlers on a daily basis, and you'll turn into the Godfather." I laughed. I looked around for Goran, but I didn't find him. Most probably, the Serb might have disappeared after the ceremony and greeting Michael. He hates to have people around. My eyes found instead Lintorff happily chatting with a brat from a noble Italian house, distant cousin to Albert, if I see correctly, a good looking guy bordering the thirties, and working as a broker in Milan. No, by the way those two were speaking, it wasn't about the Dow Jones latest rally. I know those long, caressing looks from him. I think Lintorff has found someone for tonight.

"Hey, Guntram, that's nothing. Don't pay attention." Alexei told me looking at me with compassion.

"Sorry?"

"That guy. It's a clear one night stand," he shrugged

"Alexei! I don't care what he does! He can drop... whatever!" I huffed really upset at what the Russian was hinting not so subtly.

"Guntram, I'm not blind. You're about to burst in flames out of jealousy."

"I'm glad if he gets a replacement soon. I want out of here! If that snotty Italian helps me to get what I want, I will be buying the ring for him!" I answered heatedly.

"Why are you so upset? I said nothing wrong."

"No, you hinted something. Don't cast a stone and hide your hand. I believed you were my friend," I growled at him, now openly furious as I saw the motherfucker whispering into the Italian's ear. The worse part was that he realised—I don't know how, the bastard must have a sixth sense—that I was looking at his doings, and he just lifted an eyebrow at me and smiled slyly.

"I'll tell you something as a friend. There's one thing I hate in this world, is going to a fine restaurant on a summer day, start to eat in a cooled room, and there comes one of those anorexic women, so fashionable nowadays. That bitch, who only eats a carrot per week, asks for the air conditioner to be turned off because she's cold. Well, she should eat more and not shit the rest of us because she has no fat layer left to protect her from a simple breeze."

"I don't follow you now."

"Easy. If you don't eat, let the others do it."

"Still don't get your meaning."

"If your relationship with the Duke is over like you tell us all, you shouldn't care if he fucks the Italian under the table. If you're pissed off now, it means you're still interested. So, fix the problem you have with him, and let us all live in peace. He will be more than happy to start again, and give you a second chance."

"I don't know what he has told you, but it's I who should give him a second chance. He screwed it up. Big time," I told him very incensed.

"It's been over a year and you still treat him like shit. You're both equally guilty by now. He tried to come to you several times, and you turned him over, not even giving him the chance to explain his deeds. Do you know that you're still considered as the Griffin's Consort and none of us can say a word out of place to you? Other guy would have thrown you to the trash can much earlier before putting up with you."

"There's nothing to explain. I'm tired of his lies. If you'd excuse me, I have to look for the children before they destroy something." I decided to go away before I could said something hurtful.

"Do as you like, but this is no life for either of you," he said dejectedly.

"See you," I said not even waiting for his answer.

The children were playing with Cecilia, Ferdinand's girlfriend, and I rescued her before Klaus would start to tear the small diamonds off from her purse. I think Karl was planning to attack the bird she had on the head because he was staring at her hat, waiting for her to come down to his level. Those two can be mischievous when they want.

"Hi Cecilia, may I take those two to the playground? I think they need to lose some steam before sitting them for an hour at a table," I said to her.

"Certainly Guntram. Good luck," she laughed at seeing Karl tucking my jacket to be picked up and carried to the playground. No way, little fellow, the whole idea is that you do it by yourself!

I took them both by the hands and I took one last look. This time, that motherfucker was slowly caressing the elbow of that Italian and paying all his attention to him. That boy could be your son, you pervert! He's not much older than thirty!

'And you're not even twenty-five, Guntram.' My inner messy, meddling little voice pointed out.

Disgusted beyond words I went straightforward to the swings with the toddlers, happily yelling to get something funny to do.

After the wedding banquet and the promised cake, I took them to the nursery where they continued to play with me till tea time. Jean Jacques was nice enough as to send another piece for them. At seven, people started to go away as Monika and Michael were gone to their honeymoon in the Seychelles.

By 8:30, I had them both bathed with Lissette's help and in their pyjamas. They didn't want to have dinner as they were still full with the cake, and I let them be. I had them in bed and I was reading a story for both of them, when their father entered, still dressed from the wedding. Both children jumped at him, shouting "papa", "papa". I closed the book and started to leave the bedroom when he said to me very coldly.

"Don't go de Lisle. I will be here only a minute to kiss the children goodnight. I still have to change to go out with Marcello," I swear I heard a deep satisfaction in his voice at saying that name.

"As his Excellency wishes. I hope he enjoys his evening."

"Rest assured I will do it, thoroughly," he said, gloating every word.

Chapter 5

May 23rd, 2007

Constantin visited me today to tell me that the portrait was incredible. He was deeply moved by the risk I've taken by accepting this commission.

"Your daughter was a wonderful model. I really liked to paint her," I said quietly as I was in the University's library, working on the thesis. I still don't know how he can come to Zurich, enter in this building without problems and evade Lintorff's hounds. I suspect Goran is somehow holding their leashes. Milan was not impressed at all at Oblomov.

"You captured her spirit so well. I can't stop looking at it."

"There's a favour I need to ask from you, Constantin," I said quietly, killing his exuberant mood.

"Anything you want," he replied very seriously

"We must stop any kind of contact. One of the reasons I painted the portrait was to give it as a farewell present. I have exhausted my credit here."

"Guntram, I will not tell it again. Get out of there. I can help you. The children will get over it."

"I suppose they eventually will, but I can't leave them. They're like my children."

"I understand you love them, but they're not yours. Don't you see Lintorff uses them to keep you under his boot? He will not stop till he gets you back or destroys you in the process. I know him much better than you do, and Lintorff doesn't believe in taking prisoners. You have almost finished with your school, come to St. Petesburg or Moscow for a while. Olga really appreciates you."

"And I appreciate you, Constantin. Do you imagine his reaction when he finds out that you "were messing his territory"? No, I don't want to be the cause for another riff between you two. Lintorff is my problem, and he has started to date other people. He will get tired of me soon."

"Guntram, you're hopeless. Don't evaluate him with a decent person cannons. According to your line of thought, don't you think he will throw you to the trash the minute he finds someone else? Do you really think he will respect your place in that house? Don't you want to start your own life, independently from his whims?"

"I wish nothing more than that. Please, Constantin, understand my position," I pleaded with him now.

"I don't understand it. It's crazy what you're doing. Suicidal."

"Please, as a favour."

After a long silence he spoke again "All right, I will stop any contact with you, but you must swear that the minute you go away from his side, you will call me. My men can help you to disappear if he becomes nasty too. You can't trust anybody there. Perhaps Alexei, but I'm not sure. Pavicevic is on your side, but he will not risk his men's lives."

"Goran has directly fought on my behalf. I don't want him to be in more trouble because of me."

"I know. He sees the brother he lost in you. I'm certain he will protect you with his life or send Lintorff into the next one if he lays a hand on you. I will abide with your request. For now, angel."

* * *

Ferdinand von Kleist's Diary
July 1ˢᵗ, 2007

Konrad informed me of his holidays schedule for this year: from July 15ᵗʰ to August 10ᵗʰ to Sylt. I'm glad to get rid of him for some time. I also need a holiday. I have enough of his personal life messes. This Marcello Moncenigo is simply disgusting. I see that he wants to restart his love life, but to rub the new lover in front of your older one is very low. I'm tired of telling him to let Guntram go away, and now I have to take care we don't repeat the Roger's incident all over again. Thank God, this one only wants money. We know each other for almost forty years, and he still makes the same stupid mistakes. Can't he not see that it's over? He's now into his resentment phase, punishing the lad because he doesn't bend to his will.
How can he be such an idiot?
I'll take Cecilia to the Seychelles from mid-July onward. Monika says it's a beautiful place. Everything is set for what's coming next. They don't need me here till September.

* * *

Guntram de Lisle's Diary
July 24ᵗʰ, 2007. Sylt

I'm still asking myself for whom these are holidays. Not for me, that's for sure. We arrived ten days ago, and ever since, Lintorff decided to piss me off in every possible way. I say one thing to the children to be contradicted in the next ten minutes. "Klaus, don't throw away your toys" and he says "the servants (Am I included in that category?), will pick them up." Doesn't he realise he's spoiling them? I'll speak with Friederich because he's the only one who can stop this mess.
I still don't know what he's doing here. I mean. He plays a little with the children on the beach in the morning, and then runs away to his studio to work, staying there till six or seven, when he goes away for fun. Yes, Sylt is not such a small place as I thought. Lots of rich people, a polo beach contest, two Michelin Stars Restaurants, hotels and crazy prices everywhere.
I'm trying to work as much as I can on the bloody thesis, but it's hard to concentrate with the noise the children make. This Marcello Moncenigo is also not helpful. He came by several times to pick him up, and he takes some demented pleasure in tormenting me by treating me worse than a dog. I'm not going to hang up your cloak, asshole. There's a maid for that!
Yesterday, I was in the veranda, making some sketches and it was late. The dhappy couple came home from having dinner or whatever, and I think he was cocky because he got an invitation to stay over. He came to me while Lintorff was checking

527

the children in bed.

"Still trying to paint de Lisle? You should give up, your style is very old and boring," he said casually. OK, if he wants to fight, we will.

"Do I tell you how to balance your positions in gold?" I replied.

"Right, I forgot for a minute that you went to college. Still trying to finish it?"

"Yes, thank you," I said returning to my drawings not paying more attention to him, I could feel him almost about to explode. All right time for the blow. "Are you staying tonight?"

"Yes, of course."

"I'm glad for you. Now, you're more than a one night stand. You're over the hotel phase. Your next goal should be to last till you get breakfast in the morning," I said sweetly. "It's hard, but I'm sure a skilful person like you will achieve it. The secret is, that you take nothing from him till you get the official lover status, but you're getting closer. Before that, you're only a passing fling for him. Try to get on the butler's good side also."

"De Lisle, you're out. Everybody knows it. Don't delay so much your fall and resign. It's pathetic how you crawl for his attention," he said visibly upset with me.

"His Excellency awaits for you in the car, Mr. Moncenigo." Friederich announced with great dignity, and do I see a deep pleasure glint in his eyes?

"Guess you have to work harder. So close, so far." I said. He didn't said goodbye to me.

Friederich and I were left alone in the veranda, he sat next to me, as I resumed my drawing.

"I'm only hoping this is over after the summer" Friederich said sounding very tired.

"I also want to go to my own home country," I replied softly.

* * *

July 25th, 2007

Last night I had enough of Lintorff and decided to go away for the evening. This is not working, this is slavery... I'm with the children even on weekends! I asked Lissette to cover me for the night as she was already out more than five nights. She pouted a little but agreed.

At six I went away, to a coffee in Westerland. Lissette told me there is the fun and the beach parties are incredible. Honestly, I'm more interested in the German Polo Masters in Keitum, next week. I don't know if I could escape one day to watch a game or two. However, I found a nice place with a terrace overlooking the bluest ocean you can imagine, and ordered a coffee and cake to have some peace. The place was deserted as it was too early to have dinner and too late for coffee.

It has been such a long time since I enjoyed a sunset in total silence and tranquillity. I had not realised before that I'm so close to the burn out point. Constantin was right. It's doing what he wants or kill me in the process. To parade your newest lover in front of your previous one is tactless. I should send the bastard to Hell for being so rude.

Why do I let this to affect me? I'm praying every night to get rid of him and maybe my wish would be granted. I'd better mind my own real work as Ostermann will kill me if I don't start to produce something good. My agent is like a real pimp. As the book is proving to be successful, even after Easter season is over, and we are on the fourth edition, he wants to make an exhibition in Bern with the original plates and call it something like "Childhood Memories" for next October. I know he plans to put me in a collective exhibition with other young artists in Berlin next December.

I was looking at my drawings from the previous days, when a man in his mid-thirties approached my table and politely asked if he could see them. I let him do it as I had nothing else to do.

"They're good. Do you paint professionally?" he asked, not sitting at the table.

"I don't know, really. I've sold several but no real exhibition so far."

"You should consider to make one. I have an art gallery in Berlin. Andreas Volcker is my name. You're not German. Swiss?"

"French. Guntram de Lisle," I said extending my hand and making a gesture so he would sit.

"Your name is somewhat familiar but I can't remember where I heard it."

"I'm not famous, Mr. Volcker. I only have one book of illustrations for children," I shrugged.

"That's it! I bought your book in the Modern Arts Museum!"

"What is it doing there?" I asked truly surprised.

"You must have an agent Who is it?"

"Rudolf Ostermann. I study with him or better let's say, under him," I smiled.

"Do you have more of your work with you?"

"No, just sketches. Did you say you have a gallery?"

"Yes, near Alexanderplatz. I represent several young artists. It's a pity we are full till next year, I think I've heard of you. I will give you my card and you can send me more of your material."

"My manager takes care of such things. I will tell him about your offer. At the moment, I'm here till August and can't send you anything."

"I'm here also trying to sell something to my clients. Do you want to have dinner with me?"

"All right, but we share the tab." Hell if I'm accepting something from strangers. I did it once and look, I'm still in the middle of the biggest mess of my life.

"OK, but this is my first time an artist offers to pay," he chuckled.

"Because I'm no artist," I laughed. "I'm finishing Economics in Zurich."

"You plan to be a banker? No way, hateful creatures, sitting always on top of their gold pile, defending it with claws and teeth. What do they plan to do with it? Take it to the grave? I studied Art History," he laughed.

"You have no idea how nasty they can be," I sighed but laughed also. Why the image of an old Griffin sitting on top of his gold flashed through my mind?

Andreas was a nice and pretty decent guy. He made me laugh, something I haven't done in a long time. He was not gorgeous or even attractive, but I felt at ease with him.

"Do you have a boyfriend?"

"No, and I'm not looking for one. Sorry," I said clearly (and brutally), before he would get the wrong idea. Look how many times my good breeding, politeness, got me into trouble, like with Lintorff for example. I should have gone with my first impression of him and told him to piss off. Brutally and vulgarly. My life would have been much different now.

"Wow. Straight to the point. Sure you're not training for banker?"

"I'm sorry but I don't want any misunderstandings. I'm coming out from a very bad relationship, and at the moment, the last I think about in is in romance. I want some peace."

"How old are you?"

"I'm twenty-four but I feel like forty. I was dating a man, well living with him, since I was nineteen till one year ago when we split. Let's say he cheated on me, a lot. I work for him, taking care of his children, and our working relationship is strained," I explained.

"That guy must be hitting his head against the wall. What an idiot. Cheating on someone like you?"

"He's a real banker," I said making a shrug.

"All of them assholes. Do you want to have a coffee with me another time, let's say tomorrow?"

"I have to work. The asshole is my boss, and he's already pissed off I took a night off. But let me tell you, it will only be a friendly coffee. I'm not looking for adventures."

"Yes, I got the message. I have no romantic ideas about you, just a coffee to fight the boredom of posh parties and rich widows with a lot of money to spend. I'll give you my card, and you can call me whenever you want, right?"

"All right, thank you."

At 11 p.m., the waiter kicked us out. I didn't realise we were speaking so long. We went for a drink, and continued to speak up to 1 a.m. Finally we had to part, reluctantly.

"Will you call me?"

"Only for business. I'm still too crazy. It wouldn't be fair for you," I said.

"Business is OK. I would like to see you again. Bye."

"Good bye." We shook hands like friends.

I came to the house at about 2 in the morning and I sneaked in like a mouse. I passed the foyer and was going to the stairs when a very well known voice said:

"Where were you and what were you doing to come back at this hour?" Lintorff barked from the living room. I went there and stood in front of him, sitting on a leather couch, a bottle of cognac on the table next to him.

"Dining with someone, Sire. Good night," I replied pissed off, that, he, Mr. "I'm on a permanent party", would remind me of the hour. Fuck! I'm twenty-four! Even Armin does whatever he pleases and nobody tells him a thing!

"Who and where?" he pressed.

"I don't have to give any explanations to you. Is nobody from the Order if that's your main concern."

"Does this person have a name or should I find it out by myself?"

"Whatever I do in my free time is my problem. Your questions are bordering on labour harassment, Duke. My working hours don't start till eight in the morning," I said firmly.

"You're the Griffin's Consort. Behave accordingly to your status!"

"Do not raise your voice at me Sire, I'm not your consort since a long time. Ask Monika to write a memo for the rest of the Order. Good night, sir."

"I will find out what you were doing, and I swear that if you did something out of place, you will see what is to be on the Griffin's wrong side. I will not tolerate that you behave like a slut. You have your duties to attend to and finish your schooling," he growled, his eyes almost shinning in the darkness.

"Good night, Sire. Rest well," I said going for the stairs. I'm sick of his threats.

* * *

August 1ˢᵗ , 2007

I doubted a lot about calling Andreas. Finally, I decided not to get him in the middle of my rubbish. He has to suffer a lot from his bank manager over his credits for the gallery to add on top a real Swiss banker, who has no problems to evict a full orphanage if they don't pay the mortgage.

But fate had other ideas. The bastard decided "to punish" me for my horrible crime (dinning out) by forcing me to accompany him (plus the children), to the Polo Tournament, with Marcello. Oh joy! Of course, I put my best blank face and went to the back seat of the Audi Q7 with the children as the merry couple went to the front.

With the excuse that I was concerned Klaus would end under a horses legs, the children and I went to sit to the terraces to watch the match. They were very entertained by the sport, and I have to admit that it was not so bad. A twenty-four handicap team is not ideal, but is not that bad.

"Hey, you never called me, and I meet you here? That's fate if you ask me," I froze at hearing Andreas' voice.

"Hello. I was busy. I was going to write you upon my return to Zurich. I would like an opinion from you," I said, catching with one hand Klaus before he would jump on the stranger, just to check who he was.

"These are the children? You have a handful here."

"This is Klaus Maria and the other one is Karl Maria," I introduced them. "I promise I'll write to you and send you the pictures you asked me, but now, I'm afraid I'm working."

"Good you remember it de Lisle."

Shit! Can I have more bad luck? Better don't tell me. How does he do it? He was supposed to be drooling over the Italian, getting him a glass of champagne or whatever he's supposed to be doing as date nowadays.

"Yes, I see. Send the pictures, and I'll see what I can do for you." Andreas replied looking at Lintorff in his best cold anger persona.

"Good bye, Mr...?" Lintorff said, not extending his hand.

"Andreas Volcker, from Volcker Industries. At your service, sir."

That Volcker Industries... the ones which make luxury cars and many other expensive things? When he complained about bankers, it wasn't about a difficult office manager.

"Konrad von Lintorff," he introduced himself. "Guntram take the children to the tent, it's too sunny for them." Did he used my Christian name? Of course, he's establishing his "ownership" over me in front of the other alpha male. Pathetic. Better run away before they take turns to pee on me.

"Of course, Duke. Come children, we'll go for an ice cream. I'll send you what you asked me Andreas. Good bye."

"Do it please, my travels also take me to Zurich now and then. Bye," he said unimpressed by Lintorff.

Inside the tent, I got ice cream, strawberry for both of them, in a cup and both were very busy getting their faces dirty with the things (no chance you can feed the ice cream to them any longer, "they are big now, not babies any more"), when Marcello came to gloat.

"It seems Cinderella is back in the kitchen," he chuckled. Wow, that was witty indeed, man!

"Yes, strange that the Duke throws his date away to rescue his children's nanny from a rich industrial. It took him less than three minutes to mount the attack," I smiled sweetly but he turned around and went outside, most probably to recover his date before it would start to look elsewhere.

Yes, Lintorff is a good catch only at first glance.

Chapter 6

September 24th, 2007

I'm officially now a MA in Economics by the Zurich University. My thesis was accepted today. *Does the Structure of Central Banks Influence the Effectiveness of their Interventions in the Foreign Exchange Market? Study of the Argentinean Case.* I don't know why the dissertation committee focused so much on the part where I compare the Euro system and our several types of pesos. However they liked it and even the director said that it was more for a Ph.D. than for an MBA work.

"Very detailed study. Somewhat disturbing the many holes you see in the ECB ability to react to any attack on the Euro."

I have to send a copy to Michael and another to Ferdinand. They both told me once they wanted to read it. I really don't know if this is still valid, but a promise is a promise. I will leave the copies to Monika after I speak with her about the Educational Trustee Fund. She has to close it as all is finished.

* * *

October 19th, 2007

Today was my birthday. I was surprised to receive a call from Ferdinand and another from Michael. They both wanted to have lunch with me. First, I refused, but they insisted in their own unique way. I gave up as Lintorff was away and I had the afternoon free. I miss school now.

My life is boring. I take the children to the school in the morning and then I sit to wait till they're released at four. Normally, I paint in peace, at the house or at Ostermann's studio. We have this exhibition coming and he's more nervous than I. One of these days, he will chain me to the easel, and feed me only if I paint. From four onward I take care of the boys and play with them. They're very proud to be on the "real school", not in the one "for babies". And now, they wear ties like papa and Guntram.

The lunch was at the Königshalle, of course. Where else? I wonder if they get a discount or something. I don't understand why they always go to the same place. The maître escorted me to a table separated from the rest of the dining area. Ferdinand, Michael and Goran were already there even if it was five minutes before the time. They all greeted me and wished me a happy birthday. After all you don't turn twenty-five every day.

"I read your thesis, congratulations. It's good and gave me several ideas. It's hard to surprise me nowadays." Michael praised me.

"Yes, it reinforced my faith in the Swiss Educational System." Ferdinand added. Goran remained silent. "Did it take you long to write it?" he asked casually.

"A full year. The Duke told me to start to work on it June 2006."

"Why didn't you invite us? We would have kicked Felder, in case he would have been difficult to you." Michael chuckled.

533

"Because of that. Don't kick my Studies Director. He was generous as to offer me a job at his Hedge Fund, but I refused it."

"Good, because Felder is history. Heavily hit on the crash." Ferdinand said. "But we wanted to know about your plans for the future. After all, you're now a graduate from the UHZ, most banks in the world would love to have your application."

"Really Ferdinand? Do you really think the Duke will allow it? He shouted at me like crazy when I gave my graduation papers to Monika so she would stop this account for my education."

"Guntram, that was distasteful from you. You should have done it differently, like speaking with him personally, thanking him for his support. I mean, to butter him up, just a little. But you had to send all the forms fulfilled along with a letter clearly written by a lawyer," Goran said.

"You had no idea what a week we had when he found out that you presented your dissertation, and forgot to invite him or give him a copy of it. We had to hide our ones," Michael told, unwillingly shivering at the memory.

"I'm sorry if I caused you trouble. It wasn't my intention, gentlemen."

"There's this other issue. This guy, Andreas Volcker. Is it serious?" Goran fired.

"How do you know about him? Don't tell me. Mr. Freak asked you to investigate him. Well, there's nothing between us or will ever be. He's not my type and he sees it also that way. He only wants to make an exhibition with my paintings next year. It's not my fault he has a gallery for hobby besides his many industries. It's a normal friendship. I'm not like your boss, who bangs everything that moves," I said tiredly.

"That's good little brother. The Duke is very unhappy about all this." Goran stated.

"I'm sorry for him," I said sarcastically. "What should I do? Send him a greeting card? What is he expecting me to do? Die an old man without loving anyone? Taking care of his children till they get to the University and then make the hara-kiri? Really gentlemen, you all should think in advance what you're going to ask."

"Guntram, stop defying him like that. Drop any kind of contact you have with this Volcker. He's already looking at his companies, trying to find a hole in them," Ferdinand told me. "Please Guntram, those are difficult times for everybody, many will fall, and we need him calm, cool, with a clear head. You have to help us all. One big service to the Order."

"Forget it. I will not fuck with the bastard, Ferdinand."

"Nobody is asking you something like that, my boy." Ferdinand replied, looked very shocked, but tried again. "Just let him breath a little. Stay low for the next months, till things clear up. Don't defy him like you did with Repin or this guy Volcker. Paint, take care of the children, make this exhibition with Ostermann or even start another book. If you could treat him a little better, that would be fantastic."

"Treat him better? How?"

"Well, for instance you could smile now and then, not giving the impression you want to leave the room whenever he enters, accept to dine with him and Armin, use the account with your salary, show him part of your work... you know. Small things to establish a détente." Michael suggested, his voice quivering a bit. Why?

"It's a lot what you all are asking," I said shaking my head negatively.

"Guntram, if he screws it up now, a lot of people will be in real trouble. His personal fortune and his clients are safe, the problem is the people who works at his companies. What would become of the workers if he takes the easy solution and reduces investments or simply closes the factories down? He can't fight more than one front at once." Ferdinand added almost pouting.

"We have almost no investments in America left, but we have in Latin America, Asia and Europe. The crisis will extend, and a lot of people will suffer. It's much bigger than a market plunge." Michael said very softly, sounding very concerned.

"I can't be responsible for the world's economy!"

"No, of course not, but you can give your support to one of the key factors in the world economy, my boy." Ferdinand pressed me. "Many people's lives depend on him making the right decision."

"I'm not sure. It will be not sincere from my part and he's clever enough as to realise I'm lying," I said.

"Of course, we don't ask you to be all nice to him all of a sudden. Just a little politeness. For example you could ask him for advice over the job offers you got," I stared at Michael. "All right, that one not," he continued "You can give him a copy of your thesis. It's very good and gave me several ideas to work with. Or you can tell him that you will drop this exhibition in Berlin Volcker offered you."

"That's a very good opportunity!" I protested. "Forget it Michael."

"All right, just postpone it a little. He's very cross with the guy, and wants his blood, even if you have done nothing wrong. It's very difficult to reason with him in such matters. He had still not recovered from the mess with Repin's daughter and boom, you dropped the next bomb, bullseye on the waterline. Are you related to *Grossadmiral* Dönitz?" Michael huffed.

"If your boss can't stand the fire, he should stay away from it. Get him a psychiatrist," I said through gritted teeth. They all looked at me, dejectedly.

"You promised me once you wouldn't do anything to hurt him, Guntram." Ferdinand reminded me.

"To hurt him in the sense, I'll rat you out, cheat on you or put poison in your tea!"

"There are many ways of hurting a person, Guntram" Goran said now. "You're not even interested in this man, let him go, little brother."

"Goran, I have no friends! For once, I meet somebody who could be a friend to me, and you want me to give it up?"

"Guntram, I told you all this some time ago. Do you know how hard is for a man over forty, with children, to find another job? We are only asking you to be nicer, to bury the axe." Goran finished, using that voice he has when he's one step from being upset and become dangerous.

If I don't have Goran's support I'm good as dead in here. I sighed. "I suppose I can give him a copy of the thesis and thank him for his support, but don't you think I will kiss him."

"That would be fantastic, Guntram," Goran said softly.

* * *

Ferdinand von Kleist's Diary
October 19th. 2007

During lunchtime Michael, Goran and I convinced Guntram to cease hostilities. That is a great step for all of us. I have to admit, Alexei Gregorievich is more intelligent than we all previously estimated. To press Guntram over his sense of social responsibility was a stroke of genius. Not attending the lunch so the boy would never suspect from where it comes, was another. Leaving Konrad out of it is also a good idea. Guntram is clever enough as to realise if Konrad fakes his reactions. Michael did well his part and I had no idea Goran was such a good actor when he threatened the boy.

I still can't believe he bought the story of the poor unemployed workers. He's so intelligent, almost like his father, but still believes in people's inner goodness. Jerôme was much more clever in that sense. We got Guntram to do what we want without giving anything in return! Alexei was very cunning by telling us not to offer a single thing in exchange; Guntram would have thought we were trying to bribe him and would have refused outright.

Hopefully, the boy will send this Volcker to Hell. I have enough of Konrad's ranting almost on a daily basis. What was my idiotic friend expecting? With a face like Guntram's, it was just a matter of time that another would come to challenge "his ownership" over the lad. He looks much better than his wretched uncle, but I think it's more his innocence and kindness what drives people mad about him. Oblomov told me once his boss was totally besotted over the boy, going to see him working every time he could.

It was tragic joke of fate that Repin and Konrad fell for Guntram. "We are fortune's fools," Oblomov told me once. "You Germans plot the whole day and look, one simple coincidence, and our bosses behave now like two children," I understand him now, Guntram was out on his own only once in six years, in a remote island and he came home with an industrial. I'm sure he was not even looking for him.

Let's hope the lad keeps his part of the deal because November will be very hard for all of us.

We have to stop the upcoming disaster if Konrad continues with his plan regarding Stefania di Barberini. That woman will only mean trouble for all of us.

* * *

Guntram de Lisle's Diary
October 24th

Lintorff returned yesterday from New York, and came directly from the Airport to see the children when he normally would have gone to his beloved bank. Perhaps things are muddier than the newspapers report. He was looking weary, and I could sense that he was feeling impotent to prevent something. I said nothing to him as I was debating with myself to do it or not to do it. It's hard for me to forgive him of all what he has done. He's not a person, he's a monster. But the monster has the power to ruin innocent people lives, and he would do it without blinking.

He came to the nursery at eight, when the children were already dining and preparing for bed. Both were very happy as I had given them some drawings made after the story they were reading in the school, to take to the classroom. When their father entered the nursery, both jumped on top of him and forced him to look at the pictures.

I waited for him in the corridor, still debating with myself if all this was a good idea.

"Could I have a word with you, Sire?" I asked mechanically when he left the room.

"What is de Lisle?"

"Next Tuesday, on the 30th at nine, I have to meet with the children's teacher and the principal. They would like to report on their doings at school, and I wonder if your Excellency would like to assist," I said softly trying not to sound so dry as I normally do.

"I will have to look in my agenda. Send a reminder to Monika."

"Thank you, Sire. The children will appreciate it," I whispered, unable to hold his gaze as he was inspecting me, looking for any signs of deception.

"Is that all?"

"Yes, sir," I gulped.

"Good, I'll be downstairs if you need to tell something else," he said regally, brushing me aside.

"About the exhibition in Berlin...," I started but stopped the minute I felt his eyes again over me.

"Yes, what about it?" he asked impatiently.

"I've decided to refuse Mr. Volcker's offer. We will never agree on the economical conditions, and I really don't need to do it. I will stay with the two *Meister* Ostermann already arranged in Geneva and Bern. I thought you might like to know it, Sire," I whispered. Why was I speaking so softly?

"Thank you for telling me. Good night, Guntram."

"Good night, sir."

* * *

October 26th, 2007. Friday

I was having breakfast with Armin, the chronic student, and trying to get into his thick head some accounting notions. Hopeless case. He'd better ginger up or Michael will eat his guts alive when he realises the boy doesn't understand a simple thing like how to hide your national deficits in a clever way. Since I graduated, Albert von Lintorff made pressure on his cousin so I would "teach his son" something, unless we want that the next Griffin is a "complete illiterate dunce". We are allowed to be together again and in a way it helps me to cope better with this whole situation.

"No Armin, it's not that way. Don't believe everything the teachers say. It's not the total amount what matters, is the projection what is really concerning. The Spanish went from a two percent superavit last year to an estimated six percent deficit. Their unemployment rate is climbing up at a very fast pace, and do you think they will collect more taxes to balance this? About twenty percent of their GDP is based on building houses costing twice than in Germany. Speak with Ferdinand if you don't agree with me," I was saying when Lintorff entered the room for the first time in almost a year.

We both rose from our chairs as he sat at his usual place at the table's head. I resumed my seat, without saying anything while Armin gaped at us, like the village's idiot. I kicked him under the table, and he regained his composure.

"De Lisle is right in what he was telling you. Spain will be a big headache in the coming years, no matter what their leaders say." Lintorff said nonchalantly, finishing our discussion. "Tomorrow, if the weather is fine, I would like to take the children to the zoo. Have them ready at ten," he ordered me.

"Yes, sir," I said. "Should I also come, Sire?"

"As you wish, Guntram," he answered almost kindly. "Hurry up Armin, I don't have the whole day." He shouted coming back to his usual ways.

* * *

October 27th, 2007

Today we went to the Zoo. Out of pity, I agreed to accompany Lintorff because I'm positively sure he can't manage both little monsters, and he will lose one of them in the lions' cage. Probably Klaus, checking if the lion has teeth or not. Karl is cleverer and would use a stick to prod the animal.

He left the security at home, I think, and took the monster Audi Q7 the children normally drive in. He started the engine and children's music gushed in torrents inside the car. I switched the CD off very quickly.

"I see now why Mihailovic wants a raise," he commented as he drove away.

Contrary to my expectations, both children behaved very well and were happy looking at the animals, well, those who are at "their size". The elephant or the Giraffe were too big and they didn't look at them at all. They were most interested in a group of sparrows than in the rhinos.

Around one, they were very hungry and we had to stop to eat something at the restaurant. There Lintorff drew the line, no way he would eat in a cafeteria like a student. After cutting their meat, both boys started to eat and only minded their food.

"Sire, I wanted to apologise for the way I informed you about my graduation. It was very impolite and rude, especially after all the trouble you took to put me in school," I said softly.

"For old time sake, I was expecting a different behaviour from you, de Lisle," he replied in a emotionless voice.

"I understand, Sire. Please accept my apologies, and I would like to give you a copy of my thesis. Dr. Dähler says it's good."

"If he says so, it must be worth reading it. Send it to Monika."

"Yes, sir," I said returning to my dish as both boys were looking at us, both ears up like periscopes. Snooping children!

"Do you have any work offers? Normally, someone with more than five points average and an excellent thesis, gets them."

"I have several. Two for working in London, one in Frankfurt and another here, at Dr. Felder's Hedge Fund," I said slowly. He looked at me expectantly. "I've refused them all as I would have to leave the small ones. The best was Dr. Felder's, but

538

it was a full time position from nine to eight. I will look for something part time, and work on portraits at the moment. I have several pending offers. It should be enough to support me till the next book is finished and published."

"Why did you refuse Volcker's offer?"

"We didn't agree on the money. He wants too much. I still have to share with *Meister* Ostermann, and financially it will not make any sense for me, even if I sell everything. I prefer to wait, become more known and then renegotiate with him or not," I explained. Yes, it's the truth, he wanted thirty-five percent of the price plus whatever he charges the buyer, much less than the forty percent they normally ask me, but he's a rich guy who can live from other things, and better keep the basilisk away from Andreas' business.

"I see," he said studying me more intensively than before. I had to stop Klaus from gurgling with the water, and Karl from stealing fries from his brother's dish. Four minutes unattended and they make a mess.

After lunch we went to the Rainforest dome, the amphibians and to the Otters house. At four the boys were very tired and hungry again (those two can eat a lot). Lintorff decided to take them for tea to Sprungli, near the bank and show them, after they promised to behave, his office.

I was surprised to find people working in the bank, but they were not shocked to see big boss there, with his two children. Almost all of the traders and managers were there. Ferdinand and Michael were in their offices, not happy at all to be interrupted.

"Guntram stay with Klaus and Karl in my office. I need to check on some things. Keep Karl away from my papers," he said as both boys were looking with big eyes at Lintorff's office. I noticed he had a picture of the small ones at his desk with their school uniforms. My painting from Torcello had disappeared, but in its place there was a drawing from Karl and Klaus when they were two. The rest had not changed at all.

Half an hour later he returned while I had both boys sitting on my lap and I was telling them a story to keep them away from their father's desk. He stood at the door frame, looking at me for a long time as I blushed.

"I want to eat!" Karl whined, immediately followed by his brother in his protests.

"Time to take these two gentlemen to Sprüngli. We go now, de Lisle. Get them in their jackets."

As fast as I could I put the children inside of their loden coats and took them downstairs to the car. He was already waiting at the entrance lobby fondling with his blackberry. Those things can be addictive. Karl and Klaus were so excited to have seen their father's office that they couldn't stop to jump around. It took me some time to fix them in their seats.

Fortunately, they behaved well at the café, drinking their chocolates and eating the cake without getting too dirty... well, the normal. Klaus left his chair to sit on my lap and in two minutes later, he was fast asleep on top of me. I finished my cappuccino the best I could, trying not to wake him up as Karl yawned, and fought to keep the eyes open.

Lintorff tried to take Klaus from my arms, but I was afraid he would wake up. Karl fell asleep the minute we reached the highway. I was also tired, but not exhausted like I'm usually after suffering Lintorff around for a whole day Perhaps the guys are right and I should back off a bit before I get a burn out. If Lintorff would do the same, perhaps we could reach a new compromise.

"Would you like to dine with me tonight, Guntram?"

"I don't think this is wise, sir," I refused softly.

"For a minute, I thought you wanted to ease the tension down," he snorted.

"We can't be friends, but at least we could establish some sort of détente," I said. "This silent war is leading us nowhere, sir."

"It's leading you nowhere. I'm perfectly fine with it. I will keep my game till I get real results, not a second rate deal from you. I always play to win. Your position is very weak, as you have realised by now de Lisle."

* * *

October 30th, 2007

Today was the teacher and principal meeting. I drove with the children like always in the car. I was not expecting Lintorff to show and I went with Headmistress to her office. She had a pile of my books over her desk.

"Many of the older student's mothers found out that you take care the Duke's children and wondered if you could sign their copies. There are also some from the school's library. According to the librarian the children love your book. I still don't understand why you don't advertise it more."

"I have never signed a book in my life, Ms. Meeus."

"Well, it's time for you to start. I will speak while you sign them. My secretary put a post it with the dedication on each one of them," she said truly happy.

A soft knock on the door and her secretary entered whispering something in her ear. "Oh yes, show him in," she said, rising from her chair. I did the same, almost knocking the books off.

Lintorff entered the room and shook her hand. "I'm sorry for my delay. The traffic was impossible this morning, Madam."

"Please, my Duke, do not be concerned. Mr de Lisle and I didn't start so far. I was asking him to sign some of his book's copies for the school."

"He should do it as we speak," he said, getting his own fountain pen out from his jacket. I was cornered. I mumbled a thank you, and started to write, feeling like a seven year old making the homework at the teacher's desk.

"We are completely happy to have your sons with us, my Duke. They're so well behaved and obedient. Nothing that can be compared to many of the children here. I admit we were concerned during the first year because of this young man's age, but he leads them with firm hand. It's incredible how well they obey and almost never throw a tantrum."

"They should obey their elders. It's the only way to learn their place in society."

"Not many parents think nowadays like you do, Sire," she sighed. "Both children are very inquisitive and willing to learn. Of course they're mischievous like any other three year old boys, but nothing that can't be controlled. I believe the stable environment Mr. De Lisle has provided for them is a key factor in their education.

Many of the children we have, change their caregivers constantly, and this is very counter-productive. Also that he never gives up to their whims, helps us."

"How are they doing with their subjects?" he said not caring at all at the praises she sung from me.

"Perfectly well, they work, well, sometimes is more difficult for Klaus Maria to focus, but they do it without complaints. All their teachers are very satisfied with their performances. You should receive their grades by beginning of November."

After a few questions more, and I finished signing the books (there were over twenty!), he parted.

Outside, I noticed Milan was gone with the car.

"Drive with me to the airport. We need to speak," he said coldly, pointing toward his limo. I got in the car, but he caught me by the arm, forcing me to sit next to him. The bodyguard closed the door and the driver started the engine. I had a big knot in my throat.

"I must say that I'm very satisfied with the way you have been educating our sons so far. Your dedication towards them is commendable. I agree with every word this woman has spoken."

"Thank you, sir." I said, looking at the car's floor.

"Therefore, I want a clear answer from you. Is there any possibility that you will forgive me, and return to my side? My affection for you has not faltered not even for a single day," he said with the same emotionless voice he used in Torcello the first time he declared his intentions for me.

"None," I answered without blinking. "I only want to ease down the tension among us. Nothing else. All we had is dead."

"Very well, I know what to do now."

* * *

November 12th, 2007

I was surprised when Friederich told me that the Duke wanted to see me in his private studio. After evading me for more than ten days, he wanted to see me? I know he took a flight to Rome and stayed there all the time, only to return today. This was strange and forbade nothing good for me. I ordered my pencils in their wooden box, put on my jacket and tie and went to his quarters. I knocked softly as his door and I entered. He was sitting behind his desk, his eyes oddly red from sleep deprivation.

"Sit down, de Lisle," he barked at me.

I obeyed taking my usual place in front of his desk at his private studio. I think it was more than a year and a half that I was entering in this room.

"I'm engaged to Stefania di Barberini. We will marry next March, here in Zurich. She will move to this house from December onward. I trust you will break the news to the children," he said.

I stared at him in disbelief. He? Married to a woman? I thought he was the last male chauvinist left on this Earth! I continued to gape, like a real idiot.

"You have nothing to say?"

"I'm sorry sir. Congratulations and I wish you all the best in your marriage," I replied quickly, still processing the news. Does this mean am I free to go? "What should I tell the children? I'm afraid they still don't understand the concept of marriage."

"Tell them that a woman will come to live with them and they should be nice to her. I will not tolerate any kind of disrespectful behaviour to the new Duchess," he said firmly.

"Yes, of course, Duke. When will you want my resignation?"

"The only thing you can think about is to resign?" he shouted at me, truly losing his temper and for a minute I was afraid he would jump on me to strangle me like already happened.

"I have nothing else to do in here! My presence is an insult for her! I will give you my resignation and you can put the date over it," I defended myself.

"Stefania will not take care of the children. She is to be my wife, not their mother."

"I see, Sire. If that would be all…"

"After four years of sleeping in my bed the only thing you can say is a few polite formulas? Have you no blood in your veins? You're not even cold, you're dead!" He roared again, surprising me with his outburst.

"No sir, I'm not dead. You are dead to me, since April 2006. I wish you a happy marriage. My resignation will be on your desk tomorrow morning. I'm glad that you finally accepted I'm not your consort any longer."

"You will stay and take care of our sons. I'm marrying Stefania, but she will never be their mother," he said this time with a cold and determined voice.

"The lady will not want me in the house. It's her privilege as the next Duchess to choose her servants." Yes, Lintorff, learn that the minute she's in, your absolute monarch times are over.

"I don't want your resignation, and you will keep your title as Consort. We will announce the marriage next Saturday. Dismissed."

Is there another word stronger than crazy? Insane? Lunatic? Not enough to describe him. I think I remember the expression "mental bankrupt". Yes, that would be very appropriate. He's a nuts case!

He's marrying a woman and he wants me to stay? To take care of "our" children?

What's next? A threesome? No, he would explode out of jealousy… Which one of us would he be jealous? It would be funny to find out.

I want some peace of mind. No, I need some peace of mind.

I went back to my studio to work on the sketches of the big portrait I want to make of the children. Perhaps it would be my farewell present for them.

Chapter 7

November 18th, 2007

I can't sleep or paint tonight. It was too much for my nerves. Perhaps writing helps me to cool down.

Two days ago, the soon to be Duchess of Wittstock arrived to the house accompanied by her future husband and public relations manager (Piero or Pedro della Rosa). It was late in the afternoon when she came, and Friederich made all the servants stand in line to receive her. I had both boys washed and dressed with jackets and ties (Yes, I bribed them with the promise of getting a hot chocolate on Sprüngli next Saturday and to help to frame their drawings for their father's birthday).

When I saw her, I was highly impressed; very tall, slender and with an incredible body. Dark hair and very big green almond shaped eyes. She was wearing a tailored suit with too many jewels for my taste but I'm no fashion expert as she is. Elegant moves, reminding me of a panther. Like the Angelina Jolie, yes, that's right. A true lioness. Lintorff is a motherfucker, but he has great taste in women. Friederich was less than pleased to see her, as I could say from the very thin line his lips made. She didn't pay attention to me or the other servants, focusing entirely on the children, fidgeting a bit.

"Those are your children, Konrad?" She asked him, distractedly, offering her hand to them. Both shook hands with her, and said nothing because the father was looking at them with his "no nonsense" face.

"This is Klaus Maria, the eldest, and the other is Karl Maria," he didn't consider necessary to introduce me. Good.

"They're so cute and polite."

"When they want my dear," he said, sounding like a sick love puppy. I remember that sweet, caressing tone, he uses just before he wants you in his bed. "Take the children and follow us, de Lisle," he ordered much sharply.

They went to the living room, manager included. I took both little devils' hands, praying they would behave for some more time. I could tell that Klaus was already interested in the Ostrich feathers around her neck. Lintorff helped her with her coat, lingering his touch longer than necessary. He used to do the same with me. He was showing all the symptoms of being in love with her.

"Tell me dear, who's he?" she asked, indicating me with a light movement of her head as I was busy holding the boys. No chance in Hell I would let you catch her mink or other animal coat to play Indians with it!

"Come here," he ordered and I approached him, eating my own fury at his rudeness. "This is Guntram de Lisle, my children's tutor. He takes care of them since they were born."

"I'm pleased to meet you, Madam," I said bowing my head.

"Why is he speaking so familiarly to me, darling?" she said to him, not addressing me at all. For a future Duchess, you will need you some etiquette lessons with Friederich and he will have to work very hard with you.

"When his father died, he left Guntram alone, without a family to care for him. I promised Jerôme, a lawyer at our firm in Paris, that I would protect his child. He moved with me from Buenos Aires when he finished his boarding school. He studied here at the University and worked, taking care of the children."

"How generous of you, dear. Not many would take such a responsibility. After all, he's the son of one of your employees," she said disdainfully.

Excellent, now she thinks I'm a bummer squeezing the poor banker's wallet! I wanted to smash something against Lintorff's head, but it wouldn't be nice to do it in front of the boys.

"Guntram also paints in his free time. You should be careful not to fall on his oil tubes," he added one more insult to the tab.

"That's not much, at his age you already had a doctor's degree and were managing your own companies." She said, looking at me very coldly. 'Yes, the ones you inherited from your daddy', I though, venomously. Shit! What's going on? Am I upset for the belittling remarks of a pricey slut? The more she abates me, the sooner Lintorff will let me go. He wouldn't have his wife and former flame under the same roof. He's not that crazy!

"I'm afraid, Stefania, he can't do much more. His health is very frail. Two heart attacks and he has developed a stable angina that prevents him to do much. He wouldn't last a day in the trading section!" He smirked in derogative way.

Fuck you, I'm not a bloody cripple! And I'm still in the fucking room, listening to your belittling and stupid, "cleverly made" (in your opinion), remarks. Lintorff, your education truly leaves a lot to be desired. Nobody told you about doctor-patient secrecy? No, secrecy is only for your beloved customers.

"As Artist, he only published one children's story book. He has been in several exhibitions, collectives of course, and sold a piece or two at our auctions. He makes portraits nowadays." I swear he spat the last word with contempt.

"Yes Madam, I had the honour to paint for the Vatican and for several ladies. I'm told that my best so far is the portrait of Sofia Constantinovna Repin," I replied sweetly, with my best little lamb face. I felt an immense pleasure to see his triumph ally face turned into a defeated one in less than a second. Unfortunately, it only lasted a fleeting second. He threw me a heated glare.

"I don't know her. I will look at your work at some point. I was always interested in Modern Arts," she answered pouting a little bit.

"There my dear, you will have no luck with Guntram. His style is very classical. Good for hanging in Victorian living rooms," he said.

"Indeed Sire, Marie Sophie Olsztyn bought several of my paints." There she opened her eyes. Yes, Tita is real jet set and known for her extensive modern art collection, one of the best in the world. She buys the *haute couture* you present in your TV show for collecting or fun. "I study with one of her advisers."

"De Lisle, the children are tired. Take them back to the nursery," he ordered sharply.

"As you wish, Sire," I said bowing my head and taking them away. I'm surprised they both remained so quiet.

Time to break the news to them. I took them to the nursery as it was very cold to play outside, I got them out of their jackets and ties and dressed them with jerseys. I convinced to sit in their table and we started to put their drawings in the frame they wanted to give their father for his birthday.

"Put a drawing of us also, Guntram." Karl had the idea.

"It's a present from you two. It wouldn't be appropriate."

"Papa says he likes your drawings a lot. You make one of us so he doesn't forget us," Klaus said.

"Your father will never forget you! He loves you two more than anything. He does the impossible to be with you any time he can."

"Please, one with us!" Karl pleaded.

"Doing what? You two fighting or refusing to bathe?" I asked innocently.

"NOOO. Don't be silly Guntram. One nice." Karl huffed, exactly as his father when he's crossed with Michael.

"I see. One with you hiding under the covers because you don't want to go to school?"

"He will not see us under the covers." Klaus whined as his brother sighed frustrated at the world's stupidity.

"All right I'll give you my sketch folder and you choose something from there," I conceded. I went for the thing to my room. Upon my return, both jumped at me and nearly tore the pad from my hands to look. Both sat and started to go through the pages.

"Did you like the nice lady downstairs?"

"She's not nice. She was nasty to you," Klaus stated with the same firmness his father has when he passes judgement on someone.

"She smells too much," Karl said wrinkling his nose in disgust.

"All right, it wasn't the best start for all of us, but you must understand she was very nervous, like your first day in school."

"She wasn't crying like Karl."

"I was not! You're a baby!"

"Cry baby!" Klaus mocked his brother. This was leading us nowhere. Time to remind them who's the responsible adult.

"Enough you two! No one is a baby. This lady is going to stay to live with us. She will marry your father and I would be very happy if you are nice to her. Don't you think she's beautiful? She's on TV." They both looked at me, unimpressed. All right, time to offer something better. Has their bloody father told them never to take a first offer?

"Once you know her, you will see that she's funny and nice to you. I'm sure she will like to play with you two. Your father and her will marry in March, like Michael and Monika did."

"Why don't you marry papa and she goes away? Papa says he loves you, but you're upset with him," Klaus said while he looked at the drawing of a seagull.

Fuck that bloody bastard! I was speechless for a whole minute, not knowing what to do.

"Men can't marry Klaus, besides, we don't like each other so much. Stefania is very beautiful and will be very nice to you," I said, feeling my throat dry and raspy.

"You should be friends, and we wouldn't need her. We want you to take care of us, not her," Karl stated using the same voice his father has when he tells you what he has decided something.

Stubbornness is a Lintorff trait it seems. I gave up. He's the bloody father and the bloody groom. He should negotiate with them, not I.

545

Finally, they decided over one pencil drawing of them, playing in the beach at Sylt, made during the last holidays. After some discussion, they decided to make a collage with it. I should cut the white parts off and they will place their own drawings on the right side of the picture.

On Saturday 17th, Lintorff had his birthday party, after all, he was turning fifty years old. Yes, half a century of making people's lives miserable. Impressive.

It was a black tie party for about a hundred people. I got an invitation from Friederich, but decided to stay away. It was too gruesome for me to be there. Armin tried to convince me to go, but I refused. I would only take the children downstairs for a brief greeting and then to bed. At eight, I had the boys dressed and ready, and I only wore a simple normal daytime jacket with tie.

I took a glimpse at the living room and in the centre was Lintorff with Stefania. She was wearing a deep red dress very nice and elegant. I had to nudge both boys to go to say hello to her. Both decided they would give their present on Sunday as that was their father's real birthday. Lintorff greeted his children with real affection as always, but she was as cold as yesterday. No, she's not the motherly type, but he needs a consort to parade on parties and such things, so in that sense she fulfils her duty well.

I met Ferdinand, Michael, Alexei, Goran and many others like Tita, who came from the other side of the room just to kiss me. After greeting her, I escaped with the children to put them in bed. I didn't want to be in the centre of the mess. I noticed Stefania was already making a face at me when two other bankers, members of the Order, acknowledged me. I realised already that you're the main attraction here.

I'm almost sure, she already knows the whole story about "the poor orphan Lintorff saved from poverty at his own father's pleading", but decided to let it go to avoid a scandal and keep the major prize. I hope she isn't too disappointed when she unties the package and finds the nice banker is a real piece of slime. I'm certain he will make her pay every cent she gets out of him. I would love to know about my uncle's Roger tactics on Lintorff. So far, he was the only one who showed Lintorff his place.

I put both babies, no boys, in bed and they slept quite fast. I went to my studio to paint, but the noise from downstairs was deafening. I could also not sleep so I went to the kitchen.

Jean Jacques was leading and shouting a mini army of chefs, butlers and waiters. To my surprise, (well not much), Alexei was sitting in the old guards hall, strategically placed so he would have a complete view over the battlefield.

"The man is working, Alexei," I said, sitting next to him.

"I like to watch him work," he smiled at me.

"Should you not be there? You are an associate now, not a bodyguard any longer."

"Old habits die hard, Guntram," he shrugged "Besides, it's a boring party. She's a snotty snob, didn't even smile at me. Baba Yaga," he concluded.

"She's a Barberini. If I remember correctly, you wanted to visit their crypt when we were in Rome."

"Foreboding. I wanted to see their bones scattered," he said darkly.

Michael entered in the room, looking very pale. He nearly dropped himself on the empty chair. "Our boss is crazy," he mumbled. "We're so fucked up." Michael has a very poetic way to describe situations. Good you finally realised. "Löwenstein is gone."

"Why?" Alexei asked very alarmed.

"He has just announced that he marries the whore on May 8th. Löwenstein took his wife and left the party. This is a huge mess. If we have a schism, it will be very bad, with Repin inside. He can raise people to his side in no time."

"Shit!" Alexei cursed. "Guntram you have to do something!"

"I'm not going to speak with Repin. I have nothing to do with your wretched Order."

"Not with him! With the Duke boy." Michael shouted very exasperated. "What did we ask you to do in October? Be nice to him!"

"And I was! He didn't want to have anything to do with me! It's either going to bed with him or nothing. He said something like he didn't want a second rate deal with me, because he "plays to win", whatever that means. He will play his game to the end. He's an asshole, if you want to know!"

"Guntram if she becomes Consort, we are in a mess!" Ferdinand shouted joining us with long strides. He took a chair around and sat in front of me.

"Oh yes, a Consort has so many obligations toward the Order. I was always kicked out from your meetings, and I don't know a thing about your dealings! Don't come with that to me!" I retorted him.

"She will drive him crazy. She's good for a fuck and that's all. A consort is someone who's beside you, advises and supports you! Like you did and still do part time, nowadays. It's a very important position for us, regardless of the gender. The Consort is a councillor and educates the next Griffin," Ferdinand shouted back.

"Stefania will not become Consort, or that's what he told me a week ago. She's to be his wife, but not the Griffin's Consort or the mother of his sons."

"Those were his words, my child?" Ferdinand asked me, sounding very concerned.

"Yes! I'm still the fucking Consort. That idiot doesn't understand I want out!" I cried upset to no end. I saw all of them breathing a sigh of relief. "You too? Fuck you all. You're all like your boss!"

The assholes ignored me.

"After all, he said he wants a civil wedding. I would be concerned if he would want to take the sacrament with her. Father Bruno is very upset. She got a big diamond, not the Griffin's Seal," Michael said.

"Good, The Father will tell him off tomorrow. That Jesuit has Friederich's old school." Ferdinand chuckled, truly happy. "I'll speak with Löwenstein tonight," he finished, returning to his normally self composed and aloof attitude.

"Yes, that would be the best. Guntram, don't worry we will have everything under control in no time." Alexei "comforted" me, taking my hand.

"Don't you dare to interfere! I'm praying that she kicks me out after the wedding. I'll finally move to Zurich and come back to take care of the children, if he still wants it. It's my opportunity to leave this madness, once and for all! I want also to start my life anew, like him! This pressure is killing me."

"Boy, you're so wrong if you believe for a minute that this woman could force the Duke to cast you away. He only wants her to make you jealous. It's a childish and stupid move, but, what can I say? In love and war everything goes," Michael said as the others nodded.

It's impossible to argue with them. They all withdraw into themselves and I could shout till Hell freezes over before they would even acknowledge I'm speaking. I said good night and went to bed, letting them plot who knows what.

* * *

Today, Sunday morning, I wasn't expecting anybody at the small dining room. The party finished at about 2 a.m. and it was 8 a.m. The boys could sleep till 9 a.m., when I should get them up and have them ready for Mass at 10 a.m. I served myself a coffee and sat to drink it. I needed one.

"If my uncle catches you with that coffee, you're so dead Guntram." Armin shouted happily, making me jump from my chair and almost spilled the coffee. He served another for himself. "Mass at 10, right?"

"Yes, should you not be in bed?"

"I couldn't sleep, to be honest, so I stayed up. I'll sleep better tonight," he said yawning like a hippo.

"Yes, I see. I'll kick you when we reach the Communion."

"That's my man. You look quite cool for someone who has just been stood up."

"Armin, this is over for almost two years."

"Yes, I'm the most benefited party in here. The witch will have to take my place at dinners," he shrugged. "Will you marry me now, Guntram? We can run away to Spain and do it there. You can fill out the forms," he laughed.

"No way. You're too ugly and have no degree," I mirrored his laugh.

"Armin, you will address my wife with respect in the future. I will not tolerate any disrespectful behaviour towards the Duchess," Lintorff said with his voice loaded with barely contained fury.

"As you wish, Sire." The poor guy answered very sheepishly. I rose from the table, preparing myself to go elsewhere.

"As for you de Lisle, you should not take marriage vows so lightly as it seems to be your habit. It's a sacrament," he said much more furious with me than with Armin.

What? The other started and I'm scolded? I bowed my head, biting my tongue. I will die of a perforated ulcer, I'm sure. "Throw that coffee away and remain seated," I changed my cup for a bloody tea, and resumed my place, next to Armin, sitting at his left. We all continued to take breakfast in silence.

The Barberini woman entered the room and we all stood up. She kissed him on the lips, and I turned my face away, feeling very uncomfortable to be the the third wheel.

"*Tia buenorra,*"[6] whispered Armin to me. Excellent moment to practice your Spanish, Armin. I hope she doesn't understand.

"Good morning Auntie. Can I call you like that? We are going to be family after all." Armin said with a false joviality. Lintorff threw him an incensed glare and she wasn't happy at all, but Armin didn't care much.

---

[6] It's a word play. "Tía" means Aunt, but also chippie, tramp. "Buenorra" it's a very Spanish expression for a woman who looks very hot.

"Of course, Armin," she replied, going to seat at the other head of the table... Well, Lintorff, the lady already considers herself your equal. In no time you'll find new drapes in your bedroom and new furnitures. "Oh, I had the impression this was only for the family, de Lisle."

"Of course, Madam. If you'd excuse me." Who am I to waste a good opportunity? I rose from my chair, to hear Armin saying.

"But Auntie, Guntram is family. My father simply adores him. He's always telling me to be more like him. Besides, he's the *Vicomte* de Marignac. His line is much older than our one, and I believe more than the Barberini's. He's direct descendant from the Merovingian king he was named after. Real *Noblesse d'Epée*. His grandmother is a Guttenberg-Sachsen, you'll find them in the Gotha since the First Edition. The Barberini rose to the Papacy in the XVII century, right?"

All true, but I hate to have my pedigree displayed like that. Lintorff realised how uncomfortable I was and decided to interfere.

"Stefania, Guntram was placed into my care by his father. I hold him in my highest esteem. If he works for me, it is because he insisted on it, not by my choice. You will treat him with the same courtesy you show to any other member of my own family," he said sternly.

She cast a venomous glance at me. Great, now she hates me for being corrected in such a rude way. I sat again, feeling very ashamed.

"The Guttenberg-Sachsen, are they not originally from Bavaria?"

"Yes, they are from there. Good Catholics. They married the Lintorffs on several occasions. You are right Armin, he's family after all."

"If you would excuse me, Duke, I must get your sons ready for the Mass," I said hurriedly, wanting to escape. He only nodded his permission.

After the Mass, Father Bruno decided to speak with Lintorff in private at the library. I think the priest will not buy his excuse that he doesn't marry by the Church because she's divorced (civil) nor a practising Catholic. Klaus and Karl were disappointed because they wanted to give their present to their father.

Friederich told me I was supposed to sit with the children at the table, and I felt like dying. Both children ran to their father when he left the library with the priest in tow, shouting "Papa". He picked them up and kissed them, one in each arm, and both boys hugged him, saying "happy birthday," I withdraw to the living room to leave him some privacy.

"Guntram has your present!" I heard Klaus telling excitedly. Yes, trust those two to keep a secret. "He helped us!"

"But he's afraid you don't like it!" Karl added.

"I can't say a thing till I see it. But I'm sure I'll like it, if you all together did it."

In the living room, Stefania, her manager and Armin (delighted to piss her off some more), were already sitting. I should speak with the lad. He shouldn't cross his uncle so much. It could be very bad for him. I entered and stayed in one corner. It's a miracle that said uncle "lifted" the non communication status between Armin and I two months ago.

Lintorff and the children came in and both of them ran to me to get the present. And they ran backwards to him. He opened it and remained speechless for a minute, looking at it. "It's very beautiful, thank you, Karl, Klaus. Look Stefania. Is it not a wonderful drawing?"

She came to us, walking like a cat, and looked at the frame. "Yes, your children paint very well for their age. Is that de Lisle's work?"

"Certainly, his technique is very good."

"I'm almost tempted to ask him to paint my portrait."

"Thank you, de Lisle," he said to me, in a somewhat cold voice. I bowed my head. "Darling, that can be difficult to achieve. Artists are very temperamental. He paints whatever he wants. No discipline at all. If I see correctly, he has still pending three portraits from the Ribbentrop family. You can ask, but he will start and leave it in the middle if he doesn't like it," he explained her, taking her by the arm and kissing her very softly on the cheek.

She giggled. "Would you paint me Mr. de Lisle?"

"Madame must have hundreds of portraits made by much more recognized artists than I." Fuck me, if I want to spend valuable oils, charcoal, canvas and pencils on her! I'm not a monkey! Don't models love photo shootings? "It would be very boring for you. You will have to remain still for a very long time."

The witch pouted at Lintorff. Don't you dare to get him in the middle, whore! Fight your own battles!

"It would be so nice to have a portrait of me, for the gallery of your ancestors, darling."

I can still get out of this mess. "Madam, the portrait of Elisabeth von Lintorff was painted by Rubens, the one from Christina Maria was made by Rembrandt. As you can see, you must look for a much more consecrated artist than myself. A photo from Annie Leibowitz, perhaps? Maybe Lucian Freud, he's at their level or Jamie Wyeth," I suggested.

"Botero is an option too. His prices sky-rocketed over the last years." Armin pointed out, feigning a pensive air. Boy, you have a death wish or you're very certain that
your Lintorff name will protect you from Konrad. She was already looking at him with a killer gaze and the bastard was no better. I have to speak with him later because a former top model can't be happy to be compared with one of Botero's plump girls.

"Yes, dear, my art collection is very good, but, don't you think we should give an opportunity to the young artists? De Lisle should try his luck and then we will hire a real professional," Lintorff said blocking my escape. Fuck him!

Had his two children not being present in the room, I would have told him my opinion of his superior airs.

"Guntram only paints nice people. He told us," Karl affirmed with that determined voice of his. Trust saints and children to tell the truth. My anger vanished in a second, and I had a hard time trying to control my laughter. Armin was not so successful.

"He only paints us. We are cute," Klaus said very proud, and unwillingly, saved the situation.

She was not so happy as she was forced to laugh in order to save her face. I better rescue those two before she sends them to bed without dinner.

"If Madam is willing to risk it, I will paint her portrait but I can't promise anything."

* * *

November 25th, 2007

Miss Barberini will move to the house tomorrow. She got the former Duchess quarters in the the opposite area of the castle to where the nursery is, on the second floor. They're very nice and were refurnished elegantly. I think, she got some paintings from the vault, like a Monet and a Pisarro. She also has an office as she will continue with her fashion TV program, flying to Rome once per week to record the episodes.

Armin was driving me crazy after the weekend she spent with us. Every morning, at the breakfast table, he would plead that I should "fix it" with his uncle.

"Guntram, you have to stop this nonsense. He's doing it to make you jealous! She's a gold digger!"

"Her father has a lot of money. She makes a lot in the TV and before also, when she was a model. She's not exactly poor."

"She's poor if you compare her accounts with my uncle's. She will take it all! Think on the children's fortune if she's married and something happens to my uncle! She will get all the money for herself, nothing for them! She's like the Beckham's wife!"

"Your uncle is old enough to know what to do," I replied dryly and frankly pissed off.

"*No.* My uncle is a complete idiot when it comes to you! He wants to drive you jealous so you get her out!" He half shouted sounding very frustrated.

"Credit your uncle with some more maturity. He's not a teenager like you."

"Shit, Guntram. If she comes in, I'll move out the next day. Coping with his demands in the bank is one thing, but coping with his bad mood is another. Hear my words, she will drive him crazy! She's good for fuck, not for marriage"

"In case you didn't realise, the last two years we weren't exactly living in a lover's paradise. I'm glad he starts to rebuild his life. Of course, they both should make some adjustments in their characters to make their relationship work."

Shit! Did I repeat his exact words? The ones I got when I moved in with him, back in 2002? I truly hate these flashbacks I'm having all the time, especially when I see him around her, playing the sick love puppy.

"Guntram you're a peaceful guy, a bit Zen or something like that. When you're around, he calms down, that was my father told me, and that makes a huge difference for all of us. He shouts less, doesn't fire people, does not retaliate at the smallest stupid thing. With her around, we all will get the old Konrad von Lintorff back, the one who plots the whole day, loves to shake the market only to destroy some enemies—my father still shudders at the memory of the Mexican crisis—the one who makes his employees life horrible, the cold money making machine we all know, but don't like at all. When you two were an item, he was... an endurable person. Almost nice."

Yeah, tell it to Repin and his friends. I thought, but said nothing. "Armin, it's over and I'm not jealous of her. In fact, I'm praying for their wedding. I'm concerned that she screws it up if she shows the whip too much before the marriage."

* * *

December 3rd, 2007

The new/future Duchess is here... and everybody, but me are pissed off with her. For instance, her wardrobe... 1,200 pieces, occupies all the closets in that wing of the house and she installed racks in several rooms. How can a woman have so many dresses, bags and shoes? Does she have the time to wear them all? I understand many are presents from designers, but that's a lot in my opinion. Versace, D&G, Jean Paul Gaultier, Galliano, Valentino, Balenciaga and many others also moved in with us. We're betting with Armin who gets the closest estimation of how much money she has invested. Michael organises it, but that's unfair because Monika could help him to guess. Better Lintorff works harder because Armin was not so wrong when he said she was like Victoria Beckham.

She also has a stylist and a personal shopper. Yes, I found out that there are people who spend your money for you!

However, I don't think Lintorff will be thrilled, not for money involved because he alone in Christies' can spend much more, but because she hasn't learned his golden rule "the smaller the tag, the bigger the price," he has his three tailors who come to visit him and that's all. That old Venetian man and two from England. I'm tempted to start another bet with the guys... How long till he gets a golden Rolex with diamonds as a present? Better not, Ferdinand and Michael don't like her, and they might well tell their wives to make a suggestion just to piss him off.

Friederich is still recovering from the disgust of losing his rule over the house (and seeing those racks with hanging clothes, "this is not a shop"). She brought two maids along with her and decided that the house was way too outdated, and needed a woman's touch. The china and the linen were replaced with something from Versace and Rosenthal for daily use. The poor man still has nightmares with the golden lions heads on the dishes. Lintorff said nothing, but knowing him, eating over a Medusa must not be exactly thrilling for him.

She wanted to change several of his paintings here for others he has in New York, but there he drew the line. His ancestors remain where they are and the others were bought by his ancestors.

Klaus threw up over her because of her perfume. I'm not sure about his sudden sickness, but I said nothing. She shouted at me for bringing the children to her when she was getting ready for a party and that he ruined "a Halston". Should I write an apology letter to that guy?

Two days ago, there was something like an invasion from the "Sex and the City" girls in the form of Carrie and Samantha, but not the nice good looking brunette, I don't remember her name. Her five girlfriends came for an inspection visit. The poor children were squeezed and kissed, and for a minute, I was afraid, Klaus would repeat his previous actions, this time on a bigger scale. The women stayed for tea, and I took the children away, trying to save them. She informed the others I was the tutor and some sort of an artist, who would paint her portrait... and the witches thought it was a good idea. They inspected the house making many suggestions (Lintorff would have had a heart attack if he would have heard their plans for his very classical (dull) dining room).

It seems his enlightened monarchy days in this house are over. Friederich must have told him the women were here, because he took a plane to Frankfurt that same night, never showing up.

Did Sartre not say something like *"L'enfer c'est les autres"*?

Chapter 8

December 17th, 2007

I was informed, again, to get a life for the holidays. The future Duchess decided to play the mother and take the children to… Eurodisney. I nearly chortled when Friederich informed me of the arrangements. I know for certain Lintorff hates Mickey Mouse for some dark reason. He never lets me buy anything from Disney for the babies… all good German wooden toys. Instead of the Mickey mouse, they had the *Urmel*, a German dino puppet and Jim, the train driver. They can watch the *Maus* show on Kika (Kinder Kanal), on weekends, but Donald is strictly forbidden. They don't watch TV, only DVD's with the Lintorff's stamp of approval. Klaus likes a lot the *Maus* because it shows how things are made. If I ever see again the broom maker chapter, I'll cry. The ones with the air plane or the car building were played many, many times. Their dream is to meet that mouse, elephant and duck. Pity they're cartoons.

Friederich told me, he's still upset at the idea (he has to go too), that his Excellency tried to switch it to the Augsburger Puppenkiste Theatre (the *Urmel* and many others they want to meet live there), but Ms. Barberini insisted, telling him he should update himself; that he was still in the sixties, perhaps the seventies, and there were hundreds of new things, highly educational made by professionals, he should look at. The Duke, according to her, needed a full update in the social world because he had only lived for his banks so far.

I had to suppress a laugh at Friederich's aggravated voice. After all, he had educated the Duke with such things, and "he has not done it so bad in life." Those were "American things" not German, and certainly not from "our tradition". Well that explains, why he stopped stomping every night in my hallway, before going to visit her for a whole week, after checking on the children.

However, I had to get a life for myself. Time to check with Goran "what am I allowed to do?"

* * *

December 18th, 2007

According to Goran, he would let me go anywhere in the world. Unfortunately, he has direct orders from the Duke that I should not be left alone. Honestly, Goran doesn't want to repeat the London story with Repin's wife, so I should stay in Zurich. Although he and Alexei are Orthodox, I can stay with them for Christmas and New Year. Jean Jacques offered to cook.

Not my idea of a holiday, but is better than staying in this mausoleum. I agreed mostly because the guys are good friends, and I had a lot of work for the new book, and there many ideas coming I don't know from where. I have almost no time to draw the sketches. Who knows when I will be able to paint them all.

I have to finish the portrait of the future Duchess. I already started four times because either I ruin it or I don't like it. It's her fault! She gave me so many photos of her that I'm completely lost. Also having her around, criticizing every line is nerve breaking. I can't work under such conditions! I'll move the blasted thing to Ostermann's studio and paint it there. If they like it, good, and if not, fuck you all. It's not like she's going to pay for it.

The children will go away tomorrow but they're not happy at all, I'm not coming. Lisette is also pissed off. She will have to fight with them full time. I bet that Stefania will not ruin her Versace by trying to bathe those two or risk her Galliano dinning with them.

* * *

December 19th, 2007

I "moved in" with Goran. Wartime makes strange allies. He has a big flat in front of the lake with a very nice view over the lake from his 4th floor; modern and tastefully decorated. I was sent to the guest room. He has also a cleaning lady who also cooks. I was surprised that he had so many books over warfare, politics and classical music. Guess my original idea about him was very wrong.

"Thank you having me over, Goran."

"It's always better than chasing you all over Europe," he replied and cracked a smile, but not too scary.

"I'll be most of the time at *Meister* Ostermann's studio, working. I will not disturb you much."

"You don't disturb me. Alexei is another matter. He speaks too much. You remind me a lot of my brother. He was also an artist, a very good pianist, but he passed away during the war."

"I'm sorry. I didn't know it," I whispered.

"Don't be. It wasn't your fault. I settled the score with the ones who did it in 93. He was nineteen when he died," I looked at him, but didn't dare to ask what had happened.

"I was made Captain in the Serbian Army only because I had more military training than the others and was willing to be in Krajina," he started to tell me as he indicated me a chair to sit. "We expelled the Muslims from our land with relative ease at the beginning. One guerilla group decided to take revenge upon me as I was commanding several raids against the Muslim population. They took my brother and tortured him to death. They forced him to play the piano as they were breaking his fingers. Finally, they threw his body in the forest, not even giving him the coup de grace. He died there, alone, bleeding."

"Did you...?" I just couldn't formulate the question too shocked and horrified.

"Yes, the fourteen who were in that patrol; took me three months to eliminate them all, exactly as they did to my brother. I ran out of men before I ran out of anger. My superiors decided to put me to lead some guerilla groups as I was so good for infiltration. My methods were too much for the regular Army."

"This is how I met Michael, in 1994. I was already working for the Duke, like many of my family did in the past, but I took a leave to defend my soil. Michael was commanding a unit from the German Navy, trying to stop us from smuggling weapons. He was very good and gave me a lot of trouble. Finally, he caught me, and I even had to spend one night in a NATO prison, but his superiors let me go in the morning. He was so cross and I was very impressed. I offered him a job with the Duke. It was hard at the beginning, because he and Ferdinand had a very bad start. It's difficult to follow him most of the time, but he's very good strategist. I think Ferdinand was cross that he was learning everything in less than a year and was made associate in three. Must be his astrophysics background what makes him so good at math and understanding humans."

"His sense of humour doesn't help him much. It makes you want to punch him," I whispered trying to recover some of my spirit. Did he just tell me he killed fourteen people?

"Don't listen to him. He does it to piss off Ferdinand. Do you understand now why I always tell you to leave the dead ones in the past? My revenge didn't bring my brother back and I'm who I am now. I don't regret what I did, but I would not do it again."

* * *

December 20th, 2007

I spent the day working at Ostermann's studio on the Duchess' portrait… well not the one I'm intending to give her. It's just I have so much anger and annoyance building up inside of me at being nearly forced to paint it, that I'm going to explode or destroy it with a knife. I didn't make a sketch, directly on the canvas with the oil. I inspired myself on the Lady with Ermine from Leonardo, but as there was no Ermine available for posing, I took an alley cat (nothing wrong, Audrey Hepburn had one in Breakfast at Tiffany's) and the dress is one with feathers she has from a noble designer, but if you ask me, it's a piece of shit. For jewellery I was a bit lost as I have no idea and there I knew it. "The heart of the Ocean" from Titanic.

* * *

December 23rd, 2007

I was giving the final touches to her portrait. I admit it looks a little shocking at first look. Flashy, but not trashy. However, it's not for sale. I feel so well after working on the thing nonstop. Who needs a shrink when you can paint? Ostermann will kill me for wasting my time in such a pathetic way, but now I can do her Scarlett O'Hara Portrait, copying Winterhalter style. The cream dress she chose looks very from that time. It's a Dior, I was informed, exclusively made for her and cost as much as a house. I still don't know how many slaves were needed to make the embroideries over the shoulder. That poor German must have had a horrible life as fashion painter for all the aristocracy, coping with them on a daily basis. Look at me. One simple portrait, and I can't bring myself to do it.

According to the bastard, I'm a painter "good for Victorians living rooms", so he will get something in that line.

I was giving some light touches over the *pailletes* when I heard a laugh behind my back.

"What has that woman done to you, Guntram?" It was Andreas Volcker with Ostermann, inspecting very interested the portrait.

"It's the future Duchess of Wittstock," I said formally. "Hello Andreas."

"Hello again. I said it in the morning, but you were painting, and didn't notice me," he smiled. "Is it for sale? It's very good."

"It's horrible. Kitsch. Let's say, it's only some therapeutic painting before I do the right thing," I replied showing him the picture of what I have to copy, with a miserable expression in my face.

"How many times should I tell you that you don't have to make things beautiful and elegant? Paint whatever you like. Art answers to nobody. It's one of your best."

"It will go to the trash, sir. How are you Andreas? It's a surprise to see you here."

"I had some business with the UBS and I took some time to arrange with Ostermann your next exhibition. We finally agreed on the price; only thirty percent of your sales—twenty days in April. Before you say anything, I'm only covering my costs."

"I don't know. I'm not ready or have enough material for an exhibition so soon."

"Nonsense. Ostermann showed me your portfolio and several of the pieces he has here. All of them are very good. Tita Olsztyn offered to lend me some of her pictures and I accepted. After all, it was her and my mother's idea to make the exhibition. Both of them are very close friends. I want to return to my house tonight. My mother will not let me in if I don't get you."

"Madame Olsztyn had enough of you "loafing and hiding behind your shyness." She wants to make "some profit out of her investments," Ostermann commented. "So, we pack your stuff around mid-March. Mr. Volcker is particulary interested in your latest series. The one with poor people; they're good."

"It's a pity most of your work was privately sold. Under normal conditions, it would have got better prices. But 'sales time' is over. If you're going to throw that portrait away, give it to me and I'll charge you only twenty percent of the sales."

"No, if the Duke sees it, he will kill me. Really."

"All right. Let's sign the papers and then, I'll take you for lunch," Andreas said.

I was really in a dead end. I truly wanted to make an exhibition, particulary with that series that I knew nobody would want to buy it (too social). On the other hand, I didn't want to get him into trouble with Lintorff. OK, he's going to get married, but he *hasn't given me up* so far. There's always the slight (not so slight), chance he wants vendetta because another alpha male was making pee pee on his territory.

"I'll sign after we have lunch, Andreas. There are a few things I want you to know about me," I said firmly.

We went to a small restaurant nearby. Normal place. I noticed Ratko sitting at one of the tables. We ordered the food and started to eat.

"Well Guntram, what is that thing so horrible you have to tell me? Do you have an army of Chinese painting your pieces hidden somewhere?"

I laughed. "Nothing so clever. I'm guilty for everything you see. It's about my boss, my former lover for four years, the one I work for taking care of his children. You met him at the polo club."

"Yes, Lintorff. I remember him very well."

"He's a powerful banker and still thinks I belong to him. He's jealous beyond any limits. You see that guy over there?"

"Yes, your bodyguard. You have several, but if you take care of his children, it's normal."

"That's Ratko. He takes care of me since 2004. He will inform him of our lunch or any other meeting we have. Lintorff has already been looking into your business to see if there's something he can use against you. He believes we have something going on, and the minute he finds out about the exhibition, he will go for your throat. He's merciless," I said.

"I see. Was he not going to get married?"

"Yes, to the one in the picture. She's much nicer in person."

"Yes, I can see your own jealousy there. Don't worry, I'm perfectly aware there would be nothing between us more than a professional relationship, perhaps friendship. I know it, after seeing that portrait. You're still in love with him."

"No, it's over since a long time!" I protested strongly.

"Really? Don't worry, no banker will tell me how to run my business. If he wants to fight, we will. He must also have some skeletons in his closet," he said, letting a dry laugh out. "Thanks for the warning. Will you sign now?" He said handing me the papers.

"I hope you know whom you're pissing off," I said, signing them with a sigh.

"Likewise."

Chapter 9

March 10th, 2007

I'm so glad they're gone to their honeymoon. Really. Not far away, as Lintorff has many problems in the moment, and zu Löwenstein had his third heart attack and he's not recovering well from it. The Duchess wanted to go to the Maldives (I had to look in Google to know where they are. Very expensive and exclusive. Really breathtaking place). However, beginning of March, the Duke cancelled everything as zu Löwenstein was so sick. I remember very well that particular conversation during diner. Armin was clever enough as to move out, right after Christmas, and I had to take his place when the "sweethearts" were alone, per Lintorff's direct orders and Friederich's pleading. I truly hate to be a third wheel. This new "job" as "cushion" is going to provoke me an ulcer.

However, Lintorff came back from wherever he was, after disappearing without further notice, like he normally does. The Duchess was not upset at all, as she used the three days he was away to go to Geneva and Paris for shopping. I was left in the house, taking care of the children and painting her bloody portrait. It will be ready for the fucking wedding. It's not exactly bad, but it's horrible. I mean. You can see her, but it looks like a bad copy in the Winterhalter style. The face is well drawn, the colours correct and well balanced, the bloody silk really shows as such, as well as the *pailletes* on her shoulder but it's... lifeless.

Exactly as if you paint a Barbie doll. If I would have some artistic courage, I would burn it down, but I want to get rid of the commission, no matter what. This abomination certainly can't be hung next to Rembrandt or Rubens! The Ironing Room would be more appropriate, but I'm afraid Friederich and the others servants will use it as a darts target. Who knows? Perhaps Constantin will burn it down with one of his cigarettes when he comes for his Good Friday meeting.

Enough complaining about my lack of professionalism. It's done and it's hopeless. I should better return to the ones I'm working for Andreas' exhibition.

Coming back to the story. March 1st, small dinning room, nine thirty, Lintorff on the head of the table, she at his right (he doesn't let her have the other head, only after the wedding, and in formal occasions), and I at his left, facing the Duchess. She was ignoring me as usual. No complaints at all from me.

"Konrad, dear, will you be here tomorrow? The people from the pergola will come at ten."

"Which pergola?" He asked, visibly upset at being interrupted in his thinking. Woman, you have so much to learn. If he's in a communicative mood, he will speak... if not, don't rub him in the wrong direction.

"For the wedding in the garden, Konrad," she said sweetly, opening her big green eyes.

"In the garden? Stefania we are in March! It can rain or snow. We agreed to make it inside the house. It's just the judge and some close friends, no more than eighty people."

"Yes dear, but the garden is more romantic and it will look better in the photos."

"They're only for us. Nobody else will see them and you will catch a cold with that dress you want to wear."

"No, the people from *Jet Set Today* will make some pictures of our wedding, and honestly, your stances are way too outdated to be shown."

He put his napkin over the table, his eyes stormier than ever. He took several calming breaths before he spoke. "Not all the people who own a Jet want to be in such a magazine. That's for comedians. Cancel it. The only photos I allow are those from our photographer. I will not play the monkey for the masses entertainment." Really, Lintorff, comedians can be buried nowadays in holy ground!

"I'm a well known celebrity. It's more that normal than my wedding is on a magazine. The Editor was more than delighted to have the exclusive rights and paid it accordingly."

"Did you sell our wedding's photos to a comedians' magazine?" He asked in total disbelief. Welcome to the XXI century, Lintorff. Women do whatever they please and we put our best faces. Losing gracefully is a new concept that you will have to learn to survive in your marriage.

"It's *Jet Set Today*, if you're not there, you're nobody!"

"I don't need two snobs to tell me who I am, and much less to hear it from middle age frustrated housewives, sitting in a hairdresser's shop," he answered, looking at her with murderous intent. For a minute, I was very afraid he would send her away and be done.

But that woman is more clever than I credited her for. She knows very well how much she can pull the leash. To my utter relief, she pouted and looked completely sad, like a small lamb with a pink ribbon.

"I'm terribly sorry Konrad, I thought you would love to be there. Your mother and half sisters appear now and them. They always cover the Vienna Opera House Ball and many of your friends are in their pages. Tita is mentioned almost every month. If you don't like it, I will cancel the reportage tomorrow." Now, she battered her long eyelashes. Woman, that's useless, learn it by now.

"Whatever that woman does, it's not my problem. She has never mentioned the Lintorff name on it and that should give you an idea. I will not be on any magazine, Stefania."

"I understand and respect your decision, dear, but please try to see my position. In July, I will finish my television contract and my fans will be very disappointed. I just wanted to let them know how happy I will be with a wonderful man like you."

Can I puke? Unlikely. Very unbecoming. I focused my gaze on the Medusa dish as she came to him and started to kiss him passionately. Lintorff returned her kisses with the same ardour. Friederich made a face of disgust at her "very inappropriate" behaviour... there are private rooms for that!

"All right Stefania, as it is the last time you do it, you can send some of our pictures and a press release made by our press office. I don't want reporters around me. Privacy and discretion are very important to me," he sighed. Woman, you have my undying respect for your achievement. "How are you doing with the other wedding preparations?" he asked with his false light tone.

No, you were wrong Guntram, he has not softened a bit, only retraced two steps to kick you better. She should have learned by now that when he shows so much sugar during an interrogation, you're in deep waters.

"It's a lot of work, but we will manage. Your children have already their suits, the food is ordered, the musicians hired, the judge confirmed with Monika," she told us, sweet as a bird.

"Why have you ordered food? Jean Jacques takes care of such things. You only have to tell him how many people are coming."

"I hired a catering service," she said, sounding so innocent. I nearly dropped the fork. Uh, uh. Lintorff would marry that man in order to prevent him from going away. I was disposable, he was not. Again I feared for the wedding. These two are making me live on a permanent roller-coaster, fighting and fixing it in her bedroom... if they reach it.

"What did you do? The cook will be furious! It's an insult to the man. He won two Michelin stars, much more than any catering service! He's an artist, you have to let him work free," he almost exploded.

"He's too old fashioned. We need something modern and fresh. Besides, he has so much work with the Good Friday and Easter Sunday planning. Do you know, he has already started with this?"

"I like his cooking very much. Don't upset him because he will go away, and I don't think we could replace him easily." Lintorff grunted, partly appeased.

"I have confirmed also the villa booking at the Rangali Island. Should I tell your secretary to organize the flight with your plane or do you want to take a commercial flight?"

"I'm afraid we have to cancel it. I can't go away for fifteen days at the moment. The *Fürst* zu Löwenstein is very sick and he's like a father to me. Perhaps, later we can all make a holiday there. My children like the seaside a lot," he said feigning, not so successfully, something akin to sorrow.

Yes, he has not a single merciful bone in his body. Time to make her pay for the wedding reportage, the new china, insulting the whole staff and having her girlfriends around. So far, she lost her job—since July onward, her independent woman days are numbered—her magazine wedding (no Church and three hundred guests as she wanted), bye bye romantic honeymoon (Klaus and Karl tagging along? They will put their boats in her rose filled bathtub and their father will buy them a copy of the Bismarck). Should we bet with the guys how long till she gets a monthly allowance and how much it would be?

"Dear, we planned it since January!" she whined.

"I'm sorry, but it's impossible at the moment," he said curtly, not leaving room for an argument.

"It's our honeymoon. I wanted it to be romantic and relaxing for you."

"Do you really want to spend your honeymoon in a wooden hut with a palm roof, surrounded by natives? It sounds more like Adventure Land to me. We'll go there for the holidays, with the boys. They can play pirates there."

"What are we going to do?" she whined louder.

"If you like so much the seaside we can go to Sylt. No, it's too cold at the moment. A chimney fire can be very romantic, but it's rainy. I have a villa near Cannes, sunny and not too hot at the moment. Guntram was there, he can tell you how nice it was."

"It's a magnificent property, madam, placed over a cliff." That was my contribution, feeling bad at the memory of our time there, even if when we were at odds. We went also for a weekend with the children and it was truly romantic. Honestly, that was undeserved and low Lintorff, even for you. I'm no part of your "educating the future Duchess" crusade!

"Konrad, I wanted to go to a beautiful place that reflected our love. The endless sea, shores and sky are exactly like what we feel for each other. A pure love," she said making her best big "kitten" eyes. No, puking is out of the question. Friederich also looked sickened by the mushy moment.

"One is loved because one is loved. No reason is needed for loving," It was written in the book you gave me, darling, *The Alchemist* by Paulo Coelho. We don't need a physical place to enjoy it. We can be happy anywhere we go. You will like Nice," he finished the argument.

It's official woman, you lost. You might get the title, and I do hope you have a generous prenuptial agreement because he will not give you a single cent on top of what is signed. He can be very cruel and will ridicule you till your last day. Ferdinand told me that he and Lintorff were almost bending with laughter when they read that book during a flight. Lintorff has recommended it to several of his bankers friends as the funniest thing he has read in years.

The children were the luckiest of all of us. They could attend school in the morning and return for tea time. I tried to escape several times, but she caught me. After all, I'm in "working hours". Fuck woman, I'm the tutor not your office boy! She complained to Lintorff's about not having enough support, and he ordered me to help the Duchess out of chivalry. Yeah, right. Lintorff was helping sooo much. On the 2nd, he took a plane to New York and didn't come back till the 5th, at night. I had to run everywhere with the car, looking for things she needed or visiting people on her behalf. I had to check the flowers, the stupid caterers (and argue over the champagne), without Jean Jacques help at all, and hundred of small things, nerve breaking all of them. Didn't she have a manager, a personal shopper and an assistant for such things?

She tried to train the children to carry the rings to the judge, something very simple. No chance. Klaus threw the box every time he got it and Karl just lost one of the rings. Unsuitable, was the verdict. Stefania decided that even if they looked cute, it would be better if they remained seated in a corner. I should be ultimately responsible for keeping them quiet. Honestly, I don't understand what was wrong with them as they never do such things and they behave very well in Mass. Perhaps, they're nervous to be in the spotlight.

On the night of the 6th, I presented the bloody picture to her. She seemed to be happy that I was "accurately painting the dress and her features". Well, top models are supposed to have good features. Lintorff said nothing, but critically looked at the portrait for a long time.

"After the wedding we will look for an appropriate place for it," he only said.

Nobody ever spoke a word about paying the artist, not that I would have accepted the money, but showing some appreciation is nice and won't kill you.

The night before the wedding, I was mental and physically dead. *Kaput.* I even bribed the boys with convincing Jean Jacques to make a small cake for them— he's very sore about the catering issue. Alexei had to use all his diplomacy to convince him not to resign, so they would go to bed earlier. I excused myself from dinner feigning a migraine (can't use too much that excuse, it'll wear out eventually), and went straight to my own bed, forgoing dinner and falling immediately asleep.

A sudden noise in my bedroom woke me up and I sat up in the bed, alarmed.

"You used to sleep so soundly before. It was almost impossible to wake you up, Guntram," Lintorff said with a kind and oddly warm voice. The bloody bastard was sitting on the couch I have by the window, his predator eyes fixed on me.

"Leave this room now, sir!" I said firmly, not shouting because I didn't want to wake up the children. "You have no right to be here."

"I just wanted to look at you. When you sleep, you're again the sweet and innocent boy who used to love me, not the cold, heartless man you play now."

"Get out, now. Go to your wife."

"Just one word from you Guntram, and I will stop all this. Klaus and Karl don't like her at all."

"Get out. You should be ashamed to be here. You're going to get married tomorrow, and you come to your former whore's bed?"

"You were never my whore! I loved you and treated you with the utmost respect!" he half shouted.

"You respect nothing, sir. You are unable to love. Those of us who were in your bed, are only well or better paid whores for you. Now, get out before you wake up your sons," I said, lacing my voice with all the coldness and contempt I could.

"You can lie to yourself all you want. If this helps you to continue with this foolish game you started against me, so be it. Remember, I always play to the end and I will get what I want, no matter the consequences and costs. You had your chance, Guntram. My patience with you is over. I had enough of you toying with me. My retribution can be ten times worse than yours."

"I'm also sick of you, Sire," I said in a strange mix of fury and sarcasm for the part of his Title.

"You can consider yourself warned," he said in a very cold voice, rising from the couch and leaving the room.

I couldn't sleep again. The next morning, I was tired, pale, haggard, looking very miserable in what was supposed to be my "D" Day. The Devil fuck that bastard! With a lot of work, I got both rascals ready at 11:30. Lissete stopped after the second try and she went away. I had to shout with them and give the "how to be a young gentleman" speech, perhaps a bit too harsh, but it worked because I've had not a single problem with them since that morning (four days so far). I wore the same suit I used for Michael's wedding, after a big fight with Friederich.

As the motherfucker predicted, it was raining. I decided to keep the children upstairs as long as possible and only put them downstairs for the ceremony. Anyway, Stefania was in a sour mood the whole morning and it would be better to avoid her just in case the twins decided to ruin her dress or steal one feather from her coiffure.

"Guntram, people are coming!" Karl pointed to me at around 12:00. The wedding was at 1:00.

"We're dressed. I want to go down! There's cake!" Klaus pleaded.

"All the Duchess' girlfriends are here. Do you want to be squeezed to death and get lipstick all over your faces? If we go much later, there's a chance to avoid the kissing and drooling. Why don't we make another house with the Legos?" I said. It worked because both looked at me with deep disgust, clearly shown in their faces. It's very hard to be as cute as those two are. Without saying a word, they both started to unpack the blocks from its box. It was very hard to keep my serious face.

Ten minutes later, Lintorff entered in the room already dressed. He went directly to the boys and crouched next to them, kissing them very affectionately. Maybe, I was unfair to him, he really loves his children. The rest of the world, is another story.

"I have to go now as I have to see to the guests. You two be nice and stay near de Lisle. Don't eat too much at the banquet. I don't want you to be sick tomorrow," he said and hugged them. "Take them downstairs at quarter to one," he ordered me, not even looking in my direction.

"As you wish, Sire. I will bring them back to the nursery to change them and I will take them to the movies later. I have already spoken with Mr. Pavicevic. Mihailovic will come with us."

There, he really looked at me. "There's no need to change the children for the banquet. If they get the clothes dirty, so be it," I could tell he was pissed off.

"No child has been invited to the banquet and none of the guests brought their own. The future Duchess specifically told me to take them away for the afternoon. They will eat here and have a special cake from Jean Jacques." (Yes, those two had the ears up like periscopes, better we remind them of the prize so they behave. Besides, it took me a lot of work to convince them that the banquet was a very boring thing).

"I see," he said with barely contained fury, and I realised she had informed him nothing about that. Shit! I screwed it up. Big time! There was a long pause, very long till he finally spoke again. "See that the children are happy and that they don't get wet. I don't want my sons thrown out to the streets in the middle of the rain."

"I'll be very careful, Sire." I replied very softly, hoping he would not get too mad at her.

I took the children downstairs at quarter to one, and I tried futilely to evade most of the guys, starting by Ferdinand, Michael, Goran and finally Alexei, with Jean Jacques in tow (he was invited by Lintorff's decision, to Stefania's annoyance, in an attempt to soothe the man's wounded pride. After all, he's the boyfriend of one of his Strategic Planning Division Heads). Friederich decided to leave the mess into Karl Joseph's capable hands, and took a leave for the weekend. Elisabetta and Carolina took the children away from me and decided to show them to the "other ladies" as I was looking "so bad and certainly needed to rest".

The ceremony took place in the old Ballroom, specially prepared for the occasion. The flowers were very nice and everything went without a hitch. The boys behaved fantastically, sitting next to me and looking very poised, like young princes.

Alexei was not so easy to shake away. He should be concerned that his boyfriend was about to spit on the trays when he saw what was served. "amateurs" was the only thing he said, not even touching it. I was very glad not to be invited to the banquet.

"Guntram, my friend, are you feeling well? This must be horrible for you," Alexei told me sympathetically.

"I didn't sleep well last night. I'll go away in a few minutes. I'll take the children to the cinema. We're going to watch "Ratatouille". I said quite embarrassed to be under his scrutinizing stare.

"Why bother to go out? Today, you can see it in my kitchen for free. *Connnards.*" Jean Jacques smirked, as Alexei sighed. "All right, I'll keep quiet. Do you know that the same who teaches the rat how to cook, Adrià, is the one the bitch tells me I should copy from? It's befitting. My kitchen is infested with rats," he huffed.

"Jean Jacques, please." Alexei said tiredly. "We spoke long about this."

"Klaus and Karl are dying for your cake. They behaved so well because of it," I intervened, trying to appease him.

"Obviously they get the good taste from their mothers' side," Jean Jacques replied. Alexei threw him a killer's look and I diverted my sight, totally embarrassed. "What? You think the same, but you don't say it."

"It's already a hard day for Guntram, let's don't contribute to it, uh?"

"Yes, you're right, Guntram looks horrible and it's not unexpected. Fortunately, you can escape. I left your lunch prepared last night. Karl Joseph will bring it to you."

"Thank you," I smiled at him.

"Cheer up Guntram, you'll be eating well and this will be finished soon," Alexei said to me.

"I'm fine, Alexei. I didn't sleep much; painting for the exhibition. You know how it is, you start and you forget about time. I went to bed very late," I lied.

"What you two had was bigger than life. You two looked perfect for each other. This was another house, and it was a pleasure to cook for both of you. The Duke made a horrible mistake by destroying his relationship with you. You were the best thing that ever happened to that man. I know. Now, I'm thinking of going away as I can't stand the bitch. I only stay because of you and the children," Jean Jacques said.

I spoke with them for a little longer, but around 2:00 the reception was almost finished and I took the children upstairs, as they were getting hungry and refused to eat anything that Jean Jacques had not cooked.

I was very glad to drive with Milan away at 3:30. No matter what he tells, he liked the Rat Chef a lot and enjoyed it like a child. We had a very late tea with the children and by 7:00 we were back in the Castle, both of them totally asleep in the car.

Although I was expecting the bastard to be already gone to his honeymoon, he had delayed his departure to kiss his sons goodbye.

Chapter 10

Today, Adolf zu Löwenstein came to the house, his father's condition had worsened during the night, and the doctors were not giving him more than a few hours, perhaps a day or two. The old prince had refused any sedation to alleviate the pain and wanted to make his peace with God. Father Bruno, visiting Friederich, still upset over the civil wedding, immediately went for what he needed for the last rites.

"Guntram, may I have a word with you, please?" Adolf said, taking me by the arm.

"Yes, of course. I'm sorry that you're going through these hard times. It's very hard to lose a parent."

"My father wants to see you and the Griffin together."

"I'm not sure if this would be good for him," I said, loosing my colours.

"Please, the Griffin interrupted his honeymoon and will be at our house at four. I only hope my father holds till then."

"All right. I will drive with you now," I said very quietly, not truly willing to go at all, but some things can't be avoided.

* * *

The *Fürstin* received me at the entrance of the house. She was truly sad for her husband, and I felt sorry for her, even if I couldn't feel much for the man who ordered the execution of my whole family. I hadn't the faintest idea of what he could want from me.

"He's with Father Bruno, Guntram, but he wants to see you as soon as possible," she told me while she led me upstairs, to their bedroom. The house was full of people, many already in their mourning dresses. We waited in the hallway for the priest to leave the room. When he came out, he went away with the *Fürstin*, comforting her as she started to cry.

"You wished to see me, *mein Fürst*."

"Guntram, the minute I saw you, I realised you had the Guttenberg's blood, like your father. Thank you for coming. I have not much time left, but I want to tell you that Konrad had nothing to do with your family's punishment."

"He told me that several times, but he's the Griffin, and I find hard to believe it," I retorted.

"He was the Griffin indeed, but he was incapacitated at the moment I took the decision. You see, he was in the hospital as one of the traitors attempted to murder him. He escaped with his life, but all of his bodyguards were killed. He was shot in one arm. The bullet proof vest saved his life. I decided to finish everything once and for all. We needed to stop it."

"Who attacked the Duke?"

"Several associates, all of them dead now, the ones who encouraged your grandfather's plot against Konrad. I'm about to meet my Creator, do you think I would lie to you now? I always treated you with the utmost kindness. First, I didn't want you, but when I saw you with Konrad I knew you were perfect for him."

"But he wasn't for me," I whispered.

"No, child, he's perfect for you, and that lessens my sin against you. I'm very sorry about your father's fate. He was a good man, caught in the middle of an ambitious family, like his mother was. Could you forgive me for his suicide?"

"It was a suicide, I know it now. He was very sick. There's nothing to forgive."

"Yes, my child but I feel that you think I forced his hand by threatening your life."

"Didn't you?"

"I had nothing against a seven year old, living abroad. Our laws decreed that you should have been killed, but the biggest snake had already been spared, so there was no reason to go after you. Your father's offer was unnecessary as Konrad told him. He was not even important to us. Your grandfather and Uncle Pascal were, because they were associates and traitors. Please, forgive me my child and let me die in peace."

I remained silent for a long time, debating with myself. Should I forgive him? He was truly one step from going to the other side.

"Receive our Lord in peace because I have nothing against you, *mein Fürst*. You always treated me with kindness and defended me from the others. We are in peace, sir," I said finally, taking his right hand, between mine.

"Thank you. You have a generous soul and you are an excellent Consort to our Griffin. Without you, he would have drowned many years ago."

"Good bye, Sire," I said fighting to keep my tears at bay. He only stroked my face and I left the room. Outside, Adolf was waiting for me.

"The Duke is downstairs. He was able to take a commercial flight to arrive earlier. He asks if you could wait for him."

"Yes, of course. Please tell me where."

I crossed my path with Lintorff on the stairwell, and it was shocking to see him so defeated coming up, his eyes were rimmed with red. The Duchess was nowhere to be seen. I stayed in the library with Monika and some of her cousins, all Löwensteins. We spend the time drinking some coffee, and almost not speaking. Ferdinand and Cecilia came by later.

"My father would like to see you and the Duke for the last time."

I was surprised, but I didn't want to deny him his last request. I went with Jürgen, the second child, back to the bedroom. I entered and saw that Lintorff was standing at one side of the sick man's bed.

"Konrad, never let your Consort go. Remember your promise to protect and honour him above all. Guntram has proven more than once his worth to us," the old man whispered, almost on the limit of his strength.

Lintorff came very close to me and took my right hand. I didn't pry it away because I didn't want to make a scene in front of a dying man, but his touch burned me to my bones.

"Guntram is the chosen Consort, no matter what happens between us. I will never remove his title." The bastard kissed my hand! I had a very hard time to control my desire to punch him in the face.

"I do hope he can forgive you like he forgave me, my Griffin."

"We will leave you with your family. We thank you for your services to us and we will pray for the Lord's mercy," Lintorff said coming to the old prince and kneeling at his side, to kiss his right hand. He stood up and left the room and I did the same.

It was more than six when we left the house. Lintorff was busy speaking with a lot of people and I was "parked" as usual with some of the Löwensteins and Cecilia.

"Come Guntram, we go home," Lintorff told me, and I followed him, not really willing to start a fight. His limo and Goran were there. I went in and sat, waiting for him. He said nothing, and I could feel the deep sorrow that was pouring out of him in waves. Löwenstein was like a father to him.

We were half way to the Castle, when his mobile beeped discreetly, and he took it out to read an SMS. "The *Fürst* passed away ten minutes ago," he informed me, rubbing his eyes.

"I'm sorry, sir," I whispered, taking his hand to comfort him.

Without any kind of warning, he pulled me against him as he started to cry freely, like I've never seen him before, as a child. I said or did nothing, and I let him squeeze me like a bloody teddy bear. In a few months, when all this is over, he will hear it from me. For a second, he let me disentangle from his bear hug only to continue to cry all over my chest. It was horrible as I didn't know what to do and we were approaching the house. I put my arms around his big frame, not even able to fully embrace him, and petted his head, like I do with Karl or Klaus when they fall or hurt themselves.

We remained like that for ten minutes. I noticed that we were not any longer following the normal way to the castle. Probably Goran realised what happened, and ordered the chauffeur to drive around. As sudden as it started, he let me go, and I gave him my handkerchief, like I do with the children. He took it and dried his tears, making a supreme effort to compose himself.

"Did you really forgive him, Guntram?"

"Yes, I wouldn't lie with such a thing."

"Will you forgive me at some point?"

"I don't know. You have started a new life and I want to do the same. Let me go, and we will be in peace."

"I can't let you go. You're my soul. You belong to me."

"Then you have your answer, Sire."

Chapter 11

March 21st, 2007
Good Friday

    This morning was the Dino invasion. I wanted to escape with the children to visit Elisabetta, but the father decided they should stay for the Mass and later I could take them to Elisabetta's residence for lunch.

    Already on Thursday, we had the big fight between the newly wed. The witch is still sore because her honeymoon was interrupted, her "post wedding" reportage cancelled because of the Prince's death and Lintorff forced her to remain in Zurich, not going anywhere as he, as member of the Löwenstein family, is officially in mourning. He suggested she should dress accordingly, but he nearly got the Versace china on his aristocratic head. Friederich can't still believe a woman would do that. Welcome to the XXI century, and if I remember correctly, Marianne von Liechtenstein had also an impressive temper.

    As their relationship was strained, to say the least, Lintorff decided (ordered me), to have me every night at the dinning table—after I got both boys in bed—on a permanent basis. Very bad idea if you ask me. I was not happy, and always kept myself silent.

    I don't understand him. Really. He picks a fight with a Russian mobster like Repin, has more than unsavoury customers, but he hides behind me from his wife. According to Ferdinand, he does it so he doesn't lose his temper with her, and does something we all might regret later. "I give him peace." Yes, like a dove when I want to kill him.

    As it was an "informal" setting, I had to sit at his left at the table, facing her, because he refused to let her have the other head of the table; only on formal occasions. Friederich and Dieter were serving tonight, and to her annoyance, Dieter had to run to serve us both. Is that some kind or revenge on Friederich's part to refuse to serve the Duchess? He never had trouble placing a dish in front of me.

    "Have you decided what you're going to do tomorrow, darling?" Lintorff asked in his "merry voice", the one he reserves for getting rid of you, politely, of course.

    "Don't you have tomorrow the business lunch with your associates?"

    "Yes. We have the Mass with *Pater* Bruno and lunch at around one. Where would you go?"

    "I'll stay here. If your children stay with de Lisle, I can also do it. I'm your wife and I should make the honours," she said firmly.

    "They only stay for the Mass, and as you're not a practising Catholic, the best would be for you to avoid it. It's a very boring meeting. Only men speaking about business. Nothing glamorous."

    "I'm your wife, you can't send me away," she said raising her voice.

    "Yes I'm aware, but you're a woman and not accepted in our meetings," he said very sharply punctuating every word.

    "Get out de Lisle," she ordered almost hysterically. I rose from my chair, but

Lintorff barked.

"Sit down and finish your soup."

Why this bloody fixation on always making me finish the bloody soup? Was Friederich forcing him to eat it? I looked at the butler for instructions. Piss her or him off? Good question. He made one gesture with the hand so I would regain my seat. I sat, thinking that it was not going to be a nice show.

"What is this about me being a woman? I'm your equal! You and all the pigs who come tomorrow should learn it! I work like many of you do, and I'm tired of hearing your chauvinist ways!"

"Accepting several credit cards from me didn't look very chauvinist to you," he pointed out, not losing his temper. "I'm your husband, and you, as my wife, should obey. If I tell you to go out, you should go out. Take my plane and fly to Rome, to visit your friends for example or Paris."

"Do you hear yourself? I'm not going to obey you as if we were in the Middle Ages. I'm an independent woman!"

"Madam, if you want, you could come with me and the children to the *Principessa* di Battistini's house. I'm sure she will be delighted to have you for lunch," I interfered before this would escalate more. Elisabetta would understand it, and will only turn me into her slave for the next ten years, instead of the twenty I should deserve for "bringing that vulgar woman to my house".

"Do as de Lisle says, Stefania. It's good advice. You're not welcome here tomorrow." Lintorff said. I gaped at Friederich, who looked very annoyed at their exchange. Yes, your charge needs to review his etiquette lessons.

She exploded. "I'm not going out with that good for nothing! He's just a beggar living off an asshole who thinks he's the centre of the universe because he has money!"

'If he jumps at her, I can't stop him', was the only thing I could think about. He looked at her with an incredible hatred in his eyes, and I froze.

"Madame, you're not yourself tonight. Go to your rooms and rest. I want you out, tomorrow at nine," he growled very low, nearly bending the silver fork he was clutching. She stood up, and in a fit of rage threw a glass at his direction. I closed my eyes expecting the worst.

But nothing happened. She left the room, her high heels resounding in the hallway and stairs. Dieter immediately started to pick the shards up. I had a monstrous headache and when I was going to ask to be excused, Lintorff told Friederich to serve the main dish. I knew he was one step from violence when he inquired, very politely, how were the children doing in school. I gulped and started with the story of them learning to write their vowels, preparing their school play for next May and planning to catch a rabbit on Sunday to turn it into their new pet. I noticed he visibly relaxed hearing my voice.

"Inform them that I will not let them have a rabbit. It will destroy the furniture. They have already stolen Mopsi from you."

"The dog is very happy with your children, Sire," I said also relaxing as he was calming down. "They're going to take her to school for showing after the holidays."

"This poor animal is truly earning its keep. There's another thing de Lisle, it's about their birthday. Please keep it as simple as possible. The passing of the *Fürst* is still too recent. Let them invite some friends from the school to play, but nothing more. No entertainers or activities."

"As you wish, Sire," I said. "I will inform the Duchess as she insisted on taking care of it."

Yes, that was his idea, in a sort of compensation for not letting her interfere with the Good Friday or the Easter Sunday, this year much more austere, as Löwenstein was one of the main figures of the bank, the last from the Old Guard; only a few rabbits and baskets for the children, egg hunting, but no music or theatre to entertain them. They will have to play in the playground with Karl and Klaus or run around the garden. I can well imagine myself drawing till my hand breaks.

"When will be your exhibition in Berlin?"

"From the 24th onward, your Excellency. Ostermann has already sent everything, Sire."

"Will you attend the *vernissage*?"

"I'm not sure, sir. It all depends on the boys. If they're sick like last spring, I will remain beside them. I'm not really necessary there."

* * *

On Good Friday, things were not so easy in the morning. I had the boys dressed by ten, with the breakfast in and their promise to behave in the service. It's not the first time they attend a service, but it's always their father, a member from the Lintorff family, Armin, Friederich, some servants and I; never with so many people around.

But very early, at 8:30, when I was having breakfast downstairs at the small dining room (only the brave would enter in Jean Jacques' kitchen, already nervous with the perspective of fifty tycoons in the house for lunch, tea, and dinner), Lintorff burst here, already dressed in a dark suit.

"Go with the children and stay there with them," he ordered me in a soft voice, contrasting with his harsh words and stern face.

I know better than to disobey. I caught Friederich on the stairwell, "Do you know what's going on? I've just been sent to the nursery."

"The Duchess disobeyed him."

"Do you say it like that? You're perfectly aware he can be very violent when crossed! Do something, please!"

"He will not touch a single hair from her. She's a woman. If he disciplines her, it would be in another way. Don't worry child, it's not your problem. See that the young princes are not upset if they shout with each other."

I was with Karl and Klaus trying to convince them to leave the bed when I heard some faint shouts, mostly from her. I lost my colours, but the boys didn't seem impressed at all.

"She makes papa cross," Klaus informed me, just in case I didn't know.

"Papa says he's only happy with you and us," Karl added.

"You two should mind your own business and leave the adults to their own. Now, up and get dressed. I don't want to hear any more complaints from you," I told them a bit stronger than necessary.

When both of them finally sat at their table to have their breakfasts, half dressed (I was not risking the jackets or ties), I saw her leaving the house with her car. Well, she's in one piece, I thought.

"Papa, papa!" Both were shouting and jumping to their father, standing at the door.

"Well you two are finally up. You sleep like logs," he said kissing them as they both climbed on top of him. "Today will come some friends from Papa and I want you on your best behaviour. Don't give trouble to Guntram. I will be busy till very late so we will see each other tomorrow morning. Be nice also with your Aunt Elisabetta."

They both nodded very happily "De Lisle, please tell the princess that I will be calling her tomorrow morning, but I need her to take the Duchess place on Sunday as she's indisposed. Apologise in my name to her for this rude way of asking this favour, but I will not have a minute free till tomorrow."

"Yes, your Excellency. I will sit in the backside with the children in case we have problems."

He didn't look happy at all. "I was expecting you to sit in the front with me, but it's a sensible request."

Was he thinking to sit me at the front, like I did when I was the stupid Consort? After he kicked the Duchess out, not very elegantly? *No way.* Do I have to sit with Repin and hold his hand so he gets the idea? And do I have to speak with Elisabetta for him? Shit.

The boys behaved very well at the service, as I took care to go downstairs with them only in the last five minutes before it started. I greeted a few of the members, who were more interested in seeing the children, than speaking with me. When I was leaving the chapel with them, I saw Constantin arriving with several bodyguards and Oblomov.

I went straightforward to our car, but Oblomov followed me. Milan opened the door and both brothers jumped in and started to escalate to their seats. Klaus managed to do it first and I buckled him in.

"Hello Sable, long time no see," Oblomov rumbled. I noticed Milan becoming very tense and his hand going to his jacket.

"Hello Ivan Ivanovich. Please, excuse me now. I have to go with the children."

"Boss only wants to know how are you. Put that down Mihailovic, do you want to dance?"

"Please, Ivan Ivanovich, I have two children with me. Tell Constantin I'm fine and he should not be concerned about me."

"Where's the Duchess?"

"She's away like I, This is for members only. Send my greetings to your boss."

"Very well Sable. Boss will see you in Berlin," he shrugged. "Have to work now. Bye," and he went away just like that. I had to lay my head against the metal frame of the door.

"Let's go Guntram, this is nothing for you and them. Pity I can't stay; would like to settle the score with him too."

"Is it because of London?"

"Nooo, that was nothing and approved by Goran. It's something else. New stuff," he grunted as he went inside the car. I sat on the passenger's side.

We arrived very soon to Elisabetta's residence in Zollikon. She had a very nice villa on top of a hill, overlooking the lake, surrounded by trees and a big garden, where both little devils started to chase each other, without even looking at her. I opened my mouth to scold them, but she said, "Let them be, Guntram. They're young and need to run. Your man can look after them. Come, let's go inside and you will tell me what you have been doing lately." Poor Milan, he was just promoted from chauffeur to baby sitter. He has every right to ask for a rise.

She motioned me to sit in one of the sofas in her living room.

"Now, tell everything, dear. Ostermann told me you go to Berlin on the 24th"

"Nothing is decided yet. Perhaps. The pieces are gone, and the exhibition will be open up to August 7th. Tita insisted a lot and she was very generous as to lend some of the ones she has."

"It's time you do something about your gift boy. I'm still upset you didn't give anything for this year's auction. You can still return to my good graces."

"I'm afraid that's not a very good idea. I prefer a low profile at the moment as the Duchess will be there and she doesn't like me."

"Impossible woman. I still don't understand Konrad."

"He asked me to ask you if you could take the Duchess' place on Sunday. He will call you tomorrow because today is impossible," I blurted out. She laid down against her sofa, rising and eyebrow.

"Why this sudden change?"

"The Duchess is indisposed."

"Really? Will you tell me what happened or should I force my nephew to confess, dear?

"I honestly don't know, Elisabetta. The Duke asked me this morning to take care of the children and bring them here. She was going away in the morning with her car."

"Well, you've told, let's say, a twenty percent of the truth in one go, dear. I must be losing my touch. Try again, Guntram."

"They had an argument last night and she didn't obeyed him when he told her to go away for today. I think he forbid her to be on Sunday. I don't know what transpired between them."

"My nephew is an idiot for many reasons. The main one is to have broken up with you. Marrying that vulgar woman is too much for me, but I will fulfil my duties as a Lintorff. Tell him, I will make the honours on Sunday."

Chapter 12

March 24th, 2008

This evening was the *vernissage* but I didn't go as Karl got the flu and Klaus decided to do the same. Both are in bed, with some fever and since their father is away, it seemed very bad to me to leave them alone and sick. Ostermann is there and he can bring me later the critics.

* * *

March 25th, 2008

It's impossible to discuss with that woman. I honestly tried to tell her the Duke's orders about keeping the children's birthday low, but she nearly sent me to Hell. It's your problem if Lintorff gets furious with you. I did my best. I'm not going to be in the middle when he explodes. I have enough with my own life.

* * *

March 27th, 2008

My day was totally normal. In the morning, I took the boys to school. After much pleading and cries, I accepted that they give as presents for his friends in the school, copies of my books. The fifth edition is out and this time, I'm sure we're going to lose money. I have already finished a third of the next volume, so it's very stupid to print more copies of the old one.

After a normal afternoon, helping them with their homework (have to draw their room and their favourite toy for showing), I bathed and made them eat their dinner. Around nine, they were soundly asleep in their beds and I wanted to do the same.

Friederich came to my room and told me to go downstairs because the Duke was already willing to dine and the Duchess was still in Rome, recording one of her programs. Sorry? I don't eat with the bastard, especially after he clearly threatened me with who knows what on his wedding eve.

"Guntram, please, don't be difficult. The Duke had a horrible week in Russia and China. Eat with him for all our sakes. He's so upset that I don't know what could happen tonight," he pleaded with me.

"Am I the chosen punching bag, tonight?" He only looked at me with mix of sorrow and pleading. "All right. I'll have dinner with him, but I'm not speaking to him more than necessary," I said very upset.

"Thank you my child. It's most generous of you."

He was already sitting at the table in the daily dining room. "You're late. Sit down," he barked. He certainly was in a mood. Probably Constantin pissed the bastard off. Good for him. For a second, I had the urge to shout something like "I'm late because I didn't know I was supposed to dine with an asshole." But no, I'm a polite

574

person. Fuck!

"Yes, sir. I was not notified of your presence." I took my place on the left.

"I wanted to discuss some issues regarding Klaus' schooling. I've noticed he can write following the models, but the minute he's asked to write by himself, he does it turning the letter around. Have you spoken with the teacher about it?"

"Yes sir, two weeks ago. She says it's perfectly normal to do this. This should be fixed on the first class. It's a maturity problem. Not dyslexia. Most of the children of his age do it. Karl also does it, but not so frequently, Sire," I replied.

We ate in silence till he decided to restart our merry conversation.

"Why didn't you attend your *vernissage*?"

"The children had the flu and you were away. I didn't want to leave them alone. Ostermann was there," I said nonchalantly.

"Karl and Klaus can survive one night without you. They can stay with their nanny. She's allegedly qualified for that."

"I thought it would be hard for them to be left alone when they were sick. I'm not so much into parties and socials. My manager can do a better job."

"Your critics were good for an unknown artist. Ostermann told me you sold half of the pieces."

"Thank you, Sir," I said quietly.

"I saw it yesterday. It's very different from the other, Childhood Memories. That one was ethereal, full of innocence and light, but this one was sombre, not dark, but very intense. The figures of the poor people were almost hypnotic in their beauty. The second room, the one with the landscapes and animals reminded me more of you, years ago. I bought the one with the frogs in the pond. I will send it to the house in Amsterdam."

"There was no need to buy it" (Shit, that was one of my favourites!). Did he mention he visited the other too? I thought he despised my illustrations, more or less in the Comics section for him.

"It was a pity that everything was sold out in your previous one when I visited it."

"The children have many of them and books specially made for them. There's also no need to buy anything from there."

"I see now, that forcing you to make Stefania's portrait was too much. Compared with quality of what I've seen so far, it's a very bad painting. Worthless and unworthy. I hope you you understand, that I will send this piece to another house. It's not worthy to be near real artworks."

"I understand Sire. I'm also not pleased with it. You should have hired a real artist; a consecrated one."

"Why don't you like her? She's trying her best to fit in my house. Stefania is the new Duchess, but she's treated with insolence by my own staff. The children are constantly trying to upset her and this can only come from you."

"Sir, I've never said a word against her Excellency. I've always treated her with courtesy," I defended myself.

"I've spoken with her for a long time. She doesn't feel welcome at all. She wants to start a friendship with the children, but she feels that you prevent it," I? They call her "the witch" all by themselves and she kicked them out of their own father's wedding! I opened my mouth to give him a piece of my mind, but he stopped me raising his hand.

"It would be good that she starts to relate with their friends' mothers and visits the school more. She's willing to learn her duties as Duchess. She dedicated entirely the last week to plan this birthday party, but she fears that the children will not associate all work done to her, if you are present, and think that you did it," he said.

"Sir, they're aware the Duchess has made all the arrangements. I've explained it to them, several times. I've told them that it's a surprise from her. To win a child's trust is very hard, sir and requires a lot of patience. When I was helping Father Patricio, some of the new children were not even speaking to us for several months before they decided to do so."

"Therefore, I will ask you to excuse yourself from the party," he said not hearing me at all. I was breathless and shocked. That motherfucker knows that I like this day so much since he kicked me out of the Christmas celebration. So that was his "punishment" for not preventing his wedding? What was he expecting? That I should make an entrance riding a white horse, shoot the bride and take him away with my stallion? He doesn't need a shrink. He needs an army of them.

"Klaus Maria and Karl Maria will be most upset, your Excellency."

"Perhaps. Perhaps not. There is only one way to know it. Monika has booked you a flight to Berlin for tomorrow afternoon. You can return Sunday evening. Call her tomorrow morning, de Lisle. Antonov offered to accompany you."

Fuck you! No, that's too soft. I hope all the furies from Hell eat your insides. That son of a bitch—yes, I know the mother—sent me away from my babies' birthday!

"Good night, Sir. I have to pack now," I said, rising from my chair.

"Sit. I haven't dismissed you yet," he retorted coldly.

"I should not occupy the Duchess' place any longer, sir."

"Sit down." I obeyed. "I want your oath that you will cease any hostilities or rising the other staff members against her. Your cooperation in making her feel welcome will be also appreciated."

"I will treat the Duchess with all the courtesy she deserves. I can't assure you the children will like her. They have a will of their own and their affections can't be forced or bought like in the adults' case."

"Good. I don't want to hear any more complaints of you from her or I will fire you and you will never see my sons again. There are no reasons for me to keep you any longer here as Stefania truly wants to be the Consort. You had your opportunity, but you despised it. Dismissed."

There are limits for any guy on this Earth. Even for a frightened lamb like myself.

"Friederich, leave us please," I said calmly, like the heir to the de Lisle's. We wore a crown when your ancestors were fishing and catching frogs in the Mecklemburg swamps. The butler didn't wait for him to grant his leave.

"I had the honour of meeting your mother briefly, but she described you perfectly with only one word, sir: Pathetic. Don't make idle threats sir. Bluffing is unbecoming for you. I celebrate you finally understood her Excellency's worth. She's your perfect match, Sire. I will support her in her glorious quest to be respected by the cleaning ladies. Good night." I rose from my chair, giving him one final look of contempt. Instead of exploding as I was expecting him to do, he bent his head down.

Chapter 13

Ferdinand von Kleist's Diary.
May 9th, 2008

I'm just back from the stupid charity auction my stupid cow of a former wife decided to organize twelve years ago. If they want your money, they should make an appointment, visit you and explain you the tax benefits to do so. In a way, it's less hypocritical than serving a 10,000 dollars dinner to buy rice for the famished babies in the Third World or auctioning a silly famous cow for a kiss (and you have to pay dinner for the slut later). What kind of woman lets herself be publicly sold? Only a presumptuous cow presuming in front of the others.

I did my part and bought something hideous from Junot's wife. 14,000 Francs revolutionary tax. Luckily, it was one of the first things to be auctioned, and I could escape with Cecilia to the garden, planning to return for the last twenty minutes. This is when people remember you were there. I needed my peace. Konrad, on the other hand, couldn't escape and had to endure the whole thing with the bitch sitting next to him.

We returned at nine to find the charade almost finished. I had to suppress a cry of happiness when Elisabetta von Lintorff announced a "special surprise for all of us, now that we're reaching the end of a charming evening among friends. Dr. Ostermann, please."

Two men placed another picture in an improvised easel and uncovered it. It was a truly breathtaking portrait of several of our ladies. The Van Breda's wife, Olsztyn, Marina von Ribentrop and the other one, I think was the wife of the Crédit Luxemburg CEO. She's new. All of them were sitting quite harmoniously and reading some books. Very nice. I heard several well justified gasps of admiration.

"Most of you know the artist, Guntram de Lisle. As Mr. Volcker has robbed him this year for an exhibition at his own gallery, we have decided to rob part of his work to auction for charity purposes, of course." Volcker stood up and nodded to Elisabetta and she returned the gesture likewise. "Guntram will be very pleased to know that we plan to allocate the sum obtained to a full educational program for children in the poorest areas of Buenos Aires."

Many of the women started to bid not even waiting for the husbands to authorise it. What is going on with European women? I was more than right to move with Cecilia. Latin American women are clever and know their place. Impossible not to fall for them. In Colombia, they still know how to educate a real lady.

The painting was finally sold for 75,000 francs.

The problem arose with the second one. It was a portrait from the Duchess herself, dressed with a whore's dress, a flea infested cat and that horrible blue thing from the Titanic film. Even I could recognize it. I immediately checked with Konrad, but he didn't move a muscle of his face. The Duchess was about to jump and shout.

"This one is called "Portrait of an Unknown Lady with Cat" One of my favourites so far. A very good investment," Ostermann explained to an embarrassed, but an audience barely containing their laughter.

The thing was hideous, but hypnotic at the same time. In a way like the Mona Lisa, you don't know what it really has, but you can't stop looking at it. Somehow, it reminded me that other one from Leonardo, the girl, the Sforza Duke mistress and her Ermine. Bewitching. It was not ugly, but whereas the other women showed an aristocratic elegance along with an internal beauty, this one was showing a true snob.

Yes, that's the word. Snob.

"Didn't the old lady drop it into the ocean?" Michael Dähler exclaimed very clear and loudly, provoking a collective giggle. My Cecilia had to leave the room as it was impossible for her to control her laughter. I'm sure Konrad will kill Michael on Monday, but for once in his life, he was really funny. Lucky bastard, the most acute sentence you will ever pronounce in your entire life, was heard by all our entourage.

There the frenzy started. I even bid for the thing. Couldn't resist it. Up to 23,000 Francs. Cecilia returned from the garden and took me out before I could continue. Michael reached the 27,000 Francs till Monika nearly hit him with the catalogue. Repin reached 50,000, but his wife shut him up. Brave woman. Konrad didn't say a word and much less offered a cent even if his wife was almost jumping at his neck. I wouldn't like to endure the vindictive bitch tonight. You have left her completely alone in front of our she wolves.

Finally, the only ones standing were the Olsztyn widow, van der Loo and his wife, one of the Ribentrops and Volcker. I was impressed by the price the thing reached: 99,000 Francs, almost 130,000 dollars. Volcker bought it.

I think I'll travel this Sunday to Frankfurt and stay there for a few days. Till Thursday. That should give enough time to Konrad to calm down. As Cecilia said to me in the car on the way back.

"I would love to know which thing is upsetting the Duke more. The painting or the fact that Andreas Volcker bought it."

"The second my love, the second. Volcker has a lot of guts. I hope Guntram survives this one. People will be laughing for many years. Was Celine Dion the one who sang it?"

"She has nothing she didn't ask for. You can't burst into a society. You have to win your place. If she would have been humble to us, nobody would have offered a cent for it. But she rubbed her husband's money in our faces. I hope this gives the Duke something to think about."

My Cecilia speaks little, but when she does it, she goes to the core of the matter. The minute I have the damn marriage annulment from the Vatican, I'll marry her.

* * *

Guntram de Lisle's diary
May 10th, 2008

I still don't know if I should kill Elisabetta or Ostermann. That bloody painting was out of everything. Was not to be shown or anything. Ostermann was supposed to destroy it and recover the wood from the frame! Next time, I'll destroy my own things by myself! I'm such an idiot and this time, I deserve Lintorff's punishment.

Last night, very late, Friederich came to my studio where I was painting and ordered me to go to the library as the Dukes wanted to speak with me.

I rushed there completely puzzled about the reason to call me. I spoke several times with the children into accepting her, I sang her praises, but they still don't like her. Klaus even vomited (again) his lunch over her last Sunday. I should take him to the doctor. Maybe he's not faking it and has some kind of allergy to her perfume.

When I entered, she came to me like one of the furies from Hell and crossed my face with a slap. I looked at her as she crumbled over a sofa and started to cry, heart brokenly. I thought "she found it out" and I wanted to die in shame.

"Your word means absolutely nothing de Lisle." Lintorff spat, coming toward me. "You're not even a man if you can insult and humiliate a woman like that. Your father should be very ashamed of you. He was a real gentleman."

I flinched in pain at his words. "I also regret my past with you, but my father would have understood it as it was his idea."

Lintorff looked at me as if I had lost my mind. "That damn picture of yours! The portrait you painted from the Duchess! You have humiliated my wife in front of all our friends!" he roared.

"I know it was bad, but it was decently resembling to her. You approved it."

"Not that one! Do you take me for a fool, boy?" he shouted, making me flinch with the noise. She started to cry louder than before.

I looked at him dumbfounded. I had no other picture of her! The previous four were destroyed in the process along with the sketches. "There's no other portrait, Sire," I said and immediately I got a big blow on the face from him, making me fall to the floor. A big hit, like the one I got in Venice, when he thought I was cheating on him with Fedérico. My nose started to bleed and I hurriedly took my handkerchief to contain it.

Friederich rushed in the room, shouting something in German to Lintorff and coming to me to help me stand. "I'll take you to your room, child. You will discuss tomorrow with his Excellency," he said. She had stopped crying and was looking at me with a delighted glee in her eyes.

"No. I want to know what I'm accused of. The Duke dared to put my father's name in his mouth," I said, looking at him with all the hatred I could.

"You painted a libel against my wife and then gave it to Elisabetta to be auctioned tonight! You have humiliated our name and position!"

"I painted nothing! I had to start her damn portrait more than six times and do you think I will waste more canvas on that woman?" I roared.

"It had your signature all over that damned cat! On its collar! I hate to be lied to!"

I looked at both of them horrified. Not that hideous thing! It was supposed to be destroyed! Ostermann told me he will take care of it.

"This painting was discarded in December, before Christmas. I told Ostermann to destroy it and he said he would! This thing was never meant to be sold. I presented nothing this year as I have an exhibition in Berlin at the moment. This is for amateurs!"

"How did that thing end up there and why did Andreas Volcker pay 99,000 francs for it?"

"I don't know, honestly," I whispered completely lost. She renewed her weeping, louder this time. "Madam, I will try to recover the picture. All this is a misunderstanding and I don't understand it." I said, but she cried one pitch higher, officially worsening my headache.

"My Duke, the best will be that you speak first with the Auction Organizers and his Manager. Guntram obviously knows nothing about this." Friederich interfered and for a second, Lintorff seemed to consider the suggestion.

"I'm so ashamed! I have a brilliant career and he destroyed it in one night! I'm an icon for glamour and taste and he painted me like a street whore. All our friends saw it! Fire him! None of you help me or support me. I do my best to fit in, but all of you are always plotting to humiliate me. I was much better living in Rome where people truly appreciate art," she howled.

"Madam, I will speak with Mr. Volcker, he will give it back to me. I'll offer to buy it," I said desperately. "He liked a lot one of the series hc's exhibiting. I will give it to him as it's valued twice what he paid tonight."

"You hate me and you'll do anything to ruin my reputation! What's a woman without her reputation? Konrad, get him out! Now! He's a serpent and will hurt your children!"

"Madam, that's unfair of you, and as for your reputation you should look by yourself in which catwalk you lost it!" I said, now losing my temper at her suggestion that I could damage the babies. She looked at me with true hatred in her eyes, not the usual scorn and contempt, we, the servants, get all the time.

"Get out de Lisle. Pack your things. You're fired. Leave my house tonight." Lintorff said.

"When can I say good bye to your children?" I said fighting against the choking lump at the pit of my stomach and in my throat.

"Get out. You're not worthy to be near them," he said slowly. "Friederich will send your things in the morning. Monika will take care of the financial details of your lay off."

"As you wish, Sire," I whispered, still frozen in my place, trying to understand. Did he really fire me? I would never see my babies again?

"Come child, the Duke needs to think things over. We'll speak tomorrow." Friederich said pulling me by the sleeve. I couldn't help to miss the triumphant but brief smile from her. I let Friederich take me to the main door.

"Now, it's better if you don't stay here tonight. He's too nervous and hurt in his pride. You should go to a friend's. Call Antonov, he's back."

"No, he's with Jean Jacques tonight. I will not spoil their night together. I'll go to a hotel."

"This is not good for you, child. Should I call the *Princepessa?*"

"NO, she's a Lintorff. I will only get her in trouble with him. I'll call Goran," I decided.

"Good choice. He's loyal to us."

Goran was very kind and offered his house for as long as I needed. "Nonsense, you don't go to a hotel. Let the Duke come back to his senses. That bitch drives him mad. He fired Antonov for one single remark he made when she mocked that he was gay and dating the cook. On Monday, he will fire Dähler for what he said at the auction and probably von Kleist for bidding. They already told me the story and

Michael sent me a photo of the picture with his mobile phone. Tell Milan to drive you here, I want to speak with him as he was there," he said and he hung up on me.

I said goodbye to Friederich and took the car with Milan. The man was giggling all the time and had downloaded the music from Titanic on his fucking phone. "Don't worry Guntram. We are so close to getting rid of her."

"He fired me, he will never let me see the children again."

"I wouldn't like to be the Duke when he breaks the news to the small ones. They're real little devils, like their father. Two weeks at their mercy, and the bitch will run away. They only behave because they don't want trouble with you," he chuckled. "That painting was something, boy. I'll ask the software people if they can make it into a screensaver."

"You'll be in trouble with the Duke, Milan!"

"He's in troubles with us, boy. There's a limit to what we take from him. This is not the Russian Mafia. He'd better smarten up."

Goran sent me to bed and asked me if I'd taken my pills, not even wanting to hear me. I didn't want to argue with him and went to bed, but couldn't sleep because both Serbs remained in the living room loudly speaking and laughing till 2 a.m.

This morning, after a silent breakfast with Goran and his "you look dead. Did you really take your pills?" Elisabetta von Lintorff decided to pay him a visit. I was totally shocked to see her there, standing like a princess, (Guntram, she is one).

"Thank you Mr. Pavicevic. You're a true friend of our family. Come Guntram, we have to speak with the idiot I have for nephew. I will not let him ruin his own children's lives for a cheap whore and his own idiocy."

"Madam…"

"Get your jacket. Now," she ordered me with an imperious voice. She can be impressive too.

We went downstairs, where her car was already waiting for us. Ostermann was sitting inside, at the passenger's place. "Don't worry Guntram, you had nothing to do with this. It was all my idea," he said.

"Don't steal all the credit, Rudolf. It was originally my idea. I haven't got so much fun in years."

"This picture was to throw to the trash! You promised me you will never sell it! Lintorff has every right to shoot me in the head. I've publicly humiliated his wife!"

"You said nothing about donating. It's too good to be destroyed. Worthy of Christies Modern Art Section. I'm regretting to have let Elisabetta convince me to put it in the auction. 99,000 francs. That's a record for anything ever sold there. Volcker bought it, and if he paid that kind of money, fighting with Tita Olzstyn, then you're on top of the market boy. He called me this morning to tell me one gallery from Paris and another from New York wanted to have you. You're in, Guntram. In five or seven years we will have to visit your stuff in Modern Art Museums."

"Lintorff fired me. I will never see Klaus and Karl. No picture is worthy of it."

"My nephew is a dunce, dear. No, a mule ridden by a cunning vixen. It's time he hears what we all have to say," she said, lightly squeezing my hand.

When we got to the house. She was the first to enter. "Inform the Duke I'm here," she ordered the poor Dieter, completely confused about what to do. He decided to obey her, as we stood in the foyer.

"How dare you to come in my house! Get out!" Stefania shouted from the stairs coming to us. "It's all your fault, you old hag!" I flinched at the insult to Elisabetta, but she didn't move a muscle in her face.

"Stefania. This is my Aunt." Lintorff growled coming from the library direction. She looked contrite. "I told you de Lisle to go away."

"Konrad, reserve that tone for your servants or your wife." Elisabetta said, fixing her blue eyes on him. "Your house leaves a lot to be desired if you keep *Geborene* waiting at your door, boy." Did I hear well? She just called him "boy"?

"Please Aunt Elisabetta, tell these people to leave my house. Ostermann you're relieved from your duties." My teacher only hunched his shoulders as if it were of no importance.

"So close to the Trastevere have you being living the past months that you have forgotten your manners, boy?" I saw him eating his own fury and pride when he asked her to accompany him to the living room.

We all went in tow, with Stefania coming to us. Elisabetta sat graciously in one of the big couches, beckoning me to sit beside her, in front of Konrad and Stefania. Ostermann was cleverer and sat on a corner, alone. I fixed my gaze once more in the carpet, feeling very bad.

"First of all, Guntram has nothing to do with this. As President of the Lintorff Foundation, I decided to put both pictures for auction. I was expecting our results to be very bad that night and we needed to increase the obtained amount." Elisabetta said like a queen.

"Money is never an issue for you, Elisabetta, and you know it," Lintorff growled.

"As I was saying, the portraits are both of an incredible good quality. Most of our friends have congratulated me for my good taste."

"Good taste? It's hideous. Horrible and outrageous. When my lawyers finish with you…" Stefania started to howl but...

"Konrad, hold your wife." Elisabetta smirked. "Threatening is very…" deep frown of disgust marred her face. "How would I say? It looks so much from the *Camorra*." She wrinkled her nose and I lost my colours. Did she really said what I've just heard?

"Stefania, we don't want another scandal. Please, keep your voice down," Lintorff said softly, sending a killing look at Elisabetta.

"The "Portrait of an Unknown Lady with Cat," is excellent in its quality. Many of my colleagues thought it so, not even knowing who the model was. It's the pure expression of post modern times. It captures the essence; vulgarity taking over traditional beauty cannons and equilibrium. It destroys everything we call the classical elements, but reconstructs them in a new, different way. Unique. It's a very acidic and sharp view of this society so bent into achieving instant gratification. This picture was too good to be destroyed as Guntram asked me to do. He never intended to sell it, so I donated it to the Foundation. I'm very glad that Andreas Volcker acquired it. It will be certainly appreciated there," Ostermann said.

"I will offer to buy it from him," I whispered.

"He will not sell it to you." Ostermann told me. "Why would he do it? So you give it to a woman who knows nothing about Art and can only choose a pair of shoes, to destroy it? No, he's a true patron of the Arts."

Lintorff was about to explode, but Stefania spoke before he could open his mouth. "I'm a celebrity. Many designers fight to have their names mentioned in my programme! I know more about Art than you do!"

"You have said it Madam, you're a celebrity. In two years, nobody will remember you as you're not in TV any longer. It's a short-lived fame what you have. There is no substance behind it. Nobody will remember you, Duke, in forty years, perhaps somebody will read your name on an old *Almanach Gotha*, but you will be ashes in the cemetery. But when people will look at this picture, they will know what a hypocritical, illiterate society we lived in. Guntram's name will be remembered over the years. Yours not."

"This is rubbish! He's only a bump who can't paint. Nothing else! Why are we wasting our time with this old man and his puppy?"

"He has already two portraits in the Cardinal's Gallery at the Vatican and five of his works hanging there. One of them will be added to the permanent exhibition next year. He's not even twenty-five years old. If you allow me the comparison my Duke, he's sitting in the Olympus."

"Please Rudolf, there's no need to enrage Stefania any more. Her own career was finished at that age." Elisabetta interfered. "I only want to say that if she's upset, Konrad, you should speak it with me and not take it out on Guntram. He did or knew nothing about it. Your reaction must have been a great shock for him, and I want to apologise to Guntram because I didn't carefully evaluate my actions."

"Of course I will speak with you Aunt," Lintorff retorted quite heatedly. "Ostermann, good day to you and De Lisle go back to your work."

"What?" Stefania croaked. "He painted that shit!" Elisabetta closed her eyes at hearing that word.

"Dear, the first rule for a princess is to learn to laugh at herself. If she can't do it, then she's not one," Elisabetta said gravely. I lost my colours again. "Rudolf, can you wait for me in my car? It will only take a few minutes."

"Certainly, *Princepessa*," he said bowing his head to her.

"One minute, Ostermann." Lintorff said. "If de Lisle is to recover his position in this house, there should be some changes in his status. If all this scandal was your idea, then, you will understand my request that you and him cease any kind of commercial activity. De Lisle should look for another manager if he wants to remain here. That's my condition."

I was speechless and frankly torn. Ostermann was more than a teacher and a manager. He was like a mentor, but the option was to be without my babies. No, his children. They're not mine as he showed me yesterday. "Please Dr. Ostermann, understand my decision. I've told you before that Karl and Klaus are more important to me than any painting," I whispered.

"Don't worry Guntram, I understand."

"Keep the paintings you have."

"All right. I'll send you a list with suitable replacements. Any *marchand* would love to have you."

"There's no need, sir. I never planned to be a professional. Art should not hurt people."

"People who feel hurt by Art are no people, Guntram. Good bye," he said softly, going out toward the door. I couldn't even say good bye to him, I felt so bad.

When he closed the door, Elisabetta spoke.

"Yesterday was a scandal?" She let a dry laugh out. "You have been living on a permanent scandal since you married that woman! We have tolerated your whims for a long time! Your chosen lifestyle was accepted before because you were not the first nor the last one! You always lived under the rules and respected them, but now your behaviour is outrageous!"

"Be quiet Aunt!"

"Don't you dare to use that tone with me, boy. I changed your diaper and cleaned your nose countless times! Guntram has done everything for the last two months, to get this woman accepted in our circles! He pleaded with Tita, van der Loo, Van Breda and me to invite her to our gatherings. He has spent all the credit he has earned over the years on her, at your own demand! Hear me out, boy. She's not one of us and her behaviour proves it. When I'm finished speaking with the others, you will not be received by any decent family. They will not even come to your children's celebrations! Guntram is one of us and will ever be, she not."

"Whatever I do, is by my will, no woman will tell me what to do!"

"Well Griffin, you should better start to reconsider your deeds because your paws are about to get a manicure. Move to another place with your children. If you continue with this disgraceful behaviour toward your Consort, you will be expelled from our society. Yesterday was only a warning, boy!" She roared, standing from her chair and leaving the room like a fury.

"Go back to your work, de Lisle. The children are waiting for you." A very appeased Lintorff said to me. I looked at him. "Do it now. I have to speak with the Duchess," he repeated very tiredly.

I obeyed as usual, wondering what Elisabetta had meant.

Perhaps it's true that the Griffin is just a *Primus inter Pares* like Löwenstein told me once. Why anybody will risk his life to fight against him for me? She was obviously bluffing, but Lintorff took it very seriously. Yes, he doesn't want his children shunned from society.

I asked Friederich what she had meant and he only said "Did she say that Guntram? If so, that is very bad for the Duke. He might lose everything."

* * *

Ferdinand von Kleist's Diary
May 16th, 2008

Konrad called Michael, Goran, and me for a private meeting. I was expecting that he would have calmed down from last Friday's slap on the face, but he was still enraged. He shouted long with us for bidding at the auction. When he finished his tirade, Michael got the worse part of it for his funny remark. I can't suppress a laugh whenever I remember it. My son, Karl Otto, told me that it's a line from a Britney Spears' video. We remained all silent. In honour to the many years of friendship we shared, I thought it was time to tell him the truth, but Goran was ahead of me.

"My Duke, with all due respect, you must hear us. I was not at the auction, but I saw the portrait. I will not discuss the artistic quality of it, but the background of what transpired that night."

"Pavicevic you're no part of our circle."

"I've seen it long enough as to know its rules. My family has been serving the Order for seven generations."

"Please, Goran. I should do it," I said and he only nodded. "Konrad, your marriage has been like bucket of cold water for many of us. Nobody had problems to accept Guntram, because he was discreet, polite, not meddling into anybody's business and even from "good breed", as Albert told you. Löwenstein and him supported Guntram all the time. The lad always knew his place and never said a word out of place or offended any of us. In fact, he improved your own character. Our rules do not specify the gender of the Consort, only that she or he, must be treated with the utmost respect as he is responsible for the next generation."

"We gladly accepted the war you started over him with Repin. No Mafia scum will tell us what to do," Goran added, interrupting me, with Michael nodding.

"Since your break up, you have been impossible to deal with. Truly impossible. Totally out of your senses and control," I stated expecting the explosion, but none came. Good. "I'm very glad that Elisabetta von Lintorff has given you the first touch of attention."

"The operations with SFCDOs, the gold futures rush and many other of your latest schemes only benefited part of our members. You knowingly destroyed many people's fortunes. I understand that you're still sore, like all of us, with Repin's entrance to the Order, but he's in. There's nothing we can do about it. The only reason why you're still in command is, that the Masons were badly hit, but nobody really cares about that all war against them anymore. The last two years have been a financial bloodbath for many of our peers. At some point, nobody will care if our combined assets have increased by a twenty-three percent in the last year, but they will start to ask why many of our members, situated on the top, lost everything almost overnight," I finished.

"I fail to see how this is related with Friday's events," Konrad growled.

"Easy Konrad. The boy is out of your bed, but you force him to live with you, taking care of your children. He keeps his title of Griffin's Consort, even after your marriage. There are no impediments for you to take a wife to ensure the succession, like several of your ancestors did, but she has to be from "the highest blood and virtue, never coming between the Griffin and his Consort," I quoted. "During the last two years, the Old Guard is dead. Four out of your nine counsellors are out and not replaced yet. You marry a well known high class prostitute and live with both of them. Your sanity has begun to be questioned by many of us. Your behaviour is erratic, to say it mildly, since she's here," I finished.

"Our women despise her. Monika will never sit at the same table. Forget it, my Duke. I will not order her to go there. Guntram even asked me if I could speak with my wife and the Löwenstein princess so they both will receive your wife. I will not repeat the answer to you, Sire."

"My Cecilia said something like, "if she would have been accepted, nobody would have offered a single cent for the picture," I supported Michael's argument.

"We have enough of this scandal, my Duke. No more bloodshed or attacks on the members because you're unbalanced due to a slut's whims." Goran closed the argument.

"No matter what you all think, gentlemen. All my acts will be explained when the game reaches its end. Not before, not later."

"It will be good it is soon done because our patience is at an end. Be glad it was only scorn what you got this time, Konrad. You only lead us. You're not superior to us. Leadership demands the most appropriate behaviour," I reminded him.

"Monika is also concerned because you have allowed this Barberini woman to come closer to your children. May I remind you that the education of the future Griffins is also a matter of the Order? Guntram was appointed their Tutor and has our support. Your own Tutor also expressed his concern to my wife on the ideas this woman has, and tries to inculcate on the young princes. You have also threatened the Consort to replace him with her. The Council will never accept this," Michael doubled the bet.

"Adolf zu Löwenstein already expressed his concern over all this. Remember he controls nineteen percent of the votes and you only forty-two percent. You need him to keep your position, and I doubt very much that you will get the two thirds required for your election next year. Since his father's passing, he sides with Guntram. Honour and duty before wealth was clearly written in our Code. You should learn from the boy. He's truly his father's son," I finished.

"You must end this situation, my Duke, before it's too late. It's getting out of hand, Sire," Goran summarized what we were all thinking for a long time.

"Your advise is appreciated and acknowledged, counsellors. This game will end before Christmas and a new Order will emerge. More powerful and truly dedicated to our originals ideals. I will not betray, disappoint or abandon my peers."

Chapter 14

May 24th, 2008

I still can't believe it. I'm so disgusted. I've been throwing up since I saw those pictures on my laptop. I think I will never use that thing again. I prefer folders much more, even if the computer saved my life this time.

Monday May 20th, started like a normal day. I took the children to school, early in the morning and went back to work in the house, far away from the witch, as she's in Paris, shopping. Milan drove me back as usual. He had decided to stay in the kitchen and check if he would get something good there. We both were shocked to see Lintorff's limousine parked in front of the entrance, along with three other black cars. He announced yesterday that he was flying to Frankfurt for several meetings at the ECB.

Milan parked, and strangely he checked his weapon. I looked at him in awe because he's very discreet. I saw Ratko coming to us, and they both started to heatedly speak in Serbian.

"You, in the house," Ratko said, taking me by the elbow with an iron grip. "I hope I don't have to do it," he mumbled to himself. Milan placed next to me.

When we entered, I saw Lisette crying like crazy sitting in one of the foyer chairs, another maid, Nadine, trying to comfort her whispering something very softly. Both women looked at me as if I were a monster when I passed beside them. I stopped in front of the women to ask them what was all this about, but Ratko gave me a strong shove and a "Move!" warning.

Milan knocked on the living room door and opened it without waiting for an answer and I got the second strong push from Ratko. In the room were Goran, looking very serious, Ferdinand, almost colourless, Heindrik and Lintorff himself looking like a fury from hell. There was another man, I didn't know, checking on my computer with another laptop at his side.

Lintorff stood up and directly came to me and without any kind of warning he crossed my face with a mind blowing punch and I fell to the floor. He launched himself at me to strangle me, but Heindrik and Ferdinand did their best to stop him.

I felt a huge pain in my chest and looked for the pills, swallowing one "Don't bother, your hours are numbered." Lintorff growled at me and he spat at my face.

"I fulfilled my promise! I didn't speak with or write to Repin!" I said trying to control my breathing but it was impossible.

"I will take an enormous pleasure in your dismissal. You're a hypocrite like your uncle."

"My Duke, I swear that if these allegations are true, I will take the matter into my own hands," Goran said from his corner.

"No, it's my right and duty as father."

"I haven't done anything. I stopped any kind of contacts with Volcker! Christ! You can't be so demented as to go through my things again!"

"You dared to touch my children. You're a disgusting filth. So that was your revenge against me! To hurt them? You will beg for death, when I'm finished with you. I only pray that I have enough cold blood as to make you last several days before I kill you," he said in a voice I've never heard in him, terrifying me beyond all belief.

"The children are in the school! I took them there this morning!"

"I got several anonymous e-mails with pornographic pictures of my children, taken by you. Those were distributed in those disgusting websites. Your computer is full with such material."

"All circumstantial, my Duke. I want real proof that Guntram did it. If so, I have enough cold blood to make him last a week," Goran interfered.

"What? I have nothing like that or ever done anything like that! I don't even have a photo camera. Only my mobile phone!" I took it from my jacket, and threw it to his face. He caught it easily. "You're deranged if you believe such a lie! I'm not a piece of shit like you! You had paedophile traders working for you!" I shouted back.

"Take him downstairs, Heindrik. He should not contaminate my house any longer."

The Swedish did as he was ordered, looking almost disgusted that he had to touch me. Well, welcome to the mobsters world Heindrik! You have to do a lot of nasty things! He pushed me into the cellar and sat in a chair in front of me, with his weapon out.

"Don't bother to run. I'll shoot you in a leg to make you suffer more. You're trash."

"You know me! I would never do something like that! It's a hoax!"

"You're nothing. Who would bother to set you up? The poor Duchess was crying like crazy when she saw the pictures, and showed them to her husband."

"Can you tell me what's going on? I'm not guilty of anything. You said you were my friend!"

"I find hard to believe it, but the material is there. Has anybody access to your computer?"

"Nobody, except the whole software people at the bank. All my things are monitored since 2004! I don't even have normal porn there! You can't consider some nude drawings as porn! I made them in Ostermann's studio with twenty women there!"

"Depends on who paints them."

We stayed there for some very long hours, not speaking any more, he looking at me with contempt and fury. I was feeling worse and worse, cold and with a horrible headache, becoming more and more concerned at my more than certain dismissal.

Ratko entered the room, and made a gesture to Heindrik. He pulled me from the floor without much care and almost sent me flying to the door with his brutal push. I hit the stone floor and got a small cut on my forehead.

"Boss will be cross when he finds out what you did Heindrik. Good for you that Guntram is not a tattletale. Goran too."

"Shit!" Heindrik cursed. "Be quiet about this boy," he whispered as he helped me from the floor this time more gently. I looked at him in disbelief.

Ratko took me to the library where again, Lintorff was behind his desk with my computer on top of it, Ferdinand sitting at his right and Goran at his left.

"Can you explain how this material is in your computer? Lintorff asked turning the laptop around showing me a huge photo of Karl and Klaus, naked in a lascivious attitude. I turned green, and the picture changed into another and another, all the same type. I couldn't hold myself any longer, and I threw up all over his noble carpet. I felt Heindrik catching me before I would have collapsed to the floor.

"Close that fucking thing, Konrad!" Ferdinand shouted. "Do you want to give him a heart attack? Is the tech's word not enough for you?"

"Is that the reaction from a paedophile, my Duke?" Goran asked in a very cold voice. "Relax little brother. It's a clumsy Photoshop. It's not real."

Heindrik and Goran sat me on a chair as I started to sob uncontrollably, covering my face. I was not hearing what they were saying as I could only think of the children. Who could have done something like this to them? The backgrounds were not even in the castle but in a cheap hotel room. The children never leave the house or the school.

"Oh my God, is that the school?" I whispered, dry heaving again.

Goran knelt at my side. "Listen to me. Those pictures are a hoax. Not true. Nothing ever happened to the children. They're fine, at Elisabetta's von Lintorff house in Zollikon, having tea with her. You will see them when you feel better. Now, relax because we want to know who did this to you."

"I swear those pictures are not mine!

"We know it now Guntram. Heindrik, Ratko, out," Ferdinand said, looking furiously at Konrad. "Whoever did this will be in a lot of pain soon," he barked at his friend. Both bodyguards left the room in haste.

"The technician who was here, checked your computer to see if you have originated these... pictures, but he found nothing. Of course you could have used another computer, but this one was so full of that pornographic trash, that he had his doubts. However, he checked on those pictures installation date, over 2,000, on your hard disk, and it was all done three days ago. Either you like a lot the internet or you transferred them from another computer. He checked their download date against the mirrors he has from your hard disk, and they didn't match. In his copies of your hard disk, there was nothing bad. Finally, the analysis of the children's pictures showed that they have been manipulated. He's trying to find when the original photos parts from the children were taken so we have a clue. He completely clears you from any charge. I have to offer my deepest apologies for almost believing it. These things are so disturbing that reason dies when you see them. I'm sorry Guntram, and I hope you can forgive me," Goran told me, still holding me.

"The question now is, who would be so interested as to do this?" Ferdinand asked more to himself than to me.

And I lost it there. Without even thinking, and maybe that was the reason why I caught Goran unaware, I launched at him and took his own weapon, pointing it at Lintorff. Goran almost jumped on me, but I said. "He'll be dead before you can do a thing."

"Nonsense, the safety is on," Lintorff shrugged.

"It's a Glock 17. Safe Action System. It shoots by exerting more than 2.5 kg pressure over the trigger."

"You wouldn't dare," he taunted me.

"Why not? You just nearly executed me and accused me of abusing your sons."

"Konrad, apologise to Guntram! We all screwed it up today!" Ferdinand pleaded. I think he realised I was going to do it. I just looked at the bastard in his eyes as I've never been so furious at him. Not even when I found out his betrayal.

"Guntram can't do it, Ferdinand," he mocked me. I shot.

He was right, I couldn't do it as in the last millisecond I aimed just over his shoulder, not at the head as I was doing it before. The bullet was embedded against the wall. In no time, Goran jumped on me, and took the weapon from my hands throwing it to Ferdinand. Heindrik and the other two Serbs came rushing through the door, all of them looking deadly pale.

"Get him out of here!" Lintorff shouted furiously, raising from his chair. "You will pay for this."

"Next time, you'll get it in the head, you bastard. How could you believe it? I put up with all your shit for years for the babies, and you thought I would hurt them? I'm not a piece of shit like you are!" I shouted. "I will not use poison with you, I will shoot you in in the stomach so it takes several days for you to die!"

"Guntram, go with Heindrik and Friederich, please." Goran whispered firmly holding me. "I know you're not like him or any of us, so stop this now. You're only hurting yourself," he said the last part hugging me like a child, and I started to cry hysterically in his shoulder. "Shh, it's OK, we will find the one who did this, and we will settle the score, little brother. Now you must rest. Go with Friederich. You have to be fine for the children when they return home."

I think Friederich and Heindrik more or less dragged me to my bedroom as I was still crying like a baby. I hated him more than ever.

* * *

Ferdinand von Kleist's Diary
May 21st, 2008

Monday was one of the worst days of my life. At four in the morning, Konrad called me, hysterical, from Frankfurt, waking me up. He ordered me to gather a team of my absolute trust, and meet him at the airport at 8 a.m.

"What about your meeting? You can't miss it!" I protested.

"This is more serious. Do your work!" He hung up on me! I tried to be as quiet as possible not to wake up Cecilia, but she heard me. I had to tell her to go back to sleep, and that we had some issues with Japan. I hate lying to my own wife!

I called Goran. It's his job after all. He should be awake, not I. Konrad's plane landed a few minutes before eight, but he didn't come down from the aircraft. We had to go inside, letting the poor stewardess and the pilots pass beside us as they were escaping from him.

We entered and sat in front of him. He said nothing, just turned around his computer and showed us what was on the screen.

I don't think I will ever forget that gruesome picture and the others he showed us later. How can be people who enjoy such things is beyond me. Firing squad is too kind for them. They should be left alone with Goran's men for a week. That would be suitable. Goran looked as upset as I.

Those were his children.

As a father I felt truly bad for Konrad. That was a blow below the belt. Whoever did it deserved what we were going to do, and at that point I had already some ideas. Goran could supply more, I'm sure.

"How?" I asked.

"Stefania came to me last night from Zurich, she was crying, telling me somebody sent the pictures to her E-mail account, the one she has for her fans. She couldn't believe it. They were on a website for perverts. The name of the pervert who uploaded them was "nanny sex" from Zurich."

"How did this anonymous source know they're your children, my Duke?" Goran asked. I couldn't believe it. He plays the police man now?

"They are announced as the children of a "noble banker" whose daddy likes to play with them, and I refuse to go further! Read the damn webpage!" he roared.

"I will, my Duke."

"He did it and I'm going to kill him for that. That is his revenge for his family. To destroy my own boys. I will kill him," he said with that intensity that precedes the worse storms.

"Guntram? No way Konrad, that's ridiculous. We all know him. He lives with you since six years!"

"So what? You know perfectly well he blames me for his stupid father's death! He planned all this to ruin their lives!"

"Konrad, I swear we will go thoroughly over this, but calm down and think before you do anything. Where is Guntram now?"

"At home, getting my boys ready for school." Konrad said. "Shit! On Saturday, Klaus wanted to go to sleep to his bed, and cried a lot because that bastard didn't let him do it," he said taking his head with both hands. I was feeling worse. Goran, on the other hand, was looking at the things.

"That makes no sense, my Duke. No paedophile would miss such an opportunity," Goran mumbled from his corner, still looking at the computer.

"Turn that off!" I shouted him.

"I will get to the bottom of this, but methodically. Or do you prefer to involve the police?" This man has no blood in his veins. He kills like you would open a frog in a lab; the worst kind of killer. He reminds me Zaitzev, a sniper in Stalingrad. More than fifty Germans killed in less than ten days and he never regretted a single thing.

"No. I will call Schwelm. He's very good and discreet. He should check the material, and Guntram's computer. After all, he has always made mirror copies of the boy's material. If his computer was also tampered, he should have the originals."

"Do you doubt my word? Heindrik was there also! He's still vomiting!" Konrad shouted Goran.

"Heindrik has no stomach for this job." Goran told us. "He should be behind a desk with Alexei holding his hand."

"Goran be quiet!" I shouted.

"I'll call Schwelm. Can you drive with the Duke to the house Ferdinand? I want to do some things first with these files," Goran said taking Konrad's laptop without asking.

"I swear I'll kill him slowly," Konrad mumbled.

"And I'll help you if this is true. But now, we must think with a clear head. Perhaps Goran is right. I still don't understand why your wife got it. We must trace whoever sent it."

"Are you accusing Stefania of something like that?"

"Of course not, I'm shocked she got this."

"The poor woman was hysterical. She was crying like crazy. She had to take several pills to sleep. No woman should ever see something like that."

She got this and left the children alone with the monster? It didn't feel the right thing to do. A normal woman would have called her husband home, and never leave the babies alone. I kept my mouth shut.

"Could it be a set up? When could he have done something like this? There's another nanny with him all the time, not to mention all the servants and security cameras. The place doesn't even look like the castle and he never goes alone anywhere. Milan or Ratko are with him on a permanent basis."

"Our enemies know perfectly well our resources. They wouldn't do something so stupid like that. We can discover the truth within hours," Konrad said looking at me.

"Not if we are so shocked that we act before we think. This thing can drive a man crazy. I would put a bullet on his head without hesitation. Is Guntram still Guardian of the Estate in case of your death?" I asked.

"Yes, I will remove it as soon as we get rid of him."

"I see." This boy has seventeen billion reasons to be hated. He has nothing else. No money, no friends, no enemies, except the ones he got for transitive character from Konrad. Perhaps Moncenigo is furious and wants his blood for not catching Konrad, but on the other hand, he got the Milan Office direction. The boy never interfered in the Order's affairs, and has always been loyal to us. The question is who would benefit from getting rid of Guntram. Albert? Stefania? Gertrud? Georg? I wouldn't know.

We went to the house to find it empty. Of course, the children were in school. Konrad caught the nanny, Lisette, and ordered her to go to the library. He took Guntram's laptop from his desk and went after the woman with it. That poor girl was trembling from fear. Not that I blame her, Konrad was about to explode.

The computer had no password of any kind. Strange. We both started to look, mostly were his works from the University, his thesis, E-mails from his school friends mostly related to works, some photos of the children in the garden, all of them sent to Konrad by mail, obviously made with a mobile phone. A lot of pictures from Guntram's works and many details of them, the prints for the book and some new ones but nothing more. His diary. His internet history was saved from ten days ago and there was nothing there.

"It can't be," Konrad said.

"We didn't look at "my images" folder. I said, relieved to no end.

"He can't be so idiotic. We wait for Schwelm."

"Humour me," I looked there and there was a folder, "love," I opened thinking there were old things from his time with Konrad but there were hundreds of photos of that kind. I wanted to throw up again. Konrad jumped from his seat, and cornered the woman who lost all colours when she saw the hideous things.

"How could you? You were supposed to take care of them and you let him do it!" He screamed pushing her against the wall. I had to jump to control him before he would kill her. She was sobbing something in French.

"I don't know Sire. I have nothing to do!"

"De Lisle. Did he touch my boys?"

"I don't know. He always wants to dress and bathe the children! Men don't do such things!" She cried hysterically when she took another look at the pictures.

I felt my anger boil. I was going to skin the little prick alive. Slowly. That stupid cow escaped when Goran entered the room with Schwelm and Friederich.

"Konrad, can you explain me why are you mistreating the staff?" Friederich asked with the same tone he used when we were children and into some mischief.

"Guntram abused my children! Look at his computer. He's a pervert of the worse kind!"

"I will not look at such offensive material. I know Guntram very well and he would never do something like this. I'm ashamed that you think he can. Think before you cry like a woman! Didn't I teach you better? Ferdinand, do you believe these allegations too?" Friederich scolded us.

"Get out of here Friederich!" Konrad shouted and the man left the room totally furious, like I've never seen him before.

"My Duke, Schwelm is here, he can check this thing. He brought the old mirrors he has from Guntram's computer," Goran said, bringing the man along.

"There's nothing to check. It's all very clear."

"Please Sir, we have to do it."

"Do whatever you want Pavicevic. See what kind of monster your protégée is."

"I will punish him myself Sire if this is true. Schwelm, proceed now."

The man started to look at the boy's computer and to his own laptop. He forgot that we were there.

Guntram had the misfortune to come there in that particular moment when Konrad was still furious and demanding blood. He hit the boy really hard and threatened to kill him, slow and painfully. Heindrik, on the other side, nearly broke his arm when he took him away. I was really hoping he wouldn't do anything to the boy.

All I could think was that Guntram is a good person, bordering on a total idiot sometimes because you can sell him almost anything with a teary story, look how he bought all Konrad's lies for over four years! We know real paedophiles and you almost immediately realise there's something wrong with them. It's just a matter of time you discover their secret. Guntram doesn't fit the profile.

Konrad shouted permanently that it was revenge against him. Goran was silent, the tech also, deeply engulfed in his work, and I was thinking who could have done it and how. Guntram wouldn't be so stupid as to have something like this here if he were into this. He knows everything from him is monitored. His E-mails are checked on a daily basis and he goes everywhere with Milan or Ratko.

"Everything is clean, Sire," Schwelm announced us.

"Explain," Konrad ordered him.

"Those pictures were not originated here. He has not even the software to do it. I will need more time to find the IP where they were done, but I think it would be possible to do it. It's not a professional work. My last mirror copy of de Lisle's PC is four days old. There's nothing of this. I thought perhaps he might have done it in the last week but there's nothing. I found also a back-door created three days ago. Clumsy work. I think somebody planted those images there. With your permission I will look at the pictures his Excellency gave me first. I think they're manipulated also. It might take some time."

"Do it."

Schwelm took more than three hours to check everything. I had to leave the room to make some phone calls to excuse Konrad from not showing up in the meetings and check how everything was going. Goran, on the other hand, disappeared with Ratko and Milan, perhaps to check what the boy had been doing and who he had seen. I know those two report everything to him. Konrad only called Elisabetta to ask her to take care of the children for the night, and ordered Friederich to prepare a bag with their clothes for the night. The rest of the time he sat by a window, not speaking.

I was very concerned for him. To find out that the person who you love more than anything, fucked your children in revenge is horrible. Like those fathers who kill their sons to make the wife suffer. It kills your soul.

Nevertheless, I wouldn't like to be in Konrad's place if all the things he accused Guntram of, were a lie. This boy has every right to kill him slowly. Guntram put up with a lot from you Konrad, only for your children's sake, and now you accuse him of this, without even giving him the chance to defend himself. The only one who was fair to the lad was Goran. He risked his neck for the boy. Not even I, who swore to protect him, did it.

I'm also a piece of shit like Konrad.

No, Friederich also sided with Guntram. He also thought before opening his mouth. Lord! I'm the second in command, and I was behaving like a woman? This is unacceptable!

When did we become so girlish?

"It's Photoshop. The ones from Lee Harvey Oswald were better done than these ones."

"Are you certain?" Konrad asked from his seat.

"A hundred percent, Sire. All fake, not the others of course, but he didn't do it. All was planted. I'm certain the back-door was created by infecting his PC manually. With your permission I can try to trace the origin of the mail the Duchess received, but it will take some time, and I might need to take physically away her laptop, and make some alterations to her web page's server."

"Start to work in the office. You will have her computer by tomorrow morning. Thank you for your efforts. I will not forget this, Schwelm."

"Schwelm, this remains in this room. I don't want de Lisle's reputation ruined on a gossip," Goran said.

"Of course, Mr. Pavicevic. I'll say nothing. De Lisle is a good person. I know him from the bank."

He picked up all his things and left Guntram's there, with the offending pictures. I'll ask him to clean the hard disk tomorrow. No, replacing the thing would be the best.

"We have to apologise to the *Dachs*," I said very relieved. If he would have been guilty, I would have to question many things in my life.

"I want to be sure he has nothing to do with this."

"You heard the man! Do you think he would lie? You're perfectly aware he used to work in Vice before joining us. He's the watchdog over all our men!" I was desperate. He couldn't be such a pig head! He screwed it up, big time, and he still doesn't believe it. He should go on his knees and beg for forgiveness.

No, the most decent thing to do would be to leave the boy alone; let him go away before he kills him of a heart attack or strangles him like Friederich told me he did some time ago. Guntram doesn't deserve such fate. Konrad never deserved to have a boy like him. Stefania is the perfect snake for him.

The poor lad lost it when he saw the pictures. I was afraid he would get the final heart attack right there. Konrad is a bastard for doing something like this. He knows Guntram loves the children as if they were his own. He practically lives for them, and the children love him unconditionally. They run to him every time they see him. My children never ran to me like that. In many ways, he's better than a mother. Goran swore to kill the one(s) who did this, and I will help him if he lets me.

After Guntram shot Konrad, he collapsed and started to cry. I'm glad Goran was there because he could control the boy till Friederich took him to his bedroom.

We were left alone in the room and Goran decided to go back to Zurich. I think, even he had enough for one day. Twenty minutes later, a real furious Friederich entered the room, unannounced.

"I've called Dr. Wagemann. I hope you're now proud of your deeds." Friederich informed us, looking at Konrad with contempt. "Do not judge, and you will not be judged; and do not condemn, and you will not be condemned; pardon, and you will be pardoned. Luke 6:37" Do you remember it?"

"I do Friederich. I lost my mind when I saw the pictures on his computer. I have ruined everything I've built over the last two years. He must really hate me by now."

"He can't stop crying. I hope the doctor sedates him before we have to take him to a hospital. He's heartbroken that you believed, even for a second, that he would commit such an unspeakable act with his own sons! You gave them to him and now you take them away from him? Is there no end for your meanness?"

"Friederich understand our positions as parents. You have no children. This is something that touches our most inner fibres," I defended Konrad.

"Is that your excuse for ruining a good and decent man's life, von Kleist? Will you repeat it in front of Christ so proudly like you do now? Do you always make your decisions like today? Running after the first thing you see, like a child? Then, you're not worthy of your positions. God's voice is our common sense, but you two are deaf since a long time ago," he scolded us and left the library.

"Konrad, regrets will not fix this problem. We need to find who did it. The person who designed such an attack against Guntram will do it again and next time, it will be more virulent."

"I nearly killed him. If Goran wouldn't have been here or checked with this man, I would have killed him," he whispered, sounding desperate. Now, I think he understood what he did today.

"But you didn't. Now we have to focus on how to solve it and contain the damages. That crazy nanny practically accused him without proofs. We have to get rid of her."

"Don't you get it, Ferdinand? I nearly killed the only good thing in my life! I wouldn't have my sons without him! I've hurt him, pushed him to his limits and he can't even shoot me dead."

"Bad aiming, Konrad."

"No, he shoots better than I or Heindrik. You have never seen him shooting.

He's very good, but he can't shoot an animal."

"There you have your answer. He can't shoot an animal," I tried to joke.

"No, even after all we went through, even if he blames me for his father's death, he still loves me. I have to find a way to get him back to my side before this tension kills him."

"Konrad, he hates you! You heard him!" Not again please.

"No, he doesn't hate me. He despises me, he feels nothing for me. If he would hate me, it would be easier to get him back. I have to force him to remember what we had. He has to forget that bloody family of his. They never wanted him in the first place! He's mine. What should I do? Let him go back to a Third World Country to help the beggarly people so he doesn't feel he's more miserable than them?"

"Konrad, give up. Let the lad live his own life if you love him so much."

"I can't, he's mine. I don't care if I have to force him a little like I had to do in Venice. He needs a firm hand sometimes. I let him run wild for the last two years and look now. I'm married to a slut who loves my money; he's the unhappiest person in the world, consumed by hatred, lying to himself like he used to do when I met him, and I'm on the brink of madness. This has to stop."

"Konrad do nothing we can regret later. Leave Guntram alone!" I shouted.

"I will divorce Stefania. I had enough of her. Guntram is not jealous of her. I'm certain she devised this horrible charade to get full control of my money. She'd better pray Schwelm finds nothing that links her to this."

"Konrad, she's a stupid TV slut; nothing else. For doing something like this, you need enormous resources she doesn't have. I think somebody tricked her into driving you mad, and she tried to get a part of it too. Before Guntram entered your life, there were many people mentioned in your will that have disappeared from it now. My former wife already planned and executed two attacks on him. The first one almost killed him; for the second, she trusted you to do her dirty job. Your mother would cut herself an arm so you would be hurt, especially after what you did to her husband last December. Lots of people are angry with you for your performance during the crash. How many associates did you put out of the game this time? How many more will you destroy before all this is over? Perhaps Repin had enough and decided to terminate you. How about Albert? His sons had an inheritance of over five billion, and now they have nothing, only the promise for one of them becoming Griffin, and accounts for 300 million; nothing that can be compared to before. Should I continue with the list?"

"No. I want to check on Guntram. The doctor must have finished by now."

"I'll go with you."

We went upstairs to the nursery. I remember this place. We used to play here. Many times we tried to grab the cherries from the tree, almost breaking our necks in the process. It was Albert's idea. We used to have a Märklin train for rainy days. For a minute, I wondered what had become of it. Konrad was always trying to smuggle a Rotweiller in here, but Friederich would always catch him. Guntram's bedroom used to be Friederich's and where he keeps his paints, his studio.

Friederich was standing at the lad's door. "The doctor had to give him a very strong sedative. He's with him now. He needs to sleep. Do not disturb him, Konrad."

"I only want to speak with the doctor, Friederich." He sounded really mousy. For all our sakes, we should name Friederich Elsässer honorary president. Not even

596

the old Duke or Löwenstein could put Konrad in his place when necessary. The man can still do it with me, without shouting or anything.

"Wait for him here," Friederich ordered him like only he can do it before he returned to the lad's bedroom.

The doctor came a few minutes later out. He said that Guntram had a nervous breakdown, but his heart condition was stable. It should, after all what Van Horn is stuffing him with. He should go tomorrow to the Clinic for further evaluation, but in the moment, he needed to sleep. The sedation would last till the next morning. Konrad ordered Friederich to show the doctor out, and he was not happy at all.

We both entered the room as I didn't trust Konrad at all. Guntram was sound asleep in his bed with Heindrik sitting miserably at his side. He jumped to attention when he saw us, and left the room without being asked. I think, he also feels horribly about this. We all do.

Konrad sat on the bed, and bent to caress the boy's face, removing the hair from his forehead. "He's everything I have, Ferdinand. Why can't I keep my cold blood around him?"

"Konrad, I was willing to kill him, and I love him like one of my own boys. Whoever did this, knows that any father would react first and ask later. Now, we have to focus in discovering the culprits and make them pay."

"I have to reorganize my life, this is not good for him nor for me. It will finally catch up with our children. This game he's playing is killing us both. I have to get rid of her first, and get him back with me, even if he still clings to his stubbornness. I will show him his place again," Konrad said and kissed the boy on his forehead. I don't think Guntram would be happy about it.

He rose from the bed and told me. "Do you want to stay for dinner?"

"Depends. Does Alexei's boyfriend cook?"

"I suppose."

"Then I'll stay. I'll call Cecilia. I was thinking. We can't get rid of the nanny so far. We need somebody to take care of the children till Guntram feels better."

"You're right, but I will speak with that idiotic cow. Why did she say that he always insists in bathing them? When we were in Sylt, both boys didn't want her near them and the two or three times she tried, they soaked her. Everything looks so well staged, Ferdinand."

"She's just a servant girl. They can't be too clever, if not, they wouldn't be maids. Be nice or you'll find yourself cleaning after the boys."

"I will put her in her place. I don't want her spreading lies. You do the same with Heindrik."

"It's done. We eat at eight?"

"Of course, see you."

We didn't eat at eight. Stefania returned at quarter to eight to my dismay. Why didn't she stay in Frankfurt or went somewhere else, like Paris or Milan? I don't think for a minute she had a "mother hen" strike, and decided to take care of the little ones. She's not like my Cecilia, who would be a fantastic mother.

That woman, (I know Alexei calls her "Baba Yaga", Goran and Michael prefer "the bitch", Guntram goes for "witch" and I prefer "slut" or "she devil"), went directly to Konrad's studio, where we both were working in peace, trying to catch up all the lost time with today's disaster.

"Has the police taken him away?" she shouted. I stood up, but Konrad remained seated. Bad sign for you woman, now you're in the "sluts category"; he treats his maids better than his whores.

"Of course not. It was a hoax, Stefania. He never did a single thing to my sons."

"How can you say that? You saw the pictures and the letter! If one of my fans knows it, I most probably will have to issue a press release before it reaches to the press! I have a reputation to take care of!"

"Yes dear, my children are fine at my aunt's residence. Thank you for asking," he said very sarcastically.

"Konrad, this man is a pervert! He took those photos! He must have hundreds. He must travel to Thailand every year!"

"Guntram has never been in Thailand. In fact, he threw up over your new carpet when he saw them. He had a nervous breakdown and needed to be sedated."

"It's an act! Get rid of him! Call the police. They should investigate his things!"

"We already did it, darling. One of my best software persons did it. You see, he makes copies of de Lisle's private files every week. There's nothing in the security cameras, the photos you showed me were manipulated, and the ones we found in his laptop were planted three or four days ago. I don't remember well; should be in his final report."

"You make copies of his computer? Why would you do that?"

"Industrial espionage. I can't be sure of anybody. Now, I will need your own laptop so my technicians can trace the origin of the E-mail you received. They're already working on your webpage. Should take a few days till they find who originated it."

"I sent a copy to you!"

"It's something technical that I don't understand, but they need your laptop. Don't worry, they will return it in one piece."

"It's private and I need it for working! All my scripts are there. I have photos of the upcoming collections there! If something is filtered to the press, I'm dead," she said very agitated.

"They're used to working with sensitive information. They never lost a single file so far. "

"I have my personal files in there! This is a privacy invasion! I will not let you do it."

"The person who did this is deranged and has already targeted my sons. I'm going to find who did it with your cooperation or without it. It's your choice Stefania. Tomorrow, you will apologise to de Lisle for your little scandal and believing such blatant lies."

"I will not apologise to him! He's a pervert and I have to apologise? No, forget it!"

"He's clean of your allegations, like always. Don't make me choose between my boys and you."

"He's not qualified to be a teacher. He's not even a good painter! How can you have him here? Don't tell me about your promise to his father because this is rubbish! He could control your fortune in case of your death!"

"He will do anything for my sons and he's immune to corruption, no matter what you think. Someone tried to disgrace him and almost succeeded. I will not change my view toward him. If he still wants, he can keep his job. By the way, the doctor recommended absolute bed rest for two days. You will have to take care of Karl and Klaus as I have to return to Frankfurt tomorrow morning to continue with what you interrupted."

She slammed the door. That was rude.

"That bitch did it. I'm sure now. I only need to prove it. Tell Goran to check everything she has and all her relations. I can't believe she dragged me to a brothel's fight level. Does she think I'm one of her producers or another daytime TV show hostess you can ruin by destroying her reputation?"

I could have said this is what you get for taking one from there, that she nearly succeeded, that you behaved like a hysterical little girl or something like that, but I kept myself quiet. I'm so grateful my Cecilia is a real lady, not like this one. I still don't know why he discarded that very nice woman from Sweden, a third degree cousin from Holgersen. She would have known how to behave. I still have my doubts she's from the Barberini's.

It would be good to get rid of her. The lawyers should not have many problems with it. The prenuptial agreement was very clear and auspicious to us.

"Ferdinand?"

"Yes, what?"

"Let Goran run free over this business. Don't interfere. He will know what to do."

Chapter 15

May 25th, 2008

Today, I returned to my duties full time. Klaus and Karl came back from Elisabetta's house the next day after the disaster. They were in the school in the morning and Milan and Lissette picked them up in the afternoon. Lisette still looks at me very cross and I don't blame her. I can't get from my mind the pictures I saw and she also did it. It's something that touches you in your inner core. You can't reason any more.

I should be furious at Lintorff for what he has done, but I can't. I would have done the same if I've gotten the pictures and somebody would have told me he took them. I'm disappointed that he would believe I was capable of such things for revenge. I never did anything to him before the shooting, and I still don't know why I did it. It wasn't me that day.

Friederich monitored our "peace agreement". He apologized to me and I did the same. He sounded truly ashamed of his deeds. I can't say I was ashamed, but I was not happy altogether. I asked for his forgiveness and we continued with our lives, ignoring each other even more than ever before.

Before he was dead to me. Why should it change now? I only want to do my job and be left alone.

It was totally unnecessary to make the Duchess apologise to me. I can imagine her shock when she saw the things. Poor woman even if she's a cunning witch. She called me to her office and said that she was sorry for how things turned out, that Duke believed in my innocence, but she couldn't still let everything go without having a bad feeling. She would monitor my work from now on much closer than before. Also, Lisette would be giving the orders, not I. Honestly, I'm glad I'm removed from such stress. I'm very tired and totally depressed. I spent the two free days I got from the doctor, painting alone in my studio the children and their father's portrait. It's almost finished. I didn't dare to go downstairs with the other staff members.

Jean Jacques finally got me out of my room. "If my soufflé is ruined because I was waiting for you, I swear you'll eat borscht till the next Ice Age. Come and eat with me. Two French can shut a bossy German up."

"He's Austrian, from Salzburg, and you're more than able to do it all alone."

"It's the same. Come now or I'll send Alexei to fetch you."

"I'm so ashamed my friend. I don't know why. I didn't do anything, but I feel horrible."

"That is because you're an honest person who got caught in real shit. You feel dirty from what touched you, but think on the lotus flower. They grow in the mud, but they're never stained. Show some pride to those whispering idle women. One of your cold stares and they will run away like rats."

"I have no cold stare," I protested.

"Ask the Duke, my dear. Ask the Duke," he snorted.

Not happy at all, I went downstairs and Friederich greeted me very kindly along with the other bodyguards. Heindrik was there and gave me a hug. I gave him a light punch on the shoulder, and he complained like the posh boy he is. I ate with Friederich, Jean Jacques and the bodyguards. Before finishing, Lisette had the bad idea of saying out loud, that she was going to bathe the children per direct orders from the Duchess. Everybody was silent and I could only hear my heartbeat pounding very fast.

"From tomorrow onward, starts your month's dismissal notice, Lisette. The same rule applies to anybody who ever makes another remark like that." Friederich said very slowly but clearly. "Those are his Excellency's direct orders. All of you will respect Mr. De Lisle as he outranks you and is a member of the family itself. His rank equals the Duchess."

"Let's hope not, as she's on a free fall," Jean Jacques commented.

I felt very bad when she started to cry. She was with us since the children were born! I don't care if she made a stupid remark. The only way to stop this was to speak with the devil himself.

The next morning, the 24th, I asked Friederich reconsider the lay off, but he didn't want to hear me. I asked him to speak with Lintorff, and he only replied that he was following his orders. I pleaded for the children as they like her. "I can arrange a meeting with the Duke, if you want," I nodded. Perhaps, Lintorff feels something akin to remorse from his accusations and would let Lisette stay.

I was astonished that he agreed to see me in the library almost an hour later after I spoke with Friederich. Doesn't he have to work? We're in the middle of a financial crisis like never before, and he sits around in the house?

He was working at the library, the desk full of papers and he had two laptops there. He was casually dressed, striped shirt, scarf and jacket, all in brown and grey shades. Strange.

"What is de Lisle?" He asked at me, already looking pissed off at my hesitation to speak.

"I would like that you reconsider the decision over Miss Theroux. The children appreciate her enormously, and she has been with us since they were born."

"I will not de authorise Friederich in front of his staff. He carried on my orders, and I trust you will do the same."

"With all due respect, the Duchess named her the principal caregiver for your sons, Sire. I'm not suitable for the position any longer."

"Nonsense. You're qualified for it. I want these snidely comments finished. All this was an unfortunate misunderstanding and we should leave it in the past. I don't want any of my servants spreading lies or rumours that later could hurt my children's reputation. Dismissed."

"As you wish, Duke," I turned around to leave the room, when the witch, well the Duchess, entered the room, looking absolutely furious.

"How could you lay off Lisette? How dare you to override my orders in the house? Get out, you. It's all your fault de Lisle!" She shouted at Lintorff first and then me.

"Madam," I bowed my head and moved to one side as she was going in a direct line toward Lintorff's desk.

"No, stay de Lisle. This concerns you also," Lintorff said. "Stefania, this is my house and those are my children. They are my responsibility as we clearly established since the beginning. This woman insulted my appointed tutor, and even contributed to the scandal by saying that "he always wants to bathe the children or dress them." A very strange sentence, if you want to know Stefania."

"Sire, I do it because Klaus and Karl don't want anybody else to do it..."

"Don't interrupt me de Lisle!" He shut me off, sharply. I could feel the witch gloating at my scold. "When we were in Rome, during our last holiday, she proved her incompetence as she couldn't handle the twins for simple things like bathing them or making them eat their dinners. De Lisle does it without problems, and he has no "special qualifications" like she does. If I tolerated her all this time, it was because my sons liked her, but it's over. I don't want women gossiping at my back, and the same goes for you Stefania," I blanched at his words. She looked at him, furious.

"This press release you wanted to issue about this situation, putting my children's name in your web page, is unacceptable. It has been deleted and I hope I never have to act against you because of something like this. You should be grateful de Lisle didn't read it, because if he would have released his lawyers against you for defamation, you would be paying him several millions and facing jail. Writing his name down was very stupid, woman."

I was speechless and wanted to leave the room as soon as possible.

"He's nothing. Didn't you see all those things in his own computer? Lisette saw them before all this exploded. Perhaps she wrote the anonymous letter!"

"I never had anything like that, you lying bitch!" I roared, regretting my outburst less than a second later. Lintorff rose from his chair and came to me and crossed my face with a strong slap, like the ones I used to get at the beginning of our relationship for "misbehaving" (like answering wrong to him or not moving fast enough). My cheek burned from the humiliation more than from the pain. It was nothing, compared to what I got the last time.

"Shame on you, insulting a woman. I thought you had learned better," he spat, contemptuously. Again I could see that she was more than happy. What is your problem with me woman? I've done nothing to you. Even saved your stupid marriage

"Please accept my apologies my Duchess," I said meekly.

"I accept them, but you must understand that after this it's impossible for me to have you in my service."

"Yes, Madam," I mumbled.

"But it's all right by me. As I said, the children belong to me Stefania. Don't interfere. Dismissed de Lisle."

I was not even able to look at him any more. I bowed my head again to her and left the room, closing the door. I could heard her shouting "Fire him!"

"No. He stays. I will show him his place in this house soon."

* * *

May 27th, 2008

Lisette didn't want to cope any longer with the situation and left this morning. Klaus and Karl's crying was very hard for me. I took them late to school as I couldn't calm them down before. After offering my excuses to the principal and explain her the situation, I went to *Meister* Ostermann's studio to have a little peace.

To let me have him again as my manager was the "peace offering," I got from Lintorff. Something good came out of this shit.

"Well, the prodigal son returns," he greeted me. "Start to recover the lost time, Guntram."

"I need some time to think. If you don't mind," I said very quietly.

"Come to my office. We'll speak. You look bad."

We went there and I spilled the whole story to him. He was shocked, not believing that someone could have thought that I was doing something like that. He was very glad that I could prove that nothing was true.

"I don't understand why. I have no enemies and my relationship with Lintorff is finished. She wants me out and I would love to comply with her wishes..." My mobile phone started to ring furiously. It was Lintorff.

"Yes, Sire?"

"Why did you take two hours to get the children to school? Stefania just called me about your delay," he barked at me.

"It only took the usual thirty minutes. I was trying to calm them down because Lisette was going away. They were crying so much that they couldn't be taken to school. Bregovic was with me all the time. He didn't want them vomiting inside the car," I explained, feeling very hurt that he had again believed that woman's slanders. He hung up on me, probably to check with Bregovic my story.

"What was that?"

"The Duke. His wife told him I kept the children who knows for what reason for two hours instead of taking them to school. The nanny was fired and they were crying like crazy. I had to appease them before driving. The bodyguard didn't want them in the car because they tend to vomit if they're too upset. They did it twice over the Duchess."

"Sensible little fellows. Guntram, are you still the Guardian of the Estate?"

"Yes, of course."

"Do you want to manage all this money? I can understand that she hates you because of it. In case of the Duke's death, you will manage fifty percent of his fortune."

"No, all of it. He married her keeping his properties and futures earnings out of the marital society. They have a prenuptial agreement and she will get a life pension of ten million per year if he dies. She has no access to the children's wealth."

"Think if you want to fight in the courtrooms for years with her. She can claim her rightful part of the inheritance. Fifty percent of all the money he has made from his marriage onward."

"You're right. I'm not even qualified for it. I will speak with Lefebvre to see if there's a way to nullify this. I wouldn't know what to do."

"I can always help you to spend it," he joked.

"Not even you could spend it," I laughed. "But I will not risk it because you might try to prove me wrong," he chortled, going back to the studio.

I spent the rest of the day, working on some plates for the new book, in a table near a window, getting now and them a praise from another student (or a kiss on the cheek). Ostermann's once told me that with me around, it would be impossible for him to get a rich wife. Women melt at me and they don't look at him any more. So he has to be my manager and I have to support him in his old age.

603

"I would like to be a child again," Ostermann murmured. "This one for the Bremen Musicians is very nice. Why don't you eat a sandwich with me? The witches are out till three."

We had lunch together and spoke a little about the next book. I returned to work on the Frog King, detailing the princess dress. At four he kicked me out as I had to pick up the kids from school.

Milan instead of Ratko took me to the school and both kids were happy to see me and behaved very well. They took tea in the garden and started to chase at each other, with Mopsi barking after then. One of the maids came out and told me, that her Excellency was having a headache and I should get the children away. I decided to take them to the small orchard to pick up some strawberries for their dinner. They became very dirty, but nothing that a good bath couldn't fix. Both were very happy with their harvest and I took them to the kitchen to give the strawberries to Jean Jacques. He promised to make them something like a small cake for dinner.

When they were both very entertained looking at Jean Jacques' apprentice cutting some greens at an incredible speed, Friederich entered the kitchen and told me to go to the Duchess office. Excellent! He said he would take a look on the young princes.

She told me very upset, that I was an incompetent for not being able to keep the boys quiet; that they should not be doing "menial tasks like harvesting fruits; that's for the poor immigrants from the Maghreb or the gypsies; that the carpet in the library was ruined and she will collect it from my salary.

"Of course the Duchess can do anything she wants, but do you have the Duke's permission to do this? Fining the workers is a practice long forgotten and if I see correctly, illegal."

"I have the Duke's permission, of course. He supports my every decision. Now, return to your duties."

"Madam," I said, leaving the room.

Many things can be said about Lintorff, but he was never that mean to me or mentioned money issues in front of me. But he might have changed. He believes I'm a potential child molester.

* * *

June 2nd, 2008

Again, I was caught in the middle. Stupid me! When will I learn that the best is to disappear when those two are nearby?

Coco van Breda sent a private courier to pick up some of the drawings for the new book. I was giving the man the envelope, in the kitchen, when the witch appeared to control the dinner. She looked at me, with full venom in her eyes, but went for Jean Jacques.

"Last night, dinner was unacceptable. You should do better in the future," she said. I could feel the fury pouring out from the French Chef. His two helpers and the sous chef stopped working, looking like terrified rabbits.

"Perhaps, the Duchess could enlighten me about what is acceptable" He said in his best and politest voice. I know it. I heard it a few minutes before Alexei was thrown out of his own house for a full night for asking cheese for the pasta.

"Your style is very old and traditional. Perhaps it would suit at a bachelor's house, but for me is below today's standards. Maybe you should take a leave and study the new styles, like Adriá or Arzak."

"I studied under Jean Paul Bocuse. I won the Bocuse d'Or in 1989 and two Michelin Stars for the Königshalle. I was advisor for this film *Vatel* and I'm totally convinced that this new "molecular kitchen" is rubbish for the snobs!" he exploded.

"Don't you dare to speak to me like that!"

"I speak like I want. I quit. Tell the Duke to call the pizza service tonight! You wouldn't notice the difference," he said throwing his toque and white jacket to the floor. He slammed the door and she left the kitchen very furious.

That was very bad. You don't fuck with a man's dinner, especially with this one. Lintorff adores Jean Jacques cooking. He was almost eating every night at that Restaurant before the Alexei's mess, and he pays him more than he would make if he were Chef in a fine place. Nobody gets between him and his bloody *Rouladen* and that black truffle soup.

After the children's dinner (not bad, the sous chef is also good), Friederich told me the Duke wanted to see me at the library. I took a deep breath. Hungry and pissed off. Bad combination and he had decided to take it on me. I do hope Alexei works all his charm and diplomacy to convince Jean Jacques to return... or to open a restaurant ten minutes away from this house, with delivery if possible.

Both hyenas were in the library. I went in.

"Can you tell me your working hours de Lisle?" Lintorff barked at me.

"During the school period it's from 7 a.m. to 10 a.m. and from 2 p.m. to 10 p.m., sir," I replied.

"Why did your extra activities interfere today with your working hours? The Duchess affirms that you were receiving a private courier in this house. If you want to work outside this house, do it on your free time, de Lisle. From seven to ten you're working for us. Is that understood?

"Yes, Sire. It will not happen again," I replied almost breaking my jaw with the fury.

"I don't want outsiders in my house de Lisle. You work here, nothing else."

"Yes, sir."

"Dismissed."

The witch was literally glowing with satisfaction. Wait till he finds out his beloved cook is away.

Chapter 16

June 15th, 2008

This is too much. I can't stand that woman any longer. I don't care if she's the Duchess or not. She's a witch prodding a monster against me. On the June 6th, I brought the children home from school, and when we arrived to the house for their tea time, she was waiting at us... with three journalists from Marie Claire, Vogue or whatever; one of those fancy fashion magazines.

"There you are," she told me with an imperial tone as I was taking Klaus and Karl to the nursery. "Dress the children with something more appropriate, and bring them to the garden. We need to take some photos from them."

"Madam." She hates it, she wants to be called "Duchess or *Herzogin*. "With all due respect, I was not informed of a photo shooting today. The children are tired from the school and hungry."

"It's for an important magazine and Flavio himself will take the photos." Somebody please inform me who the heck is Flavio.

"His Excellency has not informed about any changes in his not showing the children to the press policy," I said, firmly and almost losing my temper. Fuck, if I let you use them as trained monkeys! I don't believe for a minute Lintorff allowed this. He hates the press, and they're minors.

"De Lisle your job is to clean those children and bring them back in twenty minutes," she ordered me sternly. Does this woman think I'm some kind of Jane Eyre with trousers?

"Madam, I'm the legal tutor of Klaus Maria and Karl Maria. Without their father's written authorization, I can't allow you to make commercial photos of them. The magazine needs a written permission to publish them and I will not sign it. If you have this paper signed by his Excellency, I will let you do it."

"I'm his wife. I have the right to do it!"

"I don't discuss your status, Madam, but legally you're not related to them. You have not adopted them or have any power of attorney over them. Till this is changed, I remain as the one ultimately responsible for their well being in case of the Duke's absence."

"Do you refuse to obey my commands?"

"You can't order this. If you want, I'll call the Duke's secretary, and she will ask him." Yeah, Monika told me he doesn't pick up the phone from you one out of three times.

"I will tell my husband of your impertinence. You're not qualified for this position!" she shouted very vulgarly. Well, now you show your true colours. I remained passively looking at her as Klaus clutched my leg and Karl started to lose his patience with the delay with his tea time.

"I want to eat!" Karl whined, putting the big eyes he does before he starts to cry.

"Excuse me, Madam, the children need to be changed and have their tea." I said not even bothering to wait for her to dismiss me. Klaus ran upstairs with his brother in tow. I went after them.

I had to fight a little to convince them to change themselves out of their school uniforms. The poor dears wanted to attack the food without more delays. Finally, I gave up and handed one cookie to each one as bribe for doing it. They went to their bedroom and started to dress. Klaus as usual threw everything on the floor.

"Klaus, nobody is going to pick up after your mess. Put the dirty clothes where they should go," I said and he obeyed without putting much of a fight; only whining a not so convinced "*Guntram!*"

"Why does she want to make photos of us?" Karl asked, curiously. He never misses a thing.

"They're for a magazine, but Papa didn't tell me in advance. When he agrees to it, we will make them."

"I want you to paint me." Klaus informed me with his determined voice.

"Dirty like you are? No… my brushes will be scared of you. Go and wash your face and hands and maybe I'll make a drawing for you… An elephant, perhaps?"

"I want a lion!"

"If he gets a lion, I want a giraffe!" Karl immediately shouted. "It's bigger," he said to his brother totally satisfied.

"But my lion can eat your giraffe!"

I sighed. This was going to be a long afternoon and I would have to take them to the forest to play as the Duchess was having a photo shooting in the garden. "I'll draw two rhinos and no more fighting."

"And two tigers!" That was Klaus.

"And two ant bears!" Karl always chooses strange looking animals.

"I'm not turning this house into a Zoo!" I said falsely shocked. "Besides, the tigers could eat the ant bears."

"You have to draw two cages for the tigers, Guntram." Klaus told me as if it were the most obvious thing in the world. I laughed, utterly defeated.

We were having tea after, Marie, one of the new maids, served it. When I started to fulfil my promise of the paints, after dressing each one of them with a plastic apron to save the clothes from the tempera, Friederich entered quickly in the room.

"May I speak with you in private?"

"Yes. One second," I stood up and had to promise I'd be back in no time to deliver what they wanted and they should start with the tiger's cages. Both complied.

We went outside the nursery and closed the door.

"What happened between the Duchess and you? She went out like crazy to see the Duke. She told me you insulted her."

"I didn't do such thing! Just told her she can't make photos of the children without the Duke's written authorization! I denied it as their legal tutor, too. She should adopt the children if she wants to play mother for the cameras."

"I only hope the Duke allows you to explain this, because this woman can make an enormous scandal out of the smallest thing."

"What will happen? Will he fire me again? I'm dying for it. The only reason I stay in this house and put up with him, is the children. However, he showed me already they're his and I can be thrown to the trash can whenever he feels like," I whispered, not willing to raise my voice. Those little ones have very big ears.

"Guntram I will not tell you what to do, but she's a Lintorff now and the Duchess. Konrad has always been on his family's side, and respects its concept. I don't need to remind you the dangers of losing his favour. Your position is very weak, child."

"Yes, I remember. A sedative and a strong poison since there's no life for me outside the Order. Who knows if that is still valid. I'm not the Consort any longer so the "not touching rule" does not apply any more. Or perhaps, he could also convince me to jump out of a window. Is that all, Friederich?"

"Don't cross him, Guntram. You will not like the consequences if you do. He's not so keen on you any more. He married Stefania de Barberini. She can play him very easily. He believed you hurt the boys! You're here because of the children's love for you."

"Friederich I appreciate your concern. I will speak with his Excellency when he returns," I said sternly, looking directly into his eyes. He sighed as all reply, and I went back to the babies.

* * *

After dinner at seven, I convinced them to go to bed at eight. When I was reading them a story, Lintorff entered the room, very serious.

"Leave us, de Lisle. Wait for me at my private studio," he ordered, using a total indifference voice.

"Of course, your Excellency," I said and left the room as the children started to complain to their father for interrupting the tale. He efficiently shut them up with one of his looks.

As ordered, I waited for him at his studio. The witch was nowhere to be seen or heard. It's been a long time since I was in this room. Six months if I'm right. Yes, since the night he announced his engagement. Nothing had changed much, and I noticed over his desk there was only a picture of the children, none of his wife. I looked around, and there, on the facing wall to his desk, was the painting I gave him so many years ago; the one with the stream at Torcello. He used to have it at his office at the bank, but now it was here. I suppose the Rubens drawing from one of his grandmothers is back in its place. I don't know why he didn't throw my one to the trash. Strange. There's nothing among us any more. There's no reason to keep it.

"Sit down de Lisle," he ordered me, going directly toward his chair behind the huge mahogany desk. I approached him and took one of the chairs in front of him, and waited for his shouting.

"I will not tolerate any disrespect toward the Duchess. It's disgusting when a man takes advantage of his position in front of a woman. I had enough of this situation. I have already told you the consequences of such behaviour. Monika will take care of everything."

"I was only fulfilling my duty, Sire," I said calmly. I might be out, but you will learn that again she made a fool out of you. Asshole. You can't control your own wife. "I would have appreciated if his Excellency would have communicated me in advance any changes on his policies regarding the children's well being."

He looked at me a bit shocked. What were you expecting? That I cry and ask for your forgiveness? That I humiliate myself to keep this shit of a "job"? That's over since a long time.

"Explain yourself."

"Since birth, the children have never been photographed for a magazine for security reasons. If this rule has been changed, Mr. Pavicevic should inform me in advance. I only asked the Duchess if she had your written permission to do so, as that is mandatory for any magazine wishing to publish children's pictures. In my role as legal tutor, I refused to sign any. If his Excellency is not satisfied with my actions, my resignation will be on his desk tomorrow morning."

For a minute, he seemed to lose all colours as if he were shocked.

"I understand the Duchess is their stepmother and in charge of the children now, especially after your latest show of lack of trust in me. I would like you to nullify all legal power you have invested in me regarding your sons. In case of your death, the logical option is her Excellency, not me."

"I'm afraid it's not so easy to do so, Guntram," he said softly.

"I've consulted with counsellor Lefebvre, and he thinks we can do it as a private agreement, and then register it. He has already prepared the papers so your lawyers can review them. I'll send the documents to Mrs. Dähler tomorrow."

"You promised to take care of the children and remain at their side! You can't do this to them! They'll suffer horribly!" he half shouted at me.

"The circumstances regarding the original promise have changed. You had no one else to take care of them. Now, you're married, and the best for all of us is that we start all over again. The children will overcome my departure. They're only four years old."

"I refuse to sign this!"

"I don't want to have the responsibility to fight for decades in the courts with your wife for your inheritance and their custody. As a sign of respect to your wife, you should sign these documents, and transfer these rights to her."

"Klaus and Karl are our children, Guntram. You can't abandon them. They love you like a father."

"No. They are your children. I was only allowed to play with them. In the last three months you made this perfectly clear for me. Since 2006, I'm nothing more than a tutor for them, and I have tried to keep it that way as much as I could."

"What would you do? Resign and go away? You are part of the Order. You can't walk away even if you want to. You're the Griffin's Consort."

"I was the Griffin's Consort, but fortunately his acts have released me from that duty. Stefania Barberini is the new Consort. This temporary cease of cohabitation is permanent now," I clarified. "Whatever happens with my life is my sole concern, Griffin."

"Your father gave you to me, and I swore to protect you."

"Before or after you killed my grandfather, my uncle's family and pushed him through the window?" I asked, now furious, lacing my voice with all the contempt I could. He flinched just a millimetre. I rose from my chair as I had enough of this.

"I haven't dismissed you yet," I growled. "I never enforced or ordered their punishment, and you know this. Your father didn't blame me for his death! You read his letter."

"I can imagine how this letter was written. Did you or one of your underlings put a weapon on his head? He was terrified you would kill me! He would have written anything. I don't believe a single line there referring to you!" I shouted now. "You are a disgusting monster that will burn for eternity."

"I'm already in Hell since you abandoned me," he whispered, letting his head fall into his left hand, the fingers pressing his eyes as if he were utterly tired and sad.

That would have worked a long time ago, Lintorff. Now, I know better as to buy your crocodile tears. "Would you not forgive me at least? I know you won't live with me as before, but some kindness from your part would lessen my punishment, Guntram. I'm only asking for a truce in whichever terms you decide. This silent war between us is killing me slow and painfully."

"The Duke has everything in his hands to start anew, a beautiful wife and two marvellous children. I, on the other hand, was not even allowed to go away, and rebuild my own life from the shambles. Sign the papers, accept my resignation, and we will be at peace," I said, rising from my chair.

I turned around, and slowly went to the door, but he was faster than me catching my right arm with a vicious grip, jerking me violently to face him again. I looked at him defiantly, and he held my regard. "I still love you," he whispered again pulling my body closer to his own.

I disentangled my arm from his grip with a sudden and hard pull, I shoved his chest with my hands. He didn't faltered an inch, and fast as the snake he is, caught my wrists with his hands, squeezing them to the point I heard a sickening crack coming from them. He crossed my arms behind my back, efficiently trapping me as he plastered his body against mine. I tried to squirm, but the second I did it, I felt a hot pain on my armpits as he increased his applied force to stop any rebellion against him. I was helpless, again trapped in his hold, and I swear, he was enjoying it.

To my utter horror and disgust, his lips touched mine as he kissed me, forcing my neck to bend backwards as he deepened his kiss. I closed my lips as firm as I could, but he let go of them and chomped on my neck, almost biting me. It drove me crazy and I tried to give him a full header, but he pushed his weight against me and I lost my balance.

We both fell heavily on the wooden floor with him on top of me, almost suffocating me. He sat on top of my pelvis and tried to catch my wrists again before I could mount a defence against him. He immobilized my right arm while I made an effort to hit him on the face with my left hand, still free. Again, he captured it and efficiently immobilized me. He bent his head to kiss me again and I moved away my head as much as I could, trying to avoid his touch.

"Get off, you piece of shit."

"There's no way you can win this. I've tolerated long enough your rebellious nature. It's time you remember to whom you belong to," he growled as I froze upon hearing his words. Exactly like what he said in Buenos Aires, that horrible night when he decided to punish me for leaving him. I lifted my gaze towards his eyes, and I saw that determined expression he bears when he has decided something. The same he had when he "spoke" with Fortingeray or when he went away with his men to "settle the score" with the poor devils who attacked me years ago. I panicked, and I couldn't even find my voice to yell when he violently tore my tie and broke the first buttons on my shirt.

"Don't fight and you might not get bruised... too much."

Even as my vision started to be clouded, and my heart beat painfully like crazy, I tried to kick him once more, but the powerful blow I got from him nearly knocked me out. I ceased all fighting as I felt the blood from my nose dripping across my cheek. The pain on my left side intensified, and I had to suppress the urge to vomit as his hands started to undo my belt. I closed my eyes, not only to evade the reality, but to stop the room from moving around so fast.

"Konrad, please, my heart hurts," I whispered my plead, not really expecting he would stop.

He let go of my hands immediately, and removed his body from mine. I tried to sit and stand to escape, but the dizziness and pain were too strong. I buried my head in my knees, taking deep breaths in an attempt to calm myself, but it was useless.

"Where are your pills?" he asked me as he searched through the pockets of my crumpled jacket.

"In my room," I whispered feeling really bad now, closing my eyes because the dark spots I was seeing made me dizzier than before. I heard him swearing in German, and rising to go to his desk and pull a drawer violently open.

He knelt beside me and forced my jaw open and I felt the bitter taste of the pill for the high blood pressure. I started to suck it slowly as I was told to do. His arms encircled my body and he pulled me against his chest, slightly rocking me with a soothing movement. One of his hands caressed my face softly and nervously.

"What have I done? What have I done?" he said, repeating this sentence several times as his hand comforted me automatically touching me. I rested my head on his shoulder and closed my eyes as my body started to feel more and more heavy.

* * *

The sunlight woke me up in my own bedroom. It should be late as it was shinning brightly. I sat on my bed, feeling very weak and dizzy. I had no idea how I got here and why I was dressed in my pyjamas. I didn't remember putting them on. I looked at my bedside table to find it full of medications, several of them were new. I left the bed, went to my bathroom and washed my face. My left shoulder was hurting a bit and I noticed my wrists started to have that red blueish colour from the bruises. Also my left cheekbone had a large one. This one would be very difficult to explain to the children, if I ever see them again. Blaming the bathroom door could work, but the wrists part would be harder. Long sleeve shirts in the middle of June will have to do the trick. I had to suppress a soft cry of pain when I tried to rotate the right one. No drawing for some time too. I decided to return to the bed, shocked by the silence in the house. There was no school today, and Karl and Klaus should be playing in the garden.

I laid down, feeling very tired after only walking a few steps. I must have dozed because Friederich woke me up by lightly shaking me by the shoulder.

"Good afternoon, Guntram. Wake up, you need to eat something before Milan takes you to the *Hirschbaum Klinik*. Dr. Van Horn would like to make some tests on you to asses your condition better. You gave us quite a fright yesterday, child," he said in a very kind voice.

"I don't remember much."

"You argued with his Excellency and fainted. He brought you to your room and called Dr. Wagemann. He says you had a strong cardiac episode, and you need to rest for a week at least. He has left you several prescriptions, and you should feel better in no time."

"I see. Did he bring me here?"

"Yes, he was very concerned and stayed till the doctor left the house. He gave orders that you should not be disturbed under any circumstance. He helped me to remove your clothes," I felt very sick at that. I suppose Lintorff doesn't want to explain why the children's tutor had a heart attack in his studio with half of his clothes off.

"I haven't heard the children. Where are they?"

"The Duke informed them of your illness and took them for a week to Sylt. He will return on the 15th. Taking care of the little ones might be too much for you in the moment." Great, now the witch will hate me more for not being able to work and condemning her to a full week in the seagulls' company.

"I imagine the Duchess must be really upset now. The Sylt's house is far away from any entertainment."

"The Duchess is in Paris. Their Excellencies had a huge fight yesterday night after the doctor went away. Even the children were awaken by their shouting."

"Is she all right?" I asked fearfully. I know how a fight with him can end.

"Yes, don't worry Guntram. The Duke only shouted with her for misleading him. He would never hit a woman. He asked me to give you this letter. Excuse me, I'll go for your lunch," he said as he put out from his jacket's pocket and envelope and gave it to me.

"I'll go downstairs, Friederich. Don't trouble yourself," I said looking raptly at the family's coat of arms on the backside. It wasn't closed.

"You should rest as much as possible. Doctor's orders. Not moving much around, and no excitement at all," he answered me as he closed the door. I know better than to argue with him.

I took a deep breath. It couldn't be so bad if the envelope was not closed, so Friederich could approve it before giving it to me. Yes, whenever Lintorff makes rubbish, he runs to his old tutor for advice. Friederich knows much more than he tells. It's fortunate that he appreciates me like he does. I opened the letter and put out the fine paper, with his name and coat of arms engraved on the top. It was written with his elegant and thin handwriting.

"My beloved,

There's no excuse for my behaviour last night. I attacked you when I should have thanked you for defending our children's sake. Please, send the documents you want me to sign to Monika. I'll do it. I hope you can forgive me one day, Konrad"

Shit. Shit and more shit. He still calls me "beloved". Repin was cleverer and realised there could be nothing between us after our first kiss and it was consensual. That he tried his luck many times after I split with Lintorff is another story.

However, out of guilt (yes Guntram, I snorted, as if this could be possible), he agreed to sign.

I felt released. I couldn't continue any more. It was like Constantin had said, he wins me over or kills me in the process. No, Guntram, you are already dead. You shot a man, even if he's the lowest scum on this Earth. You are not one of them, like

612

Goran told you. Lintorff didn't hesitate for a second to give you to his hounds to torture you to death. You're alive because Goran saved you, not Ferdinand or any other.

What if next time, you wouldn't miss and shoot him on the head like he certainly deserves? What if you do it in front of the children? That afternoon I learned more about myself than in my whole life. I could also be a killer like them.

But I didn't want to be one and I didn't want to die either. I needed to go away. My only reason for staying had been the children, but he clearly told me that he had replaced me with Stefania. She's their mother now. Exactly as Constantin had predicted; the minute he would find someone better, he would throw me to the trash can and forbid me to see the babies. They're his, not mine. Didn't he almost fired me a second time yesterday because the witch told him I had insulted her? I was an idiot to judge him as if he were a decent person.

I'll die the minute I leave Karl and Klaus, but it's for the best. We are going to kill each other. I have no more restraints. I should have gone long time ago, when Constantin told me. I can't ruin their lives, but I can't prevent the father to so.

I took his letter and tore it into small pieces. He agreed to sign. He had thrown me out.

Perhaps I would be set free now. It was just a matter of time for the children to forget me. They're only four years old.

Chapter 17

June 16th, 2008

The children didn't return as announced, and I got a phone call from Albert von Lintorff. Hearing his voice cheerfully greeting me was a big surprise.

"My wife and I wondered if you would like to come to Turin for a week or two to take care of our biggest rascal. Armin really needs someone to show him his place," he chuckled.

"Dr. Dähler is more qualified for the job than myself, Mr. Lintorff," I replied half seriously.

"Ouch. Mr. Lintorff. You make me feel like a grandfather! I'm Albert to you! *Strolch*, I mean, Armin has a lot of troubles with his thesis. He can't sit in front of the computer to type it, and perhaps you could convince him to start to work. He's very lazy and says something about being in holidays."

"Klaus Maria and Karl Maria will return soon from Sylt and they will need someone to take care of them, Albert," I excused myself.

"My cousin decided to go to London to give you more time to recover. These things with the heart can be tricky. He spoke with your doctor, and he is concerned that the children might prove a huge stress for you. Come to Turin and you'll have some peace. I can send Armin back to Zurich if he's too nasty to obey you. Dähler will straighten him."

The Lintorffs like to do their own laundry in private; from one cousin to the other.

"I'm afraid I can't accept your invitation. I have to deliver some drawings for a children's book, my deadline is at the end of June. *Meister* Ostermann will kill me if I don't do it," was my new excuse. Yes, I have the deadline, but most of the drawings are done. Twenty out of the required ten. They should choose what the like best.

"I see. No way you can visit us? Carolina is dying to see you."

"Please send her my regards. I'll visit you as soon as I can Albert."

"Great, get better soon, Guntram," he said in a hurry, almost hanging up on me.

I returned to my work to finish this watercolour with the birds for the story. I was deeply into this when my mobile rang again.

"Hi, Alexei," I answered, truly happy that he would call me. "Jean Jacques is behaving well?" I chuckled.

"Hi Kiddo. Better keep an eye on him," he laughed. "But I didn't call for that. How are you?"

"Much better, thank you. 'Kiddo'; is not too American for you?"

"Cold War finished eighteen years ago. Anyway, I wanted to ask you if I can visit you today. I have to pick up Baba Yaga from the Airport and bring her to the residence. I would send somebody else, especially after the mess she put us all, but I would like to see you and make an inspection visit to see if you're taking all your medications," he mirrored my laughter.

"Is Baba Yaga back? I should have accepted Albert von Lintorff's invitation."

"Yeah. Shit happens," he made me almost bend with laughter with his imitation of an American accent.

"Can you give me political asylum? I promise to clean and cook," I asked half seriously. No way I would stay in the house with her. I could go to a hotel, but I would get Milan shouting after me something about security procedures, not to mention Friederich will drag me back to the house pulling me by the ear. He's very classical.

"No problem, but don't touch the kitchen. That's Jean Jacques' territory. Pack your things, and you can come with me tonight."

"Thanks a lot. You're my saviour."

"Like always. I'll inform the Duke of your whereabouts." Before I could tell him not to do it, he hung up on me. Fuck! Why all of them still treat me as if I were the bloody Griffin's Consort? It's over since 2006 and we are in 2008! Don't they write memos in this stupid Order? Lintorff still says "our children". Hypocrite!

I hope he fulfils his promise and transfers this power to the witch. I can't stand any more this situation and I don't know how I will react when I see him again. He has to return at some point to his house.

Much later at about four, two big Audis parked in the esplanade outside the new part of the Castle. Nasty Alexei, he ordered to use the place reserved for the service people. How was the sign the older *Herzog* had at his door at Güstrow? "*Lieferanten und Briefadel zur Hintertür*"? ("Deliveries and *Briefadel*—low nobility —to the rear entrance"). Alexei learns fast from his boss.

I went downstairs and found that Friederich had not formed the staff like he always does when the Duke returns home from a trip. I sighed but said nothing. He's old enough to know what's best for him. I hope the Duke doesn't yell at him for this. I stood next to him.

"Guntram, there's no need for you to receive her." Wow, just "her". Not "her Excellency", "the Duchess" or "Madam". He must be really mad at her.

"She's still the Duchess," I said calmly.

"Yes, still," he said through gritted teeth. "His Excellency has not yet reached a decision."

She entered in the foyer like a queen, this we can't deny the witch. She looks regal every time. A true lioness.

"Good afternoon, Madam," Friederich greeted her very politely. I bowed my head to her, ceremoniously.

"De Lisle come to the library with me," she ordered me haughtily.

"As you wish, Madam," I followed her.

She entered in the room and went to sit at Lintorff's desk. Brave woman, that place belongs to him, and he never relinquishes territory. She didn't offer me a seat so I remained standing in front of her as she was busy fondling with some papers from her portfolio.

"My husband decided to accept your resignation effective from tomorrow onward. You'll get your salary paid till the end of the month plus six months more as compensation. In your condition, you're a liability, and not useful to us any more He has also signed the papers transferring the position of Guardian of Estate to Ferdinand von Kleist. You're not the children's legal tutor any more. I would be very grateful if you leave this house tomorrow morning. I don't want to inflict the children the pain of seeing you going away."

I couldn't believe it was so easy. Free? I don't care if some hot associate puts a bullet on my head tomorrow. I can go away.

"Has the Duke truly signed the documents?"

"Your insolence is impossible! I will not write any recommendation letter for you! Of course, my husband signed the papers! Now, get out."

"Thank you, Madam. I'm most obliged with you. I wish you the best luck in your position as Consort."

"I'm no consort! I'm his wife and the Duchess! Impudent youth!" She shouted me back. Unprincely. She should take some lessons on the noble art of scolding the servants without looking like the fisherman's wife from Elisabetta. A dictionary would help her too. However, it's not my problem any longer. I signed the papers she held out to me without looking at them.

"Goodbye, Madam," she didn't answer me and I left the room.

I felt as If I were drunk on happiness. I will miss the children a lot. I know there will be not a single day I don't think on them, but this can't continue any longer. I can't do it. He's killing me. I have also the right to rebuild my life as I see fit. All this hatred between us will finally hurt the babies. They don't deserve it.

I went back to my bedroom and started to put my stuff together. I didn't want most of the clothes. A large majority dated from my time as Lintorff's "bed warmer", and honestly I had no use for them. I only took what I had acquired in the last two years with the sales of my paintings. I should have around 89,000 francs, enough money to support me till I'll find another job, somewhere out of Switzerland.

The account where my salary was deposited every month was untouched. It would be around 130,000 francs by now. I would have never taken money for taking care of Karl and Klaus. Lintorff can keep it and pay part of what my university costed. I sat on my desk and wrote a small letter asking Monika if the legal office could transfer the property of the house in Argentina to Karl and Klaus.

I looked around to gather my paintings, and I realised it would be too heavy to carry them all. I went to what used to be the room where I painted to say goodbye to the many things that were there; about ten or fourteen pieces. Some were relatively big. I stood in front of the finished portrait of the children and Konrad. I started it at the end of 2007, when they were almost 4 years old. I painted them playing on top of a carpet, with their favourite toys. Klaus with his teddy bear and Karl with his ant bear. Lintorff was also sitting on the floor, informally dressed, as I remembered him from our holidays in Sylt, much before the storm hit us, when he was Konrad and not Lintorff.

A Freudian or better a Jungian psychiatrist would have a nice time explaining why I painted him with his back towards me and his face (or what was the image of the nice man I met in Venice), reflected on the mirror placed on the back wall, showing the room before them. Perhaps it was too dark to have painted the whole thing only placing some light over the boys and in the mirror, reflecting the dying sunlight of a late afternoon. I truly fell in love with him in Venice and loved him even in our darkest moments till his mother killed us both.

It was a good one. Dark but good. Well balanced. This one was really worth hanging on a wall.

I sighed. It's Lintorff's decision what to do with it. It's not mine any longer.

It's independent from me. The rest he can throw to the trash.

I wrote also a small note saying goodbye note to Friederich, who was locked in the Library with the Consort witch.

The doubt hit me. She didn't know what a Consort is, and Ferdinand got the right to administrate the children's fortune if Lintorff's dead.

Perhaps, there was still the chance he had only accepted my resignation, but didn't want me to go away. No, this can't be possible. She fired me on his name. She wouldn't dare to go against him so blatantly. She couldn't be so stupid.

I called the taxi, but instead of going to Alexei's house, I will go to the bus station. Better to be on the safe side if Lintorff changes his mind.

I also deserve another chance.

Chapter 18

Ferdinand Von Kleist's Diary.
June 17th, 2008

This morning, I accompanied Konrad and his children to his house. My main reason to do so was to avoid a confrontation between him and his wife, when he would communicate her his petition for divorce. After all, "I have sufficient experience in handling these matters. Could you give me your lawyer's buffet name? They reached a good settlement for you."

"It will not work because you have a prenuptial contract. You will have to give her a minimum of five millions per marriage year and three properties of her choice, excluding the Family residence and the house in London," I explained him several times, but he didn't want to give so much to her.

We arrived at noon to find:

1. Guntram de Lisle had been fired and left the house on the 16th at 6 p.m., still convalescent when the doctor specifically said one month of absolute bed rest. I felt my blood boil. This boy should be in bed, not running around God knows where. It's almost murder to kick him out.
2. Guntram left no address. His mobile phone is switched off or without batteries.
3. Friederich had been sent into retirement to Salzburg. Fortunately, he's cleverer and went to a suite at the Eden to wait for further orders from Konrad himself.
4. Most of Guntram's paintings were destroyed per this woman's orders. Only a portrait of the children and Konrad survived the fire. One of the maids hid it because she couldn't destroy it. It's a magnificent piece. I don't know about art, but this one is very beautiful. Konrad was enraptured when he saw it.
5. The Lintorff children can cry and yell exactly as their father.

Stefania was waiting for Konrad and they both started to argue heatedly when he told her, without knowing Guntram had been fired, that he wanted the divorce, and would comply with her economical demands in exchange for her title's renounce. She exploded and refused to divorce on a mutual accord basis.

In the middle of their discussion in the library, the children burst into the room with their new nanny behind. Both were crying like crazy saying that "Guntram is not here". They are very noisy, especially Klaus Maria who accurately called Stefania "witch".

"Who gave you permission to enter my rooms?" Konrad shouted them and both shut up. "Your tutor must be in Zurich, and will return soon. Now, out. Your elders are speaking. I will speak with Mr. de Lisle about your lack of manners."

"I fired this good for nothing man. He's useless, has no qualifications for the position and does not know how to behave. There's no reason to keep him, no matter the promise you made to his father. He's twenty-five and can support himself on his own," Stefania told us. I was mute. The children started to cry again and the nanny took them away.

"Who authorised you to do this?" Konrad asked her, still calm.

"I did it as general manager of this house. You agreed he was disrespectful to me. He's fired. I paid him six months as compensation. He also signed a confidentiality agreement and another renouncing any legal claims against us."

"Out. Now," he growled looking at her. I stood up from my chair ready to intervene if he would attack her. Strangle her, perhaps. I know that look very well.

"I will not. I'm your wife and you're taking a servant's side against me."

"He's more important to me than you. You're only a well paid..."

"Konrad! No need to be vulgar!" I warned him. Say nothing or you will be in front of a divorce judge in no time, and that will cost you more than a hundred million.

"He's nobody! Not even a good artist! All the trash he left behind had to be burned and smelled horribly."

"What have you done, stupid cow?" I flinched. That alone is "verbal abuse". Two or three millions more to the tab.

"He left them behind and I ordered to clean his room for the next nanny, who will arrive in two days. She's fluent in English, French and German and has a degree in children's psychology. He even had the nerve as to leave a note for your personal secretary, transferring some hut in Argentina to the children."

"That "hut," is worth around two million dollars," he said coldly. Stupid Konrad, now you put her on the right track of your relationship with Guntram. The cow was stupid enough as to buy the story of the poor orphan almost adopted by you, in her greed to get your money.

"Why would he do that?"

"Because he's an honest and honourable person, but that's a concept difficult to understand for you. I gave him the house as a Christmas present in 2002." Konrad, I can't believe it. She will skin you alive in the Courtroom. More or less you admitted having a relationship with him! Well, everybody in Zurich knows Guntram is the Consort, so in that direction, it makes not much sense to deny it or hide it.

"You gave him a house worth two million? To that pathetic thing? Why?" She shouted, almost destroying my ears. These Italian women are good for the bed, but too loud for my taste. I prefer them mute and smiling, like my Cecilia.

"He's very special to me. He was my lover for almost five wonderful years until he decided to cease our relationship. I forced him to remain in this house for the children's sake, and to protect him from whatever may happen outside. I married you in order to make him jealous, but it didn't work. Therefore, you have outlived your original purpose in this house. Name your price for the divorce."

"That explains why you're so bad in bed. Fag. You fuck as if you were remembering the steps from a Catholic Church Handbook," she spat. Konrad looked at her without interest.

Why women are so sickeningly graphic when it comes to the sexual performance of their men? We discuss the anatomy of our partners, but leave the details for us.

"All right, I will pay you what is in the contract. Five million for one year and the three estates, under my name. You can keep the flat in Paris in the Avenue

Montaigne, the one in Rome and the small one in Manhattan. All my other properties belong to the companies. It's a good settlement for you. Take it."

"I will not! You have billions and want to give me five lousy millions? I want the house on Madison Avenue."

That particular property was valued in more than sixty million last year, without counting the artwork inside! Most of his Modern Art collection is there.

"I'll give you a pension; €500,000 per year for the rest of your life. If you marry again, it will be suspended."

Did you say €40,000 per month? You're crazy, Konrad. I give 10,000 Francs to Gertrud only because you pressed me. I had enough of that bitch for twenty-five years. I should ask for moral compensation.

"I will not accept this. You were unfaithful to me! My lawyers will destroy you."

"How I would love that to be true, alas, it is not. Guntram can't stand the sight of me," he replied dryly. "I'll raise the pension to €50,000 per month, but you will sign a confidentially agreement."

"I will not. Everybody will hear from you!"

"Stefania, nobody wants to hear about your past too. Via Condotti is so far away nowadays that it makes no sense to bring it back. Remember how we met ten years ago. Go into a golden retirement and rest from your many battles. Age is very bad for a woman of your talents. I appreciate you, and it would be my pleasure to support you. We can make all this discreetly. We divorce quietly and issue a joint press release. You would be very bored to live here, taking care of the children for the rest of your life. You're not the motherly type. If you want to play Duchess, rest assured that I will show you your duties thoroughly. You have run wild for too long."

"I will make your life a living hell when the press hears it and his too. *Banker fucks male nanny*. You'll be the laughing stock of the whole community."

"Leave Guntram out of this, whore," he grunted in that special way he has before attacking you.

"Konrad. Let the lawyers fix this. If Stefania wants to accuse you of infidelity, you can show how much money she gave to this man… what was the name? The Italian, not the French," I interfered.

"Della Rosa?"

"No. The dark one. Wait…. Francesco Rossini!"

"I remember, now. The one from the photos."

"Yes. The judge would be shocked. Perhaps your prenuptial contract could be nullified. Was not there a clause against infidelity? We can't give them to the press. Not even the Sunday Mirror would publish them! Does the "Hustler" magazine have a Society Page?" I chuckled.

She stormed out of the library. Furious. Bad loser.

"Ask Friederich to get her a good hotel for tonight. Tomorrow she can send for her things."

"Yes, I'll tell Milan to take care of this. Good riddance. I still don't know why you didn't marry that nice looking woman from Sweden."

"She was too decent to get rid of her easily. Tell the lawyers to write the documents tomorrow, and cancel all her credit cards. I want the accounts she got in my banks, emptied. We have to give her some incentives to sign."

"Of course."

"Call Goran, he should find where this foolish boy has gone now. I'm surprised he didn't go to you, like before or to Alexei Antonov's."

"Konrad. I returned him home four days after he came to me. He doesn't trust me any longer."

"In his condition he shouldn't be running around. Tell Goran to find him and bring him back home. His men should be gentle because he just came from a myocardial angina episode."

"Konrad, answer me this. Do you still love him?"

"Of course. Why do you think I waited so long to act again and married this woman?"

"He blames you for his father's death. He will not forgive you this time. Lord knows I love him like one of my sons, but perhaps you should let him go away. He's only twenty-five and could start his life all over again. This would be the most decent thing to do."

"He's confused, that's all. He was deceived by this woman into believing I fired him. Although he will never want that I touch him again, he still has an obligation toward our children. They will not suffer because of our troubles as a couple. He's their legal tutor. I only removed him only from the duties of managing their fortunes. With his heart condition, that might prove too much for him."

"Yes, and I still don't like that you transferred seven hundred million from your money to one of his accounts. This is too much."

"If he would have to support the children in the future, he will need all the cash he can have. Did he take something with him? Tell Goran to check all his credit cards and accounts moves since April 2006, including the one he thinks he hides from me."

"Perhaps its time we find out if he took much more than you think. So much money would make the Lord doubt."

"Not my Guntram. He's immune to it."

I had to spend the rest of the afternoon speaking with Goran, terribly upset his "little brother" had done something so stupid again. Yes, Guntram is a real idiot if he believed Stefania's word without checking first. However, I don't believe it. If he was fired, why didn't he ask Goran or Alexei for help, like before? The later offered him to go to his house for several days, but he took a cab to the bus station.

No. Our Guntram is not that stupid. He never believed her, but used it as a justification to escape a suffocating situation. I can't blame him. I would have done the same. Konrad forced him to his limits. How could he expect the boy would like to live under his roof, seeing him almost everyday, taking care of his children, suffering his moods and accusations, and later enduring him fucking the bitch right under his nose? I'm surprised Guntram didn't shoot him in the head, as Konrad certainly deserved that time.

True, Guntram's father's death was not Konrad's fault. Not entirely. The man was very sick, and offered his life as collateral in order to save the little one. I have the utmost respect for Jerôme de Lisle as lawyer and strategist. He always knew Konrad's weakest point and trapped him forever deluding him into believe, he was winning. He sold us at a fantastic price what was already worthless and planned his vendetta against us. I'm convinced he was the one who put me on the track of the traitors, looking for a full and final bloodbath within the Order. His only mistake was to miscalculate that his father would be so stupid as to plan to kill Konrad in a frontal attack. I agree with Löwenstein's way of addressing the issue. Jerôme had no other way out than offering Guntram to save the boy's life from the old Guard, as the lad would now belonged to the Griffin.

We should change our hostages rules. They are very outdated. There are many things nowadays that we can use as guarantees for treaties.

Konrad believes God gave him Guntram, as he saw him for the first time in Nôtre Dame, before Christmas, to top it. Perhaps. This was unplanned from both of them, and we didn't find out who he was till two or three days later at Les Invalides. It was sheer luck or divine intervention that Thibaudet was there, and accepted to pose as clerk, finding out his name.

How could Jerôme imagine that Konrad would fall like a total idiot for his boy? If that was his original gamble, I have the utmost respect for him. How could he have such a crazy idea? To give your seven year old child to your brother's former lover?

Konrad nearly killed him that night when he came to us. We both wanted to send him right there to Löwenstein's hands, but he only said "My Duke, you're perfectly aware that you will not find anybody like my brother again. Your soul is destroyed and you will never get it back. I can give you what you want the most in exchange for my son's life, my brother's and my own death," I admit the man had guts to come to us, especially after that shooting that nearly killed Konrad.

"You have nothing left. Get out de Lisle. Your line is dead. The Council has spoken."

"You still love Roger, but he despises you. What if I offer you the chance to find someone like him, but sweet and kind natured? My brother's face, but none of his faults."

"Who?" Konrad asked before I could kick the man out. I was never so pissed off with him. You were shot, betrayed and who knows what else and you still think on Roger? God, my friend was a crazy imbecile.

"My own son. Guntram. He's physically exactly as my brother. See the pictures by yourself my Duke," Jerôme said giving Konrad two photos. He just studied them, like you evaluate a horse.

"The resemblance is remarkable de Lisle, but what makes you think that the boy will accept me? Or are you giving me your own son so I can rape him in exchange from your life? Your family has no limits, really."

"You would never do it. You're an honourable man despite you're the Griffin. I can't guarantee that Guntram will like you at all. That is a risk you have to take."

"Get out. How the others kill you, it's their problem. I hope they take their time with you."

"If you don't take my offer, they will kill my child. I accept my fate, but my son has always been away from us. Since he was born. He never had contact with my family. He's not corrupted like us. Her mother was a good woman, half German. Do you want another child's death on your conscience?"

"You should have thought about it before rising against your Griffin," Konrad answered.

"Guntram is a very sweet boy. He never fights with his friends in school and likes to draw a lot. He could be a good artist. He's clever, sensitive and affectionate. Perhaps he's a little stubborn when he decides something is the right thing to do, but that would be good for you, my Duke. You need someone to gently counterbalance your dominating personality. He's very shy also."

I knew Jerôme had won the minute he was able to say the second sentence. Konrad was listening to him very carefully. Shit! "Get out de Lisle or I'll put the bullet in your head and another in your bastard's!" I roared.

"Silence Ferdinand! Tell me more about your boy, de Lisle."

"He's like his mother. A very sweet woman with a lot of patience and completely innocent. Unable to hurt anybody. I fear that his sweet nature will cause him a lot of pain in the future. In a way he reminds me to my cousin, Gerhard Guttenberg Sachsen. He spent many summers at our Estate in Poitiers."

Double shit! Konrad liked that man a lot. I think he was sort of infatuated with him at the Polo Club in Sylt when we were teenagers, but Gerhard never paid attention to him as he was several years older than us. He sent the family, the Order and everything to Hell and became a medical doctor, going to Africa or some place like that. Konrad always admired his guts and his sweet and caring nature.

"In ten years, you could have what you lost, but this time without my family's interference. Nobody but us knows of your relation with Roger. My son is twenty-five years younger than you. He should be easier to manage than my brother."

"I should see the boy before I make any decision."

"No. I will not tell where he is till you swear you will not touch a single hair on him."

"I could find out it in no time, de Lisle."

"Perhaps, my Duke. I want your oath that you will protect him from the others and will respect his decision if he doesn't accept you. His Excellency already knows how is to be in the middle of a forced relationship and would prefer that Guntram loves him by his own will. You will also swear not to touch him till he turns eighteen."

"I will not provide for him."

"You don't have to. I have already taken care of that. My son's for my brother's life."

"What about your life?"

"You can have it as a proof of my good will."

"A simple lawyer's life is worthless, not even worthy of our time. Your brother was an Associate. We should set an example," I said, but Konrad interrupted me.

"I accept. The boy for Roger's life. I give you my word with the Lord as my witness that I will protect him from any harm and if he becomes my lover in ten years, I will honour him." Konrad said to my utter annoyance. He never learns!

"I take your word, my Duke. May the Lord gives you the strength and clarity of thought to abide it."

"Where does the boy live?"

"In neutral grounds. Argentina. I have a letter for Guntram. Could you give it to him only in the case he finds out about Roger and you? I want to ease his pain as much as I can."

"I will. You have a month to fulfil your part of the deal. If you don't do it, I will give Roger to my men. They're furious for our loses."

"Good bye my Duke. We will see each other in Hell."

I was furious with Konrad when Jerôme left. "I hope you did it just to find out where the little slug is so Mladic takes care of the business."

"No. I did it to protect the boy. Killing a seven year old will not solve our problems. The Old Guard is too outdated and wasting resources. Nobody will touch the boy. As for Roger, Mladic can go ahead, when he finds him. I want to see if this one fulfils his oath. If he does, perhaps the boy would be suitable in the future."

"You are crazy!" I shouted.

"Why? If he looks like his uncle, but has none of his characteristics, he could be a good companion for me. You told me many times that Jerôme was nothing like his brothers. No one, but you, Friederich and Löwenstein know about Roger and I."

"So?"

"If I like him, I could keep him. None of you will speak."

"Konrad, you seriously should consider getting some professional help."

"Ferdinand, you're so serious that it's impossible not to pull a joke on you!" He laughed. "Really my friend, do you think I will sit and wait for ten years to get a new lover, looking exactly as the snake I want to crush? I have learned my lesson. No lover will ever come between me and my duties toward my position."

"For a minute I thought you were serious."

"I don't even care about the boy. I had enough of the de Lisles'. Roger was a great fuck and I loved him, but it's over. I have to take care of the Order now. Love can only bring havoc and misery."

But fate had other ideas. The minute Konrad saw that boy, horribly dressed like a punk, sitting in Notre Dame, following very attentively the Mass, he lost his head again. "Take care of the meeting" the idiot told me and went away before the service was finished.

I didn't want to have the boy around, but he was so besotted with him, saying that he looked like Roger de Lisle. Konrad needs glasses. Guntram was shorter, his hairs a lighter brown; his features completely symmetrical when Roger's were not, and he looked like a gentle soul from the minute I saw him. Friederich was right. This boy was nothing like his uncle. In a way he's exactly like his father, but the man had dark hair with blue/green eyes. The brown hair and the soft blue eyes must come from his mother's side or the Guttenbergs', not from the de Lisle's. When Roger entered a room, he was always the center of attention. He had a magnetic appeal. Guntram, was always trying to be the less notorious as he could. I'm sure he hated to be shown off, and would have been happier at home or in a museum.

I was relieved when Guntram finished his relationship in Buenos Aires with Konrad, but no. He would have none of it. He loved the boy like he never wanted his wretched uncle. Roger and Konrad's relationship was rocky, based mostly on sexual attraction. They would fight only to have the pleasure to solve the problem in bed. "Angry sex is the best ever", he told me once. I don't know. I prefer things more gentle. Did he love him? Konrad swears so, and ruined his own line on that belief for over twenty years. He's stubborn as a mule. I don't think it was love, only passion. However, Konrad would cut his manhood before admitting that he, like the rest of us, lets his dick rule his acts sometimes. What a goody!

Konrad likes to play the victim, too.

Why did he keep Jerôme's letter if he never had any intentions towards the boy, as he claimed? Konrad lied to me! He really considered to go after the boy! With Guntram it was real love. Konrad forwent of his selfishness to make the boy happy, and many of his actions were directed by him, in the sense he would not hurt or give him a bad impression. Before he only cared about himself and the Order.

Guntram never gave us trouble or took advantage of Konrad when he could have made a lot of money. First, I believed his protests against Konrad spending so much money on him or paying his University fees were fake. However, he never took one franc more than necessary, or sold the house in Argentina to cash it or anything like that. He never asked for money or wanted anything from Konrad. He only spent money on paints, and most of the money he made till April 2006 was given to Konrad "to pay for the lawyer", "for the school fees", "the doctor's fees" or spent on the babies. He never touched a single coin from his 4,000 francs salary. Only opened a separate account in a commercial Spanish bank, where he put the money he made selling his pieces or illustrating books. All his expenses came from there. Friederich told me he refused to have anything more from the Duke, and lived like any of the other servants. The poor man had a very hard time trying to separate him from the staff.

This lad was the best thing that could have ever happened to all of us. He gave emotional stability to Konrad, who finally produced offspring, saving his line. Pity the relationship was poisoned from the beginning. I should have never let it carry on. I should have given the boy to the Albanians when Konrad was away from Venice, but Michael prevented it by ordering Goran to protect him. Shit! I'm certain, Michael realised my plans when I almost forced Konrad to return to Zurich to fix a stupid mistake done by my team.

Guntram was too good to be true.

Unfortunately, Konrad can't live without him. He doesn't care if Guntram wants it or not. He only wants the boy in his bed (or in his own bedroom near the nursery), every night, isolated from the rest of the world. He thinks that, some day, the boy will break under the weight of solitude. I suggested him to allow Guntram to live in a small flat in Zurich, and let him come for work every day, and he nearly killed me. *No*, he wants to control his life in every possible aspect. He should be at home, playing with the children or painting. Sometimes, I think Konrad would take away his shoes so he can't run away.

I'm sure Konrad is not telling me the whole story behind Guntram's latest relapse. He did something he's ashamed of, and took the children away to hide it. I don't believe him for a minute that he did it "so Guntram can relax and recover". Shouting at him because Stefania told him that Guntram insulted her is not enough to put the lad on the brink of another heart attack.

Perhaps Guntram wanted to leave him forever, and they had a real fight. Konrad would never hurt him on purpose, but the boy's health is too frail, and the slightest miscalculation can result bad for him. Konrad must have been totally out of his mind to push Guntram so much. Only the threat to abandon him would do that. Konrad always calculates his moves. Not even, his famous outbursts of anger are true. All is an act that serves his purposes. I'm sure he does it to cover the coldness of his actions. He never loses his cold head, except with Guntram. But we can't be reasonable with the people we love. By definition, Love is visceral.

Yes, that must be. Konrad would never let the boy go, and panicked when the lad wanted to go away. If so, Guntram might have something hidden up his sleeve this time, because he already tried to escape once and failed.

Time to check what Goran found out.

* * *

June 19th, 2009

Still nothing about Guntram. How can a convalescent cardiac patient disappear without leaving any clues behind? That's beyond me. He does not even have a simple name to hide behind. If he were John Smith, Juan Pérez or Hans Mayer, it would be difficult to trace him.

He only took with him the cash he had, plus six hundred francs from the ATM at the bus station. The clothes he bought "with his own money", one sketch book, his laptop (the poor dear believes that we can't read his files any more. Somebody should tell him more about internet and hacking), and a wooden pencil box. Konrad told me that he had given him that thing in Venice, in 2002 and read whatever the lad wrote in his Diary till June 16th.

"I might have found the key to get him back, Ferdinand. I should have read that thing many months ago. Even his fury against me is feigned. He feels completely lost and in a way is looking for a way to come out of the mess he has placed himself in. "The man he fell in love with in Venice," he wrote, Ferdinand. He has already accepted he needs my guidance again. He knows he's cornered, but he's still too stubborn to admit it. He's about to break. Once I catch him, I will get him back to my side. I know how to play the game again."

Very nice theory. Pity the boy is away. Konrad will hit his head against the wall that is Guntram's determination. It's a lost battle.

He also took some photos of the children, but left the ones from his family. I can understand him. I would have burned them years ago. After all, they destroyed his life from the grave.

Only one good point. A maid, Nadine, the one who saved the portrait, remembered Guntram was always telling her about going to Poitiers to see where his family came from. She's French and knows the area, and told him how to get there. Goran should try his luck there.

On the other hand, Konrad is almost mad with concern. Guntram didn't take his medications with him. Why? I don't know. I hope this boy doesn't do anything foolish.

* * *

June 23rd, 2008

When I catch Guntram, I swear I'll beat his ass like the child he is!

Poitiers was a false lead. Nothing. Goran's men searched well. No one with his characteristics was in the hotels, hostels, rent flats or camping. He has no living relatives or knows someone related to his family. No one out of the ordinary bought his combination of medications.

What really concerns me is, that he went away without his medications. Why would he do that? I pray he doesn't have his Father's same stupid ideas.

Michael suggested Goran he should abandon the idea of looking for him under his name. He must be using an alias. He hasn't touched any of his accounts, credit cards or anything. None of his former colleagues from school or the art studio were contacted. We checked even his relations in Argentina, but nothing.

According to Michael, the best we can do is to access all databases from hospitals in Europe, looking for someone who has the same age and same symptoms. Perhaps we could obtain a list and from there to cross check it from the passengers list of that day's from the bus station. He should be running out of medications if he only took the week box he uses. He will have to go to a doctor, and unless he had some hidden money, he can't afford a private one. Pity not all passengers from bus station are registered. Only the ones who paid with credit card, so I'm afraid we will have to check all those who didn't buy a ticket in the last thirty days. Fortunately, hospitals write "Caucasian," In their reports.

* * *

June 28th, 2008

Michael is not so stupid as I thought. He got the list from most countries and eliminated those who had not asked for a second passport or lost one in the last five years… that shrunk the list to twenty-eight people out of 3,589. Goran has something to work with, finally. According to Michael, he should leave the German speaking countries out, Guntram had enough of us. We should look in France, Italy, Netherlands, Spain, Portugal, etc. That makes a sixteen person list.

Chapter 19

I need to sleep in peace for one night. I'm getting more and more tired with every passing moment. Running away is never easy and why do I do it? Because I'm a paranoid asshole. Konrad von Lintorff fired me and removed the boys' custody from me. *Finito.* It's over. I'm free.

However, the best is if I keep distance from his men and friends.

I haven't many doses left and they will finish by tomorrow. The least I need is to end in an ER because of a heart attack. I'm an idiot for not taking all the medications with me. Perhaps a pharmacist would sell them without prescriptions. I can try it, saying I lost mine and I'm a tourist. After all, they're not for "getting high".

I can't stop thinking on Klaus and Karl. I look at their photos almost hourly. I should stop it. It's done. He fired me like he said he would. It's for the best. We were going down a road of destruction. I hope the bastard takes care of them and prevents Stefania from hurting them. No, she will not bother to go after them. She only wants his money and would do nothing that could harm her chances to get it. If the children complain too much, I'm sure he will send her to Hell and look for another replacement, this time one "more appropriate" to his status. She was there "to show me my place". I didn't learn, so we both are out. Armin was more right than I credited him for. He will be a good Griffin.

I'm in Paris now. It's big, I'm French, should not be too obvious. This hostel is for immigrants and they don't want to know your name or keep a record.

I need a new identity. The minute I say "Guntram de Lisle," In a job interview I will get the Order breathing on my neck. I even left my laptop in Madrid to make them lose my track, and I'm back to the old folder style.

I have two options. Go to the police, tell everything I know and get a new identity or call Repin and ask for his help. I can't do this alone. Authorities make no sense at all. Nobody would believe me and if somebody would do, I'll be killed in less than two minutes of sitting in front of a judge. My only way out is Repin, but I don't want to start a mess or abuse his generosity. He has been a pretty decent guy with me, no matter what Lintorff and the others were always telling about him.

* * *

June 29th, 2008

I called Constantin at his private number. He picked it up. Strange, normally there's somebody else.

"Guntram, are you all right?" He said the minute he heard my voice.

"I'm fine, thank you." Does he know? How? "I need to ask you a favour. A really big one."

"Whatever you need. Why didn't you call me before? Lintorff's men are looking for you like crazy. They dared to stick their noses in my territory."

"I'm sorry. I'd better go."

"No. I know you're in Paris now. Go to my flat in Place Vendôme, 22. One of my men will wait for you there and take care of you until I can see you."

Why does everybody immediately assumes I'm a frail lady in distress? I only want one of his drug dealers contacts for medications and another of his forgers friends. Nothing else. Well, a bed without fleas would be nice also, but I can't afford that luxury. How the fuck did he know I'm in Paris? Shit.... He traced the call. Most probably he has the telephone booth's address by now.

"Constantin, I don't want to cause you trouble with Lintorff. If he's looking for me, then he will make you responsible for my going. I swear he fired me. I haven't touched anything that didn't belong to me nor spoken!" I said agitated, now afraid because he had confirmed my worst fear; Lintorff released his hounds on me for whatever reason his demented mind had. Knowing him, it could be anything ranging from not liking the ink colour or shape of my signature on those papers to being a raging bull because I signed and went away, instead of crying and begging to stay for another rape.

"Kleist called Oblomov and asked if he knew where you were. It seems you have forgotten to take your medications with you, and he's very concerned about it. Are you taking them?"

"Not since seven days ago," I heard a loud expression in Russian.

"I'm sorry. Please go to Place Vendôme and wait for me there. I'll say nothing to Lintorff until I hear your side of the story."

He hung up on me. I was disoriented. If Goran was looking for me it was only a matter of time he would find me. Running outside Europe without a fake passport was useless. The minute I'd buy an air plane ticket, they'll know where I was going. Besides, I couldn't afford one because I should use the credit card from my extra account and likely it had been discovered by now.

My only option was Constantin, and I needed my medications.

I took the metro to the Opéra and walked down the Rue de la Paix, passing the famous café and getting to Place Vendôme. Chic as usual. Number 22 was very near Chanel. At the entrance, there was a very big man, looking like Alexei. Russians must be all big. He didn't look like the doorman or like a trained ape; very big, but elegant. Not really knowing what to do I came closer to him.

"Mr. Guntram de Lisle?" he asked.

"That's me. How do you do, Mr...?

"Malchenko. I'm Mr. Repin's personal assistant in Paris. Please, come upstairs," he made a small gesture with the head and out of nowhere the real Siberian Ape appeared, taking my backpack without saying anything. Good I left my suitcase in a locker in Gare de l'Est. We entered into a big foyer and took the elevator to the 4th floor.

The place was very Parisian and lavishly decorated. Malchenko led me to a living room and offered me a seat and a tea. I was silent the whole time as he gave some orders in Russian to a butler. I drank my tea and said nothing as he inspected me with curiosity.

"I never thought I would meet the Griffin's Consort." I almost spat the tea at his face, but caught myself in time. "It's an honour, sir. I've heard so many things

629

about you. The *Fürst* zu Löwenstein used to speak very highly of you. When I was transferred to work under Mr. Repin, I saw many of your paintings. The portrait of his daughter, Sofia Constantinovna is fantastic. My wife was in love with it when she saw it in St. Petersburg."

"I'm pleased you liked it. Thank you, sir."

"Mr. Repin ask me to call a doctor for you. When would you like to see him?"

"There's no need for that. I only need to get some of my medications. If the doctor would be so kind as to write the prescriptions…"

"Certainly, sir. If you write down the names, I'll give the order," he said extending me a small leather bounded pad. I wrote down what I needed. Hope the good doctor understands German.

"Thank you, Mr. Malchenko. Do you know when I might see Mr. Repin?"

"He's in Amsterdam at the moment. Perhaps tomorrow or the day after. He says you can stay here as long as you want."

"About being the Griffin's Consort, please don't call me like that. I don't use that title any more"

"The Griffin has not changed your status after his wedding, and the marriage was never informed to the Order. Therefore you're the Consort. We are very pleased with your support to the Griffin for the last years. Most of us are glad he chose you and ensured the succession line."

"I would appreciate if you don't inform the Griffin of my whereabouts."

"I will not. I respond to Mr. Repin directly. My family is part of the Order since 1815, but my loyalty is to the Arseniev House, like always. Mr. Repin personally chose me as his assistant when he joined in 2005. I'll show you to your bedroom. It's upstairs."

As usual I got a fantastic guest room on the upper floor with a view of the square, private bathroom and big bed. There were several good paintings from XIX century.

"I'll leave you so you can rest a little before dinner."

I took a long shower, feeling more and more tired. There was a fluffy bathrobe and I put it on. When I left the bathroom there was one butler in the bedroom sorting out clothes.

"I hope they fit, sir. I could only take a brief look at you."

"Thank you. It will be fine."

All Hermès. It's nearby, around the corner so to speak. I noticed it was a little more casual style than what I normally wear. Repin's way of life is more free than Lintorff's. I think he made it to the XX century.

"Please, tell Mr. Malchenko I would like to rest till tonight."

"Yes, sir."

I put on the pyjamas, slid under the covers and fell asleep in no time.

* * *

Ferdinand von Kleist's Diary
July 4th, 2008

What was supposed to be a holiday was ruined in no time. With American markets closed, I thought I could relax at home from five onward. Konrad was away in Guang Zhou and Michael in Frankfurt. I arrived home at four, but Cecilia was not there, still working at the Foundation with Elisabetta von Lintorff. Since she got the Presidency, that woman has rejuvenated ten years, completely delighted to order all of us around and squeeze out the last cent from us.

I got a phone call from Marcel Theriault, head of the Luxury Publishing Group. They make fashion, interior decoration and society magazines. They published the photos of Konrad's wedding at Stefania insistence. Small, privately run company. He's a lower member, not even invited to the meetings.

"Von Kleist speaking."

"Good afternoon Mr. Von Kleist. I'm terribly sorry to bother you at your home but since you left the office early, I took the liberty to call you home."

"Yes. What can I do for you, Mr. Theriault?"

"The Chief Editor of one of our magazines, *Jet Set Today*, the Italian Edition, called me a few minutes ago asking me about a piece they want to publish tomorrow. He's very surprised that this would be done in this way as the Lintorff house is always so discreet and normally sends an official communiqué before anything. He says that's the way how they managed with the Duke's wedding reportage."

"I'm not informed of any press release from our companies to the Economical Press, much less about Society pages."

"It's about the coming of the next heir to the Lintorff House. Normally the Griffin would make a joint communiqué with the Duchess to announce it; having only her photos and one from the wedding is not very appropriate for these circumstances."

Scheisse! That woman is a bitch!

"You're right, Mr. Theriault. This must be a mistake. Traditionally, we don't release any communiqué after the child is born. You must withdraw this article from the magazine."

"This is the main problem. The magazine is already formatted with the Duchess picture on the cover and three full pages on the subject. It's already on the print. It will cost us a lot of money to fix this problem."

"Crossing the Griffin might be more problematic. Perhaps we could exchange the pages for some publicity from our branches in Italy."

"We have so little time. We will have to change the cover and three central pages. It will not be cheap; over 1.5 million euros in costs."

"I'm afraid I can only offer you one million without the Duke's authorisation and he's in China. You might have to publish, and then explain yourself to him." Bloody Italians, always looking for more money! Does he think I'm an idiot who doesn't know how much it would cost?

Theriault thought for a minute. A full one. "I will support your credit application for next year," I added.

"Excellent. We will change it."

"Albert von Lintorff will contact you at this number in less than an hour. Goodbye."

Fuck. Fuck and Shit. All together. I'll kill the whore myself... and Konrad for breeding without telling!

Maybe he was not breeding at all. He told me he didn't touch her since May and the mess with photos, because he had enough of the bossy bitch. I know he was fooling around with several before Guntram was so sick. Fuck! The bitch got pregnant and now wants to make it legitimate! She announces publicly so Konrad has to withdraw the divorce demand to avoid the scandal of being a cuckold.

Right, as if Konrad would care. I dialled Albert's number. He'd better be fast and work.

"*Ciao, Bambino,*" he greeted me happily. What was this techno pop music behind? Was he in a disco at working hours?

"Albert, save me your idiocy now. We have problems."

"One second," I heard him going away from the music as he said several times "*Scusi*".

"All right. I was in Tatiana's fashion show. She's modelling Prada today."

"I don't want to speak about your latest girlfriend. Your wife will kill you if you go publicly to one of her shows."

"So be it. Konrad was right. Get a young one without much experience, and you'd feel with the libido of a bunny. She makes me feel ten years younger."

"Shut up and listen! The bitch, Stefania Barberini made a three page reportage plus cover on *Jet Set Today* announcing she's pregnant from Konrad! I bought the pages and the cover. I need that you fill them with three ads from your companies. Your bank, foundation, whatever. It just cost us one million euros!"

"*Putana*! Konrad pays the million? I can put whatever I want?"

"Yes, we pay. The Lintorff's name must be really visible. The bitch should understand the message. Now, hurry up, and call this man, Theriault, and send him whatever you want. You have less than an hour!"

"All right. Do we have also the cover?"

"He has to replace it. I don't know. It's not my problem."

"Don't worry. I'll take care of it. *Ciao, bello.*"

He hung up before I tell him what he could do with his "Italian flavour". He'd better fix the mess.

Tomorrow, I'll call Konrad with the results. Otherwise, it makes no sense

* * *

July 6th, 2008

Albert did everything as indicated with only a few minor changes. One advertisement for "Carolina von Lintorff Party Service", another for the "Prima Banca Veneto Lombarda", and the last for "Princepessa di Battistini Wineries", those are Albert's disgusting wines. He even sent us several boxes to show his gratitude.

On the cover was a big photo of Tatiana in a night gown, looking fantastic "2009 Party Trends".

If Carolina kills him, it's his problem. No lawyer could save him now.

Time to call Konrad, and hear the explosion. No news about Guntram yet. All efforts fruitless.

"Lintorff."

"Hello Konrad."

"Did you find him?"

"Not yet, still working on it. I was calling you because another problem arose in your absence," I paused but he said nothing. "One magazine wanted to print the story of you having a baby with Stefania. I stopped everything, but had to buy the pages. One million euros." No need to tell him yet about Albert's use of the pages.

"I see. Tell the lawyers to stop all negotiations with her. Present directly the papers to the courts and deposit the money she will get in a judiciary account. Notify the judge. Good bye."

Chapter 20

July 3rd, 2008

I haven't done much these last days. I slept most of the time. The Russian doctor who came on the night of the 29th, called me an irresponsible foolish boy for being for so long without medications. "You have a stable angina plus one recent cardiac episode, and you run around Paris without taking your pills? Absolute bed rest for three days. Do you want to make it worse than it is? We have to control this arrhythmia you have."

I stayed mostly in the library or in my room. Malchenko is nice and cultivated, but has to work most of the time. I would like to go out but I'm afraid to meet somebody. Tomorrow, Constantin will come to Paris and we will decide what to do.

* * *

July 4th, 2008

I don't know what to do. I'm disoriented like always. Constantin does not want to help me after he got me into this mess.

He arrived for dinner, and I was surprised it was formally set in his dinning room, the big windows opened and letting the breeze enter and allowing a full view of the Vendôme Column. The room was half dark and the food was already served with champagne and no servant to be seen.

Romantic setting? You gave up that many years ago. I know your wife and painted your daughter's portrait!

"Hello Guntram, I'm glad you could join me tonight. I'm sorry for the delay in meeting you."

"Hello Constantin. I thank you so much for your hospitality."

"Take a seat, dear," I obeyed as he poured a glass of champagne and placed it in front of me. "Lintorff's men are looking all over for you. You must make a decision now. What do you want to do?"

"I can't return to him. I can't live any more with him. I need to go away. You offered me a safe conduct many years ago and I would like to use it if it's still valid."

"I was expecting so, but circumstances have changed. I'm part of the Order now. Number eight in the hierarchy. If I take the Griffin's consort away, it will be considered as treason and we will start a war again."

"I see."

"If I would take you for myself, I will also cause a war but it would be worth it, my angel. However, you don't love me or feel attracted toward me. Perhaps you could fake some passion in bed, but it wouldn't be the same for both of us. I still love you and want the best for you, but the price is too high for my organization."

"I understand. You have risked enough by offering me shelter now. Could you contact me with someone who could help me with my papers?"

"Of course I could, but I don't see how this could help. You'll get a new identity, and perhaps evade them for a few years, but in the end either they will catch you again or you will die from a nervous breakdown. The doctor was very clear to me; you need to rest. You will be permanently running, unable to make friends or start a relationship and missing your children. You will never have a normal life again or forget your old one."

"I see, but I must try. Lintorff killed my whole family and my father."

"True, but you were the collateral offered by your father to save your life and your uncle's family. According to the Order's code, you belong to Konrad, and he's forced to treat you with kindness and respect."

"What we did is called incest, Constantin. It's disgusting."

"Depending on which concept you evaluate this. You two are not blood related, therefore that's not incest in a Levitical sense. You would be political relatives if Konrad's union with your uncle would have been accepted, but it is not, so there's no link between you two. The minimum sixth degree of inbreed demanded by the Church, does not apply in this case. I remember the story of Philip IV of Spain. He married his niece, the daughter of his own brother, because his own son, who was going to marry her, died. The old king took his place to save his bloodline as he only had a daughter left. They even got the Pope's blessing in order "to avoid further conflicts between the dynasties" which is more or less what your father tried to do by offering you to Lintorff."

"I'm an independent person. Arranged marriages finished many years ago. What if I didn't like Konrad? Did he have the right to rape me till I decided to swing his way?"

"I don't know. I don't think he would have gone that far. You two met by chance to my misery, and he decided to collect the old debt. He was not even caring about you before. Didn't you live your life in Buenos Aires left to your own?"

"Are you his lawyer now?" I said, frankly pissed off.

"No. Honestly, I would like you come with me, but I realise that it would be a mess in the end. I want that you return to him and live your life as happily as possible. Think on your children's behalf. They need you and you need them too. Lintorff was very clever to have them and give them to you. You're tied to them with unbreakable chains. You will never come to me. I know it since the boys were born. I can give you two or three more weeks under my protection. I can hold Lintorff for that long, but I'll have to inform him where you are."

"Please, don't tell him. Tell Alexei or Pavicevic. They will know what to do."

"All right, I will speak with Aliosha. I hope he doesn't hang up on me, like the last time. Have you been to the Louvre yet?"

"Not yet. I wasn't feeling very fit," I said almost inaudibly, feeling sick that he was not giving an option and returning me to the monster's den.

"Well, you should. Tomorrow one of my men will accompany you. I would like to see what you have been doing so far. That portrait of the Lintorff Duchess was incredible. Very… funny. You have quite a sharp tongue, well, brush in this case."

"It was a mistake it was put for sale. The Duchess hates me for it. Ostermann and Elisabetta von Lintorff put it on the auction," I said miserably, remembering the horrible yelling I got from her and Konrad. Both together.

"A 99,000 francs mistake; I would have bought it, but my wife didn't like it so much. Why didn't Lintorff offer to buy it? Would have been a fantastic family portrait," he chuckled. "Why on earth did you paint it? You did something so delicate and full of life with my daughter's and this one was almost aggressive on its beauty; a cheap, aggressive, snob beauty."

"Ostermann named it *Portrait of an unknown lady.*"

"Yes, "Lady with alley cat and diamonds" would have been too much!" he laughed.

"The original and intended one was the Duchess in an evening dress, with the diamonds tiara and a flower bouquet; lilies and roses and a background of green leaves, something youthful and full of light, as she is. I don't know why I painted the other one. I did it in three days and then, let it to dry. I was not even waiting for the layers to dry. Ostermann took it without my permission. The original is somewhere. The Duke took it away."

"Most probably he burned it down! I would have done the same and save the world a lot of pain!"

"It was not so bad. Only lifeless, like a hundred euros portrait, nothing like Sofia's. I didn't like to do it and it shows. She came up with this stupid idea to paint her."

"You're like Sergeant. You paint the people's soul. The one you presented is exactly like her. Cheap colours, the alley cat instead of a mink and the Titanic Jewellery. I think she wanted to humiliate you, and she got burnt instead."

"And I got shouted at by Lintorff," I grunted.

He laughed openly now. "He must have had a real bad time. To be told his wife is a cheap whore in front of all Zurich's high society. No... Worse. That she's a snob no matter if she comes from the Barberini, and I have my doubts. A cheap version of Carla Bruni. I'll call Aliosha in a week. You need some time to think things over, dear."

"I think we should go to bed. Together."

He dropped his cutlery over the dish, and gaped like an idiot at me. "It will not make me change my mind, Guntram. You're not into this type of business."

"We have many issues pending since 2001. I have no relationship with anybody at the moment, and you, by the look of all this, still have romantic ideas about me. I used to think that a friendship among us would be bad for you, but perhaps one night together will help us to continue with our lives. It's the more decent thing I can do for you."

"You don't love me, just appreciate me," he said resentfully.

"You also not. You're only after an idea you have about me. Perhaps, if you fulfil your desires, everything would be easier for both of us. I don't deny you're a very attractive man. Who knows, maybe years ago, I would have fallen for you. "

"Guntram, of all people, I never expected such a proposition from you," he said shocked and doubtful.

"You see? That's a preconception you have. I ceased to be that innocent twenty year old boy, looking at the world in awe, convinced people were good and caring, many years ago. I did many things too early for my age, and missed many others more appropriate for it. I forced myself to mature for one person, twisting nature. I'm older now and I know what I want."

"It's most unexpected. I'm surprised."

"Then let's do it and be no regrets on the next morning. We need to close this part of our lives."

"You would be closing this part of your life. I will be opening another. You will never be just another lover for me," he said very softly. I took his hand and kissed his fingers. "I will be regretting for the rest of my life what could have been, but you, perhaps, will rebuild your life and find another person to love. I love you too much to deny you this opportunity," he spoke, his words coming out slowly out of his mouth. Constantin bent his body over the table to kiss me on my lips.

I responded eagerly to this almost chaste kiss. Pity he doesn't know I will never be able to rebuild my life or to love another human being. We interrupted our kissing, panting a bit, his eyes were darker than the night, full of desire for me. I smiled at him, not afraid or ashamed of it, like I used to be with Lintorff. With him I always felt restrained, fearful that I would spoil the moment by saying something stupid or behaving like a child. Yeah, I loved him so much that the smallest gesture he made, could hurt me or sent me into paradise. I cared so much about him that I lived for his smiles and kisses. Even two years after I discovered the monster he was, I still long for his touch.

I took Constantin's hand and playfully pulled him toward me. "Should we not go to the bedroom? I'm not so wild as to do it on top of the table," I said.

"You don't know what you're missing. Perhaps later," he retorted, making me laugh.

We both went to my bedroom, mostly because I wanted to feel more secure. Going to his bed felt somewhat extreme for my taste. Call me silly, but this is how I felt at that time. Standing in front of the bed we started to kiss each other, passionately. I sensed his tongue demanding to enter my mouth and I opened it as he tightened his embrace on my waist pulling me closer to his body. I relaxed myself as much as I could, closing my eyes, trying to enjoy his ministrations. After all, that was really my first gay experience. No, I'm not crazy. With Konrad everything was flowing naturally since the first time, even his forced first kiss, but now I couldn't let myself go like I did with him because I wouldn't have gone anywhere left to my own. This time I would have to take an active role, and see if I really like it for what it was.

I broke our kiss, and without splitting our locked gazes I started to undo my tie. His eyes immediately went to my hands, following every move from my fingers. I tossed the thing aside.

"Your hands, they're so beautiful," he said, his eyes following my fingers unbuttoning my shirt. I smiled at him but he didn't even realise, so enthralled he was with my hands. Unable to hold himself any longer, he took them into his and started to kiss my fingers. "They create so many beautiful things," he whispered as he started to suck my fingers one after the other.

I kissed him again and that broke the spell that was threatening to engulf me. I took my shirt off and he started to get undressed by himself. I doubted a little when it came to the belt and trousers. He chuckled softly.

"Guntram, you're still so innocent after so many years. You're blushing. Let me do it, love," he smiled, helping me to get rid of my clothes and resuming his kisses as we both fell on top of the big bed. I could feel that he was as excited as I was. He left my mouth alone and he kissed me all over my neck and chest, going downwards, making me moan and arch my back to meet his mouth every time he pried his lips away from my skin. I felt he wanted to go for the oral sex part, but I said, "No, let's do it, don't play around. I need you." He seemed a bit cross at my demand, but he pulled away from me and knelt between my legs, placing my pelvis over his tights, my legs surrounding his hips. I felt the intrusion of his middle finger inside of me as he slowly started to stretch me. Two years of nothing almost turned me into a virgin as he pointed out between ragged breaths "you're so tight, dear, almost like you do it for the first time."

He was very careful in his thrusts, trying to hurt me the least as he could. After inserting his second finger and make me moan like a whore in heat, he asked me again if I was sure of what we wanted to do. I had a hard on and he wanted reassurance?

I incorporated myself, almost sitting over his lap, my legs still wrapped around him. I kissed him this time as passionately as I could and he placed me on top of his member penetrating me in one swift move. I almost cried of the result of a mix of pleasure and pain. I started to bounce over him at a very slow pace as my arms encircled his neck and my lips started to kiss softly his neck and my tongue lick his salty sweated skin.

His eyes were the most incredible, totally darkened and full of desire. He started to pound me more strongly than what I was doing, his hand accommodating me on top of him so he could have a deeper penetration and better control over my body. I stifled a cry by biting him on the shoulder, but he didn't care at all, too busy as he was riding me.

"Would you let me finish inside you, angel?"

"We do as you like," I answered as I was feeling I was also reaching my climax.

With one swift move he put me down from his lap and turned me around. "This way is much better. I can go deeper. It will be also less painful for you," he forced me to go onto all fours and again penetrated me, this time hitting that special place that makes you go mad. His pounding was slow and he changed the angle several times, giving me an incredible pleasure by doing it. My hips started to mimic his moves and I felt his hand firmly gripping my member, playing with the tip and strongly rubbing it. His grunting in my ears made me lose all control and we both climaxed together.

We both were spent afterwards. He hugged me against his chest and kissed me again on the forehead. "It was incredible, angel. The best I had in years," he whispered in awe.

"We can still repeat it," I laughed, happy that he had it good, as I could feel he was not lying.

"Again? I thought you had to take things easy," he replied to me visibly amused at the thought that I wanted more. Man, you weren't without any for two years!

"We have to explore more your technique. Alexei told me you were incredible in bed."

"He can look like a cherub, but in bed he's an experience you won't forget easily," he said remembering him. "That cook is very lucky."

"You are not bad at all. I really would like to repeat some time later," I said, softly smiling at him. Strangely, I didn't feel restrained at all or that embarrassed feeling I normally had with Konrad. Also the need of cuddling with him wasn't so strong like after doing it with Lintorff. I mean, I always needed to bury myself into his broad chest and feel his soft caressing hands over my skin or hear him, softly whispering words of love in my ear.

Nevertheless we did it on different positions twice again. One standing against the mantelpiece and another in the shower, I gripping the best as I could, the taps.

I can't really complain. It was good sex. Really good. He has a lot of technique if I'm to judge by all the effort he put into it, and his certified experience with many lovers, including Alexei—who's not exactly a neophyte in such things—but there was something missing. Physically he's all you should desire in a lover; great body, well endowed, soft hands, and creative in bed. Much more than Lintorff as he's the only I can compare with. I had a great time, but it wasn't more than that. Sex. No butterflies flying in my stomach. No accelerated heart rate beyond the release part. No anticipation or longing, waiting for his next touch.

It was like doing it with your best friend. Good, but I can't shake the feeling of doing something wrong. Fortunately, he looked very satisfied with the exchange and we both quenched our thirst.

We spent two more days practising bed sports. I'm still surprised that he let me take the active role twice. It was nice to be on that side, but it wasn't so incredible as to repeat it. I guess maybe I'm not into girls so much as I originally believed. I wonder why the German never let me do it before. However, it's not like I'm going to ask him or do it with him.

* * *

July 13th, 2008

Today, Constantin will call Alexei and speak with him. He's gone to London to put some distance when the storm breaks loose. It's for the best. Alexei hates him, and when he finds out I was staying with him he will come and put a bullet between his eyes for not telling before… and will have his Duke's blessing for that. Last night, we said our goodbyes as we both know we will never meet again under these circumstances.

"Please Guntram, understand my reasons for giving you back to Lintorff. There's nothing in this world that would please me more than having you with me for the rest of my life, but you will hate me at some point. I could only offer you another golden prison, without your children, to protect you from Lintorff's fury. You enjoyed our time together, but you don't love me. I can see it."

"I don't love Lintorff," I defended myself. "He can drop dead," I said this time not sounding so resolute as was my original intention.

"I'm not so sure of that. Most of my performance was compared with his," I opened my mouth like an idiot. How did he realise? I was always putting my best face. He chuckled. "This is what I love the most about you. Your face shows everything. You're not polluted like the others."

"That's because I have nothing else to compare with. Come back in a few years and we will see," I growled, almost dead with shame.

"You? Playing the boy toy? Never! You wouldn't be able to do it. You're one man's love. You have found your one and perhaps one day you will forgive his lies. In a way, I can side with him. I would have done the unspeakable to keep you at my side, angel," he said kissing me for the last time.

I'd better go for a walk. I need some fresh air. The Siberian Ape I got for "protection" is a nice and quiet guy. Perhaps going again to the Orsay Museum would help. I'm tired of taking notes in the Louvre. It's horrible to have a bunch of tourist every two seconds looking over your shoulder and giving you an opinion. I know, they're nice but I'm not doing it for their applause. I don't expect a medal.

* * *

I still can't believe it. I never reached the Quai d'Orsay. I stopped much earlier, by a news-stand at the Seine's border, before reaching the bridge. I wanted to look at the newspapers as I haven't looked at any for a long time. A month.

There, like a snake, in the front page of "Paris Match" was a small photo of Stefania von Lintorff and the words "Mort tragique d'une celébrité". I bought the magazine, and went to sit in a café to read it. My Russian shadow sat next to me, looking totally bored as I was going through the pages looking for the story.

"Celebrity dies tragically"
"Stefania Barberini di Santa Croce, 37, former fashion programs hostess in the Italian Television, well known top model and third daughter of the Italian tycoon, Marco Barberini, passed away on July 10th in a tragic car crash in Switzerland."

"Her manager, Piero della Rosa, was driving the vehicle in which both were killed. According to internal police sources, the car entered in the Gotthard Road Tunnel faster than the permitted speed, colliding with a long line of trailers standing in an traffic jam. The very early hour, 5 a.m., as they both were coming back from a charity event, combined with bad weather conditions, didn't allow the driver to reduce the speed, frontally colliding. No other people were injured."

"Last March, Barberini married in a dream wedding ceremony, Konrad von Lintorff, 50, a German aristocrat, owner of several banks and companies. She was expecting a child for next winter. Her memorial service will be held in Rome."

I had to take several breaths and read the piece several times over to understand it. She was pregnant. Poor woman. She was young and to die so stupidly. One drunken driver who couldn't see a lorry. I felt sad for her, even if she never liked me at all or I, her.

Poor Konrad. He lost a child. He was very sad when he knew that only two of the three babies had survived the process, and now he had lost his third baby again. He also lost his wife. No matter the lies he told me about marrying her to make me react and that he still loved me, he liked her. He was visiting her several times per week in the night when he was around before the marriage. I crossed with him several times on the stairs, and it was a horrible moment for me. It hurt me deeply, but I wouldn't give him the pleasure of seeing me crying like a baby at how easily he had found a replacement for me.

I felt really bad for him. This must have been a great shock.

Chapter 21

Ferdinand von Kleist's Diary.
July 20th, 2008

We are recovering our normal rhythm after Stefania's death. Most unexpected. That idiot was so drunk that he could have not seen a Panzer Division. 1.7 grams alcohol! How could he drive? Why was she letting him do it? He couldn't have walked straight! There were not even brake marks on the road.

Konrad decided to bury her in her family's vault, in Rome. He had to endure the press, and show a grievous face in public. He's not happy for her death, but he's not sad altogether.

He stopped all public meetings and work for a full week, and remained with his children at home. I think he has told them nothing. They didn't like Stefania, and it makes no sense to upset them with this sad news. Klaus and Karl only want to know when Guntram will be back and when he will take them for holidays to the place "with ponies". The boys already got rid of two nannies, and number three will be running away soon, according to Konrad. They're impossible to control, even for the father. It is a mystery how Guntram could keep those two monsters in check. With him they always behaved well. Now they're two hooligans, one covering for the other. Team spirit is overvalued.

This morning, Konrad, Michael and I flew to New York. There are informal meetings with the FED over the banking secrecy and fiscal paradises law changes; just a façade for the press. This subprime mortgage crisis is very convenient for us, but it will kill many of our friends. Bernanke affirms Fannie Mae and Freddie Mac "are in no danger of failing". After several billions in, perhaps they will survive. We did relatively fine, selling from 12,000 to 14,000 even if we were called lunatics. Considering how things look, we might start to look around in 8,000 points; currencies trading, commodities and European Bonds only. The rest is in cash or gold futures. UBS-AG is in real troubles now. Bearn Sterns is dead, fortunately, and the next will be Lehman and sooner than they think.

I still don't understand why he didn't forewarn many of the Order's members. We had several casualties, and he only took care of his banks and hedge funds, increasing his personal fortune, and saving some of the middle and lower members. He's after something. He never forgave them that Repin was accepted against his advice. At this pace, Repin could destroy nothing in the Order because Konrad will save him the trouble. The funny thing is, that all of them are now eating from his hand, terrified that he will not help them to recover from the hard blow he has inflicted upon them.

He even settled the score with Marianne von Lintorff. She had her money and her husband's in a private hedge fund, established in Bahamas. Somehow her administrators heavily bet on the American Stock Market and bought CDO's like crazy (SFCDOs). Very aggressive investments in my opinion. She had huge losses by December 2007, and debts over twenty-seven million dollars.

She burst into Konrad's office one day before Christmas, totally furious. She went directly toward his son's desk and gave him a huge slap on the face. Konrad didn't react, and just looked at her with curiosity, like when we were children and he would catch a salamander and carefully study it.

"You bribed my managers into buying that rubbish! You ruined my husband!"

"This is an enormous international crisis. None of us is safe from falling, Madam."

"You're the demon's spawn! I hope you suffer in Hell like all your line."

"Hell would be a wonderful place compared to your motherly bosom. You destroyed the only good thing that was in my life. How were your words, Madam? "We are even now"."

"My husband will end in jail because of our debts!"

"You can always sell the Art collection at my house in Paris to me. Guntram always liked Meissen porcelain figures. My banks can lend you the rest of the money with your boyfriend's companies as collateral. My father's allowance should be enough as to support you, and pay the money back, if you live accordingly to your new financial situation."

She stormed out of the room. I knew nothing of this. I would have forbidden him to do something like that. One thing is to punish your greedy and stupid associates, and another your own mother. "Konrad, this is too much, even for your standards."

"It's only money. She nearly killed my Guntram, and ruined my life for something I didn't do."

"Anyway, she's only a deranged woman still grieving over her son's death. Place yourself in her shoes."

"A deranged woman should have not so much power. End of discussion, Ferdinand."

Nevertheless, in the middle of the hugest financial crisis we will ever see, no matter if we were expecting it since 2006, Michael Dähler is playing "Pinball" with his laptop.

"Would you stop it? I can't think."

"It relaxes me and allows me to think better. Some of us are truly paid for thinking," he said with his whinny voice.

"Exactly, this is why I need to concentrate on these reports from "Capital Markets" people."

"All right, we should not interfere with this delicate mental process of yours. Your brain might overload with the effort."

"Michael, you're an idiot!"

"Silence you two! Next time I'll bring Klaus Maria and Karl Maria along, and certainly I'll have more peace than with two old bickering wives!" Konrad roared at us.

We both kept quiet. He's in a bad mood since Guntram's escapade and the publication of the Banks and Financial Institutions combined losses on the subprime mortgages crisis; 435 billions. Who's such a cretin as to make debts to buy something labelled "subprime"? If you buy junk bonds you know what they are no matter how sophisticated they might look. Rule number one in this business; if you're going to invest, see if you get your capital back. That applies for industries, countries, commodities, etc. People only look in the figure beside the percentage sign.

Just when he looked appeased enough, and was returning to his own work, my mobile phone rang very loudly. Konrad looked at me, furiously.

"Von Kleist."

"Hello Ferdinand," I could have died right there, when I recognized Guntram's soft voice.

"Hello Guntram," I could feel Konrad and Michael stares fixed on me, and I made a stopping gesture with my hand lowering my gaze so they wouldn't jump on me. "It's nice to hear you again. Are you all right, child?"

"Yes Ferdinand. I'm fine. I read in the newspapers about Stefania's death. I'm sorry."

"It was most unexpected and tragic. She was so full of life."

"How is the Duke? I read she was pregnant. How is he doing, now?"

"You know Konrad, Guntram. He's deeply affected, but holding up. Would you like to speak with him? He's very concerned about you, and it will be very good for him to hear your voice, child."

"No. I don't know what to tell him. Just tell him I'm sorry for his loss and I'll pray he will recover soon from his grief. Could you please send my regards to his children?"

"Yes, of course. I'll tell him. Why don't you come and see by yourself the children? They're very sad without you. They need you." And we need you to shut them up, please!

"I've sent you a parcel with some drawings for them. They will arrive to your house tomorrow or the day after. It's a folder with illustrations of a story they liked so much, and asked me to do a week before I was sick. If the Duke thinks it's appropriate, could you give it to them?"

"Of course, I will ask Konrad." He was almost on top of me, willing to tear the phone from my hands. "Do you need anything? You left without your medications. We don't even know where you are."

"I'm still in Europe, and perhaps we will see each other sooner than you think. Good bye, Ferdinand."

"Wait!" No chance, he hung up on me. I nearly punched the 3G rubbish.

"What did he say?"

"He's fine. He wants to know how are you coping with the baby's loss and Stefania's also, but he doesn't want to speak with you. Typical Guntram. He will pray that you recover from your grief. He sent some drawings for your children to my house, and only if you allow it, I should give them to the boys. He mentioned something about seeing us "sooner than you think". End of story."

"Did he say where he was?" Michael, the clever, asked.

"Europe, but tomorrow we'll see the letter's envelope."

"Goran's people should look at it." Konrad ordered, deeply thinking. "Does he believe Stefania was pregnant from me?"

"Konrad, Guntram lives in a world full of fluffy bunnies. Of course he believes it! You were married to her, therefore, you're the father, and now you're devastated because of the baby's loss. He sounded so full of sorrow for you."

"Interesting," he said, returning to his papers.

* * *

July 24th, 2008

I would like to know where Goran and Alexei are this time. They both disappeared this morning without any explanation. When they're back, I will tell them what I think about leaving AWOL."

Guntram's parcel was checked thoroughly, and it was sent from Paris. Our people are going there... without Goran. It contained a nice folder full with nine watercolours depicting the story of *The Wonderful Musician* by the Grimm Brothers with the original German Text, written in ink at the bottom of each page, bounded together with a red ribbon.

"It's too delicate to give to the children. I will show them the book and read it, but I will keep it," was Konrad's verdict. "They're like Arthur Rackham's illustrations, but less dark; very elegant. It's understandable that he sold so many books in the past."

* * *

Guntram de Lisle's Diary
July 25th, 2008

This morning, I was drawing, well illustrating is a more appropriate term, another story for the collection of Folk's tales, Madam Van Breda wants to publish. She said as the first set was completely sold out, and she had to make five editions more, she wanted to try her luck again. People liked "Cinderella, the Little Riding Red Hood, the Little Mermaid, the Three Bears and The Sleeping Beauty." volume. I'm supposed to do it exactly like the others. "Please, keep the same quality in the drawing, so detailed and delicate at the same time. I'm thinking in translating them into English and distribute it worldwide."

As I was tired of snotty princesses, I suggested that we use animals this time. "The Musicians from Bremen", the "Frog King", "The Golden Bird", "Puss in Boots" and I'm open to suggestions. At the moment I'm with the golden bird. I think Gustave Doré and Arthur Rackham already did a fantastic job, but there are so many ugly things around for children that at least I can try to paint something that looks like a real bear or a wolf.

I'm digressing as usual. Malchenko entered the room, and announced to me that Oblomov and two other gentlemen were here to speak with me. I sighed, cleaned my hands, flattened the wrinkles in my shirt and put on the jacket.

In the living room, Oblomov, big and serious as I remembered him, was sitting with Goran and Alexei. I felt sick to see them. Goran rose from the chair and came to me, and when I was expecting the well deserved blow from him, he gave me a hug.

"Little brother. I was worried for you. How could you come here?"

"Pavicevic, not all of us share your hobby," Oblomov huffed dryly. "Let the Sable sit, we have to speak, and see how we fix this mess created by our bosses."

"Guntram. I'm glad to see you," Alexei said giving me a hug also.

"I'm glad to see you two also," I said very shyly.

"Sit, boy," Oblomov ordered me. "As you know, Mr. Repin asked me to contact Aliosha over your stay here. I did it on the 11th, but under the present circumstances, we decided to postpone this meeting till today. You will be returned to them. What they do with you is their problem, but I want to be sure that you will go back to Lintorff and stay there."

"I don't want to go to him. Please Alexei, isn't there a way out for me?"

"I'm afraid not, little brother," Goran said sadly. "The Duke wants you back. The minute he finds out you were here with Repin, it might cause a war between them."

"Guntram, perhaps it's time you hear our side of the story. The soldiers' side, not the generals'," Alexei started. "You only see the Duke and Repin fighting over you. You hear their arguments, and find out the Machiavellian moves made to ruin each other chances. So far, everything remains in a theoretical field for you. Some shouting, lies, deceptions, some well chosen words are all the things you have seen over the last six or seven years. However, we, the soldiers, are tired of this mess. We pay with our blood and our brother's blood our master's wars. You knew of Amundsen's death and Repin's man in Zurich, but those are only two from a much larger list. Related to this mess, I have already counted over forty bodies."

"As Aliosha said, if you don't go back to Lintorff, and make him believe you're going by your own will, he will come after us, and this time, it will be total war as my boss defied directly the Griffin. Repin's now a member of the Order. Instead of forty, we will be counting hundreds or thousands of bodies."

"They will clash at some point. It's unavoidable. Both want the same things, and it's not only me," I said.

"Yes, but perhaps it will happen in ten or fifteen years. As a parent, tell me, would you prevent a child to enjoy his father for ten years more?" Alexei intoned.

"No, I can't."

"Then you know what to do. Come with us. Goran will speak with the Duke, and arrange that you stay with him or with me, if you prefer. There must be a way for you two to solve your differences, and live together in peace, for your children's sake. The poor dears cry almost constantly for you, Guntram. They're convinced that you died, and their father doesn't want to tell them. Even if the father is a bastard, they don't deserve to pay for his mistakes. Come back, Guntram. Set new rules for living together, but I beg you, stop what is coming our way." Alexei begged me, sounding so terribly convincing.

"Alexei, you don't know what you're asking from me. You don't know the reasons for our breakup."

"Whatever he has done in the past, is it worth the sacrifice of hundreds of innocent lives? I don't mean us. Lintorff practically handed on a silver plate a whole Chechen village to the Russian Army to retaliate for Morozov's attack over his man in Georgia," Oblomov said sadly.

I felt very sick as I remembered that. "Guntram, nobody is asking you to love him again. We only want that you give him a second chance to redeem himself in your eyes," Alexei pleaded.

"Alexei, if you were my place, you, of all people, wouldn't ask me what you do now. Tell me this, could you forgive Constantin?"

He looked at me puzzled for a long time, and a deep frown marred his face. "Ten years ago, I would have said "no". Now, I don't know. There were some attenuating facts, like he gave me another life, and protected me from the other wolves. I could never be friends with him, that's for sure. I only want to forget him."

"This is exactly what I want. We're not so different my friend."

"Guntram, I told you once that you should forgive and carry on because living to revenge the dead ones is no life. Think on this, do you want to spend the rest of your life running away from him? You could have a new life taking care of your children."

"Goran, my only reason to stay those two years were the children. I don't care if he drops dead at this moment. In fact, my life would be easier if he does," I lied firmly, not diverting my eyes from Goran's black ones.

"That's not true. If it were so, you would have not called Ferdinand to see how he was doing after his wife's death," he rebutted me in his calm and icy way of doing things. "You still like him or even love him, but for some reason you don't want to accept it."

"I have my reasons, and they're strong enough as to hate him."

"Guntram, at some point we will have to tell him where you are, and all hell will break loose."Alexei almost sounded sorry and begging.

"Boy, if you think for a minute that I will let you cross that door, and lose an invaluable trading card for my organization, you're mad. The minute those two go away without you, I'm calling Lintorff and telling him to pick you up or better, I will put you myself in front of his doorstep. I will not risk my soldiers any more because of you," Oblomov huffed. "I accepted this conversation so they would butter you up a little and you will go and stay there, not causing me any more trouble."

"Your boss will not allow you to do so," I said firmly.

"Boy, a few nights of fucking satisfied his hunger for you. At the moment, he's glad with what he got, and it shouldn't leave this room. Perhaps in a few months, he will start again to look for you, when his latest lover is not at your level, but you don't have those months of time left."

Goran and Alexei looked both shocked, and some red crept into their cheeks as Oblomov explained my night activities.

"Go back to where you belong. You could have had much worse. Lintorff will be a good master if you behave, and none of us, much less Repin, will tell a thing about your bed entanglement with him. He doesn't need to know it. We are all at peace now."

"I'm not one of your whores, Oblomov. Whatever I did with your boss was because we both wanted it."

"Right. The moment you became Lintorff's bitch, he owned you completely. Go back to him and be glad he's not throwing you into one of our whorehouses or letting his men fuck you to death."

"Don't you dare to compare Konrad with the likes of you!" I shouted before I realised what I'd done. Oblomov smiled knowingly.

"Lie all what you want to yourself, but don't try it with me. You still defend him. You love him. That's enough for me. Aliosha, take the boy now. You have three hours to leave the country before Mr. Repin returns. I think you don't want to meet him."

"Certainly not. Tell him to miss my phone number, will you?"

"Of course, boy. Guntram, go home now and stay there. I don't want to see you in my territory ever again. Really. You have nothing to do with the likes of us. Sables are for royalty," he smiled, not offended at all. "Pavicevic, next time we see each other, we will settle our scores."

"It will be my pleasure." Goran said, giving him a disdainful look, and forcibly taking me by the elbow, lifting me from my chair. He dragged me toward the door as Alexei had to pace briskly to catch up with us.

There was a big black Mercedes waiting for us and Goran almost pushed me in. He sat beside me as Alexei took the passenger's place. "Crillon," he grunted at the chauffeur.

When we got to the hotel, only he and I descended from the car. "Alexei goes to the Airport. You stay with me, and we'll fly tomorrow. We need to speak."

He led me to a suite on the sixth floor. "I have the next room. Don't try to run, Guntram. Milan will stay with you tonight, and our rooms are connected."

I felt incensed. "What's next? You tie me to the bed?"

"No. Milan will stay at your living room. Don't cross him. Now you have to learn the story of your life for the past month. There can be no gaps, Guntram. The Duke has to believe you return to him willingly."

"I'm not going willingly. Oblomov threw me out!"

"You should never tell him about your infidelity with Repin. I don't want the London mess repeated again," he continued without caring what I was saying.

"What infidelity? We broke up two years ago. He married and noisily fucked that woman in front of me! I wanted to close a story with a person who has been in love with me for seven years and I'm unfaithful? You heard Oblomov, he's happy with several nights together."

"Do you love him? Repin, I mean."

"I don't know. I appreciate him like a friend."

"I don't go to bed with my friends."

"All right, I don't love him, but at the moment it was the right thing to do! It was just sex!"

"Good, so you don't feel any remorse?"

"Of course not! We're both adults and single! Well, I am at least. I just wanted to release the tension, and see how it was with other men."

"Did you like it?"

"I'm not answering you that!" He looked at me, freezing my blood. "All right, it wasn't bad, but not exactly thrilling. I will not repeat it. It's not worthy of the trouble," I mumbled ashamed, but he was still giving me "the look". "All right, with Konrad it was hundred times better, and I'm a bit disappointed. With the Duke, a normal one, was like the *Quatorze Juillet*. Repin is not bad in bed, he seems to have a lot of experience, but everything is mechanically done," I confessed very embarrassed.

"Good, that's what I wanted to hear. Consider this as an educational experience, nothing to be ashamed of, and forget it. Never tell the Duke. It's over and he never told you about his bed gymnastics. Don't do it again because we could not cover you twice, little brother. Now, let's review your story."

"Goran are you telling me to keep this to myself when I almost died of guilt because of a single kiss?"

"You were very young and impressionable, totally in love with him. Now you're older and wiser. For men like us, it's not a problem to do it as you don't get entangled with the whore. You said it, it was mechanical. He will never ask and you will never tell."

I had to sit on the brocade couch. These men are impossible! OK, I will keep it to myself after all, it's not Konrad's business any more who I fuck with.

Since when Lintorff is Konrad again? Shit! Oblomov is totally wrong. They're playing with me as if I were a puppet.

"Guntram, we need that you learn your part. We really don't want to fight. We're tired. Do it for all of us," he sounded like he was pleading. "If you two ever fix your problems, that is another story. He wants you back, and the children cry for you the whole time. Jean Jacques told Alexei that Klaus believes his father is lying to him. You must be dead because you left all of your clothes therefore, you're not on holidays."

"Does he think so?" I felt terrible guilty if Klaus and Karl were having such a bad time.

"They cry almost on a daily basis. They are unruly, don't respect their father, and already got rid of two nannies. They hate them and say those women want to take your place."

"How is the Duke feeling after the unborn baby's death?" I didn't want to ask about her. Most probably, he hurts over her passing but I didn't want to hear it. I would have been too painful for me.

"Like always. Putting his sternest face, and working like crazy. Since her death, he was only once in Zurich, with the book you sent. I think he doesn't want to acknowledge it." Goran sighed, sounding very sad.

That sounded very much like him. Work until you drop dead from exhaustion and don't have to think on what you lost. I pitied him. After all he's a big child surrounded by sharks and wolves, fighting the best as he can to keep himself afloat. He must be having a really bad time alone. When Löwenstein died, I was the only one who was with him, although briefly. Stefania only went to the funeral.

"Perhaps I should speak with him to see how he's coping with it," I trailed doubtfully. "I miss my children too and it's unfair to make them suffer because of our problems. I don't know if I could endure to live under the same roof with him."

"Guntram, you have the upper hand now. He's desperate to have you back, and will accept your conditions. He nearly drove me crazy this month, breathing down my neck, forcing me to look for you almost everywhere. Ask him to let you live alone in Zurich. You can always stay with the children till they go to bed, and then return to your own house."

"That might work. I love the children as much I dislike the father," I pondered. Dislike is not the exact word. I don't hate him even if I should. I feel nothing for him. That's right. Indifference. If I defended him in front of Oblomov, it was out of habit, nothing more. People should not see things where there are none.

"Good. Let's work now," he said abruptly taking me out of my reverie.

No, I'm not in love with that asshole. He ruined my life. He gave me everything and plunged me into the darkest misery without a second thought. He's a selfish bastard whose only thought is his own well-being. Like a child. As Constantin said, he saw me, took a fancy on me and decided to collect my father's debts, no matter what.

Children are selfish because they need all the protection you can give them.

However, he's more than fifty years old, and it's time he matures.
    Right?

Chapter 22

July 27th, 2008

Goran made sure that I "learned my story". After leaving Switzerland, I was going to Madrid for a full week, and from there I travelled by train to Paris where I stayed in a small hotel. I had some cash money left from some paintings I've sold recently, and I was starting to look for another job when I heard about Stefania's death. That I've called Ferdinand and sent the pictures for the children, backed up my story. I was too upset for being "kicked out" of the house, and didn't want to talk to any of them. I never realised all the gorillas were worried about me. Of course, I had my pills with me as I bought more in Spain where nobody asks if you pay cash. I swear, Goran watches soap operas in his free time. Who would be so idiotic as to believe that I, after living in Hell for two years, will be upset I was fired like a serf? Wait, serfs were never fired, they belonged to the land and their Masters; they were "put to sleep", like the dogs.

Anyway, I felt bad for leaving the children and I called Goran to ask him (let's leave Alexei out of the mess. He made some rubbish in Pakistan and the Duke is cross with him. Nothing serious), if he could "convince his Excellency" to let me come back for the children. My only condition was to live outside the castle. If I'm asking to "come back", why do I have terms?

It's the most stupid, childish and feeble story I've ever heard. Why don't we try "my dog ate my homework"?

Goran thinks it will work without a hitch. I should be relaxed, and let him do the introductory talk with Konrad. "The rest will come naturally" (?).

"For Christ's sake throw that stupid diary of yours to the trash, Guntram! No better, let's burn it in the bathroom. Good it's a spiral notebook. We can do some "editing". We keep only your sketches of Parisian things. All text is gone. You were too depressed to write."

"Remember one thing when we're in front of the Duke," he told me in the plane before landing early in the morning.

"Lie as close to the truth as possible?" I smirked.

"No. They're dead and you're alive. What's in the grave, stays there. Don't let them ruin your life, little brother. No one can live for ever full of poison like you intend to do."

He drove me to the Bank in Börsenstrasse. I was not really expected, because the nice receptionist at the entrance, dropped very unprofessionally the phone when she saw us.

"No calls, Clara," Goran growled at her going directly to the elevator, with me in tow.

"Should we not go to your office?" I asked as he pushed the "5" button.

"Guntram, don't start. You'll be fine."

"Not so sure. I'm doing this for all of you, not because I like it."

"Whatever," he said tiredly. "Do a good job."

Monika's and the other secretaries' reaction were very similar to the receptionist's. I was away, not dead, women.

"Hello Guntram. I'm very glad to see you," Monika greeted me, regaining her poise in no time, like the real queen she is. "I'm afraid the Duke is in a meeting with some people from the ECB but he will finish soon. Would you like to wait in his office?"

"Hello Monika. I'm also glad to see you. If Goran doesn't mind, I would like to wait in his office."

"I'll call Michael, dear. Ferdinand is in Brussels today."

"No need to. By the way, could you prepare the documents I left? The ones with the house transfer for the Lintorff children?" I asked.

"His Excellency forbade me to do it. I'm sorry dear."

"I see. Thank you. I hope it didn't pose a problem for you."

"Not at all, dear. Would you like something to drink? You could stay at my office, if you want. You should tell me where you've been."

"Madrid and Paris. Could you inform me when the Duke could spare a moment of his time?"

"Yes, of course."

"Ms Dähler, I would like some tea, could you send it to the meeting room? Come Guntram." Goran ordered without leaving any room for a discussion. I looked at him furiously but he was unimpressed, like always.

We sat at the big round table, our faces reflected on the polished mahogany table. We were silent and I left the tea untouched. Time passed like a slow torture. I couldn't help to think all this was a terrible mistake. I've should have gone somewhere else, never asked for Repin's help and much less agreeing with Goran and Alexei's plan. All for what? To save some mobsters' lives? They will find another reason to butcher each other in no time. No, I came here because I miss the children and I will cope with this asshole only to be with them. I did it once, I can do it again.

The door suddenly opened and there was standing Konrad, taller than I remembered him, dressed in a black suit and a blue tie. He was wearing mourning clothes for her and the baby. We both looked at each other, our eyes fixed. I didn't stand as I heard Goran doing. My throat felt very dried as my heartbeat increased his beating almost making me dizzy. I took a deep breath in a useless attempt to calm down the butterflies in my stomach.

Unable to stand his penetrating glare, I turned my gaze toward Goran, half expecting he would start the talks, but he had disappeared. Typical from the Serb. Konrad, closed the door softly and advanced toward me, reminding me of the lions when they take positions before jumping on their preys. He stood in front of me, looking at me as he didn't really believe I was there.

"I'm sorry for your loss, my Duke," I said almost inaudibly, my voice coming out raspy.

"Thank you. It was a hard blow to lose the child," he said with deep sorrow in his eyes. I felt so sorry for him. No matter if he's a bastard, he always liked children and was good to them.

"I can imagine." I went mute. I didn't know what else to say.

"Did you come on your own volition?" he asked, sitting at the chair next to me, forcing me to turn to face him.

"Yes, I did. I missed your children. I also wanted to see how you fared, Sire."

"There's no need to be so formal, Guntram. You never were my employee. I will not lie to you. I was going to divorce Stefania, but the baby prevented it. Karl and Klaus miss you terribly. They will be very happy to see you. Every night, I have to read the book you sent for them," he told me, softly, his voice quivering a little. I was speechless also, and had a hard time trying to find what else to say.

"Would you allow me to visit them?" I asked, fearfully.

"Every time you want. They need you more than me. The poor dears were very affected by your departure. Their characters changed a lot, and cry permanently for no reason at all. Everything is exactly as you left it, but your paintings. I'm afraid Stefania ordered their destruction."

"It's all right. They were not good. There was a picture of Klaus and Karl I wanted to give them."

"It's in my bedroom. One of the maids saved it from the bonfire. It's very beautiful. Would you like to come today? For the visit, I mean."

"If you don't mind, I could go in the afternoon and leave when you arrive."

"I was hoping to have dinner with you, Jean Jacques is back. We have much to discuss. Where are you staying now?"

"Nowhere. I mean, Goran has offered me to stay with him."

"The children will like if you stay with them for the night. They're very afraid of the dark these days. Please, Guntram. Do it for them."

"I'm not sure it's a good idea."

"Please, stay with us," he said taking my hand, and I let it there, my fingers hidden under his big palm. I nodded my agreement, knowing that was a mistake, but I was dying to see Klaus and Karl. "We can go now, if you want. It's time for their lunch."

"Don't you have to work?" I asked puzzled. "I'm sorry," I apologized for my outburst. He smiled at me gently, but sadly.

"Yes, I should finish some things, but I cancelled all meetings for today. Come, you'll stay in my office."

"I don't want to intrude."

"I insist," he said, raising and pulling me along. Some things never change, like his selective hearing and overbearing manners. Like many years before in Venice, I meekly followed him to his office.

It was exactly as I remembered. The place where my paint of Torcello's stream used to be was now occupied by one drawing I made years ago of the children sitting in the beach in Sylt. Over his desk there was a photo of the children, he and I. It was taken during the Christmas of 2005. I lost my colours, but said nothing. He made a small gesture with the hand, indicating me that I could sit on the coach by the window, my usual spot when I was a student. I sat there quietly, looking through the window.

Michael entered the office with a full load of folders for Konrad. I smiled weakly at him as greeting as I saw he was dying to speak with me. I turned my face again toward the window.

"You look fine Guntram," he exploded, unable to control his curiosity and eagerness any longer.

"Thank you. It's nice to see you again, Michael," I smiled back at him but sadly.

"Do you want to have lunch with us? Goran is coming along," he blurted out, not looking at his boss who, by the way, was already fulminating him with his eyes. Konrad loudly closed the leather bounded folder, and Michael slightly jumped at the noise.

"We are leaving in a few minutes. He will have lunch with me at the Königshalle."

"I see. Good bye Guntram," Michael mumbled, leaving the room fast, clutching the papers just signed without waiting to be excused.

"My Duke, it wouldn't be a good idea for me to go to this place. I have nothing else to do with its people."

"I'm having lunch with my Aunt Elisabetta. I can't postpone it."

"I can return later."

"No. I gave my permission to visit the children too hastily. I've been pondering if it's good for them or not. You come and go whenever you want, instilling more fears in them. A safe, sound and stable environment is what they need. Perhaps they will cry for a few months more, but they will finally overcome your absence."

"I understand, Sire. Good day," I said, raising from the couch and fighting like crazy to keep my tears at bay.

"I'm willing to give you a second chance, but on my terms. You will live in my house, and resume your duties as Consort. I don't want you playing their tutor on a part time basis. This permanent war we had going on for the last two years has depleted my patience and energies. You should decide once and for all what you want to do. Either you agree with this or you definitively get out of my and my children's lives."

"What am I suppose to understand as my "Consort duties"?" I spat making a great effort to control the bile rising to my throat.

"Your support in every aspect; you will remain permanently at the children's side, live under my roof, respect me and obey the orders I give. If I say you come to a meeting, you do it. No more insubordination from your part. I will not ask you, for the moment, to resume the cohabitation with me, but you will stop behaving like a servant in my own house. You will return to your previous room in my quarters. You will call me by my Christian name again, and if I ever hear you using a derogative voice like I've had to endure during the last two years, you are out."

"I will never let me touch again!" I roared.

"It's your choice Guntram. You didn't want to be my sons' tutor any longer, then you can be my Consort or leave forever."

"I hate you. You ruined my life and my family's."

"Your father jumped out of the window. He offered you to me. I didn't look for you. You came to me now, on your own will. You almost ruined my son's lives, and do you want that I treat you kindly? Were you generous to them or to me? Now, which is your choice?"

"I'll stay for them, but I swear your life will be a living hell."

"Be nice or I'll cast you away. Behave."

"I'm not a whore like the ones you like so much. I will not fake love or even appreciation for you. You disgust me to no end."

"You have expressed yourself Guntram. Happy now?" He smirked at me, raising an eyebrow as I threw him a killing glare. "It's been a long time since I see you reacting to anything I say. Pity you have a heart condition, angry sex is very exciting and rewarding."

"I hate you."

"Love and hate are closer than you think. You have ten minutes to compose yourself before we leave to meet Elisabetta. We'll see if you can behave."

"Fuck you!" I couldn't help to shout him.

"See? You're already asking for it. Was it so hard, Guntram?" He mocked me. I stormed out of the office, crossing the corridor toward the normal elevator, not his private one. I punched the button and immediately the image of Karl and Klaus assaulted me.

I couldn't leave them again. They were my babies and I had almost ruined their life. I drowned in sorrow, guilt and despair as I entered inside. I pushed again the first floor button, and had to make an incredible effort not to cry, and a greater one when a secretary joined me on the second floor. I nearly had to step on my own foot to prevent to push her aside to exit the suffocating elevator first. She softly and professionally smiled at me as a farewell gesture and I nodded.

I crossed the hall toward the entrance and there was his black limo already waiting. I stopped in my tracks, gaping at the monstrous car, looking like a coffin. The doorman ran to open the door for me, and I knew that I was at a crossroad. I could go forever and this time be really free, and die of a broken heart for not seeing my babies or I could go in and enjoy them, living with a monster. I stood there, motionless, thinking hard what to do, as the man kept the door open.

"I will not wait for you. Fix your tie," Konrad said, nonchalantly, passing beside me with his long strides. Mind absently, I straightened the collar and the bloody tie. I took a deep breath and went straight to the car. He had not entered yet, and I had to hurry to go inside before he would lose his temper for being kept waiting. I sat on the left side looking at the window, ignoring him as he took the right one.

Set my own conditions? My ass! I wanted to skin and gut Alexei and Goran together—alive and slowly. Fucking hypocrites! All was a set up since the beginning, and I was an idiot to believe them.

We arrived in no time to the elegant, exclusive and bloody restaurant. Konrad left the car first, and I went after him. He took his usual table beside a large widow overlooking the lake, but with a good view of what was transpiring in the room at the same time.

"At my left, Guntram. Elizabetta should have the right side," he indicated to me, very coldly. I complied without saying a word, and continued to ignore him as he dismissed the maître.

"After lunch we will go home and we can see the children together. I suggest you improve your mood as my Aunt doesn't have to suffer your brooding nature."

"When she comes, I will do it," I answered dryly. I had to eat my words almost a second after because she entered in the room, escorted by the Maître. I stood and smiled at her. She paused for a second when she realised I was at the same table with Konrad.

"Hello, my dear," she said kissing me softly on the cheek. "You are too old and ugly to get one," she joked lightly, addressing Konrad. I smiled again, this time truly. "I'm delighted to see you again, Guntram," she continued giving me her hand and I kissed it.

654

"How do you do, Elisabetta? You look very well," I said while she also extended her hand at Konrad, not really paying much attention to him. She took her place and continued to speak to me.

"Albert told me about your latest relapse. I hope you're feeling better after your holidays. You were under tremendous stress with the university, the exhibition and those little devils. I know it, dear. I had Albert and Konrad every summer at home. Where did you go?"

"I was in Madrid and Paris, drawing and sketching."

"It's so rare to see you socially these days, dear. You should come out more."

I didn't know what to say and I remained silent.

"I'm afraid Aunt Elisabetta, that we can't go out much. Only to business meetings for a few months. Guntram's health is frail and I'm still in mourning," Konrad intervened, looking at her directly in the eyes.

"About time you two settled your differences, Konrad. I was starting to be concerned about your good judgement since you married. It was such an unexpected move from you. It's a blessing that Guntram has decided to give you another chance," she said and also fulminated him with her blue eyes. Konrad looked down, ashamed at her slightly chiding voice.

"It's only for the children we have reached a compromise, Elisabetta," I whispered, finally accepting my fate. "I'm not sure it will work out."

"It will, my dear. I think Konrad has learned his lesson over the last two years. If you can forgive him fully for what he did to you, it should work. Take one step at a time, dear. Konrad should wait till you feel ready for more."

"I'll respect Guntram's timing in our reconciliation. I love him too much to hurt him again." Konrad said softly and I felt as if we were again in that noisy street in Venice, one late afternoon so many years ago. I looked into his eyes and for a moment, I saw again the vulnerable man-child I fell so madly in love with.

"Guntram, after the children go back to school, you have to come and help me in the Foundation. I have so many things to do and plans. I'm afraid Cecilia will leave us soon. She's getting married next May and she has to stop to prepare the wedding."

I was shocked at the news; Ferdinand marrying again? Well, they have been living "in sin" for the last six years. She laughed at my expression.

"Guntram, you need two, no, better three afternoons with Tita and I to recover what you've been missing the last two years!" she laughed. "Now Konrad, about this year contribution for the cause, I would like that you look at the figures I will be sending you tomorrow. You have the weekend to think about it but if you agree you could reduce your tax payments next year by a two percent."

"I will look at them but I was thinking more in the lines of establishing an Arts or Educational Fund in Stefania's memory." Why did that hurt me? I feel nothing for him.

"Yes, that would be appropriate. After all, she was Duchess, even briefly. I will consult with the lawyers, and see what it's best, darling."

"Thank you, Aunt Elisabetta."

I let them speak, and I dedicated all my attention to my food even if I was not hungry at all. Could I carry this on? I certainly knew I couldn't sleep with him ever again. What if he tried to kiss me? Last time he did, I nearly had a heart attack. I started to feel so tired and dizzy with my head going through several case scenarios and questions. Did he want to start a relationship again? In the office he had almost told me we fuck or you go away, and know he was saying he would "respect my timing".

Well Guntram there's only one way to know it.

"Can I drive you somewhere, Elisabetta?" He asked, taking me out of my limbo and back to reality.

"No, thank you. I have the driver with me. I'm going to return to the office. We will make the changes you suggested and present the proposal tomorrow. Tea time would be fine for you?

"Whenever you want, Aunt. We will be at home."

"Then, I'll come around four and see your children too. Good bye, dear."

We accompanied her to her car, already waiting at the entrance. After she was leaving, Konrad's appeared in no time, one bodyguard I did not know, big surprise there, jumped to open the door for him. I remained frozen on the street in front of the open door.

"Come Guntram, we will see the children now. You're doing very well so far," he said softly, his hand making a light pressure on my back. I entered the car and sat as far as I could from him. He left me alone for most of the trip, focused on a briefcase full of papers, strategically left for him.

I stared out the window, not willing to talk or acknowledge what I was doing. Without saying a word, he took my left hand and I jumped, prying it violently as if a snake would have touched me.

"I can't do this. Stop the car and let me out," I said.

"Nonsense. You're only jittery. You will get used to my touch, eventually," he refuted me, not really caring about my reaction. Again, he took my hand and I didn't withdraw it because I was too mesmerized by his eyes as he was studying me. "Karl might be upset with you. Klaus only wants you back, no matter what. It may take some time before Karl accepts you again."

"I can't do it. I will not let you touch me again," I whispered, feeling very sick and raggedly breathing.

"I'm holding your hand at the moment. I don't plan to make you mine tonight or any other night any time soon. It would be frankly unpleasant for you, and would only delay your acceptance of me. However, you will sleep in my bed, and that is not open for negotiations."

"Konrad, this is insane. We hate each other," I said desperately.

"You're calling me again by my name, that's much better. You're mistaken, I don't hate you, I love you, but I will not put up with your crap any longer."

"You call it crap? You fucked with my father and killed my uncle!" I shouted back at him, mistaking everything so nervous I was.

"I had a relationship with your uncle and your father killed himself," he corrected me calmly. "That was over twenty years ago, and again, your father never blamed me. It was your own grandfather, uncles and wives who went against me. Löwenstein ordered their execution before I could intervene and stop it. Your father did his best to save your Uncle Roger's life. Don't ruin his sacrifice with your childish notions of love. I've always treated you with the utmost respect and care, and never did anything to deserve your constant punishment over the last two years. It has never been an incestuous love, and frankly, I feel very insulted that you would believe me capable of something so disgusting."

"You're right, you're disgusting. You always knew who I was and never said a thing! You only took what you wanted. I curse the day I saw you in Venice!"

"NO, it was in Notre Dame where I saw you for the first time. I didn't know who you were until I found your name out at Les Invalides. It was impossible for me to leave you then. God placed you in my path, and I accepted you. Guntram, you almost fell in love with me instantly."

"No, I thought you were a bossy asshole for a long time," I retorted heatedly.

"Why did you paint the stream in Torcello?"

"I had too much green paint left. I wanted to get rid of it," I mumbled, furious he had so easily trapped me where he wanted.

"Watercolours don't have expiration dates, Guntram," he said in his Imperial voice.

"Fuck you!"

"You have already used that expression more than twice in a day, when before you never did. Two years of celibacy are taking his toll on you, dear?"

"Don't be so sure I was celibate. You're not the only "fuck" around here," I said feeling an enormous pleasure when he lost his colours and haughty stance. I held his shocked gaze. "You married again and we broke up two years ago. I can also restart my life."

"Who was it?" he growled, his eyes shinning dangerously.

"It's none of your business. Anyone can have an adventure now and then," I shrugged.

"Then, it wouldn't be such a problem if I fuck you tonight. You already behave like a whore."

"Takes one to know another, Konrad," I replied sweetly. "You should be glad, that I can appreciate better your exploits now that I can compare."

"You're as disgusting as your uncle," he said with all the contempt he could muster in his voice.

"Good. I'll remain in my room, if you still want me to stay."

"Good try, Guntram. You'll sleep with me. For a moment, I believed you," he ordered me, dryly, recovering his usual poise again.

He does not only have a selective hearing, but a selective understanding as well. I confessed. If he believes me or not, is his problem. Forewarned is not forearmed. I returned my gaze to my window, and he to his work.

Chapter 23

The car arrived at three at the castle. The bodyguard opened the door for Konrad, and he got out of it, elegant as always. I remained sitting in my place, still pondering if it was a good idea. He turned around and went inside the house, leaving the poor bodyguard, standing by the opened door.

"Should I drive you back to Zurich, Sir? The mountain in a dark suit asked.

"No, it's all right. Let the boss sweat a little," I answered.

He chuckled, amused. "Heindrik is right. You have a temper despite your frail look. I'm Sören Larsen; nice to meet you, sir."

It was my turn to laugh. "Dr. Dähler calls me *Dachs* at my back. I've been recently compared with a sable too; nice to meet you, Larsen."

"I think you should go in sir, before the Duke sends the cavalry in."

"Yes, Friederich can be very persistent and nastier than his Excellency himself," I smiled, remembering the old Austrian. I got out of the car, and went toward the door, where Friederich was standing, looking at me in disbelief. I was away, not dead!

"My dear child," he greeted me giving a totally inappropriate embrace. "I worried so much when the former Duchess sent you away. Why didn't you wait to speak with me? She also fired me that afternoon, but I went to Zurich to wait for the Duke. You should have done the same."

"She told me he fired me as I was useless. Nevertheless, we should not speak evil about her. She's not here to defend herself," I answered softly, sticking to Goran's idea as much as possible.

"Didn't you read the note I gave you?" he asked me looking into my eyes.

"It was from two weeks ago, written in the middle of a guiltiness burst. You said it yourself, I didn't have his support any longer. We fought that night. Horribly. I did the only reasonable thing to do, go away. "

"Reason was never your strongest feature, Guntram." Konrad intoned from the stairwell. "Come, the children will see you now. Friederich, the boy will be staying in my room. Make the arrangements."

The butler looked at me totally dumbfounded, searching for the truth in my face. I took a deep breath and climbed upstairs, where he was waiting for me, very serious. I held his regard, and he turned around and started to walk toward the nursery. He abruptly stopped and again looked at me.

"I never meant to hurt you, Guntram. Every word written in that letter was true. I don't know what Stefania might have told you, but I never removed the Tutoring of our children from you. I only transferred the financial aspects to Ferdinand because, with your heart condition, it would have been too much for you. I established an account under your name with enough funds so you could support them in case of my death," Konrad explained me. "Your cold rejection made me lose my head. Could you ever forgive me?"

"I don't know. I want to see the children," I answered feeling more desperate.

"As you wish," he said knocking on the door and opening it for me.

Klaus and Karl were formally sitting on their small table, painting with temperas, making a mess of everything. The nanny, a tall woman, was sitting with them. Klaus was the first to lift his head and shout to see me. He jumped to his feet and shed the glass of water over the nanny, and ran toward me throwing himself in my arms. Mopsi let a low growl and ran also toward me.

"Guntram! You're back! I'm so sorry, I will never do it again," he shouted, crying over my chest and clutching me with his small hands. I hugged him strong and pulled him against me as I tried to calm him down, rocking him like when he was a baby.

"Klaus, little one, don't cry. I'm not going away again. I had to stop for a while as I was sick."

"She told us you didn't like us any more and we made you sick." Karl informed us, serious as ever, from his chair, not coming to me and not leaving the brush. He resumed his painting, not looking at me any more.

"Never, Karl. I've been sick for many years, much before you were born. Sometimes my heart doesn't work well and I need to rest, and I'm not very funny, but you never did anything to me. I love you both more than my own life. I missed you terribly," I said, caressing Klaus' head. "I sent you something in the post, but I don't know if it arrived yet."

"The book! Papa reads it every night!" Klaus said. "Is it for me or for Karl?"

"For both of you, and be thankful you got it," Konrad interfered before I could say anything. "Miss Mayers perhaps, you want to change your clothes."

"Yes, my Duke," she said quickly disappearing through the door.

"Now, Guntram is back, and can make more books for you. He will be staying with you again."

"I don't want he goes away again." Karl said firmly still perched on his place.

"He will not. Papa will see to it," Konrad promised the children, sending shivers through my spine with his determination and seriousness. "Come Karl, say hello to Guntram. He wants to kiss you too."

Karl came to me, hesitantly, throwing looks at his father to gauge if his words were true. He stood in front of me, sitting on the floor with Klaus holding me for dear life, and I said as soft as I could, "would you let me give you a kiss, Karl?"

"You're not upset with us?"

"I was never upset with you two. Come Karl, let me hug you," I pleaded now. "I never meant to hurt you and I'm very sorry I couldn't say good bye to you."

He closed the distance between us, silently checking again with his father, but finally, he embraced me and gave me a kiss on the cheek. I held him close to me and kissed him on the forehead. I felt a light nudge on my ribs; Klaus was pouting because he also wanted one, becoming jealous that his brother was getting so much attention. They are always competing to see who would get more out of me. I ruffled Klaus' hair and smiled at him.

"You will stay with us forever?" he asked me.

"As long as your father wants it," I said, fearfully.

"Papa loves Guntram, and will not let him go away ever again," Konrad said in a firm voice as he knelt behind me and put his arms around my back pulling me, and the children toward him at the same time. I was so shocked, that I couldn't say anything or give him a well deserved punch when he delicately kissed me on the right cheek. "He can stay with you, playing till your dinner time. You should not tire him much. Be nice and behave."

Both children giggled, completely happy by the fact their father had just kissed me. I didn't know what to do. His kiss was still burning on my face, when he rose and walked toward the door.

"Dinner at nine Guntram. It should give you enough time to put those two in bed. Ms. Mayers should take over from seven onward," he told me from the door.

"What were you drawing?" I asked when Konrad really went away, trying to regain my poise, not very successfully as Klaus asked me "You're red like a tomato. Are you hot?"

"No, no, I'm just a little suffocated by this weather. Is wet here compared to Spain," I lied.

"What's Spain?" Karl asked immediately

"It's a place to go; very sunny and with friendly people. I was there."

"You should have come to Sylt with Papa and us. It was sunny most of the time. The other place, the city, was wet and rainy. We went to the park several times. There are squirrels there!" Klaus told me excitedly. "They shine!"

"Klaus, squirrels from this planet don't shine. Some of them have a silver colour on their backs."

"Will you make me one?" he asked putting his big puppy eyes.

"No, you two should go out in the garden. Get some sun and lose some steam. If not, there will be no way for me to put you in bed at eight," I said feeling this sense of deja vu hitting me. Bed time was always a fight, and it was much worse if Konrad and later Stefania had people in the house.

I took them to the garden where they started to run one after the other. Mopsi barked like crazy, entangling herself between their legs, and making them trip over her. That dog has no sense of self preservation. One of these days, one of them will crush her. I noticed, the bodyguard, Sören Larsen, placed discreetly near us, in the shadows. I can imagine the official story: "protecting the children".

The new nanny, Ms Mayers, Carolin, German, thirty-five, returned at five to take the children for tea time. They didn't want to go, afraid I would leave again, and we had to compromise that they will take it, silently in the garden with me. They sat seriously at the table, and behaved relatively well, not fighting over the cake or cookies or feeding the dog.

"Mr. de Lisle, you have no idea how much we need your help here," the nanny sighed relieved, her voice sounding so tired.

"They are very sweet boys. They always obey. Perhaps they cry out or destroy something while playing, but I think this is normal at four years old," I laughed.

"I've been only here for two weeks, and I was going to resign on Monday. I'm the third person in this position since June. They respect nothing, and fight everything. Their father does not help at all, only telling them off, without really caring to find out why they do it. With you here, they're completely different children. Today was the first time they sat to paint, and it was only because they were told you would be coming if they behaved."

"I had no idea it was so bad," I mumbled feeling very bad for what they had been through.

"Klaus has the ideas or starts the ruckus. Karl follows, but he's no better than his brother. He can be stubborn to an incredible point. They fight permanently with each other or with the staff," she finished.

"They were under a terrible stress these weeks. I believe the Duchess blamed them for my illness. I've taken care of them since they were born. I literally collapsed and couldn't say goodbye or explain anything. "

"I never knew her, but she was not accepted by the staff; terrible thing to die so young. Their grandmother offered to take care of them, but the Duke nearly threw his mother out of the house a week ago. His Excellency has a strong temper."

"You have no idea," I smiled. "Has he told you anything about your position?"

"Mr. Elsässer informed me that I was to continue in my position as before as you are their Tutor and will oversee over my work, sir. I will take care of the children's menial tasks, like bathing them, dressing them and feeding them. At seven, I'll start the war. When you get one in the pyjamas, the other is already naked and running away. Luckily we're in summer," she said merrily.

"Perhaps they are nicer tonight," I replied remembering that particular game of them. Of course, after the second try, I was becoming serious and they would stop it, but if they were really set on making this woman's life miserable, they wouldn't stop until total success. Like father, like son.

By six thirty there was chilly wind blowing, and I decided to make them go inside. They had shouted and ran enough for a day. Klaus wanted to be carried by me, but the bodyguard immediately intervened, and informed firmly that I could not do it due to my health condition.

"I'm sorry, sir, but those are direct orders from the Duke. They're old enough to walk."

I took both children by the hand and went inside the house. When we got back to the nursery, the boys wanted to play with me and their blocks, and we started to build a house, with some discussion over the roof colour between Karl and Klaus and if that room was the living or the stable. But they were quite civilised as they decided the horses could have a TV set and a couch. I took me a lot of will to keep the laughter to myself.

Friederich entered the room to announce to me that I was not supposed to bath or change the children. It was a heavy duty, and it would be better if I rested before dinner. Ms. Mayers should do it. I rose from my crouched position in the floor and faced him.

"Friederich, I'm feeling perfectly well and my stress' main source is not in this room."

"I agree, Guntram, this is why you should let her do her job. The Duke clearly informed me of your duties and place in this house. You're not a staff member, but a part of his family," he informed clear and loudly to me. "You can remain and check how she does it, but you will not do it."

"Thank you, Friederich," I replied curtly, dismissing him with short move of my head.

At eight, both were bathed and dressed them with their pyjamas, ready to eat their dinner, which they did without problems. They both went to bed and asked me to read a story for them. I complied and when I finished and kissed them good night,

Karl started to cry.

"Don't go away Guntram, please."

"Stay with me."

"I have to go to dine with your father. I will be here tomorrow."

"Last time you said the same!" Karl whined.

"You don't have a room. Ms. Mayers has your one!" Klaus shouted. I gulped nervously.

"There are plenty of rooms in this house. I'll find a place to sleep, and if I don't, I'll come here. Is it all right for you?"

"Where do you have your things? You have no suitcase with you," It's certainly difficult to fool Karl.

"Karl, I don't carry a suitcase along the whole day. It was in the car. Friederich must have put it somewhere and he will tell where it's. He's not going to keep my things. Besides, I left most of my clothes here. They must have been moved somewhere," I tried to reason with him.

"She burned all your paints, Guntram. Papa has the picture of we all.

"All of us, Klaus. Don't worry, they were not so good. We can make more together."

"Papa was very upset with her, much more than when we spread the ink on his papers." Yes, I remember that one. Konrad was stupid enough as to leave important documents, within children's reach, and expect they will not paint on them. He shouted at them, and true they never touched a single paper from him ever again, but he also learned to keep them in his desk, and banish the boys from there.

"They shouted a lot on the night before she left. Will she come back?"

"I don't think so, dear," I said softly, doubtfully. Maybe Konrad has told them nothing. "Now, you will sleep and tomorrow we will have breakfast together."

"You promise?"

"Yes, I do. I have to go, your father doesn't like to be kept waiting. Good night." I kissed them both again, and left the room, closing the door behind me.

Outside, in the hall, I found Friederich standing there, again.

"You have to hurry to change, Guntram. His Excellency said at nine and its a quarter to it. I have placed all your things back into your closet in your older rooms. At the tower," he said. "It's informal tonight. You don't need a tie."

"I don't think I can do this, Friederich," I said feeling more and more nervous.

"Guntram, child, do it for the young princes. It's been a long time since I heard them laughing in the garden. You're a kind hearted person, and you really should not blame him for what happened with your father. He was not responsible. The others did it before he could interfere. Those are our rules, child. I always wanted the best for you, and the Duke too. Please, my child, don't fight any longer with him."

"He has shown me how generous he is. Sleep with him or go away. Resume your consort duties, he said. I can't do it."

"You can't go back now. The children have seen you. He will do nothing against your will because he only wants a second chance with you. He regrets deeply marrying that woman."

"Stefania was never a problem between us. His lies and actions toward my family were. He was the person I loved the most in my whole life, and he betrayed me. Excuse me, I have to dress for the charade," I said a bit too harshly perhaps.

I went to Konrad's rooms. I couldn't help to shudder at seeing the door of his studio closed, the memories of his previous deeds assaulting me. I closed my eyes, and continued to the bedroom, feeling an overpowering will to throw up at seeing the big four poster bed. All my things were again exactly as I had left them, as if I had never been out of this room. I turned around and went to the bathroom to change my shirt and jacket. I removed my clothes and washed my face and hands. The only thing I could think about was, that I couldn't go on. It was too much for me. I felt very ill. I combed my hair and put on a new shirt and jacket. I had to lean on the wall for an instant to recover my spirit and took some deep breaths to calm myself down. I searched my previous jacket for my pill box, and opened it, taking the one for the night.

It was 9:10 when I reached the daily dinning room to find it empty. He can't be that touchy. I'm only ten minutes late! Fuck him! I was immediately regretting my thoughts. Again that word! I had more than enough sex with Constantin. All right, it wasn't incredible, but it wasn't that bad as to make me desire to be fucked by the German psycho! Lord, he knows how to fuck!

Shit! One single kiss and a light touching on my back, and I'm practically drooling over him, and forgetting all about my family! I'm sick, very sick in the head.

No, I'm not sick or insane. I didn't let him touch me for two years, and didn't falter not a single time, even if he made all the puppy faces he can do.

No, I'm thinking again on going horizontal with him because he's again in control of the situation, telling me what to do, and that, in a twisted way, relieves me from the responsibility of making any decision. I could fuck him, and then lie to myself telling me "he forced himself upon me" or that it was "for the children's sake". I wonder who's the biggest hypocrite of us.

Fuck! How well he knows me! He takes away all power from me so, I have no other option than surrender to him, do what he wants, and then continue doing it without any sense of guiltiness because I'm not responsible.

The worse part is, that it might work. Deep inside of me, I still love the bastard. He's the devil himself.

"Guntram, the Duke apologises, but he can't join you for dinner. He's in a meeting with Mr. von Kleist. Some problems arose in Brussels and with Lehman Brothers. He says you should eat and go to bed."

"Thank you, Friederich," I said and sat in my former usual place, the Duke's right. I ate my dinner, and went upstairs to check on the children, soundly asleep and to my room, only to remember I was supposed to sleep in Konrad's quarters.

I'm writing this on a folder I found in my old desk. He didn't change a thing even if I we broke up in 2006. All my drawers are exactly as I left them the day I went to Ferdinand's house. Perhaps, I'm killing time before going to bed. I don't want to.

"Boy, didn't I tell you to go to bed much earlier?" Konrad scolded me from the door. "It's one in the morning. Stop whatever you're doing and come."

"One minute, please," I whispered, feeling worse. He's here.

"Don't stall. I want to sleep also. Don't worry, I will not touch a single hair of yours," he said tiredly. "You're so nervous that it would be more a mess than pleasurable," he finished, going to the bedroom, leaving me there, with the words hanging from my mouth.

I took a good ten minutes before I went to his bedroom. He was already in bed, writing something on a paper, not even looking at me. I approached the bed, fearfully, and found one of my pyjamas under the left pillow. I stared at it, incredulously.

"You know what to do with this. Don't you?" he said mildly irritated. I removed my jacket, looking at the floor, and started to unbutton my shirt, my fingers entangling with each other, so nervous I was.

"Guntram, exotic dancer was never your thing, really. Go to the bathroom to change yourself before you have another heart attack!" he mocked me.

I obeyed.

When I returned to the bedroom, I couldn't help to notice how he left his documents aside, and took a good, a really good look at me. Lasciviously. He patted lightly on my side of the bed and rose an eyebrow making me turn red of embarrassment or fury. You pick one because I don't know.

"Get in. I'm not biting," he whispered.

My heart was beating very fast as I came closer to my bedside. He removed the covers, and I jumped inside, tearing from his hands, and covering with all of them up to my neck. I closed my eyes tightly when I saw his body leaning over mine, but I only felt him giving me a soft, chaste kiss on my forehead.

"Good night, *Maus*. Sleep well... if you can," he chuckled, finding my martyrdom absolutely funny. He turned around and switched the light off.

I had to bite my tongue to prevent myself from asking "are you going to do nothing, asshole?" Hard. I huffed contemptuously, and turned around. Sleep was hard to conquer that night for me. He slept like a bloody big baby the whole night, not even bothered by my constant tossing in bed.

Chapter 24

July 29th, 2008

The last two days have been strange. No, strange is not the word I'm looking for. Odd, weird, bizarre or a combination of these words would be more appropriate. On the 27th I woke up, still in his bed, with the bastard, holding me, sprawled all over me. That would explain why I had such a back pain! He's heavy, and I don't like to sleep on the bed's border just to avoid becoming a teddy bear!

"Get off!" I shouted. "Who the fuck gave you permission to touch me?"

"Do you want it so early in the morning, Guntram?" He chortled as I turned red, furious at myself for using that fucking word. *Again*! "Ah, you're already pissed off. Makes no sense."

"Don't you ever touch me when I'm sleeping! I'm not one of your whores!" I growled, tossing the covers aside and leaving the bed.

"You stop tossing around so much in the bed, and it wouldn't be necessary to immobilize you. You have to admit that you slept much better once I put my arms around you," he commented offhandedly, making me this time turn purple from shame. Yes, it's true, I've been sleeping lousily for the past two years. Must be the mattress. That's it.

"If you would spend some more money on your staff's lodging, mattresses would be more comfortable, and my sleeping wouldn't have been so bad for the past years!" I shouted very resented from the other side of the bedroom as I tried to put as much distance between us as possible.

"I must have rubbed a wrong spot because you're so feisty this morning," he said feigning a pensive air.

When I was opening my mouth to tell him which "wrong spot" he has touched, (was there a sexual connotation?), Klaus and Karl burst into the room, crying like crazy because I was anywhere to be found. They both jumped into their father's bed, fully weeping, and I felt very guilty.

"Shh, Guntram is here. He spent the night with Papa, like he used to do in the old times. Don't you see him?" He calmed them down as he petted them. Both children turned around, and saw me, standing by the bathroom door, still in pyjamas, exactly like Papa. I felt like dying.

Klaus jumped from the bed to my arms, and I picked him up as I kissed him to hide my awkward moment. Karl smiled triumphantly from the bed.

"You're not gone, but you didn't come for breakfast," Klaus whined, playing with the buttons of my pyjama and deliciously pouting.

"I overslept. I'm sorry. I'll get dressed and I'll come downstairs with you," I excused myself.

"Did you sleep with papa?" Karl asked, looking at me with his inquisitive eyes. I was rendered mute.

"Of course. From now on, Guntram will sleep with me. We have to be careful so he doesn't escape or feel sick again. Guntram wants to be friends with papa," Konrad informed the children, who looked more than happy with his solution.

"Go downstairs, and let us dress so we can have brunch all together, and then we might go for a walk to the forest," he finished, playfully putting Karl out of the bed and getting up. I was so dumbfounded at his impudence. He was using the children to trap me in whichever sick game he devised for me! How can you be such a snake?

I was so distracted with my own indignation and fighting the urge to start a real fight with him, that I didn't realise how close he was standing. He took Klaus from my arms as I thought he wanted to pick him up, but he put the child on the floor, and he grabbed my head with his hands, kissing me deeply, without giving me time to react. He kissed me deeply and truly, holding me firmly, so I wouldn't move or escape. I tried to put my head away, but the pressure exerted by his hands over my cheeks made me think otherwise. I opened just a little my mouth to breath and the beast put his tongue all the way to my throat, enjoying my displeasure. My tongue met his briefly. I don't know how long he was doing it as I could hear the children's giggles, but as suddenly has he started, he let me go. I had to lay against the wall to avoid a fall. My breath came out raggedly.

Karl and Klaus laughed and ran away.

"You're an animal! No, you're a monster! I howled. "You're worse than filth!"

"Back to classical swearing, my dear? Now, it's much better. I'm sorry I interrupted the kiss, but you see, you were getting very eager, and they're too young to see such things. Kissing is enough. It reinforces their sense of security if the parents have a stable relationship."

"I, eager? You're delusional!"

His hand went to the front of my trouser touching my member.

"One simple kiss, and you have an erection, dear. I will say that's eager. It's to be expected."

The truth was hard and I hated to hear it. "All young men have one in the mornings," I defended myself, trying to sound as derogative as I could. "It's perfectly normal, and has nothing to do with your clumsy ministrations. You're so aged that you might have forgotten what is to get one in the mornings," I finished, expecting he would explode, and we would finish this charade.

"I see," he said doubtfully. "Are you so desperate that anyone would do, including myself? You said that you preferred to be touched by a cobra than by me," he taunted me.

"The problem with you is that you don't get it up if it's not with someone from my family!" I roared. "You're sick, and the only thing you can think about is to fuck me like you did with my uncle!"

"No dear, fucking, as you say, with your uncle was like riding a real pure blooded bronco. He was amazing in bed—greedy and impossible to satiate. He always wanted more, something very useful when you're twenty. With you it is different, sweet, delicate and caring, like fucking a little lamb. You need to be petted afterwards, and love to hear sweet words whispered into your ear. Your uncle liked rowdy and even violent. It was all about dominance and power. You're not bad, but it's not the same. You will never be at his level," he explained to me, making me want to jump at his neck.

I went to the bathroom and closed the door rather strongly. I heard him laughing. Fucking bastard!

Fortunately, he was silent, busy with his newspapers and documents for the rest of the morning and left me alone with the children. We went outside to play, after brunch, with an unknown bodyguard, and remained there until tea time, when the new nurse picked them up for washing and feeding them. I had the feeling that Lintorff was after something.

At five, Albert von Lintorff and his wife, Carolina, arrived to the house for an "informal visit" and his mother was also there. I wanted to disappear, but I was more or less forced to accompany Carolina and Albert as Elisabetta decided to discuss money issues from the Foundation. The children were shown, and as usual, Carolina praised how well mannered they were and what a fantastic job I was doing with them. By seven, the children were sent away, and I had to tell them what I've been doing in Paris, what I was working in the moment, how nice my book had been, and that she had had to buy more than thirty-five copies for her friends' small children, and I should think to translate it into English.

Around eight, Elisabetta and Konrad finished their business and he invited them all for dinner, "something informal". They stayed, and as the night was warm, dinner was served in the garden. I tried to excuse myself telling the children needed to be put to bed, but Konrad's answer was, "Nonsense, Guntram. They should get used to the idea that you're not an extension of their wills nor their servant. The nanny can manage alone. She's a professional."

So I had to stay, and put my best face, not because of the guests, people I like a lot, but because of him. The main topics were the holidays and what we all should do. He stays in his bank and I stay with the children here.

"I was thinking to open the house in Nice, but perhaps Guntram would like to go to Argentina again. Karl and Klaus enjoyed immensely the ponies last time we were there, in 2006," he started as I gaped at him. What? Does he feel so comfy as to start to plan a holiday?

"Why don't you come to Turin? I already offered Guntram to come, but he had to work for that book. If you're there, perhaps Armin finds the courage to start with his thesis."

"I'll speak with the lad, and he will start to work before you know Albert" Konrad softly laughed. "I was thinking more on the lines of a family holiday, some place where Guntram could relax and the monsters destroy nothing too valuable. Where would you like to go, dear?"

I nearly drowned with the wine. Strange, I got a nice Riesling from the Mosel, exactly what I like the most. Normally I'm not allowed to drink. Fuck! He was trying to get me drunk! I left my glass over the table and sweetly answered. "I have no preferences."

"Why don't you go to Venice? After all, it was there where you met. That would be very good for both of you!" Carolina suggested very happy at her own idea. Elisabetta nodded vigorously. I panicked.

"It's not a bad idea. Perhaps we should do it." Konrad said making me feel very sick. Fortunately, he decided to start to comment on the works done in the city, and I oddly relaxed hearing his voice, speaking with a soft cadence, like I did so many years ago in that small restaurant near San Marco.

He knew all the time who I was, and Ferdinand also, nevertheless he tried to discover my personality, not to mention that he stood by me during the whole mess with the drugs, and took care of me when I was sick, not ever once complaining for the lack of sex, my tantrums over the hundreds of restrictions imposed by the doctors, the pills, the non salt diet, not going out, reducing the visits from his friends and business associates to a minimum, so they wouldn't drive me crazy. How he was always protecting me or the children, sometimes to the point of stifling you.

He was truly generous and kind to me.

He would be a fantastic match for anybody.

Anybody who's not a de Lisle, I thought looking into his blue eyes. I think he realised because the minute I was lost again in his eyes, he looked at me with his normal intensity. I looked down, ashamed.

"Guntram do you wish to retire? The doctor said you should take things easily for some time," Konrad asked, as the others looked at me with concern.

I excused myself, and left the table. He came to bed very late, smelling a bit like expensive brandy. I was afraid he would try something, but he slid under the covers and caught me like a cuddling toy. I squirmed to get rid of him, but he growled at me. "Be quiet. We both want to sleep."

* * *

Next morning, I noticed that he was away very early, and couldn't help to feel a bit lost laying there. I mean, after all it's his bed, and he doesn't like to share it. Friederich told me Stefania was never here. He always visited her in her room. I had to suffer him loudly going to her room, passing through my bedroom door, after checking on the children. I closed my eyes and slept again.

I shouted like a girl when Klaus and Karl landed on top of me, giving me a good fright. I had some troubles controlling my heart rate, and in no time, Konrad came out of his studio and was in the bedroom, sitting on the bed next to me, pulling me into his arms and checking my pulse on the neck.

"How many times do I have to tell you that Guntram is sick? You can't do this to him! Get out of here. Both of you! I will speak with you later!" Both children ran away, afraid from their father's shouting. I think they have never seen him like that.

"Konrad, it was a joke. They're children! You shouldn't shout at them," I said trying to remove my body from his hold, but once he catches something, he doesn't let it go.

"You're not their toy. They should be more careful around you and be glad that they have you. I can't lose you again," he said as I froze. His hand trailed up from my neck to my chin, firmly gripping it as his head bent down and he kissed me, softly, languidly. I was so surprised that I didn't think to withdraw from his kiss. I just let him do it as I closed my eyes. The devil is a really good kisser.

We both stopped and I was speechless and breathless. Shit, Shit and more Shit! What have I done? I let him kiss me and didn't kick his balls when he did it! My father has every right to come back from the grave and strangle me. I rose from the bed and I took refuge in the bathroom.

He didn't shout with the children and accepted that it had only been a bad joke from them. They promised not to do it ever again and I believe them. The poor dears are still very affected from what Stefania told them. She accused them of making me sick with their behaviour and told them I didn't love them any more as they nearly killed me.

Witch!

That Sunday night it was not difficult to put them in bed. They bathed without giving troubles to the nanny, and listened to their story in peace.

"I'm glad you sleep with Papa," Klaus affirmed as if it were the most normal thing in the world, in front of Nanny Carolin. I lost my colours. "He can take care of you now."

"Klaus this is nothing to discuss now," I said.

"Well, it's good." Karl supported his brother. "Papa always tells us he loves you a lot, like he loves us. He never said that about Stefania."

"I think you should go to sleep now," I ordered, mortified beyond everything, avoiding the best that I could the Nanny's gaze. I kissed their foreheads, and left the room.

She caught me at the stairwell, "Mr. de Lisle, please don't feel uncomfortable because of me. Everybody in the staff is very happy that you're back with the Duke. They say he can be a difficult master when you're not around."

"Thank you Ms. Mayers," I replied quietly. Do they still comment on everything we do in the bedroom? Are they still looking in the morning if the "master" comes out happy from the bed or not?

I went directly to the dining room without changing myself and sat there, alone, for a long time.

"There you are. You should have called me if you were hungry," Konrad said, entering the room with Friederich behind him, looking relieved that I was demurely sitting in my place. "You can serve now."

We ate in silence as I didn't feel like speaking, and honestly I was still blushing at the memory of our kiss in the morning.

"Should we go to Argentina next week? I could take two weeks off. I've decided not to participate on this joint rescue of Lehman and others."

"I'm not up to travel so much," I refused.

"I would like to have some time off. It's been a lot for me the last two months; first with your sickness and later with the baby's death."

"Yes, you're right. That was most unthoughtful from me. I'll go wherever you want to."

"You have to want it to, Guntram," he added softly. "I truly want that you're happy with me."

"How can I be happy with a man who threatens me to share his bed and uses his children as shield to kiss me?" I answered hotly.

"Show me you feel nothing any longer for me. Show me you don't care at all."

"I've said it hundreds of times, but you don't listen! You don't want to! You only want your convenience and the rest of the world can drop dead!" I roared. "You killed my father!"

"And for the hundredth time I say I didn't do it! All right, let's make a bet. I will kiss you once more, and you will promise not to bite or do any of the things we both know are wrong, and if you get an erection, you will share the bed with me. Biblically."

669

"There's nothing in the Bible to describe what you want to do! It's considered a sin!"

"It was a metaphor, but you understood the sense. If you're still flaccid, I'll let you in peace. If not, you will come on a date with me."

"I will not participate in such a childish game! What is next? We play chicken?"

"I can understand if you're afraid that you could not control yourself. It's hard, really," he sauntered.

"I have no fear. Kissing you is like kissing a cobra! There's nothing for me to win with this bed... I mean bet!" I said, now furious with myself for my stupid slip.

"I will let you sleep in the bedroom of your choosing for three weeks. Alone and undisturbed."

"I'm sure you have already planned a business trip for that time," I retorted.

"Nothing so far. Are you so afraid to get out of control with one tiny kiss? We will do it tonight, so your morning eagerness doesn't get in the middle. It's just a date. Going out, the Opera, a concert or the theatre, you can pick what you want to do, a dinner in a restaurant and going to a good hotel for some sex."

"How dare you! I'm not one of your whores! Go to them if you're so desperate! You do this to torture me. You think that now that you're in control I will bend to your will and do whatever you want. No. It's over!"

The bastard smirked. "For two years, I let you rule in this relationship and look what happened. We both were unhappy. Now, I'm setting the rules again, and one of us is happy about it. The other can join the party or not. Now, dear, what do you say? Yes or no? This is the best offer you will ever get. One kiss for three weeks of freedom; should be easy. You shout, practically all the time, that you hate me."

"I will choose the weeks and if you do something else with your hands than kissing me, I will consider that you lost."

"Agreed. I'm a fair player no matter what you tell to yourself. Shall we proceed now or we wait for dessert?"

"After dessert," I accepted. Did I do something so stupid? Yes, it seems. Guntram you're an idiot if you think for one minute that he could be sporty and fair! We finished in an eerie silence the apple cake with ice cream, the one I loved so much to have with my father.

Fuck him. No chance I will get a hard on with this memory fresh in my brain. I had to stifle a giggle.

"So, do you want to proceed now?" I pressed him as he was finishing his coffee and brandy.

"Certainly. Library?"

"Don't you want to reconsider your choice of scenario? Perhaps something romantic could increase your chances," I mocked him.

"I had no idea you needed candles and champagne. I suffice myself to make you moan and beg for my touch. Perhaps, you would like to read a report on the American dollar perspectives for next year, to curb your enthusiasm down. It would be good that we both are able to reach the bedroom," he chortled. Arrogant bastard!

Without answering, I rose from my chair and went directly to the blasted library. He came in like half an hour later and feigned some surprise to see me there.

"So. Do we do it or not?"

"My, we're eager tonight. Come here and we'll see," he said, sitting on the couch, like a king. I approached him, feeling my resolution falter a bit at his confidence. He was very certain that he would win. 'He's bluffing!' I told myself as I sat next to him.

"No biting, Guntram. Come closer, dear," he said, with his eyes fixed on mine.

He grabbed my nape with his right hand to have a better hold and to prevent any kind of escape, and I let him do it. His left hand cupped my left cheek and I leant on it without realising what I was doing. His regard softened and for a second I saw again the man I fell in love so many years ago. His head approached mine, and he started to butterfly kiss me on my neck's side, breathing slowly on my ear. That is something the bastard knows I can't resist.

I tried to disengage from his hold, but he kept me firmly in place, this time his tongue starting to play with my earlobe, delicately sucking it "You said a kiss, and now you're fucking my ear," I roared.

"Don't worry, we will get to it soon, my love," he whispered in my ear with a sexy and deep voice, making a jolt of electricity ran through my whole body. He continued to kiss me on the neck, making the hairs on my nape bristle. He placed his lips on top of mine, and reverently caressed them, not kissing me, as if he were asking permission to continue. I felt my body relaxing, completely disengaged from what my mind was telling me. Out of their own will, my lips parted and I let him kiss me this time truly deeply.

My body decided again to take a holiday from common sense, decency and intelligence, as it started to react under his soft kisses. He let go of me for a second to catch his breath and I attacked him this time, kissing him back hungrily. Konrad matched in no time my eagerness and we both started to battle to dominate the situation. I had to concede defeat when I couldn't do it more as I needed to breathe.

He let my lips go, but pulled me against his chest. "I won," he announced to me softly, without gloating or anything as I half expected he would do.

"It's unfair! Those were two kisses!" I said trying to escape, but he silenced me with another devastating kiss, almost throwing himself on top of me over the sofa. We started to kiss again like nothing in this world would matter any more.

He left the sofa and went to the floor, pulling me with him as we restarted to make out passionately. I don't know how, but he turned and in a second I was writhing against the carpet feeling his weight on top of me, exactly how I loved to do years ago. His powerful body, his magnetic aura of power attracting me and releasing me from every worry or restraint, only to long to be taken by him. My desire to do something that would drive him mad and make him lose his coldness and sense of control so he would enjoy our love as much as I did.

I felt his hand going to the front of my trousers. Getting them open and down with one single move, not even going to far away from me.

"Stop! You said a date!"

"The order of factors being multiplied does not change the product. I'll get you dinner tomorrow," he whispered, slightly rising from me to put his own clothes away. Before I could protest, he kissed me again, and I felt his manhood rubbing against me, making my hips move upwards to meet it. Without realising I spread my legs to let him nest better, like we used to do. I loved to have all his body plastered all over me, so I could feel his energy much better.

His hands firmly took my hips and he penetrated me, making me almost cry with pain as he had not prepared me or anything. It was exactly like our first time in Venice, I remembered as he kissed me again to suffocate the cry and alleviate the pain. He waited for the pain to lessen before he thrusted himself in. He started his pounding, first, very slowly and patiently, waiting for me to accommodate his shaft inside of me, till he felt my kisses becoming more urgent, and he picked up his pace.

I lifted my legs so he would have a better access and he immediately put them over his shoulders, making me moan and cry of pleasure as he knew exactly where to pound. I don't know how long we were doing it. I lost track of time as I was engulfed by desire and pleasure. I think we both came together because I felt his warmth of his fluid deeply going inside of me.

He collapsed on top of me, not withdrawing from my insides as I put my legs around his hips to keep him closer to me and restarted to kiss his face. We both laid like that for a long time.

"Guntram, I love you. You're my life, please, come back to me."

"I can't," I replied desperately, hating myself and the world because I was denied of the only person truly wonderful and perfect for me. I burst into heartbroken tears. He just held me as I cried for a very long time, trying to calm and comfort me.

Chapter 25

July 30th, 2008

After our love making we both went to bed together. In silence without touching us. I was so confused and afraid of the consequences of what we had just done. How could I do it? In less than two seconds I threw away everything and betrayed everybody after one single kiss.

I was worse than trash.

"The dead ones are as selfish as the living ones," my inner voice told me. "You also deserve to live your life."

In the morning, he left early for the bank, kissing me softly on the forehead. "We'll see each other this afternoon, Guntram."

* * *

August 3rd, 2008

Konrad took a plane on Monday evening and flew to New York. He told me he will be back around August 5th. I stayed at home with the children, mostly playing with them as their holidays are about to finish soon. The nanny and I took them yesterday to the zoo. We were back at seven and I was almost dead on my feet from running after them. I think she realised it because she told me that she will take care of the boys and get them ready for bed, and I could come back for the story time. I still don't know why everybody was saying that they're little devils. They exhaust me because they're young and energetic, but they behaved very well with Carolin today.

I went to the bedroom to rest for an hour before I would have to replace Carolin. I was laying down in bed for some minutes when my mobile started to beep. Konrad. I took a deep breath before answering it.

"Hello Konrad."

"How are you Guntram?"

"I'm fine, thank you." There was a long pause, awkward. "And you?" Yes, that sounded very stupid, but what was I going to tell him? I hate you because I went to bed with you on my own accord?

"Fine also. I'm in St. Petersburg and it's very late. I have a meeting tomorrow with some people from Goldman Sachs and Templeton. How are the children?"

"They were today in the zoo. Both are back and uninjured," I said, happy that he had found a safe topic for us. I was torn between hanging up and my wish to continue speaking.

"And the animals?"

I burst into laughter, relieved to no end to ease the tension. This sort of détente we have now is nerves breaking for me. "All back in their cages. It wasn't that bad. Ms. Mayers did a good job."

"Don't let them tire you too much. You need to get better," his voice sounded very warm and I blushed not really knowing why. Guntram! Think on who he is!

"We will stay low tomorrow. I don't think I can repeat the foe again so soon. I was in bed now, recovering for the story time," I confessed.

"Then I will tell Monika to change the arrangements. I was thinking to ask you tomorrow to take the plane, the Dassault and come to Vienna but perhaps it's better if you do it on Tuesday in the morning. I wanted to take the boys to the Natural History Museum, there's a dinosaurs exhibition from the Goby, very rare pieces," he said very slowly. "I would like to have some free time with you all, away from the bank for a few days."

"Konrad, the children will make soup out of the dinos' bones. I'm sure there are better things to do for them," I said, already imaging the disaster the whole thing could turn into.

"Well, I was also thinking on the Spanish Riding School, the several puppets theatres around here and even going to Salzburg for a day. There's also Belvedere and the Prater. Ms. Mayers should come along too. Please, Guntram, say you will come."

"All right, I'll come, but you should reconsider the Natural History Museum."

"We'll compromise with them. The Dinosaurs in exchange for the horses. Monika got them tickets for the morning trainings."

"Can you not lose just for once?" I asked him, almost laughing.

"Never if you're involved. I just can't do it," he replied very seriously. "You three are the centre of my life. Don't get too overtired around them. You're not their toy. Good night Guntram."

"Good night. I'll see you in Vienna then."

"Tell Ms. Mayers to bring some warm clothes for them. It's not very hot in the moment. Sleep well, dear."

He always has to say the last word. I don't know if I should laugh or give him a punch. "The people who sound so restrained on the phone, always set the bed on fire." Why did that phrase my old neighbour George told me so many years ago came to my mind? These flashbacks are becoming a real nuisance. The worst part is that it's not so far away from the truth. He's incredible in bed without putting any effort into it; at least for me.

Can I build a relationship based only on how good he is in bed and that I love his sons as if they were mine? Could I ever forgive him for what he did to my family? Could I forgive him for lying to me about my uncle? He would say he wasn't lying, he even told the name, Roger, only left "a few details out of the picture".

I know I will never be happy if I go away now.

How I wish my father would be here. Did he really mean it when he wrote that he prayed that Konrad would love me and cherish me? I don't know what to believe any longer.

* * *

August 5th , 2008

Putting the children on the plane was harder than I thought. I'm glad Konrad gave me one full day before travelling. Early in the morning, at eight I woke them up and with a lot of effort managed to put something in at breakfast. Carolin fought hard to dress them. They were so excited to go to Vienna to see the "white horses who can dance" and the "castle on top of the mountain". Friederich was kind enough as to take care of them yesterday in the afternoon, but I think he overdid his stories about Austria. More or less is the paradise on Earth, full with puppets, music and cakes. He should get a job at the Tourist's office.

At ten o'clock, they sat on the plane and after fastening their seat belts, Carolin and I were really tempted to tell them that 'you're supposed to wear it till the end of the journey'. Alas, we are a pair of idiots and let them move around. Marie, the stewardess had no better idea than to give them a full package of butter biscuits and there were crumbles all over the place. I'm glad the seats are leather. I think it would be easier to clean them, and that their father is not here to see them destroying his nice jet.

"I think I will drop the ice cream and lolly pops, sir." Marie sighed as I nodded. "Fortunately, we have a few hours to clean it."

"If the Duke sees this, he will never let them in again, till they turn eighteen. The other times we flew with him, we had not so many troubles."

At some point, both decided they were tired and slept. It's only an hour and a half flight! It takes longer to go to Sylt or to Buenos Aires! I don't know why they were so nervous.

When we landed and went to the private parking area, Konrad was waiting for his children, informally dressed. I was under the assumption he had to work. Karl and Klaus started to shout that they wanted to see the horses.

"No, they only perform in the mornings. Tomorrow, if you are nice and behave in the Museum," he said curbing their enthusiasm down to the point of a depression. "I will take you to the hotel, and then we will go to have lunch and to the park in front of the Museum. Ms. Mayers, drive with the children in the car," he said switching from papa to boss in less than a second.

The car with the children and their nanny drove away as we both, and two bodyguards remained discreetly away standing by a big armoured Mercedes. "Drive with me, Guntram. Enjoy half an hour of peace before facing the rest of the day," he said very kindly.

"Thank you." We drove in silence, taking the highway, "I'm surprised you don't have to work this week."

"No, my activities for the week were cancelled. My customer is facing some problems with the authorities, and couldn't meet with me. Four billion dollars tax evasion is hard to explain. I arrived last night from St. Petersburg," he started to tell nonchalantly.

"You mean, four millions," I said.

"Four billions. His companies decided to extend their fiscal benefits of eleven percent for a few years more after the Russian government set it at thirty percent. Corruption may permeate all Russian society, but once you fall in disgrace with the authorities, it's like in the Czars days. He got his family out of the country and they're in London. They will have to stay low for a few years before they touch any of their accounts in our institutions."

"Will you not have troubles if this person was evading so much?"

"None, we didn't do a thing. Tax evasion is not a crime, dear. Tax fraud is."

"You normally don't discuss your clients' troubles with me Konrad," I replied, starting to feel nervous. "Was this the reason you were in Russia?"

"No, the meeting with Golman Sachs and Templeton people was set a few weeks ago; delayed because of Stefania's passing. Business among us. I was telling you because I thought Repin was something like a friend to you. It would be twenty to thirty years," he shrugged as if it were of no importance. "Perhaps, I could arrange with the authorities to buy your paintings back, if you want, of course. It leaves me a very bad after-taste that they will be auctioned to pay debts to the treasury."

I could only gape at him, totally stunned. Constantin in prison? For tax evasion? I couldn't believe he would be so stupid. He must have much bigger skeletons in his closet than a mess with taxes. All right, four billions is not small. "Did you...?" I trailed, looking into his eyes.

"Nothing would have pleased me more, but no. It was an inside job. A change in the leadership. These things happen with monolithic structures like his own. No way to vent the internal pressure. The underlings have to dispose of the head in order to come up. Nothing like us. Repin will say nothing about his own activities if he wants to protect his family. Russians don't have this *Omertá* code, like the Italians, and families are never spared."

"I can't believe you have nothing to do with this. Since when mobsters run to the Authorities?" I whispered.

"Perhaps some of my people directed their attention to some legal aspects of the business, but they did everything by themselves. I should thank you for your indirect intervention, dear. You kept Repin's mind distracted long enough for Oblomov and the others to plot. Alexei certainly did his part, speaking with his old contacts. His fall will crown the end of the Order's purifying process. I'm hoping that several of those who sided along with this scum, will be also under investigation very soon. Revenge is a dish best served cold," he explained me.

"He's a member! You can't do this! The others will kill you!"

"Thanks for your concern, it's very touching" He said very sarcastically. "As I said, I did nothing. They eliminated their boss. The others elected him, not I. He dared to threaten Löwenstein by telling you of my involvement with your uncle. That old man voted him only to save you from that pain. Löwenstein fought against me only to save my love life."

"Repin trusted you and championed your cause in front of me!"

"You mean when you were living with him that week in Paris?" I lost my colours. "I'm touched beyond words. Perhaps, I will help his children in return. Anyway, I wouldn't have let him go away with this insult. I had enough of his constant prodding in my private life. If he wanted to fight with me, he should have done differently. Not using you as an excuse to unbalance me. Then all rules of war would have applied, even the ones from the Order."

"The poor man was in love with me, nothing else. Much before you were in my life!" I protested feeling more and more sick and worried at his coming "punishment" to me.

"He was never in love with you, Guntram. He desired you, wanted you, but never loved you. If he would have been so in love as you believe, he would have spoken to you in Buenos Aires, like I did in Venice, not going through a series of deceits to get you. He should have been forthcoming since the beginning, like me. Never make such a charade with that Argentinean boy, the drugs and the whores. He wanted to catch you for his own desires. He would have thrown you to one of his whorehouses the minute he would have satiated his quench for you. When he realised I was in love with you, honouring you as my chosen Consort, he came back after you. He wanted to drive me mad with jealousy to force me to make a mistake. Why was he after a position within the Order? To destroy us all and get our wealth. I have a responsibility toward my ancestors, I shall defend my Title with everything I have. My children's lives were endangered with this snake inside of our circle. Now, Armin has some chances to inherit it."

"Who told you I went to him in Paris?" I whispered nearly scared to death.

"The doctor who saw you, beginning of July, per Oblomov's orders. He said that you were truly sick when he evaluated you, and this is why I'm not punishing you for running to that low slag. A few days more without your medications and you would have been dead. I still don't understand why Alexei and Goran agreed to play along with his rules. Relax, I forgive you all because in a way, that was what allowed me to finish this threat to my line. You kept Repin like ten days very busy, more than enough time for Oblomov to do his part. In a way, he exchanged the information about your whereabouts for some financial advice. He was very afraid of the consequences of crossing me by keeping you. "

"And you said I was cold blooded. You have no heart."

"I do have a heart, but I'm no full of sentimentality. I love you and I want to spend the rest of my life with you. This is how I deal with my enemies and how I was before you entered my life."

"If you knew it, why did you take me back?"

"Because I love you and I can forgive one slip, considering your erratic behaviour the last two years. You even tried to tell it to me. I did it with your uncle, you did it with my worst enemy. We are at peace now, Guntram. So save me your affronted victim face because you're no better. You had your revenge too."

"How could I ever loved you? You're a monster," I whispered. "How could I even considered that you were good for me?"

"Because I'm perfect for you and you love me too, despite your protests on the contrary," he simply said. "Try to compose yourself because we're almost arriving to the hotel. You will be sharing the room with me and our sons will be down the hallway with Ms. Mayers."

"Repin didn't deserve it," I whispered again, not caring about what he was saying and feeling very bad for Constantin.

He laughed almost to the point of tears. "Didn't deserve it? The man who runs the weapons trade in the former Soviet Union, drugs, prostitution and child slavery? He must be very glad he got it so lightly and his family could escape. Guntram, you're not from this planet if you believe he could be a honest person. Forget him, he will never bother us again, my love," he finished his sentence by taking my hand and kissing my knuckles softly, reverently. I only looked at him, my eyes almost filled with tears. "We both have to forgive each other many things."

"I did it because it—" He silenced me putting a finger over my lips.

"It's in the past and it should stay there. You were confused, frightened and sick. You came back to me, on your own volition, and that's all what matters to me. Nothing else. I've also made many mistakes, but they're in the past; carved in the rocks. I can't change them even if I would like. I can only learn from them and never repeat them. You can't devote your life to some people who never saw you in your life or cared for you. Where were your uncles when you were born? Did they ever send you a postcard? No, it was only you and your father. He did his best for you, but he was very sick. I would have done the same in his place and you too. The cancer robbed him from you, not Löwenstein and the others."

"I know," I whispered painfully, feeling the old wound reopen.

"Take a look at your life for the past two years. You almost destroyed yourself in your quest for revenge. Do you realise you almost lost your children? Your health is in bad shape again, the stress is slowly killing you. I can't see you destroying yourself in such a way. Please, come out of this self destructive spiral you're in," he said squeezing my hand.

The car stopped in front of the hotel and he was the first to be out. I followed him like a zombie, not caring at all for the people around. I heard him saying something like "Tell Ms. Mayers to take care of the children for an hour. We'll go out later for lunch." I felt his hand gripping my elbow and almost dragging me to the elevator.

Again we were in the same suite he took the last time we were here, when I accepted his ring, he told me about the babies and he promised me to leave the Order. No, to reform it were his exact words. In a way he had reformed it, leaving only a few standing.

"I need to rest for some minutes," I muttered.

"Yes, of course, come to the bedroom. You look very pale. Ms. Mayers will take care of everything."

I went to the bedroom and laid down in the bed, almost falling over it. Konrad circled the bed and came closer to me. Without saying a thing he removed my shoes and forced me to sit to get my jacket out. I laid down again, this time on my right side, almost adopting a foetal position. He took his jacket and shoes off too and spooned his body against mine. For a second, I thought to jump out of the bed, but I was too tired; too tired of fighting, hating, fearing, denying and feeling utterly sad. I closed my eyes when I felt his arm across my waist, holding me, and his right hand softly petting me.

"Is there anything I can bring you?"

"No, just stay with me," I replied and he tightened his embrace. We remained like that for a very long time.

"Guntram, it's almost 12:30. We must feed the boys before they attack the complimentary fruit basket. Those things are covered with wax. Do you want to stay here?"

"No, I'll come. Just give me a minute," I replied disentangling me from his hold, unable to look at him in the eyes. I went to the bathroom to refresh. I looked myself in the mirror after washing my face, I didn't remember I was so pale. I took a glass of water and I felt slightly better. I left the bathroom and went to the living room where Konrad was already ready to leave.

"Are you feeling all right?"

"I'm only tired, Konrad; very tired."

"Do you want to stay? I can manage with them."

"No, I promised I would take them to the park."

Without any warning, he took my head with his both hands and bent his neck to kiss me, softly at first and them more urgently. I don't know why, but I closed my eyes and leaned to his body as we used to do in the past, revelling on the familiarity of his touch and body. He let me go.

"When I was with him... No, let me say it, it was never like with you. He even realised that I was comparing him with you the whole time," I confessed. He only looked at me.

"When I was with Roger, I never experienced the things I feel with you. You showed me the difference between sex and making love, Guntram," he replied.

"Can we build a relationship based only on how good you are in bed and our mutual love for your sons? I'm not sure we can trust each other ever again."

"Our sons, our children. I'm willing to try. I trust you with my life and my children's."

"I'll need some time to think about it."

"Take all the time you need. I will always be beside you and respect your decision. The only thing I ask from you is, that you don't make any decision in anger or hatred. Stay with us these days, like before, when we were a family, and then make your choice."

Chapter 26

August 5th, 2008

As promised we took both boys to have lunch in a small restaurant near the big park area in front of the Natural Science Museum. When they were finished, because I was almost not able to touch a single thing on my dish, we walked toward the Museum, crossing the big esplanade, in front of the Arts Museum. Konrad asked me if I didn't want to go to that one, but I felt it was like a sort of "treason" to leave him with the two jumping monsters alone in a museum, so I went with him to watch the Dinos from the Gobi.

Konrad understands his children much better than I thought. He didn't go directly for the bones, but he took the boys first to the Amphibians and Reptiles room, where the large array of terrariums in display, had many different and colourful types of frogs, lizards, salamanders and other animals. Karl was fascinated by the blue, black and red frogs and Klaus liked the Chameleons. The father let them run around, looking at the animals which were exactly the size of things they like, moving a lot, and hiding so they could be discovered under the leaves. After forty minutes (That's a record for the boys), of watching the animals, he took them to see the dinos in a separate room from the rest of the other halls.

He took them directly to two medium size showcases with two Protoceratops (I read the tag) in each one of them. The strange skeletons looked like a mix between a big eagle head and something like a sturdy dog body, nothing huge like you would expect from a dinosaur. Konrad picked Karl up so he would see it better. Klaus was immediately tugging from my sleeve so I would do the same.

"Doesn't it remind you of something?" He asked and both boys looked at him a little bit taken away. "It has a strong beak and a lion's body."

"It's the griffin!" Karl shouted happily.

"It can't be. Griffins are bigger and the head has no crown!" Klaus retorted.

"It is," his brother affirmed, getting ready for an argument. That can only come from his side.

"You both are right." Konrad stopped the dispute. "In the past, when people saw these bones thought that they could have belonged to a griffin, our family's animal. They never existed, of course, but it's the idea behind them what we like. As these creatures, the protoceratops, were often found when people were looking for gold, they were believed to guard treasures and live on top of the mountains."

"Guntram draw one for us. They have lions bodies and eagles head"

"And wings! They fly high!"

"Indeed, we chose them because they're strong, brave and loyal. Those are the values we stand for and defend. Nothing else. The griffin was also chosen by our Church to represent Christ, our Lord. The Lintorffs always did their best to follow these values of strength to defend what we believe in, courage to make the best decisions for the people we look after and loyalty to our family, friends and beliefs," he said as both boys looked at him very seriously.

"The head of our family is always called the Griffin, but you will have to earn this honour. To be compared with one of those creatures is a great compliment and you two will have to work very hard to achieve it."

Konrad took the children for another round, showing them the rest of the dinos while I followed them very quietly. Finally, we went outside and like many other couples, not us, we sat in the park letting the boys run around.

"I thought Armin was going to be the next Griffin and you're preparing the boys to be it," I said truly crossed at his new lie.

"Armin, if he's suitable, will act as head of the Order, which is very different than being the Griffin. That name belongs to my family, not to the Order. Even if I were to remove the Lintorffs from that decrepit group, as I plan to do, Klaus and Karl will still inherit a huge fortune from me and many companies to run. They will have to learn to do it with a Christian sense, not only looking for profit, but supporting those who have nothing. Like true Griffins. I do hope they learn from your social sensibility. Things will be hard for us in the next years; very hard for the normal people. The Order will change in the future years, once I have finished to shape it to my will."

* * *

August 7th, 2008

This morning we went to the zoo and have a nice day there. Ms. Mayers was left in the hotel to rest after spending the whole previous day with the boys at the horse exhibition and later in the Prater with Konrad on top. Poor woman, she truly earns her money!

At six, we put the children in a small puppets theatre and they were very happy with them, looking with very big eyes the whole show. When we left the theatre, Carolin was outside, waiting for us. Konrad decided to send the Karl and Klaus back to the hotel to dine. They strongly protested and pouted, but their father is insensible to children's pleads. "No, you go back with Ms. Mayers. It's more than eight. Your bedtime is long past due. Good night." Defeated, both boys decided to go with the nanny away and try to get a concession from her... good luck. Friederich chose her for the job.

"I have enough of smelling Schnitzel for a week. Do you want to go to a place with linen tablecloths?" he asked me, making me smile. Yes, I'm also tired of the fried things stench.

"I think yes. Tomorrow we go to Salzburg and it's back to the hard life of parenting for you," I replied. I was a bit shocked that after a few days away from Zurich and the normal hassle, I was starting to feel comfortable around him... 'Guntram, you were in bed with the man and don't say it was the bed... the bet! Because we both know that if you don't want, you don't want. What's more comfortable than that?' I truly hate my inner voice. It's too meddling for my taste.

"Don't mention it. How can they always ask for those things? I'm sure they don't get them at home or in the school," he complained starting to walk in the direction of the Cathedral getting me out of my daze in no time. I also hate to run after him!

"Every fifteen days, there's pizza day in the school. On a Friday, so in case they become sick, then it's our problem. Have you seen how much they run? They spend those calories," I said, almost out of breath when I caught him.

"I know. They make me feel each one of my years."

"It's not so bad. I can do it. We used to do it when they were babies."

"They were sleeping for twelve hours and drinking bottles, nothing that could be grabbed, squeezed and thrown at us. " He smiled kindly.

"The last two years were very bad," I admitted slowly remembering how they were learning to eat by themselves... and let's don't mention using the toilet.

"You have no idea how," he confessed, looking into my eyes. "We both are responsible for them, but regretting will not change it. Perhaps we could improve the ones to come."

"Perhaps, Konrad. Perhaps," I said doing my best to avoid his scrutinizing stare.

We had dinner in a small place, nothing elegant, mostly speaking about Economics as it was a much safer topic than the previous one. Around eleven, I was also dead on my feet and he decided to go back to the hotel. We went directly to the bedroom and I took a shower before sleeping.

When I left the bathroom, already changed into my pyjamas, Konrad was already in bed, looking at Euro-news on the TV.

"You could never be on holidays, could you?" I asked, smiling tiredly.

"The world doesn't take holidays. It's just the news. Tomorrow, I'll read my papers in the train."

"You? On a very public transport?" I asked incredulously.

"The children need to see a train once in their lives. I'm also thinking on sending them on a normal plane next time. Do you have any idea of why Ferdinand told me he found cookies crumbles all over one side of the seats?"

"The cookies jumped out of the box. They were truly hard to catch," I said with a neutral tone. It was the first time I joked with him in years and it didn't feel such a horrible crime.

"Harder than catching an elephant, it seems. Marie asked for a week leave."

"She has a very good life. She should be on a commercial airline; on a tourist class, full with students to know what is hard," I said lifting the covers and sliding in.

"Poor Marie, she has coped with me for the last fifteen years, and now my sons put her out of work in less than forty-five minutes. Next time, I'll send Anne."

"...and in surprising turn of events in the Caucasian Oil Ltd. scandal, Russian tycoon Constantin Repin was found dead at the Smolensk State Prison where he was sent, awaiting trial. He was charged of tax evasion for more than four billion dollars. The Russian Authorities have refused to make any comments on the case."

I just stared at the TV, not really believing it. Constantin was dead? It couldn't be! He was too clever to be caught like that! I felt the tears coming to my eyes. "Did you?" I whispered.

"No. I did not. Many people were nervous about his arrest. I have nothing to hide in my relationship with him. Guntram, I was not his sole enemy, his own people overthrew him. Perhaps, his death helps his wife and children. It could have been a suicide too," Konrad said as he took and held me in his arms. For a second, I thought to push him away, but his eyes held no deceit and I leaned my head against his shoulder, still fighting the tears.

"No matter what you say, he really loved me, in his own way," I whispered, now feeling the tears coming silently out.

"Perhaps. You can see people through the masks they wear. I realised it the moment I saw one picture you made from me many years ago, in Florence, and when I saw the portrait with the children you did during our darkest time together. Sometimes, I think you come from out of this world Guntram," he also whispered, clutching me stronger.

"Why did somebody do that? He would have never said a thing," I said, almost crying.

"One can never know. He had weapons running on every African conflict for the last ten years, most of the drugs in Russia belonged to him, he controlled the poppy seeds traffic in Afghanistan, not to mention all the Russian black market. Many people hated him and were only waiting for the opportunity to hit him. Give a forty-five and ten minutes alone with Repin to Alexei and you'll see. I'm not sad for his death. In fact, I'm concerned about the many that are now fighting to take his place. He's out of the Order and that's all what matters to me. I will make sure that none of his associates will ever come near to us again."

"I'm sorry for him. He died alone. I never wanted that for him. He was kind to me, and it was not a trick to make me jump into his bed. His wife told me he was nice to her."

"She was the one providing the physical evidence against him to the Russian Authorities in exchange for total immunity for her and her children. She has accounts by several of our associates Guntram. She tricked you into her "I love my husband despite all" charade, to make you paint that portrait. She wanted me to lose my temper and kill you, so Repin would go against me and I would have killed him. I have always wondered why she put up so much from him, but now I see it. I deeply admire her patience and strong character, but I will not take out the trash for her. You and his children must be the only ones who cry for his death."

"Perhaps it's like Ostermann said. We will be nothing in a few years, but your name will remain Guntram. Who remembers my grandmother? Everybody knows Rubens and admires him. Repin can be glad a good man shed some tears for him. That is more than he deserved."

"Everybody has somebody who cries for our deaths," I whispered.

"Of course, but most of us fade after death. I'm glad Volcker finally got that portrait from you. He will take care of it."

"You hated it!" I shouted, furious that he was lying to me so blatantly.

"I hated to be amended in front of everybody. Elisabetta had no right to do it. Not so brutally. In February, I met Volcker in a business meeting in Frankfurt. His companies were asking for cash and several of us were there. I was furious with him and ready to go against him, but he asked to speak with me in private. I was very jealous of him as he was real competition for me, much younger than I, not stained, clever and with a good position. Repin never was competition for me, as his past prevented you to love him, but this man could have presented battle. We went to a private meeting room. He only put out his laptop and showed me that picture. "Do you think that someone who paints this doesn't love you? My chances with him are zero. I only want to introduce him in the Arts circles, nothing else, Lintorff." This is why I didn't bid for the paint. I could have bought it, one single gesture from me and it would have stopped there. I didn't want it to be destroyed like Stefania would have done. Ostermann was right, it truly shows our times."

"Did you really think that? I never meant to humiliate you or Stefania. I still don't know why I painted that wretched thing. I was so furious she forced me to paint it, calling me "unprofessional" because I started four times before painting that one. I exploded in rage."

"I never wanted to hurt you Guntram, never. I only wanted to make you happy and have you with me till my death, but everything went out of control…"

"I don't know what I wanted from you in the last two years. I wanted to hurt you, but I couldn't bring myself to do it, so I despised you. I wanted to make you pay for my father's death, but deep inside me, I knew I would have been alone anyway in a year. I never met my family and they never wanted to see me when my father was alive. Perhaps, the son of poor woman was beneath their dignity, and now I wear the stupid title," I confessed.

"Perhaps your mother had no money, but if your father loved her like he did, she must have had many other qualities. I was an idiot for not taking you in the minute your father died. You would have been like a son to me, and you would have never suffered all those years in the most absolute misery for the soul. Nobody realised that you already had a heart condition! I was selfish as I only cared about my own pain, and then a coward because I killed all chances to rebuild my own life."

"We can't know how lives would have been, Konrad. Perhaps I would be already dead, thrown in a field near Moscow if you hadn't spoken with me, or still serving coffee in a Restaurant, or married with children, working like crazy and never knowing what I've missed."

"I know you don't believe me, but I swear that the moment I saw you, in Notre Dame, I knew God had given me another chance. I stood the whole Order up just to see you for a few hours more. You were… radiant but completely clueless about everything. It was like seeing an angel. The way you spoke to that Kebab vendor, making him feel important as he tried to tell you about his home country. Ferdinand shouted at me the whole night for not showing up to their meeting. We only found out who you were at Les Invalides, when you wrote your name down."

"But you were looking at my uncle in me," I sighed sadly

"No." He shook his head. "No chance, you don't look like him. You smile at people and think they're important, and this shows in the way you treat them. You're gentle even with the maids or the gardeners. You treat them exactly as you treat a billionaire. You were very pissed off when I spoke to you in Venice, you only calmed down at the Restaurant, not before. Any other person at the mention of my title or my money would have drooled on me in flattery. I told Ferdinand that you looked so much like Roger so he would take me for an obsessive person and not for someone with mystical delusions."

"You behaved like a real ass in Venice," I stated.

"I know. I was almost dying from nerves, like a teenager in love. Didn't you notice that I said my name wrong, mixing my title with my family's name?"

"Why did you bring the whole cavalry around? Ferdinand and Heindrik?"

"I didn't. They came by themselves," he huffed visibly upset. "Ferdinand was very concerned. Michael not. The first night you came to my bed, I was so shocked that I couldn't sleep. I felt so miserable that I had hurt you so badly, leaving the fears from my past to ruin our relationship. You were such a frail creature, almost like a child and yet you came to me for comfort and protection. I realised there, how alone you were in the world, if you considered that I was the only person who had been kind to you. I didn't know what to do with you. I only knew that I needed you more than anything I ever did. You were so innocent and pure, that I was terrified that I would contaminate you with my own life. You were my greatest source of happiness Guntram. Nothing scared me more than losing you. That week you were in the hospital, it was the closest thing I had to Hell."

"I tasted it when I met your mother," I whispered.

"Do you think you could ever forgive me for lying about my past with Roger?"

"I've forgiven you because of your children. Living with you again will be difficult. It's too much what we did to each other. I need more time to think," I slowly said, realising that this was the first time he had truly apologised for his lies.

I came closer to him and snuggled in his embrace. I don't know why I did it. I just needed to feel him again. We stayed like that till we fell asleep.

It was very early in the morning, the sun was just coming up, when I woke up, still in his embrace, my face buried against his chest, my hands supported by his rising chest. I looked at his face, bathed by the growing light for a long time, sleeping like a child, and I knew that there could be no other person for me in the whole world. It was him or nobody. We both needed each other not only because of the children but for our own sanity.

I very lightly stroked his cheek with the back of my fingers, half expecting one of his psycho jumps on me, but he continued to sleep. Boldly I stretched my neck to reach his lips and softly kissed them.

"Guntram, what are—?" I silenced his words with another kiss, intertwining my arms over his neck and softly pulled him toward me. He started to respond to my kisses.

I could feel his weight settling against me as he tried to shake the sleep off. His still dulled eyes, like a child, making a supreme effort to understand my actions, were so tender. "Don't think, Konrad, just feel," I whispered, my brain not really willing to admit what we were about to do but my heart was more than ever willing.

"Do you really want it, *Maus*?" He whispered in my ear, his low voice laced with desire making me shudder.

As my only answer I softly pushed him away from me to force him to lay on the mattress. He was taken aback but said nothing as my hands started to unbutton his pyjama top and my mouth was over his left nipple, sucking it hard, while my hands travelled all over his chest. Lord, I had forgotten how wonderful his skin felt to me. I needed more. I lifted myself from his body and still kneeling beside him, my bottom over my calves, my hands went to the buttons of my own pyjama, slowly opening them.

He just looked at me in awe, trying to understand what was going on but I smiled at him weakly and all his doubts vanished. His large hands took my ones away from the buttons and he unfastened the remaining ones, sliding the shirt while he caressed my back, lovingly almost afraid that this was a dream and he would wake up from it. He took my head into his hands and I took his right hand and I put it against my lips, kissing its palm.

I started to suck his fingers making him close the eyes and moaning, looking

685

lost in the sensations, just exactly as he was when were together in the past. I found his pleasure gesture one of the most endearing and erotic sights I've ever seen, encouraging me to do more.

My left hand went down to the front of his trousers and I took his already fully erected member, making him jump a little. I hushed him and not waiting any longer, I lowered my head to his shaft and I started to lick from the base to the top.

I was so distracted with sucking its point that I didn't realise that he had also put down my own trousers and was caressing me slowly but urgently. I jumped a little at his finger's intrusion but I continued to suck harder as he began to stretch me slowly and carefully.

When he was near his climax, I put my mouth away from his member, losing some drops and regained my initial position, my own member also painfully up. We both look at each other, not really knowing what to do next, hesitating at our next move. My upper teeth slightly bit my lower lip and my tongue moistened them again.

He sat on the bed and kissed me shyly at first but as my mouth opened, and my tongue welcomed his one; his kisses became more urgent and ragged. He pressed me against his chest as I put again my arms around his neck, feeling dizzy at his ravishing kisses.

I had to suppress a desperate cry when he disentangled himself from me and almost forced me to turn around and grab the silken headboard of the bed, still on my knees. Somehow he had managed to get some lube and I shuddered at its cold contact inside me. He penetrated me with one swift and decided push, making me gasp from pleasure, but one of his hands kept me firmly in place as it grabbed my hips. He surrounded my chest with his right arm, also effectively trapping me but I didn't care, I only wanted to feel him. Wild and unrestrained in his desire for me.

Konrad started to move inside of me very slowly, setting the pace with the powerful rocking of his pelvis as I was completely pliant and submissive in his arms. He kissed the left side of neck and my mouth searched for his mouth, returning his kisses. His hand left my hips and took my member, starting to pump it with the same pace he had set.

We climaxed together and I collapsed into his arms, looking for a warm embrace. Konrad pulled me against him and softly petted me while he murmured "*mein kleines Kätzchen,*" In my ear, breaking my heart again into pieces. I disengaged myself from him and he let me slide under the covers, turning my back to him. I felt his weight also settling beside me, his arm holding me by the waist and pulling me closer to him.

We said nothing for a long time.

I just lay, spent, next to him, feeling the warmth of his body. "Perhaps we still could be friends," I whispered not able to stand the tension any longer.

He turned me around immediately and sat on the bed, looking at me with clear fury written all over his face.

"Friends? As fuck buddies? Never Guntram. I'm too old and too conservative to settle for that. I want you to be my mate, my companion, the father of our children. I want what we had before; a real marriage with all its joys and miseries. I want to come home, a real home, like the one I had with you, to hear you telling me about your day, what the boys were doing or destroying and saying that you love me. I want to be able to tell you what I've been doing, whom I've met or what I plan for the future. I want to spend the nights with you in my arms. I want to grow old with you next to me. I don't want an amiable relationship between us and a good fuck twice per week. This is not for me nor for you," he said very heatedly, as he jumped out of the bed. "What we just did was a mistake if you're not ready to really forgive me and love me again."

He slammed the bathroom door making me flinch with the noise. I looked at my watch; 7 a.m., time to really wake up and face the world.

Chapter 27

August 8th, 2008

Around 8 a.m. I gathered enough courage as to leave the bed, shower and dress, making myself ready to face him again. I was completely disoriented. Did he still want what we had so many years ago? Did I want it also? *No*, I wanted it, the question was if I could do it again, without feeling guilty, every minute he was not there to chase the ghosts away.

He was in the living room, reading something in his laptop. I noticed he had not ordered breakfast or called the butler.

"Do you want to have breakfast with the children?" I asked, still mortified with what had just transpired between us.

"I'm not hungry. You eat with them if you want," he replied dryly, not really prying his eyes from whatever he was reading.

I crossed the room and knelt beside him, touching his arm, well grabbing it as he wanted to put it away from my touch. "Konrad, I was not playing with you if you think that. I'm afraid that what went between us is too big for me to overcome it. I can't forget it," I said softly.

"Nobody is asking to forget it. It's impossible, but it's time you start to live for yourself not for the others, not for me, not even for the children. Whatever you do from now onward, must be your decision," he said visibly upset at me.

"I didn't want to hurt you this morning, Konrad, no matter what you think. It's too much what you're asking from me."

"I'm only asking you to be my partner in this life. I don't want a good slut in my bed like you're proposing now. I want that you are my Consort for the good and the bad things this life has. You're old enough to understand the concept now."

"Don't you think you're straining my goodwill too much? It's four years of permanent lies what you're asking to be forgiven plus two other more of making my life a living Hell," I replied now upset with him.

"You were not exactly an angel to me or showed me the smallest mercy. This morning you gave me hope to rebuild my life with you, but not even ten minutes later you destroyed everything with only one sentence."

"It's not my fault that you have the emotional intelligence of a seven year old, Konrad. I was like you, but you forced me to mature with your betrayal. I'm not the boy you picked up in a Venetian square or a French Cathedral, living for you and kissing the floor you were standing on. I'm much older, cynical and aware of where I am standing and with whom," I said firmly. "You said it once, young ones forgive easily. My youth finished in April 2006. You say you want something like a marriage with me, but I don't think you know what a marriage is. It's two people. Two. Making decisions together, not one of them bossing around and setting conditions and rules for the other. I will not take it. I don't want it any longer. I'm through with that. Now, you think Konrad if you're truly ready for a marriage like that," I finished, raising myself from my crouching position, not really expecting an answer from him.

"I do."

"What?"

"I do want it. You and I together as equals."

"We'll see. I'll go to check on the children," I replied, going to the door. He said nothing and returned to his work.

After some fighting to calm the boys down, we finally got them in the car, with the nanny and I drove with them to the train station. Konrad would be joining us later. He had to work. Getting the children in the train was difficult, but not impossible as they wanted to see the lockers, the box offices, the trains, the platforms, the clocks, etc. I had no idea that there were so many exciting things in a train station. The two bodyguards were on the brink of a collapse when they put them in the first class compartment with Ms. Mayers.

They nearly jumped on the train controller to check everything the poor man had. After that, I had enough and needed some fresh air. I went out and closed the door, nearly bumping into Alexei.

"What are you doing here?" I asked not really shocked. "Family Holidays" had just been transformed into "Business Meetings".

"Escaping the big meeting. Ferdinand, Michael, some others Executives and Goran are also here. Next two compartments. This thing looks like the Glacier Express to Davos," he laughed loudly at seeing my crossed expression.

"Good to know," I smiled. "Any neutral grounds?"

"Next compartment on your left. It's ours, but nobody is in there as they're all packed in the other two. It's safer to speak here than in a hotel room," he said as he opened the door to let me in.

"You're different since Paris," Alexei said as he sat in front of me. "Goran is updating the Duke on the Russian situation," he added still studying me very carefully.

"I'm living with Lintorff and the children. They make me very happy," I replied curtly and looking very interested at the landscape.

"You were in bed with him! That's it!" he shouted.

"And people say confidence is not disgusting, Alexei," I mumbled. "Keep your voice down! The children are on the other train compartment with their Nanny!"

"That woman already knows you two share the bed and not because he has no money to pay for another room. When Jean Jacques told me, I couldn't believe it," he said happily. "I'm very glad you two finally sorted it out. I was very concerned for you. It was almost like you enjoyed your pain."

"Keep it down, will you? I still don't know."

"All right. I'll say nothing, but it would be so good for all of us that you two would give each other a second chance," he sighed.

"Alexei, can I ask you something?"

"Depends on what, Guntram," he said softly.

"I don't know what to do. You're the only person I know who has a relationship like mine. I'm afraid that if we start all over again, he will be as he was in the beginning and I don't want that if I make the huge sacrifice he wants from me."

"Guntram, my relationship with Jean Jacques took a lot of time to build. Since 1996 and we still fight like the first day. This will never change. We both had to leave things behind in order we could be together. I have to bite my tongue every time he invades my kitchen and he has to do the same when I ran away to buy something at McDonald's. You both will have to give up and try to find and equilibrium and remember, it will only be an equilibrium, nothing solid, something that can change at any moment."

"I don't know if I can trust him. The minute he feels he's in power again, he will be like before and I could not control him any longer," I whispered.

"Guntram, for the past two years, you showed the man his place. Shit, you're frightening when you're set on making somebody's life miserable. You never faltered, not for a second. He almost lost his sanity with your punishment. Look all the stupid things he did; he married that woman, dated that Italian asshole, was nearly kicked out of his position as Griffin for not respecting you, destroyed half of the associates because they sided with Repin, went into a second war with him. I still don't know how he managed to win so much in so little time. He recovered everything the minute you came back from Paris. I'm still trying to understand what the fuck transpired in the last two weeks."

"He knows what I did with Repin, Alexei. He knows you were there also."

"And he didn't kill you?"

"No. Repin was never "serious competition" for him. In fact, he used this distraction to plan his final blow against the man, with Oblomov. He let me be with Repin so I would realise that I still loved him and kept his enemy distracted. Oblomov informed Konrad my whereabouts before Constantin asked him to contact you. I believe, Konrad used Oblomov's fear of a full scale confrontation to his benefit," I confessed, feeling very sick.

"He's a better general than I thought," he said with real admiration for his boss. "Look Guntram, there are no guarantees in love. All princes can turn into frogs and vice versa. Whatever happened in the past, should remain there. You can't change it. Just think if you really love him. If you do, give him a kick in the ass and continue to love him. If not, go away. This time for good."

"Thank you Alexei, you're a good friend."

"You also. Don't tell him the part of the kick, will you? He might take it literally, you know how these Germans are. I have to go back to the meeting. Everything is a mess inside the Order, many running like little ducks to the Duke for help and forgiveness."

"He's back in power it seems."

"And how... Many will pay dearly. He's cleaning the Order, making it smaller, but more efficient. I think he finally learnt that the mammoth we were riding was too big, clumsy and in a way very similar to the Soviet Union."

"Do you know how things are in Russia now?"

"Oblomov is facing serious competition from the others. Might take a few years till the situation is stabilized. The Duke clearly said we will not go there. We have to focus here in Europe and Latin America. He will not fall in the temptation of over expanding."

"Not very reassuring what you tell me."

"This is his game, Guntram. Let him play it because he knows it better than any of us. I'm still trying to understand what happened in the last year. Michael is highly impressed and a little pissed off that he was not fully informed."

We heard a knock at the door and there was Heindrik. "Guntram, the Duke wants to see you. Now," he said, immediately disappearing.

"Well, you heard the Master's voice," I said grinning.

"Don't piss him off, *Dachs*." Alexei smiled back.

"I already did it this morning," I shrugged.

Heindrik and Larsen were "standing guard" in front of the compartment where Michael and Ferdinand were sitting with Konrad. All of them busy with their laptops. I still wonder how he can transform a small place like this into an office and from where came those two? Larsen opened the door for me and I entered.

"Ah, Guntram. Several things arose this morning and I can't accompany you and the boys today. I have a meeting in Salzburg and you will have to excuse me. Monika has sent you a dossier with things to do with them and some tickets to see the puppets there."

"They're very good!" Michael said almost without thinking. "I mean, I saw them many years ago, but the quality should remain," he corrected himself as the other two looked at him disapprovingly.

"As I was saying, we will remain for the night and will return to Vienna tomorrow noon."

"All right, I'll manage with Ms. Mayers... Konrad," I could see the other two pretending to be busy with their laptops, but listening to every word we said. Both let a collective gasp of relief out at hearing me using his Christian name. "Where are we staying?"

"Salzburg's Sacher Hotel" He said with a mortified face. "There's nothing else available at such short notice. It will be crowded."

"Is it appropriate?" I asked while looking at the folder.

"There's nothing else, I said," he retorted mildly upset.

"To take the children to *The Magical Flute*." After all, it's *the* Masonic play. Friederich will have my head when I return home," I said sweetly.

"Can't have everything in this world. Don't explain the symbolism and we all be fine. Do you prefer to go to *The Sound of Music*?" He told me with sufficiency after exchanging several hesitant looks with the other men. I guess they didn't think about that small detail.

"*Non*. It's all right, Konrad. I'll take care of them."

"I'll see you tonight, Guntram. Don't let them jump over the cakes," he said returning to his things. I smiled at Ferdinand who was carefully looking at me and left the compartment.

The train had a bar, but it was already crowded with several associates. Getting a coffee proved a hard task and I asked a cappuccino to go for Carolin. The poor woman was already in that compartment for two hours with the boys.

"Hi Guntram," Ferdinand said shyly, but blocking my way out of the restaurant.

"You told him!" I said seriously.

"I said nothing about anything. Only what you told me, that you were in Europe and that the book would arrive for the children," he defended himself and I laughed at him.

"Who would have said that I could make you nervous?" I joked. "Sorry Ferdinand, it was a bad joke. You told him about the plane."

"Guntram. It was a pigsty what I got. There were even greasy fingerprints on the windows," he protested loud and energically.

"I know," I chuckled at his horrified expression.

"How are you?"

"I'm fine, but what you want to ask is how are we. I don't know. We are not fighting an open war like in the past and we had eased down a lot of the tensions, but nothing more. It's true that we share the bed as everybody seems to know by now, but sex is not the solution to all problems. We are in relative peace. Fragile."

"That's already a big improvement my boy. A real one. I'm glad for you two. He looks like another person since you came back." He told me with a soft voice, smiling in a fatherly way.

"I have to take this to the nanny. She must be dying," I said embarrassed and unwilling to continue the talk.

"Boy, this is nothing compared to what we saw in July. Nothing. Those children shout exactly like their father. Three nannies down. Friederich lost all his credit with the employment agencies. I don't know how you do it."

"I do nothing. They're nice boys, they were just nervous and afraid. Stefania told them that I was sick because of them."

"I'm glad for what happened to her," he said very seriously. "One thing is to fight with you and Konrad and another to get the small ones in. Bitch!"

"She's dead, don't speak evil about her, Ferdinand. Let's think on the future."

I went back to my compartment with the children and gave the coffee to her, and she was looking very happy to be "released" for a few minutes. She went away as I showed the folder to the children.

"Papa has to work a lot today. Perhaps we will see him at dinner, perhaps not. We will staying in a hotel in front of a river. It's very nice. I was there before."

"We have no pyjamas!" Karl pointed out.

"Well, we will get one for you after we see the puppet play at 2. Ms. Mayers will help us to choose."

"I want to see dinosaurs! A griffin!" Klaus said very excitedly.

"Perhaps there's a griffin in the castle, at the top of the mountain. It's a real castle for knights," I said, letting him sit on my lap.

"Make us one Guntram!" Karl asked.

"Dinosaur or griffin?"

"Griffin… and a unicorn! Klaus added.

"I'm not your slave," I replied dryly.

"Please Guntram, please," both said now.

"That's better," I said taking their colours and started to draw, while Karl leant on top of my shoulder to look better.

When we finally got to the hotel, I left the two bedroom suite for the nanny, so she could have some peace and took the one bedroom for us. She was shocked and the hotel manager decided that if we could give him one hour more, he could have ready the presidential suite for the Duke. I accepted and thanked the man. I asked him to tell the butler to unpack when our things would be arriving. I wanted to take the children out to run a little before sitting them for lunch.

It seems that the news about Konrad's bad temper reach even Salzburg.

We went around the city, to see the puppets, had tea at some small place looking over the castle and I made them run up and down the hill that leads to the Castle. We visited it and they liked at lot, comparing many things with the furnitures they have at home. Many tourists looked at us astonished.

692

By eight o'clock we returned to the hotel and I met Sören at the lobby. "They're still in meetings, at the winter garden. They have already asked for dinner to be served at ten there. Don't wait up for the Duke."

I took the children for dinner in one of the hotel restaurants, making them promise they would behave as they would be sitting "with the grown ups" and they would eat without complaining. They insisted on changing their clothes and getting a tie "like papa", if not, they would not go. Ms. Mayers and I had a very hard time trying to suppress our laughter, when we complied. They behaved very formally, eating everything even if there was no "children's menu". I let them have a piece of that chocolate bomb that the Sacher cake is for desert. Both loved it and it was exactly "as Friederich said," I think he scored several points there.

At nine thirty, they were in bed and didn't even care for the story so tired they were.

"Good night Ms. Mayers."

"Good night, sir. I'm truly glad you're here. They're delicious children when you're around—obedient and polite. It's a real pleasure to work with them."

"Thank you."

When I reached my own bedroom, there were two sets of the three bears representing the staff (maid, doorman and cook) and a small card "with compliments from the Sacher Hotel," I suppose they're for the children. Six guys more at home. I was too tired to do more and I went to bed to write yesterday's and today's events.

* * *

August 12th, 2008

We left Salzburg on several cars on the morning of the 11th, three days after the original plan. I was almost not seeing Konrad in Salzburg as he was in several meetings, coming only to sleep very late and leaving very early, barely exchanging a few polite words with me. I have no idea what they're after, but it was like seeing all the Dino meeting from Good Friday, split in smaller doses over two days. I was out of the hotel as long as I could, because most of the Dinos or their offsprings knew me and were coming to greet me. As if I could do something if the Griffin is cross with you!

I was sent with the children and the nanny to a big Q7 and we drove back to Vienna to the same hotel and the same rooms. Konrad was driving to the airport with the young Löwenstein and Ferdinand in one of his monster limousines.

When we arrived to Vienna it was already four o'clock and I decided to take the boys to the Schillerpark nearby. I sat on a bench as they were very busy chasing each other. Looking at them I felt a big constricting knot in my throat. Here was where he told me we were expecting them and where he gave me the ring. It was the beginning of one of the happiest times in my life. I think I never was so happy like at that period.

No, never.

I missed that happiness. Truly. I wished that both my babies will ever enjoy it like I did, if only briefly, but they should have the opportunity to know it.

Perhaps my father wished the same for me when he remembered my mother.

Yes, maybe. I do it as a parent.

"You're here." Konrad's voice surprised me.

"Yes, the boys needed to lose some steam," I replied, strangely embarrassed as he sat on the bench, almost touching me.

"It was very kind of you to take care of our children these days. Did they have tea already?"

"Not yet. I was going to take them to," I whispered.

"I'll do it so you can rest a little."

"You must be also tired," I replied very quickly.

"Yes, but this was originally a family vacation. I'm sorry it was interrupted by the Order's affairs. I will take them also to *Stephansdom* to thank our Lady. It all started here and oddly finishes here. It's almost like a sign."

I looked at him, puzzled at his words. "I can't follow you."

"I told you, many years ago, in this same place, that I would change the Order to make it again as it was originally designed by our ancestors, a guild of knights prepared to defend our beliefs and our Church; ready to help our brothers in need, not making profit out of their misery. It took me five years, but it's done. You also accepted me as your husband."

"That was one of my happiest moments in my life. The other was when I saw your children sleeping in their car seats for the first time," I murmured dreamingly as he looked me in the eyes. "I wish they could feel this too."

"I couldn't tell which one was the happiest time for me. All of them were joyful in one or another way. I was only happy to see you, but it's over now, really over," he said with a deep sadness and I couldn't say a thing.

Both boys saw their father and came to us to jump over him and me. He jovially told them that he would take with him for tea so I could rest a little.

I went back to the hotel, almost dragging my feet. Even it was the same suite as before, it looked strange, gloomy. He had finally understood it was over and I felt like dying on my insides. I realised that I didn't want it to be over. I never did. I wanted to punish him, but not that he would leave me. I sat by one of the big windows, overlooking the street, watching the tramways pass and the sun going away. The only thing I could think of was, "I'm sorry, *Papa*. I can't do it any more. I don't want to."

Konrad and the children returned to the hotel very late. It was around nine o'clock. Klaus and Karl entered the room shouting and running, almost jumping on top of me. The were absolutely excited and happy.

"Papa bought us a cake!"

"A big one, all for us!"

"We ate it, and put some cream on top of it."

"Slow down, I don't understand. Did your father buy you a cake before dinner?" I asked still dazed with their shouting and jumping around. Why was I seeing four children when there are only two?

"In a hotel like the one we were in. We sat at a table with the adults!"

"It had apricot jam inside and chocolate all over it."

I saw Konrad entering the room also, looking slightly guilty. I fulminated him with one look. "Did you buy a full Sacher cake for the children?"

"We are in Austria. Where else would you get it truly fresh?"

"Rumour has it that there are three kilos of pure chocolate in each one of them! Are you out of your mind? What were you thinking? NO, you clearly were not thinking!" I shouted him, totally frustrated at his irresponsibility. Fortunately for him, the nanny entered to pick the children up, and took them for their bath.

"Ms. Mayers don't give them dinner. They just had something." Konrad said with all the dignity he could as I was fuming.

I kissed the children goodnight as they were still under the chocolate rush, praying inwardly that they wouldn't give a very hard time to Ms. Mayers. Friederich will not be happy with us if we lose another nanny.

"Guntram don't be so mad at me. They really enjoyed it. It was just a cake. Small size," he justified himself very sheepishly.

"I hope you still consider the situation enjoyable when your romantic night with me goes to hell as our children vomit on top of our bed, feeling completely sick," I answered sweetly.

He looked at me, shocked by my words. He smiled at me, his eyes filled with a light I've not seen in a long time. He took me in his arms and kissed me delicately as if he wouldn't believe it was true. He cupped my face for a long minute as my eyes mirrored his adoring look.

"After vomiting they should be all right. One tea, and they can go back to bed, my love. Nothing we couldn't handle together," he shrugged, making my smile broaden.

Konrad fumbled with the pocket in his jacked and got a small box, opening it with one hand, his eyes not leaving mines not for a single moment. He took my left hand, and once again, he put the red griffin's seal on my finger.

"Forever."

"Till death do us part, Konrad."

"I will do all what I can to make you happy," he said, taking my head between his hands, after kissing me.

I put my fingers over his lips and whispered. "No, we have to build our happiness together. Everyday. You and I as equals. None of us should think he's responsible for everything."

"Yes, my love. I swear to do my best to change my ways. For our children."

"For us, Konrad. For us. Nobody else," I whispered standing on my tiptoes to kiss him deeply.

Finis

Printed in the USA
CPSIA information can be obtained
at www.ICGtesting.com
LVHW011911300823
756644LV00005B/202